I0772370

Kingdom of Smoke and Starlight

THE ONCE SEVEN KINGDOMS
· BOOK TWO ·

ABIGAIL EHRHARDT

Content Warnings

This book contains subject matter that might be difficult for some readers, including death, violence, discussion of past sexual threat, references to past abusive relationships/domestic violence, quick mention of animal death (not a pet), and brief mention of stillbirth.

For those who are afraid to let themselves heal. It's all right to stop picking at your scars.

PART 1: MIDNIGHT

Chapter 1

Analia couldn't force herself to move.

She stood on the stairs leading to the Ash Castle roof, only aware of the Devourist's cold, sucking mouth on her neck. The zap of Deardryn's magic. Pryanth's lips across her cheekbone as he promised to kill her.

She knew they were only memories. But they played on an endless loop in her mind, chipping away at her until all that remained was the empty shell staring at the door before her.

She didn't know how long she'd been standing there, just two steps from the top. She only knew that she'd stopped feeling the ache in her feet a long time ago. She didn't feel the burn of Pryanth's pendant squeezed in her fist, buried in her gown's hidden pocket.

There was just the stillness, the hollow feeling inside.

And the sudden sound of approaching footsteps.

Analia's magic roared. She pivoted on her heel, drawing her dagger and pressing her back to the door. She would not let them take her. Never again.

Ember and Cadmus emerged from the gloom around the bend. They immediately halted a few steps below when they spotted her dagger; one she couldn't bring herself to immediately sheathe.

But it was her brother, wearing a fine gray jacket threaded with orange, yellow, and scarlet. Ember, dressed in a sleek green gown with her light brown hair braided over her shoulder. There were no honey eyes, golden magic, exposed gray bone.

She was home. She was safe. Still, Analia's hands shook as she finally slid Aaron's dagger back through her belt.

She'd adopted his habit of never going anywhere without it, even tucking it beneath her pillow at night as he had. It was always in reach, even when the nightmares had her jolting upright in bed, barely able to choke back her scream as she remembered all those hands.

Cold, dead hands. A slim tan hand to the heart. Hands pinning her against Pryanth's bed frame. Her own hand, gripping her dagger so tight her fingers ached. Sometimes, that pain was the only thing that slowed her pulse—although that was rarely followed by her falling back asleep.

Now, Cadmus's blue eyes reflected the light from a nearby sconce as he watched her uncertainly. Ember, however, shoved past him without a care in the world.

"I knew you'd be up here," she said.

"Yes," Analia forced out. "That's always a safe bet."

She didn't add that, just like every time she'd visited since returning to the Ash Kingdom, she hadn't managed to step foot outside. Instead, she turned to Cadmus. "Is it time?"

"Just about," he confirmed.

"I see he tracked you down, too," she went on, glancing at Ember.

"And he had the audacity to tell me I would've been late if he hadn't."

Cadmus made a noise of protest. "You were so late to the last meeting, you showed up thirty minutes after it ended."

"I was going to be on time!" Ember protested. "But then some nymphs wanted to show me their new greenhouse and how they're using mirrors to direct sunlight—"

"And you were late," Cadmus finished.

"You can't be late if you never show up," Analia mused.

Ember pointed a triumphant finger. "Thank you!"

Analia forced a smile as Ember and Cadmus bickered on. It was all a part of the game they'd been playing the past six weeks: Cadmus trying not to pry, Ember acting as though nothing was wrong until told otherwise.

They weren't the only ones who'd noticed that they'd seen the Princess of Ash off to the Sun Kingdom, but someone else had returned in her stead. Someone whose broken pieces no one knew what to do with—least of all herself.

All she could do was focus on remaining calm as Cadmus extended his hand to her.

Cadmus. Her brother. She was home.

So why was she relieved he pulled her into the darkness instead of walking back through the castle corridors with her? Corridors she once knew so well she could run through them in the dark, but now only felt haunted.

Analia shoved the thoughts aside as they reemerged in a back alleyway near the square. Midafternoon sunlight slanted across the open space before them, dappling the heads of the crowd that had formed beneath the Council Building's balcony.

Some stood in groups, others leaned against statues. All, however, wore distinctly pinched expressions, their voices the low buzz of an impending swarm.

"It's almost over," Ember said softly, noting Analia's furrowed brow. "After today, it will all be over."

"This part, at least," Analia muttered.

Ember and Cadmus exchanged a look. They'd been doing that a lot lately, as if in the time she'd been gone, they'd become a unit. Analia reached for her enka flower bracelet, her chest horribly hollow.

Not seeming to notice, Ember gave her shoulder a squeeze. Then, she slipped into the crowd, undoubtedly going to stand with the other apprentices.

"We should get up there," Cadmus said, nodding to the balcony. There was only one chair, front and center. A low platform stood beside the door leading into the building, the handful of Ash Royals from lower branches already seated on the curved bench atop it.

Analia knew she should feel exhilarated looking at that balcony. But there was only a heavy weight in her stomach as she said, "Let's just get this over with."

Cadmus looked like he wanted to speak. Clearly thinking better of it, he wordlessly squeezed her hand, then shadowjumped them up to the balcony.

The moment they reappeared, Analia could feel her people's eyes latch on to her. They moved along the near-black fabric of her gown, over to the phoenix pin against her chest; down to the simple woven belt where her dagger hung.

It was such a familiar assessment. But as Analia took her seat in the center of the bench, Cadmus on her right, she kept her expression unreadable.

She'd spent enough time cowering and silently seething because of her people. She refused to let them see her flinch ever again. Even if, with every passing day, it was getting harder to do so.

Throughout the six weeks she'd been home, she'd felt herself trying to curl inward once more. Not irresistibly. But every routine she settled back into felt haunted by the scared little girl who had once enacted them, to the point she was starting to fear there was no escaping her. Not while in Ash, at least.

Analia blinked hard as the massive clock tower across the square tolled the hour. It was time.

An unsettling quiet fell over the crowd as the door to the balcony slid open.

Ronun was the first to emerge, dressed in his usual black-and-gray robes. But no one paid the interrogator any mind. All attention was on the shackled prisoner that shuffled before him.

Brenn.

Her father had seemed to age a decade in the cell he'd been kept in. His soiled gray tunic hung off his once solid frame. His red hair had grown longer, now falling into his sunken, hollow eyes.

With every step, the chains connected to his wrist and ankle cuffs rattled against Analia's nerves. But Brenn didn't seem to notice. He didn't even spare the crowd a glance as Ronun ushered him toward the lone chair.

It was only when he was forced to sit that he seemed to focus. He twisted his head, quickly locating Analia in the small group of Royals to his right.

For the briefest moment, Analia thought she caught something like desperation in her father's eyes. Then, he raised his cuffed hands in a mocking wave.

Analia tensed. And Brenn's damper cuffs shifted down, revealing a black, asymmetrical star tattooed on the inside of his left wrist.

Analia's eyes widened. She leaned forward, trying to get a better look, but Ronun grabbed Brenn by the front of his tunic and twisted him forward.

Analia quickly turned to Cadmus, "Did you see—"

"Yes," he breathed, eyes narrowing.

Before Analia could respond, Ronun cleared his throat. All attention snapped to him, but Analia's gaze remained fixed on the back of her father's head. Her uncle's killer's head.

It should have sunk in by now. But as the trials went on, as the events of that day were retold over and over again, the realization didn't dim.

Instead, it burned, hotter and hotter until she could feel her fury branded into her soul. Hot enough that as Ronun—deciding to ignore the residual hum of voices—began his speech, every thought of that marking eddied out of her mind. All she knew was the blaze of her magic as Ronun finally told the Ash Kingdom the full story of what had happened to their late king.

Previously, Brenn's trial had been kept private, no one wanting to create a stir. But that hadn't stopped the rumors from leaking out the castle like a toxic vapor, moving from street to street until Analia doubted there was a single person who didn't know of Brenn's betrayal.

The outrage had been steadily building throughout the weeks. Now, that quiet hum of voices evolved into a furious buzz as Ronun displayed every one of Brenn's crimes like a bloody corpse on a doorstep.

But still, Brenn did not flinch. Not even as Ronun finished his speech and beckoned Analia forward. As next in line to the throne, she was the one who got the final say as to what to do with her father. And looking into his face, all she felt was rage.

She wanted to burn him to ash. She wanted him to suffer until he knew every single hurt he'd ever given her.

Slow. Painful. Ruthless.

It was nothing less than he deserved. If the roles were reversed, he wouldn't hesitate a second.

Analia gripped her dagger hilt, struggling to quell her flames. Then, she turned her back on Brenn to address the crowd.

"For six weeks," she called, "I've allowed my father to plead his case. Out of the fairness my uncle preached, I gave him every opportunity to justify his actions. Yet, no person who has heard his testimony has found any shred of defensibility for his crimes."

Analia's gaze swept over the motionless crowd below. "It's tempting to say we should sentence him to death. A life for a life. But my father doesn't *deserve* the comfort of an afterlife."

There came a sharp inhale behind her. Analia ignored her fellow Royals. Instead, she turned to Ronun, whose level gaze felt like the final confirmation she needed.

"Contact Scarsthain immediately," she said. "Tell the warden to prepare an Eternity Cell."

Analia could have heard a pebble roll across the square.

Located on the border between the Moon Kingdom and what was once Star territory, Scarsthain was the highest security prison in Elefthia. It was home to the foulest, most deadly of creatures, locked away in utter darkness: no contact, no noise, no stimulation of any kind. Just the prisoner and the recess carved from bone that each cell was set in.

Most beings were sentenced to torture. But the Eternity Cell was imprisonment for however long the Crystal, the gods, whatever force, decided to keep the prisoner alive and rotting.

It was a fate believed to be determined by something greater. Mercy or suffering.

Standing in that silence, Analia knew she should feel a blaze of triumph, justice, anything. But as she turned to go, there was only guilt for the father Brenn had once been to her.

"Wow," Brenn drawled into the silence. "What a queen. Abandoning her people, killing her husband when she didn't get her way, and coming back here to condemn her own father so she can take the crown."

Brenn settled back in his seat, his voice dropping to a mutter. "At least my crimes had the kingdom in mind."

The crowd's attention swung back to her. Analia didn't know if she wanted to scream or sob.

How did he always do this? How did he always find a way to spin the truth like a loose thread on a tapestry, leaving her no room to argue, her silence only reaffirming his tale?

Analia slowly turned to face her father, forcing herself to hold his gaze. "Pettiness is unbecoming on you," she said, her voice remarkably steady. Then, not waiting for a response, she walked through the door. And all she remembered of her descent down the stairs to the entryway was the silence.

The silence in her own mind, the silence of the crowd she'd walked away from. She knew it wouldn't last for long. Indeed, the moment she stepped outside to a reluctant squadron of soldiers waiting for her, the silence erupted.

"Go assist your squads," she told her guards, not breaking stride. "They'll need your help escorting Brenn out more than I will."

The guards nodded stiffly before retreating back toward the Council Building. All except one.

"Anna." Rois made to touch her, the look in his eyes something she hadn't seen since he'd told her he'd chosen the guard over her.

"That's an order," she snapped, stepping out of reach.

Rois winced, but he knew better than to argue. He quickly disappeared back into the square, leaving Analia to compulsively rub the silky petals of her enka bracelet as she watched the chaos unfold.

Everyone was so angry. Angry at losing Accalon, angry with his killer. Angry with the queen they were about to inherit.

Princess Analia Valarus and her midnight flames. Flames that had been rumored—and now confirmed—to have burned her husband to ash on their wedding bed. Never mind she hadn't tried to summon them since that day. They still snarled through her nightmares, scorched through her veins.

They were a part of her. And if she was willing to kill Pryanth, where did it end? She probably belonged up on that stand as much as Brenn. But instead, she was trying to take the crown?

Analia's magic roiled, but she shoved it down. Then, turning on her heel, she began the long walk back to the castle.

Aeley was waiting for her in the castle entryway. Her mother had decided to forgo Brenn's sentencing, opting to stay back at the castle with Lucilla instead. Analia couldn't have cared less if her mother attended, but she was quietly relieved her twelve-year-old sister wasn't forced to witness their father's condemnation.

"So?" Aeley asked, blocking Analia's path to the stairs.

"Scarsthain," she said flatly. "Eternity Cell."

Aeley brought shaking hands to her face. "Holy Crystal above."

Analia's flames crackled, but she shoved them back.

"What's done is done," she said, stepping around her mother.

"You could have stopped this!" Aeley spat, following her up the stairs. "You could have spared him from that fate!"

"He killed my uncle!"

Aeley's hand shot out, icy fingers latching on to Analia's wrist. "He tried to love you, Analia. He tried. And he made a mistake—"

Black sparks flew from Analia's skin. Aeley yelped and snatched her hand back, but Analia didn't care.

Her mind was bathed in flames, screaming to burn the woman that stood before her. Taking everyone's side except hers, just as she'd always done.

Aeley took in Analia's flushed cheeks, her chest as it heaved for breath. "Are you ever going to forgive?" she asked. "Or are you going to be angry for the rest of your life?"

Analia expected her control to finally snap. Instead, her fury slowly funneled out, leaving her voice cold and empty.

"I believe it's a parent's job to teach their child to forgive. Perhaps you should have considered teaching me that when I needed you to."

Aeley's blue eyes flashed. Analia didn't care.

She turned and headed off down the hall, her mind utterly blank until she reached her chambers. Closing the door behind her, she sank down onto her bed and buried her face in her hands, not trying to stop her tears.

She was so, so tired. Tired of the anger, tired of her family, tired of the emotions that slammed against her like an endless wave.

Analia didn't know how much time had passed when her door quietly slid open. She looked up, hurriedly wiping the stray tears from her face.

To her surprise, it was Lucilla—dressed in a simple gray gown, her golden hair loose around her shoulders—hovering in her doorway.

"Come to tell me you hate me, too?" Analia asked.

Lucilla flinched. Guilt sank its claws deep into Analia's stomach.

Husband killer. Father's condemner. Lashing out at innocent little girls. Crystal spare her, what was happening to her?

Analia made to apologize. Before she could, Lucilla silently crossed the room and wrapped her arms around Analia's middle.

Gods, her grip was so tight. Just like the skeletal arms of the Devourist, clamping her arms to her sides, its mouth pressed to her neck—

"I'm sorry he was so mean to you," Lucilla said into her shoulder.

Analia's heart twisted. She shoved the memories aside, Pryanth's pendant digging into her side as she held Lucilla tight.

"You have nothing to be sorry for," she said fiercely.

"But I knew."

"Lucilla, look at me."

Lucilla complied, tears in her blue eyes.

"What happened to me was not your fault, understand? I will not have you blaming yourself for any of it. All right?"

Lucilla ducked her head, pressing her face into Analia's shoulder once more. "I just want to help," she whispered.

"I know," Analia sighed, smoothing a hand down Lucilla's hair. "I know you do."

She was one of the few that did.

Chapter 2

Analia didn't know how much longer her patience would last.

The morning following Brenn's sentencing, she woke gasping for breath, her cold sweat carrying the icy touch of Pryanth's hands. It had taken hours for her pulse to slow, even longer for her to settle her magic.

During that time, she'd been relieved no one had come to hound her. But as the sky slowly lightened outside her window, there still came no word. No bombardment of messages, no family members to bicker with, not even a summons to breakfast to ignore.

With a sneaking suspicion, Analia descended to the Council Chamber, just to find all six councilmen in session. Without her.

Now, their arguing voices throbbed against the headache building in her temples.

Most of the conversation revolved around her surprise decision to condemn Brenn—which she hadn't informed them of. As far as they'd been aware, she had landed on execution, and she'd simply failed to correct them.

But Analia didn't offer any explanations. Instead, she sat back in her seat, quietly observing just as Accalon had taught her.

That, however, meant listening to them as they bickered round and round. Leaving Analia to absently stroke the silken petals of her bracelet.

It wasn't the first time she'd been tempted to test Aaron's claim that if she called for him, he'd come. If she was honest, there hadn't been a single day that had passed since he'd left that she hadn't considered it. She'd almost done it, too, just a few weeks prior on Accalon's birthday.

Her uncle had always made it a point to spend the day with his family. But his evenings were always reserved for her.

Every year, they'd smuggle whatever leftovers there were from his dinner feast up to her turret, where she'd ask for stories from the time before he was king. She always ended up snuggled against his side, drifting off to the smell of smoke and ink as he shadowjumped her back to her chambers.

This year, however, she'd spent the entire morning curled up in bed, unable to move as the grief slammed into her over and over. She could barely clench her fingers around her bracelet, just needing something, anything to hold on to. And the door immediately flew open.

For the briefest moment, she felt a flicker of hope. But it was promptly slashed as she looked up at her mother's thoroughly unimpressed expression.

Barely sparing her a glance, Aeley informed her that Ronun needed her immediately. Then, she turned on her heel and left. And Analia's fingers slowly slid from her wrist.

Now, Analia shoved the memory aside, the part of her mind tracking the councilmen's conversation sensing an opening.

"There's no going back on my decree," she said. "The moment you do that, you create a division of power and completely undermine our authority."

"You should have informed us of your decision," Councilman Ganze snapped, seated directly across from her.

She wasn't surprised he was the first to speak. Ganze was the longest-lasting member of the council. It was his one true claim to power in a world dominated by Royals, and he made sure he wielded every last shred of it.

Analia said, "This decision was mine alone to make as next in line—"

"That crown isn't yours yet," Councilman Laird interrupted. Always the first to follow in Ganze's shadow.

"Was I supposed to come to you for permission?" Analia scoffed. "Even though the council is only comprised of advisors with no legal say?"

"We have more say than you do," Ganze said. "Unless you'd finally like to take the crown."

Analia's hand tightened around Pryanth's pendant in her pocket.

There were no more reasons she could stall her ascension. Based on the looks of anticipation on the councilmen's faces, they had been waiting for this moment.

"You still hesitate," Councilwoman Marie murmured, tucking her red-brown hair behind her ear. "You cannot have all the power and none of the responsibility, Your Highness."

Analia clamped down on her retort. She glanced at the paintings on the Chamber walls, finding the image of Azar at the peak of Mt. Vasolus, encased in golden flames. Her ancestor. Her birthright.

But did she even want it? Did that even matter?

"If I become queen," she said slowly, "will we finally start to make moves on Sun?"

The room erupted into a flurry of voices, just as it had every other time she brought up Deardryn. And just like every other time, Analia struggled to hold back her flames.

"How many times must we tell you?" Ganze demanded. "We have no proof!"

"I got a confession out of her!" Analia shot back, her flames winning out as she pushed to her feet. "She confessed to killing Baylen, just as Brenn confessed to killing Accalon, and that was enough to charge *him*."

"You had multiple witnesses for Brenn's confession!" Laird argued, also rising. "But you were the only one to hear Deardryn's. If you are going to rally support for a war, you need something more substantial than just your word."

"Especially since Deardryn has an abundance of evidence against you," Marie added, a single point of calm in the chaos. "Her son was burned alive on his wedding night to an Ash Royal. Her temple has been destroyed by flames."

Analia bit back her words just in time. She'd told the council her magic had destroyed the temple, not wanting to reveal the true, silver-laced reason. That wasn't her secret to share.

But Analia refused to let that lie back her into a corner. She was *tired* of corners, especially in this gods-damned castle.

"Are you saying we're supposed to let Baylen's death go unpunished because Deardryn can spin a more compelling story?" she asked.

"You already killed Pryanth!" Ganze said. "You got your justice. A life for a life."

"Your Highness," Marie broke in smoothly, "we must look at the bigger picture. If this were any other time, our declaring war on Sun would elicit no reaction from the remaining kingdoms. Now, however, Deardryn has formed a tenuous connection through her murders. Just enough that if she requested alliances, the other kingdoms might respond."

"And they wouldn't respond to us if we told them the truth?" Analia demanded.

"Why would they believe us over Deardryn when she has all the evidence?" Marie asked. "Deardryn's story is far more likely to garner support than ours, meaning if we went to war with Sun, we could very easily be surrounded by enemies."

Silence settled across the table. No one, not even Analia, could argue with that.

Slowly, reluctantly, Analia sat back in her chair, her magic guttering in her veins. Even as the remaining councilmen nodded magnanimously. As if they'd already won.

Ignoring the other councilmen, Analia looked to Marie—her last hope for reason. "Deardryn is a threat to every kingdom in Elefthia," she said. "Surely they would want retribution for the lives she's taken."

Ganze began, "You can't prove—"

"Surely," Analia continued over him, "it is our responsibility to warn the kingdom that is still in danger."

"King Sylas is still under the impression Deardryn saved his husband," Marie explained, lacing her fingers atop the table. "Not only will Deardryn have more proof than us, but he will naturally be more inclined to believe her."

"But what if we get proof?" Analia asked. "What if I go back to Sun and get the rings?"

"That might work," Marie said over the sudden mutters. "But that's assuming you can even find the rings. And from everything we know of Deardryn, there is no chance she would leave them in a spot you could easily get to.

"Beyond that, you are now a wanted criminal in her kingdom. Any person who sees you would report your presence to the Royals immediately, and we cannot risk you."

"So, we do nothing?" Analia asked, no longer caring if the desperation bled into her voice. She finally looked to the other councilmen, all of whom averted their gazes.

"Our best option is to wait," said Laird eventually. The flush had faded from his weathered face, replaced by a heavy exhaustion Analia felt in her bones. "As soon as Deardryn attacks Moon, we'll have all the proof we need."

"And a collection of kingdoms furious with not just Sun, but also us for not informing them," Analia countered, leaning forward. "We can't try to outmaneuver Deardryn. She's already far too many steps ahead for that.

"The fact that we haven't heard so much as a whisper from her in six weeks isn't a sign of her being unnerved. It means we're so far behind her that we can't see her next move, and informing Moon is the least we can do to catch up."

"Informing Moon will get us nowhere," Councilwoman Tris argued.

Analia's gaze moved from face to face, but she could see there was no winning this battle. There was only one card she had left to play.

"And when I'm queen," Analia said, half choking on the word. "If I decide to ignore your counsel, what happens?"

"If you ignore us," Ganze said, folding his arms, "then you will be starting a war as a new queen without the backing of the council. And that will make things very, very difficult for you."

Analia swallowed a frustrated sob.

She wasn't even queen yet, and already the council fought her on everything. Didn't they see there was nothing left of her for them to trample? Nothing but her relentless flames and the secret measures she'd already put in place.

It was the thought of those measures alone that had Analia pushing back her chair. "My ascension will occur in two weeks."

Then, with a heavy heart, Analia exited the chamber.

Not looking back.

Not thinking she could stomach what she'd see if she did.

Chapter 3

Dimitri was not enjoying himself.

The central Moon Kingdom was built on and around a massive bog. Wide wooden boardwalks stretched across the peat, connecting the various platforms that held storefronts, taverns, even some performance halls. But the predominant feature was the mud.

So much fucking mud. It thickened the air, clung to his skin. It even squelched beneath his boots as he trudged across the boardwalk, the wooden planks bouncing with every step.

"'Go to the Moon Kingdom' they said," Dimitri muttered, his hood up and head down as he avoided the milling citizens. "'It'll be easy' they said. Gods-damned Crystal-forsaken fucking liars."

The first week or so hadn't been terrible. He'd managed to make it across the Star Kingdom in a matter of days, thanks to the brief riding lessons Aaron had given him back in Ash. But no amount of tips could have prepared him for the bandits that infested the outer layers of the Moon Kingdom.

Everywhere he turned, there seemed to be a new crew on the prowl. For a time, he'd managed to outsmart them as he zigzagged deeper into the kingdom. But then one of them managed to skewer Dimitri's horse through the ribs with an arrow, and he'd been certain he was a dead man.

Fortunately, Analia had given him a sizable stash of gold before leaving. Coming out on the other side, all he had was his poetry collection, a letter Analia had given him "in case of emergencies," and the few gold pieces he'd managed to hide in the lining of his boots.

Then, there was the walking. So much walking. Even now, the blisters on his heels burned as he finally left the boardwalks behind and started up a steep, forested hill.

It was almost over, though. He could see the dark spires of the Moon Castle through the trees. All he had to do was give Sylas Analia's message about Deardryn, and someone would jump him home. Wherever that was.

Dimitri winced. Shoving the thought aside, he stepped out of the trees, just to come to a grinding halt.

"Crystal fuck me," he muttered.

Before him loomed the massive, polished black wall surrounding the Moon Castle. Sylas, however, apparently hadn't been content with magical wards and a gate. He had to add three massive gatehouses spaced out across the wall.

They were made from the same black stone, the closest one painted with a large, pearlescent full moon. Dimitri would have bet all the gold in his boots the other gates had crescent and half moons on them. Even if they didn't, there was no missing the guards that patrolled the wall between them.

Gods, all he wanted was to plop down on a nearby boulder and call it quits. But knowing there was nothing else to do, he sighed and headed off.

The gatehouse remained silent as Dimitri made the short walk up to the Full Moon Gate. Even when he paused a foot away from the iron bars, nothing stirred.

"Hello?" he eventually called. "Is someone going to raise this thing for me or what?"

"Unlikely," a male voice drawled, sounding as though Dimitri wasn't the first stray he'd shooed away that day.

"I have a message for your king."

"Truly? And who are you to be given such an honor?"

"The person that has a message for your king. Now let me in."

Dimitri rattled the portcullis. Finally, the guard emerged from the shadows. Bronze hair fell across his forehead in waves, partially obscuring a wreath of purple pine needles tattooed above his eyebrows.

Bracing one chainmail-clad forearm on the window ledge, he gave Dimitri a once-over. Then, he snorted. "Get lost, street rat."

Street rat? Dimitri looked down, taking in the mud spattered across his boots and pants. His dark gray cloak didn't look much better, either. Maybe he had a point.

Dimitri folded his arms. "My message is from Princess Analia Valarus."

He might look disheveled, but he was a Royal messenger. He was powerful. Important.

The guard burst out laughing. Dimitri scowled as he doubled over, gripping the window ledge for support.

"Of all the Royals you could pick," the guard wheezed, "you go with the dud Princess of Ash?"

He choked on a fresh wave of laughter. Dimitri's ears burned. He gripped the gate rods, "You think you'll still be laughing when you're beheaded for diverting a Royal message?"

"Gods, you're stubborn." The guard wiped a tear from his cheek. "Fine. Show me this 'message' you have."

Dimitri took a breath, ready to retort. But he hesitated.

"Come on," the guard said, snapping his fingers. "Let's see it."

Dimitri silently cursed Analia and her schemes.

"She didn't write it down," he said, the heat spreading from his ears to his face.

"Oh, come on! You outline this elaborate scheme to get through the castle gates, and you don't even come prepared?"

"It's sensitive information," Dimitri protested. "She didn't want to risk it getting into the wrong hands."

"Get lost, urchin," the guard laughed, turning away.

Dimitri tugged on his cloak, his mind a storm of curses. If this guard wouldn't let him in, he would have to try the other gatehouses—although why would they be any more likely to let him in? This was his only chance.

Dimitri tugged even harder, and something shifted in his cloak pocket. He reached inside, his fingers wrapping around the thin envelope Analia had given him.

"Wait!" Dimitri said, waving the envelope overhead. "Fine, look. Here it is."

For a few moments, Dimitri thought the guard would ignore him. Then, with a sigh, his bronze head popped out of the window.

"You expect me to believe that's real?"

"Come down here and look at it then."

"Crystal spare me." The guard retreated back into the gatehouse, complaining loudly about street rats and their pathetic schemes. By the time he appeared on the other side of the lowered portcullis, spear over his shoulder, Dimitri was vibrating with rage.

"Here." He shoved the envelope against the bars. "See. Royal sigil. Now lift the fucking gate."

The guard narrowed his eyes. He swiped the envelope with one hand, the other rubbing the stubble along his jaw as he turned it over.

"It seems real enough," he finally said.

Dimitri reached between the bars to take it back.

"Now let's see what your princess has to say."

"No!" Dimitri lunged forward. The guard ripped open the envelope, withdrawing a single piece of paper.

"To whomever this may concern," he read, leaning away from Dimitri's grasping hand. "This messenger comes bearing correspondence from Princess Analia Valarus. The message itself is only meant for Royal ears. Now let him through, guard."

Dimitri's protest sputtered into a snort as the guard looked up, outraged.

"Nice fucking try," he spat. He ripped the letter in half, Dimitri letting out a gasp.

He drew his spear with one hand, attempting to force Dimitri's arm back through the portcullis bars with the other. But staring at the ripped letter at the guard's feet, Dimitri's temper finally peaked.

"Listen here," he hissed, pressing his face to the bars. "I don't give two copper shits if you think I'm lying. I have a message for your gods-damned king. So, get your rusty ass back up to your gatehouse and open this fucking gate."

As it turned out, the guard didn't enjoy being told what to do. By the time reinforcements arrived, he was jabbing his spear through the gaps in the portcullis, Dimitri taunting him right out of reach.

"What is the meaning of this?" bellowed a tall, bearded man with dark brown skin from the gatehouse.

The guard yanked his spear back. "This urchin is trying to force entry into the castle—"

"I have a message for the king from Princess Analia—"

"It was a forgery—"

"It had the Royal sigil!"

"Quiet!" the man bellowed.

Dimitri and the guard cringed.

"Tavian," the bearded guard barked. "Did this man have a sealed letter?"

"Well, yes, but—"

"Did the wax seal match the Royal's kingdom he described."

"It did," Tavian admitted, "but why would he have something like that?"

"He ripped it!" Dimitri tattled, jabbing his finger at Tavian.

Tavian started to protest, but the bearded guard stomped his foot.

"Why he has it isn't our concern. If the message is for His Majesty, and it's authentic, then he'll decide what to do with it."

"So, ha!" Dimitri said.

A vein throbbed in Tavian's temple. He turned away from Dimitri, "But Byron, sir—"

"You can either escort him inside, or patrol the slums for the next week."

Not long later, Dimitri swaggered through the raised portcullis. Byron came down to join Tavian's escort, giving Dimitri a full view of the black snake tattoo coiled around his ear—what was with these guards and their tattoos?

Dimitri was tempted to ask as they pushed through the heavy castle doors, but he was quickly distracted by the entryway.

It was like he'd entered a cave. Countless ornate lanterns sat in nooks in the stone wall, casting a hazy purple glow across the room. Multiple layers of balconies lined the walls, curving around a glass chandelier shaped like the phases of the moon. Directly below, a massive fountain softly burbled, its rim curved like flower petals, waters sparkling with tossed-in stones.

Dimitri was quietly impressed. The guards marched him between moonstone pillars to a curving staircase, a pair of passing servants dressed in black rough-spun uniforms casting them furtive looks. But for once, Dimitri didn't mind the stares. Not as the anticipation built in his veins with every flight of stairs they climbed.

Finally, someone would put an end to the Old Hag and her schemes. After years of tormenting Dimitri, she would get a taste of what it was like to lose everything. And he would know it was in part because of him.

They turned down a final purple carpeted hall. Dimitri's ears pricked as voices drifted from up ahead, one low, flat, and bored. That had to be Sylas. It was time.

The three reached the end of the hall. To the right, an ajar door led into a massive sitting room, the hallway continuing around a corner to the left.

Dimitri peered into the room as Tavian made to knock.

A dark-haired man with brilliant green eyes sat in a window seat directly across from him. He rested his finger against his lips as he watched the pair on the couch in front of him, one a black-haired man with pale skin, the other a woman with golden hair.

Tavian's fist collided with the wood, just as the woman laughed.

Ice slid down Dimitri's spine.

The woman turned her head.

And Dimitri took off running.

"Hey!" Tavian yelled.

Dimitri barreled around the corner and down the hall, frantically searching his pockets for the bracelet Aaron had given him. He had to warn Analia. He had to escape. Crystal spare him, how was she here?

Dimitri was about to turn a corner when something slammed into the back of his head. He stumbled, and a hand grabbed his arm from behind.

Dimitri flailed, straining to take another step. He'd just felt the silky petals of his bracelet when another hand grabbed his free arm, jerking it away. The bracelet fell to the ground at Dimitri's feet, hopelessly out of reach as he was yanked to a halt.

"I knew you were a street rat," Tavian hissed in his ear.

"You don't understand!" Dimitri gasped, trying to break free.

"Save it for interrogations."

Dimitri's breathing accelerated as Tavian's grip was replaced by Byron's. He was trapped, helpless as Byron dragged him away. He could only watch as Tavian bent down and scooped up his bracelet.

Something flickered deep in his gut, but he desperately shoved it back down.

Deardryn had infiltrated Moon. He had no way to tell Analia. And he had no idea if the Sun Queen had spotted him.

Chapter 4

The weeks leading up to Analia's coronation were a haze of activity.

The council was mainly concerned with preparations, squawking loudly and frequently about how little time they had to organize such an event. Analia pointed out that they would have more time if they stopped calling enough meetings to permanently adhere her to her chair, but they ignored her. If only the kingdom and its whispers would do the same.

It was almost unnerving how little things had changed, although she should've expected it. Why should the kingdom change when she was the one that had left? Left to infiltrate an enemy kingdom, solve their king's murder, come into her magic, do everything they had demanded of her.

Yet, Warack still sneered in her face when she ordered him to prepare extra patrols for her coronation. She, in turn, told him he was an insolent brat who could either do as she said or find somewhere else to swing his sword.

Warack was just starting to retort when Rois shoved between them. Snapping something at the other guard, he grabbed Analia's arm and half dragged her away. He made it down three corridors before Analia managed to wrench out of his grip, flames flickering across her hands.

She wheeled on him, waiting for him to call her out. But Rois's voice was gentle as he asked, "Are you all right?"

Analia's flames leaped. "Stop coddling me, Rois!"

Rois took a step back. "I'm only trying to protect you."

Analia didn't know if she wanted to scream or sob. Even after that display, he still saw her as the mouse who had left the Ash Kingdom almost six months before.

Analia clutched Pryanth's pendant in her pocket, forcing her magic to wink out. "Some flames deserve to be stomped out."

Then, not waiting for a response, she turned and headed down the hall, something heavy settling in her stomach.

The morning before her coronation, Analia's dreams were stalked by the Devourist. It bore down on her, its mouth on her neck, memories flashing before her eyes—

Analia jerked upright in bed, barely able to choke back her scream. Her eyes darted around the room, taking in her familiar surroundings, the early morning light streaming through her window.

But her grip didn't loosen on her dagger. And knowing she couldn't stay in this Crystal-forsaken castle a moment longer, she shoved out of bed and went to find her brother.

Analia leaned back against the marble tombstone carved into a pair of wings, her fingers moving across her old, child-sized harp's strings.

It was incredibly uncommon for an Ash King or Queen to have a tombstone. The kingdom believed rulers were meant to be released on the wind, which was why they were burned to ash by Mt. Vasolus.

But that tradition didn't extend to the citizens, and Analia figured if whatever remained of Accalon were to linger, it would be around his wife and child's grave.

The lush grassy hill that sprawled before her was located in Flickerwood, the town right outside the central kingdom that Arienne had grown up in.

For all of that day, Analia played her harp. Played until the sky was flecked with stars, played until every shred of fury and heartbreak had been channeled into her songs.

"I just don't know what to do," she finally whispered, tipping her head back toward the darkening sky. A sad, lonely piece of her waited to hear Accalon's response. But the only sound came from the breeze and the ruffle of peace lily leaves from the pot beside her.

She didn't know who had left the plant. She assumed it was someone from Arienne's family, but she didn't know them well enough to be certain.

After Arienne's death, her family had wanted nothing to do with Accalon or the Royals. They didn't care there was nothing he could've done, didn't care he never stopped loving her. All they knew was their daughter and grandchild were dead, and the man who swore to protect them wasn't there when it happened.

Analia's heart gave a slow, aching squeeze as she remembered the devastation in Accalon's eyes every time he brought her on his monthly visits to the hilltop. Together, they would arrange new flowers and polish the marble, Accalon doing his best to hide the guilt that was slowly eating him alive.

"Someone is still looking after them, Uncle," Analia said softly. "You don't have to worry. They're taken care of, just like I'm taking care of your people."

Analia's fingers drifted over the strings. "They loved you so much. Almost as much as you loved them. I think they could have loved me, too, if it weren't for Brenn."

Analia's fingers stumbled. "I tried so hard. I tried to rise again, above their scrutiny. And I think they've been trying, too. At least, they have in these past eight weeks. And I know I just need to be patient... But Uncle, I'm so tired."

A tear traced its way down her cheek. "You fought so hard for your people. Every day. And I want to fight for them. But I don't... I don't think they want me to."

Analia let her harp fall, trapping one of her legs. She wrapped her arms around herself, tears flowing thick and fast.

"I don't know what to do," she whispered. "I just don't know what to do."

There was no winning. Either she ruled over a people that still didn't trust her, likely never would, and battled with councilmen over every *single* decision. Or what? What other option was there?

Analia was so lost in her thoughts that she didn't immediately notice she was no longer alone. Ember and Cadmus sat on either side of her, Cadmus gently lifting her harp and setting it aside. Then, both their arms were around her, holding her tight enough her ribs ached. And for the first time in eight weeks, no memories from Sun assailed her as she cried into Ember's shoulder.

"I don't know what to do," she said, the soft fabric of Ember's healer robe damp beneath her cheek. "I just need someone to tell me what to do."

"I can't do that, Anna," Ember whispered, her thumb moving back and forth along her shoulder. "This is your decision."

"He would be so proud of you," Cadmus said. "No matter what choice you make."

A fresh sob clawed up Analia's throat. Cadmus leaned his head against hers, murmuring something as it finally tore free.

That was all she'd ever wanted. She could handle the councilmen, the lingering mistrust and disdain of her people. But the thought of disappointing Accalon, of making the wrong choice...

"I miss him," Analia whispered. "I miss him so much."

"I know," Ember said, her own tears running free. "I'm so sorry, Anna. I'm so, so sorry."

Cadmus pulled both of them closer. And it was a long, long time before Analia finally leaned away, her entire body aching as if the grief had dealt a physical blow.

But Ember and Cadmus didn't ask any questions. Ember only retrieved Analia's harp from the grass, her blue-gray eyes glassy as she tucked it under her arm.

She was too exhausted to panic as Cadmus lightly gripped her shoulder, his other hand reaching for Ember.

So many hands. But that also included Accalon's hands: ruffling her hair, squeezing her own. Maybe even guiding Cadmus to come retrieve her that night earlier than he'd promised.

And as Analia closed her eyes thirty minutes later, her dagger clenched in her fist, she knew what she needed to do.

Chapter 5

Standing in the Healer Temple, the four Ash Kingdom archmaster healers glowering down at her, Ember knew she'd messed up.

The temple was fashioned from swirling green stone. A massive mosaic of the human body stretched across the floor, complete with organs, bones, arteries, and veins. The heart had been turned into a dais that the archmaster healers sat upon, each of their chairs in a different chamber and angled to face Ember.

When she'd first been summoned to the temple six weeks prior, she'd only been able to stare at their chain belts.

Golden roses for Mellaine, Archmaster of Herbology. Silver scalpels for the Archmaster of External Healing, Symonne. Reena, Archmaster of Internal Healing, had links designed like steel vertebrae. And shimmering black loops for Hollyn, Archmaster of Mysteries.

The strongest healers from each specialty. And Ember had been stunned when they informed her that her xenol research would be rewarded with a medical mystery marking and a trial. One that she hadn't told anyone about, even as the weeks of accusations and ridicule had her wanting to break down the same way Analia had earlier that night. But if this meeting went well, they would finally put everything to rest.

"You wished to see me?" she asked, clasping her hands before her.

She wasn't surprised by their frowns. Still, her gaze darted to the statue of Rosala behind them.

The goddess wore long green robes, her face partially obscured by a golden mask carved with roses and vines. Somehow, she made Ember feel worse.

"From the start of your trial," Hollyn said, "we let you know our verdict would come after His Majesty's."

"Your list of crimes is extensive," Reena said, reclining in her seat like a throne. "Stealing samples from the school—"

"I only stole one sample of xenol," Ember interjected.

Reena's ice-blue eyes flashed. Ember squeezed her hands tighter, struggling not to give her a look of her own.

The blonde healer had always been her least favorite of the archmasters. Not only was she the youngest to ever join their ranks, but she never let anyone forget it.

"That's true," Symonne said. "And you refused to tell us what you were doing with said sample. Just as you did not inform us when Princess Analia gave you a living specimen. Instead, you conducted unauthorized research, lied to your superiors, and contacted healers from other kingdoms without permission to further your investigations."

"That's not the full story," Ember protested, not for the first time.

"Do you deny any of this?" Hollyn asked serenely. It was no wonder she was the master of medical mysteries: no one could ever read her smooth, ovular face. Combined with her silky black hair and obsidian eyes, Ember didn't know if she was enthralled or terrified.

"Princess Analia trusted me with that sample," Ember said.

"Did she tell you not to share her information?" Reena asked. "Did she specifically swear you to silence and forbid you, an apprentice, from bringing this to your master healers?"

Ember's head whipped from side to side. She wished Analia was there, Cadmus even. The two most powerful Royals in the kingdom were on her side. But since the healers strictly kept their affairs internal, she was left to stand alone.

"Princess Analia couldn't let this information spread," she said, pulling at the neck of her robes. "She couldn't risk anyone finding out about her mission."

"Your duty is not to one person," Symonne told her. "Even if she is a Royal. You swore an oath to Rosala. Your loyalty, your service, your duty is to the goddess and all the people you swore to heal and protect. We are a neutral party, but you allowed yourself to become entangled in a political game that had nothing to do with you."

"Analia risked her life to get that plant to me! If my job as a healer is to protect and heal, doing anything to risk that secret would completely violate that oath."

"Are you saying you don't trust us to uphold our own oaths?" asked Mellaine softly.

Ember had hoped, being a fellow herbologist, that Mellaine would be on her side. Yet, Mellaine's rich brown eyes were stern, unyielding.

Gods, why were they doing this to her? Why did they drag her before them over and over again just to tell her what a horrible healer she was? Didn't they know she'd been told that every day for the last thirteen years?

"Please," Ember said, moving up the rib cage. "I thought I was doing what was right."

"And that is an admirable pursuit," Mellaine said, shooting a warning glance at Reena. "Unfortunately, it came at the price of breaking your healer's oath."

Her words tingled down Ember's spine. No, she couldn't have broken her oath. She was only helping her friend. That couldn't have been the wrong choice, an unforgivable choice. But Ember's lungs struggled to fill.

"Archmaster Mellaine, please," she pleaded, knowing she was her only chance. "Yes, I didn't tell any of you about my investigations. But that wasn't violating my oath, it was a mistake."

"Do you truly believe it was a mistake?" Hollyn asked. "That if you could go back, you wouldn't make that choice once again?"

"Even though you claim to believe that choice was upholding your oath," Reena chimed in.

Ember's heart pounded throughout her body. She could practically hear her fellow apprentices' laughter in the crackle of the everflame torches. *Stupid human herbologist healer.*

"The council has come to a decision," Hollyn said, tracing the shimmering loops of her belt.

Ember wanted to scream. She wanted to march on to the dais and demand they hear her. But she couldn't move.

"The council has decided," Mellaine said gently, "that the service you did for this kingdom does not outweigh the crimes you committed to do so."

"Your apprenticeship at the Ash Kingdom Healer School is officially suspended indefinitely," Symonne said, "with reintegration into the Healer School pending demonstrations that you have accepted and learned from your erroneous behavior. For the time being, Dane has offered you a full-time position at his apothecary."

The council continued to outline her punishment, but their voices fuzzed out in Ember's ears.

She had been so close. All she needed was one more ring, and she would have achieved her dream of being a full healer. But with a handful of words, the council tore down her world.

It didn't matter it was just a suspension, not an exile. Her ability to heal, at least lawfully and in the name of Rosala, was completely out of her hands. She couldn't even have Analia or Cadmus order them to give her back her healing privileges.

Ever since the beginning of the Royals and healers, they had sworn to trust each other's judgments and stay out of the others' affairs. She could tell them of her trial and the outcome, but seeing as she'd violated her oath to help them? Ember could not—would not—inflict that guilt, that feeling of powerlessness on them.

She was on her own. She always had been. But she'd never felt it so keenly before.

Hollyn asked her a question, but she didn't hear it. Instead, she looked to the statue of Rosala.

Many believed her spread arms to be her attempt to hold back her elder sister, Kierra, and younger sister, Elladine, the goddesses of life and death, respectively. When Ember had knelt at her feet when she was officially named a healer, she had thought her arms were welcoming. Now, she felt as though Rosala was shepherding her toward her condemnation.

She had been chosen by Rosala. At ten years old, without a drop of Blessed blood, Rosala instructed the Crystal to gift her with magic. They had recognized her potential, her value, her worth. And now, the healer council was trying to take that away? Claim they knew better?

"What do you think you're doing?" Reena spat.

Ember hadn't realized she'd climbed onto the dais. She only knew the white-hot wave of indignation that barreled through her insides, burning away everything in its path. And she welcomed it with relief.

"When I solved this mystery eight weeks ago," she said, pivoting on her heel to face them all, "you gave me my medical mystery ring. You rewarded my efforts; you recognized my skills. And now you're *punishing me* for those very reasons?"

"Ember," Mellaine said, "we just discussed this. If your good deeds are to be rewarded, that also means your misbehavior must be punished."

Her hand grazed Ember's sleeve, and Ember jerked away.

"Brenn was found guilty of assassination!" she exclaimed. "He evaded all forms of detection for months. Even if Analia had all the information she collected from Sun, it was my identification of xenol, its effects, and its reaction with wine that solidified the case. He would have escaped justice if it weren't for me, yet my crimes outweigh that?"

"Your pride outweighs that," Symonne snapped.

Ember's temper guttered.

"The pride that had you, an *apprentice* with only two rings at the time, work in secret instead of asking for help," Symonne went on, her rich brown fingers tapping her thigh for emphasis. "The pride that has you on this platform, raging about your successes to an audience that won't acknowledge them to the degree you want."

"Do you think I would risk my friend, my kingdom, for pride?" Ember asked. But her voice was growing weaker.

"No," Hollyn said. "But that's because we don't think you even considered that that pride could have created a risk."

Ember opened her mouth to argue, but Mellaine raised a hand.

"You are talented, Ember," she said. "But you are still an apprentice. You can't do everything by yourself."

If that were true, then why had everyone forced her to do so?

A lump rose in Ember's throat, and that terrified her most of all. She took a few slow steps back, her eyes moving from face to face.

"Is that all?" she asked, her voice fizzling out into something flat, empty. The last defense she had.

Hollyn touched her mouth, partially obscuring her frown. She nodded. Ember nodded back. Bowed to each healer in turn. Then, she turned and strode off the platform, back through the temple, forcing her mind to settle into the steady, even echo of her footsteps.

One step after the other. That was all she could do.

Ember pushed through the apothecary door. She barely remembered moving through the empty aisles, only aware that her knees didn't give out as she reached her back room.

She crossed to her devinroot box, pinching off a fuzzy orange leaf and bringing it to her nose. The sharp smell sent a wave of cold clarity through her mind. One that had her releasing a long breath as she sat at her desk.

She would figure this out. She always did. But that didn't stop her from putting her head down on her desk, barely muffling her sob as it finally broke free.

Chapter 6

T he morning of Analia's coronation dawned cold and cloudy.

Analia reached for another hair pin, half of her deep red hair already twisted in intricately coiled braids atop her head.

Usually, her maids would have taken care of such things. Ember, however, had marched into her chambers first thing in the morning, just in time to brazenly close the door in Lynette's and Mardie's faces.

When Analia had asked what Ember was doing, she replied, "Helping." That, however, only seemed to include lounging on Analia's bed and providing the occasional comment as Analia got herself ready.

She could tell something was off with the healer. Yet, whenever she asked, Ember quickly changed the subject.

"You missed a piece," Ember said, finally rolling to her feet and padding over. "Right in the back. Your hood's going to mess it up anyway, but at least you'll have the pins as evidence that you tried."

She plucked a pin from Analia's vanity and expertly slid it into place. "Perfect," she said, patting Analia's hair. "Beautiful as a queen."

Analia knew the words were supposed to be comforting. But they did nothing to assuage the dull, persistent ache in her chest that had started up the night before.

"Have I thanked you for last night?" she asked, eyes on her mirror.

Ember's reflected face softened. "That doesn't require a thank you."

Analia's gaze dropped to her phoenix pin, still resting on the vanity. "I need you to tell me I can do this," she said. "I just need to hear one person tell me I'm not making the biggest mistake of my life, because I don't think I can—"

"Anna." Ember nudged Analia around on her stool so they were facing one another. "This kingdom is lucky to have you as their queen. You risked your life to go to the Sun Kingdom to get their justice. You've fought for them with everything you have. There is not one thing you haven't given to this kingdom. This title is yours."

She *had* given everything. And they had taken it without a second thought. Taken until she had nothing left, and that still wasn't good enough for them.

"You are already their queen," Ember said. "This ceremony only makes it official. All you have to do is be introduced, summon some fire, recite a stuffy speech some councilman wrote Rosala knows how long ago, and then we can hide in my back room and play until our fingers bleed."

Ember squeezed Analia's shoulders. "Nothing will change, I promise."

That was what she was afraid of. But Analia forced a smile as she grabbed her phoenix pin. "Thank you."

Ember took the pin from Analia's fingers, attaching it to her dark gray robes for her. "You can do this," she said for a third time.

Analia nodded. But her pin felt as heavy as Pryanth's pendant in her pocket. She could do this—she *would* do this.

So then why were her lungs constricting? Why did Ember's words feel like a cold knife scraping down her spine, and why was the thrashing wind outside shrieking *wrong, wrong, wrong.*

It synced to her pulse as Cadmus entered—also in his dark gray robes—and offered his hand to her.

Wrong, wrong, wrong. It chased her through the darkness as Cadmus shadowjumped them to the foot of Mt. Vasolus, a crowd already formed at its base. It pounded through her blood, stirred her magic awake, built and built and built until she was choking back a scream.

Ember and Cadmus exchanged a look. Then, Cadmus guided Analia back into the shadows of a nearby building, blocking the crowd from view with his body.

"Everything will be all right, Anna," he told her, carefully pulling her hood over her hair. "You just have to breathe, and take it one step at a time. Can you do that?"

Analia squeezed her eyes shut. All she had to do was walk down the magically guarded aisle through the crowd to where the councilmen waited to introduce her. It was a part of the ceremony that only occurred when there was no body of the predecessor to burn. She could handle that.

But she couldn't make her feet move. All she could think about was how icy her people's disappointment would be.

But the music had begun. Cadmus gave her a quick hug, then nudged her forward. And Analia felt her feet move, the shrill cries of flutes and slinking rasp of strings taking up the chant. *Wrong, wrong, wrong.*

She wasn't a queen. Not to her people. Even with magic, she was a smudge on her kingdom's reputation; a collection of useless shards encased in skin and bone.

Still, the crowd tugged her forward with invisible hands, weighed down by expectations they knew would never be met. At the end of the aisle, the council watched her with tight expressions.

They didn't want a broken queen. A queen who had to have her younger brother shadowjump her to the top of the volcano because she couldn't do it herself.

It would be just another hand on her body. Deardryn's palm against her chest. Pryanth's arm across her throat. The Devourist pinning her, its mouth on her neck. Everyone touching her, trapping her, breaking her; jumping her to the top of the volcano where she would have to let the furious tirade of her magic loose, not knowing if she could reel it back in.

Analia reached for her bracelet, the silken petals sliding between her fingers.

She couldn't run. This was her duty. But that didn't stop her eyes from searching.

She just needed one friendly face. Someone to give her one Crystal-forsaken look of confidence she could hold on to.

But there was no one. No face that wasn't strained, ranging from uncertain to downright hostile.

Analia broke from the crowd.

A single voice hissed behind her, "Dud princess."

Analia froze.

Dud princess. That was all she was. All she'd ever be.

Ganze made an impatient gesture, saying something that was snatched away by the wind. But it was Ronun, standing on the edge of the crowd, that caught her eye.

The kingdom interrogator. Her uncle's top adviser. The man that, despite his stiff demeanor, had given her the tiny validation and honest counsel she had so desperately needed.

Now, staring into her eyes, he gave the smallest shake of his head.

Analia didn't think as she turned back to the crowd.

The music snapped to a halt.

The crowd shifted.

Analia raised her voice over the wind that flung back her hood and sent her robes swirling. "What are we doing?"

Silence.

Analia could feel the councilmen's gazes scorching through her robes, but she ignored them. Instead, she let the thoughts that sliced straight to her core at her aunt and cousin's grave finally tumble free.

"This is one of the most important moments for any kingdom. This is the moment that decides our future, and no one is happy with this direction. Not me, certainly not you."

Her eyes swept the crowd, unsurprised by the lack of objection. "A people need to have trust in their ruler, faith in their leadership. But I've never been able to garner that respect from you. First because of my lack of magic, and now because of what that magic has done.

"You deserve to be ruled by someone you respect, someone you trust. Not the person chosen for tradition's sake."

Analia turned. She finally took those last five paces toward the line of councilmen, just to lift the obsidian crown from the black velvet box Marie held in both hands. The crown was slick as blood, but she held firm as she moved to the side of the motionless crowd where Cadmus stood, his blue eyes wide.

"Cadmus should be your next ruler," she told them. "He's who you want. He's who you trust... who you love. So claim him."

Analia reached up, settling the curved crown atop her brother's head. It was only to him that she whispered, "Take care of them."

"Anna..."

"I am not your queen," Analia said, still looking at her brother. "I never have been, and I never will be. I'm sorry."

Analia touched the woven stems of her bracelet and thought a single word. Then, she turned.

She felt as though she were in a dream as she passed through the stunned crowd. No one moved to stop her, no one moved at all. Not until she made it to the edge. And with that first step outside their ranks, it was like a seal had been broken.

The crowd slammed into movement, voices clashing, colliding. And Analia ran.

Her feet pounded on the cobblestone streets, every loose stone stabbing through the thin soles of her slippers. What had she done? Crystal spare her, what had she done?

It didn't matter. There was no going back. No changing this. Not when the fear of what lay behind her had her flames leaping dangerously close to the surface. All she could do was run, faster and faster, through winding streets, around lines of stores, weaving through the statues of past rulers.

The Phoenix Gate finally came into view. Analia skidded to a stop, gripping the bars and doubling over as she tried to catch her breath.

Her eyes darted, the wind whipping her unraveling braids around her face. But nothing stirred around her.

Seconds, minutes ticked by. Analia looked up into the phoenix's dark eyes, her heart pounding against her ribs.

And she remained alone. Completely, utterly alone.

True, undiluted terror turned her body to ice.

It hadn't worked. The bracelet hadn't worked. She was trapped, nowhere to go, left to the kingdom's mercy.

Analia raised shaking hands to her face.

A slow, mocking clap sounded behind her. Analia whirled. And from across the street...

"Never a dull moment, Analia darling."

Chapter 7

I t took Analia a long moment to remember how to speak.

Aaron stood in the shadows of the alleyway across the street, looking as though he had been molded from the midnight sky.

The tan had faded from his skin. His jacket couldn't decide if it was black or midnight blue, the edges embroidered with silver threads. His fitted black pants were tucked into leather boots—which Analia would have bet her entire kingdom's fortune had daggers hidden inside.

He was an undisputed predator of night and shadow, his network singing the soft, lethal melody of nightmares.

Before Analia's flames could so much as flicker, he flashed a smile. "Miss me?"

Analia's shoulders relaxed. That wryness, combined with the messy dark brown hair and starlight eyes? That was all Aaron.

"How long were you watching?" she asked.

"Oh, not long." Aaron rocked back on his heels, his smile growing. "I only saw what came after you touched the bracelet, which mainly included a lot of running. Your endurance is astounding—"

"Why in the name of the Crystal didn't you stop me?"

"I wanted to see how far you could get."

"I hate you," Analia muttered.

Aaron's eyes sparkled. He put a dramatic hand to his chest, "Oh, Analia, how you hurt me. And after I came all this way when you called for me."

"You mean it actually worked?"

"That, or I have remarkable timing."

Analia snorted. She looked to her bracelet, then to the uneven road that separated them. She could feel the distance between them like a gash across skin, but neither of them moved to mend the gap.

"You're really here," she said, half to herself. Why couldn't she move?

"In the flesh," Aaron confirmed, spreading his arms. Not taking that step. "Although I almost wasn't. I tried to jump straight to the gate where I left you, but the wards didn't appreciate that—neither did I, by the way. I might as well have run face-first into a stone wall, and my big head doesn't protect against that. I ended up jumping to the volcano and following you back here."

"Why didn't you stop me?" Analia repeated, shifting on her feet.

Aaron's expression softened. "Because it looked like you needed to run it out," he said. "And who am I to tell you when to stop—"

Aaron's words cut off with a grunt as Analia barreled into him. He stumbled back a step, his arms immediately wrapping around her and pulling her close.

"Now that was the reception I was looking for!" he laughed.

Analia rolled her eyes, not caring he couldn't see. She could feel the slick, gliding melody of his network across her senses, blocking out the distant echoes of voices—cheering? She didn't care. Not as she inhaled metal and spice and finally felt her flames settle inside her.

There were so many things she had to tell him. Yet, as she opened her mouth, only one word came out. "Hi."

Aaron chuckled. He brought his mouth close to her ear, his voice like velvet across her skin. "Hello, Analia."

Analia pulled back to look at him. Aaron quickly released her, that same soft smile he had given her the last time she'd seen him touching his mouth. His Phoenix Gate smile.

"I see you dressed for the occasion," she commented, her eyes moving along the embroidered threads of his jacket.

"Only the finest for your coronation," he said. "Although I take it that didn't go as planned?"

"You could say that."

Aaron noted her fingers toying with her pin. Then, he turned to sit on a nearby bench, "You want to talk about it?"

"There's not much to explain," Analia sighed, moving to sit beside him. "My taking the crown would have only ended in disaster. And even though everyone knew that, me saying no created its own disaster."

"That's usually how things go."

"I suppose." Analia drew the toe of her slipper through the gravel. "I was barely able to show my face in the kingdom. Now, I won't be able to so much as walk the castle halls without being ridiculed for disrupting tradition, creating chaos, whatever else they'd like to hurl at me."

Analia's mind flashed to the marble wings, and her throat tightened.

"So you called me," Aaron said, oddly distant, "as a fail-safe?"

Analia shoved his shoulder. "I called you, smartass, because I thought you would know what to do. Even if that meant talking me into going back to that Crystal-forsaken volcano."

"Because I always have an opinion?"

"And they're usually right," Analia sighed. "Annoyingly so."

Aaron laughed under his breath, the slight tension leaving his shoulders. "It seems to me," he said, leaning back against the bench, "you already made your choice. Now, you're just trying to figure out how to live with it."

"I have no idea how," Analia admitted.

The voices from the coronation still echoed in the distance—were they coming closer?

Analia's hand found her dagger hilt. Whatever happened at Mt. Vasolus was over. They were all on their way back, furious that she'd not only escaped the corner they'd shoved her in, but that she'd found her own way out.

"I never wanted this," she blurted. "I know I could be a good queen, but I don't care if I have the title or not. None of that matters when Deardryn is still on the loose, and that title gets me no closer to stopping her."

The Ash Royals would shadowjump back to the castle in a matter of seconds. Aaron would have to leave. She was on her own—always alone.

"You could come with me," Aaron said, so quiet Analia almost didn't hear.

"I what?"

"You would never be able to tell anyone what you saw," he said carefully. "You might not be able to leave, in order to protect that secret. But if your goal is uncovering Deardryn's plans, I will help you."

Tingles ran down Analia's spine. "You will?"

"I will. So if that's what you want, come with me."

Aaron's offer seemed to solidify each time he made it. Now, he offered his hand, his silver eyes intent as they locked on hers.

Analia hesitated. Could she truly leave behind her kingdom, her uncle's kingdom, and never look back? Could she abandon them over a little adversity?

Footsteps sounded on the other end of the street. Analia's flames roared.

"Go!" she hissed, her head whipping back toward Aaron.

Aaron didn't hesitate. He melted into the darkness, his hand still outstretched to her. Analia's heart pounded in her ears.

"Of course it's you again."

Aaron froze midjump. Then, he solidified once more, a dazzling grin splitting his face.

"Careful, Ember," he purred. "You keep that up, and I might start to think you actually like me."

Ember tossed her hair, coming to sit on Analia's other side. "I think you like yourself enough for the both of us."

Aaron laughed. Ember reached across Analia to playfully ruffle his hair. But Analia couldn't move.

That panic, just at the sound of footsteps, was like being back in Sun. Constantly looking over her shoulder. Never safe, always on guard.

Crystal spare her, she couldn't go back to that. Especially not as Ember explained how Cadmus had ascended Mt. Vasolus. How he was crowned king. How the council was furious with her. Everyone hated her, rejected her, trapped her.

"Here," Analia said, interrupting Ember's recount. She slid the enka flower bracelet from her wrist, pressing it into Ember's hand. "If you need me—if you need us—use the bracelet."

"Anna," Ember said, eyes bouncing between her, Aaron, and the bracelet, "what are you—"

"I'm leaving," Analia said. She could have sworn Aaron sucked in a breath behind her. "I can't stay here, Ember. Not when the council refuses to act. Not when…"

The words were a bitter clog in her throat, but Ember nodded in understanding. And Analia felt a momentary swell of love through the turmoil as Ember didn't try to change her mind. She only asked, "What do I tell everyone?"

Analia hadn't thought that far. She looked to Aaron, her eyes wide.

"You tell them she left," he said. "She left of her own free will, forfeiting her Ash Kingdom citizenship and swearing on the Crystal and the gods she would reveal no kingdom secrets, nor swear fealty to any of the six kingdoms."

"An outlaw," Analia breathed.

They weren't unheard of. Most lived a solitary, nomadic life, drifting from kingdom to kingdom, taking up jobs as beggars, mercenaries, and the like.

"They'll try to hunt you down," Ember warned.

"No, they won't," Analia said. "Not with that oath. The only person who would try is Cadmus, and the council would fight him for the resources."

Ember dropped her gaze, unable to deny it.

"You can still change your mind," said Aaron softly.

Analia looked to Ember, her heart squeezing at the thought of leaving her. But Ember would be fine, she had a new friend. Perhaps a better friend. And Analia had instincts that screamed *Go, go, go.*

"I'm coming," she said.

Aaron didn't look satisfied like she'd anticipated. Instead, his eyes dimmed as Ember pulled Analia into a hug of farewell, Analia keeping a careful leash on her flames. She told Ember only Cadmus could know the truth, and Ember nodded, squeezing Analia tighter.

Finally, Analia pulled away. She pretended not to see the tears Ember blinked back, her own heart crumbling even more.

"I'm sorry," Ember whispered. Not for anything she'd done, but for everything else.

Analia opened her mouth, but no words came out. Ember gave her a watery smile, then made a shooing gesture.

Aaron took Analia's hand, and her eye twitched. He immediately started to let go, but Analia tightened her grip. Then, with a final farewell to Ember, not knowing if she would ever see her friend again, she nodded to Aaron. And only hesitating a moment, he pulled them into the shadows.

As the Ash Kingdom faded around her for the final time, a tiny sob rose in Analia's throat. Not for her home, but the home she could have had. The kingdom that held the last echoes of her uncle.

But Analia didn't loosen her grip on Aaron's hand.

For a long time, they remained in the cold, empty darkness of the shadows. Longer than she expected.

Eventually, there came a bump, like a carriage wheel rolling over a pothole.

Then, the darkness seemed to thicken. It congealed around her like old, clotted blood, trying to stop her, consume her.

Analia's flames swirled. Aaron pulled her closer, snarling something under his breath.

And abruptly, they were through. They rocketed forward, stumbling out of the darkness and back into the world.

Analia quickly regained her footing, her flames on high alert as she glanced around. But she was only in a bedroom.

The walls were lined with dark wood paneling. Across from her stood an ornate wardrobe and set of drawers, each glinting with silver detailing. A matching side table sat beside a large bed covered in dark blue bedding, the headboard carved with twining lilies. Off to the side, an open door led into a stone-tile bathing room.

Aaron released her hand. He sank down on the bed, groaning softly as he buried his face in his hands.

"Are you all right?" Analia asked, moving to kneel beside him.

"Fine," Aaron said. "Stupid, but fine."

"What happened?"

"I decided to shadowjump all the way across Elefthia, then immediately jump back with a passenger."

All the way across Elefthia? Where in the name of the Crystal were they? Regardless, "Stupid," Analia agreed.

"Stupid indeed."

Analia shook her head, but she couldn't stifle a rising sense of awe. She didn't think any other Royal could have done that—maybe not even Accalon. How much power did Aaron have?

Analia's eyes moved around the room once more. Aaron looked up, starting to speak, but he immediately cut off as Analia stiffened. For her eyes had finally made it to the window across from the bed. And the kingdom that lay beyond it.

Chapter 8

Analia's entire being went numb. She didn't remember rising to her feet, crossing to the window, pushing aside the thin silver curtains.

Beyond a simple wooden gate, smooth stone streets wound between what looked like countless civilian homes, decorated with bright, glittering accents. A scattering of people moved about their days, the majority of the crowd farther out where the tasteful homes were replaced with tall, sleek buildings.

Numerous people passed between walls that Analia could have sworn were coated in graffiti. Paused to talk on the steps of—was that a music hall? It was too far off to tell, beyond a river with a gleaming white bridge spanning across it.

"That's Pearl Bridge," Aaron said, his voice tight as he came up behind her. "There are a cluster of rivers that branch off the lake to the northwest, and we designated a special bridge to each created sector.

"That one's called the Mirage. Theater, music, art, dancing."

"What is this place," Analia breathed. She didn't dare tear her gaze from the window, didn't dare move at all.

"This is my home," Aaron said softly. "This is the Starlight Kingdom."

Every thought faded from Analia's mind.

"Anna?" Aaron asked uneasily.

Analia's grip tightened on the windowsill. Aaron's hand grazed her back. And Analia's flames erupted.

Aaron swore. He snatched his hand back, stepping away from the black fire that flickered across Analia's skin.

"Anna," he said carefully, "I know it's a lot—"

Analia took a step back. Then another and another, retreating until she could sit on the bed, barely having the presence of mind to not burn the fabric.

What had she done? Crystal spare her, what had she done?

"Anna—Anna, breathe."

She'd become so good at looking over her shoulder. But she'd dropped her guard around Aaron, who hoarded secrets like an assassin hoarded blades.

Aaron pulled the curtains shut. He stepped directly into her line of sight, silver eyes demanding. "Analia. Breathe."

Analia sucked in a deep breath, tears burning behind her eyes. But the fire licked them away, licked away every thought that wailed she was trapped again. She had abandoned her kingdom. Her *uncle's kingdom.* Her *uncle.*

"You need to start explaining," she ground out. "Now."

Aaron didn't so much as flinch. But he couldn't hide his exhaustion as he sat on a dark blue settee tucked in the corner, his hand dragging through his hair.

"This kingdom was established long before the Shattering," he began. "A secret project of Talitha's. When the Star Kingdom was destroyed, the survivors came here."

Analia's flames curled around her shoulders, their heat bringing a flush to her cheeks. "And you couldn't have warned me?"

Aaron looked away.

"I was expecting some random clan you had assimilated into or a band of outlaws—"

Aaron's head whipped back toward her, "Because all Star Royals are savages, right?"

"Because I never know with you! Every time I think I know everything, you clobber me with another secret out of nowhere!"

"I couldn't tell you this!" Aaron exclaimed, silver light flickering around him. "This isn't about you, Analia. This is about my people. No matter how much I trust you, I couldn't risk them."

"Your people, who have been hidden here for centuries. And you haven't told anyone?"

"How could I?" Aaron demanded. "You've heard the legends, how we've been painted. If we told anyone we still existed back then, they would have come here and destroyed us. And the longer we waited for things to calm down, the less we could reappear. We would've been seen as a threat—as you're so excellently demonstrating, by the way. It would mean war all over again."

"And yet," Analia said, "that didn't stop you from insisting I come with you. Are you simply incapable of sharing your secrets, or were you just hoping they would trap me, too?"

"'Trap you'?" Aaron thudded back against the settee, disbelieving.

"I can't exactly leave now."

"You agreed to come!"

Analia's magic flared. Before she could speak, Aaron gave a sharp jerk of his head.

He took a long, steadying breath. Then, with a display of supreme control over his magic, the silver light winked out.

"I told you the parameters around coming here," he said, remarkably calm once more. "You said yes. You took my hand. I'm not keeping—you are not trapped here. And if you truly want to leave, I will take you back."

Aaron waited. But all Analia heard was the tiny voice in her mind, wondering what she had done.

The fight seemed to drain out of Aaron's body. Slowly, he rose from the settee, heading for the door. Yet, his hand lingered on the doorknob.

"This is your room for as long as you want it," he said. "The hatch that leads to the roof is down the hall on the ceiling."

Aaron cast her one last searching look, clearly looking for a reason to stay. One Analia desperately wanted to give him.

But fear from her past clamped icy shackles to her wrists, forced a frozen bit between her lips. And it stomped her already burning, crumbling soul into a few more pieces as Aaron finally slipped out.

Analia didn't move at the sound of a commotion on the other side of the door. She dully noted male voices, one louder than the other, abruptly cut off by a series of thuds as if he'd been pushed down a set of stairs.

Gods, just add whoever they were to the list of people who thought she was a monster.

The thought had the last of her flames winking out. She dragged herself off the bed, her feet seeming to carry her into the bathing room of their own accord.

The geometric tiles were pleasantly cool through her slippers. Dark stone counters and shelves were stocked with towels and a collection of soap bottles, as if this room had been waiting for her.

Analia tore off her robes, kicked off her slippers, suddenly unable to stand the feeling of the stiff fabric against her skin. She stepped into the deep tub that had started filling on its own, grabbing a bottle of jasmine-scented soap and scrubbing it into her hair.

She understood why Aaron had to keep this kingdom a secret. But holy Crystal above, if he could keep an entire kingdom hidden for centuries, what couldn't he hide?

She knew he would never purposefully hurt her. But then again, did she? There was a time she would have made the same excuses for Brenn, Pryanth, Deardryn. All of them had started out perfectly kind, just so they could tear her down into nothing.

Every. Single. Time.

Yet, knowing all of this, she still found herself wanting to trust Aaron. But with her history, could she trust that cycle wouldn't turn again? Could she trust her own instincts? Crystal spare her, what had she done?

Analia eventually hauled herself out of the tub, wrapping herself in a fluffy white towel. She didn't bother combing out her hair, didn't bother checking to see if there were any clothes inside the wardrobe—knowing Aaron, there certainly were. She simply crawled into bed, her eyes drifting to the still-covered window. Aaron's home.

Analia pressed her face into her pillow. And she didn't try to stop her sobs.

Chapter 9

Aaron sat at his dining room table, nursing a mug of tea and praying to the Crystal his head would stop pounding.

After the utter disaster that was the day before, he'd left Analia's room to find his brothers lurking outside the door. Branten wasn't a surprise—just as it wasn't a surprise when Aaron shoved him down the stairs for eavesdropping. Mor, though?

Aaron hadn't bought for one second Branten had dragged him along. But that didn't stop him from accepting Mor's invitation to train and drink the whiplash away.

He just didn't understand what had happened with Analia. He knew the kingdom would be a surprise, even a shock. But how had she gone from hugging him tight enough he could barely breathe to looking at him like he might slit her throat?

Aaron shoved the thoughts aside at the sound of approaching footsteps. He glanced up, barely able to keep his expression smooth as Analia paused in the doorway.

He'd already noticed the hollows beneath her cheekbones. He'd thought she felt skinnier when he hugged her, but now he would have bet he could count every rib under her silky blue shirt. A blue that brought out the varying shades of gray in her eyes, almost enough to distract him from the shadows that lay beneath them, but not quite.

Gods, what had happened to her?

"You found me," he said pleasantly.

Analia's wary gaze moved from the table laden with fruit, toast, and eggs to the windowsill filled with enka flowers. "Where's everyone else?" she asked.

"I told them to stay away for now. Give you a chance to get your bearings before releasing that particular shitstorm."

Analia nodded, her shoulders relaxing slightly.

"You can sit," Aaron invited, gesturing with his mug to the five empty chairs. "There are no traps on the seats. They were all on the stairs, so you seem to have evaded them."

Analia snorted. Aaron offered her a smile, holding his breath. Finally, she crossed the threshold, easing into the seat across from him.

"I'm assuming," she said, "since all the traps were on the stairs, you haven't poisoned the food?"

Aaron speared a melon ball with his fork and popped it in his mouth. His alcohol-soaked stomach roiled, but he swallowed and spread his arms wide.

Analia's lips twitched. Aaron perked up, but she quickly schooled her expression and took a single piece of toast.

"You can have more than that," he said.

"I'm not that hungry."

"Is that why I could count your ribs?"

Analia's head snapped up, "You cannot."

"Really?" Aaron drawled, leaning back in his seat. "Want to take off your shirt and prove it?"

Analia's eyes flashed. Aaron gave her a lazy, mocking grin.

Come on, erupt. Show him that fire.

Analia quickly forced her temper back down, that careful control sliding back into place. And Aaron fought the urge to demand where in the name of the Crystal his friend had gone.

He took a long sip of tea, placing the mug back on the table a bit harder than necessary. They both looked up at the thunk, their eyes locking.

Aaron could see his own frustration reflected in her eyes. But beneath that, there was no mistaking the fear. The fear of a woman who had fled her coronation, desperate enough to take the first out she was given.

A slow, heavy wave of disappointment rolled through Aaron's chest. He raised his hands in surrender, his heart aching as Analia returned to her toast.

Silence.

"I'm assuming," Aaron finally said, "you have questions for me."

"Will you actually answer them?"

Aaron fought back a wince. He deserved that one. Him and his "clobbering secrets." Especially with how many remained.

"I suppose," he said slowly, "you'll have to ask and find out."

Analia considered. "Where are we exactly?"

"The Wild Lands. It's true a large portion is saturated with the Ancient Ones' magic, but we're in one of the untouched pockets."

Analia nodded, not looking terribly surprised. She nibbled her toast. "Will you tell me the full story?"

Aaron didn't have to ask which one. He ran a hand through his hair, his throat tightening around the words. But she deserved to know this story, he'd known he would have to tell it the moment he offered her his hand back in Ash. Nevertheless, it took Aaron a moment to finally pry the words free.

"This kingdom was first established at the end of the Blessed-Human Civil War. Your history has you believe the Blessed conquered the humans and were kind enough to sign a treaty of human rights. What Talitha made sure to scrub out is the fact that the only reason that war came to an end was because she and the major players on the human side came to an agreement. In addition to said rights for all humans, Talitha also gifted a select group a portion of the secret, untainted section of the Wild Lands. Completely secure, hidden, and free from all Blessed rule. They just had to tolerate a secret base for her own kingdom nearby."

Aaron spooned eggs onto Analia's plate. "This safe haven has existed all throughout history, hidden from prying eyes. So, when the Shattering War began, my father took no chances. He quickly—but inconspicuously—started shepherding people to this kingdom.

"He wasn't planning for a permanent displacement. He was just trying to save as many lives as he could... especially after what happened to my siblings."

Aaron's grip momentarily tightened on his fork, but his voice remained steady. "My father found out about the other Royals' plan to attack the castle an hour before it happened. He used every last drop of magic he had to shadowjump as many castle occupants here as he could. He had no chance of escaping when that blast finally came, but his bone fragments were the only ones to be found because he saved everyone else."

"But if he'd already gotten everyone out, why did he go back?" Analia asked.

"My mom thought he wanted to make sure he'd really gotten everyone. But most of us believe he sacrificed himself to cover his tracks, that he hoped if the Royals found his remains, they would have no reason to suspect they'd failed and start looking for us."

"And you've been here ever since?" Analia asked.

"And we've been here ever since," Aaron confirmed, not breaking her stare.

The story was far from over. A fact that, judging by the tilt of Analia's head, she was all too aware of. But there were no flames in sight as she asked, "How has no one found this place?"

Aaron's muscles slowly relaxed. "Wards," he said, spearing another melon ball with his fork. "To any outsider, it appears as a random rocky cliff face: no place to disembark, no civilization. And the wards are tied to the Star Royal bloodline. As long as there's one of us alive, the wards hold."

"Just like the wards around the Ash Castle," Analia mused.

"Indeed. Although," he added, half to himself, "I'm curious as to how my wards affected you with your sensory abilities. You can still sense, can't you?"

Analia's hand flew beneath the table, undoubtedly clenching around her dagger—the dagger he gave her.

"It was just a question, Anna," Aaron said, a bit sharper than he intended.

Analia's eyes flashed. Aaron's magic roiled. And Analia looked away.

There came a long, tense pause.

"Yes," she finally mumbled. "I can still sense the different magics."

"Well, all right, then."

Silence.

Aaron was contemplating ripping his own hair out when Analia paused, forkful of eggs halfway to her mouth. She stared down at her fork, then her half-empty plate, then accusingly at Aaron.

Aaron didn't think he could take another round, but he gave her an innocent smile.

"When did you do that?" Analia asked.

Aaron shrugged. And his heart nearly stuttered to a stop as she rolled her eyes, something like amusement flashing across her face.

"Is this what it feels like to be mothered?" she asked.

"Grandmothered, actually. When I was small, Ethelind would do that to me whenever I was pouting and claimed I wasn't hungry."

"I wasn't pouting," Analia whined.

"No," Aaron said. "You were anxiously protesting."

Analia scoffed, but she ate another forkful without complaint.

Finally, the tension seemed to slacken. Not completely. Just enough for Aaron to feel like he could actually fill his lungs.

"I know it's a lot to take in," he said quietly. "But this isn't a place you need to run from, Anna. Give it a chance. You might just come to love it here as much as we do."

Analia nodded mutely. Aaron had to fight not to sag in his seat. Instead, he pushed to his feet, heading for the front door.

"I need to be going," he said over his shoulder. "I have a council meeting to try and stay awake through."

"What am I to do, then?" Analia asked.

"Whatever you wish." Aaron turned to look at her fully. "This place is not a prison."

It was everything he wished he'd said the night before. Now, with tempers cooled, the sentiment finally seemed to sink in as Analia bowed her head. "I know."

Aaron offered one last hopeful smile. Then, he passed out of the dining room, through the entryway, and finally out the door.

Aaron slumped back against the exterior of his house. That was certainly progress. But if this was how Analia reacted after seeing the kingdom, then how in the name of the Crystal would she react after seeing Surce's tapestries?

A gentle breeze ruffled his hair, the sound of laughing children echoing in the distance.

One step at a time. That was all he could do. But as Aaron faded into the shadows, he couldn't stop himself from wondering if this had been a mistake.

Chapter 10

Prison was not what Dimitri was expecting. Yes, it was cold, dark, and stank of human waste. But the worst part was the boredom.

At first, he entertained himself with his poetry collection that the guards hadn't bothered to take. Then, he practiced his writing in the dirt on the ground with his finger.

After about thirty minutes, Dimitri was over it.

In the following days, he tried to engage the chainmail-clad guards when they dropped off his meals, but they didn't so much as look at him. It reached the point he was actually grateful when the green-eyed man finally came to his cell.

Now, Dimitri sat in a small Council Chamber, having been washed, scrubbed, and dressed in a simple deep green doublet and pants. The two men from the sitting room faced him across the table, Dimitri having learned the green-eyed man was King Sylas's husband, Patryclas, and nothing more.

He figured their smothering silence was supposed to be intimidating, perhaps a pointed indication he should speak. But Dimitri's mouth had gone completely dry.

He was no Royal. He didn't know how to play this political game, especially now that Deardryn was involved.

"I think," Patryclas finally said, "a good place to start is your name."

The last thing he needed was Deardryn hearing his name around the castle—especially if she hadn't spotted him in the hallway. Not to mention Sylas's bored, unimpressed look was far too familiar not to sting.

But Analia needed him.

"Dimitri," he said, warily drawing out the syllables.

"And your last name?" Patryclas asked.

"Don't know."

Sylas asked, "How do you not know your own name?"

"How do you let foreign Royals into your castle?" Dimitri shot back.

He expected a retort. But Sylas only reached for his wine glass with a tattooed hand, his black eyes scrutinizing Dimitri with unnerving consideration.

"You saw me speak with Deardryn," he said. A statement, not a question. "And more interestingly, you recognized her as the Sun Queen."

Dimitri's hands tightened around the edge of his seat. Patryclas shot Sylas a puzzled look. Sylas, however, only had eyes for Dimitri.

"You, a nameless boy from Sun, come with a message from Princess Analia Valarus of Ash. How does this come to be?"

Dimitri should have been relieved. If Sylas hadn't spotted him that day, it was unlikely Deardryn had. But Dimitri still couldn't help but squirm as he said, "You've already spoken with her. I'm sure she told you everything."

"Why do you think Queen Deardryn would say anything involving you?" Patryclas asked.

"Why don't you look surprised I think she would?"

The faintest smile flickered across Patryclas's lips. Sylas remained inscrutable.

"So," Dimitri said. "What'd she tell you?"

"I thought you were the one with a message for me," said Sylas.

"I am. But if it has to do with the Old Hag, and you're suddenly having late-night castle talks with her, I'd rather keep my head attached to my body."

"Clever," Patryclas murmured, resting his finger across his lips. Sylas, however, only took a long sip of wine.

Gods, what was the Moon King thinking? Dimitri tried to read his expression, but all he saw was the faint contraction of his thick brows.

Finally, Sylas said, "Deardryn told me she learned Patryclas was poisoned with xenol at our last Solstice Ceremony."

Patryclas shot him a quick look.

"Apparently, it is an ancient plant only grown in my territory, with information being so scarce she could only find a damaged page of research in her library. Between that and the Royal deaths, she fears this could be a sign of someone targeting the kingdoms, and has requested to use my resources to expand her research."

That was it? Where were the accusations against Analia? The attempts to discredit her story before it could reach Moon?

Dimitri looked between the kings, but Patryclas's green eyes were firmly fixed on the loose thread he'd discovered in his dark red sleeve.

He had to be missing something. Regardless, he wouldn't let the Old Hag snag an ally, even if it was just through research.

"Now, I believe you had a message for me?" Sylas said, twirling his goblet between his fingers.

"Oh, I have a message," said Dimitri.

Then, he told them everything: Deardryn summoning the Devourists, her Royal magic rings, how she poisoned Patryclas to earn their trust and then killed her own nephew to evade suspicion. He was careful to avoid revealing his bastard bloodline, Analia's magic, and Aaron's identity.

"That's what really happened," he finished, gripping the edge of the table and leaning forward.

He didn't know what reaction he was expecting. But Sylas only tilted his head at Patryclas. Patryclas rubbed his knuckles across his forehead, then gave a shallow nod.

"Interesting," Sylas murmured.

"I thought something seemed peculiar about Deardryn's peace marriage," Patryclas said. "The emotions between Analia and Pryanth felt too... bitter. But then with the guard..."

"Aaron," Dimitri supplied.

Patryclas nodded thoughtfully. "I thought I was misreading. But there was no mistaking when I looked at him after I was poisoned."

"Trust me," Dimitri said, "it was obvious to everyone even without an empathy Blessing. The only person that didn't notice was Analia."

Patryclas's eyes sparkled.

"If I had known we'd be gossiping," Sylas muttered into his goblet, "I would have suggested we meet out by the boardwalk with the schoolgirls."

"Don't mind him," Patryclas said conspiratorially. "He's just disgruntled because he's the last to find out about all of this."

"As lovely as it is that you two are bonding," Sylas said loudly.

Dimitri realized he'd been smiling at Patryclas and quickly straightened his expression. He turned to Sylas, "So, what are you going to do?"

"Nothing."

Dimitri almost fell out of his chair. "Did you not hear me say she tried to kill Patryclas?"

"I did." Sylas stretched. "A no-name boy from Sun comes with news from Princess Analia, who has poked the Dragoness and fled. Yet that very Dragoness tells me a different story."

"So, you're going to believe her?" Dimitri demanded.

"No."

"And you won't believe me?"

"No." Sylas reached across the table to take Dimitri's untouched wine. "I grew tired of political theater over sixty years ago."

Patryclas coughed into his fist.

Sylas frowned. "You don't believe me?"

"Of course I do," Patryclas said immediately. "I was just thinking you've only been king for twenty."

"Exactly." Sylas downed his stolen wine, missing the wink Patryclas gave an unamused Dimitri. "I have one person telling me one story, and another telling me the complete opposite. So, I'm going to wait until I have more information."

"And you're going to let him?" Dimitri asked Patryclas. "You're going to let the queen who tried to kill you wander about your kingdom without saying anything."

Patryclas took a breath, then glanced to Sylas. The Moon King narrowed his eyes in challenge, Patryclas shaking his head in frustration. But Dimitri was well beyond that.

"So that's it?" he demanded, shoving to his feet. "You're going to sit and do nothing like a gods-damned coward—"

A column of shadows slammed into Dimitri's chest. He flipped over his chair, sliding across the floor and slamming into the wall with a mind-rattling thud.

"I could have your tongue for saying that," Sylas said contemplatively.

Dimitri gagged as shadows crawled down his throat, thick and cold and consuming. He could feel the panic rise inside him. The same panic that had burst forth in Gritta's all those years ago—no. Not again. Dimitri desperately choked it back, struggling to speak.

"Dimitri," Patryclas said, his hand on Sylas's arm. "What are you trying to accomplish?"

"For you to do something about Deardryn!" Dimitri spluttered, shadows writhing across his tongue.

"And how is what you're doing helping?"

Dimitri cringed. There was nothing he could say to that. And Analia, the one person that believed in him, would pay the price.

Still, he could barely force out his words. "It's not."

"And what do you think will?" Patryclas prompted.

Dimitri bit back a mumbled list of complaints. He turned his aching head toward Sylas, who peeled the shadows back from Dimitri's mouth expectantly. "I'm sorry I called you a coward."

Sylas smirked.

Dimitri muttered, "Even though you are."

"Dimitri," Patryclas warned.

"Fine, I'm sorry!" Dimitri threw up his hands. "I was just... angry because Deardryn keeps getting away with hurting and manipulating people. Can I get up now?"

Sylas considered. Patryclas squeezed his arm and gave Dimitri an approving nod. Dimitri wanted to crawl under the table and die.

"I never said I would do nothing," Sylas said, shadows creeping back across the floor. "I have two stories, each with its own threat. The smartest option is to allow Deardryn to come to my kingdom and do her research. While she's here, I can find out which story is true."

"It's the most strategic option," Patryclas agreed.

Dimitri pushed himself into a sitting position, ready to argue. Patryclas's cautioning gaze locked on his.

For a moment, Dimitri wavered. Finally, he let his protest bubble back down.

Sylas was going to do something. They had a plan. That was all he could ask for. And as Sylas and Patryclas continued talking, Dimitri settled into something like relief.

It sank into his muscles as he picked himself off the floor, Sylas jerking his head in a dismissal. He even remembered to bow at the last moment before slipping out the door, letting it thunk shut behind him.

"So, you survived after all," Tavian said from where he lounged against the opposing wall.

"I know," Dimitri said. "It's almost like you were supposed to let me speak with them."

Tavian flipped him a rude hand gesture. Dimitri didn't even care as Tavian shoved off the wall, ordering him to follow.

He'd done it. He was actually free now.

He'd dreamed of escaping the Sun Castle for so long, a part of him had started to believe it would never happen. But here he was. And once again, he found himself not knowing where to go.

"Dimitri!"

Dimitri glanced back as Patryclas hurried after him. "Would you like to scold me some more?" he asked.

Patryclas reached his side. He waved away Tavian, who sauntered off without protest.

"Incredible," Patryclas murmured. "You're drowning in despair, and yet you keep fighting."

"I'm not despairing," Dimitri snapped.

"No?" Patryclas cocked his head. "What would you say you are, then?"

Furious.

Dimitri continued down the hall without comment. Maybe he could find an inn for the night...

"Stay here, Dimitri."

Dimitri choked on a laugh. "Why would I do that?"

"Because you're a foreigner in this kingdom. The moment you step outside the castle gates, the Moon guard has every right to track you down and relocate you back to Sun."

"They wouldn't bother. Plenty of people drift between kingdoms, there's no law saying we can't."

"None of them could spread such a dangerous tale."

"Fine," Dimitri said, "I'll keep my mouth shut. Happy?"

Patryclas put a hand on Dimitri's arm. Dimitri jumped so hard his shoulder knocked into a picture frame. Patryclas quickly removed his hand, a faint line forming between his brows.

"What do you want, Dimitri?" he asked. It wasn't a rebuke, but a genuine question. One that sent a different kind of jolt down Dimitri's spine.

"I don't know." He turned dismissively, finally stepping into the entryway.

"Maybe you should find out," Patryclas suggested, still following. "And in the meantime, you could stay here. Work in the castle—"

"I'm not a fucking servant."

"No," Patryclas said, unflinching. "You don't have the temperament for that, do you? Is that why you don't know what you want?"

Dimitri's hands clenched around the slick rim of the fountain. He knew he should shrug off the offer. Even as he was painfully aware staying was the only option he had.

After all, he was running out of gold. And only an idiot would choose a rickety inn bed over a castle mattress. Besides, he had to make sure Sylas kept his word.

"Fine," Dimitri said, eyes on the water. "I'll stay. But I work in the library, not as a gods-damned servant."

Patryclas leaned against the fountain beside him. "You must believe yourself to have a great deal of power if you can demand your position."

"I'm important enough for you to come after me and try to convince me to stay."

The corner of Patryclas's mouth lifted. "I'll make a deal with you," he said. "If you can prove to me you are a loyal subject in the next three months, I will grant you citizenship and the freedom to do what you please in my kingdom."

"What's the catch?"

"By the end of those months, you must tell me what you want to do with that freedom."

Dimitri's skin prickled. Yet, he couldn't see any harm in agreeing to Patryclas's request.

"Fine," he said.

"Give me your palm."

Dimitri warily did as ordered. Patryclas unsheathed a dagger from his belt, the leather hilt decorated with a pale crescent moon, the blade slender and curved.

"Hey!" Dimitri jerked his hand back. "I said you could have my hand, not stab a hole through its center."

"This is how we make oaths in my kingdom," Patryclas explained.

"By skewering people?"

"You don't need to be afraid, Dimitri."

"Stop telling me what I feel!"

Patryclas smiled to himself. "These blades are called scarsworn daggers." He drew the tip across the palm of his hand, which was decorated with thin white scars. "They are only created in the Moon Kingdom forges. The Blessed workers enchant the blades with their binding magic, and it's activated by the blood of each swearer."

He pressed the flat of the tip against the well of blood in his palm, then curled his fingers beckoningly. Dimitri glanced over his shoulder, past the softly burbling fountain to the castle doors. Then, he warily extended his hand.

Patryclas drew the flat edge of the blade in a swirl on the inside of Dimitri's wrist. Immediately, there came a flurry of tingles, Dimitri's eyes widening as the blood sank into his skin and turned into a deep purple heart.

"The mark will turn black once the promise is fulfilled," Patryclas said.

"It doesn't go away?"

"I'm afraid not."

Dimitri's mind flashed back to all the tattoos he'd seen throughout the kingdom. Interesting.

"Your turn," Patryclas said, offering Dimitri the blade, hilt first.

Dimitri didn't hesitate. He slashed his palm, barely feeling the sting as he collected the blood and snatched Patryclas's hand. Swirling the blood on Patryclas's wrist, he watched as the smear shifted into a purple outline of a sun with radiating beams. Dimitri quickly looked away.

"Welcome to the Moon Kingdom," Patryclas said.

Dimitri scoffed, shoving the blade back in Patryclas's hand. "I want my bracelet back."

Chapter 11

Analia remained in Aaron's house for a week. She knew she could leave and explore the kingdom—Aaron had practically invited her to do so. But that offer indicated a degree of trust she flinched away from, even as his words echoed through her mind.

This place is not a prison.

The house was built from dark, polished wood. Thick blue carpet covered the second-floor hall, numerous bedroom doors lining either side. On the first level was the dining room, kitchen, and arched entryway. But the main attraction was the sitting room: dark couches and armchairs; a low, sleek table; massive stuffed bookcases separated by a black marble fireplace.

In an adjoining side room, Analia discovered an old, dusty harp, its tuning hammer discarded on a nearby stool. Then, she played. She poured her heartbreak, loneliness, fury into every song, her mind turning over every decision she could've made that final day in Ash.

She knew she couldn't have ascended the volcano. Ruling over a people that resented her would've ended in disaster, just as staying would've resulted in the council or Cadmus forcing her to take the crown. As much as it killed her to admit, both she and Cadmus could take care of Accalon's kingdom, but only Cadmus could make them happy.

She'd had to leave.

This place is not a prison.

Aaron was quick to pick up on her patterns—especially after he accidentally snuck up on her and she almost torched him with midnight flames. He easily batted her magic aside, looking more intrigued than anything.

"Let me know if you want company," he said, turning to go. "Even if it's the silent variety."

While Analia never called on him, Aaron made it a point to return from his kingly duties to nudge her into the dining room at every meal. He never failed to talk and smile as if nothing had changed between them, even as Analia could barely force herself to respond. His only expectation was she clear her plate, and then she could return to her harp without protest.

This place is not a prison. But her mind was starting to feel like one as she ran through scenario after scenario.

By the early hours of the seventh day, Analia decided there had only been two options: go with Aaron, or remain in the Ash Kingdom.

There was no one left to protect her in Ash. She had no chance of earning their forgiveness. Even if she put everything aside, did her people want her to be in the Ash Kingdom? Did *she* want to be in the Ash Kingdom?

Analia's hands slowed on the harp, that final thought ringing in her mind. Did she want to be in the Ash Kingdom?

What she wanted was to figure out what Deardryn was planning, and she couldn't do that from Ash. And Aaron had said he would help her.

In that regard, it didn't matter if she wanted to be in Ash. If she wanted to stop Deardryn, she had to stay where she was.

Go with Aaron. She had made the right choice. So then why did her fingers linger on the strings? Why did her stomach give a vicious twist as there came a knock on the door?

"I like that song," Aaron said by way of greeting as he stepped inside.

"Were you listening to me?" she asked.

"I like to hear you play."

His unabashed honesty had Analia's cheeks burning.

"You know," Aaron said, sitting on a stray stool across from her, "this harp was originally my brother's. It was supposed to help with his dexterity, but then we realized he has no sense of rhythm."

Analia's lips twitched. "That explains the dust."

"Just as my presence explains the food awaiting us." Aaron rose to his feet, offering his hand with a flourish.

Analia hesitated. But remembering her decision, she allowed Aaron to pull her to her feet and lead her out the door.

A aron sat across from Analia at the dining room table, unable to wipe her tiny smile from his mind.

How long had it been since he'd seen one of those? Since she willingly came to a meal, and he didn't have to pry the words from her mouth?

He'd suspected something had shifted when he woke not to the sound of her usual scorching melodies, but something softer, almost haunting. But that distant look lingered in her eyes as she pinched off pieces of her muffin.

"Knock knock," he said, reaching across the table to tap his spoon against her temple. "Anybody home?"

Analia's gaze sharpened as she leaned away. "Aaron, that was in your mouth."

"I'm sorry, you're right."

With a wicked grin, Aaron moved the spoon to graze the corner of her lips. Analia swatted his hand away, that smile flickering to life again.

"Aren't there places you need to be?" she complained.

"Well, there are certainly places people would *like* me to be today. Meetings, with councilmen who would like to chew me out—"

"Are you in trouble?"

The genuine concern in Analia's eyes had Aaron's heart skip a beat—was that a flash of guilt as well? Regardless, he waved a dismissive hand. "I can handle them."

Analia didn't look wholly convinced. Aaron sipped his tea, determined to remain casual.

"Since you got to ask a question," he said, "does that mean I can ask what you've been contemplating so hard?"

Analia fiddled with her muffin wrapper. Aaron was just starting to think she wouldn't respond when she said, "I was trying to decide if I was making the right choice."

Aaron hesitated. "Have you come to a conclusion?"

"I think so."

This woman and her cryptic answers were going to be the death of him. But Analia didn't follow up that statement with a request to return to Ash. And there was no amount of hard-earned skepticism that could stop the hope from stirring in his chest.

"Then you, Analia, have impeccable timing."

"Why's that?"

"Because all of my family have returned, and they're demanding I feed them—you don't have to attend," he added quickly, clocking the slight tense of her shoulders. "Or, you can come, but decide to leave at any point, no questions asked. It's your choice."

"I'll come," Analia said, pinching another piece of muffin.

Aaron didn't have a name for the flood of emotion he carefully kept off his face. Something that felt oddly similar to longing.

A floorboard creaked behind the closed door. Aaron's eyebrow twitched up.

"Before you officially commit to dinner," he said, a bit louder than before, "I feel as though I need to warn you about my family. Laness in particular. She's extremely nosy and has no sense of personal boundaries. Isn't that right?"

Right on cue, the dining room door flung open. Analia jumped, a thin geyser of black flames spouting up from her hand.

Aaron's magic surged, but with a look of panic, Analia abruptly stifled the flames. The same look of panic from when she'd almost burned him in the sitting room.

Before Aaron could pursue the thought, Laness—looking as unconcerned as ever—bounced into their midst.

Like most nymphs, she was noticeably shorter than the average human. Delicately pointed ears peeked out from her thick, chin-length brown hair. The varying shades of green in her eyes had always reminded Aaron of dappled sunlight through a canopy, her slitted pupils the one area of shadow. Today, she wore a white shirt—dirt-stained as usual—and flowing peach-colored pants.

Aaron couldn't blame Analia for leaning back slightly as Laness placed her tan hands on the table and beamed. "Analia! It's about time Aaron stopped hogging you."

Before Analia could respond, Laness rounded on Aaron. "And *you*."

Aaron let out the smallest of sighs.

"What were you thinking?" Laness demanded.

"Well, currently I'm lamenting I trusted Branten to keep his mouth shut."

"You were already pushing it jumping across the entire continent to get to Ash. But then you just had to go and jump all the way back? With a passenger? With no breaks in between?"

"I figured if I would have to rest anyway, why not rest at home?"

"You're lucky you *made* it home. What would you have done if your magic gave out and those shadows booted you out in the middle of nowhere, huh?"

"That wasn't going to happen," Aaron protested.

Laness shook her head. She turned to Analia, muttering, "Boys," as if it were the worst insult she could think of. Then, she plopped into her usual seat, snatched a muffin, and popped it in her mouth.

Aaron rolled his eyes. "Anna, meet Laness. My spymaster, collector of secrets, overbearing pain in my ass."

"Don't forget pastry connoisseur," Laness chimed in.

"How could I possibly?" Aaron winked at Analia, and a cautious amusement flickered in her eyes.

Turning to Laness, she said, "I'm assuming the enka flower bracelet is yours?"

Laness beamed. "It is! My very own invention."

"How do they work?"

"Think of them like a bridge. Each bracelet acts as the endpoint on either side, with the flowers allowing us to conduct messages back and forth."

"You must have a lot of messages to sift through," Analia said, eyes drifting to the abundance of bracelets stacked on each of Laness's muscular arms.

"Tell me about it. These aren't even the half of them. I can tap into any enka flower across Elefthia and determine what's going on in its surroundings as well.

"I'm juggling so much noise—for you, by the way," she said with a haughty glance at Aaron, "That I can barely sift through all of it. I only had time to check yours was still active and you hadn't called out for Aaron."

Laness made a dramatic gesture with her muffin. Aaron could have hugged her right there as Analia slowly relaxed back in her seat.

"That's incredibly useful," she said.

"That's what I'm saying!"

Aaron shook his head. "Do you have anything to report, Laness, or were you simply trying to insert yourself into our conversation?"

"First off," Laness said, "I did not try. I succeeded." She took a bite of muffin. "And second, I always have news, but it can wait until tonight."

Breakfast didn't last much longer after that. Analia was the first to go, murmuring a farewell before slipping out the door. As soon as she was gone, Laness let her cheerful mask slip into something more resigned.

"So that's her."

Aaron sighed. "That's her."

"What can I do?"

"I don't know," he said, running a hand through his hair. "That was definitely progress, but I don't know how to help her. I don't know what's going on with her."

"Well, that second one is easy," Laness said, grabbing yet another muffin. "She spent four months in an enemy kingdom, every second wondering if she was about to get caught and executed. She got married off to a monster of a prince, just to lose control of her magic and kill him, nearly died herself at her mentor's hands, survived to be tortured by her past, and finally, condemn her own father. That's a lot."

She only knew the half of it. Aaron had only told his family the bare minimum upon returning home. He'd told himself it was out of respect for Analia's privacy, but deep down, he knew there was a part of him already hoping she would come and tell her story herself. But now?

"I keep wondering if her being here is only making it worse," he murmured.

He'd known that final day in Sun would leave a mark. He himself hadn't been able to relax for weeks after all his time in Sun, his jaw still tightening every time he remembered how he'd been surrounded by his family's killers.

But he'd failed to consider just how corrosive that stain could be for Analia. And if her being here was just adding to the list of things she had to process?

"Don't go giving up on her like that," Laness said, throwing a balled-up muffin wrapper at him. "You were an utter disaster after the war, and look how far you've come."

"Thanks for the reminder," Aaron muttered.

Laness threw another wrapper at him. "Trust me," she said, "all things considered, Analia's response is to be expected."

If anyone would know that, it was Laness. Aaron bowed his head. "You're right."

Laness's expression softened. "You've had a long time to learn just what an invasive weed the past is," she said, rising and heading for the door. "It's easy to forget sometimes how long it takes to adjust to that. Just give her time."

Aaron's guilt grew even heavier, keeping his head lowered as Laness exited. Gods, if Analia was anywhere near that black, bottomless pit he had been in...

His eyes moved across the table, taking in the burned muffin wrapper resting at her seat.

Something clicked in his brain. Something that had him pushing to his feet and sliding a note under Analia's door a few minutes later.

If Analia was truly in that pit, then she was the only one who could drag herself back out. But that didn't mean he couldn't offer a hand. Especially when he knew one way to make that climb just a little bit easier.

Chapter 12

"What do you think?" Aaron asked.

He and Analia stood on one of the many waterside walkways that curved throughout the kingdom, the river gently burbling beneath their feet. He'd shadowjumped them there immediately after lunch, knowing it was close enough to walk, but too excited to do so. Especially as Analia took his hand without protest, only asking where they were going.

Now, her smoky-gray eyes swept over their surroundings, her head tilted to the side. "Why is it so empty?" she asked.

Plenty of people moved through the streets behind them. But the walkway they stood on was completely barren, not even hosting a few tables and chairs like many of the others. It was wide-open space, stretching as long as Aaron's dining room.

"Because," Aaron said, leaning back against the railing. "This section of walkway isn't meant to be a place where people stop to chat."

"What is it then?" she asked, her eyes narrowing.

Aaron held her gaze. "A place for magic training."

Analia blanched. She backed up a step, eyes darting along the wooden planks that creaked beneath their feet, across the railing, over to the rest of the kingdom. But Aaron remained perfectly calm.

"Most," he said, "if not every Blessed in this kingdom has found their way to this spot when learning to harness their magic. Not just because every inch of wood has been magically reinforced and wards protect the kingdom, but also because of the river."

Analia's eyes flashed to the water. "What do you mean?"

"Well," Aaron said, "we've found it's incredibly useful when someone's magic gets out of hand. Either because the water is enough to extinguish the magic, or the surprise at being tossed in is enough to startle the wielder into reclaiming control. Branten in particular loves to rile me up, just so he has an excuse to throw me in."

He took a step closer, lightly gripping her shoulders. Analia flinched but didn't pull out of his grip.

"I know it's unnerving," he said, forcing her to meet his gaze. "All that power buzzing through your veins, having no way to release it for over a week. You must have been out of your mind trying to suppress it."

He couldn't believe it had taken him so long to figure it out. Especially when he was all too familiar with the fear widening her eyes.

"I can't," she whispered, so faintly he barely heard.

"Yes, you can," Aaron said, squeezing her shoulders. "It's just one quick release, just like they teach you your first day of training."

"I can't," Analia repeated, hand tightening around something in her pocket.

"Even if I promise to throw you in if anything goes wrong?"

Aaron winked, but Analia's expression didn't falter.

"One quick release," he repeated. "You can do that."

But Analia's muscles had completely locked, her wide eyes staring, staring, staring.

But why? It had been six weeks, this should have been second nature for her. Unless...

"They haven't been training you," he said slowly.

Analia's face twitched.

Frost crackled through Aaron's veins.

"How have they not been training you?" he spat. "Everyone in that hypocritical, impossible kingdom tore you to shreds because you didn't have magic. And now they don't so much as lift a finger to help you train when it *does* come?"

"Drop it, Aaron."

But the cold was relentless as Analia wrenched out of his grip.

"Did you even try to find someone to train you?" he demanded. "Or were you going to let them turn you into a pretty piece of ornamentation for their throne?"

"You mean how you're trying to turn me into your latest problem to fix?" Analia shot back.

"I'm trying to help you!"

"I don't need you to help me!"

"What happened to you?"

Analia flinched. Aaron didn't look away. Not from the face of the woman he had—no, he couldn't go down that path. Not after what happened last time with Liss. But there was no denying the incredibly strong and resilient and beautiful woman before him also had a part of her that had stopped trying to climb back out of that dark, bottomless hole.

"You are wasting away before my eyes, Analia," Aaron said, his voice raw. "You don't get to tell me not to care about that."

He reached out, taking her trembling hands in his. "Just tell me what I can do. Tell me how I can help you."

"Aaron, there's nothing for you to do!"

Aaron realized it wasn't fear, but fury shaking Analia's hands as she ripped them back. She made to turn on her heel, but he grabbed her wrist.

"No," he spat, "don't tell me it's fine. We've gotten far past that game."

"I'm not fine!" Analia yelled. "I know I'm not fine, but I don't know how to fix me and I'm trying to fix me and you demanding to know what you can do isn't helping, so *back. Off.*"

Analia twisted free and shoved him away. It wasn't until the smell of singed fabric swirled between them that her eyes widened, moving from the scorch mark in Aaron's deep blue tunic down to her hands still wreathed in midnight flames.

Aaron's heart pounded hard enough he thought it might bust through his rib cage. But it was with a frosty calm that he said, "That. That right there is why you need to train your magic. If you don't release it, it will only build, and build, and build. At that point, you won't have a choice if it explodes."

"How do you know," Analia demanded, fists clenching as she extinguished her flames.

"Because it happened to me."

His words thudded between them like a chunk of ice.

Something flashed across Analia's face. Then, she furiously shook her head.

"Fine," she hissed. "You want magic?"

She shoved out her hand, palm up. A miniature geyser of flames burst forth from her palm, disappearing almost as quickly as it came. "Happy?"

"Yes," Aaron said matter-of-factly. "That's the first time I've seen some life in your eyes."

Analia glared.

"You need to blaze a lot hotter if you want to burn me," he told her. "Let me know when you want to erupt."

Analia held his stare. Then, she wordlessly turned on her heel. And Aaron didn't try to stop her as she stormed off the walkway and into the kingdom beyond.

Aaron leaned back against the railing, trying to calm the magic that churned in his own network. That was not how he'd intended things to go. Not at all.

Analia marched through the kingdom streets, gulping down air as she tried to smother her flames.

She had been so close. She'd agreed to go to dinner with Aaron and his family. She'd survived her meeting with the slightly overwhelming Laness. She hadn't even flinched when Aaron slid that note under her door, saying they were going on an adventure.

So. Close. Then she burned it all to the ground. And the flames still flickering across her hands didn't care.

Analia sucked in a slow, deep breath, the air sweetened by the nearby bakery.

She couldn't keep doing this. She couldn't—wouldn't—revert back to the person who burned Aaron at every opportunity, just because she was afraid. She could be as broken and miserable as she wanted, but she wouldn't drag Aaron into her chaos.

Especially not after she'd seen the heartbreak in his eyes as he demanded to know what had happened to her. If only she knew.

Analia squeezed her hands into fists, smothering the last of her flames. Slumping against a nearby building, she tipped her head back toward the setting sun. Almost dinner time.

Instead of heading back toward Aaron's house, she briefly closed her eyes, then ventured into the shopping district before her.

Analia did her best to avoid the larger clusters of people coming in and out of the buildings around her, slightly taken aback by the lack of stares she received.

It was certainly a crowded kingdom, thrumming with the songs of countless magic networks. But there was also an unmistakable sense of peace as people talked and swapped friendly smiles.

Aaron truly had been preserving a sanctuary. And Analia was a sucking, swirling cloud of darkness in its core.

Maybe she should go back to Ash after all. Spare Aaron, his people—

Analia paused outside a small dress shop, her eye caught by one of the gowns in the display window.

At first, she thought it was a simple black dress: tight, stretchy, short. But upon closer examination, the fabric rippled, the simple black melting into shifting patterns of midnight blue and deepest purple, sparkling with what looked like a million tiny stars.

Before Analia knew what she was doing, she pushed through the shop door.

As far as she could tell, the shop was empty, the only sound her quiet footsteps as she wove between racks of gowns toward the window. She reached up, the gown slipping through her fingers like water.

"Mesmerizing, isn't it?"

Analia whirled, clamping down on her flames.

The woman that stood before her was a statue forged from bronze. Her long, wavy hair was a few tones darker than her skin, her eyes paling into a piercing topaz. She wore a sparkling black gown of her own, cascading down her tall, lean frame and pooling at the floor in a collection of silver and white beads.

She tilted her head, a knowing glint in her eyes as if she could see straight through Analia to the writhing flames within.

"The gown has been enchanted by my own magic," the woman continued. "The fabric and the coloring remain the same, but each beholder sees a different constellation of stars."

"That's incredible," Analia said, forcing her hands to unclench.

"It is. Although I believe I have something that is far more to your liking in my back room. Would you care to join me?"

Analia shifted on her feet. There was something about this woman that reminded her of Deardryn. They had the same easy calm, the unreadability that tempted Analia to dart out of the store and never look back.

But where Deardryn was analytic, this woman was placid. Inviting.

Analia nodded, and the woman's lips curved in a faint smile. She turned, her skirts whispering on the ground as she drifted through the racks, waving for Analia to follow.

Analia expected to be led to a side door, perhaps a barred-off section. What she didn't expect was to round the small counter in the back of the shop, just to come face-to-face with a curtain of hanging beads. Descending from the ceiling on what looked like a million threads, they sparkled in varying shades of palest blue, green, silver, and white.

The woman didn't pause before sweeping through the beads, disappearing into the space beyond. Analia hesitated, sensing the faintest pulse of a magic field. With a hand on her phoenix pin, she poked her head into the beads. Then, she immediately pushed all the way through, the beads feeling more like a whisper of air than actual material against her skin.

The circular room on the other side of the curtain was impossibly large. A massive loom sat in its center, the beginning of a project in the works. A single stool sat before the loom, a long, ornate bench set a few feet behind it. And along the walls, taking up every inch of space, were hundreds upon hundreds of tapestries.

There was no set size, style, even theme of the images displayed. Yet, they all came together to create a patchwork story across the walls.

"Welcome to my studio," said the woman, running a hand down her loom.

"How is this room contained in that tiny building?" Analia asked.

The woman's faint smile grew. "This room isn't actually a part of my shop. It's completely separate, with the beads we passed through acting like a doorway."

"Just not to the other side of the shop," Analia mused.

She took a step deeper into the room, eyes sweeping across the tapestries. Some, she had no problem deciphering.

A massive frost-covered mountain. A bloody battlefield, the churned-up dust tinged with silver, the focus directed down on the soldiers' boots. The scroll she and Aaron had retrieved from the Sun Kingdom, clasped shut by seven metal rings.

Other tapestries remained a mystery: a tornado of swirling colors. A close-up of a rough gray stone, a single crack running down the center. And interspersed through it all were images of an incredibly familiar face.

"I take it you are, in fact, intrigued?" the woman asked.

Analia tore her gaze from a tapestry of Aaron's neck, his damper chain clearly in view. "Did you create all of these?" she asked.

"These and many more."

"That's incredible," Analia said. "Each tapestry is positively flawless..."

Analia's words trailed off. She had been turning about the room, trying to soak in every image she could. Just to look to the wall directly above her head and to the left. Right into her own face.

Chapter 13

The tapestry took up a sizable section of wall. Even if it hadn't, Analia would have had no trouble recognizing her wedding night.

The delicate pearl straps of her dress. The sparkling gold neckline. The chain of Pryanth's pendant. The storm of midnight flames.

Analia's hand drifted to her throat, feeling the betrayal, heartbreak, despair, something solid as she backed up—someone—

"It's me," said Aaron, gripping her shoulders. "It's only me."

Aaron steadied her, then quickly stepped away. A part of her noted how her flames hadn't surged. But the thought was drowned out by the image of her own haunted eyes, the swirling flames.

Analia abruptly turned her back to the tapestry, bile burning in her throat.

Aaron had swapped his scorched tunic for a simple black shirt, his deadly gaze now fixed on the seamstress. She could have sworn he muttered, "Meddler," under his breath, but if the seamstress heard, she didn't let on.

She casually prodded her working thread, commenting, "This tapestry finally seems ready to be woven."

Aaron's answering glare was a thing of nightmares. One that had a lump lodging in Analia's throat as she looked to him. "Did you describe that to her?" she asked.

A part of her knew her flames should be leaping. But all she could muster was a dull sense of hurt. Of all images he would want to immortalize...

"Oh no," the seamstress said. "I wove that far before he witnessed it."

Analia blinked. "How long, exactly?"

Aaron's face went deathly pale.

The seamstress tilted her head. "Perhaps half a century."

Analia stared. One, two, three heartbeats. Aaron looked as though he were bracing himself for that eruption he had mentioned.

But Analia was calm. Perhaps too calm as she turned to the seamstress. "Who are you?"

"My name is Surce," she said, folding her hands in her lap.

"My second-in-command," said Aaron tightly.

Finally, Analia's body seemed to thaw. "How could you have woven this half a century ago?" she demanded.

Surce flashed Aaron a smug look. Aaron ignored her, remaining on high alert. Still, there were no flames as Surce picked up her working thread and began.

"My mother was a nun of Ferin, the god of time and prophecy. She was completely and utterly human, descended from the original group Talitha granted freedom to live within the Wild Lands. Eventually, she found herself pregnant.

"My mother refused to say if she broke her vow of celibacy or if something more nefarious occurred. Many believe my father to be one of the Blessed residing in the Starlight Kingdom, due to my apparent Blessing from the Crystal. As a result, the humans wanted to send me away, but my mother fought to keep me with her.

"As I became older, my mother introduced me to the loom. Most of my tapestries were what one would anticipate from a child. But there were a select few that felt as though I had a second set of hands guiding my own: selecting the threads, deciding the pattern, informing my hands how to move. And every single one of those tapestries depicted a truth yet to play out.

"For decades, my tapestries were dismissed as coincidences. But as more and more came true, the humans became suspicious. I tried to control the tapestries, not wanting to incur the wrath of my people, but there was no stopping my Blessing that so replicated that of the very god my mother worshipped. Just as there was no destroying or hiding my creations. And my attempts to do so were my downfall. Especially when the humans discovered a tapestry depicting the death of their king.

"When it came true, the humans declared my gift was a curse. They said my tapestries weren't predicting the future, but designing it. And you can understand how designing the death of the king was unacceptable."

Analia's stomach sank.

"The mob came for me in the middle of the night. They decided in payment for my crimes, I would be put to death. They had just tied me to a stake, ignoring my pleas as they lit their torches, when Aaron and his brothers stormed the Human Kingdom and saved my life."

Surce dipped her chin to Aaron, who had tears in his eyes. "Aaron then gave me a choice," she said, her hands moving across the loom. "Remain in the Human Kingdom under his protection, or come with him to the Starlight Kingdom. And though it pained me, I returned with him."

Silence settled across the studio. A silence that reached straight through Analia's chest and squeezed.

"I'm sorry," she finally whispered.

Surce gave a casual flick of her wrist. "Do not waste your sympathy on me," she said. "Yes, it pained me in the moment to leave my people, but I knew they would kill me if I stayed."

Analia understood that perfectly well. Except it wasn't her people that would kill her, it was the guilt.

Analia's body froze. A distant part of her mind heard Aaron and Surce still speaking, but all attention zeroed in on that final thought. The thought that somehow yanked every worry, every uncertainty she'd had the past week, into a near-blinding focus.

It wasn't fear making her question. It was guilt, sinking its claws deep into her stomach, not because she had abandoned her uncle's kingdom, but because she was relieved she had escaped it.

This place is not a prison. Six little words that almost brought tears to her eyes, whose echoes trailed her through every melody.

She had always felt trapped: trapped by expectations, trapped by her past, trapped by her desire to honor her uncle. She was even trapped by her relief that Cadmus could fulfill that wish, and Deardryn's scheme was the perfect excuse she'd needed to flee. Not just the Ash Kingdom, but the version of herself she had come to despise.

This place is not a prison. She could be free if she wished. And the guilt from that wish had been eating her alive.

Analia struggled to focus as Aaron turned to her, the lethal swirl of his network subsiding. "How did you find this place?" he asked.

"I brought her here," Surce said smoothly, swiveling on her stool to face them fully. "Laness informed me of the state of her wardrobe, and we agreed intervention was required. I was getting her measurements."

Aaron raised a brow, but Analia didn't deny it. His eyes did a casual flick across the walls as if checking for something, his shoulders relaxing slightly as he took in the tapestries. Before Analia could wonder, he was turning away, offering Surce a clipped farewell.

The seamstress gave an airy wave, telling Analia to expect a delivery the following day. Analia thanked her, then hurried to catch up with Aaron.

She passed through the beads and back into Surce's shop, her eyes landing on the black dress just as she was about to leave. Her mind drifted back to the thoughts it had jerked her out of.

Could Surce have truly brought her here? Did she want to be in the Ash Kingdom?

Analia touched her pin as she slipped out the door, Aaron waiting for her on the other side. Without a word, he led the way back through the streets, Analia stealing glances at him from the corner of her eye.

He, too, had come looking for her, even though she could still see the tension from their fight in the set of his mouth.

"So," she eventually said, drawing out the word. "You knew?"

Aaron nodded, not looking at her. Analia didn't think she wanted to know the answer to her next question, but she couldn't help but ask. "Was that the only reason you helped me in Sun?"

"No." His eyes finally met hers. "That tapestry might have shown me what you're capable of—and I don't just mean your magic. But you showed me just as much that day in Accalon's chambers. And I wanted to help you see that tapestry into fruition."

Gods, that was all he'd been doing on the walkway. Not fixing or changing her, but pushing her. Never giving up on her.

"I'm sorry," she said, her voice cracking.

Aaron's expression softened. "Not only do I forgive you," he said, "but I'm sorry, too."

"Why are you sorry?"

"Some of the things I said to you weren't exactly kind."

"That doesn't mean I can bite your head off."

"No," Aaron said, smiling slightly. "But I understand why you tried."

He did understand, didn't he? He'd told her as much that day on the fountain back in Sun. And she'd practically thrown it back in his face.

A tear rolled down Analia's cheek. Gods, when she wasn't screaming, she was sobbing.

Aaron's eyes followed her tear as it fell. Waving her over to a nearby bench, he asked, "You want to talk about it?"

"Not yet," she whispered, sinking down beside him.

Not while her flames still sizzled. They could torment her all they wanted, but she would not give them a chance to hurt Aaron. Never again. Even if that meant disappointing him now. But Aaron seemed to register the quiet promise laced through those words: *soon, though.*

Another tear slipped free. This time, Aaron caught it with a gentle sweep of his finger.

"I want you to be here, Anna," he said, eyes fixed on his rescued tear. "But if that's not what you want, if that's not what's best for you, I will take you home."

Analia knew he meant it. Which meant he was willing to jeopardize his kingdom, his everything, if that's what it took to help her.

He *trusted* her.

"We have a dinner to go to," she said, her decision settling in her chest.

Aaron made no attempt to hide the emotion that flooded his face. Crystal spare her, had she truly become so wretched that simply having dinner with his family meant so much?

That black wave rose up once more.

Aaron stood from the bench, offering his hand. And Analia held on tight as he pulled her to her feet.

Aaron led the way back to his house, only a hint of apprehension in his voice as he talked about the various establishments they passed. He stopped at the bakery Analia had noted earlier, quickly emerging with a box smelling of chocolate.

"You know," Analia said, "you haven't told me who's going to be at this dinner."

Aaron brightened. "Well, you already had the distinct pleasure of meeting Laness and Surce, but you'll also get to meet my brothers."

So, she *had* heard two voices outside her door that first day.

"Your non-blood brothers," she clarified, following Aaron across a bridge made from sparkling onyx.

"Indeed. I've already told you about Branten, who is my Master of Arms."

"Why does a hidden kingdom need a military?" Analia asked.

Aaron's expression darkened. "For the moment we're no longer hidden."

Analia shivered.

"But there's also Mor," Aaron went on, his face clearing quickly. "He's actually the reason we're having this dinner now. He had to spend the last week in the Human Kingdom and only just got home."

"Does that mean the humans aren't a part of your kingdom?" Analia asked.

"They are," Aaron said carefully. "I told you how this started out as a hideaway for the humans, a way to get away from the Blessed—minus the few people that maintained Talitha's base. Well, when a kingdom's-worth of Blessed showed up, they weren't exactly thrilled.

"At first, there was peace. An incredibly brief peace, and then there was war. There were... a lot of casualties on both sides. But eventually, my family prevailed, and out of respect decided to allow the Human Kingdom to remain separate, but still under Star authority. I'm still their king, but I prefer to let Mor rule over them and handle the day-to-day."

What types of "casualties" caused the flash of pain across his face? Before she could ask, they reached the house.

Aaron opened the wooden gate, pausing as he caught sight of her raised brows. "What?" he asked. "Have the flower beds offended you? I'll admit, Laness has a tendency to go overboard, but I wouldn't tell her so unless you'd like some vines to flip you on your ass."

Analia smiled slightly. The flower beds lining the walkway up to Aaron's front door were rather aggressive, with a myriad of blooms creeping around a wooden bench and coiling through the front porch railing. The air was heady with rose, jasmine, geranium, and countless other floral scents Analia couldn't name, floating on the twilight breeze. It felt like a dream, a fairytale.

"I was only thinking about how you live in a house," she said. "Not a castle. And a rather small house at that."

"There's a bigger house I lived in when I was young," Aaron said, casually hooking his arm over the gate. "I have a habit of punting my family over there when they're being annoying. But after the war... all that open space was just a reminder of how empty it had become."

"That's how it felt after my uncle died," Analia said. "Like that castle, and that kingdom, too, stopped being my home the moment he was gone."

Her confession seemed to hang in the air between them.

"Well," Aaron said, offering his Phoenix Gate smile, "that just means you can start looking for a new one."

Somehow, that smile, that thoughtful tinge to his voice, had her confession drifting away. She followed him through the gate, that question whispering through her mind once more.

Did she want to be in Ash?

Chapter 14

Even though Analia had already met two of the four expected dinner guests, she couldn't help her relief when she found only one person waiting in the dining room. He sat with his back to the entrance, only allowing Analia to see narrow shoulders and short, golden-brown hair.

"Why am I not surprised you're the only one on time?" Aaron griped, crossing to the table and clapping the man on the back.

"I reminded Branten on my way over," said who had to be Mor, his voice soft and smooth. "Although whether he'll remember that I reminded him is unlikely."

Aaron snorted and tossed the pastry box on the table. "You should have reminded him he was the one who demanded we have this dinner in the first place."

Mor laughed under his breath as he turned in his seat.

His face was ordinary in an oddly pleasing way: lightly tanned skin, straight nose, a scattering of freckles across his right cheekbone like a tiny constellation. He wore a pristine dark blue jacket decorated with silver buttons, looking every bit the king Aaron claimed he might as well be. Especially as his assessing hazel gaze met Analia's.

Before her flames could flicker, he smiled—a truly kind, beautiful smile—and rose from his seat.

"Analia," he said, offering his hand. "I'm Mortimer, but everyone here calls me Mor."

Analia took his hand, about to speak. Then, her eyes darted down.

Mor's hand was entirely made from gold. His fingers were warm and smooth to the touch, giving a quick squeeze before releasing hers.

"Incredible," she murmured. "The gold has been looped into your magic network."

Analia ripped her gaze from Mor's hand, horrified. "I'm sorry, I shouldn't have—"

"No," Mor laughed, his expression relaxing. "You're saving me the effort of trying to insert it into conversation."

He returned to his seat, pulling out the one beside him. "The magic from my network is what enables mobility. It's still stiffer than flesh, and it took time to create any semblance of dexterity, but it's certainly more helpful than a stump."

Analia's cheeks burned, but she took the seat Mor offered her. "I didn't know magic could do such a thing."

"I'm impressed you were able to sense that it could."

Analia waited for him to inquire how. But he only took a sip from his wine glass, giving her space to elaborate if she wished.

Instead, Analia looked to Aaron quietly leaning against the windowsill. He quickly schooled his expression, but Analia had caught the warmth in his gaze.

"Mor's being modest," he said, coming to take the seat on Analia's other side. "He has a tendency of waving that thing about at every opportunity."

Mor casually straightened his jacket. "I've found that people's initial reactions are excellent demonstrations of their character."

Analia's insides squirmed, but she couldn't help but ask, "What did my reaction say about me?"

Mor's answering smile was kind. "That you'll fit in around here just fine."

To Analia's surprise, her flames settled.

"And guess who created that hand?" Aaron asked.

"How would I..." Analia's eyes flew wide, "Don't tell me..."

"Oh yes," Aaron said, his face pinched. "Our new drug lord friend, Marcos. Now that was a delightful surprise."

Analia was about to ask how he knew for sure when the front door banged open.

"How many times have I told you not to use my trees as targets?"

"Laness, it's been *decades*," a deep male voice drawled. "Don't make me do that math."

An absurdly tall, muscular man stomped into the dining room, his entire body encased in black leathers that glinted with metal reinforcements. Analia barely registered his crooked nose and reddish-brown hair when Laness stormed in after him.

"You injured my trees!"

"With the hilts, not the blades."

"You bruised the bark!"

"Bruises are good for you," Branten said, taking the seat across from Analia. "They toughen you up."

Laness flicked her wrist. The enka flowers on the windowsill behind Branten flashed out, the purple-and-black stems wrapping around the back of the chair and flipping Branten to the ground with a thud.

"There," Laness said. "Now you can toughen up together."

With a huff, she took her seat beside Branten's. Grinning, he righted his chair with one hand, the other reaching for the pastry box Mor nudged toward him.

"Look, Laness," he said, fishing out a chocolate croissant and waving it under her nose. "Rosalina's. Hi, Anna," he added, as casual as a friend she'd known for years.

Analia didn't have time to react as Laness looked to her. "You see what I have to deal with?" she asked, nevertheless swiping a pastry.

Analia raised an eyebrow at Aaron. He gave her an innocent look, then nudged her beneath the table.

"Decades," Mor sighed. "They've had this fight for decades."

"You would think at some point Branten would learn to sit somewhere else," Aaron said. "But we've given up trying to train him."

Surce breezed through the door, "Particularly after how long it took him to learn basic table manners."

Settling in the seat across from Aaron, she nodded to Mor. He flicked his golden hand, and a moment later, steaming plates of potatoes, green beans, and chicken glazed with honey appeared on the table with a soft thrum of magic.

Analia turned to Mor. "How did you do that?"

"My Blessing revolves around relocation," he explained. "There are some limitations, but I'm able to move most objects in my general area. All of this was just waiting in the kitchen."

Analia had countless questions, but she was distracted by Branten examining the unusually large napkin that had also appeared in front of him.

"Why?" he asked.

"For the mess," Surce explained gently.

Laness cackled.

"Give me a break, woman," Branten complained, piling his plate with potatoes. "Not all of us grew up in fancy temples or licking silver spoons."

"You shouldn't mind that last part," Aaron said as he offered Analia the green beans. "You much prefer licking other things."

Mor choked on his wine. Branten tipped back his head in a laugh, "And I've gotten no complaints."

"Because there's no one *to* complain," Laness retorted.

"Decades," Mor repeated as Branten and Laness squabbled over serving spoons.

"I don't know how Surce has tolerated us for so long," said Aaron.

Surce hid her amusement in her jewel-encrusted goblet.

"Decades," Analia said, her grip a bit tighter than necessary as she cut into her chicken. "You must have known each other for a long time."

The brothers exchanged a look. Mor took a bite of potatoes, and Aaron gestured to Branten with his wine glass.

"Aaron said he already filled you in on how we all got here," Branten began, "so I won't go through all that nonsense. What's important is my mom was already dead from the plague that had been sweeping our war shelter before King Hester was able to jump us here. My dad thought we'd gotten out before either of us could get infected, but his symptoms came on slower than usual, especially for a human. He was a tough old bastard though, managed to fight it off for almost six months before dying. And that left me alone on the streets when I was four.

"Now, today, we have funds and programs and shit to try and prevent us street rats from being, well, street rats. But this was in the early days of evacuations, and everything was a fucking disaster. Everyone was just trying to survive, so I did the same.

"For four years, I fought, stole, and lied my way to the top of the street gang I was in. By that point, I'd learned how to survive, and I'd learned how to not get caught while I did it."

"Until you destroyed a clock tower," Surce murmured.

"Not very surreptitious," Laness agreed through a mouthful of chicken.

Branten's face reddened. "I told you it was an accident. Mostly."

"You still got caught," Mor pointed out.

"By Ethelind of all people," Aaron agreed, eyes sparkling.

Branten shuddered. "All you need to know is there might have been a very loud crash from the clock tower, followed by yours truly scuttling out the back where Aaron's grandmother and queen at the time was waiting for me. And I nearly shit myself right there when she gave me her famous death stare.

"She told me I'd been causing enough trouble on the streets, and either I could pay for the long list of petty—and sometimes not so petty—crimes I'd committed, or I could drag my sorry ass to the Underground."

"What's the Underground?" Analia asked.

The brothers exchanged another look, this one far more muted than before.

"We're not quite sure how the Underground exists," Mor finally said. "You can think of it as an underground network of tunnels that stretch all across Elefthia, although the pathways below don't mirror those above."

"There's some sort of magic," Branten said, "that allows the tunnels to shift however they like, meaning you can enter the Underground here, take a few turns, and then end up all the way in the Wind Kingdom."

"As far as we're aware," Aaron said, "we're the only kingdom to have discovered the tunnels. Thus, one of my ancestors decided it was the perfect secret military camp."

"Completely ruthless," Branten said. "Filled with troublemaking children looking for an outlet. So, naturally, Ethelind assumed I would fit in just fine. And that's where I met Aaron, who'd already been down there for over a year at that point."

Aaron waved an airy hand, promising another time. Analia didn't miss how his grip tightened around his fork. Deciding not to push it, she turned back to Branten. "Is that when you beat the shit out of him?"

Branten choked on his chicken. Laness thumped him on the back, the two collapsing in laughter. Aaron shook his head, and even Surce swapped a smile with Mor.

"He was so quiet," Branten said, wiping a tear from his eye. "The Underground must have been beside themselves after getting their hands on him. His presence alone created competition, and competition created fighters. And I knew beating him would be the easiest way to establish myself."

"He won that first round," Aaron admitted. "But for the next year, we took every opportunity we could to knock the other around. I don't think there was a single day that either of us wasn't bruised, bleeding, or pissed off because of the other. And of course, our trainers did nothing."

"Bruises make you tough," Laness mimicked.

Aaron said, "As long as no one was dead and no one got caught in the act, they didn't care, so there was no reason to stop."

"So, about a year in," Branten said, reaching for seconds, "Aaron and I were brawling in some abandoned tunnel or another. Somehow, I knocked his head back into a protruding stone, and he just lost it.

"Up until that point, we'd been fighting with blades and fists, with my Blessing enhancing my speed, strength, and reflexes. But Aaron is *loaded*. I'd somehow snapped his damper chain, and he blasted me all the way down the tunnel. And that was when I decided he was going to be my ally."

Laness and Surce exchanged an exasperated look. Aaron's eyes dimmed as he dropped his gaze to his plate.

"That was around the time I showed up," Mor said with a quick look to Aaron. "I voluntarily came to the Underground when I was nine. I had just lost my hand, and I didn't want to be helpless."

Analia had countless questions. But Branten cut in, "Despite being a bastard, Stumpy here was one of the only boys down there who wasn't considered riffraff."

"'Stumpy,'" Mor repeated, vaguely offended.

Laness peered into Branten's glass. "He isn't even drunk yet!"

"Creativity is truly fleeting," Surce sighed.

"Oh, far from it," Aaron said, seeming to shake himself off. "This is just Branten's bruised pride making a reappearance because Mor knocked his ass to the dirt with said stump."

"I got him first," Branten protested.

Laness rolled her eyes.

"When Mor arrived," Aaron said, fighting back a grin, "Branten was quick to go after him. He was particularly fond of targeting the new boys because they had the most possessions to swipe.

"I found him in one of his usual haunts, and he told me how he'd jumped Mor, and grabbed all his stuff before he even knew what was happening. I then grabbed Branten by the ear and dragged him after me as I looked for Mor. When I found him, I gave him his stuff back and said he deserved a chance to fight back."

"And then he clobbered me," Mor said.

Branten winced, but Mor brushed it aside with an easy wave of his golden hand.

"I tried to stick to myself," he went on, "embarrassed by my struggle to fight with one hand, but Aaron quickly found me again. At first, he offered to help me, and I refused. So, instead, he goaded me relentlessly."

"Sounds familiar," Analia muttered. Aaron gave her a dazzling smile.

"He even got Branten to come and jab at me," Mor said. "But I refused to rise to the bait. Until one day, I snapped. I don't even remember what Branten said. I just know I whipped around and smacked him upside the head with my 'stump' hard enough he fell to the dirt."

Laness cackled. Aaron and Branten swapped proud looks.

Smiling himself, Mor went on, "And all Aaron said was, 'Don't drop your elbow next time.' Then, Branten got up and told me to do it again. From that point on, they helped me train."

"We had become a unit," Aaron said. "One that persisted even when we were finally released from the Underground."

"The moment we emerged," Branten said, "Grandma Ethy was waiting for us, looking all expectant as she told us we would be coming home with her. She hadn't gone through all the work of getting our sorry asses out of trouble just to release us back to our usual mischief. So, we moved into the big house with Aaron and Elspeth—"

"Wait," Analia said, turning to Aaron. "If your mother was still alive at this point, why was Ethelind queen?"

She'd thought all this time Ethelind's coronation had been out of necessity, with the previous Star Queen dead for reasons Analia still didn't know. But if Elspeth was alive and Aaron too young to rule, it didn't matter that she wasn't a Star Royal. The crown should have been hers.

Aaron opened his mouth, the table suddenly gone quiet. He glanced around, his face softening at the looks his family gave him.

"After the war," he said carefully, "my mom found herself with little interest in ruling. Since I was too young at the time to take the throne, she asked Ethelind to step in."

Aaron's gaze met Analia's. Just for a moment, he allowed her to see those same broken pieces he'd shown her in the Sun Castle armory.

Analia looked down at his hand on the table between them. Her own hand twitched.

"Elspeth was a gem," Branten said.

The clink of silverware started up once more. Aaron looked away, and Analia grabbed her glass instead.

"She and Ethelind treated us like their own children," Mor agreed fondly. "But we only had a few years with them until the war with the humans broke out."

"We were all sent out into the field," Branten said. "Aaron had his own squadron because Star Royal. I also had my own squadron because *obviously*. And Mortie was bounced between the battlefield and the war tents because Ethelind quickly realized he was better at politics and strategy than Aaron.

"We fought for some time, praying to the Crystal that the others were all right. Aaron in particular had a way of scaring the shit out of us, especially when he was captured—"

"We don't need to get into that," said Aaron firmly.

"But that's where we met," Laness complained.

Aaron flashed her a warning look. Laness flicked a piece of bread at him.

"Aaron and I were prisoners at the same time," she told Analia. "I wouldn't have survived if he hadn't taken me with him when he escaped." She glanced at Aaron. "Happy?"

Despite her easy tone, Analia didn't miss the flicker of tension in Laness's expression as she reached for the pastry box. Nor did she miss how Laness didn't volunteer how or why she'd been captured.

"And we've already discussed how Aaron and I met," Surce said, folding her napkin. "But I don't believe we have heard your story, Analia."

Analia's flames stirred as all eyes moved to her. She looked to Aaron, who shrugged.

"I only told them what I had to when giving my report."

Analia didn't begrudge him that. Still, her words were clipped, precise.

"For twenty-two years, I had no magic. And my father turned my entire kingdom against me as a result. The only person I had was my uncle, who was murdered by my father, his brother, in order to take the throne. And somehow, in his death, my uncle's magic passed to me."

Analia forced herself to meet each of their stares. "Somehow, his magic allows me to sense all other magics, not just Ash Royal magic."

No one looked particularly surprised.

"Was that part of your report?" she asked Aaron.

"Only because we assume it has to do with you being Deardryn's key," he said apologetically.

"That plus the scroll we still can't open," Branten muttered.

"And dragon lady is on the move," Laness said, tipping back in her seat. "That servant friend of yours finally gave me an update. My gods does he think loud. Especially when I startled him by responding."

"Is he all right?" Analia asked.

"He's fine," Laness assured her. "Angry, irritable, but fine. But you're not going to like what he said."

Laness proceeded to explain how Deardryn had infiltrated Moon, Analia's stomach sinking further and further.

"I still think we should just send someone in to kill her," Branten said. At some point, he'd completely deconstructed the empty pastry box and was now folding it back together. "You can take out as many lackeys or conquer as much territory as you like, but the war doesn't end until the big man's dead."

"But who can we send?" Laness asked with the air of having this argument many times. "Even Aaron barely survived the last time they fought. Half-functioning network or not, she'll be expecting him now, and we can't lose him."

Surce added, "Especially since even if he does defeat her, we can't guarantee he can retain his anonymity in the process."

"Branten has a point, though," Mor said thoughtfully, taking the box Branten was beginning to rip into pieces. "Even if we destroy her rings, there's nothing stopping her from creating more. We'd be trapped in a game of constant defense, although complete offense doesn't have much promise either."

"Which means there's only one option," Aaron said. "We find whatever she's after first."

"And then what?" Branten muttered.

"Stop her from using it against us," Aaron said, as if this were perfectly logical.

"But how are we to do that?" Analia asked.

"We utilize my tapestries," Surce replied. "I can't promise a direct answer or specific location, but the threads are finally willing to speak to me."

Surce's eyes flicked to Analia so fast she wondered if she'd imagined it.

"How long until it's done?" Aaron asked her.

Surce thought for a moment. "Two weeks."

Aaron nodded. His family's assessing gazes shifted to Analia.

Somehow, she knew this was the moment that would not just establish her relationship with Aaron's family, but how they viewed her overall.

Her mind flashed back to the last time she had come face-to-face with Deardryn, her golden magic ripping apart her mind, her soul. She might be the key, but that didn't mean Deardryn wouldn't destroy her when she was done.

"If we're going to be tracking Deardryn," she said, "then I'm going to need to train."

Aaron's twitch of surprise was so small she almost missed it. He looked to her, about to speak, but Analia turned to Branten.

"Will you teach me to fight?"

Aaron snapped his mouth shut.

Branten rubbed his hands together, a grin slowly stretching across his face. "You think you can handle it?"

"I suppose we'll have to wait and see."

Analia had been completely defenseless in Deardryn's temple. If she couldn't get a handle on her magic, this was her next best option.

Laness nodded vigorously. Mor flashed her a look of understanding, then glanced down at his golden hand.

"We start at sunrise, then," Branten said, pushing back from the table with a stretch. "Don't come crying to me when you're more bruise than flesh."

Dinner was quick to break up after that. Aaron told Laness to fill Dimitri in, and he waited downstairs with Analia until everyone had left.

"Well," he finally said, heading for the stairs, "you certainly impressed tonight. Although that just means those four now feel entitled to harass you at their leisure."

"I think I can handle them," Analia said, trailing after him. "Although after everything you all told me, I wouldn't have expected them to be so... warm. Happy."

"Don't let them fool you," he said. "The brightest lights have the darkest pasts."

Aaron casually opened Analia's door and bowed her through. Did he not realize what he'd just revealed about himself? About her?

"So," Aaron said, drawing out the word as he leaned against her door frame. "What do you think?"

Analia didn't hesitate. "I think Branten is going to kick my ass tomorrow, and he's going to enjoy it."

Aaron tipped back his head in a laugh. A true, delighted laugh as he said, "Undoubtedly."

As Aaron bid Analia good night, she felt that question rise up once more.

Did she want to be in Ash?

Analia smiled, that final thread drifting away.

Aaron quietly closed Analia's door behind him. He leaned against the wall, his hand coming to rest against his chest.

Gods, how could one little smile have him hoping history didn't have to repeat itself? How could it convince him that bringing Analia to his kingdom wasn't a mistake, but the best choice he could have made.

And as he headed to his own room, Aaron was determined to make sure she knew her choice to stay was just as good.

Chapter 15

Ember sighed dramatically, tossing her book onto the table in her back room. It had barely been a week since her banishment, and she was already bored.

She'd read all the books she'd smuggled from the Healer School. She'd organized her back room—which mainly consisted of opening drawers, delightedly finding various objects she'd lost, and then closing the drawers without moving anything. She'd learned two new songs on her harp, helped countless patrons, and pinched off so many leaves from her devinroot that she swore it was giving her the proverbial evil eye.

But Ember refused to cave. Eventually, the healers would realize just how underwhelming her fellow apprentices were. Then, they would have to come back to her, at which point she would triumphantly, but graciously—and maybe even a little smugly—accept their offer for her to return.

If only it were that simple.

Ember rubbed her face, the typical midafternoon lull creating a near-painful quiet. Rosala spare her, she needed to be around something other than leaves. Something that could actually talk back to her.

Ember marched through Ash Castle corridors, having made the executive decision to close the apothecary early. She'd spent more than enough time inside to know the castle forward and back, most people not even sparing her a look anymore. She wasn't, however, expecting the arguing voices beyond the Council Chamber's ajar door.

"It's my kingdom, too, Cadmus!"

"I know it's frustrating, Lucilla, but—"

"I'm a Royal! Just like you! I should get to help!"

Lucilla stood with her back to Ember, hands on her hips as she stared down her brother across the table.

"There's nothing you can do, Lucilla!"

"Because there's nothing you'll *let* me do. You're no better than Mother."

Cadmus made to speak, but Lucilla turned on her heel. Ember ducked back behind the door, remaining hidden as Lucilla stormed down the hall.

For a few moments, the Council Chamber was silent. Eventually, Ember cautiously peeked around the door. Cadmus had moved to rest his fingertips against the painting of Mt. Vasolus, his expression troubled.

Ember cleared her throat. Cadmus startled, then pivoted to face her.

"Is this a bad time?" she asked.

"Even if it was, I don't think that would stop you."

"That it would not." Ember flounced into the chamber, taking a seat at the long council table. "I see you're having sister troubles."

"More than you know," Cadmus sighed, coming to collapse in the seat beside hers. "Lucilla hears just enough to know something's wrong, but she refuses to accept there's nothing that a twelve-year-old can do."

Ember's eye twitched. "There has to be something."

"Nothing she wants to do," Cadmus muttered, shoving the obsidian crown back on his head. "The kingdom is confused, Em. Some people think I should have the crown, others think it belongs to Analia. No one knows what to make of our broken tradition, and I have no idea how to make that tension subside."

"All because of Analia," Ember said bluntly.

Cadmus sagged as if realizing what he'd been implying.

"I understand why she had to give up the crown," he said. "I'll personally singe anyone who tries to claim otherwise. I just... I just don't understand why she had to leave."

Cadmus looked away, blinking hard. "I thought we were finally becoming a team. A good one at that. But then she left. She didn't even say goodbye, and I have no idea if she's all right."

Ember's heart squeezed. He had every right to be frustrated that he'd been left with Analia's mess to sort out. But the crack in his voice was that of a grieving brother, not a king.

"Come here."

Cadmus didn't protest as Ember leaned across their chairs, pulling him into a hug.

"Analia is fine," she promised. "She even gave me an enka bracelet so we can all stay in contact."

She tapped the bracelet around her wrist for emphasis. Cadmus swallowed hard, his head dropping down to her shoulder.

"You'll tell me as soon as something changes?" he asked.

"You're king now. You could very easily order me to do so."

"Not when I know I don't have to."

Cadmus remained where he was a few moments longer, seemingly collecting himself. Finally, he pulled away, Ember quietly watching him as he wiped his eyes. Gods, he was barely nineteen, left to carry not just his family's turmoil, but an entire kingdom's worth.

"You know," she said, "Lucilla isn't the only Ash Royal with a big heart."

Cadmus laughed slightly. "My father would say that makes me a weak king."

"And your uncle would say it makes you a brilliant one." Ember touched his arm, forcing him to look at her. "Analia didn't want to leave you. Especially not without saying goodbye. But we both know she couldn't have stayed here after rejecting the crown."

"I know," Cadmus sighed. "It would have been chaos if she stayed, and it's chaos now that she's gone. I just... Ember, I don't know how to be a king."

"I believe that's why you have councilmen."

"They're just as divided as the rest of the kingdom."

Cadmus shoved back his crown, his expression mirroring Analia's before her coronation. Lost. Afraid. Alone. The curse of the crown.

"Hey," she said, nudging him with her foot. "Your people chose you to be their king because they trust you. They've loved you your entire life, and they have no reason to stop now. You are their king. And you are more than capable of ruling, as terrifying as it seems."

Slowly, some of the tension faded from Cadmus's expression. He absently rubbed his knuckles across his temple, "Maybe you should write all my speeches for me."

"I would if you would do the accompanying poses."

"I don't think anyone could pull them off as well as you."

"That's a given."

Cadmus's lips flickered in a smile. "Thanks, Em."

He leaned forward and kissed her cheek. Ember wrapped her arms around herself as he rose and moved to examine the paintings.

She'd never had much of a family. Her father was a mystery, and her mother had left her with the healers as soon as Ember was chosen in order to join a traveling performance company.

But at some point, she'd found a new family in Analia and Cadmus. And she hadn't realized how much she'd been missing them.

"So," Cadmus said, "I assume Dane doesn't know you temporarily closed shop."

"Why would he?"

Cadmus laughed. "How's your apprenticeship going?"

His question might as well have smacked her between the eyes.

How could she tell him that in solving his uncle's murder, she may never be a healer again, and there was nothing he could do about it?

Cadmus glanced over his shoulder.

"Painstakingly tedious," Ember blurted. "Nothing unusual."

"Master Lenzi's testing your patience," Cadmus said, eyes back on the Mt. Vasolus painting. "She knows it's only a matter of time before you get your final ring."

"Yes," Ember said, jumping to her feet. "You're probably right. You know, I should actually be going. Apothecary and all."

Cadmus nodded distractedly as she darted for the door. She couldn't lie to him. It was the exact reason she'd been avoiding him: she was no match for the guilt.

Ember reached for the doorknob, just as something brushed against her awareness. Something faint, but familiar enough to have her pause midflight.

"Cadmus," she said, turning and trailing her hand along the wall as she approached him. "What's behind here?"

She tapped the painting of the Crystal, held aloft in the Defiants' hands.

"Nothing," he said. "It's just a wall."

"Then why do I sense plant residue?"

Cadmus's eyebrows shot up. He moved to her side, bringing his face close to the wall.

"These cracks are deeper than all the others," he said after a moment. "I wonder..."

He pressed his palms to the wall, turning and sliding them until there came a faint scraping noise. Ember pressed closer to see as Cadmus twisted and pulled the stone wall apart, splitting the image of the Crystal into three pieces.

Ember began, "What in the name of Rosala's saggy left—"

"Don't finish that," Cadmus grunted, opening the gap as wide as it would go.

Ember reached into the narrow gap before he could stop her. Feeling around, she latched onto something dry and crispy and pulled it out. Cadmus's eyes widened.

"Looks like we found where Accalon hid his xenol," Ember said, the dead leaves crinkling in her fingers.

Cadmus peered into the hole. "There's something else."

He reached inside, needing both hands to drag out a massive, age-worn book. Its leather cover was falling apart, the gold-stamped words so faded Ember could barely read them.

"The Complete History of Elefthia." She snorted. "I'd expect nothing else."

"That's not all," Cadmus said. He pulled a loose piece of paper from between the pages and flipped it around for her to see.

"A hand-drawn map of Elefthia?" Ember tossed the xenol back in the hiding spot. "I suppose it matches the history theme."

"Look at the top right corner," Cadmus said, tapping it with a finger.

Ember's eyes widened as she spotted the tiny black phoenix in flight.

"It looks like a wax seal dipped in ink," she said.

"That's what I was thinking," Cadmus said. "What does this mean?"

"I have no idea," Ember said brightly, swiping the map from him. "But I think we should figure it out."

Especially if that meant she had something to do while waiting for the council to redeem her. Maybe it would even result in a reason for them to welcome her back.

It was a solid plan. So then why did Ember's insides squirm?

PART 2: TWINKLE

Chapter 16

Analia jolted out of her nightmares as her bedroom door flew open.

Laness bounced inside, carrying an armful of woven bags overflowing with various fabrics. Barely looking at Analia's dagger and flash of midnight flames, she dumped her load in front of the wardrobe and got to work unpacking the clothes Surce had promised.

Analia tried to pay attention to Laness's cheerful talk of colors and styles, but her eyes kept returning to the enka bracelets stacked on her muscular arms. She'd said she hadn't paid attention to Analia's bracelet. But what had she picked up when she *did* check in? What had she done with that information?

Analia's questions were left to rot inside her as Laness tossed her a bundle of clothing. Quickly changing, she followed Laness downstairs and out the sliding glass back door.

Where the front yard was taken over by flower beds, the back was an expanse of grass. Laness led Analia off the lightly furnished porch and into a grove of birch trees, the two quickly coming upon a hollow in the center that had been converted into a training arena.

"She comes after all," Branten announced. He wore his black fighting leathers, his face gleaming with sweat as he continued his set of lunges in the hollow's grassy center.

"Don't start, Branten," Mor said wearily, lounging on a thick patch of moss near the hollow's shady edge.

Laness wished Analia luck. As she headed back up the slope, she made sure to nudge Aaron—who appeared to have dozed off in another patch of moss—with her boot as she passed. Aaron made a noise of protest, which Laness ignored.

"Long night?" Analia asked him.

"Aaron isn't a morning person," Mor explained.

"I'm still a delight to wake up to, though," Aaron yawned, sitting up and giving the patch of moss beside him an inviting pat.

"So you've told me." Analia hesitated a moment, but she moved to sit beside him.

"Unless you're his training buddy," Branten griped. "Then all he does is complain."

"I can kick your ass at noon just as easily as I can at dawn," Aaron said.

"Want to prove it?" Branten asked, coming to a stop. "Give Analia a little taste of what she should look forward to?"

Aaron sat up straight, his eyes glinting. "Weapons?"

"Fists and feet, brother."

Aaron's answering smile was positively wicked. He rose to his feet in one smooth movement, dusting the scraps of moss from his shirt as he sauntered forward. "I'll try to leave him in one piece for you, Anna."

"I thought you just spent seven months learning how to fall on your ass," Branten laughed.

Mor sighed. "And so it begins."

Aaron and Branten gave him a rude hand gesture. Then, in unison, they began to circle one another, still hurling taunts that only got fouler by the second.

"This part might take a while," Mor told Analia, scooting closer. "Those two have been training together for so long, they know all each other's moves."

Analia nodded, stealing a glance at Mor from the corner of her eye. "So what are they doing now?"

"Looking for an opening."

Mor made to continue, but his brows twitched up. At first, Analia thought he was staring at her clothes: a thin blue shirt and darker blue leggings. But Mor's eyes had landed on the dagger at her hip.

"Aaron gave you one of his daggers?" he asked.

Analia shrugged, her flames crackling as the surprise in Mor's eyes verged on disbelief. Before either of them could say more, Branten made his move.

The hollow came alive with the thud of fists and feet, the two moving so fast Analia could barely track them.

"Is it always like this?" she asked.

"Branten won't be like this with you," Mor assured her quickly. "Not at first, anyway. Those two are just constantly pent-up and like to take it out on one another."

Branten let out a grunt, Aaron cursing a moment later.

"Aaron's a fantastic fighter," Mor went on, eyes on the fight. "Always has been. But Branten is something else. Growing up on the streets, you obtain certain instincts that just can't be replicated."

"What about you?" Analia asked.

Mor smiled slightly. "I've always found the best attack to be the one you don't see coming."

A cool breeze combed through Analia's hair. Suddenly, she could imagine it all too clearly: Mor's calm, quiet voice in her ear as he sliced a dagger down her spine.

No, not *her* spine. But it finally sank in that Mor, who seemed so kind and considerate, had trained in the same darkness as Branten and Aaron.

Analia made to say more when Branten shouted her name.

Her flames leaped.

Aaron's head whipped toward her.

And Branten tackled him to the ground.

"Clever," Mor murmured.

"That wasn't fair," Analia said, her grip painfully tight on her dagger.

"A fight is never going to be fair," Branten said, still on top of a glowering Aaron. "It will never be balanced. One person is going to have better training, better instincts, better conditions. Relying on fairness doesn't make you honorable, it makes you dead. You hone the advantages you've got, use them without hesitating—"

A wave of silver starlight slammed into Branten. He flew back, Aaron landing on top of him a moment later with a feline grin.

"Case in point," he said. "I win."

"You would have been dead already if I weren't being such a magnificent teacher."

Branten shoved Aaron off him, and Aaron rolled to his feet. He winked at Analia, then moved off to where a pitcher of water sat on a small wooden table.

"All right, Anna," Branten said, beckoning her forward. "Your turn. Don't say I didn't warn you."

For the next hour, Aaron and Mor trained on one side of the hollow, while Branten ran Analia through a series of exercises on the other. He was a surprisingly good teacher, knowing when to encourage her for one more push-up, and when to let her call it quits and move on.

By the end, every muscle in Analia's body trembled, even her toes. But as Branten passed her a cup of water, she could have sworn her flames didn't push quite so hard against their leash.

"Same time tomorrow?" he asked.

Analia looked up into his dark brown eyes. This time, she didn't think twice.

"Yes."

Chapter 17

Dimitri immediately brightened as he followed Patryclas into the castle library.

Violet stained-glass windows encircled the space, baskets of hanging plants descending from hooks beside long, dark curtains. Yellow and green footprints marked the thick gray carpet, winding through aisles of bookcases and around scattered armchairs and tables.

It definitely wasn't as large as the Sun Castle library. But it was cozier, more inviting.

"You like to read?"

Dimitri startled, realizing he'd been skimming his fingertips over book spines as he passed. "A little."

"I've always loved the way they smell," Patryclas said, his footsteps muffled as he continued through the stacks. "My mother's family owns a bookshop, and every time I smell parchment I think of my years hiding between shelves, delighted every time I could finish a sentence by myself."

"You couldn't read?"

"It can still be a challenge today. My mind likes to rearrange letters and words. Early on, I would struggle through a sentence, just to reach the end and realize I had no idea what I'd just read."

"I used to memorize the words my half brother would read aloud during his lessons," Dimitri murmured. "Just so I could pretend to read his books later."

"You taught yourself to read?"

A jolt ran down Dimitri's spine. He snatched his hand away from the book he'd been straightening, horrified by the words that had slipped past his lips. Almost as horrified by the feeling of peace that had allowed them to do so.

"You can't blame me for being curious," Patryclas said, not glancing back as he continued through the aisles. "You speak like a commoner, but you have the gall to insult a Royal to his face. You can read, but you didn't learn in school." He smiled over his shoulder. "You are incredibly fascinating."

Dimitri glowered, but he was oddly pleased. "Does that mean you'll finally tell me what we're doing in here?"

"No," Patryclas said, rounding the corner. "But she will."

Gods-damned Moon people and their "No, but" responses. Dimitri marched after Patryclas, a list of complaints on the tip of his tongue. Just to come face-to-face with a blank wall.

But something tingled across his skin. Patryclas nudged him forward with his fingertip, and just like with Deardryn's garden, the wall shimmered away as he stepped through the magic.

A curved bookcase surrounded the intimate space. A scattering of large red pillows lined its base, a heavy desk with built-in shelves and drawers seated in the center.

"You have a hidden book nook?" Dimitri exclaimed.

"No," came a high, female voice. "I have a hidden book nook."

A woman around Dimitri's age rose from one of the pillows. She had a pale, heart-shaped face, creating a striking contrast with her deep green eyes and long, curly dark brown hair. As she came closer, Dimitri realized the pattern on her dress resembled rows of book spines.

"Pardon me, Sabi," Patryclas said. "But I believe your nook is within my library within my castle."

"Whatever you say, Uncle P," Sabi said, spreading her hands in a sarcastic curtsy.

Dimitri snickered. Patryclas glanced to him, then rubbed his face. "I'm almost afraid to leave you two alone together."

"You're leaving me?" Dimitri asked, just as Sabi demanded, "You're leaving him?"

"Don't pretend you're surprised." Patryclas urged Dimitri forward with his fingertips. "Dimitri, this is my niece, Sabi. Sabi, this is the new assistant I promised you."

"Is he?" Sabi didn't sound convinced. She drifted closer, making a slow circle around Dimitri. "Well, I suppose his eyes are sharp—yes, with the classic reader's squint. And those slim fingers are perfect for page flipping..."

Sabi came close enough Dimitri could smell lavender. He'd barely tensed when Patryclas shooed her back. "Personal space, Sabina, he's not one of your books you can press your nose against."

Dimitri barely registered Sabi's indignant response as he retreated a few steps.

How had Patryclas learned his discomforts so fast? Why was he scolding his own family to reinforce them?

"This nook is only accessible to me, Sylas, and Sabi's team," Patryclas explained.

"Which means just us," Sabi said.

Patryclas smiled at Dimitri, then smoothed down Sabi's hair. "I'll leave you to your work," he said, turning to go. "Sabi, try not to run this one off."

"If he flees, that means he wasn't good enough."

Patryclas sighed as he disappeared back into the library. Left alone, Dimitri and Sabi eyed each other warily. For a few long moments, neither of them spoke.

"If I look beneath your pillows," Dimitri finally asked, "will I find the bones of your past assistants?"

"Only the ones who displeased me."

Dimitri snickered, and Sabi's expression relaxed.

"Well come on," she said, snapping her fingers as she passed him. "We've got work to do."

Turned out, Dimitri's job was binding books.

"I take care of all the copying," Sabi said, lifting a hefty stack of papers from beneath her desk and thudding them down before Dimitri.

"Why do you get to do all the fun stuff?" Dimitri whined.

"Because I'm the most logical option."

"Says who?"

"Says my Blessing."

Before Dimitri could respond, Sabi tapped his shoulder. Dimitri jerked back, but Sabi had already bent to touch the carpet. Instantly, the gray darkened, taking on the same black as Dimitri's doublet, down to the blended burgundy threads.

"It's the same," Dimitri marveled, raising his arm to examine his sleeve. He'd quickly discovered that he enjoyed the form-fitting clothes of the Moon Kingdom—far more than his stiff servant's uniform.

Sabi beamed. "My Blessing is replication," she explained, running her fingers through the carpet and turning it back to gray. "I can copy any pattern my magic touches, then transfer it somewhere else. If you think about it, words on a page are just another pattern, meaning—"

"Meaning you're faster and I'm the binder," Dimitri sighed. He plopped down at the desk and sulked.

He thought he could at least read while he pretended to work, just as he did in Sun. Gods, what had he been thinking, promising Patryclas?

"Amazing," Sabi said, dramatically falling into the seat across from him. "When you pout like that, you look exactly like Princess Marcella. Did you hear she and the sentinel are fighting again? The one with the pine wreath?"

"Tavian?" Dimitri's nose wrinkled.

"That's the one! I never understood that pair. She's so innocent and absentminded, and he's just..."

"Annoying?" Dimitri supplied.

"Don't lump him in with us."

Dimitri's lips twitched. He dropped his gaze to his stack of papers, his shoulders slumping with a sigh. "You have a cover yet?"

For the rest of the afternoon, Dimitri fell into a rhythm: check page numbers, place cover, bind, next. It was a surprisingly slow process, although he suspected the variety of tools Sabi had passed him that thrummed with magic sped up the process considerably. Sabi flitted in and out of the space with various books in tow, but he paid her little attention. Instead, his mind wandered back to his time in the Sun Castle library with Analia.

He never thought he'd come to miss someone, let alone acknowledge it. But those late-night research sessions had been the first time he hadn't been completely alone. Even when they read in silence, she was company. And he'd felt the loss of that these past few weeks like a missing limb.

Patryclas wanted to know what he wanted? He wanted to help the one friend he had. And, well, he supposed there were worse things he could be doing in the meantime.

At some seemingly arbitrary time, Sabi declared his shift was over. Dimitri meandered back through the library, rolling his stiff neck and shoulders. He was just opening the door, intending on finding Patryclas to pester him about dinner, when he heard voices echoing down the hall.

"I never knew that."

Dimitri jumped back behind the door, his heart pounding. Crystal spare him, not *her*.

"And I've never heard you claim not to know something," Sylas muttered.

"Well," Deardryn laughed, "there aren't many wraiths in my kingdom to study."

Dimitri shuddered. Even the wraiths who worked as servants in the castle made the hairs on his arms stand up.

Thankfully, most preferred to possess the recently deceased human bodies offered as vessels instead of walking around in their spectral forms. But those all-black eyes and the cold that radiated off of them were worse than unnerving. Especially since he'd read legends that said not all wraiths waited until a body was deceased before claiming it. Yet, no human or Blessed in the kingdom seemed to give them a second look.

"I would be honored to learn more of your kingdom's history and culture," Deardryn went on.

Dimitri pressed himself against the wall as the footsteps approached.

He didn't have enough time to make it back to Sabi's nook. Even if he tried to hide in the stacks, he knew it was only a matter of time before she spotted him. He was trapped.

"You should attend our Full Moon Festival," Sylas said. They were just paces away. "I'm sure you will find plenty to analyze."

Dimitri held his breath. The Old Hag better not be ready to start her research now. They reached the door.

And without pause, they continued down the hall. Still talking amicably.

But Dimitri's pulse didn't slow. It pounded throughout his body, his nails digging into his palms.

So, Sylas wasn't just allowing her into his library, but into his traditions as well? Dimitri swung the door open, intending to do what, he didn't know. What he wasn't expecting was to bump into Patryclas on the other side.

"I was looking for you," Patryclas laughed, steadying Dimitri. "Sabi has a tendency of not releasing her helpers."

"Why is she here?" Dimitri spat. "Why is Sylas talking about wraiths and history and festivals when he's supposed to be interrogating her."

Patryclas's eyes moved first to Dimitri's flushed face, then to the group of servants huddling at the end of the hall. "Come with me."

"But—"

"Dimitri…"

"Fine."

Dimitri stomped down the hall after Patryclas, silently fuming. He knew the Moon King wouldn't speak until they were in private. But Patryclas surprised him once again.

"How do you expect my husband to interrogate Queen Deardryn if she isn't here?" he asked.

"But Sylas said—"

"His Majesty," Patryclas corrected, pushing open a door. "If you're going to prove a loyal citizen, you must show your king respect."

Dimitri flexed his tattooed wrist as Patryclas ushered him into a private study. That Crystal-forsaken oath was already coming back to bite him. He didn't argue, though, as Patryclas gestured for him to sit.

"He still doesn't have to be inviting her to festivals," he grumbled, sinking down onto a cushy blue couch.

Patryclas didn't immediately respond. He stepped over to a side table with a teapot and mugs, keeping his back to Dimitri as he poured.

"Skirmishes have been breaking out across Moon Kingdom territory," he finally said. "Nothing major, but Deardryn says the same has been happening in Sun. Do you take sugar?"

"What?"

"With your tea," Patryclas said. "I know the Sun Kingdom has a sweeter palate."

Dimitri mumbled an affirmation, completely at a loss. First Patryclas was sharing confidential information, then asking his tea preferences? What game was he playing?

Dimitri scrutinized his face as he turned, a mug in each hand, but he appeared completely earnest.

"What are you saying?" Dimitri asked.

"It's all a result of fear." Patryclas moved to hand Dimitri a mug, then sat beside him. "Someone, or something, is killing Royals, the most powerful beings in Elefthia. And the citizens are lashing out. Some due to fear, others to take advantage, but many because they are trying to regain control in a world that doesn't make sense anymore."

"So, Sy—His Majesty, is trying to make an alliance?" Dimitri asked.

"That and keep an eye on her." Patryclas fingered the rim of his mug. "Sylas never wished to be King. Even now, he delegates everything he possibly can. But he has always loved his home. And though he would never admit it, seeing his people in distress is destroying him.

"Deardryn's proposal goes beyond finding the killer. It provides an opportunity for strength—as unconventional as it might be. And Sylas refuses to take away that hope of safety, even if that means dealing with Deardryn for now."

Dimitri took a long sip of tea, the temperature just cool enough not to burn. He didn't think there was any cure for the resentment bubbling deep in his stomach. But there was something about the soft cadence of Patryclas's voice, the warm chamomile moving through his body, that had him relaxing.

"You don't trust her," he said slowly.

"I never claimed to," Patryclas said. "There's something odd about her emotions, like they're laced with shadows."

"But His Majesty *does* trust her?"

"I don't think Sylas truly trusts anyone. But being suspicious has never stopped him from doing what's right for his kingdom."

"So what?" Dimitri asked, draining his mug. "You're keeping me around as a reminder?"

"You certainly don't let him forget."

Dimitri was oddly pleased by the amusement in Patryclas's eyes. He looked at his mug, then down to his feet.

"I'm sorry I snapped at you," he muttered.

"I know," Patryclas said. "And I forgive you."

Dimitri didn't expect those words to ache. He let Patryclas take his empty mug and set it on a nearby table, his gaze fixed on his now empty hands.

He knew what Patryclas was doing, what he was offering. It was the very thing he had told himself all his life that he didn't need, just for Analia and Aaron to show him he craved it.

Connection. Company. So then why did he find himself shrinking back from the opportunity to have more?

Outside, Dimitri heard Deardryn laugh. At least he knew one thing for sure: he couldn't keep scuttling around this castle.

Chapter 18

"**C**admus," Ember said, "I love your uncle, but sometimes, that man made no gods-damned sense."

The two sat in the otherwise empty Council Chamber, *The History of Elefthia* flipped open on the table between them.

In the weeks since discovering Accalon's hiding spot, they'd taken turns reading through its contents. Ember had finished in a matter of days, seeing as she had nothing else to do. Cadmus, however, had needed far more time, seeing as he had countless things to do.

As the title suggested, the book covered the history of Elefthia, starting at the Ancient Ones' rule and ending at the Shattering. It had been further broken down into history by kingdom—which had promptly caused Ember's eyes to glaze over.

"It's not like there's some super-secret information in here," she went on, flipping through the pages. "We learn most of this during our history lessons. I guess the customs and significant landmarks from other kingdoms are new, but the mysterious power of Scarsthain isn't exactly hide-in-the-wall worthy."

"Especially since it's not the only copy of the book in the kingdom," Cadmus said. "I found three more in the library in a matter of minutes. Although none of them had these."

He tapped the top right corner of a page, where three circles had been drawn together to form a triangle. It was one of many symbols Ember had noted during her read, some pages having multiple markings crammed in the corner.

"I knew those had to be handwritten," she mused.

"At first, I thought they were bookmarks," Cadmus said, sliding his notes away from a candle with a dozing fire sprite. "But then why would he use different symbols?"

"It's definitely an annotation," Ember said. "He has no other notes scribbled in the margins, and if none of the other books had the symbols, they have to be the reason he hid the book."

"Especially if he created the added confusion of putting the marker at the top of the page instead of beside the referenced text," Cadmus agreed.

The fire sprite stretched.

"I copied down all the symbols," Cadmus went on, pulling out his sheet of sketches and placing it on the open book. "I still don't know if the symbols themselves represent anything, but I think they're a code of sorts—careful, little one."

The fire sprite had hopped off its candle to look at Cadmus's drawings. Ember caught a faint whiff of smoke as Cadmus gently nudged it away, a corner of the page scorched by its fiery little hand.

"Oh, Cadmus, look," she said, hand over her heart as the other pointed to the table. "It left tiny waxy footprints! That's adorable!"

The fire sprite beamed. Hopping over the book, it landed on the back of her hand, its little feet not quite hot enough to burn. It gave her a tiny wave, and delighted, Ember waved back.

"Em, focus," Cadmus said, fighting back a laugh.

"You're just jealous," Ember crooned, cradling the fire sprite to her cheek. "You *wish* you could leave adorable tiny waxy footprints."

The fire sprite tittered and stuck out its tongue.

Cadmus shook his head. "You two are a bad influence on one another."

Grabbing the candle, he brought it close to Ember's hand. The fire sprite amiably returned to the crackling wick, leaving Ember to wave goodbye as Cadmus placed the candle back on the table.

"As we were saying," he said, struggling to maintain a straight face. "If we're going to find out why my uncle hid this book, we need to decode the symbols."

Ember sighed dramatically, then pulled Cadmus's sketches closer. He'd clearly taken great care in replicating the symbols, even though most were just a collection of rudimentary shapes.

"Usually," she said, "I would say eleven codes isn't too bad. But with each clue being a page long?"

"I know," Cadmus said, resting his chin on his fist. "I tried to start looking for themes, but I don't have the time. The council is insisting on having round-the-clock meetings, and it seems like everyone needs the king's approval to do something."

"I can work on it," Ember offered.

"What? No, this shouldn't be all on you. This is my uncle's mystery, and you have plenty of work to do between training and the apothecary."

"Don't worry about it," Ember said quickly, gripping her hands under the table. "This is the time of year when Dane is bored enough to come in and work his shifts. I'll just skim when I'm not busy, no extra work at all. Promise."

Cadmus bit his lip.

"Come on," Ember said. "We both know I'm going to do this whether you protest or not. You might as well just accept my help."

Ember extended her hands and wiggled her fingers. Cadmus opened his mouth, glanced at the book, then shook his head.

"Sometimes," he said, "I think you're the only true friend I have." He closed his sketches between the pages of the book, then handed it to her. "Thank you."

He turned away to collect his things, missing Ember's forehead wrinkle. Rosala curse her, she hated lying to him. But she hated the idea of telling him about her sentence even more.

Sliding the book under her robes, she headed for the door. To her surprise, Cadmus followed a moment later.

"You heading out, too?" she asked.

"I want to restart my uncle's tradition of walking through the kingdom," he said. "I think it might be helpful if my people can actually see and speak with me. Even if they have nothing particularly kind to say."

Ember tilted her head as he adjusted his crown. He was facing a kingdom's-worth of turmoil head on, while she did nothing about her banishment. And yet, she expected things to change?

"You are a wonderful king, Cadmus," she said, touching his arm. "We are lucky to have you."

Cadmus looked as though he was lost for words. Finally, he mouthed a thank you, then quickly turned to open the door for her. Ember glanced back to say goodbye to the fire sprite, but it had disappeared.

Ember and Cadmus found Lucilla sitting on the entryway floor, playing with a group of fire sprites. She didn't speak as they passed, her lips pursed.

"I see she's still holding a grudge," Ember said, stepping through the castle doors.

"So it seems," Cadmus sighed. "I just hope someday she'll understand why I did it."

Ember didn't respond. The two remained quiet until they reached the Phoenix Gate, Ember glancing over to find Cadmus lost in thought.

"Hello?" She waved her hand in front of his face. "Anybody in there? Is this what it's like when I get distracted?"

Cadmus flinched, then dragged his gaze to her face. "Sorry," he said. "Lately, I can't stop thinking about all the time my father spent at Mt. Vasolus when he was king."

What did that have to do with anything? Before she could ask, Cadmus shook his head, his expression clearing.

"Thank you," he said. "Not just for the book."

He briefly touched her shoulder. Then, he strode off down the street, Ember watching him go.

Something was definitely going on with him. But was it kingdom-induced stress, or something else?

Shrugging to herself, Ember turned in the opposite direction. She knew Cadmus would talk to her when he was ready. In the meantime, she had an apprenticeship to get back into.

The sun was just beginning to set when Ember arrived at the outdoor marketplace. Each type of goods was housed under its own uniquely colored pavilion, the individual sectors coming together to form a massive arc along the edge of the square.

Ember headed straight for the green fabric roof of the produce sector. A small crowd of people had already formed inside, wandering through the wooden racks of fruits and vegetables.

Ember waved to people as she wove through the aisles. She'd always loved coming to the market. There was something about the constant hum of voices, the fresh smell of growing things that never failed to brighten her mood. That is, until she spotted the group of green healer robes across the way.

Ember ducked behind a group of humans as the healer apprentices approached, baskets of fruit swinging from their wrists.

It wasn't the first time she'd been confronted with her fellow apprentices since her banishment. A group of particularly snobbish girls had waltzed into the apothecary a few days before, their voices dripping with false concern as they asked why she wasn't in class. She didn't remember the breezy excuse she'd given, just that she had to clutch her churning stomach once they had left.

Honestly, Ember didn't give two copper shits if the apprentices or anyone else didn't like her. But that didn't mean she enjoyed how most of her class already jeered at her for her specialty, the fact that she was human. She didn't want to consider what they would do if they found out about her suspension.

But mercifully, the apprentices passed without noticing her. And their opinions were about to be irrelevant as Ember finally spotted a familiar head of gray-streaked dark hair and emerald robes.

Swiping an abandoned basket, Ember moved to the end of the healer's row. She kept her eyes on the fruit display as she slowly shuffled down the rack, eventually bumping into the healer with a yelp.

"Master Lenzi!" Ember exclaimed, jumping back. "I didn't see you there!"

The woman turned, revealing the copper skin and orange markings of her old master healer.

While all apprentices learned the four areas of healing together, they also received one-on-one training with a master healer in their specialty. Ember had been thrilled to be assigned to Master Lenzi. A fellow human herbologist, Lenzi was stern, demanding, had soul-crushingly high expectations, and was the best teacher she'd ever had. She was also incredibly consistent—not only with her shopping schedule, but also the look of mild exasperation she gave Ember now.

"Ember," she said warily, "what are you up to?"

"Why must I always be up to something?" Ember asked. "Why can't I just be thoroughly engrossed in examining these lemons—"

"They're grapefruits."

"See, and I would have realized that if I hadn't been so distracted by how happy I am to see you."

"Uh-huh." Lenzi took the grapefruit from Ember's hand and dropped it in her own basket. "I'm not letting you back into the school."

"But why?" Ember whined.

"Because you clearly haven't learned your lesson."

Ember's eye twitched.

"If you think about it," she said, following Lenzi into the next aisle, "that lesson is almost irrelevant. They told me I needed to ask for help because I'm only an apprentice. But I was able to solve the xenol mystery, which means I already had the medical mystery skills. So, all of my efforts were really focused on internal healing, which means I have to have mastered that, so really, I have all the skills of a full healer, just not the markings."

Ember thought her speech was pretty convincing. Lenzi, however, shook her head, dropping a red pepper in her basket.

"Sometimes," she said, "your arrogance is astounding."

If only she knew how flimsy it really was.

"Come on," Ember said, trailing after Lenzi. "You know you miss me."

"I do. You were one of my most promising students. Although your refusal to accept the consequences of your actions is making me reconsider that."

Ember flinched back into a spice rack.

Lenzi glanced over her shoulder, her expression softening. "Tell me you understand why you had to be punished," she said. "If you can do that, then I will go to them myself and request your immediate return to the school."

It was a simple enough request. After all, Ember knew she had broken the rules, she could admit now it was fair she had to be punished to some extent.

But she knew that was just the topsoil of Lenzi's request. Just as she knew it was the layer beneath that had her mind refusing to move, her words forming a solid mass in her throat.

Master Lenzi gave her a knowing look. She shifted her basket to one arm, her free hand coming to rest on Ember's shoulder.

"Give it some time," she said. "You'll get there."

With a quick squeeze, Lenzi turned away. As soon as she disappeared into the crowd, Ember sagged against the rack.

Rosala spare her, how delusional had she been? The archmaster healers weren't going to change their minds on their own. She couldn't win with arguments and technicalities.

Her only way back into the school was admitting they were right. She was a proud, reckless, easily disposable human herbologist healer.

Maybe if she wasn't so gods-damned prideful she would be able to march into that temple and spew those words like an empty offering. But even the thought felt like dropping every weapon she had before the battle was even fought.

But what was she fighting for? What would remain of her if she did cave and her pride was stripped away? Somehow, those questions scared her even more than the possibility of never being a healer again.

But Ember didn't have time for hypotheticals or uncertainties. She had to focus on what she *could* do.

Touching the heavy book in her robes, she marched out of the marketplace.

Chapter 19

The two weeks Surce needed to finish her tapestry flew by in a blur.

Analia spent much of that time training with Branten, her first couple sessions leaving her so sore she could barely move. The rest of Aaron's family was never far away—one reliably sprawled on the couch at all times. When she mentioned it to Aaron, he scoffed, calling his family a bunch of strays she could tell to scram at any point. But she never did.

Exactly two weeks after the family dinner, Aaron found her playing Mor's old harp. She'd discovered her flames were always at their quietest after training or when she played, to the point they didn't even flicker when Aaron invited her on his errands. So, tentatively, she agreed.

For the rest of the afternoon, Analia followed Aaron through his kingdom. They started at the district across Onyx Bridge, which his people had dubbed the Pulse. It mostly consisted of the shopping district she'd discovered, but Aaron told her it was also the core of the kingdom's nightlife, with numerous places to eat, drink, gamble, and dance.

As they moved from building to building, Analia was surprised by how many people approached them, even just to say hello. Aaron always brightened in response, calling each person by name and often stopping to briefly chat.

Every time, she braced herself for the moment attention shifted to her. But while there was wariness in most faces, there was also a friendly curiosity as they smiled and waved. It wasn't until they reached the silver bridge and what Aaron called, "The tiny boring business sector," that she finally broached the subject.

"Why don't they hate me?" she asked.

"Why would they?" Aaron asked, startled.

"Because your kingdom has been hidden for centuries, and I'm an outsider. I'm the biggest threat to their safety."

"True," Aaron admitted. "That's why I made a public address during your first week telling my people I brought someone home with me. And while I understand that might frighten them, even anger some, I assured them our secret is safe with you."

"And they believe you?"

"They trust me," Aaron said, pausing before the silver-and-white Council Building. "And now, they'll decide if they trust you, too."

Aaron cocked his head toward the building, but Analia shook her head.

"How do I prove that?" she asked, plopping down on a nearby bench.

"By being yourself." Aaron headed for the door, calling over his shoulder. "One of the advantages of being cut off from the other kingdoms is we don't uphold their prejudices. All my people want to know is how much you care about their kingdom."

Analia mulled over his words as she waited for him outside.

They should've felt like reopened wounds. Instead, as she watched Aaron's people pass, she felt oddly lighter.

To them, she wasn't the dud princess, the foreign infiltrator. She was no one. No one besides a friend of their king whom they clearly adored. And the realization was... freeing.

"Do they know what you did for them?" Analia asked when Aaron eventually reemerged.

Aaron's harassed expression morphed into surprise. "No," he said, pausing beside her bench. "As far as they're aware, I was off on business those seven months. And I plan on keeping it that way."

He gestured for Analia to rise, and they headed off once more.

"But why not send Laness into Sun?" she asked. "Or even Mor? If Deardryn had caught you and discovered this place..."

"You saw her power, Anna. Half-functioning network or not, she nearly killed me. Multiple times. And she would have definitely killed anyone else I sent in."

Aaron's gaze grew distant as they stepped back into the Pulse. "It was a gamble. But I knew we needed the scroll, and there were only two options. One, I send someone in, they get caught, they're tortured for information, my kingdom is revealed, and I lose a friend. Or, I go, same risks apply, but fewer bodies in the end."

The two turned a corner, a riverside walkway spreading out before them. Groups of people sat talking around circular glass tables, children laughing and shrieking as they ran through piles of red and gold leaves.

Aaron paused to watch for a few moments, his expression softening. He truly loved his people. And they had no idea how many dents their king, their shield, endured as a result.

"You must have really missed this place," Analia murmured.

Aaron sighed. "More than I can say."

Analia made to touch his arm.

"Aaron, Aaron!"

The two quickly turned, Analia's hand dropping to her side. A boy no older than five charged up the street toward them, copper curls bouncing against his forehead.

Aaron brightened. "Hello, Brookston," he said, kneeling as the boy skidded to a stop before him.

"Look what I can do!"

Without warning, Brookston fired a punch toward Aaron's face.

Analia flinched.

Aaron easily caught the tiny fist in his hand, grinning at the smack. "Well done!"

Brookston beamed. "I didn't hit with my pinky this time!"

"I noticed that." Aaron looked up at Analia, his eyes sparkling. "Aside from overseeing my military, Branten has helped establish some of the orphan programs he mentioned at dinner. And Brookston here just started the training aspect offered."

Analia's pulse hadn't returned to normal, but she casually tucked her hair behind her ear. "Should I be surprised Branten has little boys coming to punch you in the face?"

Aaron laughed. Brookston, on the other hand, seemed to notice her for the first time. Blue eyes widening, he shuffled closer to Aaron.

"Who's that?" he whispered, more than loud enough to be heard.

"That's Analia," Aaron whispered back. "She's a friend of mine."

"That's her?" Brookston stole an obvious look at Analia, who pretended to be engrossed in examining a window display. "She's pretty."

"Oh, Brookston, she's positively heartbreaking."

Analia fought back her blush.

Aaron gave Brookston a nudge. "You should say hi."

Brookston's eyes darted back and forth between Aaron and Analia. Finally, seeming to steel himself, he looked up. "Hello."

Analia's heart melted. "Hello, Brookston."

Brookston excitedly hopped from foot to foot. He glanced back at Aaron, who nodded encouragingly.

"Aaron told us you're special to him," Brookston blurted.

Aaron made a strangled noise. His eyes darted, looking as though he didn't know if he wanted to flee or clap a hand over Brookston's mouth. Analia, meanwhile, felt the constant, heavy knot in her chest begin to unravel.

Brookston's wide eyes bounced between them. "Was I not supposed to say that?" he asked.

"No, it's fine," Analia reassured him. "Aaron is special to me, too."

Brookston's face lit up. He tugged on Aaron's jacket sleeve, "See? I helped!"

The last of Aaron's shock seemed to shatter as he let out a laugh. "You've been spending too much time with Branten."

Analia quietly watched as Aaron said goodbye to Brookston, playfully shooing him back down the street toward a group of children. It took her a moment to realize that throughout their entire interaction, her flames hadn't so much as flickered.

"So," Aaron said, a mischievous grin on his face as he rose. "I'm special to you, huh?"

"You already knew that," Analia said dismissively. She headed off down the street once more, Aaron falling into step beside her.

Now that she thought about it, though, she hadn't exactly made that clear to him lately. If anything, she'd done the opposite.

She felt for her flames, which once again only started to crackle under her attention.

For so long, she'd only thought of them as a constant, indiscriminate blaze. But could it be, all this time, they were simply responding to her?

Looking for reasons to push Aaron away. Waiting for the unpredictability that had allowed Pryanth and Brenn to pierce straight through her heart. Even when his every look, every word, had her heart whispering, *I know you.*

"Analia," Aaron said in a singsong voice. "Where have you disappeared to?"

Analia refocused. They'd stopped on an empty section of walkway, the river's rolling current just loud enough to mask their voices to those nearby.

"I was thinking," she said slowly, "that children seem to like you. First Loliette, the orphan girl from Sun, now Brookston."

Aaron laughed, leaning back against the railing. "It's my undeniable charm."

He flashed a grin. And for the first time, Analia noticed the tension around its edges.

Gods, he didn't deserve this. She couldn't let her flames, let herself, keep punishing him.

"You know what I was also thinking?" she asked.

Aaron shook his head.

"That I can count the people who haven't betrayed me on one hand." Analia looked down at the river, feeling Aaron's gaze on her face. "It seems like every time I begin to trust someone, I find a new knife to my back.

"Accalon was my one constant, and then he was murdered by his own brother. And when I tried to find that consistency in Pryanth, he said either he'd take me against my will, or he'd kill me."

She'd never said that part aloud before. But as the words slipped free, the fist constantly squeezing her throat finally seemed to slacken. Even as a ribbon of starlight flashed across Aaron's knuckles. Yet, he remained quiet, letting her continue.

"You, Dima, and Ember," she said. "You're all I have left. And when you showed me this kingdom, all I could think was it was one more thing I hadn't seen coming. You were one more person that could stab me in the back."

"Never," said Aaron hoarsely.

Tears pricked behind Analia's eyes. "I just need to know I can trust you. I know you would say I can, even if I can't, but I... I can't lose you, too."

Aaron's careful composure cracked. He slid his hand across the railing, his fingertips grazing hers. The chasm in Analia's chest yawned even wider.

"Have I ever told you why I want to be king?" he asked.

Analia shook her head.

"It's because I am intimately familiar with the hatred Elefthia has for my family. Those who were around throughout the Shattering War remember as well. But *every-one* here knows this is a safe place. And while I have no idea how long this peace, this safety, can endure, I will do whatever it takes to preserve it. Even if that means becoming the monster the kingdoms believe I am."

He shifted so she was forced to look at him, his silver eyes intent. "You are now a part of that safety, Analia. You can stay here as long as you wish." He rested his hand on top of hers. "And I am not going anywhere unless you tell me to."

Analia didn't trust herself to speak. Aaron moved closer, close enough she could smell metal and spice as he promised, "You can trust me."

The sincerity in his eyes had her knees shaking. But beneath that sincerity was a glint of challenge. She could trust him, but could he trust her? Trust her to not run away?

Analia nodded. Aaron's fingers tightened around her hand.

And abruptly, they were gone as he looked over her shoulder.

"Well," he said, pushing off the railing, "I believe we're about to be summoned."

Analia looked down at her hand, now oddly cold, then stuffed it into her jacket pocket. Before she could ask, Mor emerged from the crowded streets and headed for them.

"Is it time?" Aaron called to him.

"Surce wants us all at the big house," Mor confirmed.

Analia asked, "Does that mean she finished the tapestry?"

Mor nodded, offering his golden hand to Aaron. Taking it, Aaron slid his other arm around Analia's waist and pulled them into the shadows.

A moment later, a wide-open dining room solidified around them. And for the first time in a long time, Analia didn't immediately step out of Aaron's grip.

Chapter 20

The big house's dining room was made from pale, polished wood. A massive oak table and matching chairs took up the majority of the space, with a second smaller table pushed into the far corner. It was there Branten and Laness sat, hunched over the chessboard between them.

Aaron and Mor exchanged a look.

"What?" Analia asked.

"Just watch," Aaron said.

A minute ticked by in silence, then two. Neither Laness nor Branten moved a piece.

Analia made to speak, just as Laness threw up her hands with a groan. Branten let out a victorious whoop, Mor laughing under his breath as he took a seat at the table.

"What was that?" Analia asked.

"That," Aaron said, crossing to a cart holding various liquor bottles, "was a duel between the two finest military strategists in my kingdom."

Behind him, Branten gloated as Laness tried to jab him with a pawn. Mor twisted around in his seat to catch Analia's eye, his head tipping back in a sigh.

Analia's lips twitched. "I'm assuming Branten's knowledge comes from his Underground training," she said, taking the seat beside Mor's, "but what about Laness?"

"Laness was trained by the DovenU," Aaron explained. "A tribe of the deadliest female warriors in all of Elefthia."

"I've never heard of them."

"They're another secret, protected establishment of my ancestors." Aaron returned to sit on her other side, thunking down two heavy bottles on the table. "Their base is located east of here in Mt. Lanula and is guarded by my magic—although they remain independent from my kingdom."

At the side table, there came a clatter and a curse as chess pieces spilled to the ground.

"Put your toys away, you two," Surce said, breezing through one of the three arched doorways with a tapestry under her arm. "We have business to discuss."

Branten looked up from the floor, "Does that business involve food?"

"We've been waiting for hours," Laness complained.

"You mongrels need to learn how to feed yourselves," Surce said.

Mor laughed under his breath as he flicked his golden fingers. An assortment of food containers appeared on the table, smelling of something spicy.

Laness darted for the table. Branten made to follow, but Surce gestured for him to help her pin the tapestry to the wall.

"You seem to be feeling cryptic today, Surce," Aaron commented, pulling a box of what was revealed to be chicken and rice toward himself and Analia.

Mor began, "It's certainly turning into a grand—"

He froze, hand half-extended to offer Analia a fork. His eyes fixed on the tapestry as Surce and Branten stepped back, Aaron's face paling as he did the same.

"Why in the name of the Crystal did you create that?" Branten demanded.

Surce smoothed down her burgundy dress. "Because that is where we need to go."

Aaron and Mor swapped a look and shuddered. As Surce moved to the table, Analia finally got a good look at the tapestry.

Most of the chamber depicted was coated in shadows. Countless runes were carved into the stone walls and floor, many outlined in various colors. Long iron chains pooled around the center of the tapestry, disappearing into the densest clump of shadows. So dense all she could see was a pair of white, slanted eyes with a sliver of a pupil.

"Aaron," Analia said, her flames unusually calm. "What is it?"

Aaron dragged his gaze from the tapestry, his expression haunted. "The worst possible outcome."

Analia's stomach did a slow roll.

For a moment, the only sound was the scrape of chairs as Branten collapsed into his seat, Surce following suit. Then, Laness picked up a fork, put it in Branten's hand, and pulled a box toward him.

"Eat first," she ordered. "Then, you three explain."

"No," Mor said, rubbing his temples, "we can explain now."

Branten glowered. Aaron gestured with his fork for Mor to go on.

"For context," Mor said to Analia, "there's no set amount of time a person stays in the Underground. Once every three months, every person who believes they have finished their training is brought to the same place. Then, they're told to run."

"Run where?" Analia asked.

"Wherever the Underground likes," Branten said. "The Underground's magic lets it do whatever it wants. Change your path midway through, throw up a wall, a surprise turn or two. My favorite was the giant-ass chasms out of fucking nowhere.

"Sometimes they're just illusions. But every time, your instincts are the only thing that keep you alive while running."

Aaron said, "Most people decide to run the final trial alone. It's hard enough surviving your own trials, let alone someone else's. And since each failure to escape puts you lower in military ranks, going alone is your best option.

"But Branten, Mor, and I decided to stick together. No one was going to get left behind in the darkness, and no one would be alone in open air."

"And that's when we found that charmer over there," Branten said, gesturing over his shoulder with his fork.

"You never told us this," said Surce.

"Why do you think?" Branten muttered.

"You could feel the power the moment you stepped inside," Mor murmured, having barely touched his food. "Strong enough you could feel the hum in your bones."

"What happened in that chamber isn't important," Aaron cut in firmly. "All that matters is that creature is dangerous."

"So, naturally," Branten said, "we booked it out of there."

"And we made it out of the Underground on our first try," finished Mor dully.

Laness frowned into her food box. "And that's the creature we have to go find?"

Analia glanced back at the tapestry and shuddered.

"This can't be our only option," Branten protested.

Aaron turned to Surce. "What were you thinking when you wove the tapestry?"

Surce scooped up the last of her rice. "I was searching for the path forward."

"It makes sense," Mor admitted. "Whatever that creature is, it does possess an un-orthodox amount of knowledge."

No one looked particularly happy about that.

"Well," said Laness, closing her box, "it's the best lead we have."

Surce mused, "Although I'm not pleased with how little information the tapestry provides."

"Well," Analia said, "at least we know I have to be the one who talks with it."

Aaron's head whipped toward her.

Branten—who had been tipping back in his chair—clattered back down. "What?"

"I need to be the one to talk with the creature," she said. "We don't know what type of information it can give us, let alone will. And if we're going to be asking about Deardryn, and we're assuming her key is *my* sensory abilities, I might have follow-up questions none of you would think of."

"She has a point," Laness said, tapping her fork against her lips.

"But she's only been training for two weeks," Branten protested. "In order to ask her questions, she needs to get to the creature first, and the Underground will be ruthless."

Surce said, "The tapestry refused to be woven until Analia arrived for a reason, I can feel it."

"We can't just send her in there," Branten insisted.

"Not alone," Mor agreed.

"Which is why I'm going with her," Aaron said, setting his fork down decisively.

Analia looked to him quickly, but his face was unreadable. She, however, had no problem interpreting Mor's and Branten's expressions as they protested.

"It's not up for debate," Aaron said, raising his voice over theirs.

"Then let us come with you," Branten pleaded.

"You shouldn't have to face it alone," Mor agreed.

"Absolutely not," Aaron said. "The more people we bring in, the more tests the Underground will throw at us."

Branten and Mor looked away.

Gods, what horrors had those three been exposed to while trapped in those tunnels? What horrors was *she* going to be exposed to?

"He's right," Laness said reluctantly.

Surce nodded, and Aaron pushed himself to his feet. He glanced to the tapestry one last time, then down to Analia.

"Are you sure you want to do this?" he asked, softening a fraction.

Analia wanted nothing more than to say no, don't send her into that underground death trap. But she'd survived the Sun Kingdom. She'd survived her own kingdom. And for perhaps the first time in her life, she was needed.

Analia nodded.

"Then we leave tomorrow morning," Aaron said. Not waiting for a response, he strode from the room, the door clicking shut behind him.

The five of them exchanged a heavy look. Eventually, Surce quietly rose to her feet, going to take down her tapestry. Laness followed her a moment later, the two quickly disappearing through another door with tapestry in tow.

"And then there were three," said Branten, having bounced back remarkably fast.

"Make that two," Mor said. Collecting the empty boxes, he tossed them in the corner bin where they disappeared with a quick thrum of magic.

"What? Mortie, no! We should do something, shake it off."

"Not this time, Branten."

Mor offered Analia a small smile of farewell, then slipped out the door.

Branten sighed dramatically. "Of course, it's on me to gather the family."

"Branten," Analia said, "I think you should leave them alone."

"Not tonight," he said. "With what's to come tomorrow, leaving them alone will only result in sulking and hiding."

Oh gods, Analia knew that look. It was the same face he made when she begged him to reduce her number of lunges.

"What are you going to do?" she asked.

Branten grinned, his heavy boots clomping as he strode toward the door. "You'll see. You're helping."

T he next ten minutes consisted of Branten sprawled on a thoroughly annoyed Mortimer's bed, loudly hemming and hawing until Mor kicked them out. He did grumble something about getting changed before slamming the door, though.

"And that's one," Branten said, marching off.

"You really think you can get all of them?" Analia asked, hurrying after him.

Not stopping as he passed, Branten hollered into the dining room, "Laness! We're drinking tonight. Wear something cute."

"Like I'm ever *not* cute," Laness replied.

"Grab something for 'His Majesty' and Anna while you're at it."

Laness yelled a confirmation, and Analia raised a questioning brow. Branten only grinned. "That's two."

"How are you going to get Aaron?" Analia asked, following him down a narrow hallway.

"I'm not," he said, pausing outside the last door on the right. "You are."

Analia took a hasty step back. "Why me?"

"Because Aaron's in his mom's room, which means he's in full-on brooding mode and I don't want to deal with that."

"So I have to?"

"Would you rather get Surce?"

Analia winced. Now that was an argument she knew she had no hope of winning.

Branten patted her shoulder. "I've taught you all I can. Go forth, my apprentice."

Analia rolled her eyes. Branten trudged back down the hall, leaving Analia to toy with her phoenix pin.

Aaron sat on what used to be his mother's bed. He could never decide if the room and all its memories were a form of comfort or torment.

The ghost of her voice. The faint smell of lilies and river air. The countless times he'd sat with her because she refused to see anyone else.

All he knew for sure was he was drawn to the spot every time the raging storm in the back of his mind shoved to the forefront.

Aaron let out a shuddering breath, dropping his head into his hands.

He'd known the moment he saw the tapestry he was going back into the Underground: his home, his prison. He could handle that. But how was he supposed to face the voice that still hissed through his nightmares? How was he supposed to drag Analia into that?

A soft knock came on the door. Aaron's nails dug into his scalp, but he called for them to enter. To his surprise, it was Analia who stepped inside a moment later.

He wasn't a fool; he knew she had reached out a hand on that walkway. But he'd also learned the hard way just how easily an extended hand could be ripped away. Analia had reiterated that fact.

Yet, there she was, closing the door behind her. Glancing around the lightly furnished room decorated in silver and lilac.

"Branten has decreed we're to go out tonight," she said, coming to sit beside him.

"And I suppose you were charged with retrieving me?"

"Something like that."

Analia offered him a tentative smile, but Aaron shook his head. "Not tonight, Anna."

He shifted to face the window, waiting for the inevitable lift of the mattress. But Analia stayed where she was, close enough he could smell smoke and the jasmine soap she used to wash her hair.

"Branten told me this was your mom's room," she said softly.

Aaron glanced back at her, noticing her fingers toying with her pin. Her uncle's pin.

"It is," he hedged.

Analia was quiet for a moment. "What happened to her, Aaron?"

Aaron immediately looked away. "That's a long story."

"One that's worth telling."

No. Aaron couldn't pry that story loose. Not when an army of knots was already destroying his insides.

"Another time, maybe."

"Aaron." Something in Analia's voice had him glancing back. "You can trust me, too."

There was that hand again. The one that had offered the story of her wedding night, the memory alone having his fingers flex around the duvet.

Finally, Aaron said, "My mom was forced to watch, helpless, as her children were murdered. Then, she lost my father. In the span of a month, my mom lost everything except me... And then I disappeared into the Underground for over a decade."

"You came back to her," Analia pointed out.

"Physically, maybe," Aaron muttered. "The Underground breaks you, Analia. The military would say it rebuilds something stronger, and in a lot of ways, they're right.

"But that didn't stop the pain in my mom's eyes when she saw me stumble out of the Underground, beaten and bruised. And I can't... I can't be the reason someone feels that type of pain."

Analia made to speak, but Aaron shook his head.

"I can't let my family see... I won't have them needlessly worry about me when I know I will be fine by tomorrow. I can't do that to them, too."

There. They were even. She'd tried, she'd failed, she could go with a clear conscience. Crystal only knew Liss always had after his mother came up.

"Aaron." Analia leaned toward him, forcing him to look at her. "You don't want anyone to worry about you?"

Aaron nodded slowly.

"Then don't give them a reason to worry. Show them that you had your moment, you collected yourself, and now, you're as all right as the situation allows. And come out with us."

Analia gave him the same challenging look he'd given her on the walkway. One that told him she cared enough to come, but she also respected him enough to leave if he asked.

Aaron wavered.

Analia extended her hand to him. "I want you to come."

Slowly, Aaron's body seemed to thaw. He took her hand, her fingers lacing through his. Not pulling away.

Somehow, she had that beaten-down hope in his chest stirring once again. Enough so that twenty minutes later, he was dressed in his embroidered black-and-blue jacket, waiting downstairs with the rest of his family.

His black mood still clung to him like a piece of dead skin, but as Analia joined them, as he took in her beaded dress whirling in shades of silver and white, he found himself murmuring, "Shooting star."

As he followed his family out the door, Aaron decided maybe he could trust that hand after all.

Chapter 21

Analia sat in a circular booth between Aaron and Mor, severely regretting her decisions.

The dance hall was dimly lit, the live band magically amplified so loud the cushioned booth vibrated with every drum beat. There were no smoke rings that hung in the air, but the room was hot from the mass of bodies—so many bodies. Writhing to the music, crammed around tables as they drank and gambled.

The moment Analia stepped inside, she thought she might jump out of her skin. Aaron took one look at what had to be sheer panic on her face, then steered her over to the hidden corner booth, where he turned a small silver dial in the center of their table. Immediately, a soft thrum of magic expanded outward, forming an invisible bubble around their booth and quieting the music to a more tolerable level.

Mor decided to join them, the rest splitting off to dance.

As Aaron and Mor took bets on how they thought Branten would get them kicked out that night, Analia forced herself to breathe. She could do this. She had to do this.

"Oh," Mor said suddenly. "Look, Surce is on the hunt."

Aaron perked up, then hummed in approval. "She has good taste."

Analia squinted, trying to follow their gazes. Eventually, she spotted Surce on the outskirts of the dance floor, talking with a tall, fair man and a petite woman with curly hair.

"Which one?" she asked, the first thing she'd said all night.

"Both," Mor said, eyes still on the trio.

Analia coughed on her water. Aaron smirked.

"Surce not only enjoys the company of both men and women," he said, "but often, at the same time."

"Really…" Analia glanced back to Surce, who ran her fingers along the man's arm.

"She certainly knows what she likes," Mor mused. He turned back as a curvy woman in a bright blue dress bustled up to their table, her golden hair braided around her head like a crown.

"Your Majesty!" she beamed, bowing to Aaron and flashing Analia and Mor a friendly smile. "We haven't seen you around here in some time."

"I just couldn't stay away, Jesmine," Aaron said over the music. "How's Leah?"

"Oh, she's wonderful! Thrilled to see you, too. She actually requested I come snag you so she can talk to you about the ale trade."

Aaron gave Analia a questioning look. Stifling her surprise, she nodded, and Aaron slid out of the booth and through their magic bubble, saying he'd be back shortly.

"How do you have trades if your kingdom is hidden?" Analia asked Mor.

"You'd be surprised how many people aren't trading with who they think they are." Before Analia could inquire further, Mor shook his head. "Crystal spare us, he's gambling now."

Analia craned her neck, just spotting Branten as he sat down at a long, crowded table. "I take it he's not very good?"

"No," Mor sighed, "he's excellent. I've never met someone who could read and deceive people as well as Branten."

"And that's a problem?"

"It's a problem because he doesn't know when to stop. I wouldn't be surprised if one of these days, he tries to gamble my hand."

Analia smiled slightly, her eyes moving down to the golden hand Mor rested on the table. "Can I ask how you got that?"

"I've been wondering when you would." Mor turned to face her fully. "My mother was from the Human Kingdom, but she and her friends loved to sneak into the Starlight Kingdom to get a glimpse of the magic. Naturally, she quickly fell in love with one of the Blessed. As soon as my grandparents found out, she was forbidden from ever seeing him again. But a few months later, they realized she was pregnant."

Analia's stomach did a slow roll.

"From the start, my grandparents were on high alert for any sign of Blessing. They were hopeful I was a Demiblessed the Crystal utterly ignored. And though they tested me, neglected me, berated me, I never showed any sign of magic. But that didn't stop their paranoia.

"Finally, when I was nine, my grandfather decided I needed to prove myself, once and for all. And that night, he cut off my hand."

Analia sucked in a breath. Mor briefly squeezed his eyes shut.

"They didn't realize no Blessing would be enough to regrow a hand. But there was no doubting my wound began to clot far faster than it should. It would be some time before I discovered the true nature of my Blessing, but that was when my grandparents banished me from their home, and their kingdom. And the Underground was the only place I had to go."

Analia didn't have a name for the emotions that had her flames burning hotter, hotter, hotter.

"You must hate them," she said.

Mor's face was resigned as he reached for his ale. "Not at first. For a long time, there were a lot of excuses for them, trying to find one little reason not to despise the few people I had. But then when the anger did hit..."

"Explosive?" Analia asked.

Mor winced. "You could say that. Aaron and Branten would definitely say that."

"Aaron would definitely say that about me, too."

Mor fell quiet. It wasn't Aaron's silence, designed to nudge people into talking. It was contemplative as he, too, looked over his past, his golden fingers idly tracing the rim of his cup.

Analia leaned back in the booth, her gaze fixed on the softly glowing stars painted on the ceiling. "It feels..." She struggled for the words. "It feels like every last shred of emotion I've tried to shove down is now erupting all at once."

"Ah, the emotional kickback," Mor said, nodding sagely. "Burning through all the buildup before you can start fresh."

So, she'd been right earlier that day about her flames responding to her. Which meant all that fury—or, at least, a portion of that fury—was hers.

She was angry with Ash. Angry with Pryanth and Deardryn. Angry with herself because she'd left the Ash Kingdom, yet she still clung to every lesson and pattern it taught her.

"I just don't want to hurt anyone else," Analia murmured.

Mor touched her knee under the table, drawing her gaze back to him.

"We all have scars, Analia," he said. "Just at different stages of healing. Everyone gets that here."

Analia blinked hard. Her gaze drifted across the crowd, spotting Branten heading their way. For the first time, she noticed how his eyes never stopped moving, as if he, too, couldn't quite turn off the instinct to search for danger. That same instinct had Analia's eyes shifting to the side, noticing a girl with warm brown skin and eyes staring directly at her.

The girl's mouth drifted open as their eyes locked.

The back of Analia's neck tingled. She turned to Mor, who quickly reassured her there was nothing to worry about. Before Analia could decide if she'd imagined the tension in his voice, Branten reached them.

"All right, Mortie," he said, reaching out to tap Mor's golden hand. "You handling this one?"

Mor's expression cleared. "Will a pinky do?"

"Perhaps," Surce mused, approaching the table with Laness close behind, "he can use what's left over to purchase himself some common decency."

Aaron laughed as he, too, reappeared. "Now why would you want to go wasting Mor's pinky gold like that?"

"Besides," Branten said, "I'm full to bursting with decency."

"Oh," Laness said, "is that what we're calling bullshit now?"

"That's going to make things confusing," Analia mused.

All five of them, even Surce, gave her surprised, yet pleased looks.

"The good news," Aaron said, reclaiming his spot beside her, "is Branten is *only* full of shit."

Branten didn't deny it as they all crammed into the booth.

As the night continued on, Analia turned over the fact that she'd come to this kingdom to escape Ash. But perhaps this kingdom wouldn't be such a bad place to stay after all. Maybe, she just had to try.

As Aaron's leg brushed hers under the table, she decided she could.

By the end of the night, Aaron was thoroughly drunk. Not on alcohol, but on every one of Analia's comments, her smiles, the way the distracted look had finally cleared from her eyes.

"We're going to the Black Dragon," Laness said as she led the way out the dance hall door. Branten was already halfway down the street, swaggering toward the tavern around the corner. "Any of you coming?"

Mor shook his head, saying he had a council meeting in the morning. Surce had already disappeared with the man and woman she'd been "hunting," leaving Laness to raise her brows at Analia and Aaron.

"What are you going to do?" Analia asked him.

Aaron tipped his head back, hands clasped behind him. "I think I want to take a walk."

"Can I come?"

That drunken buzz peaked. "Always."

Analia shook her head at Laness. The nymph shrugged and headed after Branten, the tiny crystals in her indigo dress sparkling in the streetlights. Mor waved before leaving as well, and Aaron turned to go in the opposite direction.

"Are we going anywhere in particular?" Analia asked, falling into step beside him.

"You'll see."

Aaron led her through the night-darkened kingdom. It wasn't the fastest route, but he knew Liss would be out that night. Even though the pain that lanced through his chest every time he saw her had dulled, he still found himself subconsciously avoiding crossing her path.

"Mor told me about his hand tonight," Analia said.

"Did he?" Aaron was undeniably pleased by the quiet outrage in her voice.

"I don't know how he could go back to them, let alone rule over them."

"Mor has always had an ability to set things aside," Aaron explained. "He can see things from every angle, and somehow has the pragmatism and forgiveness to realize he's the best fit for that role."

Certainly better than himself.

Aaron's eye twitched, but Analia didn't seem to notice.

"Speaking of Branten," she said, tucking a lock of hair behind her ear, "has there ever been anything between him and Laness?"

"Never," Aaron said with a laugh. "Those two are merciless to one another, but it's born out of loyalty, not romantic chemistry. They would destroy each other if they became anything more than friends. And we've arrived."

Their path opened up on a gravel lakeside at the northwest edge of the kingdom. The water sparkled in the darkness, its smooth surface reflecting the starlight like a massive mirror.

The few people that visited only came during the day, most preferring to steer clear because of the constant guard patrols. But the guards were currently across the lake, meaning it was just Aaron, Analia, and the stars.

"Beautiful," Analia breathed.

Aaron offered her a hand down the steep slope, leading her toward a tall, arched bridge. "Just wait until we reach the top."

Aaron trailed his hand along the stone railing as they climbed, acutely aware that the last person he'd brought to this spot was Liss. He hadn't planned on ever bringing someone back after that. But as they reached the peak, as Analia's face lit up, the tightness in his lungs eased.

"You can see everything up here," she exclaimed, moving across the bridge.

The Starlight Kingdom spread out below them, a collection of dazzling lights, sparkling bridges, and rivers that wound through it all like a network of veins.

"And if you look across the bridge," he said, taking Analia by the shoulders and turning her, "you can see the Human Kingdom."

It didn't look like much in the dark. The humans preferred a far more modest settlement, especially since they refused to use any of the Starlight Kingdom's magic.

"And that?" Analia asked, turning in his grip to look over the side of the bridge.

"That," he said, "is the rest of Elefthia."

Just on the other side of the lake, Aaron could feel the tingle of his wards. But beyond that was a collection of forested ridges, cut through by winding ravines. Somewhere past them was the Moon Kingdom, but Talitha had been careful to make sure there was a large portion of Wild Lands between them.

"Do any of the major rivers run through those ravines?" Analia asked, pointing into the darkness.

"Clever girl. That's how we manage what little trading we risk."

"And the wards are enough to keep anyone from finding this place?"

"Well," said Aaron, releasing her shoulders to rest his elbows on the railing, "no one here wants to leave, so there's no risk of word leaking through my people. Our few merchants have earned the greatest amount of trust I'm willing to give, and even then, precautions have been taken so they can't reveal our secret. As for the humans, they've all been warned what will happen to them if they dare."

Aaron paused, the look on Analia's face telling him he didn't need to elaborate just what those warnings entailed.

"As for outsiders," he went on, "there have been a few people throughout the centuries that have stumbled upon us, but interrogations always found it to be an accident. Then, they were executed to keep the secret with their corpse. Many by my own hand."

"Why not enact the same precautions you give the merchants?" Analia asked.

"Because there are Blessings that can prevent accidental slipups, but there's no way to stop someone from willingly sharing our secret."

Aaron waited for Analia to call him unreasonable, cruel even. But she only turned in a slow circle, her dress rustling in the breeze as she drank in the view.

Eventually, she looked back at Aaron—who tried to hide how he had been drinking in a completely different view. One that involved the curve of collarbones and dip of her waist.

"Does that mean you've captured me so I can entertain you on your watch duty?" she asked.

Aaron laughed. "I captured you, smartass, to show you Ethelind's favorite spot."

"Is it really?"

"She'd always come up here, hands on her hips, surveying her kingdom below. Positively regal."

Aaron watched from the corner of his eye as Analia registered the past tense. He braced himself for her to ask, but Analia surprised him once again.

"She must have been a wonderful queen."

Aaron scoffed. "She was the most difficult, reluctant queen there ever was."

"What do you mean?" Analia asked, obviously amused as she came to lean beside him.

"Ethelind was on my father's side of the family, but she had no interest in ruling, politics, none of it. So, she did everything she could to delay her bleeding, and then when it did come, she scuttled off to the DovenU before anyone could marry her off."

"I was wondering why I didn't recognize her name from history," Analia said.

"She disappeared before she could be carved into it," Aaron confirmed.

"It's almost funny how Royals seem to have a tendency of doing that," Analia mused. "Ethelind, the Defiants."

Aaron nodded thoughtfully. According to legends, the Defiants had apparently disappeared after their rule because they thought it was the only way to completely transfer their authority. He'd once thought it was an extreme approach, but after taking his own crown, he could understand.

That, however, wasn't a story he could tell at the moment, so he only shrugged and continued on. "Ethelind trained there for centuries, rising through the ranks, eventually becoming their queen. The only reason she came back was because the kingdom had burned to the ground, and she said she wouldn't leave her people to a grief-stricken widow and a babe who didn't know his ass from his kneecap."

Analia snorted. Aaron grinned.

"You know," Analia said, her voice softening, "I think I've learned more about you in these past three weeks than I have in all the time I've known you."

A slow, deep ache pierced Aaron's chest. "I never wanted to keep secrets from you," he said quietly.

"I understand why you had to."

"Well," he said, unable to stop himself from shifting closer, "now that you're here, there's no reason to hide."

"I don't think you would be you without a few secrets," Analia said thoughtfully.

Aaron fought back a flinch. *Clobbering secrets.*

"I've had to keep so many secrets," he said, tracing a groove in the rail with a fingernail. "Secrets from my mom so she wouldn't worry, secrets in the Underground to survive, secrets as a king.

"It's like... it's like I've spent my life walking along the lakeside, collecting stones to throw. Yet, when it's finally time to release them, my hand won't open. It can't because I've been holding on for so long that my fingers don't remember how to uncurl."

Just that admission had his throat closing around the words.

"Maybe you just have to start small," Analia suggested. "One finger at a time."

"Maybe," Aaron murmured, unconvinced.

Analia shrugged. She fixed her gaze on the kingdom once more, a faint smile on her lips as she took in the sparkling lights.

The first and only time he'd brought Liss to the bridge, she'd spent maybe five minutes looking around. Before he knew it, she was complaining about how cold she was and insisting they go back down. But Analia?

"I missed you," Aaron whispered.

So much for starting small.

Analia looked at him quickly.

Aaron became acutely aware of how close she stood. But there was no flash of heat as her voice cracked, "I missed you, too."

Something heavy seemed to dissipate from Aaron's shoulders. He reached over, ruffling her hair. And it was a long, long time before he finally shadowjumped them home.

Chapter 22

Dimitri stepped into the empty masquerade shop.

He'd spent the last two weeks under shadowy hoods, braced to find Deardryn waiting for him every time he rounded a corner. The only reason his nerves weren't completely shot was because he'd heard rumors long ago about Blessed who had the ability to change people's appearances. It had taken him hours of research and pestering an uneasy Patryclas, but finally he'd found this shop, tucked away in a back corner of the square.

Now, Dimitri glanced around the small studio, his brows rising at the lavish couches and gold-trimmed walls. Expensive.

"Sun Kingdom," someone purred. "Don't get many of those around here."

Dimitri's jaw dropped. A slim, tattooed man descended a narrow back staircase, his footsteps light despite his leather boots.

His features weren't particularly striking: dark eyes, mahogany hair, light brown skin with a hint of stubble on his jaw. But his tailored doublet screamed luxury, the red velvet so dark it almost appeared black.

"What makes you say I'm from Sun?" Dimitri whined.

"Your coloring says it all." The man stepped up to Dimitri and touched his hair. "You mostly see fair hair in the northern kingdoms—although Wind is typically more silver than gold. I suppose you could be from Ash, since there is no olive in your skin. And yet…"

Dimitri flinched as the man turned his face from side to side. "Yes, I can see the ghost of your tan. Which means it's more likely that you are, in fact, from Sun."

Dimitri pulled out of the man's grip. "Not everyone in Ash is pale."

"Which is why my little game isn't infallible. You just happened to be the walking paragon of a Sun citizen."

Dimitri edged back, his nose filled with something dark and earthy.

Gods, if this stranger could recognize him that fast, it was a miracle Deardryn hadn't caught him.

"That's why," he said, "I need you to change my appearance."

"Me?"

"You saying you're not Rayner?"

A slow smile crept across the man's lips. "I see my reputation is spreading."

Reluctantly. Patryclas had told Dimitri numerous times nothing good would come from him visiting the masquerader. The only reason he'd caved and given Dimitri the shop location was because he could feel how acute Dimitri's anxiety had become.

"All right, then," Rayner said, moving deeper into his studio and circling around a curved counter. "What will it be, then?"

"Whatever this gets me." Dimitri dumped a handful of gold pieces on the counter with a quiet clink. It was the last of what Analia had given him, but if it would spare him from Deardryn, it would be worth it.

Rayner pulled the pile toward himself with long, elegant fingers. He took his time sifting through, eventually leaning his elbow on the counter to prop his chin in his hand.

"I can change one eyebrow."

"What!"

"It should really only be half, but that would reflect poorly on my business."

"Why the fuck do you think you're so expensive?" Dimitri demanded.

"You know why. You wouldn't be here if you didn't." Abandoning Dimitri's gold, Rayner meandered over to a collection of abstract paintings on the wall. "It's rare enough to find a Blessed who can change his own appearance. But someone who can also change others?"

Sensing the impending monologue, Dimitri slumped into a cushioned chair.

"Many of my fellow masqueraders put their Blessing to nefarious purposes," Rayner explained. "Assassins, spies, con men. But my interests have always been smaller. The stray freckle, the accidental ink smear. Each individual second holds massive potential. And it only takes one minuscule change to catalyze an entire chain of events."

Well, this screamed bad idea. Dimitri's eyes moved along the curving purple lines that ran across the back of Rayner's neck, disappearing beneath his doublet.

"You like it?" he asked, pivoting to catch Dimitri's eye.

Dimitri immediately looked away, "Like what?"

"My tattoo." Rayner popped open his top buttons, revealing the purple ink swirling across his chest. "It's rather ostentatious, but what else do you expect from a Royal?"

"You made a bargain with Sylas?" Dimitri asked, leaning closer despite himself. A bargain that wasn't fulfilled based on the color.

"I didn't have much choice in the matter," Rayner said, moving to take the chair beside Dimitri's. "As soon as I entered the kingdom, I was, shall I say, cornered into making a bargain. My loyalty and promise not to use my Blessing for nefarious reasons in exchange for protection and my shop."

"So what's the loophole?" Dimitri asked bluntly.

Rayner laughed, soft and wicked and delighted. "Well, I can hardly be blamed for my clients' actions if I don't know what they plan to do with their new appearances."

"Especially if you forget to ask."

Rayner grinned. Gods damn it all, now Dimitri had to like him.

"Well," Rayner said, crossing his ankle over his knee. "I gave you a story. I believe that entitles me to one of yours."

Dimitri's nose wrinkled, but Patryclas's words echoed in his mind. *How is what you're doing helping?*

Dimitri paused. Thought for a moment. Then, he casually leaned back in his seat. "You don't want my stories."

"I don't?"

"They're all hypotheticals. Like how I'm hypothetically trying to change my appearance to deceive the visiting queen."

Rayner's eyes sparkled. "In that case, you'd better tell me something else while I work."

Dimitri struggled to hide his hope. "You better be talking about more than an eyebrow."

"For free? No. But I'll make you a bargain."

Dimitri choked back a groan.

"I'll give you one month," Rayner said. "My magic only lasts a week, so you'll get four free refreshes. After that, I'll continue to work for free in exchange for a book."

"What makes you think I can get you a book?" Dimitri deadpanned.

"The ink staining your fingers." Rayner reached over and flipped over the hand Dimitri rested in his lap, revealing his darkened fingertips. "Something tells me you're not writing to correspondents on the daily."

Dimitri snorted. "Fair. What book?"

"A Lifetime of Faces: The History of Moon Royal Appearances."

Dimitri couldn't stop his grin. "What are you planning to use that for?"

"A safeguard in case a certain oath were to go sour."

Gods damn it all. Now Dimitri really liked him. And it was for that very reason he was reluctant to form any sort of contract between them.

But he'd spent twenty years hiding from the Old Hag. He'd escaped her kingdom, had escaped *her*. She didn't get to force him to bow his head any longer.

Dimitri met Rayner's gaze. "Deal."

The exchange of tattoos was quick and precise. Dimitri shook out his hand as the tingles dissipated, what looked like a pane of shattered glass now tattooed in purple across the underside of his wrist.

"Well then," Rayner said, scooting his chair in front of Dimitri's and rubbing his hands together. "What do you think? Full sailor's beard? Although I must say, I do like your weaselly features. Perhaps a gruesome scar."

"Just make me blend in," Dimitri said, suddenly queasy.

Rayner sighed, "Such a waste. All right, close your eyes."

"Why?" Dimitri demanded, leaning away.

"I'm not going to hurt you. You have the book I want. Just close your eyes."

Dimitri pressed his lips into a line. Rayner smirked. And ears burning, Dimitri closed his eyes.

Rayner's touch was surprisingly gentle. He trailed his fingertips across Dimitri's face, the warmth of his skin spreading slow and thick as honey.

Over his jaw. Up to his forehead. Down the slope of his nose.

Dimitri's insides squirmed at the contact, but he forced himself to hold still. Even as Rayner's fingers trailed down his throat, coming to stop in the center of his chest—why was he lingering?

"Done."

Dimitri's eyes snapped open. Rayner remained disconcertingly close as he examined his face, Dimitri shrinking back in his chair like a hissing cat.

"I mostly left your body alone," Rayner said, ushering Dimitri out of his chair. "Why buy a new wardrobe if you don't have to. Especially when it was your coloring giving you away. Now look!"

Rayner spun around a full-length mirror with a flourish.

The man staring back at Dimitri was a total stranger. His dark blond hair was now black and wavy, the top longer than the sides. The ghost of his tan was replaced with a pale complexion, with his pointed features now fuller, harder.

Dimitri felt like he was outside his body. He touched his face, and the stranger mirrored his movements. It felt so wrong—uncomfortably so. Especially since it was still his own amber eyes staring back at him.

"What about these?" Dimitri asked, pointing at his eyes. His father's eyes.

Rayner looked affronted. "Sorry," he said. "The eyes are the one thing my magic can't change. The best I can do is glamor eye drops, but they're not cheap and you don't seem like the type who wants to squeeze magic into your eyes every day."

Dimitri screwed up his face. He'd inherited one undeniable thing from his father, and it was the one thing he couldn't get rid of.

Something flickered deep in Dimitri's stomach, but he stomped it out. Make that two things he couldn't get rid of.

"Well?" Rayner put his hands on his hips. "You could at least compliment my work. Eyes or not, you're still unrecognizable."

Dimitri blinked distractedly.

Rayner scoffed. "Don't bother. Just get me my book."

Dimitri allowed Rayner to usher him back through the shop. He thought he just caught the ghost of a smile on Rayner's lips, but then he shut the door.

Dimitri wandered around the square, unable to stop himself from touching his face.

He hadn't taken any time to explore since arriving in the kingdom—he'd had no desire to do so in the first place. But now, he felt a surprising urge to use his newfound freedom.

The square truly was beautiful. Fuzzy moss crept along walkway railings and building facades. The air was still thick with the smell of mud, but there were also small colorful flowers blooming on the sedge, some even attracting groups of butterflies. Tamarack trees lined the bog, tall stalks of grass interspersed throughout their ranks.

He'd always pictured the Moon Kingdom as a dark and forbidding place. But if anything, it was green and lush, the laughter in the air almost... welcoming.

And of course, that was when Dimitri spotted a familiar golden head on a perpendicular boardwalk.

Instinctively, Dimitri ducked under an overhang. Then, he grinned to himself. Definitely worth the gold.

Dimitri watched from a distance as Deardryn studied a statue of Mahina, the Moon Kingdom's Defiant. Eventually, she turned and continued on her way, completely oblivious as Dimitri headed off after her.

He didn't dare move close enough to overhear as she stopped to talk with various people. But he had no problem spotting that gods-damned sapphire pendant that he'd had to scrub innumerable times hanging around her neck. The one he'd seen her draw Mist magic from just months earlier.

Why would she be wearing that now?

Deardryn moved to an open platform where a little girl sang and danced, her ragged clothes splattered with mud. Dimitri leaned against a railing, pretending to examine the moss as he caught pieces of the song.

"When three by three by three align, the sleeping shadows will untwine."

What kind of song was that?

Dimitri looked up in time to see Deardryn say something to the little girl, who chirped something in response. Deardryn patted her cheek, then continued down the boardwalk.

Dimitri wavered. Then, he pushed off the railing and approached the little girl, her caramel eyes flashing gold in the sunlight.

"Hello," he said, straining for cheerful.

"Hi!"

Oh gods. Dimitri barely knew how to talk to children, let alone enthusiastic ones.

"I saw Queen Deardryn Oshar came to listen to your song," he said.

"Uh-huh." The girl chewed on a dirty thumbnail. Dimitri fought back a shudder.

"She must have really liked it since she came to talk to you afterwards."

The girl nodded, her wide eyes fixed on him expectantly.

"Well?" Dimitri asked, losing patience. "Is that what she said to you?"

"Oh!" The girl clapped her hands with understanding. "She asked who told it to me."

That was an interesting question.

"What did you tell her?"

"That my papa told me. And his papa told him, and his papa told him, and his papa told him—"

"And his papa told him?" Dimitri guessed dryly.

"Actually, his aunt Shiri told him, but my mama said we're not supposed to talk about her. But her papa told her, and—"

"I get it," Dimitri cut in, fisting his hands in his pockets. "Let's skip to the last papa."

"Well, he was an adventurer. He wanted to map out all of the Wild Lands, dark magic and all. And one day, he saw a nice big rock. And that's where he read this song."

"On a rock," Dimitri deadpanned.

The girl nodded sagely. "A really big rock."

"Uh-huh."

The girl chattered on, and Dimitri fought not to roll his eyes.

He'd wasted too much time with her to catch up with Deardryn. But why had Deardryn stopped to talk to this girl in particular? And why couldn't he get those lyrics out of his head?

Chapter 23

Analia's flames would never get used to people barging into her room first thing in the morning.

"Does anyone knock around here?" she complained, trying to rub her nightmares from her eyes.

Aaron paid her no mind as he headed for her wardrobe, the metal reinforcements on his fighting leathers glinting in the early light.

"Get dressed," he said. "We've got a bit of a hike ahead of us."

Analia grumbled under her breath as she slid out of bed. She didn't miss the tension in Aaron's shoulders, but he remained remarkably composed as he grabbed her a black tunic and pants.

"Why aren't we shadowjumping to the Underground?" she asked, coming up behind him.

"Wards," Aaron said, moving to her set of drawers. "The Underground doesn't permit direct magical access."

Aaron pulled out a pair of white lace underwear. Examining them, he put them back and exchanged them for a different pair.

"I'm sorry," Analia said, snatching the bundle from Aaron's arms. "Were the first pair not to your liking?"

"In my head, you're always in black."

Analia huffed, heading for the bathing room. "You have no shame, do you?"

"Oh, my shooting star," Aaron said through the door she'd closed behind her, "I don't think you would like me nearly as much if I did."

Analia paused, midway through pulling on her tunic. She'd thought he'd said she'd looked like a shooting star the night before, but he'd been too quiet for her to know for sure. Now, as she finished getting dressed, she was oddly pleased.

She stepped back into the main room, but the flicker of amusement she'd heard in Aaron's voice was nowhere to be found. He only held up a pair of fighting leathers, identical to his own. Analia raised a brow.

"I'm not taking any chances," he said. He beckoned her closer, then set to work helping her into the leather armor.

Aaron's hands were quick and efficient. He tugged on a surprising number of hidden straps and buckles, occasionally asking if something felt tight enough. To Analia's surprise, her flames didn't so much as flicker as he knelt before her, his hands brushing her hips, sliding down to her thighs as he slid a collection of thin daggers into cleverly concealed slits in her leathers.

Analia crouched to tie her boots, her hand accidentally brushing his as he reached for the same one. Just for a moment, the distracted look cleared from his eyes. He flashed his Phoenix Gate smile. Then, he quickly tied her other boot and helped her to her feet.

"Not a perfect fit," he said, studying her carefully. "But we didn't have time to get you measured for your own pair."

"It feels good," Analia said, swinging her arms experimentally. The leather was tight, molding to her body like a second skin. Clever slits had been made around her joints, allowing for greater mobility.

Aaron rocked back on his heels, his silver eyes assessing. Stepping closer, he adjusted the metal reinforcement on her left forearm.

Analia expected him to move back. But he remained just inches away, his eyes searching her face.

"You ready?" he asked.

He didn't sound ready himself. Analia nodded, taking his hand. And as they faded into the shadows, she knew she was ready to try.

Aaron would never understand how something could feel so familiar, yet so unsettling at the same time.

He and Analia emerged from the shadows in a dense wood. Tall, slender trees sliced into the sky like an army of swords, the ground a tangle of undergrowth. The air was completely stagnant, not so much as a whisper of wind interrupting the silence.

"Where are we?" Analia asked. She'd spoken at a normal volume, but her voice still sounded unnervingly loud in the silence.

"The outskirts of my kingdom," Aaron said. He gestured for her to follow, then headed off.

The hike up to the Underground entrance was a grueling one. It was mostly uphill, overflowing with hidden ruts and undergrowth that could twist an ankle if not careful.

Aaron's body had no problem staying on alert, guiding Analia away from the most treacherous sections. But his mind was elsewhere, caught up in the memories that flashed across his awareness like a lightning storm.

"Do you think we'll run into anyone training in there?" Analia asked, breathless from the climb.

"No," Aaron said distractedly. "We have no business with them, so the Underground will do its best to keep us separated."

He scanned the trees up ahead for the tiny opening, attention lapsing once more.

"That must be a relief," Analia went on.

"How come?"

"You won't have to worry about me wandering off with another poor, moody warrior man."

Aaron's eyes finally slid to her, something primal stirring in his veins. "You can do as you please."

"Oh, I'm aware," Analia said, looking up at him from the base of the boulder he'd climbed. "But I wonder, do you think he, too, prefers black?"

Aaron's attention locked on her. "And we're back to the underwear," he murmured.

Analia shrugged. She started to pull herself up the boulder, but her foot slipped.

Aaron caught her hand and helped her up. She made to step away, but Aaron's grip tightened.

He knew she was taunting him. But that didn't stop the hum from traveling through his blood, sharpening his senses to a wicked clarity.

He guided her closer, leaning in to murmur in her ear. "Is this the part where you tell me you enjoyed the feeling of my hands on your thighs?"

Analia's breath caught.

Aaron felt suspended in time.

And Analia patted his chest and slipped around him.

"I see you're padding your fantasy," she said over her shoulder.

Her touch seemed to burn straight through his leathers. He pivoted to watch her continue up the hill, having to suppress far more appealing thoughts as he called after her, "I do believe you started it."

Analia made a rude hand gesture behind her back. And somehow, that lightning storm settled into the background as Aaron chuckled and headed after her.

It wasn't long before they broke from the trees. They entered a sandy clearing, completely dominated by a large, garnet-encrusted boulder in its center.

"This is the place?" Analia asked, eyes trained on the boulder as if she could sense the roiling magic within.

Aaron nodded. "This was where Branten, Mor, and I first stumbled out."

Memories tapped on his awareness, but he forced them back as Analia looked at him.

"We don't have to do this," she said.

Earlier that day, Aaron would've been tempted to take her up on her offer. But she'd cared enough to provoke him back to the present; a simple kindness that, at some point, he'd stopped expecting. *Not worth it.*

"No," he said, "we have to go. But I appreciate you pretending otherwise."

Not giving himself time to think, Aaron crossed to the stone and placed his palm on its center.

The boulder rumbled. Aaron felt Analia come up beside him as it split down the center like an opening mouth, just large enough for a person to squeeze through.

Aaron fought back a shudder at the familiar smell of cold, damp earth. He turned to Analia, catching her shifting from foot to foot.

"You're going to have to trust me in there," he said. "No hesitation, no second-guessing. If I say duck, duck. If I say jump, jump. Even if it looks like there's no reason to, or we're about to run into a wall, or fall into a pit—you have to trust me."

"All right," she said, eyes on the opening.

"Are you ready?"

"Are you?"

Aaron made a face. Analia took his hand and squeezed. He squeezed back.

Then, he led the way through the entrance. And the ground immediately disappeared beneath his feet.

Analia yelped as she was dragged after him, the two tumbling down, down, down.

They finally landed at the bottom in a tangle of limbs—one Aaron would have thoroughly enjoyed in other circumstances. Now, he immediately sat up. He scanned the tunnel, only seeing packed earth and sconces that disappeared into the darkness ahead.

"Are you all right?" he asked, turning to Analia.

"I'm fine," she said, also sitting up. "I'm assuming that wasn't supposed to happen?"

"No," Aaron said, staring up at the sliver of light above their heads. "Usually, that's a downhill corridor."

Thankfully, their leathers had absorbed most of the impact. But if Aaron had any uncertainty as to whether the Underground was messing around, it was gone now. Especially as the entrance above rumbled shut.

"Run?" Analia asked, the same way she'd ask what the weather was.

"Run," Aaron agreed. Without further comment, he hauled her to her feet, and they took off.

Aaron didn't know how long they ran. He let instinct take over as they swerved through tunnels; leapt across caverns they should have never been able to cross; wove around spires of black, glimmering stone.

He didn't register how the tunnels shifted from dirt, to stone, to obsidian glass. He let everything drift away besides Analia's hand in his, allowing him to feel when she flinched—*flinched?*

Aaron glanced at her quickly, spotting the thin line of red across her cheekbone. He made to slow, but Analia's grip tightened. "Don't stop."

And they ran on. With every trial, he could feel the Underground zero in on Analia like a hunter on a bull's-eye.

Clearly, it knew she hadn't come to be one of its recruits. She was just an outsider, trying to use its tunnels for her own gain. And regardless of Aaron being with her, the Underground was going to show her the consequences of that choice.

"You can test her all you want," he growled under his breath, hauling Analia up a steep stone staircase. "But I'm not leaving her, and I won't let her fail. So, just show us the creature."

He could have sworn the Underground snarled in response. But escaping on his first try all those years ago must have given him some merit, for after dodging a volley of flying stones, they reached the end of the tunnel. And the Underground finally dumped them into an antechamber.

The two staggered to a stop at the entrance, gasping for breath. Analia slumped against the wall, but Aaron stayed on alert, scanning their surroundings.

The antechamber was carved from smooth black stone. Bronze braziers sat beside two massive pillars that looked suspiciously like bone, an intricate archway atop them. And beyond that arch was a familiar set of steel doors.

"I'm assuming this is the place," Analia said, finally catching her breath.

"It is," Aaron said, stomach sinking. "How's your cut?"

"Fine." She wiped the blood from her cheek with the back of her hand. "Something flew past too fast for me to see what it was. I promise, it's nothing, let's go."

Aaron studied the scratch a moment longer. Satisfied, he stepped aside. Then, together, they spun the massive silver wheel on the door, and stepped inside.

The chamber was just as Surce's tapestry depicted. The black stone shimmered with a rainbow glow, following the lines of the carved runes. Iron chains spiraled into a knot of shadows in its heart.

Even though he knew it would happen, Aaron's stomach lurched as the door slammed shut. And brilliant white eyes blinked open within the darkness.

"Prince of Starlight," the creature drawled. "Has no one taught you manners?"

Its voice was like a dagger scraping along Aaron's bones. He rocked back on his heels, letting his face smooth into a bored, unimpressed mask.

"Well," he said, "the only manners I learned were stealing another boy's cloak and not slitting his throat is an unnecessary kindness. I suppose we could implement those rules, but you don't appear to have a cloak."

The creature let out a hiss of a laugh. Then, just as Aaron knew they would, the shadows peeled back like the skin of a fruit, revealing the huddled form in its core.

The creature vaguely resembled an adult human. Instead of skin, black scales encased its body, seeming to swallow the rainbow light of the runes. It had hands and feet, but the limbs themselves were more serpentine, lacking obvious shoulders, elbows, and knees.

"Aaron Stelingente," it purred. "Insolent as always."

It turned to Analia, about to speak, but its eyes widened a fraction. It looked first at her cheek, then down to her wrist, its slit nostrils flaring.

"Second generation," it mused. "Fascinating."

Aaron made to interject, but it went on. "Princess Analia Valarus, why would you keep such deplorable company?"

Analia didn't appear to be listening. Her eyes moved across the runes that covered the floor, walls, and ceiling, lingering on the spots that glowed.

"Overwhelming, isn't it?" the creature asked. "All the magic in this chamber."

Aaron bit back a curse. He'd felt the thrum of magic the moment he stepped inside. But with Analia's Blessing?

"It's Royal magic," she said, oddly serene as she crouched to examine the runes at her feet. "All seven have been infused into these runes, although the Star magic is so much fainter."

"Someone must have really wanted you locked up," Aaron commented. "Care to share why?"

The creature reluctantly returned its gaze to him, a forked tongue flicking out to lick its lips. "Because I have knowledge. And knowledge is the most destructive force in the world."

Aaron fought back a shudder. He remembered those white eyes seeming to stare into his soul: dragging out his fears, dissecting them with a wicked curiosity.

"If you have knowledge," Analia said, rising once more, "that means you should know why we're here."

"I do."

"So what do you want?"

Aaron's hand went to his dagger, but the creature threw back its head in a cackle. "Oh, I like you, Princess of Ash. You're jaded by your past. I wonder when you'll realize just how much has been taken from you."

Analia took a step back, hand flying to where her phoenix pin usually rested against her chest. "What do you—"

"Just tell us what Deardryn's after," Aaron cut in.

"Well, you're no fun," the creature said, shackles clinking as it shifted. "But you remember the price, don't you? A secret for a secret."

Ice trickled down Aaron's spine.

"What could you want with secrets?" Analia asked. "I thought you knew everything."

"One would think that," the creature mused. "I suppose you'll simply have to think hard."

The creature fixed Analia with its soul-searing stare. Analia took a step back, her face draining of color.

"Hey," Aaron said, picking a pebble from the ground and flicking it at the creature. "Knock it off."

The creature let out a soft hiss. It focused on Aaron once more, Aaron struggling not to look away as Analia let out a tiny breath.

Finally, the creature made a noise of disgust. "I don't want a secret from you, princeling. You have so many you could get away with telling me your left pinky toe is crooked."

"Now, how did you know that?" Aaron purred.

"I want a secret from you," the creature said, focusing on Analia once more.

For a long moment, Analia didn't speak. Aaron wanted to call the whole thing off, grab her hand and keep on running until they reached fresh air. But Analia squared her shoulders, looking directly into the creature's eyes.

"For twenty-two years," she said, "I felt like I was barely holding myself together. But now that I've finally fallen apart, I have all these pieces I don't know how to put back together again."

"Fascinating," the creature murmured. But its eyes weren't on Analia. They had moved to Aaron, who felt an iron-clad fist squeeze his heart.

It took everything he had not to reach for her hand, not sure who he would be trying to comfort in doing so. But Analia's chin remained high. "Your turn."

The creature studied the two of them for a moment longer. "The answer you seek is within the scroll you stole from the Sun Kingdom."

"The scroll won't open," Aaron said, picking his nails.

"That's because the scroll can only be opened in the presence of its sister scrolls. Once all three scrolls are reunited, I think you'll find Analia will have no problem opening them."

"And you're not going to tell us where the scrolls are," Analia guessed.

"Oh, I think you should have an easy enough time," the creature said. "Not only did Talitha create the scrolls, but she was the one who hid them. I'm sure the secret must have been passed down."

Aaron certainly hadn't been informed of any secret scrolls. Analia made to speak, looking annoyed, but Aaron shook his head.

"Don't bother," he said. "That's all we're getting out of it."

The creature clicked its tongue, but Aaron ignored it. He turned to go, not feeling inclined to offer a farewell, much less a thank you. Yet, as Analia made to follow him out the chamber, she looked back.

"Why can I sense all the different magics?" she asked.

Aaron knew he would regret it, but he paused.

The creature flashed a wicked grin. "Because you're special."

"Not special enough for you to be helpful," Analia grumbled.

The creature's smile grew. "Now you might just be someone to watch out for, Princess. Although that pendant in your pocket already proved that."

Analia went rigid. Her hand flew to her pocket, hidden beneath her leathers.

"You are special, Analia Valarus," the creature said, "but that doesn't mean things will be easy. Questions may be free, but answers always have a cost."

Analia didn't move. Aaron grabbed her burning hand and pulled her through the door without a backward glance.

The steel door slammed shut behind them with a resounding clang. Aaron loosed a long, shaky breath, his body cold despite the braziers. But Analia didn't pause, continuing almost mechanically toward the exit. Deciding not to push it just yet, Aaron followed.

Time had clearly moved differently in the Underground, for it was already dusk when Aaron and Analia emerged. The Underground ushered them out the same entrance they'd come through, clearly eager to rid itself of an intruder.

Analia, however, didn't seem to notice. She released his hand and headed for the trees, something dark and ominous settling in Aaron's stomach.

"Analia!" he called, hurrying to catch up. "Analia, what's wrong?"

"Please," she said, half stumbling down the hill. "Please just let it go."

Her words were a kick to his gut. After all the progress they'd made, she was shutting him out again?

"Anna, please," he begged. "What pendant?"

Analia made to respond, but her foot slid out from under her. Aaron grabbed her elbow, her leathers uncomfortably hot as he steadied her.

"Just *talk* to me," he pleaded, turning her to face him.

"I can't!" she exclaimed. "If I talk about this now, I'll just burn you, too, and I can't do that, Aaron."

"What do you mean, burn me too…"

Aaron's words trailed off. His eyes dropped to where Analia's pocket would be, remembering the last time he'd seen her burn someone.

"It's Pryanth's," he said slowly. "You still have Pryanth's pendant, don't you?"

Analia gave him a miserable look. And the tentative hope in Aaron's chest crumpled.

"Why?" he whispered.

"Aaron…"

"Why in the name of the Crystal would you want to hold on to that?"

Analia's flames flashed across her leathers, but she didn't respond.

Gods, when had he become such a fool? He'd known she'd developed feelings for Pryanth. But he'd also seen the hurt, disgust, even fear in her eyes toward the end, culminating in her finally killing the bastard.

But it had only been two months. Two gods-damned months since she was in Pryanth's arms, his lips on hers, hands on her body, branding her face.

Aaron thought he might be sick as he asked, "Are you still in love with him—"

"No!"

Somehow, that didn't make him feel any better. "Then why keep his pendant?"

"Aaron, I'm not going to fight with you," she said, stepping out of his grip. "I'm not going to explode over something that is none of your concern. So please, just drop it."

A part of him noted how a few weeks before, she would've let those flames erupt. But that didn't stop the dull ache from radiating through his chest. *Not worth it.*

"I'm sorry," he forced out.

"Me too."

Neither of them spoke as they made it down the hill, Aaron silently jumping them back to the house where his family waited. He could tell by their faces they knew something happened, but they all had the good sense not to ask.

Aaron briefly filled them in, saying they would talk more in the morning. Then, he headed for his room. He didn't know if he was relieved or disappointed as the minutes ticked by, and there came no footsteps, no knock on his door. There was only the faint sound of Analia playing what might as well have been her harp.

It was a new song, one that Aaron's limited music knowledge had him realizing was in a new key. He could have sworn the hurt and frustration laced through those notes had his magic stirring in response.

He just didn't understand.

Chapter 24

Analia knew the nightmares were coming for her that night. She looked up into Pryanth's face, her flames ripping free, his scream ringing in her ears—

Analia jerked upright in bed. Her eyes darted around the room, her hand clutching her dagger hard enough to hurt.

She didn't immediately smell the smoke. But when she finally looked down, taking in her scorched bedding, the last of her composure shattered.

Analia curled in on herself, vaguely noticing she'd managed to keep her clothes from burning. But that wasn't enough to stop her tears from overflowing, that black wave rising up, up, up.

A quiet knock came on Analia's door. She tried to silence her sobs, hoping whoever it was would think she was asleep, leave her alone.

But the door opened, and Aaron was sitting beside her, his hand smoothing down her hair as he murmured, "It was just a dream. Just a bad dream."

Gods, why had he come? Why be so kind after she'd caused what she could have sworn was devastation in his eyes on that hill, too ashamed to explain it away.

"I'm sorry," Analia said through her tears. "I'm so sorry."

"What, for the bedding?" Aaron asked, his hand moving down to her back. "Please, did you see that color scheme? You just gave me an excuse to finally replace it."

No, not for the bedding—although she could add it to the list. She was sorry for everything. So, so sorry.

"You know," Aaron said, scooting closer, "sometimes, it helps to open the window."

Analia peeked up at him. Aaron gestured with his free hand, and the window across from her bed slid open on its own. A cool breeze swirled through the room, kissing her burning skin until her shoulders dropped.

"That's it," Aaron murmured, his other hand squeezing her knee. "Slow, deep breaths. You're safe, I promise."

Gods, she didn't deserve his comfort. She didn't deserve anything from him.

But she couldn't stop herself from leaning into him, desperate for something, anything to hold on to.

And Aaron didn't pull away. He tucked her against his side, murmuring into her hair until her shaking subsided.

"How do you feel?" he finally asked.

"Nauseous," Analia said.

Aaron looked down at the remains of her bedding. "I'll be right back."

He squeezed her shoulder, then rose and slipped out the door. Analia had barely finished wiping her tears when he returned, carrying a bundle of bedding he promptly dumped on the floor. Then, he nudged her to her feet and guided her over to the settee.

Analia silently watched as Aaron stripped the bed, tossing the ruined bedding into the hall. Before she knew it, he'd remade the bed and had come to retrieve her, going so far as to pull back the silver duvet for her.

"Better?" he asked.

Analia nodded, curling into a ball. Aaron reached out as if to brush the hair from her face. At the last moment, his hand jerked to touch the dagger she still clutched in one hand.

Analia waited for him to take it away. But it was understanding in his eyes as he said, "Let me know if you need me."

Analia nodded once more. This time, Aaron softly closed the door behind him as he left.

And Analia stared at that door for a long, long time after.

The family congregated at the big house the following morning, but the conversation wasn't fruitful. No one had heard of any secret scrolls. They decided doing some digging couldn't hurt, though. In the meantime, Aaron said he would write to the DovenU, figuring if Ethelind had known anything, they were the best place to start.

Analia remained at the dining room table as the group split off, picking at a lemon-blueberry muffin. She'd spent the entire meeting waiting for Aaron to mention the night before, point out how if she'd mastered her magic, it wouldn't have happened. But he never did. If anything, he was aloof, as if still reeling from their argument.

Analia pushed back from the table. Tossing her wrapper in the magical disposal bin, she headed off to find him.

She finally located Aaron in what appeared to be a lavish library. She padded over to a collection of recliners, Aaron seated in the furthest one to the left.

"We'll have to get you a chair of your own," he said, not looking up from what Analia assumed was the letter he was reading over. "No one here is particularly fond of sharing, but I think Mor will forgive you just this once."

He gestured to the seat next to him, and Analia gingerly perched on its edge. She waited until he was done reading before asking, "So how's the letter?"

"As good as it's going to get," Aaron sighed, folding it up. "The problem is, the DovenU aren't officially a part of my kingdom. So, no matter how glorious a tale I spin, we're more than likely going to have a wait on our hands."

"Even if you use your breathtaking smile and undeniable charm?"

Aaron let out a surprised laugh. "Sadly, I can't account for taste."

He rose, crossing to a nearby table filled with tall black candles.

"I never got to tell you thank you for last night," Analia said quietly.

Aaron waved a hand, "There's no need—"

Analia finally caught his eye. "Thank you."

Aaron softened. "You're welcome."

Analia looked away as Aaron flopped back into his seat.

"How did you know what was happening in the first place?" she asked.

"Well, you sent off a bit of a magical flare. That, and I could smell the smoke."

"Wonderful," Analia grumbled. She finally slumped back against the dark blue velvet, listening to the quiet rasp of Aaron striking a match. "You didn't have to come, you know."

"Of course I did."

"But we were fighting."

"No, we were arguing."

"What's the difference?"

"A great deal of things," Aaron said, carefully dripping the wax on to his envelope. "But the important part is, no matter how bad the argument, I'm always going to come."

He looked up from his letter to meet her gaze, and Analia swallowed hard.

"I didn't mean to make us argue," she mumbled.

"Oh, Analia," Aaron laughed, "arguments go both ways."

Analia made a face. Aaron grinned, returning to his letter and stamping the wax with his family sigil: a filled-in constellation of the Crystal.

He was so unconcerned. And yet, he'd asked her over and over why she kept that pendant.

"Why do you care so much about the pendant?" she asked, genuinely curious.

Aaron's shoulders immediately slumped. He ran a hand through his hair, taking his time before speaking.

"When I realized you were holding on to Pryanth's pendant," he finally said, "there were a lot of emotions. None directed at you. But at the core of it all, I was jealous. Jealous because after all the monstrous things Pryanth did to you, you were able to forgive him enough that you wanted to remember him."

Aaron looked up from his sealed letter, something fragile in his starlight eyes.

The kindest, most hated man in Elefthia. Constantly flashing his bloodstained claws the past few weeks, daring her to agree as if he thought it were inevitable.

"You're not a monster, Aaron," Analia said softly, shifting in her seat to look at him fully.

Even if he was, he certainly wasn't the worst one in the room.

Aaron didn't look convinced. "But I can be," he said. "I already told you, if it means protecting the things I love, I will become the worst monster of all. And while I stand by the decisions I've made, I'm not sure anyone else can."

Analia reached out, her fingertips barely able to graze his arm. "Has anyone told you," she asked, "that you are worthy of being forgiven?"

Aaron's expression shuddered. He dropped his gaze to his letter. "I do believe you told me, once upon a time."

"Then allow me to remind you."

Aaron kept his face averted. Analia retracted her hand, automatically reaching for Pryanth's pendant in her pocket.

"I think," she murmured, half to herself, "that lonely, scared Ash Princess would have fallen in love with the first person who showed her an ounce of kindness. But that doesn't mean I forgive him. And that's not why I hold on to the pendant."

Aaron finally looked at her. As Analia pushed herself to her feet and headed for the door, she wondered if those thoughtful eyes could read that forgiveness was the exact opposite reason she kept that pendant.

Reaching the door, Analia turned back. "Are we good?"

Aaron flashed his Phoenix Gate smile. "My shooting star, we always were."

He was completely earnest. No mental games, insisting he was fine while holding their spat over her head.

Slowly, the knot in Analia's stomach began to unravel. She offered Aaron a soft smile of her own. And as she closed the door behind her, she could have sworn she saw Aaron touch his chest.

Chapter 25

Analia tumbled down the training hollow's slope, landing in a heap on Aaron's usual patch of moss.

"And I'd say that's that," Branten said, appearing at the top of the slope.

Analia glowered.

It had been a few days since Aaron wrote to the DovenU. Just as he suspected, negotiating a time to visit had turned into a tedious event, leaving Analia with plenty of time to train.

Slowly but surely, she was making her way through Branten's regimen. Most of her work was focused on building up her strength and balance—"The most important part of fighting is your footwork," as Branten constantly reminded her. But as time went on, all she could hear was the creature's voice hissing through her mind, her flames burning so hot in response she had to beg Branten for something new to do.

She'd expected him to argue. Instead, something like understanding passed over his features.

Thus, their game began: if Analia could evade Branten for fifteen minutes, he would up her training.

"How long did I last?" she asked.

"About eight minutes."

Analia groaned.

"It was a good effort," Branten said, coming down the slope and offering her a hand up.

"You were playing me the entire time!"

"Of course I was," Branten scoffed, yanking her to her feet. "But that doesn't mean you didn't do well."

"Maybe," Analia muttered, heading for the small table where a pitcher of water always sat. She could feel Pryanth's pendant weighing down her pocket; the creature's voice reminding her what would happen if she didn't get stronger.

"Today wasn't a failure, Anna," Branten said, coming up behind her. "It was just another training exercise. One that gave you a new weapon for your arsenal."

"That being?"

"Always be aware of your surroundings." Branten reached around her, filling a cup for himself and downing it in one go. "You did everything right. You were quick, you were patient, and you waited until I was distracted and my center of gravity was off.

"But you lost track of your surroundings. You didn't notice I had turned your back to the hollow, so you had no reason not to jump back when I made to shove you. And you had every reason to be surprised and lose your balance when the ground was no longer level."

"I should have known that," Analia muttered.

"Well, now you do. And you also know that not only can you use your surroundings to your advantage, but your enemy will sure as shit try to use them against you."

Analia met Branten's gaze. Level, no hint of judgment. She nodded slowly, her flames relaxing.

"How many do I owe you?" she asked, moving to reclaim the wooden pole Branten had incorporated into her workouts.

"Well," he said, perching on the table, "I believe we were about halfway through before you started running your mouth."

Analia snorted. Obediently, she lifted the pole, her muscles aching as she sank into a squat.

"So how do you do it, then?" she asked. "How do you remain aware of everything?"

Branten circled her, checking her form. He nodded in approval, and Analia pushed herself up.

"You do that by always moving. Staying alert. And finding someone you trust to watch your back. Back down."

Analia thought her muscles might turn to liquid, but she lowered herself once more.

"That's never worked out well for me," she murmured. The only people she seemed to find were ones that stabbed her in the back.

"Me neither," Branten said.

Analia had lost track of how many times she'd seen that same flicker of lonely uncertainty on her own face. Yet, Branten's expression quickly cleared, replaced by something softer, more appreciative.

Analia pushed herself back up, flipping her pole around to lean on it.

"How do you do it?" she asked again.

"It takes a long time," Branten said, going to retrieve his own, far heavier pole. "Growing up on the streets, you might have your accomplices, but you know everyone has to put their own interest above everyone else's. That's the only way to survive.

"But I've spent the past century with this family, and not once have they failed to protect my back. Even in the times when I didn't want or need them to."

He raised his pole, Analia mirroring him as he sank into a squat.

Find someone you trust to watch your back. The words echoed through her mind as she finished her training for the day. But as she made her way back toward the house, she didn't feel like she'd found an answer. If anything, it was just another piece she didn't know what to do with.

Analia sighed, leaning against the railing of the stairs that led to her room.

Once, she would have already been on her way to the roof. Yet, there she was, still unable to take that step.

"You know," said a voice in her ear, "most people find actually climbing the stairs to be incredibly helpful."

Analia barely spared Aaron a glance. "I was admiring the dent in the banister."

"Hoping it was my head that made it?"

"Among other things."

Aaron laughed. "My shooting star," he crooned, sliding an arm around her waist, "how cruel you become when you're sore."

The floor beneath Analia's feet began to fade. She quickly stepped out of his grip, "I thought you said you wouldn't coddle me."

Aaron reemerged from the shadows, his head cocked. "That I did," he admitted, leaning back against the railing. "All right then, go on. Prove me wrong."

Aaron made a shooing gesture. Analia flashed him a withering look. Then, gripping the railing, she hauled herself up the first step.

"Very good," Aaron drawled. "One down. Only about thirteen to go."

"Crystal strike you down," Analia muttered, muscles screaming.

"Such a proud girl you are," Aaron went on. "You do know it will hurt far more if you tumble back down?"

"Yes, and then I will have proven your point."

"Don't be ridiculous," Aaron scoffed. "I would catch you long before that happened."

Analia paused, halfway up the stairs. He would, wouldn't he? She pulled herself up another step, the wood slick beneath her sweaty palm.

"Although," Aaron said, "I must admit. I am enjoying the view."

Analia twisted around.

"Ah," Aaron said, eyes meeting her own. "But this one is far better."

Analia was momentarily taken aback. She glanced over her shoulder, summoning a look of puzzlement.

"What?" Aaron asked.

"I would have thought for sure there was a mirror behind me."

Aaron's face split in a wicked grin. "Cruel," he repeated. He melted into the shadow of the staircase, reemerging at the top.

As Analia half climbed, half stumbled up the remaining steps, he didn't offer her his hand. He rocked back on his heels, letting her finish what she'd started. And though she thought she might collapse, Analia finally dragged herself on to the landing.

"Look at that," Aaron said. "You proved me wrong, once again."

He sketched a dramatic bow. But that wasn't humor in his eyes. It was respect.

When was the last time she'd been given that?

Aaron rested his hand on her back, guiding her into her room.

"I will say," he went on, "I still think my way was far easier, but I suppose I can understand wanting a little pain with my pleasure."

"Why must you always ruin it?" Analia muttered.

"All I'm saying is there are plenty of ways to unwind after training. Some more enjoyable than others."

Analia's head whipped toward him. Aaron traced one of the lilies carved into her headboard with a fingernail, his smile having her mind flashing back to his hands on her thighs, his voice in her ear asking if she'd liked the feeling.

Analia's cheeks flushed. She turned to her bathing room, ready to slam the door in his face. Then, she noticed the sound of running water, as if Aaron had instructed his magical house to start the bath the moment he realized she was sore.

Slowly, Analia's temper cooled.

"Thank you," she said.

Aaron offered his Phoenix Gate smile. "Any time."

Analia slipped into her tub a few minutes later, trying not to moan as the hot water ran over her aching muscles.

It was such an unnecessary kindness. One she doubted Pryanth would have ever thought to do for her.

Even in the beginning, when he brought her tea in Ash, when he kissed her in the Sun Castle library, called her the flame to his life. It was out of his own interest, not hers. And she'd known this. So why had she clung on anyway?

Analia eventually climbed out of her tub. She picked up Pryanth's pendant from the counter, the gold flashing in the light.

When had she come to expect so little? How could so little hurt so much? Not just when she had it, but when it was gone?

Find someone you trust to watch your back.

At least she knew one thing: that had never been Pryanth.

Aaron lingered outside Analia's door, unable to wipe the smile from his face.

Gods, he'd missed that. Feeling like he didn't have to brace himself after every word. Crystal knew he'd spent enough time playing that game with Liss—although by that point, they were barely speaking unless they were screaming.

He'd barely kept a straight face when Analia pointed out the dent Liss had kicked during some fight—what was it even about? Knowing them, something as trivial as what to have for dinner, resulting in their usual spiral out of control, then avoiding each other until someone cracked.

He'd been gearing up for that cycle to turn again after their spat on the hill, regardless of him going to check on her. But into the library she'd come, that hand extended once more.

She always surprised him.

Aaron headed off down the hall, spotting Branten loitering at the bottom of the staircase.

"She's going to kick your ass someday," the warrior informed him.

"I don't know what you're talking about," Aaron said lightly, thumping Branten on the side of the head as he stepped into the sitting room. "Although, should I ask why she had moss in her hair?"

"Analia took a tumble during training," Branten said, moving to sprawl on one of the couches. "I'll give her credit, she thinks fast on her feet. Good instincts, too. Well, besides thinking she could take me."

"What?" Aaron whipped around, "Did you—"

"Oh, relax, I didn't do anything. Well, nothing major."

Aaron gave him a look.

"Gods, brother," Branten chortled. "You're hopeless, aren't you?"

"Mind your business," Aaron said, turning to the bookcase. He thumbed through the titles, his mind wandering back to the hillside.

He had been too hasty. Not just in his reaction to Analia's comments, but in thinking that maybe she could have—

Aaron's hand spasmed around a book spine. He quickly banished the thought.

The point was, he didn't feel hopeless—even though he knew better.

There was just something about Analia. Something about her smile in the library, the look on her face as she thanked him for the bath, had him unable to suppress his hope.

"Shouldn't you be at a council meeting right about now?" Branten asked.

Aaron scoffed. "*Should* being the operative word."

Finding the book he wanted, he retreated to stretch out on the couch perpendicular to Branten's. As soon as he opened it, he coughed on a cloud of dust.

"*A History of Blessings,*" Branten said, reading the cover. "Don't tell me you actually told them why you're postponing all your meetings."

"Of course not," Aaron said, flipping through the old, crackling pages. "I won't have their propensity to drag their feet over every decision put this kingdom at risk."

"I still don't know why you don't disband them."

"Because," Aaron sighed, "as long as I keep them out of the big decisions, they're actually helpful with running the small-scale. Although they've been sniffing around Analia."

"What?" The couch springs squeaked as Branten shoved upright. "You can't be serious!"

"It's fair," Aaron admitted. "If I were them, I'd want to know why a foreign princess was special enough to have our king not only reveal himself, but also bring her here."

Aaron didn't have to add that the council was already miffed he'd only told them he was going away on business, leaving Surce in charge. They were *especially* miffed he had returned seven months later with a vague story about a scroll he only disclosed out of obligation.

"Too bad," Branten said. "Aaron, with her power..."

"I know," said Aaron grimly. "Which is why I'm doing everything in *my power* to keep them away from her."

"Good."

Aaron finally looked up, something warm stirring in his chest.

Branten had every right to resent Analia, even after she was brought to the kingdom and their secret was safe once more. But the fact that he and everyone else had not just taken her in stride, but had opened their arms to her?

Branten gave Aaron a nod of understanding. Aaron swallowed hard, looking down at his book once more.

"You know," he said, "you could help look for clues instead of lolling on my couch like an oversized ingrate."

"I've never been good at that fancy book-reading whatever," Branten said. "Laness would tell you it's because I can't read."

Aaron grabbed a coaster from the nearby table and threw it at him. Branten dodged, not pausing as he continued, "I've been asking around, though. Seeing what people know about Talitha and the overall history of the time."

If anyone could naturally strike up a conversation as random as that with a stranger, it would be Branten.

"Anything come up?" Aaron asked.

"Well, that's the interesting part," Branten said, swiping a stray pen from the table. "There's no end to the things people have to say about Talitha herself. That she was a fair ruler, a blunt speaker, crazy stuff about how when she was mad, the sky would darken to night. At this point, I wouldn't be surprised if she shit gold to fund the orphans."

"Don't talk about my million times great-grandmother like that," Aaron said, not looking up from his book.

"Well, here's the real interesting part," Branten said. "When you ask people about the war and the Crystal, suddenly everyone has the exact same story. The Defiants nabbed the Crystal from the Ancient Ones, used it to release magic into Elefthia, and then it disappeared at some point in history—which is straightforward enough. But no matter how in-depth people got, there were no variations, no extra or forgotten details, nothing."

"That's oddly uniform for a story that occurred so long ago," Aaron commented. "Don't get ink on my couch."

"It's oddly uniform for any story," Branten said, continuing to dismantle his pen. "Not even Sentos, who's told that story about his naked streak to freedom during the Shattering a thousand times, has told it the same way twice. But we've got the bastards at the bottom of the ale barrel saying the same thing as the boys I'm training, and I know they haven't been talking."

Aaron mused, "And it's the same story outlined in the children's book Analia used to read in Ash, and I found in Sun."

"Weird," Branten said, examining his dislodged ink cartridge.

"Definitely unusual," Aaron agreed. Although what it meant, he couldn't say.

The brothers split up not long after that. Aaron remained on the couch, only faintly registering the sound of the side room's door opening and closing as he read. At the sound of harp strings, he looked up.

She was playing in that key again. The one that had his magic reaching toward her. But looking at the closed door, Aaron rose and moved in the opposite direction.

Not today. But someday, maybe.

Chapter 26

E mber stood atop a ladder in the nymphs' greenhouse, soaking in their applause.

"She's healed!" Levidia declared.

"The great plant reviver graces us once again," Galena said, bowing deeply.

Ember beamed as the other nymphs cheered and giggled. Giving the massive philodendron she'd just healed a pat, she scrambled back down to the floor.

"This place is really coming along," she said to Levidia as the rest of the nymphs dispersed.

In just the few weeks since its opening, the greenhouse had gone from an empty glass enclosure to a jungle of plants of all species and colors. They'd even balanced the humidity, to the point Ember had to replace her robes with a sleeveless lavender shirt and leggings.

"Isn't it?" Levidia grabbed Ember's hand, towing her up a curved staircase. Once we figured out where to actually put the shade curtains, the plants have been flourishing. Well, except for the gloxinias. Their leaves were scorched and Lel won't let me hear the end of it."

"How bad could they…" Ember's voice trailed off as they reached the top. "Levidia, *no.*"

A row of fuzzy gloxinias huddled beneath a countertop scattered with gardening tools. Yet, even that shady spot hadn't been enough to protect the leaves from massive brown spots.

"It wasn't my fault!" Levidia said, her swirling blue eyes widening innocently. "I wasn't even supposed to be tending to this section."

Ember shook her head, crouching beside the plants. "Tell Lel I'll have them fuzzy and green again in minutes."

"This is why you're our favorite human,"

Levidia kissed the top of Ember's head. Then, she bounced away, dramatically flicking her long brown braids as she announced Lel could put the vein in her forehead away.

Ember laughed to herself as she rested her hand on the nearest plant. The ease with which she healed the nymphs' plants was a welcome change of pace.

So far, she was struggling to make any connections with Accalon's symbols. She'd flipped through every page, making note of how many times each symbol showed up and what topics were included on their respective pages.

Some symbols were easy enough to decode. The three circles making the triangle referred to the three major mountains of Elefthia: Vasolus, Raegyr, and Lanula. She thought she had a good idea for the remaining symbols, but the spiraling circle was throwing her off. Sometimes it appeared on pages referencing the Crystal, other times the Gods, sometimes the Ancient Ones, and other times a random location like Scarsthain.

Ember moved to the next gloxinia, her ears pricking as a group of nymphs wandered past with watering cans.

"He really does remind me of his uncle. He has that same thoughtful look in his eyes."

"Better than the contempt in his father's," a second agreed. "That pugnacious fireball nearly burned our kingdom to the ground."

"For all we know," said a third, "Princess Analia's midnight flames would have done the same."

Ember bit her tongue and inched closer.

"She and Brenn were still the rightful rulers," a fourth one pointed out. "And Analia didn't seem so bad. A little sullen, maybe."

"But Cadmus is wonderful," the second nymph said.

"He told me he liked my rose bush when he visited last week," the first whispered confidentially.

The nymphs tittered.

"But good king or not," the fourth interjected, "does the crown belong to him?"

"Why are you so stuck on that?" the second one complained.

"Because it's tradition," the fourth insisted. "The kingdoms have only been as stable as they are because those Royals finally found a system that works. Who knows what kind of damage they could do to our wildlife if those traditions fall apart."

"Think of what damage they could do with a corrupt Royal on the throne," two countered.

The four nymphs dissolved into a round of squabbling, which quickly turned into a shoving match. Ember ducked to avoid an arc of water from a swinging watering can, then stood and stomped forward.

"All right," she said, shoving between them with arms outstretched. "Put the gardening supplies down. Otherwise, your plants will be staying brown."

The nymphs reluctantly quieted. They cast each other haughty looks, one nymph in a blue frock still tightly gripping a shorter nymph's hair.

"Good," Ember said, lowering her arms. "Now, you with the—wow, that is a beautiful frock. It looks just like a cloudy sky."

"Isn't it stunning? I got it down the street at the new seamstress's shop—"

The shorter nymph loudly cleared her throat.

"Oh, right," Ember said. She gave the nymph with the frock a pointed look, and she reluctantly released her shorter friend.

After a few more remarks, the nymphs scurried away, smiling and laughing as if it never happened. Ember wearily returned to her gloxinias. If that was what the nymphs were like, she didn't want to imagine what Cadmus was trying to deal with.

Even so, she felt oddly weightless as she resumed her healing. Those nymphs had stopped the moment she arrived. There was no battle for attention, or respect, or approval before they listened to her. It was all already hers. And the novelty of that feeling had Ember wanting to cry.

Ember dusted the dry soil from her hands, healing complete. She was just about to wave Levidia over when the greenhouse door opened below.

"Hello, Your Majesty," someone chirped. "The peace lilies are on the right."

Ember brightened. She craned her neck for a sight of Cadmus over the railing, ready to interrogate him on his plant choice—wait, that wasn't red hair.

"My thanks, as always," Aeley said, reaching for a peace lily on the nearby shelf. "Your new location is lovely, Galena."

Galena beamed. There was a quick, familiar exchange of silver chips, and then Aeley was gone. Galena turned back to her conversation as if nothing had happened.

"Galena," Ember said, rapidly descending the stairs and tapping her on the shoulder. "What was that?"

"I know," the red-haired nymph said. "I think three silvers is nowhere near enough for my beauties, but Levidia told me we're trying to make a profit, not a haggling house."

"You just interacted with the King's mother and didn't so much as bat an eye."

"So?"

"The last time you saw a Royal, you tripped over a plant pot and then hid in your garden for a week."

Galena's face turned as red as her hair. "Accalon startled me! Besides, I've been selling peace lilies to Aeley for years. It's hardly an unexpected interaction."

"Years," Ember repeated.

What use did Aeley have with so many peace lilies? As far as Ember knew, there were none in the castle garden, and she'd never seen any in the castle.

She glanced over at the shelves of peace lilies. Although each pot was a different color, they were the same cylindrical shape, with rows of curving lines crisscrossing to form an X in the front.

It was a unique design. One she'd seen recently.

"How often does Aeley get them?" she asked.

Galena shrugged as she pruned back a leggy plant. "About once a month."

Ember's mind buzzed. Why was Aeley leaving peace lilies at Accalon's wife's grave?

"Tell Levidia I'll be back in a couple days," she said, then hurried out.

Ember caught up with Aeley at the Phoenix Gate.

"Aeley!" she called, skidding to a stop behind her.

Aeley barely glanced back. "Where is your respect?"

"Your Majesty," Ember corrected begrudgingly. "What are you doing with that peace lily?"

"The same thing everyone does with a houseplant."

"Not everyone leaves houseplants at Accalon's wife's grave."

The temperature dropped a dozen degrees. Slowly, Aeley turned to face Ember, her blue eyes frosted over. Ember swallowed hard.

"I lived in this castle with Arienne for three years," the king's mother said, terrifyingly quiet. "I knew her for three years before that. I got to know her, befriend her, walk through every step of bringing a child into this world with her. And it's because of her I can't go a single day without thinking of the pain of losing that child."

Ember inched away from Aeley, her eyes dropping to the hands she clenched around her plant pot. Gods, she'd marched over here, so consumed by the possibility of a clue that she hadn't even stopped to consider...

"Her loss impacted you, too," Ember said softly.

Aeley's expression shuddered.

Ember went on, "You were only trying to pay your respects."

"Someone has to remember her and the child that was lost." Aeley's voice cracked. She quickly turned away, marching through the gate without waiting for a response.

But Ember unthawed under a sudden flash of heat.

"Wait," she said, lunging forward to grab Aeley's arm. "You go through all this effort for a deceased child, and yet you can't show your own a drop of compassion? How could you do that to Analia?"

Aeley wrenched out of Ember's grip, *"Analia."* She seemed to catch herself. "Stay out of Royal affairs."

Ember took a step back. Aeley slammed the gate between them with a clang and marched off toward the castle. Ember stared after her, the disdain for Analia slicing through her own insides.

It was no wonder they'd become such close friends: they'd both spent their lives hearing they would never be enough. But while Analia had retreated inward, Ember had exploded out.

She was a force of overwhelming confidence and hard work. There was no room for fear or failure. Not when she had to prove everyone wrong—because she was terrified they were right. She wasn't enough. She would never be enough. And she was so tired of fighting.

Ember dug in her pocket, pulling out a crumpled devinroot plant. She couldn't remember when she'd started carrying them around with her, just that the sharp, familiar smell seemed like the only thing holding her together.

She leaned her forehead against the gate, tracing an engraved spiral on one of the rods as she waited for the devinroot to wash the pain away.

It was such a tiny detail. An oddly familiar one, too.

It wasn't surprising, though. Accalon had always been endearingly meticulous. Ember would have bet fifty gold pieces he'd gone so far as to make sure that little detail was on the painting in the Council Chamber—wait.

"It's a map!" Ember exclaimed, bursting into the thankfully out-of-session Council Chamber.

Cadmus jerked out of his chair, stammering questions she didn't bother answering. She headed straight for the painting of the Phoenix Gate, her eyes scanning—yes, there. She might have been fighting a hopeless battle with the healers, but this gods-damned mystery was just about to take a massive step forward.

"The symbols don't just categorize ideas in the book," she said. "They're also scattered across these walls. The topic of each symbol is a clue to which painted location has the same symbol."

"Ember, slow down," Cadmus said. "I can barely understand you."

Ember thought her mind was about to explode. She impatiently waved him over, eventually grabbing him by the sleeve when he was in range to hurry him along. "Look!"

Cadmus took an infuriatingly long time to study the wall. Finally, his eyes widened.

"You're a genius," he said, laughing as he pulled her into a quick hug.

Ember nearly overflowed with giddiness, the emotional whiplash sending her mind spinning. It was progress. She was finally, undeniably, doing something right.

"I made a copy of my sketches," Cadmus said, ushering her toward the table and pulling a page from a nearby pile. "If you mark down whatever themes you've found, we can start searching—"

"Already ahead of you," Ember said, snatching a discarded pen and starting to scribble. "Have I told you how much I love and loathe your uncle?"

Cadmus laughed, looking over her shoulder as she wrote. "Even with all this," he said, "it's still not going to be easy. That symbol was smaller than a fingernail. It's going to take some time to find all of them."

"That circle triangle is on the three major mountains," Lucilla said, peeking around Ember.

Ember and Cadmus whipped around.

"When did you get here?" Ember demanded.

"A few minutes ago," Lucilla said, smoothing her pale pink gown. "You left the door open."

Cadmus shot Ember a look. Ember stuck out her tongue.

"What are you talking about, Luce?" Cadmus asked, turning back to his sister.

"It's on the mountains," she repeated. "Look."

Lucilla took Cadmus's hand and led him around the room, Ember trailing behind. At the painting designated to each mountain, Lucilla traced her finger around the tiny triangle of circles, nearly invisible against the mountains' rocky faces.

"How did you know that?" Cadmus asked, mystified.

"Uncle Accalon used to bring me in here to teach me our history. I think he liked looking at all of his paintings."

"Sounds like him," Ember said. Cadmus elbowed her.

"I had to stare at Mt. Raegyr's painting for so long," Lucilla said. "Eventually, I just noticed it. Uncle told me I had excellent eyes," she added proudly.

"But how did you find the others?" Ember asked.

"I snuck in when the council wasn't in session," Lucilla said, moving to perch on the edge of the table.

"But why?" Cadmus asked.

Lucilla shrugged. "I was curious. I thought maybe it could be a secret puzzle from Uncle."

"A puzzle," Ember mused, moving back to their list of symbols. She beckoned Lucilla closer, "Have you seen any more of these—"

"Ember," Cadmus warned.

Ember glanced at him as Lucilla approached. His face remained perfectly calm as he joined them, but Ember could feel the faint heat radiating off his body.

"That one's on the Phoenix Gate," Lucilla said, ignoring her brother and pointing to the spiral.

"On the wall?" Ember asked.

"And the actual gate," Lucilla said. "I tried to carve a backward one next to it with my magic so it would match, but the metal wouldn't let me."

"You get into all kinds of trouble, don't you?" Ember said.

Lucilla grinned. "It's easy when you're the littlest Royal. As long as you're sweet and innocent, no one pays attention."

Ember laughed.

"You might as well let me help," Lucilla added, looking at a frowning Cadmus. "I'll just send the fire sprites to eavesdrop on you again if you say no."

Fire sprites—Rosala curse her. No wonder that fire sprite had been so curious. Cadmus cursed under his breath, undoubtedly realizing the same thing.

"So," Ember said, "what I'm hearing is it would be a waste of valuable time to try and stop you."

Lucilla clasped her hands. Cadmus bit the inside of his cheek.

That tired, hopeless look was back in his eyes. The same look he'd had when talking about Analia. The sister he'd failed to protect. The sister he could no longer make it up to.

"You can't protect her forever, Cadmus," Ember said softly. "Don't make her feel like she can't do anything."

Cadmus deflated. He turned to study his notes, not looking at either of them as he said, "We'll have to move fast. The council has a block of meetings lined up, with the first one in fifteen minutes."

"Well," Ember said, "then you better start moving, Your Majesty."

Chapter 27

"You throw a punch like that, Anna, and all you're doing is breaking your hand."

Analia scowled. She and Branten stood in the training hollow, a red training dummy newly set up in its center.

Branten took her fist in his large, calloused hand. "You keep this thumb inside your fist, you break it. You don't keep your wrist straight, you break it. You hit with your pinky and ring fingers, you break them."

"So," Analia said. "I did nothing right."

"You had excellent footwork."

Analia scoffed. "So, what do I do, then?"

Branten released her fist, raising his own for her to see. "Your thumb goes on top of your pointer and middle finger knuckles," he instructed. "Punches are precise, and you hit on an exhale with the second knuckles on those first two fingers."

"Why an exhale?" Analia asked.

"Try it and find out."

Analia raised a brow, but she turned back to the dummy. She checked her footing, then, shifting her fingers into the proper position, she loosed a breath and struck. Immediately, she could feel her punch was harder, stronger.

"Why do you always have to be right?" she complained.

Branten chortled. Moving around her, his fist flashed out with a brutal thud. "I'm just that good."

"Humble, too," Laness said, descending into the hollow with Aaron, Mor, and Surce close behind.

"I see you still haven't invested in a proper place to sit," Surce commented, the weak sunlight bringing out the golden threads in her scarlet gown.

Branten looked as though he were about to retort, but Analia turned to Aaron. "What are you all doing here?"

"Family meeting," Aaron said, stretching out on his usual patch of moss. "I finally settled on terms with the DovenU and doubted Branten would cut training short to come listen."

"Damn right." Branten turned back to Analia. "Fifty punches, you start over every time your form slips. Go."

Analia gave Branten a look, but she complied.

"You better be giving her water breaks," said Laness.

"Stop fussing," Branten said, going to sit on the edge of the table. "What'd the slayer ladies say?"

"We're to meet tomorrow morning," said Aaron.

"That sounds about right," Laness said, plopping down beside him. "They have all the power, and you have no time to prepare."

"Were there any stipulations?" Mor asked.

Analia caught Aaron's expression darken from the corner of her eye. "Their queen wishes to meet Analia."

"Me?"

"You've still got thirty punches," Branten told her.

Analia fixed her footing and continued. "What could their queen want with me?" she asked.

Aaron muttered, "Knowing her? Anything."

"No one in that mountain would lay a finger on her," Laness said firmly.

"I know," Aaron said. "But it's still Analia's choice."

Analia didn't pause her punching as she felt their eyes land on her.

"If that's what it takes to find the scrolls," she panted, "I'll go."

"I'll come, too," Laness offered. "They might be more willing to help if I'm there."

"I'm going as well," said Branten, the finality in his tone having Analia glancing at him. He gave her a brief nod, and something in Analia's chest softened slightly.

"So," Mor said, tapping the cluster of scattered poles he'd collected into alignment, "that leaves me and Surce to hold down the kingdoms."

"Yes," Surce mused, "I have a good feeling about this."

"Then tomorrow it is," Aaron murmured.

Analia could feel his thoughtful gaze on her as she rounded out her punches. But she wouldn't flinch away from this. She'd been stared at in Ash, whispered about in Sun. The DovenU Queen wanted to judge her for herself? Fine.

Analia slammed her fist into the dummy for the fiftieth time, breathing hard. It took her a moment to smell the smoke, to look down and discover she had burned away her wrappings.

Analia's shoulders slumped. She pushed the hair that clung to her sweaty forehead aside, glancing around. Only Aaron remained in the hollow, watching quietly from a few feet behind her.

"Where did everyone else go?" she asked.

"Back to the house," Aaron said. "Branten and Laness wanted to discuss diplomacy strategies, and I told him I'd stay with you."

Analia hadn't even heard them leave.

Aaron's eyes moved down to her hands. Analia tensed, knowing what was coming next.

"Your elbow started to drop toward the end," he told her.

"It did?"

Why wasn't he calling out her flames?

Aaron stepped closer. "May I?"

Analia nodded slowly. She turned back to the dummy, her senses pricking as she felt Aaron come up behind her. He rested one hand on her hip, the other sliding down to her forearm.

"Line up your first two knuckles with your forearm," he murmured in her ear. "Elbow in, wrist straight. Exhale. And bam."

Aaron drove her fist into the dummy with a quick, solid jab, his chest brushing her back as he moved with her. "Just like that."

Analia nodded. She expected him to release her and step away. But Aaron remained perfectly still, the slick glide of his network brushing along her senses.

There was something steadying about his presence. It allowed her to close her eyes, momentarily relaxing back against him. Then, she snapped out her arm, her fist slamming into the dummy.

"Perfect," Aaron murmured. His fingers trailed down her arm, curling around her elbow before finally dropping away.

Analia's flames stirred. That had been one of Pryanth's favorite compliments in the beginning: perfect. She had tried so hard to believe him, but his words always bounced off her like a stray pebble. But now?

Analia turned to face Aaron, momentarily surprised by how close he still stood.

But she didn't back away. Because he had said it like a fact, looked at her like it hadn't cost him anything to say so. And Analia's burning flames settled into something warm.

Find someone you trust to watch your back.

"Cool downs?" she asked.

Aaron blinked as if dazed. Then, with a quick nod, he backed away.

Analia lay down on a cushy swath of moss, Aaron kneeling before her. He took her heel in his hand and slowly stretched her leg back, smirking as he commented on her flexibility. Analia threw a fistful of moss at him.

As they continued, her mind drifted back to Pryanth.

Why was it when he was alive, she had no problem feeling the sting of his words, the burn of his slap. Yet, in his death, she didn't feel free. She felt herself mourning those moments of sunshine.

Gods, why couldn't she have seen through him faster?

aron left Analia at the foot of the stairs, shadowjumping off to Crystal knew where. She hauled herself up the steps, vaguely noting how her muscles didn't ache as much that day.

This time, instead of stopping at her room, she kept walking.

Analia's feet sank into plush carpet, her eyes scanning the ceiling. There. Right where Aaron said it was. The hatch to the roof.

Still, her heart flinched. She quickly turned away, her eyes landing on the door to her right, which had been left ajar.

She'd assumed it was another bedroom when first exploring the house. But peering inside, she spotted a familiar curtain of beads.

Before she knew what she was doing, she stepped through the open door and through the curtain.

Analia wasn't surprised to discover Surce's studio on the other side. Nor was she completely surprised to note the seamstress was seated at her loom, looking at Analia like she had been waiting for her.

"Hi," Analia mumbled, glancing away from that topaz stare. Why had she come?

"I was wondering if you would discover my doorway," said Surce. "Please, come in."

Analia obediently moved to sit on the bench behind Surce's stool. "I've been wondering how you come and go so quickly."

"My doorways aren't quite as efficient as Aaron's shadowjumping, nor Laness's ability to appear wherever there's an enka flower, but they are sufficient."

"I didn't know that about Laness."

"She can only go so far with each jump, but it's nevertheless an ability that makes her an excellent spy."

Surce gave Analia a tiny smile, then turned back to her loom. It wasn't a dismissal, but Analia was certain if she rose from that bench and left without another word, Surce wouldn't mind at all.

Instead, Analia remained seated, quietly watching Surce work, her magic enabling several invisible hands to weave alongside her. Eventually, Analia rose to explore the tapestries on the wall.

"I don't recognize any of these," she commented. Bracing herself, she looked to where her wedding night tapestry had hung, just to find a depiction of a harp, its frame painted green and stained with bloody fingerprints.

"Some are the same as that initial day," Surce said, not looking up as she waved to the tapestry of a cracked gray rock. "But you are correct, most have shifted. The beads aren't just a doorway, but also a curator, choosing which tapestries to display based on which individuals pass through."

"So, these tapestries were picked for me?"

"You and me," Surce said. "I have no doubt if we were to leave and only you passed through the beads, you would see something different."

Analia could have sworn she caught a glimpse of knowing on Surce's face, but she quickly looked away. "Come," she said, waving Analia over. "My magic may infuse these threads, but that doesn't prevent them from getting tangled. I could use your help."

There was magic in the threads? Analia double-checked, but she only sensed the magic in the beads and Surce's network, reaching out in various directions as it guided her threads. But nothing from the threads themselves. Interesting.

"You should get an assistant," Analia said, moving to Surce's side and picking up a spool of thread.

"I've tried over the centuries," Surce said, "but none of them were able to handle getting a glimpse of the future."

"Even your family?"

"Oh, *especially* them," Surce laughed. "Those four are notorious for either fixating on what they see, or trying to force what they expect will happen."

"So," Analia said, "you do everything? Weave, interpret, and keep the family in line?"

"Especially the final point."

The two shared a smile.

"The future is a lonely place," Surce said, sobering as she turned back to her loom. "It's obscured by fog, sometimes unbearably flexible. Oftentimes, my readings are erroneous, but our subsequent actions are what enable the actual outcome. Other times, it's our own desire to rebel against the future depicted that allows it to unfold. And even more frequently, the tapestries merely guide us to a fork in the timeline, and it's left to us to decide which path to choose. It's a concurrent certainty and unknown most aren't able to cope with."

"But you can?" Analia asked.

"Most of the time. In the moments I can't, I remind myself I'm doing this for my home. For the people who took me in and claimed me as their own after decades of being alone.

"With all that being said, I'm curious. What do you make of this tapestry?"

Analia studied Surce a moment longer. She couldn't imagine how much strength it required to forge a home out of such solitude. Thoroughly impressed, she peered down at the loom.

The tapestry was near complete, displaying what appeared to be a mountain peak. The tip seemed to be coated in something like steel, a small gaping hole in the threads slightly below it.

"Is this for our trip to the DovenU?" she asked.

"Precisely."

"How are you going to fill in that hole?"

"I'm not," Surce said simply.

"What?" Analia demanded. "Why not?"

"Not all holes need to be filled, Analia."

"But how will you complete it?"

"That's not important," Surce said, moving down to what Analia assumed was the final row. "What's important is we can see the full picture. The hole might be blocking a crucial detail, it might not. But the threads decreed the hole was necessary, and thus, it remains."

Surce finished off the tapestry with a flourish. Expertly removing it from the loom, she held it up for inspection.

"Yes," she mused, "the threads do enjoy your presence."

Turning, she headed for the beads. "Come. I suspect everyone is waiting with bated breath."

Analia obediently followed Surce back through the beads. Reaching the upstairs hallway, she paused at her bedroom door, waving Surce on without her.

As soon as the seamstress was gone, Analia slipped inside, bringing her hand to her aching chest as she stepped into her bathing room.

She could practically feel every crack and broken piece beneath her palm, radiating out from the hole her uncle's death had sliced through her heart. A hole she'd so desperately tried to fill while in the Sun Kingdom, even when it hurt to do so.

Analia pulled Pryanth's pendant from her pocket, its magic field thrumming beneath her fingers as she stared at her tired reflection.

So many things had nearly killed her. But she had survived. Just as Aaron had promised.

A knock sounded on her bedroom door.

"Analia," Aaron's muffled voice called, "please tell me you're coming to lunch. Laness and Branten won't stop bickering, and Surce keeps trying to talk to me about thread counts."

Analia's fingers flexed around the dangling chain.

"What a hard, hard life you have," she replied.

"This isn't even the fun kind of hard," Aaron complained. "Please, my shooting star, don't subject me to them alone."

Analia's reflected face softened. She looked to the door, back down at the pendant. Then, fingers shaking slightly, she let the pendant fall, the chain pooling around the golden heart on the counter like the creature's shackles.

Find someone you trust to watch your back.

Analia turned away from the pendant, its magic field a heavy knot in the back of her awareness. As she joined Aaron and he ruffled her hair, she wondered if maybe, just maybe, she'd had someone all along.

Chapter 28

The day they were to meet with the DovenU, Analia and company gathered in the dining room first thing. Well, Laness, Analia, and Aaron gathered first thing. Branten waited until the last minute to swagger through the doors—which no one seemed particularly surprised by.

What was surprising was how Laness shoved Aaron's arm aside as he reached for Analia, saying it was her turn to magically transport her.

Now, Analia braced herself against a tree trunk, her eyes squeezed shut as the world tilted beneath her feet.

Laness struggled to smother a laugh. "I probably should have warned you about the dizziness, huh?"

Analia mumbled something about that being nothing like shadowjumping.

The usual empty darkness had been replaced by thick, earthy air. It squeezed around her as she rocketed forward, a sharp tug on her gut abruptly jerking her up into the world as if she had been racing across underground root networks.

Now, she tentatively opened her eyes.

They'd appeared in a lush, sunny glade. Tall stalks of grass waved lazily in the breeze, their clumps decorated with enka flowers.

"Is this the place?" she asked.

"Not quite," Laness said. "This is the closest enka flower patch, but the border is just up ahead."

That explained the slick glide of Aaron's magic in the near distance. Finally feeling steady enough on her feet, Analia pushed off her trunk and followed Laness into the woods.

"I can't believe this is the Wild Lands," she said, undergrowth crunching beneath her boots. "Our legends say it's all barren, inhospitable land, saturated with the Ancient Ones' magic. But this...?"

"Beautiful," Laness agreed. "Although it's strange," she added, half to herself. "Being back after so long."

"How so?" Analia asked.

Laness was quiet for a few steps. "The last time I made this walk was right after the war. Aaron had suggested this place might be good for me after everything that happened, but it was Branten's pestering that finally got me here."

Laness ducked under a branch, her voice becoming thoughtful. "Sometimes, I think I wouldn't have been able to make it if he hadn't taken that walk with me."

Analia watched as Laness examined a patch of thorns, eventually finding the best spot to step down with her boot. "I take it you didn't just come here to learn how to fight."

"That was part of it," Laness hedged, waving Analia forward. "But this place isn't just a military tribe."

There was a part of Analia that didn't want to ask. But she knew Laness was giving her an opening, even though she couldn't meet her eyes as she did so.

"What is it, then?" she asked softly.

"A sanctuary," Laness said on an exhale. "A place for any woman who has nowhere else to go."

Laness headed off once more, the rustle of the thorns snapping back into place seeming to finish her thought. *Including me.*

Analia looked down at her boots as she followed. "Aaron didn't tell me that."

"No," Laness said. "He wouldn't have. Aaron might keep his secrets, but he holds just as tightly to everyone else's. And the trauma, healing, and releasing in that mountain wasn't his to share."

Laness tossed a smile over her shoulder. One that was almost believable. But Analia was all too familiar with the wariness that tightened the corners of her eyes.

"You would think with how much Aaron talks," she said, "he wouldn't have any secrets left."

Laness nearly choked on her laugh. Clearly, Analia wasn't the only one who dreaded other people's pity. But as they finally emerged from the trees, she couldn't help but wonder what had happened during that war.

"Took you long enough," Branten called.

He and Aaron stood a few feet away. Mt. Lanula loomed behind them like a massive arrowhead, its nearby boundary softly thrumming against Analia's mental shield.

Laness marched forward, hands on her hips. "That's rich, coming from you."

The two quickly dissolved into their usual squabbling. But there was a careful assessment in Branten's eyes as they went back and forth. Judging by Aaron's softened gaze, she wasn't the only one who noticed.

"So," he said, stepping to her side. "I see you survived your initiation."

Analia winced, her nausea momentarily resurfacing at his words. As Aaron laughed at her expression, she gave herself a moment to take him in.

His embroidered black-and-blue jacket. The daggers at his belt. Those starlight eyes that held so many secrets.

But she wasn't angry he hadn't told her the truth about the DovenU. If anything, she respected him more for protecting that secret. Just as he'd protected her own.

"It was exhilarating," she said. "But I think I'll stick to shadowjumping."

Aaron's face was a mask of wicked satisfaction.

"In that case," he purred, sliding his arm around her waist, "that can be arranged."

"You'd like that, wouldn't you?"

"Oh, my shooting star, let's not pretend this is just about me."

Analia made a squawk of protest. Aaron grinned and tugged her braid. As he turned away, Analia struggled to straighten her expression.

"All right, children," he said, clapping his hands. "Are we ready?"

Laness cut off midsentence. She exchanged a vaguely offended look with Branten, but the two showed no sign of their usual zinging retorts as they nodded to Aaron.

"Good." Aaron loosened the leash on his magic, power rumbling around him like an impending thunderstorm. "Let's not keep our friends waiting, then."

Not waiting for a response, Aaron stuck his hands in his pockets, then stepped right over the border.

"Crystal spare us," Laness muttered.

Analia barely had time to take a breath when something tickled her mental shield. Her eyes shot to the left of the mountain, Branten and Laness moving to stand behind her. Still, it was a few moments before she could make out the two women silently prowling toward them.

The woman on the right was stocky, with dark blonde hair braided down her back. The other was tall and lean, with dark brown skin, high cheekbones, and long black hair falling over her shoulders in twin braids. Each wore skin-tight, hooded bodysuits, the fabric shifting colors to perfectly camouflage them to their surroundings.

Aaron returned to Analia's side as the Dovenesses—as Laness called them—reached the border. The blonde woman hung back, allowing her companion to stalk forward. Despite having no magic network Analia could detect, power crackled through the air as her eyes met Aaron's.

"Your Majesty." She dipped her chin, not breaking his stare.

Aaron rocked back on his heels. "Hyla. Leona." His eyes slid to the side, briefly acknowledging Leona before making their way back to Hyla.

"So," Hyla said, drawing out the word. "This is her?"

Her dark eyes latched on to Analia like a viper, but Analia kept her chin high. "I can speak for myself."

Hyla arched a thin brow, her attention shifting to Laness. "Welcome home, sister."

"It's good to be back," Laness said, completely earnest.

Hyla dipped her chin in acknowledgement, her gaze finally moving to Branten. Her nose wrinkled. "You brought *him?*"

"I'm happy to stay outside if you think it's best," Branten said.

Hyla looked less than impressed. "You all will be remaining outside."

Analia swapped a perplexed look with Laness. Aaron, on the other hand, only rocked back on his heels. "Inform your lady that won't be happening."

"Lady Zinia made it perfectly clear she only wished to see Analia," said Hyla.

Aaron's magic thrummed. "I'm not sending her in alone."

The quiet ice in his words sent chills down Analia's spine.

Hyla didn't appear so much as fazed. "You have no choice," she said.

"At least let me come," Laness said. "I may not live here anymore, but I'm still a member of the DovenU."

"You may travel with us if you insist, but only Analia will meet with our lady."

"All right, hold on," Branten said, taking a step forward. "Let's just take a second—"

In a blur, Hyla planted her foot in Branten's chest. He flew back, landing on the gravel with a thud.

"Stay on your side," she snarled.

Aaron's power surged. The Dovenesses tensed, Laness immediately shifting to stand in front of Analia.

Crystal spare them, this was not going to end well.

Analia glanced back at Branten. And the look of utter bewilderment on his face had her choking on a snicker.

"My, Branten," she said, voice dripping with sarcasm. "How the mighty have fallen."

Aaron and Hyla stiffened.

But Laness burst out laughing. She doubled over, barely managing to force out her words. "That was amazing!"

Leona quickly joined in, her hand falling away from her weapons belt.

Branten pushed himself into a sitting position, something like wonder in his eyes as he looked over Analia's shoulder. "Hyla, was it?"

Analia turned in time to see Hyla roll her eyes. She exchanged another long, challenging look with Aaron. But slowly, the two relaxed, Aaron's magic settling once more.

"So," Hyla said briskly, "will Analia be coming with us or not?"

Aaron made to respond, but Analia stepped forward. "I'll come."

"Anna," Aaron murmured.

Analia glanced back. Aaron's unreadable mask remained in place, but she could see the resolve in the set of his jaw. One that told her he was willing to do whatever it took to make sure she didn't have to go in alone if she didn't want to.

For a moment, Analia couldn't tear her eyes away. But she wouldn't let what little peace existed here dissolve.

"I'll be all right," she promised, sounding more confident than she felt.

Aaron bit the inside of his cheek. But he nodded, his fingers brushing hers as she moved past him and crossed the border.

Leona came forward, and Analia lifted her arms as the Doveness patted her down. She'd left Aaron's dagger at home, knowing it would send the wrong message if she brought a weapon. There was nothing for them to find—

"What's this?" Leona's hand darted into Analia's jacket pocket and pulled out Pryanth's pendant. "Oh, pretty!"

Analia felt something like a kick to her gut. She'd put the pendant in her pocket out of habit that morning, but that didn't stop her from wanting to snatch it back.

Yet, as her fingers flexed, Laness's words softly echoed in her mind. *Trauma, healing, and releasing.*

Slowly, Analia forced her fingers to relax.

"Keep it," she said.

Leona cocked her head. "Really?"

Analia could feel Aaron's eyes on her as she nodded. Leona shrugged. Then, she slipped the pendant over her head and around her neck.

"You're welcome to wait here," she said to Analia's group. Hyla made a face, but Leona ignored her. "We'll bring Her Highness back when she's done speaking with our lady."

"Fine," said Aaron coolly. He turned to Laness, "Go with them."

Laness hopped across the border. Hyla's eye twitched, but she turned and headed back toward the mountain without comment.

Analia cast Aaron one last look. Then, she hurried after Hyla, her eyes drawn to the flash of gold around Leona's neck.

And for the first time in she couldn't remember how long, Analia felt like she could fully take a breath.

Hyla led the way around the mountain, only pausing when they were out of Branten and Aaron's sight. Analia braced herself for the grueling climb ahead. But as it turned out, there was none.

Hyla touched a nearby rocky outcrop, the outline of her hand briefly glowing purple. Then, the rock dissolved, revealing a hidden passageway into the mountainside.

Hyla marched through without a backward glance, Leona offering Analia a crooked smile before following. Sensing the magic ahead, Analia edged into the tunnel, Laness taking up the rear.

The path before her was completely dark. Analia somehow couldn't tell if she was moving uphill or down, but before her nerves could get the best of her, the short tunnel opened up.

The mountain had been hollowed out into a massive cavern. A honeycomb of passageways climbed up the mountain walls, disappearing into the darkness far above. Countless orbs of light zipped through the air, casting a rainbow glow across the chamber. And directly before her, groups of women were engaged in sparring matches, moving impossibly fast.

Hyla quickly dismissed Leona, telling her she had chores to attend to. The disgruntled Doveness trotted off, Hyla briskly striding away in the opposite direction.

"Chores?" Analia asked Laness as they hurried after Hyla.

"We all have to pitch in around here to keep things running," Laness explained. "From the most skilled warriors down to the women who are still learning to fight."

"Everyone's equal," Analia mused.

Even if that were the case, Hyla certainly acted as though she were important. She didn't so much as move through the crowd as the crowd moved around her, everyone quick to get out of her way. Even the orbs of light avoided her path.

"What are those?" Analia asked as they stepped into a tunnel.

"Winllows," said Laness. "Many believe them to be the spirits of Dovenesses who have passed. Or, at least, fragments of their spirits."

"Since our tribe is hidden," said Hyla, "these spirits are the ones who travel across Elefthia, finding those in need of our refuge and guiding them here."

"They'll also help you get to the higher levels if you're nice," Laness added.

Analia was about to ask how when Hyla paused before a massive stone door, carved with whirling, abstract designs.

"We have arrived," she said. She knocked on the door three times, followed by four slow kicks to its base.

There was a pause. Then, one solid, ringing knock came from the other side of the door.

Analia's flames guttered.

"Our lady will see you now," Hyla said. Not giving Analia time to steel herself, she opened the door and unceremoniously shoved Analia inside.

Immediately, something like a heavy hand slammed down on her flames. She stumbled back, the magic in her network dwindling, dwindling, dwindling.

"Wipe that look from your face," came a voice from deeper in the chamber. "Your magic will come back to you."

Analia's eyes darted around.

The entire chamber was built from polished black onyx. Not the smooth, unmarred variety of Onyx Bridge, but carved with intricate designs she'd only seen in the Sun Kingdom.

Even the furniture was built from onyx, which included two throne-like seats with a low table before them. Seated in the throne to the right was a small figure, dressed in loose gray-and-white robes. Her hood was pulled up, only allowing Analia to see the tip of her nose, steely-gray eyes, and broad, calloused hands resting in her lap.

"I know," Analia said, surprisingly calm as she bowed to Lady Zinia. "This chamber's a damper." One that was apparently strong enough to latch on to her through the soles of her boots.

Zinia clicked her tongue. "So, he's blabbered to you about dampers. Is there anything that boy king hasn't told you?"

"I found out about dampers on my own," Analia snapped. She immediately made to apologize, but Zinia waved a hand.

"Don't take it back if you don't regret it. That won't fluff my feathers, it will only insult me more."

"I didn't mean—"

"Yes, you did," said Zinia. "You're loyal to him. That's a good thing. Now sit, I'm tired of you hovering."

Analia warily approached, her final spark winking out as she rested her hands on the back of the empty chair. "Is everything in this chamber carved from onyx?" she asked.

"Your eyes can answer that question."

"They can't tell me why."

Analia braced herself for another tongue-lashing. But Zinia sat back in her seat and folded her hands.

"I have no interest in political pissing matches or who outranks who. In this chamber, with both our networks neutralized, we are simply women. And that is how we will talk."

Interesting. Analia finally sat, and Zinia gave her a look of approval. What in the name of the Crystal had she gotten herself into?

"Lady Zinia," Analia said, "I'm not going to waste your time. I know Aaron already wrote to you—"

"He did," Zinia interrupted. "But I want to hear everything from you."

There was no arguing with her. Analia swallowed hard. Then, she explained everything: Deardryn, the creature, the scrolls.

"Which is why we need to know if Queen Ethelind told you anything about the missing scrolls," Analia finished.

Zinia considered. Crossed and uncrossed her ankles. Gave a long, feline stretch that had Analia about to jump out of her skin.

"Yes," Zinia finally said. "Ethelind left the scroll with me."

Analia perked up. "Does that mean you'll give it to us?"

"No."

"What?" Analia leaned forward in her seat, "Lady Zinia, if we don't get the scroll—"

"You waltz in here," Zinia said, "an unknown foreign power, expecting me to hand it over because you're claiming the world is breaking apart. I don't think so. Not when Queen Ethelind trusted me to keep that scroll safe."

Phantom flames burned across Analia's skin. "Lady Zinia," she said, struggling for calm, "I understand why you see me as a threat to not just the Starlight Kingdom, but to your tribe. But Deardryn is an immediate threat."

"I'm aware."

"And I know you don't trust me. But you do trust Laness and Aaron. So, if you won't give it to me—"

"I won't," said Zinia. "But I will allow you to earn it."

There it was. The perpetual, unappeasable demand of the Ash Kingdom. Prove yourself.

Analia eased back in her seat, drawing out her words. "What did you have in mind?"

"One trial," said Zinia. "Scale Oharrah's Point and retrieve the bronze disk at the top. Return it to me, and I will give you the scroll."

"That's it?" Analia asked.

"That's it," Zinia confirmed. "Do you accept?"

There was no room for debate. Only a yes, or a no.

Analia's hand drifted to her now-empty pocket. "I do."

Chapter 29

Aaron couldn't stop glancing at Analia as they circled around to Oharrah's Point. She hadn't protested when he ordered Laness and Branten back to the house—although that could be because she was still recovering from her magic slamming back into her network.

He had to admit, that was clever of the warrior queen. But it hadn't stopped the ice in his veins when Analia first emerged, pale and shaken.

"I know you want to ask," she said, catching his eye as he glanced at her once more.

Aaron's lips twitched. He took in her black-and-silver jacket, rousing the wicked satisfaction he felt whenever she wore his kingdom's colors. But that was nothing compared to the fact that those jacket pockets were now empty.

"You gave up the pendant," he said.

He'd told himself he'd come to terms with Analia carrying it around. But his breath still froze in his lungs as she told Leona to keep it.

"Laness told me what the DovenU really is," she said, skimming her fingertips along a tree trunk. "A place of trauma, but moving on as well. And I thought... I thought I could give it a try."

Countless questions buzzed through Aaron's mind. But as they crested a small hill, one particular memory shifted to the surface.

"You said forgiveness wasn't the reason you kept the pendant," he said slowly.

Analia didn't immediately respond. The breeze pulled a tendril of hair free from her braid, and Aaron fought the urge to tuck it behind her ear as he waited.

"Pryanth said he loved me," she finally said.

Aaron tensed.

"I tried so hard to convince myself that I loved him, too. Or, at the very least, that I could someday. Even after..." Analia's voice choked off.

"Anna..." Aaron reached for her.

"But he was only filling a void," she said, stepping away. "The one my uncle left behind. And that pendant was a reminder that regardless of how I felt, I killed the man who said he loved me."

Something seemed to rip in Aaron's chest. She had been carrying that around with her all this time?

"Oh, Anna," he murmured, lifting a branch out of the way for her. "That wasn't love. I know your father and that gods-damned kingdom taught you otherwise, but that wasn't love."

"I think that was my problem," she said, half to herself. "All I've ever known is chaos. It's miserable and heartbreaking and unpredictable. But it's also familiar. Comforting, even. And at some point, a part of me gave up on finding anything else."

Aaron reached for her arm, pulling her to a stop. He turned her around to face him, Analia giving him a puzzled look.

"I need you to know," he said, eyes intent on hers, "that you don't deserve any of the torment you've endured. Not from Pryanth, not from the Ash Kingdom, not from your fucking father. What they did to you was *inexcusable*.

"The only thing you deserve is the endless, unconditional love your uncle had for you. So don't stop until you find that, all right? Promise me."

Tears shimmered in Analia's eyes. She nodded, but Aaron didn't release her.

"Tell me you know what they did to you wasn't your fault," he said, his voice cracking. "Tell me you know you deserve to have survived and escaped. That love is supposed to make you whole, not leave pieces in its wake."

Aaron waited to see the same denial he'd felt when his family had explained the same thing to him. But Analia only flashed a small, tired smile. "I know."

"You do?"

"Well, I'm starting to." Analia's eyes momentarily dropped before returning to his. "Do you know why I was able to give up that pendant?"

Aaron shook his head.

"Because I realized it was never something to hold on to." She touched his cheek, then stepped out of his grip. "I know everything you're telling me," she went on, heading off once more. "I just don't know when I'll be able to believe it, too."

Aaron realized he was still rooted to the spot, his fingertips touching his cheek. "That's all right," he said, dropping his hand and heading after her. "You have decades of evidence that says otherwise. Sometimes, you need to experience it to believe it."

"Maybe you should just tell me what to look for."

Well, there were countless directions he could take that conversation, some more chaste than others. Before he could respond, the two broke from the trees.

Oharrah's Point rose up in front of them. It was the shortest of Mt. Lanula's three major peaks, but it was also the steepest.

"Unfortunately," Aaron said, "I believe that will have to wait."

"Why do you look disappointed?" Analia asked, eyes on the mountain. "Now you get to watch me as I walk away."

Aaron let out a surprised laugh. "That sounds like permission."

"I didn't think you needed it," Analia said over her shoulder, heading off.

"That I did not," Aaron murmured, his gaze drifting down. "You should know," he went on, "I've always been better at showing than telling."

"Really?" Analia turned back. "Does that mean you'll *show me* why you're such a delight to wake up to?"

Their eyes locked. Aaron's body tightened, a buzz starting deep in his veins. He waited for her to shrug it off, look away—why wasn't she looking away, why couldn't he look away?

A gust of wind blew into them.

Analia jumped, her eyes finally releasing him.

Aaron's heart seemed to trip over itself. He desperately shoved down every thought that threatened to bubble to the surface; thoughts of smoke and jasmine, the spot where her neck met her shoulder beneath his lips, his teeth—stop.

"Of course," he said, focusing on her left eyebrow, "you have to survive this trial of yours first. Then, you can have me all to yourself."

Analia gave him a haughty look. Then, she turned and marched off.

Thank the Crystal. Not just because she would need to be fired up to make it through this trial, but because Aaron wasn't certain he would have been able to walk away himself. Not as he leaned back against a tree trunk, unable to wipe the look in her eyes from his mind.

A nalia trudged toward the mountain, trying and failing to suppress her smile.

Sometimes, Aaron was too much of a flirt for his own good. It was starting to reach the point where she couldn't tell when he was amusing himself or actually being serious. Regardless, she wasn't expecting that moment to feel so... enjoyable?

She enjoyed feeling like she had control. She enjoyed being the one to initiate, even if it was just for fun.

So many of her interactions with Pryanth had been dictated by him: when he touched her, how he touched her, the direction of their every interaction. He'd had all the power. And he'd punished her every time she'd tried to take it back.

But Aaron? Aaron not only offered her that power, but he followed her lead when she decided to take it.

But she would have to figure out what to make of that another time.

Oharrah's Point loomed tall and steep before her. The closest handhold in the gray rock was above her head, and seeing no other option, she stretched up on her toes. She was incredibly pleased with how smoothly she was able to pull herself up, but there was a long way to go.

Analia slowly made her way up the mountain face, remembering the history Laness and Hyla had told her on their way out.

Apparently, the DovenU had existed long before they found Mt. Lanula. At that point, they'd been a small band of women, constantly on the run from their pasts. It was a long time before they stumbled on Mt. Lanula, although it didn't become hospitable until Oharrah, the first warrior queen, scaled this peak and proved herself to the mountain.

Analia didn't know what that last part meant. But that didn't stop her from constantly looking around. Especially as she noticed the thrum of magic coursing through the rock beneath her.

Yet, the mountain remained perfectly still as Analia climbed, the rising sun baking the back of her head.

Eventually, she took a break about halfway up the mountain. She lifted her sweaty face to the wind, choking back a groan as she saw how far she still had to go.

What was the point of this? All she was proving was her physical strength. Why did that matter?

Analia sighed, reaching for another handhold. She'd become so accustomed to the thrum of magic that she didn't immediately notice that the mountain had started to rumble. She only looked up when a shadow fell across her face.

Just in time to see the boulder thundering toward her.

Analia yelped. She jumped to the side, her hands scrambling for a hold as she slid down to a narrow shelf a few feet to the side. The boulder tumbled past a moment later, close enough to graze her arm.

Analia pressed herself against the mountain, her heart pounding. She shifted her weight, reaching for a handhold. And the shelf crumbled beneath her feet.

Analia lunged for the handhold. She dug her fingers in, her nails breaking as her feet dangled in open air.

Crystal spare her. She only had one handhold. Her fingers were starting to cramp.

Analia gritted her teeth. She kicked at the rock, shoving herself up, up, up, just managing to reach a second handhold. But Mt. Lanula was just getting started.

Analia scrambled up the mountain, dodging boulders and dirt slides, desperately clutching handholds that shrunk to mere scratches. Her fingers were sticky with blood. Multiple times, her sweat-slick palms slipped on the rock that vibrated so hard it almost threw her off.

She just had to reach the top. She chanted those words over and over in her mind, letting out a scream of frustration as gravel stung her eyes and she slid back down.

She had come too far to fail. She had survived too much to be taken down by a gods-damned mountain.

A chunk of debris slammed into her from the side. She crashed into the mountain, black spots dancing across her vision as she bashed her knee, her temple. She tried to tighten her grip on her handhold, but the rock smoothed over. Analia scrabbled for a hold, her hands scraped raw, her body sliding down as the mountain shuddered.

She. Was. Not. Done.

Analia wedged her boot in the crack where a boulder met the mountain. Then, flinging her stinging hands over the top, she stepped up with her other foot, hauling herself over the final boulder with a curse.

The top of the peak flattened into a decently sized bluff. Across from her, tucked into the wall of the next peak, was a low, shadowy cave. The disk had to be in there.

Analia marched forward, spitting out gravel, her last shred of control beginning to fray. And it positively snapped as there came a dragging sound from inside the cave.

Analia dove out of the way, just as a massive pincer flashed out and sliced the air where she'd been standing. She rolled to her feet as the creature emerged.

It vaguely reminded her of a scorpion. Except this scorpion was the size of Aaron's dining room table, its body glinting with what looked to be an iron-coated shell marred with slash marks.

Before Analia could blink, it whipped a long, barbed tail at her. Analia jumped to the side, just for a pincer to snap at her waist. She rolled under it, desperately searching for a plan.

She tried to edge around the scorpion, but it weaved with her, its small black eyes locked on her. Guarding its home? Waiting to attack? It didn't matter. Analia had no weapons, no advantage, no plan.

Her flames crackled, but she shoved them down. She was too exhausted to manage them, to stay in control—gods, she could not lose control.

Something whistled in Analia's ears. She jerked back, but the scorpion's tail sliced through her jacket sleeve, just grazing her skin beneath. Seeing an opening, it lunged, Analia letting out a shriek as she jumped aside, her back foot meeting empty air.

She was trapped. There was nowhere to go. No one to save her. She was helpless—no. She had promised herself she would never be helpless again.

The Princess of Ash may have had nothing to work with, but that wasn't true anymore. This was her chance to not just survive, but finally fight back. And she was tired of being afraid to do so.

Analia ran forward. The scorpion reared back on its back legs in surprise. Analia dove forward, under the swinging pincers, somersaulting under its iron-clad belly and through rows of legs.

The scorpion slammed back down, but Analia was already on the other side. She raised her foot, catching the scorpion's whipping tail on the sole of her boot. Then, she tumbled into the cave.

The first thing that hit her was the smell. Analia threw her arm over her nose, choking on the stench of decaying flesh. Carcasses littered the cave floor, ranging from small birds to rodents.

The scorpion hissed behind her.

Analia hurried deeper into the cave, bones crunching under her boots, eyes scanning—there. All the way in the back, a flat bronze disk the size of her palm glinted on a high shelf set in the stone.

The scorpion's pincer grazed her calf. Analia lunged forward and snatched the disk. She whipped around just in time to see the scorpion launch itself at her.

Analia pressed her back to the wall, eyes darting for an escape—gods, there was nowhere to go.

She slid down the wall, her arms coming up to protect her head.

Something clicked at her back. She felt the wall slide up. An air current hit the back of her neck.

She didn't pause. She spun into the passageway, immediately met by a steep decline.

Analia rocketed down the dark, narrow passageway as if on a massive slide, her body barely slowing as she slammed into each winding turn. She clutched the disk to her chest, waiting for the scorpion to follow. But its outraged hisses rapidly faded behind her.

After a few long moments, light shone up ahead. She tumbled out of the passageway, reemerging at the foot of the mountain.

Analia braced her hands on the ground, coughing up dirt and dust, her skin sticky and stinging from bloody cuts. She didn't know how long it was before there came the crunch of footsteps, a pair of boots stopping before her. Analia looked up, struggling to catch her breath.

"So," Aaron said. "How'd it go?"

Chapter 30

It took Analia a long moment to process his words. Then, she scrambled to her feet and shoved his chest, "Where in the name of the Crystal were you?"

"Here," he said, infuriatingly nonchalant.

"The whole time?"

"This was your trial, Analia. I couldn't get involved. Besides, you didn't need me."

Analia made to retort, but Aaron grabbed her hand. In a blink, they were standing before the carved door leading to Zinia's damper chamber, Aaron telling her he'd be at the border as he disappeared once more.

Analia was left to splutter in the corridor, his words echoing in her mind. *You didn't need me.* At least one of them thought so.

Not bothering with Hyla's combination of knocks and kicks, Analia shoved through the door. She was almost relieved when her flames were snuffed out.

"Don't you knock, child?" Zinia demanded from her throne, not so much as glancing up.

"I figured since you almost killed me, we could call ourselves even."

Analia came to stand before the warrior queen, offering her the disk.

Zinia shook her head. "Almost killed you, please. You almost killed yourself, plodding through the trial like some thick-headed mule."

"How did you even see it?"

Zinia waved a hand. "You should have had no problem dealing with the scorpion at the top. You could have melted its armor, or even cooked the beast inside the shell. Instead, you refused to use your magic."

Heat flashed up Analia's spine. "And yet, I still got the disk," she said, throwing it down on the low table a bit harder than she meant to.

"Interesting," Zinia murmured. "Even dampered, your magic still controls you."

Before Analia could respond, Zinia rose from her throne and crossed to the far wall. "You have extraordinary power, Analia. An unprecedented gift. And you are squandering it."

Analia's heart thundered in her ears. "Does that mean you're going back on our deal?"

"No." Zinia slid aside a section of the wall, revealing a hidden compartment. Reaching inside, she withdrew a scroll, identical to the one from the Sun Kingdom.

"I stand by my word," she said. "You may have gotten the disk, and you may have great potential, but don't be mistaken. That trial was a failure."

The word reverberated through Analia's body. Either not noticing or not caring, Zinia slid the section of wall shut and crossed the room, pressing the scroll into her hands.

"Come to me when you are ready to master your magic."

Master her magic. The same demand Aaron had made on the walkway, right before she scorched a hole through his tunic and proved his point.

Yet, Aaron hadn't brought it up since. Even when she left herself wide open. She'd thought he was respecting her decision. But now, staring into Zinia's eyes, a different kind of fire roared with realization in her chest.

Analia nodded stiffly. She might have thanked the queen, she might have walked out without a word, she didn't know. Nor did she know how she managed to make it back through the mountain, her released flames joining her temper's conflagration. All she knew was the wind that whipped against her burning skin as she emerged from the tunnel, her eyes immediately locking on Aaron waiting at the border.

"Did you know?" she asked, preternaturally calm as she stopped before him.

Aaron rocked back on his heels. "Know what, exactly?"

"You told me you couldn't intervene because the DovenU made it my trial. But when have you ever done something just because you were told to?"

"Analia, you didn't need me," Aaron repeated.

"Because of my magic," Analia said. "Because you knew without your help, this trial would finally force me to either use my magic or face the consequences."

Aaron met her gaze, unflinching. "Yes."

Analia's control snapped.

"What gives you the right?" she spat, flames sparking across her skin as she advanced on him.

Aaron held his ground. "Look at yourself, Analia. Is this what you call control over your magic?"

He shadowjumped a few feet back, a ribbon of starlight poking her in the ribs like a cold, taunting finger. Analia's fire sparked before she could stop it, the thrum of the colliding magics drowned out by the howling wind.

"I was fine!" she seethed, desperately trying to rein in her magic. "Everything was fine until you stirred it awake, it was under control—"

"It was consuming you! That's why I didn't help you, and I would do it again."

Aaron shadowjumped to Analia's right, a silver spear poking her shoulder. Analia choked back a scream as she scrambled away.

She just needed a moment to calm down, regain control. But the words flew from her lips, hot and fast.

"It's my magic! You don't get to choose what I do with it. It's my choice!"

"And what choice is that, Analia?" Aaron shadowjumped around her, taunting silver pokes flashing out from all sides. "Is it the choice to ignore the power you have? To hide from it? It's certainly not the choice to control it with how much you're leaking out."

Analia tried to dodge, but Aaron was too quick, her magic screaming for release with every collision.

"Do you think it's easy?" she yelled. "Having this much power? You have no idea what it's like trying to control it."

"I know exactly what it's like." A whip from the left. "I know *exactly* how not easy it is." On the right. "But I still fought back."

"I'm trying!"

"You gave up!"

The wind screamed.

"Even after your uncle was killed," Aaron said, "you didn't stop fighting. You found your magic, you escaped Sun. But you *gave up.*"

A wave of silver barreled toward her head-on. And Analia blasted it aside as a lifetime of self-loathing bubbled over.

What happened to you? You gave up.

Aaron sent another volley of silver spears, Analia's flames demolishing them before she could even think.

"Stop it!" she screamed, trying to back away, trying to shove her flames back down.

Aaron reappeared behind her, so close she could feel his breath on her ear. "Make me."

Analia whirled. Aaron retreated a few steps, raising a shield forged from starlight.

"Break through," he challenged, something like devastation in his eyes. "You want to prove to me that you have control over your magic, that I'm wrong? Then break. Through."

The wind gave a mighty gust. Aaron's eyes widened as he staggered. And seeing her chance, Analia tackled him to the dirt.

Aaron's shield remained intact as she landed on top of him, giving his face a silver hue as she leaned in.

"You don't get to choose when I use my magic," she hissed. "You don't get to back me into corners and force me to bend to your will. No one does."

That was what everyone had done to her all her life. The Ash Kingdom decided she was worthless. Pryanth decided she was his to possess and break. Deardryn decided she was her pawn to poke and test and forge.

And she had *let* them.

"Exactly," Aaron said, eyes locking on hers. "Not me, not the Six Kingdoms, and not your magic. So fight back."

Analia did. She slammed her hand down on the shield above Aaron's face, midnight flames spreading across the surface like deadly paint on a canvas. She could feel his magic singing through her bones, but he let the shield dissolve.

Analia's hand landed on Aaron's wind-chilled cheek. He looked at her, braced for the burn.

But she'd managed to extinguish her flames just in time. Especially since Aaron hadn't flinched away, as if he was willing to let her burn straight through him if she wanted.

Slowly, the wind died down.

Analia stared at her hand on Aaron's cheek, her heart pounding against her ribs. She could feel every place his body lined up with hers, the remnants of their magic flickering around them like the last sparks of a lightning storm.

"Anna," he said, looking up at her. "You did it."

Analia scoffed. She rolled off him, quickly checking the scroll was still in her belt. Remarkably, it remained unharmed.

"Let's just go," she muttered.

Aaron sat up, offering his hand. "I *am* sorry," he said.

Analia took his hand. "Just another secret, right?"

That was a low blow.

Aaron quickly pulled her into the shadows, but she still caught his flinch. A distant part of her knew she would regret that. But as the dining room came into focus, she didn't care.

She tossed the scroll on the table—ignoring the group of four seated around it—and marched to her room. She just caught Branten ask why they always came back pissy and Aaron's snarled response before she slammed her door.

Chapter 31

T he Starlight Kingdom's tradition with the river had some legitimacy.

Analia stepped into her bathtub, the icy water hitting her like a jolt to her spine. The flames recoiled from her mind, steam hissing up around her as she slid down the wall into a sitting position. And Analia wanted to cry.

That had been too close. Far, far too close.

Her control hadn't been that near to dissolving since her wedding night. And if Aaron had pushed just a little bit harder?

Analia shuddered, dragging her knees to her chest.

Aaron claimed he understood, that releasing the beast beneath her skin was the only way. But his magic didn't require a whip of xenol to tame it. It wasn't a constant roar in his ears, thirsting for blood, for vengeance, for ash.

If Aaron truly understood, he would know that monster needed to be locked away. Because while Analia had allowed Brenn, Pryanth, everyone, to bend her to their will, she'd allowed her magic to break her. And she could never allow it to do that again.

Analia climbed out of the tub, her hair sending icy rivulets down her back. She'd just shrugged on a fresh shirt when there came a knock at her door.

"It's me."

Analia's eyebrows shot up. She moved to open the door, "Since when do you knock?"

"Since Aaron told me I have to," Laness replied, stepping inside.

Analia fought back a wince. "I'm guessing he sent you?"

"No," Laness said, going to perch on Analia's bed. "I just wanted to check in."

"Did you." Analia stole a look at the enka bracelets on Laness's wrists. Laness, in turn, took in Analia's dripping hair and folded arms.

"You want to talk about it or forget about it?" she asked.

Analia looked away.

"Fine then," Laness said, hopping to her feet. "Let's go."

"Go where?" Analia asked warily.

"You'll see," Laness said, heading for the door. "Don't worry, he's not downstairs. He left. Now, come on."

Analia was tempted to brush her off. But Laness turned in the doorway, hands on her hips, and Analia reluctantly followed.

Laness led Analia through the house that was now mercifully empty. Pushing open the front door, she hopped off the porch and came to a stop beside an overcrowded flower bed as if showing off a grand treasure.

It didn't look like anything special. Honeysuckle maybe?

"Why are we stopping?" Analia asked.

"Because," Laness said, dropping to her knees, "we're gardening."

"Gardening?"

"Yes, gardening. I might keep an immaculate garden, but that doesn't mean there aren't weeds that try to invade."

"We're gardening," Analia repeated, sure she was missing something.

Laness nodded impatiently, eyes on her work. "Feel free to be as angry with the plants as you like. Not only can they take it, but most are magic, so they'll also forgive you."

She pulled out a weed with a soft rip, holding it up for Analia to see.

Analia deflated.

"I'm not angry," she said, eyes on the scraggly roots. "I'm exhausted."

"Well, the plants can take that, too."

Laness tossed the plant into a nearby wooden wheelbarrow, then patted the ground beside her. Analia released a long breath, sinking down to her knees. Then, together, they got to work.

For the rest of the afternoon, Analia fell into the rhythm of weeding: find, pull, toss. The two didn't talk much outside of, "Do I pull this?" and "Toss it with the rest." That, however, didn't stop the glances Laness stole from the corner of her eye.

They had started off infrequent, mostly checking Analia was actually pulling a weed and not a flower. But as the sun descended lower in the sky, and Analia required less assistance, she still caught the occasional look. It wasn't concern in her eyes, or even worry. It was curiosity.

Analia's gaze returned to Laness's bracelets, their conversations swirling through her mind. *I just wanted to check in.*

"Laness," she eventually said. "What exactly did you sense from me while I was in the Ash Kingdom?"

Laness's shoulders slumped. She sat back, running her dirty palms down her thighs as she said, "My bracelets don't work universally. The bracelet you wore was made specifically for Aaron, so it forges the strongest connection when he wears it. Well, it should, but the bastard learned how to block me out."

"That sounds like him."

Laness laughed, but quickly sobered. "When Aaron split the bracelet, he didn't damage the magic, but the bracelet wasn't made for the people who put them on."

"What does that mean?"

Laness bit her lip.

"You still felt everything, didn't you?" Analia asked quietly.

Laness fiddled with a pulled weed. "Mostly."

Analia felt as though she'd been stripped down to her core.

"I didn't have direct access to your mind," Laness added quickly. "It was like I could feel the earth rumble, but I couldn't tell why."

"Did you tell him?"

"No," Laness said, fast and firm. "The only thing I told Aaron was you called to him and you needed help. Nothing he couldn't have seen for himself; I'll swear it on whatever you like."

Laness held Analia's gaze, her face wide open and earnest.

Analia wanted to believe her. But there was also a part of her that felt violated.

She hadn't given Laness permission to rifle through her mind. She wouldn't have put the bracelet on in the first place if she'd known what it entailed. But Aaron had withheld that information from her, too.

Just another secret. Just another person playing with her emotions. Perhaps she should show Laness what was making the ground quake, burn her so bad she wouldn't want to wander through her mind—what was she doing?

Analia's hand tightened around a plant, her nails piercing the stem. How were her flames already back?

"Anna?" Laness asked uncertainly.

Analia forced her hand to open. The weed fell to the grass, thankfully unburned.

"I believe you," she rasped, turning to hide her face. "I believe you."

Gods, she couldn't keep doing this. Not when her flames recovered faster than she did.

"Do you know why he never told me how the bracelets work?" she asked, her voice raw.

"Honestly?" Laness asked. "I think he knew I wouldn't rifle through your mind, and with everything else going on, it didn't even occur to him that it was something worth mentioning."

It was such a simple explanation. And Analia knew it was true.

She nodded slowly, Laness hesitating before asking if she wanted to keep gardening. Analia's body ached from hunching over for so long. But with a quiet rush of gratitude, she nodded and returned her attention to the weeds.

All Aaron felt was ice. It chilled his blood, frosted over the hole Analia had pierced through his heart. *Just another secret, right?*

He barely registered her dropping his hand and storming away. Only faintly heard Branten's question before he snarled back and told Surce to take the scroll.

Then, he spun on his heel and stalked through the house, out the door, down the back porch steps. And he wasn't surprised in the slightest to find the hooded figure waiting for him in the training hollow.

"What do you want?" Aaron snapped.

He tried to walk past her, but she stepped into his path. "Try again."

"What do you want, Your Majesty?"

In a blur, Zinia whipped a dagger from her robe and whacked his knuckles with the flat of the blade.

"Insolent boy," she said, prowling about the hollow.

Aaron rubbed his stinging knuckles, silver light rising around him. Zinia didn't even spare him a glance.

"So," she said, "that's the girl you risked this kingdom for? She's certainly a spitfire. Pretty, too. You've always had a weakness for women who can hand your behind to you."

"Don't start," Aaron snapped. "I'm not an incoming girl you can poke until they break."

"Oh no, you prefer to do the poking—"

"Stop."

"Is that what it was? You two rolling in the sheets while in Sun—"

"Enough."

"You couldn't find anyone else here? Although I suppose if that temper of hers is any indicator—"

"Enough!"

A silver, swirling storm rose up around him. Zinia didn't flinch. She stepped aside, her voice firm as their eyes locked. "Release it."

Aaron didn't hesitate. He slammed his magic into their side table with a mighty crash. Wood chips flew across the hollow, propelled by the silver cyclone still swirling in the aftermath.

Aaron's chest heaved, but he didn't try to reel his magic in. He let it pour out of him, an endless tirade of wrath and hurt and heartbreak.

He didn't know how long it took for the ice in his veins to thaw. But slowly, his heart rate steadied; his breathing returned to normal.

"Better?" Zinia asked.

Aaron nodded mutely.

"Half-witted boy," she muttered, pacing once more. "So wrapped up in this hunt, *this girl*, you forget to release."

"For all the things you say about her," Aaron said, "she also completed your trial."

Zinia waved her hand, "Yes, yes, plenty competent and powerful, too. Which some would say only puts a larger target on this kingdom's back."

"I stand by my decision to bring her here."

"Oh, I know. And you should. If what that girl told me was true, you need to keep her as far from that Sun viper as possible, for all our sakes. But that doesn't erase the risk. Especially with that power of hers."

"I know," Aaron sighed. He moved to clean up his mess, although it mainly consisted of surviving splinters and chips of glass from the pitcher.

"Why haven't you been training her, then?" she demanded, pivoting to watch him. "You of all people should understand the danger that comes with letting that much power go unchecked."

"She doesn't seem to want anything to do with it," Aaron said. "She's trying to fight it."

"She's failing," said Zinia bluntly. "Are you telling me you can't take her in a battle of wills?"

"Why do you think I didn't step in today?"

She snorted. "Stubborn, too. When you inevitably provoke her breaking point, I'll be happy to take her in."

Aaron ducked his head.

"Oh, you two are fine," she said dismissively. "You needed a square kick to the rump to finally face your powers. That's all you did today."

Aaron bit the inside of his cheek.

He'd known Analia would be furious when she inevitably put it together. But he wasn't trying to pick one of the constant, petty fights he and Liss had been infamous for. It was a fight worth having, even if Analia disagreed.

"She'll realize it soon enough," Zinia said, softening a fraction. "Then, she'll thank you for it."

That wasn't the point.

A shard of glass pricked Aaron's thumb. He looked down at the bead of blood, then summoned a quick flash of magic to destroy the last of the debris in his hand.

"Regardless," he said, rising to his feet, "that still leaves us with the problem of Deardryn. And there's more now."

Aaron quickly filled her in on Branten's observation, the warrior queen pausing her pacing to listen.

"Yes," she mused, "that hoodlum makes a fair point. Why didn't you have Analia discuss this with me?"

"Because you and I both know the reason you summoned her wasn't to talk politics."

Zinia shrugged, not trying to deny it. Aaron rolled his eyes.

"You know my tribe is neutral ground," she said, folding her arms. "I've interfered enough by giving you the scroll."

"All I'm asking is you talk to your girls," Aaron said. "You have people from all seven kingdoms at your disposal. I just want to know if this uniformity is a byproduct of our isolation—"

"Or if something more nefarious has occurred," Zinia finished.

Aaron briefly closed his eyes. "I want you to be able to stay neutral," he said quietly. "Your girls have been through enough. The last thing I want to do is put them in a position where they might have to fight against their old homes. But if Deardryn succeeds?"

"I know." Zinia sighed, adjusting her hood. "We shall convene soon."

"Thank you."

Aaron bowed his head, and Zinia turned to go. Pausing, she glanced back. "Your Majesty?"

Aaron looked up.

"Don't blow it."

Aaron knew she wasn't talking about the scrolls.

"Go back to your mountain."

Zinia gave a dry, tired laugh. Then, she strode off into the trees, her footsteps making no noise on the carpet of dead leaves as she disappeared.

"Old bat," Aaron muttered. But he couldn't ignore how his insides squirmed at her words.

The truth was, he'd known he and Analia would come to blows. And a part of him had been relieved.

Aaron moved to the corner of the hollow, where Branten haphazardly stacked his training gear. Dragging out one of Analia's training dummies, he backed up across the hollow, methodically drawing his daggers and sending them flying through the air.

He'd spent the entirety of Analia's trial leaned against that tree trunk, unable to stop replaying that look she'd given him. Just as he was unable to stop the warmth from spreading across his entire body. It had kept him rooted to the spot as the trial went on, knowing he was not only forcing Analia to face her magic, but he was also sparing himself the torture of wondering when that feeling would be ripped away.

Aaron retrieved his daggers. Returned to the opposite end of the hollow. Threw.

He wasn't afraid of things falling apart—it had happened far too many times for him to fear it. What he was afraid of was rebuilding, just to discover it was possible. Leaving him to wonder what else could have been salvaged if he had simply tried.

But he and Analia had always worked through ice and flame and darkness. Together. And there were far more pieces intact than broken.

Aaron paused his throwing, looking up at the sky that had deepened to twilight. He knew what he had to do.

Chapter 32

Aaron stood in the center of Analia's room, looking over his handiwork.

He'd come in from the training hollow to find everyone gone, Analia and Laness just visible out the front window as they weeded. For a few moments, he watched, fingertips pressed to the glass as he sent Laness a silent thank you. Then, he turned away, knowing this would be his best chance.

Now, Aaron stretched, spotting the bedspread from the corner of his eye. He'd felt completely helpless that night as he watched Analia sob in a ring of smoke and ash, just wishing there was something, anything he could do.

But there was, and he'd done it. He just hoped someday, she could see it that way, could forgive him for the moments he'd gone awry.

The back of Aaron's neck tingled. He turned, finding Analia quietly watching him from the open doorway.

Dirt stained the knees of her fitted gray pants, matching the spots on the cuffs of her blue-and-white jacket. She no longer looked as though she were about to scorch him on sight, but tension still crackled in the air between them.

Looking over his shoulder, Analia's eyebrows rose. "What is this?"

"I thought you'd want to play," Aaron said. He stepped aside, giving her a full view of the harp he'd moved up from the side room.

Analia took a half step inside. "You moved the harp upstairs?"

"It's your harp."

Analia wavered. Finally, she fully stepped inside, Aaron turning to watch as she drifted over to her harp. Her hands slid over the wood frame he had dusted and oiled, pausing where there used to be a snapped string that he had replaced. She retrieved the tuning hammer from the nearby windowsill, quietly testing a few strings.

Aaron knew he should speak. But when he opened his mouth, there were no words on his tongue.

Crystal spare him, this was a bad idea. Just a failed attempt at a peace offering that was clearly not ready to be received. He made to silently slip from the room—

"Do you ever wish you could go back in time and change what you've done?" Analia asked.

Aaron paused. "When I was younger?" he asked, sinking back down on the bed. "Constantly."

Analia nodded to herself, settling on the stool before her harp. "That's all I've been thinking about since escaping the Sun Kingdom."

Her fingers moved across the strings, softly playing in that original key. "I wish I could go back in time and see through Pryanth. Solve everything faster to avoid him. Maybe even find a way into the kingdom without being betrothed to him. Because I know I never loved him, but that doesn't stop the feeling that I failed myself while I was with him."

"Anna," Aaron said gently. "None of that was your fault."

"Maybe," she said, unconvinced. "But even then, I failed myself when I lost control and killed him."

Aaron knew from experience there was nothing he could say to that. All he could do was let her talk, his eyes on her fingers as she played.

"It's too much, Aaron. Too much power. Every second it's screaming in my mind, creeping closer with every nightmare until I feel like I'm about to explode."

"I won't let that happen."

"But it's already happened," she said, twisting on her stool to face him.

Yes, it was fear in her eyes. Not just of her magic, but what it had already done; what it could do again.

"That's why we'll practice," he said, rising from the bed and crossing to her. "We practice until you can turn your magic on and off in your sleep."

"But what about between now and then?" she pressed. "What if something goes wrong?"

"It *will* go wrong if you don't train."

Analia dropped her gaze to her hands, not agreeing, but not arguing either. Tentatively, Aaron stepped closer, her knees brushing his thighs. Still, she did not meet his gaze.

"Analia," Aaron sighed, "I shouldn't have let things progress that far on the border."

"I almost destroyed you," she whispered. "And you would have let me."

Something heavy thudded into Aaron's chest.

"I know," he rasped. "Gods, I'm sorry. I just hope you know I wasn't pushing you to hurt you, or frighten you, or whatever else. It was because I completely, wholeheartedly believe releasing your magic is something you need to do. Not just for your own safety, but those around you, as well."

"I know," Analia whispered.

A lump formed in Aaron's throat. "Please," he said. "Don't end up like me. Don't learn that lesson the hard way."

Something flashed across Analia's face, too quick to read.

"I don't want you to be right," she said. "And I'm terrified of you being wrong."

"Sounds complicated," Aaron said, earning a faint smile. "I'm not asking you to not be afraid," he went on, sobering once more. "I'm not asking you to dive head-first into your magic, either. I'm only asking you to try it my way."

A soft wave of starlight rolled forth from his hands, swirling around them in a protective cocoon.

"Are you willing to do that?" he asked, sliding his arms around her waist, lightly resting his hands on her back. "Are you willing to try?"

Analia's fingers curled around her pin, but her voice was steady. "How?"

That uncontrollable warmth flickered in his chest. He looked down at her on her stool, a smile tugging up his mouth as he asked, "Did you ever venture down into the kitchens in your fancy castle?"

"Of course."

"Do you remember how the head chef added salt to each dish?"

"What does that have to do with anything?"

"Indulge me."

"He poured the salt into his palm, then pinched some from the pile with his other hand," Analia said, as if it were obvious.

"Exactly," Aaron said. "And that's what you're going to do with your magic. Just reach into the flames, and take a tiny pinch."

Analia didn't respond. Aaron was almost certain she was going to refuse, but then she raised her cupped hands between them, summoning a ball of black flames the size of a large peach. Crystal spare them all if that was a small pinch.

"A little smaller," Aaron said, keeping his tone light. "Try letting some of the magic sift away like salt between your fingers."

The fire shrunk rapidly.

"Careful," he said. "It's far easier to release the magic than it is to reclaim it—there."

Analia looked down at the grape-sized ball of flame in her palm. "Now what?" she asked.

"Now," Aaron said, "you hold it until I tell you to stop."

Analia's expression hardened.

The exercise took more power than what one would assume. In order to keep her ball of flames the same size, she had to constantly refuel it. It took a great deal of precision: adding the same amount of power that was draining out—something Analia seemed to quickly grasp when her flames flickered, then rose to double the size before shrinking back down.

"Aaron," she said, a bead of sweat running down her temple. "Aaron, they're screaming."

"I know," he said, lightly flexing his hands on her back. "Just a little longer. I've got you."

Analia squeezed her eyes shut, but she kept the ball of flame alive. Aaron watched her carefully, the heat of her flames bathing his face.

His years on the battlefield had not only taught him how to push his soldiers, but how to know when they were about to break. Right when his face began to burn...

"All right," he said. "Stop, put it out."

Analia immediately complied. She brought shaking hands to her face, seemingly unable to speak. Aaron stepped closer, ready to hold her up, but she recovered quickly.

"Better?" he asked.

Analia nodded mutely. Aaron let his magic wink out.

He knew this was his moment to go. He should leave her to the same relief he had felt in the hollow just a few hours before.

But Analia dropped her hands from her face. Relaxed against his hands. And one of those hands traveled up her spine, his fingertips skimming along her shoulder, her neck, coming to curve around her cheek. The same cheek Pryanth had struck.

Analia's face twitched.

Aaron immediately pulled away—what had he done?

Analia caught his hand, pulling it back to her cheek. As if she wanted to erase Pryanth's phantom brand from her skin. As if, after seeing the destruction a fraction of Aaron's magic could wreak, she still trusted his hand to do it.

Aaron brushed his fingertips against her skin, at a loss for words. He simply watched, mesmerized, as Analia sat with that fear.

"I'm sorry I threw your secrets in your face," she said. "I don't care how angry I was. You didn't deserve that."

She let her hand drop, leaving him to cradle the side of her face. This time, she didn't flinch. She didn't back away. She leaned into his touch, closing her eyes as his thumb stroked along her cheekbone, smoothing over the hole in his heart.

"How about we both agree we're sorry and forgive the other," Aaron suggested.

"I think I can do that."

"Good."

For a few moments, they were quiet, Aaron terrified to so much as twitch.

"Aaron?" she finally said.

"Yes?"

"I did it."

There were endless interpretations of her words. And Aaron felt a mounting sense of pride, respect, for every last one as he agreed. "You did."

Analia's smile was the most beautiful thing he'd ever seen. In that flash of a moment, he became acutely aware of his body. How he stood between her thighs, his hand resting against her cheek. How it would be so easy for him to lift her chin, just the smallest amount, and trace that smile with his lips, taste her victory on his tongue.

But he also remembered her flinch.

He dragged his gaze from Analia's mouth, noting how she'd gone completely still.

Gods, what was he doing? She had just poured her heart out to him. A heart that had been broken and twisted and tossed aside. Yet, there he was, trying to give her one more thing to deal with.

"Let me know when you're ready to train," he said, almost choking on the words.

Then, he let his hand drop. He stepped back, ignoring the aching loss of the pressure of her thighs around his, and headed for the door.

"Aaron?"

He glanced back.

"Don't stop pushing me," Analia said.

That look in her eyes. Crystal spare him, he was doomed.

Aaron's voice was hoarse. "Likewise."

Then, he slipped out the door and buried his smile in his hands. Not today. But someday.

Chapter 33

Dimitri had established a routine in the Moon Kingdom. His days were bookended by meals with Patryclas and Sylas—the latter still unenthused by his presence. A handful of Moon Royals also attended, allowing Dimitri to scope out not only the most powerful people in the castle, but also the ones Sabi was constantly gossiping about.

Every day, he reported to the book nook, where Sabi was a never-ending stream of chatter. It didn't take long for him to realize the reason her assistants never lasted was because none of them could keep up with her mind.

She easily memorized pages of text and spewed them back out at top speeds, bouncing from high-level mathematics to wraith culture in a single breath. Every time Dimitri asked a follow-up question, her face spasmed as if she were astonished he wasn't begging her to stop.

But Dimitri liked her endless facts. He liked when she caught him skimming instead of binding and asked if he found anything interesting. He even liked when she asked questions about himself, as if he was the latest subject to catch her fascination—although she hadn't even blinked when he changed his appearance.

On the fifth day of every week, Dimitri meandered down to Rayner's shop to refresh his disguise. He expected these meetings to be quick, business-like. Yet, they always ended up talking long after Rayner's work was done, the two shifting from topic to topic with almost unnerving ease.

"Why did you agree to this so easily?" Dimitri asked one day, his eyes shut as Rayner worked.

"Because," he said, voice soft with concentration, "I'm lonely. And you're just twisted enough to enjoy my company."

Dimitri didn't know what to say to that. He knew the feeling, though. The way loneliness silently crept up on a person. He hadn't even noticed it himself until it had wrapped him in an invisible cocoon.

For years, he'd been trapped in the worst kind of prison, permitted to watch the world around him, but never to make contact. No one could. But that feeling when someone finally managed to reach through?

"And you fascinate me," Rayner said.

Dimitri's eyes popped open. "You know nothing about me!"

"That's the point," Rayner said, tapping Dimitri's chin. "I can see from the look on your face that you understand, that you're thinking about something, and I know you'll never tell me. Honestly, Dimitri, I've never met someone who so shamelessly pries for information, yet avoids sharing anything themselves."

Dimitri didn't think he was supposed to be flattered by that, but he was. "Don't act like you're some personal-detail dispensary."

He waited for Rayner to shrug it off. Instead, the masquerader cocked his head. He sat back in his chair, thoughtfully drumming his fingers on the armrest. Finally, he announced, "My favorite color is green."

"Inspiring," Dimitri drawled.

Rayner smirked. "All right, then. Tell me yours."

"Seriously?"

"I'm waiting."

Dimitri's sigh could have shaken the building. He flopped back in his chair, "I don't know, red?"

"Why?"

"Oh, fuck off."

Rayner caught the nearby book Dimitri threw at him. "My favorite color is green because it reminds me of the moss in the square and that I'm home." He nudged Dimitri's foot with his own. "Your turn."

Dimitri glowered, and Rayner gave him a lazy smile. Somehow, he was the only person completely unfazed by Dimitri's sharp tongue and even sharper personality.

The reminder never failed to have him squirm. But perhaps that unshakable serenity made Rayner the perfect person to tell.

"I never had anyone to celebrate my birthday with," Dimitri began, studying his nails. "The only acknowledgement or gift I've ever gotten is a red knit blanket someone left on my bed when I was five. And I still don't know who left it."

He didn't add how it was the first time he'd ever felt seen, cared for. He didn't need the extra pity. But Rayner nodded to himself.

"You certainly are a red," he mused. "Although you look best in green."

Dimitri scoffed. "You would design me an entire new wardrobe if you could."

"And you wouldn't wear any of it just to spite me."

Dimitri shrugged. And Rayner's answering grin had the rising ache in his chest sinking back down.

Despite the tentative contentment Dimitri slipped into, Deardryn was still a constant looming presence. Not only were her appearances becoming more frequent, but she was no longer the only Sun person in the kingdom.

On more than one occasion, he spotted familiar Sun soldiers in the castle halls: Lev, Dannel, Andrik. Thankfully, none of them spared him a second look. But Deardryn's increasing grip on the kingdom, and Sylas for that matter, had his stomach sinking.

He also realized, as his due date with Rayner approached, his shattered glass tattoo began to itch insistently. Fine, he got the hint.

Three days before the book was due, Dimitri meandered into the book nook. Sabi paced the tiny space, her nose buried in a book on Moon Kingdom architecture. Checking she wasn't looking, Dimitri crept around the table.

Sabi kept all records of book requests in a small leather book, hidden on one of the shelves beneath her desk. The problem was, she hated it when people touched her things. Just last week she'd swatted him upside the head for borrowing one of her pens.

Dimitri glanced at Sabi, still consumed in her book, then eased into her chair. Bending down, he caught sight of countless stacks of books—all of which she would notice if they'd shifted even an inch. He just had to find the records and add Rayner's book to the list—there.

Dimitri swiped the book from the lowest shelf. Just for his boot to knock against the chair as he leaned.

"What are you doing?"

Dimitri bonked his head on the desk. Crystal strike him down, he'd poked the dragon.

"That's my chair."

Dimitri rubbed his head as Sabi marched over, nostrils flared. He had no time to write in the book—

"And that's my book!"

No chance of hiding it, either. Crystal spare him, he was about to become some of the bones hidden beneath her cushions.

"I was just checking the book list," he said.

"Why?" Sabi swiped the book from his hand. "It's mine."

"Cool it, grabby, I was just checking you got the book Patryclas requested."

"Uncle P didn't request a book."

"Yes he did," Dimitri said, his mind racing as he fled to his own seat. "Yesterday. He came in here while you were looking for that book on ancient archways out front."

"What?" Sabi turned in a flustered circle, eyes darting. "He didn't tell me he wanted a book. Why didn't he tell me—why didn't you tell me?"

"I thought you knew!"

Dimitri squirmed as Sabi fretted. He didn't like lying to her, didn't like using Patryclas. But as his tattoo flared with a fresh wave of itchiness, he knew he had no choice.

"What was the book?" Sabi asked, finally turning back to him.

A Lifetime of Faces, Dimitri said. *The History of Moon Royal Appearances.*

"Why would he want *that?*"

Dimitri shrugged, hoping Sabi would rush off to find the book. Instead, she stayed put, tapping her fingers against her lips.

"So," she finally said. "Instead of asking me if I'd gotten the request, you decided to snoop through my things."

Dimitri's ears burned. "I'm nosy, too."

Sabi scoffed. "Don't touch my things."

Tossing her book on the table, she swept out of the nook. Dimitri sat frozen in his chair.

He hadn't even considered asking her to make a copy for him. Not when that would require having a certain level of trust in Sabi. But she had left her book unattended on the desk, so she clearly had that trust in him.

When Sabi reentered the nook, book under her arm, Dimitri was unable to meet her eyes. Even as she copied the book in record time and slid it over to him to bind.

"I'm sorry I swiped your book," he mumbled.

"What?" Sabi barely looked up from her copying. "That's all right. I already forgave you."

Dimitri hunched over his book, an unexpected ache piercing his chest.

She didn't hate him. She wasn't walking away. Even though his fear that she might had nearly catalyzed her to do so.

"Thank you," he said quietly.

Sabi flicked her hand in acknowledgement.

Dimitri remained quiet as he bound Rayner's book. As soon as it was ready, he brought it over to the pile of books he'd already completed. Most of them were for the library itself, with the number of borrows and requests for a title increasing the number of copies Sabi created. Some, however, were requested by people who would like to keep their copy instead of return it, at which point Sabi and Dimitri would get a small commission outside of their castle stipend.

Dimitri idly thumbed through the pile, breathing in the comforting smell of parchment. He'd spent so much time checking page numbers and binding each book he practically had each title memorized. Although, now that he was looking at them...

"Sabi," Dimitri asked over his shoulder. "What's with the history craze?"

"They're orders from Queen Deardryn."

Dimitri pivoted all the way to look at her. "Really."

"Oh yes," Sabi said through a plastered smile. "Her Majesty is fond of making bulk requests and then retrieving the books as needed, all without telling me which books she needs first, which creates a disastrous schedule..." Sabi realized she was tugging her hair and quickly stopped. "But it's my pleasure."

"Uh-huh," Dimitri said, mind racing as he stared down at Rayner's book.

Deardryn came from a kingdom full of hidden texts. She could learn whatever she wanted about the Moon Kingdom back home. Why go through the effort to get the texts here? Unless she had already searched through her texts on Moon and had failed to find something. Something she suspected was here.

"I can go deliver this book," he said. "My shift is almost over."

"Good," Sabi said. "If you happen to see Princess Marcella on your way out, preferably holding my book on horse riding, feel free to wrestle it from her. Rumor has it she's been studying up to impress her sentinel."

"Are she and Tavian on again?"

"She clearly wants them to be."

Dimitri snorted. It wasn't until he was halfway to Rayner's that he realized he was still smiling.

Hours later, Dimitri sat at a corner table in the library. He'd successfully delivered the book to Rayner, resulting in his shattered glass tattoo turning black with a flash of heat. Without hesitation, Rayner brandished his bronze scarsworn dagger, and with a purple lock on the front of Dimitri's shoulder and a key on Rayner's, their new bargain was set.

Now, he studied Deardryn's order history—which Sabi had given him upon asking—the matching books stacked beside it.

He knew Deardryn wasn't the type to randomly request a book from the shelf. She was methodical. There was a reason she chose the second book after the first, and the third after the second. He just wished he could figure out why.

Dimitri tapped his pen against his teeth. She jumped from history, to legends, to a guidebook on landmarks. Was she just looking for the best way to assimilate into Moon Kingdom culture?

The library door softly opened. Patryclas waved to Dimitri as he passed, his arms full of books. If anyone could solve this puzzle, it was Patryclas. But Dimitri couldn't force his mouth to open.

"Uncle P," Sabi said, appearing from nowhere and snatching his books, "what are you doing? You're a king! You're supposed to demand I send someone to retrieve these."

"But then when would I get to see you?"

Dimitri stared intently at the pair. Notice him. Come over. Ask what he was doing; give him no choice but to explain.

"I'm sorry we were so late in getting your book to you today," Sabi said.

Dimitri's heart froze. That was not the attention he wanted. Especially since Patryclas would have no problem sensing the tornado of guilt behind him.

Gods, he was dead. Either after Sabi skewered him with her fancy pen collection, or Patryclas relocated him to the Sun Kingdom for causing trouble.

He should have told the truth—he shouldn't have made that gods-damned oath.

"No apology necessary," Patryclas said, clasping his hands behind his back. "I know you're incredibly busy with Queen Deardryn's requests."

Dimitri turned his back to the pair, pressing his palms against his eyes. Patryclas had to know it was him. Why didn't he say anything?

Behind him, Sabi and Patryclas talked a few minutes more. Finally, Patryclas made to go.

Dimitri looked up as Patryclas approached, braced for the rebuke.

"Good night, Dimitri."

Dimitri stared. There was no sign of anger, even suspicion, in Patryclas's expression as he passed. Why? Was Patryclas... protecting him? What had he done to deserve that?

Patryclas reached the library door.

This was his moment to ask for help. But Dimitri only stared, wide-eyed. What if he said no? How would he figure this out if he didn't speak?

Patryclas twisted the knob.

"Patryclas?" Dimitri croaked.

The king turned back. "Yes?"

Dimitri took a deep breath. "Can you help me?"

Dimitri didn't know what reaction he was expecting. But there was no denying something stronger than relief rolled through his body as Patryclas smiled. "Of course."

He returned to Dimitri's table and took the seat across from him. "This wouldn't have anything to do with the stack of books you have acquired?"

Dimitri slumped in his seat. "Maybe."

"Just as it might have something to do with the mysterious book I never requested?"

Dimitri slumped even lower. "Maybe."

Patryclas laughed. "What can I do for you, Dimitri?"

Dimitri had the strangest urge to cry. Quickly composing himself, he said, "I'm trying to find the connection between legends and history."

"Legends *are* history," Patryclas said immediately. "They're just the parts that people aren't completely certain of."

"Are there legends about landmarks in your kingdom?"

"Oh, countless." Patryclas leaned back and rubbed his chin. "Let's see, there's a grove of trees in the south where the only living lunar hawks can be found."

"I've read about those," Dimitri said. "Their feathers don't *actually* glow in the moonlight, do they?"

"Undeniably so," Patryclas said. "There's also a famous battlefield from the Shattering War that people claim to be haunted by the ghosts of the fallen. Oh, and there's a statue of Mahina that radiates a strange, undeniable magic."

Dimitri perked up. He'd seen Deardryn stop to examine the Defiant's statue the day he first met Rayner. Grabbing the landmarks book, he flipped through the pages, looking for other places he'd seen Deardryn wandering about.

"What about the Arch of Paralia at the entrance of the central kingdom?"

"Ah, the Spider Queen." Patryclas nodded. "It was said she knew every rumor that whispered through her streets. She constructed the arch herself to let everyone know as soon as they entered her kingdom, there was nothing she wouldn't see. Many describe feeling a cold magical tingle as they pass under it."

Dimitri nodded to himself, remembering that very sensation when he'd arrived. So, Deardryn was tracking down locations that had legends of mysterious magic. He still didn't know why, but if he could stay on her trail...

"So," Patryclas said, reaching across the table to tap Dimitri's purple heart. "Have you thought more about what you want?"

Dimitri slid his wrist away, but he didn't try to hide his smugness as he said, "I want to stop the queen."

"That's what *Analia* wants."

"What, we're not allowed to want the same thing?"

"People can want many things," Patryclas said. "I want to know what only you want."

Dimitri opened his mouth, thought better of it, then turned to organize his books. "Why do you care so much, anyway?"

"Because I was you, once."

Dimitri looked up. Patryclas tipped his head back, the purple glow of the nearby lantern bathing his face.

"For a long time, I was afraid of the future. I was first in line to receive my mother's bookshop: a boy unable to read and without her copying Blessing. Instead, I had my father's ability to feel everyone's emotions: the judgment of my struggle, the fear of what might happen to their legacy, the empathy for my situation.

"I became consumed in managing their emotions, not just for my own sanity, but out of concern for the people themselves. And eventually, I lost myself in it. And the moment I saw you, I knew you, too, were lost. Maybe not in the same way, but at some point, something or someone forced you to give up on what you want."

Dimitri couldn't move as Patryclas leaned toward him.

"No one deserves to feel that. The despair of losing your purpose. Especially not you."

"I'm not special," Dimitri breathed.

"No. You are remarkable. You are exceptionally bright. You are unwaveringly loyal to Analia. Sabi claims you are the fastest learner she's ever met. And you are one of my favorite people, just for being you."

Dimitri didn't know if he was breathing. He could feel each of Patryclas's words form a crack running down his chest. But it wasn't a fracture in a pane of glass. It was a long-forgotten door finally inching open.

"Find your purpose, Dimitri," Patryclas said, rising from his seat. "It doesn't have to be large or grandiose or even something that anyone else would care about. It just has to be something you want to strive for. Something that makes you want to be alive."

He squeezed Dimitri's shoulder. And it wasn't until Dimitri was about to fall asleep that night that he realized he hadn't flinched.

Chapter 34

Analia ran her fingers along the polished rail of Pearl Bridge, finally taking her first steps into the Mirage.

She'd wanted to come ever since spotting it out her window that first day. Yet, as she slowly ventured deeper into the kingdom, she'd always found herself shying away.

But that morning, she'd fallen back asleep after waking from her nightmares. She'd had a good training session with Branten—who spent a large chunk of time bemoaning the mysterious disappearance of their table. She'd come inside to find Mor dropping off a stack of papers for Aaron, and he'd mentioned the exhibit going on in the Mirage.

"It's on my way to the Human Kingdom," he said. "I could walk with you."

Somehow, that was enough. They'd talked the entire walk over, Mor giving her a friendly wave as he left her at the bridge. Still, it took Analia a few heartbeats to actually step foot on the shining pearl. But as soon as she was across, she couldn't believe she'd waited so long to come.

The Mirage had the same components of the equivalent sector back in the Ash Kingdom: music halls, painting studios, display after display of statues, jewelry, tapestries, and everything in between. But where the Ash Kingdom was highly organized, the Mirage was a creative explosion.

Analia wandered down streets that had been painted into a starry sky. Every exposed wall was plastered with paintings, the street corners occupied by dancers and other live performances.

With every step, Analia grew more and more certain her uncle would have loved it there. She rested her hand over her pin, a deep ache piercing her chest, but she continued on without pause.

She didn't miss the curious looks as she wandered past music halls thrumming with countless styles of music. She did her best to catch their eyes and smile, some returning the gesture, others not. Some came forward to introduce themselves.

It was small, but it was progress. And Analia cradled it close to her chest as she found a weapons display. Now, this had Aaron written all over it.

Analia examined a row of decorative sheaths, her mind drifting back to the night before. How Aaron had loosely wrapped his arms around her, letting her know that he knew she didn't need him, but he was there if she wanted him.

He truly did believe in her, in ways so few ever had. She just didn't know if she had the courage to take that final risk he was asking of her. Even though when sitting on that stool, his arms around her, the predominant feeling she'd had was safety.

"You should get that one."

Analia turned to face the woman who had spoken—holy Crystal above, she was stunning.

Golden-brown hair fell in waves around her shoulders. Her eyes were a vivid blue, brought out by her black form-fitting bodysuit, accented with silver to match the scabbard at her hip. There was a small birthmark on her right cheekbone, which resembled a heart as she smiled.

"You can't walk around with a naked blade," she went on, eyes lingering on Aaron's dagger. "That, and sheaths can make a great accessory."

"Stylish and deadly," Analia said.

The woman grinned. "My thoughts exactly."

She leaned in front of Analia, filling her nose with the smell of nutmeg as she plucked a sheath from the table. "Now this one has potential."

The sheath was made from soft leather. Thin silver threads wove across the glossy black surface, coming together to embroider a row of stars along the edges.

"It's beautiful," Analia said.

"Take it, then."

Analia hesitated, thinking of her empty pockets. Aaron had told her numerous times if she needed anything, she only had to charge it to his accounts, but she was still reluctant to spend his gold.

"Don't worry about that," the woman said breezily, seeming to read Analia's thoughts. "These are all free samples specifically made for the exhibition."

She pressed the sheath into Analia's hands, clearly not taking no for an answer. Especially not as Analia slid her dagger into the sheath.

"Perfect fit!" the woman declared. "It was meant to be."

"And you showed up just in time to notice," Analia agreed.

"It's a skill of mine," the woman said with a wink. Then, with a wave and "Happy Exhibition Day!" over her shoulder, she breezed back into the crowd.

Analia ran her fingers over her new sheath. Taking note of the business on the sparkly plaque farther down the table, she figured it was time to head home. She didn't make it far, however, before a familiar voice called over the noise.

"There you are."

Analia turned, waiting for Aaron to catch up. "Were you looking for me?"

"My shooting star, I'm always searching for you." He reached her side and ruffled her hair. "I was hoping you would get to see this. I would've brought you myself, but I lost track of time and forgot it was happening today."

"Mor told me this morning."

"And you've already acquired a souvenir." Aaron nodded approvingly to the sheath.

"More like was forcefully gifted."

"That sounds about right." Aaron guided Analia into the crowd with a hand on her back. "I'm glad my dagger has found such a happy home."

As they continued back through the crowd, Analia's mind flashed back to the strange looks both Mor and the woman had given her dagger.

"Why is it so surprising to people that I have one of your daggers?" she asked.

"Well," Aaron laughed, "Branten would tell you it's because I love my daggers more than some mothers love their children. I've also been informed I'm unreasonably possessive with them."

Analia smiled big enough her cheeks ached. All that, and he'd still given it to her without hesitation.

"How can they tell it's yours, though?" she asked.

"Unsheathe it," Aaron invited.

Analia complied, realizing she'd never fully examined it before. She was intimately familiar with the worn leather hilt. But as she studied the silver blade, she finally noticed all the fold lines. They radiated out from the center of the steel like petals of a flower, each layer adding dimension to the one before.

"Beautiful," she said.

"And deadly."

The two reached Pearl Bridge.

"Is there anything else you'd like to see?" Aaron asked.

"I think I saw everything by the time you found me."

"Good," Aaron said, the hand on her back sliding so she was in the circle of his arm. "Because I was looking for you for a reason."

Analia yelped as they faded into the shadows. Aaron chuckled, pulling her closer before reemerging in his side room.

"I thought you said you liked shadowjumping," he teased.

"When I have a bit of warning," Analia complained. "Did you seriously jump us home instead of walking five extra minutes?"

"I like doing this," Aaron said, lightly squeezing her hip before heading deeper into the room. Analia stared after him, needing a moment before she could follow.

Aaron had clearly been busy. A long table covered in stacks of paper now sat where her harp used to be, the wall behind it plastered with notes written in Aaron's looping handwriting.

"I see you've transformed the place," she commented.

Aaron bent to retrieve a fallen note. "I'm a visual thinker."

"And what exactly have you been thinking so hard about?"

"The Unleashing," he said. "Mor got me the last of everyone's research today, and I've been driving myself insane going over it all."

"And?"

"It makes no sense," Aaron declared, dropping into one of the two chairs at the table. "I've looked through everyone's notes covering books, historical documents, and art, even interviews with my people. Yet, somehow, while every story about Talitha is never told the same way twice, everyone has the exact same information when discussing the Unleashing."

"Are you serious?" Analia asked, sitting beside him. She'd noticed an odd uniformity within her own research, but she figured it was due to the sources she was picking through.

"Various details are forgotten or omitted," Aaron said, "but there is no variation in the story. No unusual details present in some accounts, but not others."

"But that doesn't make sense," Analia said. "No story has been perfectly preserved for days, let alone centuries. The nature of word of mouth alone..."

"I know," Aaron said, rubbing his temples. "Which is why I need you."

Analia didn't expect to enjoy those words as much as she did. "How so?"

"I need fresh eyes," Aaron said, rising from his seat. "I've been looking at these papers for days straight, and I don't trust my mind anymore. I need you to go through everything and tell me if you see anything I haven't already scribbled on the wall while Branten drags me off to training."

"I think I can handle that," Analia said, reaching for a stack.

"Oh, my shooting star, you don't give yourself enough credit." Aaron leaned over her shoulder and whispered in her ear. "Thank you."

Then, he faded into the shadows, not catching Analia's flush. Turning to her stack of papers, she got to work.

It took the rest of the afternoon and a good chunk of evening to get through all the notes. The work quickly became monotonous, her mind drifting back to Aaron no matter how hard she tried to focus.

He'd told her back in Sun he had no information on the scroll. All he'd known was he needed it for his people, and that had been enough for him.

Yet, he'd revealed himself to Deardryn to try and save her, putting those very people at risk. He'd even escaped the temple with her, assuming he had lost the scroll. But why?

Analia rubbed her eyes, setting aside the last page of notes. Finally, she returned to her room. Just to find Aaron sprawled in her bed, offering her a lazy smile.

"Really?" she asked, deadpan.

"I'm your reward." Aaron spread his arms, assuming a dramatically seductive expression.

Analia's composure cracked. "You're ridiculous," she said, heading for her wardrobe.

"In the most charming of ways."

"That's one way to put it."

Analia caught Aaron's grin in the mirror.

"Were you able to make it through everything?" he asked.

"I was," she said, pulling out a nightgown. "But I didn't find anything new."

"I was worried about that," Aaron murmured.

"I've been thinking, though," Analia went on, stepping into her bathing room to change. "Every telling of the story talks about how the Defiants rose up, climbed Mt. Raegyr, and confronted the Ancient Ones. But it becomes incredibly vague after that point.

"They say Talitha stole the Crystal, but not how. They don't even say how she knew to steal it in the first place. Then, the only other time the Crystal is mentioned is to say it disappeared sometime during Talitha's rule."

"What are you suggesting?"

"I don't know if I'm suggesting anything," Analia said. "I just don't understand how you lose an all-powerful Crystal."

"Ah," Aaron said. "So, what you're suggesting is that it was hidden."

"You say that like you've had the same thought."

"It's certainly crossed my mind. But then, there's the immediate question of—"

"How could seven people hide the Crystal without the location leaking out," Analia finished, stepping back into her bedroom.

Aaron straightened slightly as he spotted her black-and-silver nightgown. His eyes did a quick flick from head to toe, lingering on her exposed shoulders, the hem that brushed the curve of her thighs.

"That's assuming," he said, his eyes traveling back to her face, "that it was all seven that hid it."

Analia's eyebrows shot up. "You think Talitha could have hidden it on her own?"

"I'm thinking a lot of things," Aaron said. "Like how Deardryn preaches peace, yet she was willing to kill a Royal from every kingdom to get her rings. Rings that would theoretically allow her to sense not just her own magic, but all Royal magics. Concurrently, if she puts them on all at once. And I don't know about you, but I can only think of one object that would have that type of magic field. And it's been completely lost to history."

Ice skittered down Analia's spine. "You don't think she's hunting the Crystal…"

"I think we need to get those scrolls open."

Aaron settled back against the pillows, apparently having run out of conspiracies to share. Analia, however, felt all her questions turn into an ache behind her eyes.

It made complete sense. If the Crystal was able to Bless any type of magic, that meant all those magics had to be contained in its magic field. She assumed that would mean, even if Deardryn only had her own magic to hunt with, the Crystal would be included in whatever she could sense. But by searching with multiple types of magic, she could create a filter. And there were only so many objects that could fit the criteria.

It at least explained why Analia was her key: she didn't need any rings to create that filter. But why would Deardryn want the Crystal in the first place? What use could she have for it?

At least one thing was for sure.

"You're still in my bed," she said.

"You know," Aaron said with a stretch, "most women are delighted to find me in their beds."

"And they're just as delighted to wake up to you."

"That's the second time you've brought that up," Aaron murmured. "Tell me, would you rather I show you why with my fingers, or my tongue?"

Analia's heart might have skipped a beat.

"Please," she said, moving to place her dagger on her bedside table. "Like you could get me into bed—"

Aaron's hand shot out. He gave her wrist a quick tug, his arms coming up and around her as she half stumbled, half fell on top of him with a yelp.

"Huh," Aaron said, pulling her fully on top of him. "Would you look at that."

"You are far too pleased with yourself," Analia complained.

"Oh, certainly," Aaron agreed. "And growing more pleased by the second."

He shifted beneath her, and Analia realized she was still on top of him: one hand on his shoulder, the other on the pillow beside his head. The hard planes of his stomach and chest were perfectly lined up with hers, close enough she could feel his heart beating.

Aaron winked. Analia rolled off of him with a huff, Aaron sliding his trapped arm up her back and around her shoulders. He shot her a quick look as if checking for permission. But Analia had already relaxed against his side.

"So," she said, tapping his calf with her foot. "How many lovers have you had in this position?"

Aaron's smile turned crooked. "One or two."

"Uh-huh."

"Usually, there's a lot less clothing, though."

Analia swatted his cheek, and Aaron made a noise of protest.

"For someone with such acclaimed generosity," she said, "I'm surprised no one has stuck around."

Analia expected a flippant response. But Aaron's face fell.

"There was one girl," he said, sobering disconcertingly fast. "About half a century ago."

Analia felt her own smile fade. "What happened to her?"

"I went too long without releasing my magic," Aaron said, fixing his gaze on the ceiling. "The humans had been demanding more of my resources and less of my control. I was out in the training hollow with her when Mor came to me with yet another demand, and I ended up obliterating one of Branten's training dummies.

"Mor was completely unfazed. But when I turned to her, all I could see was the horror in her eyes. And when I went to talk to her about it later, the conversation ended with her telling me, 'Not worth it' as she walked out the door."

Aaron's hand flexed around her shoulder. Analia propped herself up on an elbow, an iron-clad fist squeezing her heart.

"What was her name?" she asked.

"Liss." That one syllable held infinite emotions. But Aaron only nudged her back down beside him. "After that, I realized the danger my magic and infamy would create for a partner or child. And it's hard to want to keep looking after that."

He didn't sound upset by this fact. He was resigned, as if it were a simple truth he had accepted long ago. One Analia couldn't wrap her mind around.

"How has no one tried to stick around anyway," she murmured.

"Why, my shooting star," he asked, turning his head toward her. "Would you like to take the risk?"

He gave her a long, searching look. It was the same look he'd given her when they first met, his gaze sliding through every wall, caressing along her heart, settling in her soul.

She'd flinched away from that look in Ash. Now, she couldn't help but wonder what he saw.

"Do you remember the day we escaped the Sun Kingdom?" she asked.

Aaron nodded.

"You revealed yourself to Deardryn. You left the temple thinking the scroll was gone. And when I asked you why, all you said was because you saw what was important, but I still don't know what that means."

The corner of Aaron's mouth lifted. "It means," he said, "I was sent to the Sun Kingdom to find a scroll. One I assumed was important in some way. But I *knew* you were important."

His thumb moved along her collarbone, right above her heart. She knew he didn't mean important to Deardryn's scheme, or even important to finding the scrolls. She was important. To him. Enough to take the greatest risk imaginable to not just himself, but his kingdom.

"Training starts tomorrow," Analia said.

Aaron's face flashed through so many emotions she couldn't keep track. Settling on pride, he said, "All right, then."

For the briefest moment, his arm tightened around her, pulling her close. Then, he was sitting up, telling her she better not have gotten ready for bed without having dinner first.

Analia half-heartedly protested as she followed him down to the dining room. And it wasn't an accident when, later that night, she fell asleep on the pillows that still smelled of metal and spice.

Chapter 35

Ember didn't know which annoyed her more: the councilmen's insistence on having a meeting every Rosala-forsaken moment of the day, or Accalon making the symbols in the first place.

Between herself, Cadmus, and Lucilla, they'd manage to search most of the walls during the gaps between council meetings. Interestingly, despite the book having eleven symbols marked throughout, they'd only found two of them on the walls: the three circle triangle and the spiral.

They already knew the triangle corresponded with the mountains, and after a few searching sessions, Cadmus figured out the running thread between the spiral categories was magic. That, however, didn't make them any easier to find.

"I've been thinking," Ember said, tapping her fingers on the painting of Scarsthain.

"I thought I sensed something vibrating," Cadmus said from the opposing wall.

Ember snorted and rubbed her nose. Lately, her devinroot had been leaving it dry and raw—which was new. Same with her jitteriness, as if her body was trying to keep up with her racing mind.

"Ember?"

Ember blinked hard, struggling to focus. "Right. Well, I was thinking if we haven't found any of the other symbols, instead of scanning every single painting, we could just focus on the ones that are linked to the spiral and circle triangle symbols."

She'd been thinking about it all night, pacing around the small barracks-like room all healer apprentices were housed in, methodically inhaling her devinroot when her mind would wander.

"That could work," Cadmus said, moving to the table. "We just have to go through all your notes and label each reference."

"I already did that," Ember said, zipping around the table and thrusting her notes into his hands. "I already cross-listed the number of symbols we found and where with the mentioned locations and people in the book—see, why aren't you looking? If you just look between the columns, you can see the only location we haven't found a symbol with is Scarsthain—probably because the paint is so dark and the stone is crumbling, but if we can verify it's there, we're done!"

Ember beamed up at him, her body buzzing. Cadmus, however, took his time flipping through her notes, a small crease between his brows.

"What?" Ember asked, her eye twitching. "Did I miss something?"

"No, Em, not at all, this is incredible. It's just... how have you had time to do all of this?"

Ember felt as though an expanding bubble had been popped in her chest.

"This is an important mystery," she said. "Why wouldn't I make time for it?"

"You shouldn't if it means ignoring your apprentice duties."

Ember pulled on her healer robe, the soft fabric suddenly feeling horribly abrasive against her sensitive skin. From the devinroot?

"Cadmus," she began, but he shook his head.

"You're so close, Ember. You just need one more ring, and then you have your dream. You can't sacrifice that for a mystery that two other people are helping you with."

No, that dream had been taken from her. She had to solve this mystery. It was all she had left.

"Em," Cadmus said, unbearably gentle. "What's going on with you?"

"Nothing," she said, her hands curling into fists in her pockets. She wouldn't let the emotion in her chest bubble over. She couldn't have Cadmus look at her with disappointment when she was so close to solving this mystery and then everything would be fine—it had to be fine.

"Ember."

Cadmus set down her notes and took a deliberate step toward her. Ember backed into a chair, her entire body tensing for impact as he touched her arm.

"You can trust me, you know," he said.

Ember looked up into his eyes. And his undeniable sincerity had the entire story finally exploding past her lips: her weeks of trials, the council's decision, her suspension.

Cadmus's face flashed through countless emotions. But all he said when she finished was, "What can I do?"

Those four little words decimated what little resolve she had left. She sank down into her chair, hiding her face in her hands as she said, "I just need to hear someone else say everything will be all right."

"I'll do you one better," Cadmus said, moving behind her chair to squeeze her shoulders. "I have no doubt in my mind it will be all right. We will fix this, Royal-healer separation or no."

Rosala spare her, she hoped that was true.

"What did they say you have to do?" he asked.

"Confess that I know all of my oath-breaking behavior was wrong. Admit I made a mistake and now understand I can't do everything by myself."

The words burned like acid on her tongue. But to her surprise, Cadmus laughed.

"That's all?" He shifted to kneel beside her. "Em, that's easy. None of us should have been working on that case, let alone by ourselves."

"You don't get it." Ember pushed to her feet, furiously blinking back tears.

"No, you're right," Cadmus said, rising as well. "You understand healer politics better than I do. What's left for you to do, then?"

"Nothing," Ember said flatly.

It took Cadmus a moment to realize what she meant. Then, his eyes widened. "You haven't been doing anything?"

Ember headed for the paintings, "Don't start, Cadmus."

"Ember," Cadmus said, rising and chasing after her, "you're a healer. You were chosen by the Crystal despite having no Blessed blood, and instead of fighting for your dream, you're here wasting time with me?"

"The archmaster healers are being ridiculous."

"And so are you!"

There it was. The truth. The truth she had always known. But Rosala spare her, it sounded so, so much worse out loud.

"When does this end, Ember?" Cadmus asked.

"When the healers admit they were wrong." Her voice was so small.

"And when is that going to happen?"

Ember didn't respond. She couldn't. Not when Cadmus's words dragged forward her every doubt like a prisoner on an execution block.

"Admit it, Ember," Cadmus said, stepping up beside her. "You are fighting a hopeless battle, all for the sake of your pride."

"Of course it's because of my pride!" Ember snapped, whirling on him. "My pride is all I have left.

"You're a Royal, Cadmus. You are the gods-damned king, chosen by your people. You have no idea what it feels like to walk into a room and immediately have to prove yourself. That has been my life for the past thirteen years since the Crystal not only Blessed me, a human, with healer magic, but herbology magic of all specialties."

"Why do either of those things matter?" Cadmus asked.

"Because the Crystal only chooses elitists with gore complexes to be healers. They view human healers as less than because they think our lack of Blessed blood weakens our Blessings. Herbology is thought of as the weakest Blessing because we focus our healing through plants instead of our own magic, but we're also viewed as threats because with those plants, we can become proficient in multiple areas of healing."

Ember despised the look of understanding that crossed Cadmus's face. She sharply pivoted to examine the Scarsthain painting once more, her fingers shaking as she dragged them along the rough stone.

"This battle," she said raggedly, "has nothing to do with me being stubborn. It has everything to do with the fact that no matter what I do, it is never enough for the healers, and I'm terrified they're right. I can't let them be right about this because then what else are they right about? How much of the respect that I've had to *claw* for will they take away from me if I let them win?"

Ember felt as though she had been rubbed raw. She glanced at Cadmus from the corner of her eye, but he only shook his head.

"For all the beauty this kingdom creates," he murmured, "it has no tolerance for flaws."

"Is that what I am?" she asked tiredly, her finger drifting up to the heart of Scarsthain. "A flaw?"

"Not at all. But I think this kingdom has taught you that you are."

Cadmus trailed his fingertips down her arm. "My uncle told me when his mother discovered he had bright blue flames, she was terrified. All other Royals before him had been Blessed with traditional colors like orange, red, and gold, and she had no idea how our kingdom would react to such an overt deviation.

"But Uncle never minded. He went so far as to break another tradition by working in the mines because he loved the craft and wanted to get to know his people. And to this day, he is the most beloved Ash King in history. You know why?"

Ember shook her head.

"Because he didn't let the kingdom's judgment rule his life. Especially when there was nothing he could do to change the color of his flames. Instead, he did what felt right to him, and that drew more people to him than any 'normal' colored flames could. And he also got the satisfaction of becoming the superior of every person that tried to shove him down."

Ember sniffed, her finger pausing on the painting. Cadmus leaned into her line of sight.

"I know these are vastly different circumstances," he said. "I know those healers at the school are going to be relentless bumps in your path, and for that, I am truly sorry. But right now, the biggest obstacle you have to deal with is your caring what they think."

Something in her chest gave a long, rolling ache. Somehow, once again, Cadmus had seen the connections that no one else had.

"I know," she said quietly. "I just don't know what to do about it."

"For starters, you can allow me and Lucilla to help you with this puzzle."

"I can do that," Ember said. "Although I already found the last symbol."

Cadmus looked to her finger on the wall, the spiral barely distinguishable in the center of the prison's cracked, shadowy center. He opened his mouth, scoffed, then shook his head. "You are infuriatingly smart sometimes."

Ember laughed slightly. "I could say the same to you."

She wiped a tear from her cheek, giving him a pointed look. Cadmus shrugged a hand.

"It will be all right," he promised, softening once more.

Ember's shoulders slumped. She allowed Cadmus to usher her over to the table, feeling completely drained, but the slightest bit lighter as well.

"Now that we've confirmed all the spots," Cadmus said, shuffling through their papers, "we just need to figure out what to do with them—"

The door burst open behind them.

"The sprites say Ganze is coming," Lucilla said, darting into the room.

Ember cursed.

"He's ten minutes early," Cadmus said, too distracted to shoot Ember a disapproving look.

"I sent Rois to derail him," Lucilla said, nudging between them to look at their notes.

"What did you tell him?" Cadmus asked.

"That it was for Analia. He'd do anything for her. He's in love with her."

Cadmus's eyes widened. He looked to Ember, who just shook her head.

"You know too much," she said.

Lucilla shrugged a dainty shoulder. "So, what are we doing?"

"That's a great question," Ember said, pulling out a seat and plopping down. "Currently, we're staring at a bunch of symbols and locations with no clue what to do with them."

"Have you tried sketching them out on this map?" Lucilla asked, brandishing the map Accalon had tucked inside his book.

"No," Cadmus said. "We don't know what that's for yet. We shouldn't ruin it."

"Can't we just get a new one if need be?" Lucilla asked.

Ember made to list all the reasons that was a bad idea, but nothing came to mind. She glanced at Cadmus, who seemed to have reached the same conclusion.

"Is this what it feels like to be humbled?" she asked.

"No," Cadmus sighed, grabbing a pen from the table. "It's just what it feels like when a twelve-year-old is smarter than you."

"I'll be thirteen in the spring," Lucilla said cheerfully. She swiped Cadmus's pen and got to work, happily chattering as she did so. Cadmus smiled down at her, his hand on her shoulder.

His words were still a persistent ache in Ember's chest. But as Lucilla drew, they seemed to take hold inside her like an anchor.

Maybe proving herself to the healers wasn't as important as she thought. Maybe the battle for that acceptance was worse than not having it. But where did that leave her with her suspension?

Before she could think on it too hard, Cadmus stiffened. Ember and Lucilla looked to him questioningly, but Cadmus's gaze was fixed on Lucilla's completed drawing.

"How did you make that?" he asked, his face pale.

Lucilla looked to Ember uncertainly. She'd drawn connecting lines between each location, forming a curved, asymmetrical star.

"I just connected the dots," Lucilla said. "I started with the first place the first symbol in the book was talking about, then moved to number two, and then the next until it was all of them."

Cadmus released a long, hissing breath.

"Cadmus, what's going on?" Ember asked.

"Anna and I have seen that mark before," he said. "Tattooed on the inside of our father's wrist on the day of his sentencing."

Ember's heart stuttered. Lucilla's wide blue eyes darted between Ember, Cadmus, and the map, her mouth starting to tremble.

Before Ember or Cadmus could speak, a fire sprite zipped through the door's keyhole. Alighting on Lucilla's shoulder, it whispered in her ear.

Lucilla quickly collected herself. "Ganze is coming."

The three launched into action. Cadmus gathered all their papers, passing them to Ember to slide beneath her healer robes. Then, they scattered from the Council Chamber, Lucilla disappearing around the corner as Cadmus reached for her.

"She'll be all right," Ember promised.

Cadmus nodded. Ember made to slip away, but Cadmus stopped her with a hand on her arm.

"We have to contact Scarsthain," he said, his voice low.

We, not *I*. Even after all that in the Council Chamber, he wanted her help.

Ember nodded. Then, she slipped down the corridor, just as she heard Ganze greet Cadmus.

Chapter 36

Analia met Branten in the training hollow, just to discover they weren't alone. Aaron stood off to the side, his bare torso gleaming with sweat as he pulverized a training dummy. He paused to give Analia a nod of greeting, then returned to his training, allowing her eyes to wander down his sculpted back.

His muscles flexed with every movement like steps of a dance, coordinated with the melody of his network.

Graceful. Beautiful.

But it was the straight white scars that stretched across his back like lines on a war map that had her unable to look away.

Her flames snarled. Even as Branten called her over, they wanted to burn whoever had done that to him to ash. And as Analia moved through her exercises, she knew if she ever found out, she would let them.

The moment she finished her routine, Aaron appeared at her shoulder, his scars now hidden by a white shirt and dark jacket. Sliding his arm around her waist, he offered a farewell to Branten and a "Fair warning" in her ear. Then, not wasting a moment, he whisked her into the shadows.

"I'm assuming this means training starts now," Analia said, blinking as they reemerged. The quiet lakeside spread out before them, the rocky shore completely deserted.

"Clever girl." Aaron moved to sit against a long, flat rock beside the water, flashing a smile that promised nothing but trouble.

"What are you up to?" Analia muttered, sinking down across from him.

"Any other time, the answer would be schemes and debauchery. But today, I'm simply looking forward to a magnificent display of flame and rage."

"What does that have to do with training?"

"Everything." Aaron leaned back against the rock. "You've had magic building up in your network for Crystal knows how long. You are a bonfire, Analia, and it's far easier to tame a candle."

Analia's fingers spasmed around her pin. "What are you saying, Aaron?"

"I'm saying you need to let your magic out. All of it. Burn through as much buildup as possible so we can start training with a clean slate."

No. She couldn't let those flames rip free. There would be no stopping them, no controlling them.

"Can't we do more of the salt pinching exercise?" she asked.

"We could," Aaron said. "But then we would be here all day, all night, and I wouldn't be surprised if you started accumulating more magic than you were releasing."

"But I thought the point of training was learning how to control my magic."

"Why are you stalling?" Aaron asked, genuinely curious.

"Because I don't want to hurt anyone!" Analia exclaimed. "I don't know if I can reel it in once I've let go, and if someone happens to come down here—"

"They won't," Aaron said. "As soon as you told me you wanted to train, I closed the lake to citizens. I even put up the same wards that are on the walkway that will prevent your magic from reaching the kingdom. You should be able to sense them if you don't believe me."

Analia did believe him, but she reached out anyway. She immediately found the tingle of magic, wrapping around the perimeter of the shore.

"What about you?" she asked.

"I'll be fine," he said, starlight flickering around him. "Do you trust me?"

Analia nodded.

"Then let go."

Analia's head bowed as if pulled by an anchor. Remembering their conversation on her bed, she closed her eyes and tentatively reached for the well of flames inside her.

Immediately, they thrashed against her control, reaching for open air.

Analia jerked away. Maybe if she let out a little at a time instead—

Something pinged off her arm. She opened her eyes, looking down at the stinging circle on her arm, then to Aaron. "Did you flick a pebble at me?"

"You were flinching away."

"I was not."

"Analia, I spent enough time on that bench in Sun to know when you're truly trying."

Analia flashed back to the Ring Room. Failure after failure after failure. Pryanth screaming in her face, just for her to run after him and listen to him berate her once again.

"Don't go there, Aaron," she warned, heat spreading across her body.

"I was the one that sat with you," Aaron said. "Day after day. Just the two of us, because the prince that said he loved you couldn't be bothered to show up."

"Aaron—"

"And your teacher? The one who said she believed in you? She was only forging you into a tool. Even then she couldn't show up for you."

"Aaron—"

"They abandoned you when you needed them most. Just like everyone else."

"Aaron, stop." Analia scrambled to her feet and backed away, heat pulsing off her body in waves. She tried to take a breath, tried to force the storm of flames back under control.

"You did it again," Aaron said, flicking another pebble at her. "You can't flinch away."

"Stop flicking pebbles at me!"

"You have to feel the anger, Analia."

"I'm not angry."

"No, you're furious." Aaron rose to his feet, his eyes blazing. "You're furious with me for pushing you to do this. You're furious with the Ash Kingdom for allowing themselves to be poisoned against a child. You're furious with Pryanth for convincing you that he loved you, even as he put an arm to your throat and promised to kill you. You're furious with yourself for feeling like you should have done more, and you're furious that you know there was nothing you could have done, but you still feel ashamed. Feel the fury, Analia."

"I can't," Analia sobbed, midnight flames flashing across her skin.

"Yes, you can," Aaron told her, silver light swirling around him. "There's nothing here you can hurt or destroy. It's just you, me, and a lifetime of injustices. So, let them burn."

Her flames screamed their approval. They thrashed against her control, burning until her back was drenched in sweat. And it just kept coming.

It was too much to control. Too much to hold in. Too much anger roiled to the surface to be shoved back down.

"Aaron," Analia whispered.

Aaron's gaze was as firm as his voice. "Let. Go."

Analia's control snapped. Flames erupted from her body in a furious column of black and blue. They shot toward the sky, spilling out of her like memories on a journal page.

Brenn calling her a duckling. The look of collective disdain on her coronation day. Deardryn blasting her with magic. Faces, words, every loving touch she'd ever experienced that was cold with lies and decay.

She had never loved Pryanth, but he'd never loved her either. Love was a word to him, a weapon. One he never used to fight for her. No, *she* fought: fixing every argument, smoothing down every bristle, swallowing every emotion she had until she thought they would break her from the inside out. And in return, he jabbed, and he jabbed, and he jabbed.

She had been powerless. She'd had no magic. But now she had her uncle's flames roaring through her veins. And there was no bringing them back under control.

Aaron dove over his rock just in time. He threw his arm up against the wave of heat, his magic churning as he stared up at Analia's conflagration.

If it were any other person, he would've shoved them into the lake by now. That, however, would shut off the magic, and she needed to get all of it out. But Crystal spare them all, Aaron had only experienced a releasing this powerful once before. His own.

Aaron tentatively extended a tendril of magic, hissing and jerking it back as soon as it made contact.

"Anna," he called, coming to crouch on the rock. "Anna, I know you can hear me. Just like you did the last time your flames got out."

He sent another ribbon of starlight prodding at the flames, gritting his teeth as they collided. But he held firm.

"You told me you couldn't stop the flames, and I don't want you to now. But do you remember what you told me after that?"

Aaron pushed against her fire, feeling the slightest give. "You told me you knew you couldn't stop your flames. But you couldn't let them hurt me, either."

Two simple statements that had been etched into his heart.

"Do you remember that, Anna?" Aaron asked, giving another push, the flames giving another inch. He slid off the rock, taking a few steps toward her. "You couldn't let them hurt me. And I won't let them hurt you, either. But you have to let me help you."

He gave a final shove, the flames bending inward to create a narrow tunnel. Then, knowing this could very well be his death, Aaron encased himself in magic and stepped inside.

He shouldn't be able to breathe. He shouldn't be alive in the first place. But Aaron stumbled after his magic, eyes squeezed shut and body teetering on the verge of overheating.

Soon, he found a huddled form with his foot. He fell to his knees, his fingers thankfully remaining unscorched as he touched her back. Then, heart pounding, he leaned forward to speak in her ear.

"Well, see. That's your problem. You're completely tense." Aaron dragged his thumbs up either side of her spine, keeping his voice conversational. "Don't worry, I can help with that. In many ways, actually, but we'll stick with this for now."

He moved her hair aside, his fingertips brushing the back of her neck. "Can I help you?"

He was almost certain she couldn't hear him. But after an unnerving pause, she gave a fraction of a nod.

Aaron nearly slumped in relief. Instead, he got to work massaging the coiled muscles in her neck, keeping his tone light.

"The interesting thing about your magic is it's incredibly similar to blood. Most of the time, it's able to flow freely, regardless of if you're consciously pushing it along. But that doesn't mean you can't block the flow."

His hands slid down to her shoulders. "It's like when you fall asleep on your arm, just to wake up to it tingling. The pressure stopped the blood flow. You'll have to ask Ember about the tingling, my seven-year-old self got distracted before I could ask. But the same concept applies to your magic.

"If you tense up, the magic is going to tense as well. If you want your magic to flow, you need to relax into it. Don't try to direct it or stop it or control it in any way."

Aaron had no idea if she was listening, but he kept talking anyway. Slowly, he loosened the knots in her muscles, her shoulders finally relaxing beneath his hands.

"That's it," he murmured, resting his chin on her shoulder. "No holding back."

He squeezed her arms, moving down to her clenched hands. "See, now, Branten would be thrilled to note your thumb is on the outside. But for this, you need to relax. No fists today."

Analia shuddered, leaning back against his chest.

"There you go," Aaron said, finally straightening her fingers. He rested her hands against her stomach, placing his magic-chilled hands atop hers. "No controlling, no fighting. Just let it flow all the way out. It will be over soon."

Truthfully, he had no idea when it would be over. All he could do was run his thumbs along the backs of her hands. Lean his head against hers as she started to shake.

Slowly, painstakingly slowly, the flames died around them.

Aaron opened his eyes. The vestiges of their magic flickered around them, black and silver sparks winking out as Analia's body temperature faded back to normal.

Aaron let out a sigh of relief, pulling her closer.

And Analia shoved away hard enough he fell back on the stones.

A nalia hid her face in her hands, unable to stop her tears.

She couldn't deny the relief at having her magic drained to empty. But those first couple seconds had been eclipsed by a scorching, undiluted wrath. She'd had to shove Aaron away, terrified of what she might do.

Now, she felt him come to kneel before her. She tried to back away, but Aaron made a soft noise of protest. And Analia didn't have any fight left in her as he gathered her to him once more.

"I killed him," she choked out.

"I know," Aaron soothed.

"No, I *killed him*." The words tumbled past her lips, sharp and fast. "I lost control. I killed him. I should regret what I did, but a part of me doesn't because even though I didn't love him, I was desperate enough to be on the way. And the only thing more terrifying than what he could have done is the fact that I don't know if I would have stopped him. *That's* why I kept that stupid pendant. To remind myself that I am a monster that doesn't regret killing someone."

There it was. The ugly truth that had been blackening her heart, laid bare between them like a rotting corpse.

"Analia," Aaron said, terrifyingly calm, "he was going to kill you."

"He was drunk!"

"Doesn't matter! He was going to, just like he slapped you when he was sober."

"But he didn't!"

"Because you did what you had to do to survive."

"I *lost control.*"

There was no word for the destruction that rampaged through Analia's body.

Aaron studied her for a few long moments. Then, he released her, scooting back a few feet—gods, even he couldn't stand to touch her.

The thought had barely formed when Aaron encased himself in a column of starlight. It blasted toward the sky, slamming against her mental shield in an astounding wave of power. And Analia could only stare as he began.

"The first time I lost control, I was seven. In my kingdom, it's custom to wear our dampers when mastering our Blessing due to the destruction a slip can cause. Yet, after my family was killed, my mother insisted I stop wearing mine.

"Part of me thinks it was her grief talking. Most of me thinks it was her fear that she would lose me, too. The only thing I know for certain is I was four years old, drunk on a power I barely understood. And somehow, I made it three years before the repercussions caught up with me.

"I was playing in the streets with a group of friends when another boy came storming up to us. Before I could ask him to join us, he got in my face, screaming that he'd lost everything because of me. I tried to apologize, but he shoved me to the ground.

"I barely registered the pain as my head hit stone. But when I brought my hand up, and my fingers came back red and sticky…"

Analia's stomach sank. "Did you…"

"Kill him?" Aaron asked, a jagged piece of glass. "No. But I would have if Ethelind hadn't shown up and practically choked me with my damper. When my senses faded back in, the boy was sobbing as my grandmother tended to him, blood gushing from his nose, his skin tinged gray. I don't know how long I stood there, staring, but Ethelind finally snapped at me to go home and wait for her there. I immediately fled, too ashamed, too much of a coward to so much as learn that boy's name.

"When Ethelind arrived home, she first rounded on my mom, telling her this was exactly what she was afraid of if I didn't wear my damper. She then told me this could never happen again, and she dropped me off at the Underground the next morning. And it was five years before I even considered touching my magic again."

Aaron let his magic wink out, his face twisted with grief. Analia made to speak, but Aaron shook his head, coming to kneel before her once more.

"You told me once that I was worthy of being forgiven. That applies to you, too."

He lifted her chin, forcing her to look at him. "I can't tell you who deserves to live and who deserves to die. But I *can* tell you no matter how much you torture yourself, you can't change what you did to Pryanth, nor can you change what Pryanth did to you. What you can do is master your magic. Learn to control it, otherwise Pryanth won't be your only casualty."

Two silent tears streamed down Analia's cheeks. "I don't want this power," she whispered.

"But you have it," Aaron said firmly. "This feeling is never going to leave you, Analia. Instead of allowing it to force you into living in fear, let it be a reminder of what happens when you're not careful."

Aaron brushed the hair from her face, his hand coming to rest on the side of her neck. "You told me I'm not a monster," he said, "and I'm telling you the same. So, either we're both monsters, or neither of us are."

Once, Accalon had explained how if someone struck a foundational support beam in just the right spot, the entire structure could come toppling down. Analia had a split second to register how Aaron's words made a direct hit. Then, her last pillars of control fell.

Tears spilled down her cheeks, hot and fast.

"Please," Aaron whispered, his arms tightening around her. "Please forgive yourself. You don't have to do it now. Just believe that you can do it someday."

Analia cried harder. Aaron whispered a warning and faded into the shadows. They emerged on his rock a moment later, Aaron pulling her onto his lap as her fingers spasmed around his jacket.

And she sobbed. Not just for herself. But for Pryanth. The man that hurt her, that tried to love her, that she made excuses for, that she forgave, that she killed.

"You will survive this," Aaron whispered into her hair.

Analia didn't know how. But he'd promised her the same thing back on her turret, and he'd been right.

"Gods," she said, "I have to stop crying into your chest."

"I can cry into yours, next time," Aaron offered.

Analia hiccupped. Aaron eased back, just enough to look at her.

"I told you," he said, "I'm here any time you want a cathartic wallow. That wasn't a one-time promise. At this point, I'd be offended if you didn't include me."

Analia gave him a wobbly smile.

"I'm right here," he told her, resting his forehead against hers. "I want to be here. And I'm not going anywhere. I promised you that, too."

He brushed the tears from her cheeks, not taking his eyes from hers until she nodded. Then, he nestled her against him once more. Even as Analia quieted, as her body relaxed into his, he didn't pull away. And neither did she.

Eventually, Analia took a long, steadying breath. She peeked up at him, her eyes moving over his face.

The sharp angles of his cheekbones and jaw. The soft curve of his mouth. His eyes that sparkled with starlight, looking back at her with an emotion she didn't have a name for.

Her gaze drifted down...

"Oh gods," she said, clapping a hand to her mouth. "Aaron, your shirt."

A noticeable tear stain marred the chest of Aaron's white shirt. Aaron blinked, seemingly struggling to process her words. Finally, he looked down. Studied the situation.

Heat crept across Analia's cheeks, over to her ears and down her neck. She scrambled off his lap, the beginnings of an apology on her lips.

Aaron burst out laughing. He fell back on the rock, laughing so hard his entire body shook.

"Oh, Analia," he finally got out, wiping a tear from his eye. "You have no idea what kind of war you just started. I almost feel bad for you, although it's your own fault for challenging my title of champion wallower. Your tunic might not even survive."

Analia hid her face in her hands. "Let's just go home."

Aaron, still laughing, pulled her to him once more. "I'm proud of you," he told her as they faded into the shadows. "My torrential shooting star."

They reemerged in Analia's room. Analia immediately shoved him away. Aaron flicked her temple, laughter trailing behind him as he strolled out of her room.

Analia gave his back a rude hand gesture. But when she caught a glimpse of her red, puffy face in the mirror, there was no denying her smile.

Chapter 37

Dimitri lounged on a couch in Rayner's shop, loudly sighing as the masquerader admired his newly changed appearance in the mirror for the eighth time.

"You have no patience," Rayner chided, fluffing his shoulder-length black hair.

"And you look like you've been lost at sea for six weeks," Dimitri retorted.

"It's the scruff, isn't it?"

Dimitri sighed even louder, covering his face with his poetry collection. It was the night of the Full Moon Festival, the distant music telling him it had started back around Rayner's fifth appearance change.

"Relax, Dima," Rayner purred, coming toward the couch. "We have plenty of time. And I've finally settled on my appearance. See?"

He knelt beside Dimitri, lifting the book from his face.

Dimitri's eyes traveled up Rayner's black-and-gold tunic, briefly pausing on the purple tattoo peeking through the top undone buttons. Finally, he reached Rayner's face.

Dimitri shoved his shoulders. "You look exactly the same as you always do!"

Rayner fell back. "Not true! My normal hair is brown with a faint copper hue. Now, it's auburn. Speaking of which." Rayner ran his fingers through Dimitri's dark hair. "Are you sure I can't change anything? Even a little streak of blue right here?"

"No." Dimitri jerked to his feet, unsettled by the tingles that had trailed down his scalp to the base of his spine. "Let's just go already."

"Fine," Rayner sighed, following him to the door. "But only because you agreed to wear that green doublet. It does such lovely things to your eyes."

Dimitri's head whipped around. Rayner slipped around him and out the door, flashing a smirk as if he just won a point in a secret game.

Oh, absolutely not.

Dimitri marched after Rayner across the boardwalks, a retort fizzing against his lips.

"I must admit," Rayner said before he could speak, "I wasn't expecting you to be so eager to attend tonight."

Dimitri paused. Considered his response. Considered again. Then, begrudgingly, he let his retort bubble back down.

"It's all I've been hearing about the past three weeks," he said instead. "The parade of lights, the moon dance."

"Don't forget staying up until dawn."

Dimitri hadn't forgotten. Just as he hadn't forgotten Sylas's invitation for Deardryn to join them.

Ever since discovering Deardryn's interest in magical landmarks, Dimitri had been playing catch up. He'd spent every spare moment identifying magical landmarks in his book and visiting the ones he suspected Deardryn had already hit. He hadn't been able to figure out what she was looking for, but after carefully asking around, he was confident she hadn't found it yet.

The last location on his list was the Wraithhouse: the largest religious sanctuary for wraith-kind in all of Elefthia. Now *that* he wasn't looking forward to.

"There it is," Rayner said.

Dimitri hadn't noticed they'd left the square behind. He quickly brushed the thoughts aside as they merged with a sizable crowd, all heading for the glowing archway at the base of the festival hill.

Water lilies and other marshland flowers wrapped around the frame, sparkling with the dusting of snow that had fallen that afternoon. Countless strands of glowing white feathers cascaded down like a curtain, softly brushing their heads as they filtered through.

"Are those lunar hawk feathers?" Dimitri asked, head craned back.

"They are," Rayner said. "They always molt their feathers at the full moon, and some unlucky bastard is in charge of collecting and threading them all year."

He reached up as they passed through, pulling two strands free. Looping one around his neck, he settled the second strand around Dimitri's.

"Look at that," he said, adjusting Dimitri's strand. "You're blending in more and more."

Dimitri ran his fingers along the soft, downy feathers, noting the feather chains wrapped around people's wrists, necks, and hair. To his surprise, he recognized many of their faces, either from the castle halls or the kingdom streets. Even more surprising were the smiles he got as people passed.

Something soft, delicate, seemed to bud in his chest. He turned to Rayner, his words sticking in his throat. "I think... I think I like it here."

Something like indecision flashed across Rayner's face. Before Dimitri could be sure that was what he saw, Rayner reached out and tapped his temple. "In that case, you should turn around."

Dimitri did as suggested, and his eyes widened.

The crowded hillside was alive with thousands of tiny lights, ranging from feathers to lanterns in every hue. Music drifted down from the top of the hill, where a statue of Mahina reached up toward the stars.

"I'd almost forgotten how beautiful it is," Rayner said, half to himself.

"Weren't you here last year?"

"I stopped coming a while ago. There are only so many times you can come to this festival alone before it becomes monotonous. And since it's unwise to trust someone like me..." Rayner's eyes cut to Dimitri significantly.

Dimitri fiddled with his feather strand. Did he trust Rayner?

Once, he wouldn't have had to consider that question: he didn't trust anyone. But now?

"You mean as untrustworthy as a foreigner who has to hide his identity?" he asked.

Rayner's face flashed through emotions in quick succession: amusement, hesitation, regret, longing.

"And you claim I'm impossible to figure out," Dimitri muttered.

Rayner smiled to himself. "And yet, your relentless buzzing energy never fails to cut through the monotony."

Dimitri's face flushed. He ducked his head, mumbling, "I don't buzz."

Rayner laughed. Plucking one of Dimitri's feathers, he sauntered off up the hill, calling over his shoulder. "Come on, my fellow outcast. I know you enjoy stroking your feathers, but the entertainment is supposed to be up here."

"Really?" Dimitri shot back. "And here I thought the entertainment was attached to your mirror."

He marched after Rayner. Yet, as he reached his side, Dimitri couldn't maintain a straight face.

The two slowly worked their way up the hillside. They wandered through stands selling lanterns and candles, through display after display of pastries that Dimitri happily accepted samples from. Throughout it all, he kept his eye out for a familiar head of golden hair.

"You know," he said, licking leftover frosting from his fingers, "this entire festival is completely backward."

Rayner dragged his gaze up from Dimitri's fingers. "How so?"

"The Moon Kingdom is all about shadows and shit, not light."

"Where do you think shadows come from?" Sabi stepped out of the crowd before them. She wore a gown of silver chiffon, her dark brown curls decorated with lunar hawk feathers.

"Since when do you emerge from your cave?" Dimitri asked.

"Since my victims stopped having the courtesy of coming to me."

Rayner laughed under his breath.

"Have you heard?" Sabi asked, leaning in conspiratorially. "Apparently, Princess Marcella had quite the Royal tantrum when she spotted a dress identical to hers in the crowd tonight."

"Really?" Dimitri snickered. "Did she forget to return her book again?"

"Oh, she returned it. *Bent.* Top right corner. Do you know how long it took me to fix that?" Sabi tossed her hair. "This little outfit change only took minutes, though."

"You should talk to Rayner," Dimitri griped, shoving him forward. "The only thing he can do in minutes is stare at his reflection."

"I don't remember you minding when you were poking through my book collection," Rayner drawled.

Sabi perked up. "Book collection?"

"Don't bother," Dimitri said. "It's pitiful."

Rayner shrugged unapologetically. "You know," he said, his gaze running down Sabi's gown, "if you're going to insult me, you should at least introduce me to your friend first."

Sabi flushed and stuck out her hand. Dimitri, however, was distracted by a familiar golden head over her shoulder.

Deardryn stood on the outskirts about thirty feet away, dressed in a gown of deep blue velvet. Patryclas and Sylas stood beside her, their heads bowed in hushed conversation. Eyes narrowed, Dimitri started to edge around Sabi.

"Come on!" she said. "The moon dance is about to start!"

Before Dimitri could react, she grabbed his hand and towed him toward the group forming on the hilltop. He reflexively reached back, catching Rayner by the wrist.

Dimitri didn't know if there was a point to the moon dance, but as the music picked up around him, he didn't care. Time seemed to blur as he, Sabi, and Rayner danced with the crowd, the measured steps of the Sun Kingdom nowhere to be found.

This was wild. This was free. Surrounded by the heat of hundreds of bodies, music lacing through his blood, pounding in harmony with his pulse.

Rayner eventually passed him a paper cup whose contents burned all the way down, settling in a warm glow in his stomach. Grabbing their hands, Sabi ordered them to close the circle and took off running. They spun round and round, not stopping until Dimitri was dizzy and drunk and stumbling with laughter.

He felt like a child.

He felt alive.

And those were a familiar pair of black eyes.

Dimitri blinked, struggling to clear the swirling lights from his vision. Locating Deardryn once more, he turned his attention to the wraith sitting against Mahina's plinth. Alone.

"I'll be right back," he said.

Sabi and Rayner raised their cups, barely paying him any attention.

Dimitri stumbled through the crowd, eyes locked on Magnar, the warden of the Wraithhouse. If he was lucky, he might be able to cross the Wraithhouse off his list without having to slip away to visit. Then, he would finally catch up with Deardryn.

But Dimitri could still feel the drunken haze across his mind as he reached the statue. Just as he could feel it in his words as he offered a cheerful greeting.

Magnar looked up as he slid down beside him. "You seem to be enjoying yourself."

Dimitri touched his fingertips to his flushed cheeks, not even minding the cold radiating off Magnar. "I am. My friends gave me too many of these"—he raised his empty cup—"so I thought this would be a good resting spot."

Dimitri plastered a drunken smile on his face. Magnar made a noncommittal noise, then turned back to his own cup. A soft breeze blew across the hillside, rustling Magnar's cloak enough for Dimitri to catch a peek of the pink pearl dangling around his neck.

"Hey," Dimitri said, elbowing him. "Did you see we have a surprise guest?"

Magnar stifled a groan. But as he followed Dimitri's gaze, he perked up slightly. "Ah, yes, Queen Deardryn. She mentioned she would be attending tonight."

"You talked to her?" Dimitri leaned closer, widening his eyes with awe.

"She came to visit the Wraithhouse about a week ago."

Bull's-eye.

"Wow. What did she talk about?"

"What do you think she asked about in the Wraithhouse." Magnar touched his fingertips to Dimitri's shoulder, lightly shoving him away. "She wanted to learn about wraith culture and the lore behind our pulsepearls."

"You mean these?"

Dimitri reached for the pink pearl—maybe he *was* drunk. Magnar yelped, simultaneously swatting Dimitri's hand away and jerking back.

"That's it," he said. "I'm leaving."

Rising to his feet, he dusted off his cloak and swept back into the crowd. Dimitri slumped back against the plinth, locating Deardryn once more. So, she was back to asking about wraiths. But what could she possibly want with them?

"Why are you on the ground?" Rayner asked, suddenly standing above him.

"Don't you know people will step on you?" Sabi asked beside him.

"I bet Magnar wants to step on me," Dimitri mumbled.

"Magnar?" Rayner plopped down beside him, intrigued. "What have you been up to?"

"Oh, nothing," Dimitri said. "Just drunkenly snatching at his pulsepearl."

"Dimitri!" Sabi sat on his other side, hand over her mouth.

"What?" Dimitri whined.

"Pulsepearls are the core of wraith magic," Rayner explained. "Not only are they said to be born from those pearls, but they allow the holder to magically relocate to any location where there is another pulsepearl."

"Those pearls are their life source," Sabi said. "They're incredibly protective of them."

"I've known wraiths to kill just for looking at them too long," Rayner said.

"And you tried to grab one?" Sabi swatted the side of Dimitri's head. "Stupid!"

"Is that why I always see the wraith servants with them?" Dimitri asked, absently rubbing his head.

"Some leave their pearls in a protected area so they don't have to constantly worry for their safety," Rayner said. "There's a magically guarded display in the Wraithhouse."

Sabi and Rayner continued talking, but with a jolt, Dimitri sat up straight. He'd been absently scanning the crowd as they talked. And he just managed to spot Deardryn and a golden Sun guard slip away down the hill.

Finally, she was on the move.

"I have to go," Dimitri said, scrambling to his feet, ignoring his friends' protests.

Dimitri shoved through the crowd, struggling to keep Deardryn in his line of sight. She wouldn't escape. He would not let her get yet another step ahead.

Deardryn and her guard reached the bottom of the hill. Casting a quick look around, they stepped onto a forest path as casually as a pair taking a midnight stroll. And silently, Dimitri headed after them.

Dimitri scurried through the darkness, the moonlight illuminating the two figures up ahead. He could just make out enough of their hushed conversation to realize the Sun guard was Andrik, but what was more interesting was the right turn they made when the path forked.

Where were they going? The central kingdom was in the opposite direction. All that was out this way was the river.

Was she going to use the currents to drown out their words? Well, she could try, but Dimitri was right behind her.

Just as he suspected, the two turned off the main trail and carefully picked their way through the undergrowth to the riverbank.

What he wasn't expecting was the rowboat that waited for them.

Dimitri tiptoed to the edge of the woods, the currents mercifully drowning out the slight crunch beneath his boots. Still, he held his breath as he crouched down behind a mossy boulder.

Was she shipping Andrik back to the Sun Kingdom? Why not just shadowjump him? Indeed, Deardryn faded into the shadows, but she reappeared a moment later with three more guards.

Dimitri's heart pounded in his ears. He had to do something. Once they were on that boat, there was nothing he could do.

Dimitri inched around his boulder, a twig snapping beneath his knee.

Deardryn's head whipped around. "What was that?"

Dimitri froze, not daring to breathe.

He couldn't outrun the guards. He could try to hide in the darkness, but with these woods, there was no telling what rustle might give him away. He was trapped.

"Probably just a squirrel, Your Majesty," came Andrik's voice.

"What squirrels roam the woods at night?"

Dimitri dug his nails into the mossy stone. She was so close. The moon was so bright.

"Stay on guard," Deardryn said.

Dimitri remained frozen, listening to the thud of boots and rope as the Sun soldiers prepared the boat. He couldn't flee. He couldn't get closer to investigate. He couldn't do anything.

The realization drove through his stomach like a spear point. He had nothing. Not even a clue as to where they were going, which meant Deardryn was even more ahead of him than he realized.

The boat splashed into the water. Dimitri peeked his head out as Deardryn placed what appeared to be a golden pendant in Andrik's hand, then stepped back and watched as the boat took off—why were they heading south?

For a long time, she remained where she was, eyes on the river. Eventually, the sound of the Sun guards' splashing oars grew distant, finally fading into silence. Only then did Deardryn melt into the shadows, leaving Dimitri alone on the riverbank.

Dimitri thudded his forehead against his boulder. He waited for the usual lash of anger to explode from his stomach, wash everything away in a wave of fury. But there was only a slow-building pressure: reaching up from his heart, squeezing around his throat, forcing him to his feet.

Dimitri didn't know how he found Patryclas. He just knew his feet carried him to the quiet corner where he and Sylas sat on the grass, shoulder to shoulder.

"Who's upset you now?" Patryclas asked, obviously amused as he played with Sylas's fingers.

Dimitri didn't trust himself to respond.

Patryclas glanced up at him, lips parted to speak. Then, his expression froze. Turning, he whispered something in Sylas's ear. Then, he rose from the grass, Sylas casting them a curious look as Patryclas ushered Dimitri to a secluded bench at the base of the hill.

"Dimitri," he said, voice firm as he sat beside him. "What's wrong?"

The pressure was building. It contracted inward from all sides, pressing against the layers of walls he'd built between himself and the world until they tilted inward, one by one.

"Dimitri."

He couldn't speak. Silence was all he had left.

Patryclas gripped his shoulders, green eyes demanding. "Dimitri, talk to me."

"I can't do anything right," Dimitri breathed. He didn't feel his lips move. "I couldn't be a legitimate child. I couldn't escape the Sun Kingdom on my own. I can't catch Deardryn, even though that was the one thing Anna asked of me. I am *powerless.*"

"Dimitri—"

"Don't tell me it will be all right," Dimitri said, snapping back into his body and jerking away from Patryclas's hand. "Don't tell me we can fix this or it's not that bad because it is, and I don't know what to do."

Dimitri's breath raked through his lungs. His mind spun. He couldn't regain control, he couldn't calm down—why couldn't he calm down?

"Dima, breathe," Patryclas ordered, placing his hand on Dimitri's back. "Put your head between your knees—that's it. Now inhale."

Dimitri sucked in a long, deep breath, his lungs screaming as they stretched.

"Now exhale."

Dimitri deflated, feeling the life woosh out of his body. Over and over. All he could do was cling to Patryclas's words because there wasn't anything left inside him not broken or frayed or bleeding.

He wanted to crawl out of his body. Just wanted everything to stop.

But slowly, he could breathe without instruction. He could breathe.

Dimitri leaned back against the bench and touched his face, his shaking fingers coming away damp. He was completely, utterly exposed. And there wasn't enough left of him to care.

"Has this happened before?" Patryclas asked, his hand still on Dimitri's back.

"Once," Dimitri rasped. At Gritta's. Dimitri shoved down that same expanding glow in his stomach.

"Everything is so big," he said, wiping his nose on his sleeve. "Every emotion, every drop of anger is so big that I can't fucking take it anymore."

Patryclas rubbed his chest; the exact spot Dimitri's own chest ached. Crystal spare him.

Dimitri expected the guilt to pull him under. Instead, the ache seemed to fade, just a little bit.

Before he could question it, Patryclas opened his arms.

Dimitri stared.

"What?" Patryclas asked, slightly teasing. "Have you never been hugged before?"

Dimitri's very being went still.

Analia had hugged him when he left the Ash Kingdom. Deardryn's younger sister Saura had hugged him once when he was small. But that was only because he'd barreled into her, sobbing with terror as Pryanth chased him through the corridors. Beyond that?

"Well, no wonder," Patryclas murmured.

Dimitri stiffened, but he didn't fight as Patryclas wrapped his arms around him.

"I don't need your pity," he mumbled.

"I know," Patryclas said. "But you can have my affection."

"I don't want it."

"Of course you don't. You've never been shown how wonderful it can feel."

Dimitri started to protest.

"It wasn't your fault, Dima," Patryclas murmured, stroking his hair.

Dimitri flinched as if struck.

"Whatever you've done in the aftermath, it doesn't justify being isolated as a child. You've been paying for other people's mistakes all your life. But it was never your fault."

No one had ever said that to him before. And those words had something dangerous, something fragile, deep in his chest finally collapse.

Dimitri squeezed his eyes shut, unable to choke back the sob that clawed up his throat.

It was so much easier to blame the world for the rejection, hatred. But no matter how hard he tried to deny it, he knew he was the common thread. He was the problem.

He was the one that was unlovable.

Yet, love was all he felt as Patryclas held him tight. And it destroyed him all the same.

Dimitri didn't know how long it took for him to catch his breath. He gingerly pulled away, the tenderness in Patryclas's eyes feeling like a bruise across his heart. But Patryclas ducked his head, not allowing Dimitri to look away.

"All those big emotions, Dimitri?" he said. "They're not all bad. That's why we keep them around. Even if the good ones are the hardest to let in sometimes."

"I want this one to go away," Dimitri mumbled.

"All right, then," Patryclas said. "You have your first answer. Now you just need to figure out what will make it do so."

Dimitri sniffed. Patryclas squeezed his shoulder, letting his hand linger.

As Dimitri sat with that little gesture of comfort, all he could hear in his mind was six weeks. Six more weeks, and all of this would be taken away from him. The acceptance, the affection, delivered so forthrightly he had no choice but to accept them. No choice but to relax into Patryclas's touch.

No, he did have a choice. The choice to enjoy this feeling while it lasted.

And as Patryclas kissed the top of his head, Dimitri thought maybe it would be safe to do so.

PART 3:
SHOOTING STAR

Chapter 38

In the days that followed what Aaron dubbed "the magnificent display of flame and rage," Analia was consumed by training. Not just with Branten, but Aaron as well.

At first, Aaron tried to follow a standard Ash Royal training regiment, starting with lighting a candle. Analia, in turn, summoned a ball of flame that reduced said candle to a pool of bubbling wax—which was oddly satisfying.

After that, each lesson started with a release of magic, Aaron surmising she accumulated magical buildup far faster than average. The releases were nowhere near as intense as that first day on the lakeside, but it still left her shaking in the aftermath, her body searing with rage before mercifully ebbing to more tolerable levels. Then, her true training began.

"It's the same exercise as the one I taught you in your bedroom," Aaron said, lounging against the same large rock from before. "Take a pinch of magic, hold it, release. Except this time, there's no adjusting the initial size. You either match what I show you, or you put it out and try again."

"What do you mean, show me?" Analia asked, seated on the rocks across from him.

Aaron picked up a stone the size of a child's fist and presented it to her like a piece of fine jewelry. Analia rolled her eyes.

"It's precision work," Aaron said, tossing the rock into the water with a splash. "If you're going to master your magic, you need to master how much you draw forth. Summoning a massive flame and then shrinking it down to what you need wastes too much time. It's a reaction. To win, you need to act."

"Makes sense."

"All right then." Aaron sifted through the rocks beside him, coming up with a pebble the size of his thumbnail. "Your first model."

He passed Analia the pebble. Then, he folded his hands in his lap, staring out across the lake with a look of serenity.

"That's it?" Analia asked. "No poking or prodding?"

"You need to learn how to call on your magic without your temper," Aaron said. "It's a crutch—an extremely effective crutch, but not an infallible one. Although," he added with a smirk, "if it's poking and prodding you're after, you only need to ask."

"It's been that long for you, huh?"

"My wicked shooting star, what a scathing tongue you have."

"Something tells me you can handle it."

"Depends," he said, leaning forward. "What part of me is handling it?"

Analia licked her lips. "What part would you like?"

Aaron's eyes dipped to her mouth. "You're stalling."

He looked away, the momentary intensity in his gaze sending tingles across Analia's skin. Shaking her head, she tunneled deep inside herself, imagining her hand pinching a spark from the pool.

Immediately, her flames roiled. They thrashed against her control, demanding more be set loose.

"Too big," Aaron said.

Analia blinked down at the ball of flame that filled her palm. She cursed, quickly extinguishing it.

"Try again," Aaron invited, as if they had all the time in the world.

Analia took a deep breath through her nose. Then, she reached for her flames once more. Maybe if she couldn't stop the excess flame from escaping, she just had to compensate for it.

"Too small," Aaron said.

The flame at the tip of Analia's finger was the size of a pinhead.

"You're not helping," she complained, extinguishing her flame.

"Don't let them win," was his only response.

Attempt after attempt, pinch after pinch, Analia exposed herself to her magic. Every time, Aaron informed her how it was too big, too small, far too large.

Analia tried everything she could think of to bend her magic to her will. But her flames weren't something to be tamed. She'd learned that on her wedding night.

Analia tensed—no. She had to let her magic flow. She couldn't fight it. Not when releasing everything she had in a mighty eruption, and not when pinching a tiny candle flame.

Analia squeezed her eyes shut. Then, she finally sank into her magic.

Wave after scorching wave slammed into her, but she didn't resist. She was a piece of driftwood tossed around on a stormy sea, feeling the rage but not allowing it to spill free.

She waited until she became accustomed to the swirling heat. Then, she thrust out her hand. She took what she needed, letting the rest wash over her.

"Perfect."

Analia opened her eyes. And in the center of her palm, right beside her pebble, was an identically sized ball of midnight flame.

Analia let her flame wink out, looking up to the sky now sparkling with stars. Had it really taken her all day just to do that? Crystal spare her, she didn't know how she was going to survive this.

Analia was about to voice the thought aloud when she spotted the radiant look on Aaron's face. And exhausted, she reached for her flames to do it again.

Aaron was quick to flip-flop Analia's schedule. Branten graciously agreed to switch to night training—especially since that meant he could raid Aaron's dinner table whenever he wanted. Aaron, in turn, shadowjumped Analia to the lakeside every dawn, allowing her to burn through her buildup first thing in the morning instead of trying to contain it until the end of the day.

Despite not being a morning person, he never complained about their arrangement. Even when she told him they could train later, all he said was, "Keep holding your flame."

As the days went on, Analia slowly eased into her magic. But she still felt a twinge in her gut every time she reached for it. It wasn't the sense of loathing that came with Pryanth's memory, but something else. Something she couldn't put her finger on.

"We're being summoned," Aaron announced one morning.

Analia paused her attempt at his latest challenge: radiating magic. He'd told her to think of it as the heat from the flame, allowing her to constantly release small amounts of magic without conjuring a spark—although it did seem to increase her body temperature.

"Who's summoning us first thing in the morning?" she asked, unfolding herself from the ground to join him on his rock.

"Laness." Aaron pushed back his sleeve, revealing his new enka bracelet. "Apparently, Surce has news that requires immediate attention."

"Sounds exciting."

Aaron's eyes sparkled. He reached for her, his breath warm against her cheek as he offered a warning. Then, he pulled her into the shadows, reemerging in his kitchen.

For a room Aaron seemed to barely use, it was surprisingly inviting. Sunlight streamed in through a large window above the sink, lighting the wide-open space that was painted in soft neutrals. Laness, Branten, and Surce sat upon matching wooden stools around a central island, various tea-making supplies scattered across its surface. Mor stood at the wood stove, tending a sizzling pan.

"I didn't know you cooked," Analia said, moving to take a seat at the island.

"I'm the only one allowed to touch the stove," he replied.

"'Allowed'?"

"You want to explain that one, brother?" Branten snickered as Aaron returned from hanging up their jackets.

To Analia's surprise, Aaron flushed. "I got distracted."

"You fell asleep on the couch!" Laness exclaimed.

"Like I said, distracted."

"Long enough for your creation to be reduced to charcoal," Surce murmured.

Aaron scowled as he came to sit beside Analia.

"This bastard filled the entire house with smoke," Branten chortled. "Even after we opened every window and door, the house still reeked for days."

Laness said, "We locked him inside until the smell was gone so he could think about what he'd done."

"Oh really," Analia said, swiveling on her stool to face Aaron. "So, all the food when it was just the two of us?"

"Provided by many of the restaurants in my kingdom," Aaron sighed, reaching for the teapot. He filled the two remaining mugs on the island, Branten's eyes widening in horror as he slid the first toward Analia.

"Don't look like that, Branten," Analia chided. "Now we know that Aaron isn't good at everything after all."

Branten threw back his head in a laugh. "What do you mean, 'after all'?"

"We have a *list*," Laness agreed.

"Don't pretend like you two are any better in the kitchen than I am," Aaron accused.

Laness and Branten exchanged an affronted look, then raised their mugs at the same time.

"That does *not* count," Mor said, not even glancing at them.

Aaron jabbed a triumphant finger. Laness and Branten protested over one another.

"And with that stimulating debate concluded," Surce said, raising her voice slightly, "we have more important things to discuss."

Laness and Branten begrudgingly fell silent as Surce pulled a folded tapestry from a pocket in her gown. She unfolded it on the island before them, revealing an image no larger than a place mat. The threads shimmered with a metallic silver sheen, the numbers "19, 20, 1, 18," forming a square in the tapestry's center.

"Am I supposed to know what that is?" Branten asked, squinting down at the image.

"It looks like a vault door," Laness said.

Aaron looked as though his tea had been turned to lemon juice. "Are you saying the scroll has been there the entire time?" he asked.

"Perhaps," Surce said. "Or potentially a clue to its location. For how big of a discovery this could be, the size of the tapestry is rather off-putting."

"But what is it?" Branten asked.

Mor abandoned his pan to take a quick look at the tapestry. His eyebrows rose. "The Royal vaults?" he asked, returning to the stove.

Branten swore. Aaron stirred a spoonful of honey into his mug, hard enough tea sloshed over the sides.

"What am I missing here?" Analia asked, gently taking the spoon from his hand.

Accalon had taken her to see her own family's vaults on numerous occasions, telling her she needed to appreciate the privilege she had. They had wound through the cold, dark catacombs beneath the Ash Castle, Accalon unlocking the various steel doors to reveal the riches within. Nothing that would have her glower into her tea like a certain Star Royal was doing.

"The Star Royal vaults are not unlike any other Royal vault," Surce explained. "Located beneath the Council Building, they contain the majority of Aaron's family's wealth."

"And they can only be accessed with council approval," Aaron muttered.

"You don't have unrestricted access to your own possessions?" Analia asked.

"Well," Aaron conceded, "I could very easily kill them and take the keys. But my ancestors wanted some degree of a safeguard to dissuade reckless behavior. If one would be desperate enough to kill said council to get into the vault, that would create a whole new host of problems that many don't want to deal with."

"But the scroll can't be in there," Laness said, tapping a corner of the tapestry. "It's far too obvious of a hiding spot."

"Although it was our awareness of that very fact that prevented us from searching there," Mor pointed out.

"That and the councilmen," Aaron muttered.

"What do you have against the councilmen?" Analia asked.

"I hate the councilmen," Aaron complained. "They're all pompous pains in my ass."

"More importantly," said Surce, "they are not fond of you."

Analia shot Aaron a look. "What did you do?"

"Nothing!" Aaron protested, just as Branten laughed, "What *didn't* he do?"

Aaron threw a tea bag at him.

"While Aaron has a gift for charming those he likes," Surce explained, "he is utterly incapable of charming those he does not."

"He's great at infuriating anyone and everyone, though," Laness said.

"Especially the councilmen," Branten agreed. "They just love it when he pretends to listen to their advice, just to completely disregard it whenever the family disagrees."

"Which is frequently," Mor clarified, his golden hand struggling to open a jar of jalapeños. Analia moved to help, but Branten caught her eye and gave a minuscule shake of his head. Mor readjusted his grip, the lid coming free with a pop.

Branten beamed. He quickly schooled his expression as Mor glanced back at Aaron, who mumbled, "I need a buffer. Someone they actually like."

"Which means Mortie or Surce," Branten said, putting his elbows on the island. Surce promptly pushed them off.

"You're forgetting an option," she said.

Aaron tensed. Branten and Laness swapped a look. Analia looked down at her mug, inhaling warm, peppermint steam. Her uncle's favorite.

"You mean me," she said.

"The council has been wanting to meet you," Aaron admitted.

Analia wasn't surprised. "In that case," she mused, "I would certainly sweeten the deal."

"It's going to take more than just your presence," Mor told her. "Access to the vaults is the only bargaining chip they have. They're not going to give it up easily."

"Fair enough." Analia rose to help Mor pass out plates. "And I'm assuming even with Aaron granting me permission to stay here, the council is prepared to create friction if they don't like me?"

No one responded. Analia wasn't fazed. It was no different than dealing with the Ash council.

"When's the earliest I can meet with them?" she asked.

"Tomorrow," said Aaron flatly.

Mor's fingers brushed hers as he passed her a plate. She looked up at him, reading the quiet concern in his hazel eyes. Not for the mission, but her.

"Tomorrow it is," she said.

She flashed Mor an appreciative look, then moved to hand her plate off to Surce. With that decision made, the conversation was quickly dropped.

Despite the unease around the following day, Aaron's family bounced back fast. Analia discovered Mor was an incredible cook, to the point she, Branten, and Laness squabbled over who got the last omelet he'd stuffed with peppers, onions, and cheese. Even Aaron relaxed once he got some food in him.

Eventually, everyone cleared out for the day, leaving Analia alone with Aaron in the kitchen.

"Do you really think letting the councilmen see me will be enough for them to let you into the vault?" she asked, hopping up on the island.

"That depends," Aaron said, leaning against the opposite counter with a wicked grin. "How much are you willing to show them?"

Something ancient, something long-buried and dangerous stirred in Analia's chest. "Are you suggesting I climb into bed with one of the councilmen so you can get your way?"

"Of course not," Aaron scoffed. "Although some of them are rather good-looking, if lacking in mental faculties. Perhaps that could be your final hurrah to getting past Pryanth."

"Funny," Analia said, casually swinging her legs. "I would have thought you would want that badge of honor."

Aaron's eyes darkened. They trailed over her face, somehow feeling like a physical caress across her temples, her cheekbones, the curve of her lips.

"That's yours to bestow," he finally said.

Analia's pulse quickened. Before she could respond, Aaron pushed off the counter.

"Don't be mistaken," he said, closing the distance between them. "If you chose to give me that badge, I would take it in a heartbeat." He stepped between her thighs, bracing his hands on the island to either side of her and leaning in. "I, however, would be spending far more time proving I was worthy of said badge."

"And you are so confident that you could," Analia murmured, tilting her face to look at him.

"And you still haven't told me if I'll be using my fingers or my tongue."

Aaron lightly traced the outline of her lips with a finger.

Analia's breath caught.

And Aaron was gone.

He faded into the shadows, Analia just managing to catch something like panic on his face before he disappeared. Then, she was left alone on the island.

Analia brought a hand to her lips. She could still feel the vibration of his words in her bones, the heat of his gaze on her mouth.

It was just a game. So then why had her toes begun to curl?

Analia gave a sharp jerk of her head. Arrogant, lecherous Royal. She hopped off the island, brushing aside his words as she headed for the door.

Chapter 39

The Council Building was not what Analia was expecting.

The wide entryway was made from a brutal gray marble. A central staircase made from sparkling glass twisted up to a second-floor balcony, surrounded by metal hallways that carved deeper into the building. The overall look was surprisingly harsh, only enhanced by the line of heavy metal doors Aaron led her toward.

"I can't wait to hear their comments on my punctuality," he muttered, shoving through the door. He wore his usual black-and-blue jacket, his mood having improved marginally since they'd gone out to train that morning. Even now, Analia could feel his magic churn as they continued down a collection of narrow carpeted halls.

"I wonder," she said, toying with the dainty pearls stitched into her lilac gown. "Do you think if the councilmen fell off a sun dragon, they, too, would bounce?"

Aaron scoffed. "Is it wrong of me to hope they wouldn't?"

"Depends on who you're talking to."

The ghost of a smile flickered across Aaron's lips. "You're trouble."

"And you haven't told me what exactly the council is expecting from me."

"They just want to see the reason I exposed myself to Deardryn," Aaron said dismissively. "It has less to do with you than it does their ever-mounting dislike of me."

"Does that mean you told them I was important?"

Aaron's smile grew. "If you must know, smartass," he said, pushing open another door, "I told them I wasn't going to let you fight alone. Even if that meant not letting you die alone, either."

The air whispered out of Analia's lungs. Aaron didn't seem to notice as they rounded the final bend, entering a hall flanked by doors. A woman with short blonde hair and delicate features sat on a nearby wooden bench, her hazel eyes locking on Aaron as they approached.

"Are they inside?" he asked.

"They are, Your Majesty," she said, her voice a husky purr. Her eyes blatantly traveled down his face, his chest, all the way to his boots and up again.

Analia struggled not to roll her eyes. But as Aaron pushed open the door carved with an elegant 114, she could have sworn he gave the woman the barest hint of a wink.

Something like a bee sting burned behind Analia's sternum. Before she could figure out why, the door thunked shut behind her. And five sets of eyes immediately snapped to her.

The council room was lined by a wraparound counter. The thick maroon carpet and dark wood paneling should have made the room feel cozy, but the large rectangular table in the center of the room was anything but. Its sturdy, polished wood was painted black, the silver stars of the Star Kingdom sigil carved into its surface.

Seated around it, dressed in long black jackets with silver star-shaped buttons, were the councilmen. The two women and three men made no attempt to hide their shock as they watched her—although, was that hunger in the closest man's dark brown eyes? Before Analia could decide, he said, "You brought—"

"Councilman Jasper," Aaron purred, cutting him off.

Jasper scowled, accentuating the vicious scar that curled from his left temple down to his square jaw. "You arrive after all, Your Majesty."

"You make it sound as though I'm late," Aaron said, taking his time as he guided Analia toward the head of the table. "Seeing as though this meeting can't start without me, I'd say you're all extremely early."

Crystal spare them, Surce was right. Analia tried to hide her dread—although there wasn't a drop of surprise in any of the councilmen's expressions.

"We were only wondering where you've been," said a man with a drooping silver mustache.

"Well," Aaron said, "I've spent most of my life in this kingdom, but I recently ventured into the Sun Kingdom, as you know, and then there was that brief stint in Ash—"

"Today," Jasper cut in, exasperated.

"Ah."

Aaron raised a brow at a man with shaggy brownish-blond hair, seated to the right of the head chair. He quickly rose, scrambling to find a new seat.

"Well," Aaron said, helping Analia into the vacated seat before taking his own, "I was bringing you a gift."

Aaron spread his arms. The councilmen's eyes flashed back to Analia, taking in her expression, scrutinizing her features. Analia studied them in return.

She could sense all five of them had a magic network. The woman across from her was the youngest of the group by far, with long auburn hair and azure eyes. Beside her was the shaggy haired man struggling to hide his wonder, followed by Jasper, Samuel, and finally a Blessed woman old enough to have wrinkles etched into her dark brown forehead. All closed doors, and Aaron was only nailing them shut.

But Accalon had trained her for this moment. He'd brought her into the Council Chamber as a child, showing her how silence and questions and details could be wielded as deftly as any weapon or healing salve.

This was her battlefield. And Analia intended to win.

Analia let the silence hang for a few heartbeats. Then, she turned to the shaggy-haired man. "And I thought Ash council meetings were hostile."

The councilman let out a surprised laugh. "Princess Analia," he said, "you have no idea."

Ignoring the older councilmen's rigid postures, he reached a hand across the table toward her. "Councilman Iphen, at your service."

"It's a pleasure," Analia said, clasping his hand.

"Oh, the pleasure is all mine," Iphen said, lightly squeezing her fingers before releasing her. "I've been wanting to meet you for some time now—"

"Yes," said Jasper. "We were starting to wonder if we ever would."

"I'm honored by your interest," Analia said, holding his icy stare. "But forgive me, I've only caught half your names."

She turned her back on him, offering the auburn-haired woman an apologetic smile. Just as she hoped, the woman introduced herself as Jeneva, prompting the rest of the table to follow suit: Iphen, Jasper, Samuel, Marion.

"I know you all must be incredibly busy," Analia said once they were done. "I'm hoping I won't take up too much of your time. But before we get to that, I'm sure you're wondering what I'm doing here in the first place."

"The thought has crossed my mind once or twice," Iphen said, casually tipping back in his seat.

"If once or twice means constantly," Jeneva said, shoving him back down.

"Yes," Jasper said, "I'm sure you have quite the tale to spin."

If only she didn't.

Turning to Aaron, she asked, "Where do you think I should begin?"

Aaron fingered the embroidered threads of his jacket. "I've personally found starting at the beginning to be incredibly helpful."

Analia kicked him under the table. Turning back to the council, she took a breath to speak. But her words lodged in her throat.

This wasn't some random story. It was hers. Her mangled, bloody pieces they demanded she scatter on the table for them to examine and dismiss as they pleased.

Aaron's foot found hers under the table. She shot him a quick look, but his face remained completely unreadable. Even as he sent a ribbon of magic to stroke the back of the hand she had clenched around her chair like an icy thumb.

Calm. Reassuring. Believing in her.

Not giving herself time to think, Analia began.

She talked about her life in the Ash Kingdom: her lack of magic, the rejection and shame, every wonderful detail she could remember about her uncle. Aaron rested his knee against hers as she reached his death, but Analia's voice only cracked slightly as she moved into her time in Sun. She was careful to only provide the necessary details regarding her magic. And by the time she reached her return to Ash, her coronation, and Aaron's offer and stipulations, Jeneva was wiping her own tears, Iphen's jaw was slack, and Marion gave her knee a single pat.

"I fled my uncle's kingdom," Analia said, "fully understanding I would never be able to speak of what I saw. That I might never be able to leave at all. But I've spent the past two months acquainting myself with this kingdom, and I hope you believe me when I say I have no intention of harming it."

Analia finally sat back in her seat, trying not to sag. She hadn't intended to talk for so long. But once the floodgates had opened, the entire story had tumbled out.

Now, no one spoke at all. The council only stared, expressions ranging from shock to awe.

"Are you aware," Jasper finally said, "that we have executed every other foreigner to discover our kingdom?"

"That's enough," Aaron said, terrifyingly quiet. At some point, he'd moved to the counter, where a pitcher of water sat. He filled a glass, setting it before Analia as he retook his seat.

Analia took a grateful sip, her throat still scratchy as she went on. "From what His Majesty has told me, none of those people had any reason to be loyal to the kingdom, and every reason to escape."

"And how are we supposed to know you don't fit that very mold?" Samuel asked.

Analia could practically feel him squeezing one of her pieces between his fingers.

"Samuel, were you not listening?" Iphen demanded. "She already fought for this kingdom in the Sun temple when she risked her life to retrieve the scroll."

"A scroll we still have no information on," Jasper interjected.

Iphen flashed Analia an exasperated look. Analia let her lips twitch before composing herself once more.

Jeneva piped up, "She also had three weeks in the Sun Kingdom and two months in Ash to reveal His Majesty, and she didn't."

"And," Marion said, folding her gnarled hands on the tabletop, "she swore on the Crystal to renounce her kingdom and never swear fealty to any of the other five kingdoms."

"Which doesn't include this one," Analia finished.

She hadn't noticed Aaron's clever wording until retelling it—although she hadn't mentioned how he hadn't forced her to actually swear the oath, ensuring she could return to Ash if that was what she wanted.

"I am more than happy to swear whatever oath you like that I mean no harm to this kingdom," Analia said. "I have no intention of being a threat. But Deardryn is."

She glanced to Aaron, who gave a resigned nod. Analia proceeded to explain everything they knew of Deardryn's plans and their theory that she was hunting the Crystal.

"This isn't a vague, petty scheme," Analia said, leaning forward. "It is a real, immediate threat to the peace that has been cultivated in this kingdom for centuries, which is why we need to get into that vault."

"Why are we only being informed of this now?" Marion asked.

"Enlightening discoveries were only recently made," Aaron said smoothly.

Analia sank back in her seat, hoping that was a sign he was finally stepping in. Jasper, however, kept his dark eyes fixed on her.

"Which discoveries are you referring to, Your Majesty?" he asked. "The fact that this princess proved herself capable of enemy infiltration, assassination, and successful conviction of her own father? Why should we believe that behavior won't follow her here?"

"Don't threaten my life and it won't have to," Analia said flatly.

The corner of Aaron's mouth quirked. "Seems like a reasonable request to me."

"Don't try to deny her being here puts us at a greater risk," Samuel said.

Guilt sank iron-tipped claws into Analia's stomach. Especially as Aaron didn't disagree.

Marion added, "You also failed to inform us of Deardryn's threat to us until now. And yet, you are asking for our trust? How are we to know there isn't more hidden information fueling this request? Information that might be leading you to make one of your historical risky decisions that could result in even more harm befalling this kingdom."

Marion's calm rationale sliced deeper than any of Jasper's or Samuel's ridicules. Judging from the brief tension in Aaron's mouth, he realized he had dug himself into that hole. But he raised his chin.

"I know none of us are particularly fond of each other," he said. "But we all share the same goal of protecting this kingdom. And every one of you knows I would do anything to do so. Even if that means destroying myself.

"I wouldn't have brought Analia to our home if I had any reservations. I know that despite this, you still look at her and see an outsider, a princess of another kingdom and an inherent threat to our own. But I am telling you I trust her explicitly, and all of you should understand what kind of weight that statement holds.

"It's with that same gravity that I tell you, if you truly sit here with the kingdom's safety in your hearts, the best way to ensure that is by letting us into the vault."

Analia stared at Aaron as if seeing him for the first time. The arrogant, smart-mouthed warrior. The flirtatious, achingly compassionate friend. And the passionate king willing to do whatever it took to accomplish what he thought was right.

A man whose scars marred his body on the inside and out, yet he still trusted her. Explicitly.

Analia barely registered the other councilmen agreeing to confer on the matter. Inviting them to stay in the attached suites instead of jumping home and back, since they didn't know when they'd come to a decision. She only saw Aaron nod once before rising to his feet.

Their eyes locked. Analia felt a thrum, as though the lowest string on her harp had been plucked deep in her gut.

"Your Highness!" Iphen popped into her line of sight, sketching a deep bow. "I would be honored to escort you to your suite."

Analia tore her gaze from Aaron. "Yes," she said. "That would be wonderful."

She rose from her seat, allowing Iphen to grip her by the elbow and lead her out the door. As he led her down the hall, she was painfully aware of the softness of his hand, no hint of callouses against her skin. She glanced back, expecting to see Aaron following.

But he had dropped down on the bench beside the blonde woman. He leaned toward her, whispering something in her ear that had her giggling and playfully pushing him back with a hand on his chest. A hand that lingered there as she said something in response. Aaron smirked, his eyes dipping to her mouth.

The sting behind Analia's sternum resurfaced with a vengeance. She looked away, letting Iphen pull her around the corner.

Iphen led her through narrow halls; up curving stairs; through so many doors Analia couldn't keep track—not that she tried to. Iphen didn't seem to mind, though. He talked enough for the two of them, interspersing his admirations of her story with random facts about the rooms they passed.

He honestly wasn't half bad. He was just so… bright. He was cheerful, carefree in ways Analia didn't think she ever could be. Not after everything she'd seen, the subsequent darkness in her heart she had thought she recognized in Aaron.

But perhaps Aaron's own darkness made him crave the light. Maybe he wanted soft, pretty blonde women who smiled easily and flirted unashamedly. After everything he'd been through, could she begrudge him that?

Iphen paused before a seemingly random door on the top floor. "This will be your room for the time being," he said. "His Majesty's private suite is across the hall."

Analia nodded, thanking him for the escort. He promised to retrieve her the moment they came to a decision, assuring her he knew the council would see reason. Analia plastered a smile on her face the entire time. But the moment she slipped inside her room, her expression fell.

Analia barely spared her tasteful suite a second glance. She sank down on her bed, her head bowing forward and into her hands.

She didn't know how long she sat like that. It wasn't until she heard the door across the hall open and close that she even realized what she'd been waiting for.

Analia's shoulders slumped.

She'd thought Aaron would come to see her, debrief on the meeting at the very least. But he didn't.

She knew she should just go knock on his door. But she was completely unwilling to find out if he wasn't alone.

Analia sighed, sinking back against her pillows. She had just started to think that maybe, despite all of Aaron's smiles and friendliness and charm, he was just as lonely as she was.

But perhaps Aaron liked being alone. Maybe she could, too.

Chapter 40

T he sun slowly sank outside Aaron's window as he sharpened his daggers, waiting for the council to come to a decision.

Despite all odds, that had been one of the tamest meetings he'd ever sat through. Jeneva rarely gave him problems—she might be the only one he liked—and Iphen was more of a nuisance than a threat. He wasn't worried about either of them. No, the deciding vote would come from Marion, and as usual, Aaron had no idea what to expect from her.

Even if they did agree, he wouldn't take the credit. That belonged to Analia and Analia alone.

Gods, she'd been mesmerizing in that room. She'd mentioned to him once how her uncle had a gift for holding people's attention, and clearly, she'd inherited that talent. He just wished he had a chance to tell her so.

After leaving Vivienne, Aaron had passed Iphen in the halls, the councilman saying Analia wished to rest until they were summoned. He wasn't surprised, the poor girl had been poked and scrutinized for hours. But that didn't stop him from immediately rolling off his bed the moment he heard a knock on Analia's door.

Aaron entered the hallway moments after Analia. He tried to catch her eye, but Iphen pointedly stepped between them, his back to Aaron.

"I've been sent to inform you we've come to a decision," he told her.

Aaron's brows crept up. Analia didn't look at him as she asked, "That being?"

"I'm to escort you inside the vault immediately."

"Really?" Analia brightened marginally. "I'm glad we were able to win over Marion."

Clever girl. Aaron offered her a wink, but she didn't notice as Iphen ushered her down the hall, the councilman not so much as acknowledging Aaron. And Analia didn't look back.

Something cold and heavy lodged in Aaron's stomach. He headed after the pair, quickly coming up on Iphen's other side and leaning in.

"Never turn your back on your king again," he whispered as he passed. He didn't bother checking Iphen's reaction. He didn't want to look at the man at all as he led the way back to the council room, that cold weight in his gut growing heavier with each step.

Marion was waiting for them outside when they arrived. With a silent nod to Aaron, she led the group to the end of the hall—which appeared to be a dead end. Yet, the moment she pressed her palm to the wall, the image shimmered. Slowly, the magic peeled back, revealing the hidden door and stairwell beyond.

Together, the group descended the dark, gloomy stairwell to the Royal vaults. And all Aaron could focus on was the murmured conversation behind him.

He'd thought Analia had been unusually friendly with Iphen during the council meeting, but he'd assumed she was trying to make a good impression. Now that he thought about it, though, Analia's eyes had continually gone back to Iphen while she was talking. And Aaron would never forget how she had walked out that council door with him, no looking back. Just as she'd done in the hallway.

Finally, they reached the bottom of the stairs. Marion pushed open the ancient stone door before them, leading the way into the antechamber beyond.

A faint glow emanated from the purplish stone, casting most of the tiny chamber in shadows. Vivienne lounged behind a carved wooden desk, the single door behind her etched with spiraling numbers. The moment they stepped inside, her eyes found Aaron.

"Your Majesty," she said, bowing her head. "It's a pleasure to see you in my domain."

Aaron forced a smirk, leaning against her desk. "Vivienne. How many times must I tell you it's a crime the council is hiding you from the light of day?"

He knew he was laying it on thick. But Vivienne had always been a drunken fool on compliments, and this time was no different.

"I suppose you'll just have to come visit me more often," she said, looking up at him through her lashes. "I'm sure you can think of an excuse or two to have the council let you in."

Her fingers rubbed along the length of her pen. Aaron tried not to shudder. He had no problem remembering those fingers running down his arm after the council meeting. But he forced his smirk to grow as he stepped back, allowing an openly judging Marion to come forward and authorize his visit.

Turning to lean against the desk, Aaron let his gaze skate over Analia and Iphen, coming to examine an extremely fascinating chip in the wall. So fascinating, he barely registered Iphen's honey tone. He certainly didn't hear Analia's responding laugh—laugh?

Aaron's heart slammed to a stop. He quickly turned his back to them once more, gripping the desk so hard his fingers ached.

"What?" Vivienne asked, self-consciously touching her hair.

Aaron didn't respond. He couldn't respond. Because Analia. Just. Laughed.

He'd never heard her do that before. His mind couldn't stop replaying it, obsessing over the way it bubbled out of her, as if she hadn't expected Iphen to say anything that could—

Aaron felt as though he'd been sent into freefall.

He'd been acutely aware of the possibility when he brought Analia to his kingdom that she might never reciprocate the emotion rapidly building in his chest. What he hadn't considered was her finding someone else.

"Your Majesty?" Vivienne asked.

But Analia had every right to make that choice. That was the entire reason he'd gotten himself tangled in this emotional turmoil.

But Crystal spare him, it had been torturous enough watching her walk around with Pryanth's pendant, wondering if a part of her still harbored feelings for a dead man. How was he supposed to come to terms with, let alone survive, watching her give herself to someone else?

"Aaron?" Vivienne asked uncertainly.

But this wasn't about him. If he truly cared about her, he should be able to support her, no matter what her decision was. Even if the sound of Iphen murmuring to her grated against every single one of his nerves—

"Is there something on my face?"

Aaron's hands clenched around the desk. Then, he let instinct take over.

"Apologies," he crooned, leaning in close, tucking a stray lock of hair behind Vivienne's ear. "I must have lost myself in possible excuses."

Marion snorted. Aaron's eyes darted to her, then back to Vivienne. "I don't think she approves," he said confidentially.

Vivienne tossed her hair. Marion made to move past the desk, but Vivienne waved her off with a breezy hand.

"Don't worry about that, Councilwoman," she said, rising to her feet and pulling out her own ring of keys. "I can take care of them."

Iphen made to protest, but Aaron harshly reiterated the message. Analia touched his arm and murmured something to him, then stepped away. Aaron leaned back as Analia approached, but Vivienne still managed to stroke his cheek before twirling away. She strutted over to the door, pressing a purple-glowing palm to the center of the number spiral, missing the glare Analia shot her back—what did that mean?

Aaron followed Analia through the door, frost crackling through his veins.

The vault was carved out of a large, subterranean rock. Chunks of garnet sparkled in the turquoise light, cast by the hundreds of tiny glowworms inching across the ceiling and walls.

Aaron caught a glimpse of the crease between Analia's brows, undoubtedly triggered by the abundance of magic fields. He opened his mouth, just as Vivienne's hand curled around his arm.

Aaron fought the urge to shove her off. Instead, he kept his voice steady as he answered her countless questions, his eyes scanning the doors. No, no, no—there. 19, 20, 1, 18.

"This is it," Aaron said, cutting her off midsentence. "My apologies, Vivienne, but you're not permitted to enter."

Vivienne pouted. "But *she is?*"

Analia's face was uncharacteristically blank.

"She's nonnegotiable," Aaron said firmly.

Vivienne made to protest more, but Aaron gently extracted his arm and stepped away.

"Oh, don't do that," he teased, nudging up the corner of her mouth with his thumb. "You know you're stunning when you smile."

Vivienne beamed, bouncing back fast enough Aaron had whiplash on her behalf. By the time she tossed him the keys and sashayed out of the chamber, she seemed perfectly unperturbed.

"Definitely no one like her," Aaron murmured.

"You should tell her that when you meet up for one of your excuses," Analia said casually, taking the keys from his hand.

Aaron's head snapped toward her. Before he could respond, Analia jammed the key into the hexagonal crystal knob and shoved open the steel door. Just to reveal an empty chamber.

"No," Aaron muttered, prowling through the door. "You cannot be serious."

He couldn't have subjected himself to the council, Vivienne's relentless touches, and Iphen's *Iphen-ness,* just for an empty chamber.

"Aaron, look," Analia said, kneeling before what he'd thought was a random crack in the center of the floor. "There's a magic field."

Analia dug her nails into the stone, scrabbling for a hold. Aaron moved to help her, but the stone wouldn't budge.

"Use your magic," she said.

Aaron wreathed his hand in starlight and pressed it to the stone. Immediately, there came a click. The stone easily slid aside. And Aaron and Analia stared down at the folded note tucked into the shallow hiding spot.

"Not the scroll, then," Analia said, sitting back on her heels.

Aaron didn't respond. He retrieved the note, his mind growing colder, colder, colder. Especially as he unfolded it, just to find a string of nonsensical symbols.

"What?" Analia asked.

Aaron was distantly aware of her fingers brushing his as she took the note, his hand falling limply to his side.

"A clue, then," Analia said, folding the note. "That's not terribly surprising. Surce figured as much after seeing the size of the tapestry."

"Yes," Aaron said, his voice cold to his own ears as he looked away. "Feel free to inform your councilman my wrath won't be destroying the building."

Analia's eyes narrowed. "What do you mean, 'my councilman'?"

Aaron could practically feel how thin the ice was beneath his feet. Yet, the words tumbled past his lips anyway.

"Analia, you've been flirting with him all day."

"Of course I was," Analia said, exasperated. "You practically told me to do so, and he was the easiest ally we could get. Far easier than you trying to force your way in here."

"So all of it was for what, the good of the team?"

"Yes. And I would have told you all of that if you had bothered to even look at me before going to fool around with your precious Vivienne."

"What?" Aaron fell back on his heels. "Analia, she's the vault keeper and was giving me bedroom eyes since I walked in."

"So, it's fine for you to flirt for information but not me?" Analia demanded, rising to her feet.

"If you'll recall," Aaron said, rising as well, "*she* was all over *me*. Do you think I enjoyed that? Getting pawed at, just so she could go home and brag to her friends about how she fucked the Star King because he needed information?"

Analia's hand flew to her phoenix pin. "You took her to bed?"

"I didn't even *touch* her."

Analia cringed. Aaron's heart ached.

"I knew she could be helpful with getting into the vault," he went on, stepping closer. "So, I sat with her and let her touch me while I tried to get as much information as I could. By the time I got back to my room—which she was not invited to—Iphen informed me you didn't want to be disturbed."

"I never said that," Analia said immediately.

Aaron made an exasperated noise. Of course Iphen had interfered.

"Regardless," he said, "I was planning on telling you before we met with the council once more, but you were always with Iphen. Avoiding me, turns out. There was no other time to talk to you alone before we reached the vault, and Vivienne was there, and I flirted with her to get her to kick the other council members out. It was *meaningless.*"

"Is that what bothered you?" Analia asked, stepping close enough Aaron could smell smoke and jasmine. "Not knowing if it was meaningless with Iphen?"

"It bothered me that it wasn't meaningless enough for you to *laugh* with him."

Analia stared, close enough her chest brushed his as she inhaled. "What do you—"

"In all the time I've known you, Analia, I have never heard you laugh. I have never seen you happy enough to do so. But apparently, Iphen was all you needed."

He turned away, raking a hand through his hair. "You stood from that table today and didn't even hesitate to walk out with him because you felt safe enough to do so. Iphen is a gnat who's content if people kiss his ass until it shines, but he's safe. He will never know how it feels to have someone he loves deem him only worthy of sex because of the target on his back and the power in his veins."

Aaron snapped his mouth shut. He retreated across the chamber, bracing his palm against the stone.

He hadn't expected those words, shouldn't have let them pop out. But now, all he could see was Liss turning her face away. Sliding out of his bed and out the door.

Not worth it, not worth it, not worth it.

It took Aaron a moment to register the quiet footsteps. A few more to realize they weren't heading for the door like so many had. Instead, they came closer. And there was no trace of anger in Analia's voice as she asked, "Does that power look like this?"

Aaron didn't want to look. He didn't want to have to try and pull himself together, didn't want to see the pain in her eyes if he failed.

Analia's fingertips grazed his arm, so lightly he barely felt it through his jacket. As if she no longer knew if it was all right to touch him.

Something sharp dragged through Aaron's chest, and he turned to face her.

Analia raised her hand, flames sparking to life across her fingertips. Flames her kingdom had berated her for never having. Flames that never would have come to her if she hadn't lost her uncle. Flames that looked exactly like what Aaron was talking about.

"You didn't hesitate to summon your flames," he rasped.

Even as she'd relaxed into training, there was always a flash of hesitation across her face before she summoned her magic. But not this time.

"You know why?" she asked.

Aaron shook his head.

"Because I have an excellent teacher."

Analia extended her hand to him, flames licking down her hand. Hesitantly, Aaron wreathed his own hand in starlight, interlacing their fingers. Flames warming ice, ice cooling flames.

"So," she eventually said. "What I'm hearing is we both jumped to conclusions today."

Aaron's head drooped. "That sounds about right."

"Have you noticed we have a tendency of doing that?"

"Unfortunately. Something tells me we should stop."

"Well," Analia said, eyes on their hands, "I was actually thinking we could jump to just one more."

"And what would that be?"

Analia offered him a tentative smile. "That we're both sorry and forgive the other."

Aaron sighed, bringing their hands to his cheek. "My shooting star, that is always a safe place to jump to."

Analia kept quiet, leaning into him slightly. And Aaron wondered if she, too, were wishing it didn't have to hurt so bad when they landed.

Vivienne gave Aaron a little wave as he and Analia eventually returned to the antechamber. Aaron barely had time to acknowledge her before Marion was stepping forward, asking what they'd found. He reluctantly showed her the note, making a point to slip it back in his pocket when she was done examining it.

The council didn't need to worm their way into his investigation. Especially not the one that immediately headed for Analia.

Aaron tuned out Iphen's voice as he fussed, Analia's tone perfectly polite. Even as she wiggled her fingers at Aaron behind her back.

The tightness in his chest eased a fraction.

She knew him too well, understood him in ways no one else had. Certainly not Liss—oh gods.

Aaron felt like he'd been struck between the eyes. Quickly wrapping up his conversation with Marion, he reached for Analia, barely remembering to whisper a warning before shadowjumping away. All he could hear was fragments from their fight in the vault.

His icy tone. Him, refusing to let it go. Looking for reasons to be angry because that was one of the only emotions Liss knew how to make him feel.

That entire argument was him and Liss all over again. But Analia wasn't Liss.

That final thought bounced through his mind as his family gathered for a late dinner. They passed the note around the table, Surce saying it resembled an ancient code she should be able to crack in a few days.

Aaron folded and unfolded the note as everyone wandered off, his mind stuck on those three little words.

Analia wasn't Liss.

Which meant he knew what he had to do. Still, it was close to midnight before he had the courage to drag himself to his feet.

Chapter 41

Aaron stepped into the sitting room, mug of tea in each hand.

He knew Analia would still be awake. What he wasn't expecting was to find her sitting on the couch with Mor and Surce. Talking. Not about the Crystal or the note. Just talking, like they did this all the time.

A slow, heady wave of affection rolled through Aaron's chest. He was actually faintly disappointed when Surce and Mor noticed him in the doorway. The two excused themselves, Mor patting him on the back as he passed, Surce following with the most eloquent look of *Don't fuck this up,* he'd ever seen.

"Is that for me?" Analia asked, nodding to one of the mugs.

"It is," Aaron said, coming to sit beside her. "Consider it a peace offering."

Analia accepted the mug, smiling to herself as she breathed in the steam. "Peppermint. Did I ever tell you that was my uncle's favorite?"

"No," Aaron said. "Although that explains why you always smile when you drink it."

Analia's smile grew. "Aaron Stelingente, have you been watching me?"

"I already told you I'm counting your smiles."

"And you are suspiciously lacking one while saying that."

Aaron ran a hand through his hair. "That's because I have to tell you something..."

"And you can't uncurl your fingers?" she guessed.

Aaron nodded.

"Aaron," she said, "you don't have to tell me anything. I promise, we're all right."

"But I want to tell you," Aaron said. "I just..."

Aaron's fist tightened around his mug.

He knew exactly what he wanted to say. The words were right there, sliding up his throat, quivering on the tip of his tongue. But he didn't know how to set them free. He only knew how to swallow them back once the opportunity had passed.

"Aaron." Analia rested her free hand on his knee, her voice calm, precise. "What do you want to tell me?"

There it was. A direct question. A reason to speak. And as soon as the first word was out, they were all tumbling free.

"If you had asked me a year ago, I would tell you Liss was the only woman I've ever loved. We met around ten years after my mother died, when I was in the midst of drowning my grief in blood, sex, and alcohol. All of which wouldn't stop while I was with her.

"But that first night when we met at The Black Dragon, I thought it would be our only night. Yes, she was beautiful, could hold her ale with the best of them, and knew more ways to kill a man than I did, but I wasn't interested in anything beyond the physical.

"To avoid being completely crass, I'll just say we enjoyed that first night enough that one night became two. Then three, then five, and soon, we were consistently finding ourselves in each other's beds. We both reiterated numerous times it was only sex, nothing more.

"But at some point, we started talking before, after, in between. She told me how she'd inherited her family's weapons shop after her brother, the only family she had, was killed in the war with the humans. I told her bits and pieces about my mother. And slowly, we stopped reminding each other.

"Suddenly, I was going to visit her at work. She was coming to train with me. We were united in grief and rage. And unsurprisingly, we were caught in the other's blast zone."

Aaron stared down into his mug, the peppermint turning sour on his tongue. Analia lightly squeezed his knee.

"Our first fight happened when I slept through our dinner plans after a council meeting. She eventually stormed over here, found me asleep in my bed, and shook me awake. The two of us went back and forth until she finally yelled I had abandoned her just like her brother, at which point I pulled her into my bed and showed her otherwise."

Aaron winced, but Analia's grip didn't waver.

"I picked the next fight after she barely spoke to me for three days because she was busy with her shop, which also ended with us in my bed. And somehow, that became our routine. The sex was a large component, but more importantly, I think it was because all that grief and rage needed an outlet.

"By the time we reached the point where I let my magic loose around her, we were barely speaking unless we were fighting. So, when Liss walked out the door, saying the danger of my magic made our arrangement not worth it anymore, I let her go. But it wasn't long until I was desperately trying to get her back."

"Why?" Analia asked. There was no hint of judgment in her voice, but Aaron still couldn't look at her.

"Because for the ten years after my mom's death before I met Liss, I was numb. So horribly numb and hollow that I didn't even remember what it was like to feel. But Liss made me feel, more than I thought possible. And after living so long with nothing, just to find someone who melted the ice until my blood was boiling? I was terrified of giving that up.

"So, we talked, and we reverted back to our initial arrangement: just sex. But this time, I was in love with her, and the only thing I could think of when I was with her was her voice, telling me over and over again: not worth it. Always at its loudest when I would go to kiss her afterward, and she would always, without fail, turn her face away. Because I was not worth it."

Aaron's voice cracked on the final words. It had been decades, but he could still feel every single one of those tiny cuts to his heart. *Not worth it.* But it was Analia's hand falling away from his knee that had the lump rising in his throat.

Gods, what had he done? He'd just given her every reason to back away, repeat history all over again. He. Wasn't. Worth it.

Analia set her mug on the table before them. Aaron braced himself for the moment she stood, walked away.

Analia wrapped her arms around him, pressing her face to his shoulder. Aaron stared, uncomprehending.

But Analia didn't try to commiserate with him. She only hugged him tight, letting him know she was there, that he had something to hold on to if he needed.

Aaron felt as though he'd shed a heavy suit of mail. He finally brought his arms up and around her, letting smoke and jasmine brush the past away.

"There's not much to tell after that," he said, sounding more tired than he expected. "Liss and I naturally started drifting, and my family had a few choice words and ultimatums we can get into later. But eventually, Liss and I parted ways, and we haven't spoken since. And that's the full story. I just... I just wanted you to know it."

Aaron sank back against the couch, feeling as though a hand had reached straight through his chest and plucked out something vital. But still, Analia did not release him.

Gods, he'd almost forgotten the relief that came with someone else holding him together. He hadn't been lying when he'd told Analia he was a champion wallower; he just hadn't mentioned how he wallowed alone. That a companion in his grief was a comfort he didn't allow himself to have.

Even now, he kept his arms loose around her, neither drawing her closer nor preventing her from pulling away. And once again, Analia surprised him.

"The first time I smiled after my uncle's death," she said against his shoulder, "was in the Ring Room when you mocked me about my flame and rage. Today was the first time I laughed in I don't remember how long, and it wasn't because of Iphen. It was because he said something so absurdly saccharine that even though you were barely paying attention, it still shattered your unreadable mask into the most disgusted look I've ever seen."

Analia finally pulled back to look at him. And Aaron was taken aback by the fury in her eyes as she said, "You are worth more than sex, Aaron. So, so much more."

Aaron had never realized how badly he needed to hear someone else say it.

"My shooting star," he sighed, ruffling her hair.

Analia gave him a small smile. One that finally had Aaron confident he could disentangle himself without falling apart. Just as he made to gently nudge her away—

"Wait," Analia said, touching his arm. "Stay until you finish that?"

Aaron followed her gaze to his half-filled mug, resting beside hers on the table. A new kind of ache pierced his chest. Deep, delicious, warm.

Aaron retrieved his mug and sat back against the couch, drawing her with him. "Always."

The two stayed on the couch long past the point when both mugs sat empty on the table, bouncing from the Crystal to kingdom gossip without pause. Analia eventually rested her head on his shoulder, sending a flurry of tingles up Aaron's arm.

Yes, she definitely wasn't Liss. And as the two finally peeled themselves off the couch, that realization settled in his chest.

Chapter 42

The weeks after the Full Moon Festival flew by in a blur.

Dimitri threw himself into research and landmark visits, especially when Aaron's nymph friend shared their Crystal theory. He still hadn't found anything substantial—although hopefully, that meant neither had Deardryn. Still, the lack of information had Dimitri's insides slowly twisting tighter, to the point Patryclas pulled him aside in the hallway one night after dinner.

"Are you all right?" he asked.

Dimitri hesitated, absently rubbing the purple heart on the inside of his wrist. It was the first time the two had a moment alone together since the festival, Patryclas's schedule having become packed with his various kingly duties.

A part of Dimitri had been relieved. He didn't know how to face Patryclas after falling apart in front of him; after hearing Patryclas validate him and parts of his past he had no reason to know about.

Yet, staring up into Patryclas's face, the king didn't look at him any differently. If anything, the faint line between his brows was downright familiar.

Dimitri let his hand fall to his side. "I've been worse."

"You have, haven't you," Patryclas murmured.

Dimitri shrugged. Thinking the conversation was over, he made to slip around Patryclas and continue down the hall. But Patryclas put a hand on his shoulder.

"If you *do* get worse," he said, "even just by a little, I'm here. No matter what I'm doing or might be in the middle of. If you need me, you come find me. All right?"

Dimitri opened his mouth, but no words came out.

For so long, he'd only known words to leave a bruise. But somehow, Patryclas made them sound like everything he needed to hear.

Trusting Patryclas knew exactly what he was feeling, Dimitri gave a small nod, then quietly slipped down the hall.

As the days passed, Dimitri still made little headway on his investigation. Yet, instead of seeking out Patryclas, he found himself wandering down to Rayner's shop. Even when Rayner was busy with a client, he lounged on the couch, flipping through his poetry collection.

Despite hours of eavesdropping, he still didn't understand Rayner's business. Some people wanted full disguises. Others wanted a different nose. No one was given the same pricing. The only consistent thing was Rayner's consideration and enthusiasm as he talked about all colors, shapes, and sizes.

"My job isn't to transform people into a nonexistent universal beauty," he explained one day. "People come to me because they want a change. They want to leave something behind, or find something new, or to feel like the person they've always wanted to be. My job is to help them find that person, even just for a little while."

Eventually, Sabi started joining Dimitri on his visits to Rayner's shop. Rayner had apparently made quite the impression on her during the Full Moon Festival, and by the end of her first visit, the two had realized they shared a mutual enjoyment of using their Blessings on one another. Dimitri in turn enjoyed providing his unsolicited commentary.

Now, he lay on Rayner's couch, watching Rayner highlight Sabi's hair in front of his mirror.

"You know," Rayner said, running his fingers down a curl, "changing appearances, disguises? We could be unstoppable. We could *make* someone unstoppable."

"We could make a second Princess Marcella," Sabi enthused. "The original wouldn't know what to do with herself."

"What do you have against Marcella anyway?" Dimitri asked, reaching for his book on the floor.

"Me? Nothing."

"Ah," Rayner said, "so you have something *for* her."

Sabi blinked. "I what?"

"He's asking if you want to get in her pants," Dimitri called.

"What?" Sabi's eyes flew wide.

"Well hold on," Rayner said. "I was also asking if you want her to get in *your* pants."

"Why? Why would you ask that?"

"It's fine if you do," Rayner told her, fighting back a laugh. "Just as it's fine if you don't. I was just curious."

"Well, I... I guess I've never thought about it." Sabi cocked her head, puzzled. "I've never really thought about that in general. Princess Marcella simply intrigues me. No, don't!" Sabi batted Rayner's hand away as he started to darken her hair. "I like it."

Rayner shrugged, completely unfazed. "I must say," he said, moving toward the couch, "you know an awful lot about everyone."

He lifted Dimitri's feet, settling them on his lap as he sat down. Dimitri's eyes shot to him over his book, Rayner flashing that same secretive smirk from the Full Moon Festival. Dimitri rolled his eyes. But he didn't pull his feet away.

"I don't know everything," Sabi said, oblivious as she admired her reflection. "You overhear a lot working in the castle—although twenty-one years later and people still bewilder me."

"We do tend to follow a lack of logic," Rayner mused, playing with Dimitri's laces. "Especially those of us who live in castles."

Dimitri let his mind drift as the two went back and forth, Sabi eventually coming to sit on Rayner's other side. For perhaps the first time in his life, he felt perfectly content. Even as Rayner's hand wandered up his boot, his fingers brushing his calf—maybe especially so.

It was almost unnerving. But that could be the fact that, in a matter of minutes, he would have to pull away.

He had one last spot to check from his landmarks book: the statue of Darmanten, god of day and night, located in the town right outside the kingdom. He just wished he knew if Deardryn had already visited.

"Hello? Dimitri?"

Dimitri blinked as Sabi tapped the sole of his boot. "Quit it," he said, pulling his feet away. "I'm not an egg you can crack."

"Well, it'd be nice if I could crack an answer out of you."

Dimitri glanced to Rayner.

"Sabi asked if you were heading back to the castle with her," he drawled.

Dimitri wanted nothing more than to say yes. But he shook his head. "I have to go somewhere else."

"Where?" Sabi and Rayner asked in unison.

Dimitri hesitated. There was no doubt their help would be invaluable. But could he drag them into this mess and risk them getting charged with treason?

Rayner's hand slid up to Dimitri's knee. He looked up, taking in Rayner's glittering gaze, Sabi's look of mounting impatience. Maybe they should get a chance to decide for themselves.

"I have to check out the nearby statue of Darmanten," he said, sitting up. "You can come. If you want."

Dimitri braced himself for their questions.

"Well then hurry up," Sabi said.

Dimitri stared.

"I know where we can borrow some horses," Rayner said with a stretch.

"Borrow or steal?" Sabi demanded.

"They won't be missed."

Sabi huffed. She slid off the couch and marched toward the door, "Come on, then."

Rayner smiled to himself and rose. Dimitri pressed his fingertips to his own grin, then followed.

Finding the statue was quick and painless. According to Sabi, the town's main attraction was their flower maze, a massive garden that occupied both wetlands and dryer soil, allowing for a myriad of flowers to grow. It also had the statue of Darmanten standing in its center like a ten-foot sentinel.

"I've always wanted to see this!" Sabi exclaimed, jumping off her horse before it came to a complete stop. Hiking up her skirts, she marched into the snow-dusted garden, leaving Dimitri and Rayner to secure their horses to the garden fence.

"That woman is unstoppable," Rayner murmured.

Dimitri adjusted his leather gloves. "She likes architecture."

The two of them crunched after Sabi, who took great care to touch every frost-coated shrub in her path.

"This statue was the first statue of Darmanten ever constructed," she told them. "It's said Darmanten is the only god that exists in both our and the wraiths' pantheons of gods. Consequently, both folk have exerted a great effort to maintain the statue for millennia."

"Maybe that's why it's said to give off a tingle when you touch it," Dimitri said.

Sabi hummed thoughtfully. The three rounded the final bend, stepping into the center of the garden where Darmanten's statue stood. They approached from the side, allowing Dimitri to see the face on either side of the statue's bronze head.

On the back was the face of morning: soft lines, pouting lips, and friendly eyes. In contrast, the face of night had a square jaw, his brow and nose strong and prominent. In this depiction, night was in control, meaning it was he who held the Scepter of Light aloft in his bronze hand.

"It's even more magnificent in person!" Sabi said, hurrying forward. "Look at the delicate construction of the scepter! These lines and angles!"

Sabi happily ran her fingers along the statue as she circled around it, still analyzing.

"You feel any tingles?" Dimitri asked.

"Tingle what?"

Dimitri shook his head. He moved to the statue's plinth, resting his gloved fingers against the bronze. Nothing.

"Try without the gloves," Rayner suggested, coming up behind him.

Dimitri pulled off his glove with his teeth. He touched his fingertips to the icy metal thigh. Still, there was nothing.

Something colder than the winter air started to curl in his stomach. He looked to Rayner, who shook his head as he touched the statue's knee.

"Sabi?" Dimitri called, his voice sticking in his throat. "Do you feel anything?"

"I feel bronze," she said, coming around the corner on his right. "No tingles, though."

"This makes no sense," Dimitri muttered, prowling around the statue. "It was in the guidebook. It has to have magic."

Had he been wrong about Deardryn's thought process? It wasn't impossible. He clearly was missing something with that gods-damned boat.

Had all this been a complete waste of time? Or had the magic come from the Crystal after all, and Deardryn had gotten here first, and she got it, and the magic was gone, which made Dimitri's entire mission a failure, a fucking failure, and there was nothing he could do once again—

"Touch the statue," Rayner whispered in his ear.

Dimitri hadn't heard him approach. He hadn't realized he'd stopped moving in the first place.

"Focus on the cold against your fingers."

Rayner took Dimitri's hand and pressed it against the statue's knee. Cold raced across his palm, startling him back into his body.

At some point, his breathing had become fast and shallow. His heart pounded throughout his body, his skin unbearably hot, his mind racing fast, fast, fast.

Crystal spare him, it was the festival, Gritta's Inn, all over again. Why couldn't he stop falling apart?

"Make your exhales longer than your inhales," Rayner murmured. "It can help."

Dimitri couldn't bring himself to respond. He sank down to sit on the statue's plinth, wrapping his arms around his knees and hiding his face. Rayner sat beside him.

Gods, he hated this. He hated losing control, hated the relentless spiral of his thoughts, hated feeling like he was trapped in his body.

Inhale, exhale.

He just had to figure out what was going on. Magical tingles didn't just disappear for no reason. Either they never existed, or whatever caused them was taken away. He just had to figure out which. Which meant he needed a plan.

The knot in Dimitri's stomach slackened slightly.

If something was causing the tingles, there had to be a sign of it left behind. He just had to investigate the statue. Then, he would either find it, or find something was missing. That was all he needed to do.

Dimitri blinked hard. Lifting his head, he stole a quick look at Rayner, who still lounged against the statue beside him.

"Better?" Rayner asked.

Dimitri nodded. He quickly turned his head away, something hot prickling across his skin.

"Hey." Rayner leaned around Dimitri to look at him. "Panic, despair, and I have been friends for a long, long time. Don't be ashamed they found you, too."

There was something dark and haunted in Rayner's eyes, but his gaze was steady. Dimitri's lips parted.

Bootsteps crunched around the corner. "Hey, have you two…"

Sabi froze in her tracks. She looked to Dimitri, curled on the plinth, then to Rayner. "Are you—"

"He's fine," Rayner said, rising to his feet.

Sabi didn't miss a beat. "Well, I think I solved your tingle problem."

Dimitri didn't dare to hope. But he hauled himself to his feet as Sabi headed back the way she came. He glanced at Rayner, his words clogging his throat. But Rayner only passed him his fallen glove with a wink and headed off. And the knot in his stomach loosened just a little bit more.

Sabi waited for them at the front of the statue, hands on her hips. "Take a look at the centerpiece of the scepter," she said.

Dimitri squinted. The scepter itself was long and thin, carved sunbeams wreathing around the phases of the moon. A fist-sized prism sat on top, which enabled Darmanten to shift between his forms. And inset in its center was a small pink pearl.

"Is that a pulsepearl?" Dimitri asked.

He scrambled on to the plinth and stretched, but he was too short to reach. Rayner laced his fingers, giving Dimitri a boost as he stepped into his hands.

"Can you reach?" Rayner grunted.

"Yes." Dimitri fiddled with the pearl, but it remained locked in place. "It's stuck, though."

"Oh, there must be a lock mechanism!" Sabi said, clasping her hands before her. She rattled off its intricacies at top speed, Dimitri understanding about half of what she said. He felt around the base of the pearl's socket, eventually feeling the catch through his glove.

"I got it." He flicked his finger, and the pulsepearl popped free.

Sabi cheered as Dimitri hopped down. The three huddled together, peering down at the pearl in Dimitri's palm.

"Oh!" Sabi said. "Look look look! See the stripe of white? That means this pearl's wraith has passed."

"It's actually authentic?" Rayner said, disbelieving.

"There were likely protections placed around it while the wraith was alive," Sabi said, rolling the pearl in Dimitri's palm with a finger. "But now that they've passed, both the protection and the pearl have lost their magic."

"Which explains why the magic is gone from the statue," Dimitri said.

He passed the pulsepearl to Sabi and plopped down on the plinth. That at least explained the magic. It also connected back to Deardryn asking about pulsepearls. But what could she possibly want with the wraiths?

"So," Sabi said, dropping down beside him. "Are you going to tell us what this is all about yet?"

Dimitri looked up at the face of night. Once, he, like everyone else, had found his expression to be harsh, even cruel. Now, he thought there was something inviting about the faint smile on his lips.

Dimitri asked, "Have either of you heard when three by three by three align—"

"The sleeping shadows will untwine," Rayner finished.

"How do you know that?" Dimitri asked.

Rayner picked at his nails. "It's on the door of Scarsthain."

Scarsthain. The only place in the guidebook Dimitri hadn't checked yet. He'd figured there was no point: it was open to all kingdoms, which meant Deardryn had free access to its knowledge. But maybe that wasn't the case.

"Do wraiths have anything to do with Scarsthain?" he asked.

"They're the wardens," said Rayner.

Crystal fuck him. "I have to tell you something," Dimitri said. Then, he told them everything about his investigation.

"Wow," Sabi said once he finished.

"I knew I liked you for a reason," Rayner mused.

Sabi went on, "I knew you were poking around Deardryn, but I—"

"How did you know!" Dimitri exclaimed.

"Please, you think I didn't notice you were going through her book orders?" Sabi brushed the snow from her boots. "I'll tell you, Dima, you may know how to keep a secret, but your face doesn't."

"My magic could help with that," Rayner offered vaguely. "Although I might have to take away your nose. And your eyes. And your mouth."

"Great," Dimitri snorted. "You practice on yourself and let me know how it goes."

"Well," Sabi mused, "if he does succeed, then he would have no way of telling you... oh." Sabi nodded sagely. "I understand. That was funny."

Dimitri laughed. Sabi tentatively joined in, realizing he wasn't laughing *at* her.

"Why are we discussing Scarsthain?" Rayner asked, his lips twitching.

"Because Deardryn is researching it," Sabi said.

"Again," Dimitri said, "how do you know that?"

"She just requested a book on wraiths, which guard the prison, you were talking to Magnar during the festival, and now we're here finding dead pulsepearls because you're tracking Deardryn. It's amazing how far common sense can get you."

Sabi rose to her feet, examining the statue's knee socket. Dimitri tapped the plinth, his mind racing.

"What I don't get," he said, "is why Deardryn hasn't swiped the Crystal if she knows it's there."

"The prison isn't owned by the Royals," Rayner explained, turning his back to Dimitri as he examined a single blooming bush. "The wraiths allow us to store enemies away, but no human can come and go as they please. You need permission first."

"How do you know so much about Scarsthain?" Sabi asked.

"I've spent a lot of time with wraiths."

His tone left no room for follow-ups.

"In that case," Dimitri said, a bit too loud, "Deardryn must be waiting on that permission."

"So then, how do we get there first?" Sabi asked.

A warm sort of ache moved through Dimitri's chest. He watched as Sabi waved Rayner over, ordering him to do the "hand lift thing" so she could replace the pearl.

Patryclas's voice echoed through his mind. *What do you want?*

"How 'unstoppable' are you two feeling?" he asked.

Chapter 43

As the days went by, Aaron felt like a drunken fool. The kind whose blood sang through his veins; the kind that woke up inexplicably happy; the kind that smiled for no reason. Except there was a reason.

She had already been a constant spark in the back of his awareness; one he had spent so much time trying to temper. But now, that spark was melting away what little resolve he had left.

During council meetings, he replayed how Analia's face had lit up when he presented her with her first pair of fighting leathers. As he researched the Crystal, his mind drifted to her smile; the curve of her thighs beneath her nightgown; the arch of her back as she stretched for a book on the top shelf—that was usually when he put his head down and groaned.

Even when walking through the kingdom, he revisited their interactions over and over. Especially the morning of her twenty-third birthday.

Aaron had been prepared to covertly check on her throughout the day, knowing it was going to be a rough one. But she'd come to him herself, plopping down on the couch beside him and saying she missed her uncle.

Selfishly, Aaron didn't know what he loved more: the fact she'd turned to him for comfort, or the hours they'd sat, his arm around her and her head on his shoulder as she talked about Accalon.

In some wicked twist of events, mornings became his favorite time of day. Getting to pull her close as they shadowjumped to the lake for training, her body immediately relaxing into his. Even when he had to step away, his disappointment was swept away by the fierce wave of pride as their training progressed.

Analia had quickly mastered pulling forth the precise amount of magic she desired. Consequently, they had moved on to manipulating that amount. Larger, smaller, hold, release, summon, release, Aaron ordered her at increasing speeds until a sweat broke out across her brow.

It had taken Analia some time to match her pace to his without error. But during their last session, she'd ended it with a look of triumph after having flawlessly completed Aaron's routine.

She was slowly mastering her magic. And Aaron was rapidly losing control of his heart.

The first snow of the season began at the end of one of their training sessions. By the time Aaron returned home that evening, the snow had stuck to the ground, crunching beneath his boots as he crossed his backyard and hid behind a birch tree.

The training hollow had been shielded against the elements centuries before, allowing Analia to continue her nightly training. Indeed, it wasn't long before Branten trudged past. Analia followed a few minutes later, just to yelp as a snowball hit her shoulder. She whipped around, immediately spotting Aaron grinning at her around his trunk.

"You!" she exclaimed.

Faster than he expected, she scooped up a handful of snow and hurled it at him. Aaron ducked behind his tree just in time, quickly returning fire. Analia shrieked and darted away.

The grove was quickly flooded with laughter and flying snowballs as they chased each other through the trees. Scooping up another handful, Aaron faded into the shadows, coming out right behind her.

He'd intended to make a direct hit. But the snowball dropped from his grasp as he slipped around her, grabbing her hands. "You're warm!"

Analia yanked her hands back, "You're freezing!"

"I can't believe you've left me to languish in such inhospitable temperatures."

"You've been out here for five minutes."

"Why are you so warm?" Aaron asked, inching closer to the heat radiating off her skin.

"Magic release." She grabbed his hands, pulling him down with her as she sat in the snow. "The more I release, the higher my temperature seems to climb."

"Fascinating," Aaron murmured. "I'd thought you felt warmer than usual after training, but you're well beyond feverish right now."

He dropped one of her hands, pressing the back of his to her burning forehead. "But how do you already have this much magic to release?"

"I have no idea," Analia said, bringing her warm hands to his frozen face. "But it's increasing with every training session. Like instead of finding the bottom of the well, we're just digging it deeper."

Aaron was careful to keep his expression neutral. "Are you worried?"

"A little," Analia admitted. "Deardryn told us about Gavare and how people thought he was a leaky cup, but what if I'm the opposite? What if I'm an overflowing cup, and training is somehow only filling it faster?"

She shifted her hands, anxiously searching his expression.

"I don't think I have an answer for you," he said. "All I can assume is training might be filling your cup faster, but that magic is inside you regardless. You have to decide whether you want to wield it or suppress it."

Analia deflated, her hands falling to her lap. And Aaron couldn't wipe the image of midnight flames from his mind, reaching toward the sky in an endless tirade.

Could one vessel truly contain so much magic? Could it survive—no. Aaron could not, would not, think about that. Not when Deardryn had said this was Accalon's magic, and he'd survived for centuries.

If xenol was what it took, Aaron would hunt down Marcos himself. He would infiltrate the Moon Kingdom where it grew if he had to. He would give her a damper if necessary.

"Don't worry," Analia said, misinterpreting his tension as she patted his arm. "I'm still going to train. You might just have an uncomfortably warm stray hogging your couch."

Aaron's eyes flicked to hers, then down to his flexing fingers. "For someone so uncomfortably warm," he said, "you still managed to get snow stuck in your lashes."

"Really?" Analia blinked furiously, only succeeding in looking thoroughly bewildered.

Aaron's lips twitched. "Look up."

Analia complied, and Aaron leaned toward her. He carefully swept his thumb along her lash line, wiping away the snowflakes that clung there.

Just another quick, innocent gesture. One that should have been followed by him sitting back.

Instead, his eyes slid down to hers, wondering what would happen if he didn't. What would happen if he pulled her closer instead? What would have happened if it wasn't his thumb, but his lips that skimmed across her lashes?

Analia turned her face away. Aaron jerked back hard enough his neck ached.

"What about this side?" she asked.

It took Aaron a few thundering heartbeats to realize what she meant. Finally, he dragged his gaze to the eye she had angled toward him.

"No," he said on an exhale. "You're fine."

"What?" Analia fell back in the snow. "How was it only on one side?"

"I don't know how you do it."

Analia made an exasperated noise, throwing up her hands.

Somehow, despite every calcified emotion that had come to weigh down his heart, Aaron laughed. Analia gave him an affronted look, which only had him laughing harder. He looked up at the stars, still grinning as he shook his head.

"Tell me," he said, leaning back in the snow. "Did Accalon ever teach you about the constellations?"

Analia brightened. "He did." She leaned back beside him. "Turns out, your kingdom isn't the only one with legends around the stars."

"Oh?" Aaron wondered just how much of his kingdom's legends she remembered. But Analia's face gave nothing away as she went on.

"My uncle's favorite legend took place right after the Unleashing. With the Defiants in their new positions of power, they had to divide Elefthia between their kingdoms, which naturally roused countless squabbles between them. But it was said Azar remained unusually quiet.

"Eventually, the other Defiants asked him what section of land he wanted, to which he replied, 'I want my home.' The other Defiants, understandably confused, asked where that was, and Azar shrugged and told them he'd know when he found it.

"Azar then gathered his closest confidants and most trusted warriors, and together, they struck out across Elefthia. They traveled for weeks, Azar's companions repeatedly asking if this was the place, or if they were getting closer. But Azar always shook his head. And every night, his gaze was drawn to the sky, noticing three stars that seemed to glow brighter than the rest."

Analia pointed to the sky, drawing a triangle between three brightly glowing stars, moving down as if tracing the pole of a torch. "Azar decided they were to follow the path of those stars. Eventually, he came upon Mt. Vasolus, at which point he stabbed his sword into the earth and declared the volcano to be the heart of his kingdom. After the Ash Kingdom was officially established, he dubbed those three stars the Twinkling Torch, a constellation that any Ash citizen could follow to find their way home again."

Aaron couldn't bring himself to look at her. "Do you miss it?" he asked.

Analia thought about it. "I miss the kingdom my uncle got to see. I miss the sconces and the creativity and the fire sprites that always found their way onto the Great Hall's candle wicks. But everything else?"

Analia sighed, drawing in the snow between them with a finger. "I love my uncle. But I've known for a long time that if I followed that torch, it wouldn't be leading me home."

Aaron had to remind himself to breathe. "Does that mean you wouldn't go back if you had the opportunity?"

"I think I'd like to go back at some point to see Ember and my siblings."

"Any time, Analia. You say the word, and I will bring you back."

"I know," Analia said. "I just hope you'd linger, because I have no desire to stay when that visit is over."

It took Aaron a second to respond. "You don't?"

Analia shook her head. "For so long, that thought felt like a betrayal of my uncle's memory, like I was defaming the thing he cherished most when I should've been maintaining it."

"That kingdom was not the thing he cherished most," Aaron told her firmly.

Analia's mouth trembled. "I think that's just it," she said. "My uncle loved me, and he loved his kingdom, but we didn't love each other. So really, leaving was the only way to preserve everything he loved."

"Does that mean you don't regret coming to my kingdom?" Aaron asked.

Analia was quiet for a long moment. Finally, she looked over at him. "I think it's the best decision I've ever made."

Aaron felt as though his entire being was infused with torchlight.

"Good," he said.

Not today, but someday. And maybe someday was even closer than he thought.

Although that would also mean another "someday"—one that had become inevitable the moment Aaron first saw her in the Ash Kingdom—was also approaching. In that regard, he didn't know what terrified him more: the fact that the time to release that one, irreversible secret might be drawing near, or the possibility that it may never come.

"What's wrong?" Analia asked, peering into his face.

Too perceptive.

"Well," Aaron said, recovering quickly, "while your control over your magic is lovely, it has also made it so we're lying in one massive puddle."

Analia blinked. She looked down, taking in his point.

"Huh." She looked at herself. Looked at Aaron. "Good thing my leathers are waterproof." She sat up, patting him on the head. "I would hate to be you right now, my soggy, moody warrior man."

Aaron let out a surprised laugh. "Is that to be my nickname from now on?"

"Until I think of something better," Analia said, strolling back toward the house.

"Really?" Aaron rose, shadowjumping so he could fall into step beside her. "Do enlighten me, my shooting star, as to what you've left on the cutting room floor."

"That's my problem," Analia said. "I don't think you can be contained in a shooting star. That head of yours is just too gods-damned big."

Analia didn't notice Aaron's grin as she opened the door. Someday. Some fucking day.

"Oh, Analia," he began. Just to freeze as he spotted Laness waiting for them.

"What's wrong?" Analia asked, spotting the paper Laness anxiously folded and unfolded in her fingers.

Aaron asked, "Did Surce decode the note?"

"Aaron," Laness said miserably, "I'm so sorry."

With those four little words, Aaron found himself unable to feel the heat radiating off Analia's skin. All he felt was the cold winter air, pushing through the cracks in the porch door, leaching through the glass.

"What does it say?" Analia asked.

Laness's shoulders slumped. "Surce said it's with the humans."

Aaron barely heard Analia ask what that meant. Barely heard Laness's response. All he knew was something cold and dark thudded into his stomach.

"Dinner," he ground out. "Two hours from now. Let everyone know."

Laness nodded quickly. Analia turned, reaching for him. But Aaron faded into the shadows, reemerging in his mother's room. It was only then that he let the curse rip from his throat, his magic shattering the closest windowpane with an ear-splitting crash.

Shards of glass rained down on the hedges outside, but Aaron didn't care. He only collapsed on his mother's bed, curling in on himself as if that could protect him from the destruction in his chest.

The humans. It always came back to the fucking humans.

For the entirety of those two hours he'd given himself, Aaron kept his eyes on the window. He watched as the glass shards—Blessed by a glassworker in the Mirage—floated up from the hedges and fit themselves back into place. Soon, the entire pane was reassembled, even the web of cracks smoothed away.

Aaron released a shuddering breath, burying his face in the pillows. If only it were that easy.

Chapter 44

Ember never thought she'd go anywhere near the most ruthless prison in Eleft-hia. She thought that was a perfectly reasonable goal to have. Yet, there she was, devinroot numbing her mind as she followed Cadmus and their wraith escort, Rolla, through the rocky passage to Scarsthain's entrance.

The prison was built into a cliff face, the only access point a narrow ledge far above a frothing river. Due to the prison's wards blocking all forms of magical entrance, they hadn't been able to shadowjump inside. Instead, each kingdom's Royals had been given a pulsepearl to summon one of the wardens whenever a prisoner needed to be retrieved or, in the rarer case, a visit needed to be made.

It had taken weeks for Cadmus to gain approval to enter the prison. Apparently, the wraiths made few exceptions, even for kings with traitorous fathers inside.

"I hate it here," Ember muttered, bumping her shoulder on one of the tight, narrow turns.

"Well, Em," Cadmus said ahead of her, "it's about to get a lot worse."

Taking a final turn, they emerged in a packed-earth chamber. Torches lined the walls, casting shadows over a large, rusty metal door.

"This is the entrance," Rolla said, turning to face them. The female wraith was dressed in long dark robes. She kept her hood pulled up, only giving Ember a glimpse of pale skin and all-black eyes.

Reaching into her robes, she withdrew a slender knife. The silver hilt was carved into a serpent head, the long, thin blade split at the tip like its tongue.

"What is *that?*" Ember asked.

"It's the prison's key," Cadmus said. Accepting the weapon, he pricked each finger on his right hand, then knelt to press his hand to the dirt. "Scarsthain doesn't rely on locks that can be picked or broken. Instead, these blades allow the prison to taste everyone who enters."

"That way," Rolla rasped, "it knows who to keep in, and who to flush out."

Rosala spare her. Rolla took the blade from Cadmus and thrust it at Ember. She flinched away from the sharp tip pointing at her face, but hesitantly accepted the hilt.

Pricking her fingers, Ember knelt beside Cadmus. The moment she touched her fingers to the dirt, she could have sworn the ground latched on, greedily sucking down her blood like roots in wet soil. Ember's stomach churned, but she kept her hand where it was.

"Good," Rolla said. "Now rise."

Cadmus and Ember did as ordered. Then, without further comment, Rolla slid open the rusty door with a bone-chilling squeal, not glancing back as she stepped into the darkness beyond.

Left alone, Cadmus turned to Ember. "You ready?" he asked.

How was he so calm? How was he ready to step through that door without hesitation, whereas Ember could taste bile rising in her throat?

"If we die," she said, wiping the dirt from her hands on her healer robes, "my ghost will find your ghost and kick its ass."

Cadmus snorted. He took her hand, his fingers sticky with blood. Then, he led the way through the door.

For a moment, all Ember felt was the cold. It pressed in on all sides, reaching deep inside her until even her magic was snuffed out.

Cadmus's hand briefly tightened around hers. Ember blinked rapidly, the darkness shifting to reveal the hallway before them.

It looked as though it could be in any civilian home: gray carpet, high ceiling, a staircase at the other end that faced a collection of doorways. Rolla waited for them at the farthest one, having retrieved a torch from one of the many sconces lining the walls.

As they approached, Ember realized words had been etched into the door's wooden face. *When three by three by three align.*

Ember struggled to read the rest. But as soon as she passed through the door, it no longer mattered. Nothing mattered. Nothing besides her certainty that she was going to die.

The walls were made up of a collection of bones. They fit together to form cell doors every few feet, Ember's stomach heaving as she realized she could distinguish the recent bones from the old. Screams and moans leaked through the cell doors, some terrifyingly human, the most horrific cells the ones that were completely silent.

Rosala spare her. She needed her devinroot. She needed fresh air and to escape the feeling that the prison had locked on to her pounding pulse.

Ember scratched her markings, her skin unbearably itchy.

"It's just the magic, Ember," Cadmus breathed in her ear. "Don't let it overwhelm you."

He squeezed her hand, painfully tight. When had she started shaking?

She took a slow, deep breath, ignoring the sickly sweet scent. She was a healer. It was her job to stay calm and collected. Cadmus needed her just as much as she needed him.

Ember focused her attention on her feet as they descended deeper into the prison, counting her steps.

One, two, three, breathe. One, two, three, breathe. One, two, three—bloodstain?

Ember looked up, taking in the broken cell door and empty cell beyond.

"What's that?" she whispered. Intrigued, calm. Not afraid.

"That was Ren Inferita's cell," Cadmus breathed, his face pale. "In the three millennia this prison has stood, he is the only one to have escaped."

Ember found that oddly comforting. "How'd he do it?"

"No one knows," Cadmus said. "We only know it happened a little less than a century ago—"

Rolla whipped around and hissed. Ember jumped, silently mouthing apologies until she turned back around. Cadmus and Ember exchanged a look, but they kept their mouths shut.

Rolla led the way around a few more winding turns. Finally, they paused before a seemingly random cell.

"This is his?" Cadmus asked.

In response, Rolla tapped the center of the cell with her dagger. The bones shifted with a rattle, forming a small window. Ember peered inside, only able to spot a huddled form in the shadows and a splash of red hair. She looked to Cadmus, but his expression was unreadable.

"You have ten minutes," Rolla said. "I'll be watching."

Cadmus nodded once. Accepting the torch, he pressed his blood-smeared fingers to the door. There was a click and a grind as the door slid open. And without hesitation, Rolla shoved them inside and slammed the door.

The first thing that hit Ember was the smell of human waste. She glanced behind her, but the window had disappeared. If only that were true about the man chained to the ground, staring at the opposite wall.

"I know you're not real," Brenn said, his voice barely a whisper. "Go away."

"Father," Cadmus said, stepping closer, "it's me."

"You're not real," Brenn repeated, slightly louder this time. "Go away."

"Father—"

"No!" Brenn screamed as Cadmus touched his shoulder.

Cadmus jerked away as Brenn flailed, his voice getting louder and louder. "No, no, no!"

Cadmus tried to soothe Brenn, but it only seemed to upset him more. "Father, please—"

"No!" Brenn's fist connected with Cadmus's jaw. Cadmus stumbled back, his expression crumpling as he looked to Ember.

"Can you help him?" he asked.

Ember didn't know how without her magic, but she nodded anyway. She moved in front of Brenn, taking in his sunken eyes and cheeks, the yellow tinge to his skin.

Gods, what sort of nightmares triggered this reaction? What kind of torture plagued his mind? Did anyone deserve this kind of punishment?

There was no time to wonder. Ember brushed the thoughts aside, letting her instincts take over.

"Brenn," she said soothingly. "This isn't an illusion."

"Don't lie!"

"If this wasn't real, wouldn't we be tormenting you? Wouldn't you be in pain by now? We haven't done that. This is real, look."

Ember caught one of his hands, bringing it to her wrist. "That's a pulse. I'm alive and not hurting you."

"You're just waiting until I let my guard down," Brenn said, his eyes wild.

"All right, then," Ember said, surprisingly calm. "Let's just wait, then."

Ember gestured for Cadmus to join her. "We'll sit right here where you can see us for as long as you like. All we want to do is talk."

Ember sat back against the wall, Cadmus easing down beside her. He leaned the torch against the wall on his other side, then rested his hands palms up on his knees.

For a few long minutes, Brenn panted and struggled against his restraints. Ember could feel their precious time trickling out, just as she could feel the heartache Cadmus could barely contain. But she remained still and quiet.

Finally, Brenn's struggling petered out. Slowly, he eased back on his haunches, something settling in his eyes as he looked at his son.

"Cadmus?" he rasped.

Cadmus nodded, unable to speak.

"I was hoping for Aeley. I thought she would have... after everything we've been through—that I *put her* through—I thought she had finally..."

Brenn's voice trailed off, his gaze drifting up. "You have your sister's crown."

Cadmus startled. He touched his obsidian crown as if he'd forgotten it was there. Brenn let out a dry, bone-chilling laugh.

"Look at you, Cadmus. Stealing your sister's crown, just as I stole my brother's. I never would have thought you'd have the spine to follow in my footsteps."

"We are nothing alike," Cadmus spat.

"No," Brenn said, "because I'm in here, and you're still up there. Alive, breathing fresh air."

Brenn leaned in close. "How does that feel, Cadmus? How does it feel to be free? How does it feel to wear a stolen crown on your head and know you got away with it?"

Cadmus cringed away. "I didn't steal Anna's crown. I didn't murder my family for power."

"It's exhilarating, isn't it?" Brenn said as if he hadn't heard. "You're so drunk on power that it almost feels normal. Yes, there's the guilt that lingers from the moment you made your decision. The grief as you go through with it; the hatred you have for yourself every day following because what if there had been another way?

"But the moment you put that crown on your head..." Brenn's head fell back. "We were on the brink of war. We would have been destroyed if my brother stayed in power. But I was a good king. I put my kingdom, its survival, first. I did my duty."

"You betrayed your kingdom *and* your family," Cadmus spat.

"Oh, you love the crown," Brenn said dismissively. "You love the power. It's all right to admit it."

Something flashed in Cadmus's eyes. Fear, despair, rage, Ember didn't know. But that didn't stop her from swiftly stepping in.

"We're not here to talk about crowns, Brenn."

Brenn's crazed gaze slid to her, sending a chill down her spine. "I know you," he said. "You're that human healer bitch my pathetic Analia used to trail—"

Cadmus gripped Brenn by the shoulder, turning him back to face him. "You don't get to speak about either of them like that."

For the first time, the fact that Cadmus was an Ash Royal, the Ash King, sank in. He was powerful. Deadly. And Brenn stared at him as if he could see right through him to the wall.

"Analia," he said again. "It always comes back to fucking Analia."

"Yes, it does," Cadmus said. "Because she's the one that noticed the mark on your wrist."

Brenn's eyes bulged. "No."

Cadmus reached for Brenn's wrist. Brenn scuttled back, his ankle chains limiting his range. "No!"

Ember put a hand on Cadmus's arm to stop him, but the heartache in his expression had hardened. He moved after Brenn, dodging his flailing limbs and grabbing his arm. Brenn shrieked, but Cadmus ignored him as he dragged his arm forward and shoved down his cuffs.

"It's here," he said over his shoulder. "Look."

Ember shifted uncertainly, but her curiosity won out. Grabbing the torch, she crept up behind Cadmus and peered over his shoulder. Yes, that was undeniably the same mark Lucilla had drawn tattooed on Brenn's wrist, his skin red and raw from his cuffs.

"What does it mean?" Cadmus asked between gritted teeth, struggling to restrain his father.

"You know," Brenn panted. "You hear it calling to you. Starting as a whisper in the back of your mind, evolving until it devours your every thought."

Cadmus stiffened slightly. "You mean Mt. Vasolus."

Ember blinked. Brenn cackled.

"So, you do hear it," he said. "And yet, you don't know what it means. Are the whispers that faint, or are you just a coward?"

Ember fought the urge to jab the torch into Brenn's face. But Cadmus was eerily calm. "Tell me what it means."

Brenn snatched his wrist back and cradled it to his chest. "Why would I do that?"

"Because you have no leveraging power and a lifetime of this cell to look forward to."

"And you need answers bad enough to come here."

There came a single hard knock on the cell. Time was running out.

Cadmus gave Ember a questioning look, and she shrugged. He turned back to his father. "What do you want?"

"Kill me," Brenn hissed. "Kill me. Take it all away. The cell, the silence, the torment. Take it all away."

Ember's chest ached, but not for Brenn. She shuffled around to see Cadmus's face, but he only rubbed the bruise blossoming across his jaw.

"Tell me what the mark means," he finally said.

A wild grin spread across Brenn's face. "Tell me why you want to know."

"Because it showed up in Uncle Accalon's private research."

"Ha!" Brenn threw back his head. "Of course it did. That man was obsessed with magic. Magic flows, magic types."

"Like different Blessings?" Ember asked.

"No, types," Brenn said impatiently. "Healer magic, Royal magic, Blessed magic—"

"But they're all the same," Cadmus said. "Just different Blessings from the Crystal."

"If you say so," Brenn muttered.

Ember's eyebrows were becoming dangerously high. There came another knock. Out of time.

"So," Cadmus said, looking back to Brenn, "it has to do with magic."

The cell door shuddered.

"It's the call of the mountain," Brenn said. "Now hurry, before they open the door."

Brenn lifted his head, exposing his throat. Cadmus considered his father for a long moment. Then, without a word, he rose to his feet.

"Wait," Brenn shrieked, trying and failing to rise.

Cadmus gestured for Ember to follow him.

"You promised!" Brenn wailed.

"No, I didn't," Cadmus said, heading for the door. "You should have listened more carefully."

The door slid open. Brenn lunged against his restraints. "Kill me! Kill me kill me kill me, you worthless excuse of an heir! Kill me!"

Cadmus took Ember's hand and helped her through the door. He glanced back, giving his father a final pitiless look. "Enjoy your 'exhilaration,' Father."

Then, he slammed the cell door shut, cutting off Brenn's scream of rage. Ember looked up at Cadmus, but he shook his head.

Together, they silently followed Rolla back through the prison and into the entryway. Ember nearly sagged in relief as her magic reentered her body, but still, Cadmus did not speak. He remained stiff and silent as they made their way back through the ravine trail, finally reaching the point where he could pull them into the shadows.

A moment later, Ember blinked in the return of light as Cadmus's bedchamber solidified around them. Cadmus immediately dropped her hand, releasing a long, hissing breath as he slumped back against his pillows. After that far of a jump, Ember couldn't blame him.

"Cadmus," Ember said gently, sitting beside him on the bed. "Let me help you."

She reached out to touch his forehead, but Cadmus pulled away. "Ember, no. Your suspension."

Ember's hand froze, a small, wounded noise clogging her throat. He was right. She couldn't help him. Not in the name of Rosala. Not without breaking her oath even more.

Ember pulled her hand back, something splintering in her chest. But judging by the look on Cadmus's face, her pain was not the most pressing matter.

"So," she said, her voice thick. "That was a lot."

Cadmus nodded, his eyes closing as Ember brushed the hair from his forehead. What was she supposed to say to someone who just witnessed their father's torment?

"He was right about Vasolus," Cadmus mumbled.

"What do you mean?" Ember asked.

"It's been whispering to me. Ever since I put on the crown, I can't stop thinking about it, about how Father spent so much time there when he was king. It's calling me."

Ember thought back through her time with Cadmus. How she'd caught him staring at the painting of Mt. Vasolus multiple times, his comment about the volcano as they split up at the Phoenix Gate.

She knew this couldn't just be a coincidence. But instead of feeling elated, the hairs on her arms stood up.

"Cadmus," she said, "this feels like a really bad idea."

"It's the next clue Accalon gave us."

"How do we know it's a sign to go there and not a sign to stay away?"

"I thought you of all people would be the first to go," he said, turning to curl up on his side.

At one point, that would have been true. But now, she couldn't get Brenn's words out of her mind, the way he'd spoken about not just Analia, but Cadmus as well.

How many times had she told Analia not to care what her father said? Yet, there she was, caring too much about what her fellow healers thought. And if it was only her drive to change their minds propelling her to that mountain when every instinct screamed for her to stay away...

"Promise me we will do more research before making a decision," she said.

Cadmus mumbled something into the pillow. Ember prodded his side.

"All right," Cadmus said a bit louder.

He settled back against the pillows with a huff, and Ember thought the conversation ended there.

"Thank you for coming with me," he said softly. "I couldn't have done that without you."

Ember touched his shoulder. Telling him to get some rest, she rose from the bed and quietly slipped out the door.

It was instinct more than anything that had her glance up and down the abandoned corridor outside. Just as it was instinct to retrieve the scrap of devinroot from her pocket and bring it to her nose.

She didn't remember exactly how long it had been since her last dose—two, maybe three hours? It didn't matter, since she only used it when she needed it.

Sure enough, the sharp, leafy scent had the last of the prison's chill fading from her bones, her scattered thoughts coming back into alignment.

They might be at a crossroads with Accalon's mystery, but at least she knew the path she needed to travel now. She just hoped she was brave enough to walk it.

Chapter 45

Analia took her seat at the dinner table, Aaron's family unnervingly silent around her.

After Aaron had left, she'd spent a good chunk of time restlessly pacing the house. Mor had taken one look at her when he arrived and nudged her into the kitchen, distracting her with stories from his day as she helped him make dinner. But still, her mind churned. Even now, everyone completely ignored the steaming bowls of stew before them, all attention locked on the empty chair beside Analia's.

He had only been gone for two hours, but she still missed him. At some point, she'd started to miss him every time he was gone.

She missed his easy laugh. The way his smile turned crooked after firing a quip he was particularly proud of. The pressure of his hand on her back as they walked through the kingdom, the touch to her arm in greeting, the brush of his fingers as he freed her hair from her cloak—had he always touched her so much? Or did she only notice now because she had become just as aware when those touches were gone?

Somehow, she'd become completely attuned to his presence. Not like with Pryanth where she was waiting for the thunderclap. It was like finding her favorite constellation in the sky.

Aaron chose that moment to arrive. Everyone looked up as he pushed through the door, his face pale and exhausted. But his gaze didn't waver as he took his seat and ordered Surce to tell him everything she knew.

Apparently, the note was to the point, only promising that the scroll was in the Human Castle.

"I've been ruling over that kingdom for half a century," Mor said. "I'm not doubting your translation, Surce, but if I haven't caught wind of it by now, there's little chance I could find it."

"Well," Laness said, drawing out the word uncertainly.

Aaron's eyes narrowed. "Well, what, Laness."

Laness put up her hands. "I was only thinking it doesn't matter if Mor can't find the scroll because we know someone else who can."

All eyes flashed to Analia.

"I could find it," she agreed, idly stirring her stew. "Assuming it's also clasped with the same magic rings. I'd just need to get into the castle."

"Even if you can't get it," Laness said, "You could tell Mor where it is."

Branten chimed in, "He could grab it and then swap it with a fake."

"And they'd never know the difference," Analia finished.

"This could actually work," Mor mused. "We just have to—"

"Enough." Aaron dropped his spoon with a clatter.

They all looked to him, expressions ranging from shocked to confused.

"Aaron," Laness began gently, but Aaron gave a sharp jerk of his head.

"You're all forgetting one crucial detail," he said, reclaiming his spoon in a white-knuckle grip. "We have no safe way to get Anna into the Human Kingdom. She's a stranger to them. No matter what role or reason I assign her, the humans will immediately be on guard and security will be tightened ten-fold."

Analia's excitement fizzled out.

Laness squirmed in her seat. "Well…"

"Well, *what*, Laness?" Aaron ground out.

"Aaron, you know there's one role that you can give Analia."

"Laness," Aaron warned.

"You know," she pressed, "there's nothing they can do if you say she's your betrothed."

Analia's hand jerked, splattering stew on the table.

Aaron sent Laness a vicious glare. "Out of the question."

"Why?" Laness demanded, slapping her hands on the table. "It's perfect! If it's a recent betrothal, you have every reason to bring her."

"She has a point," Mor murmured, passing Analia a napkin.

"I told you," Aaron said, "the answer is no."

Analia tried, but she couldn't suppress her wince. Aaron immediately turned to her. "What's wrong?"

"I'm all right," she said, eyes on the table as she wiped up her spill. "My pride just isn't as indestructible as yours."

The table went quiet.

For a moment, Aaron stared at her, confused. Then, his eyes widened in alarm. He swore, leaning toward her, the rest of the table looking away.

"Allow me to make myself perfectly clear," he said, all sharpness gone. "It would be my honor to be betrothed to you, pretend or otherwise. I just don't see this scheme ending in anything but disaster."

Analia ignored the soft glow in her chest. "Walk me through it, then," she said.

Aaron sighed, his knee leaning against hers. "This scheme wouldn't be a one and done situation. It would be incredibly suspicious if I only brought you to this one meeting, and then the humans never saw you again. Just as it would be suspicious if any humans snuck into my kingdom and discovered my people had no idea you were queen.

"The only way to pull off this lie is if you become permanently bound to my kingdom, and even then, there is an infinite list of ways our story could unravel."

"You and Anna could always have a spectacular separation," Branten piped up.

Aaron didn't even spare him a look. "I promised you my kingdom was a safe place for you. I don't want to jeopardize that by trapping you in a lie with a high probability of falling apart."

Analia blinked hard. "Aaron," she said, "you don't... Thank you. But all of our other options are just as flimsy."

Analia braced herself for his reaction. But Aaron only bowed his head, running his hand through his hair. "Go on."

Crystal Bless that man.

"There are innumerable roles you could assign me," Analia said, "but there's one flaw at the core of all of them. I undeniably look like an Ash Royal. I'm at the top of an enemy kingdom's political ladder, and the humans will be outraged you brought me into their home."

"I know," Aaron said. "That's why I want to keep you as far from them as possible. For your own sake as well as my kingdom's."

"For your kingdom's sake," Analia argued, "you need to get that scroll. And I am the only one that can track it."

Analia held Aaron's gaze. Finally, he braced his elbow on the table, leaning his temple against his fist and gesturing with his other hand for her to go on.

"We both know I have the best chance of getting the scroll," she said. "And we both know there are risks that come with that. But if I'm your betrothed, I have no reason to be a threat to their kingdom's secret."

"The humans still won't like it," Aaron said.

"Oh, undoubtedly," Analia agreed. "But there's nothing they can do about it. No matter how much they loathe it, that type of bond can't be disrespected. It's the precise reason I was betrothed to Pryanth before entering the Sun Kingdom."

Analia's tone had been matter of fact. But Aaron's face fell.

"I don't want to put you through that again," he said, his hand tightening around the back of his chair. "Pretend or not."

Analia softened. "Oh, Aaron." She reached over, gently prying his hand free from his chair. "This would be nothing like that. I want to be here; I want to do this." She interlaced their fingers. "And you are nothing like Pryanth."

Aaron looked up at her, something unbearably fragile in his eyes. She squeezed his hand, acutely aware of how his warm fingers fit between hers.

It was such a contrast with the blaze of Brenn's fingers behind her ear; Pryanth's unpredictable icy words. But perhaps it was that contrast that allowed her to recognize, appreciate, the consistency in Aaron's warmth. A type of warmth she had given up on. A type of warmth she did not want to let go of.

There came a delicate cough. Aaron quickly pulled his hand from Analia's, both of them twisting to look at Surce.

"If I may," she said, smoothing a crease in her deep purple gown, "there are more questions that will arise based on Analia's heritage."

Aaron, looking flushed, waved for her to continue.

"Naturally," Surce said, "the humans will wonder why Aaron would be consorting with someone from outside our bubble, and a Royal at that. Does that mean we're not hidden anymore? Are there alliances happening that they're not aware of? Those types of questions, if left unanswered, could very well lead to another rebellion."

"Which means," Laness said, gesturing with her spoon, "if Analia is walking into that kingdom, there has to be a special reason."

Aaron rubbed his temples. "And you all think a betrothal is the only way to do it?"

"Unless we're completely overthinking this," Branten said. At some point, he'd folded their entire stack of napkins into an army of swans.

"What do you mean?" Analia asked.

"Well," Branten said, "we know you *look* like an Ash Royal. But outside of that, would the humans know you're an Ash Royal?"

"Are you suggesting a masquerader?" Surce asked.

Branten shrugged. Laness and Surce swapped intrigued looks. Mor, however, slumped lower in his seat.

Aaron's eyes latched on to him. "What aren't you sharing, Mor?"

Mor's gaze flicked guiltily along the table. "It would be an interesting plan," he admitted. "But the humans already suspect that she's here."

Aaron's magic flashed, highlighting his family's shocked reactions in silver. "When were you planning on telling me this?" he asked, icy calm.

"Do they know that it's her?" Surce asked sharply.

"There are rumors," Mor admitted. "One of the humans snuck across the bridge the night we were at Leah's. She caught a glimpse of Analia through the crowd—Aaron, I'm sorry."

Analia's mind flashed back to the girl that had been staring at her across the dance floor, Mor quickly trying to brush it aside.

"Oh gods," she breathed.

Aaron gripped the edge of the table. "And you didn't find it prudent to inform your king?"

"I wasn't going to tell you until it was relevant because I knew you would worry unnecessarily."

"How do you know it would be *unnecessarily?*" Aaron demanded, shaking off Branten's hand on his arm.

"Because this is my specialty," Mor said, unflinching. "Few believed the rumors as is, and I planted information to dissuade the rest. I promise you, Analia is safe."

Slowly, Aaron relaxed back in his seat, his eyes still frosted over.

Mor turned to Analia. "That being said, I'm sorry I couldn't keep you out of this situation in the first place."

"This wasn't your fault, Mor," she told him. "It was only a matter of time before word got back to the humans."

Mor bowed his head.

"Well," Branten said, "that just means Anna has to go as herself."

"Now how'd you connect those dots?" Aaron grumbled into his wine.

"It's always easier to show a man what he expects than convince him of something else," Branten said simply.

"It's inevitable they'll see me with you at some point, Aaron," Analia said. "Even if you take away the question of where your betrothed is, we'll still have to contend with rumors spreading once more."

"And my plan," Laness piped up, "is the best way to get ahead of that moment."

"Careful, Laness," Aaron sighed. "I'd rather not have to scrape bits of your head off my walls because it popped."

Laness folded her arms. "It wouldn't kill you to admit I'm right."

Aaron threw one of Branten's napkin swans at her. Laness dodged, and Surce swatted it aside before it could land in her bowl.

"What do you think?" Aaron asked, turning to Analia.

"I think this is up to both of us," she said. "But it has a greater impact on you. This arrangement might prevent you from ever marrying someone you truly care about."

Aaron smiled faintly, his eyes doing a slow scan over her face. "I'm not worried about that."

Analia stifled her prick of disappointment. She'd almost forgotten how he'd said his magic and Liss had convinced him to stop paying attention to such things.

"Well," she said, pinching her thigh under the table, "I already told you I would be in. That makes it your call."

Aaron's shoulders slumped. He ran a hand through his hair, the rest of the table quiet.

"Are you sure?" he asked, one final time.

It should be a difficult decision. This was massive, life-altering. But Analia didn't feel an ounce of regret, doubt, even fear as she looked up at him.

"Aaron Stelingente," she said, flinging a dramatic arm around his shoulders, "I would be honored to be your betrothed."

Finally, Aaron's stony expression cracked.

"You're ridiculous," he told her. In a blink, he leaned in and pressed the smallest kiss to the corner of her mouth. "Done."

Branten whooped, the table breaking into a smattering of sarcastic applause. Analia fought the urge to touch her fingertips to her mouth.

"That's it?" she asked.

Aaron tapped her nose. "Don't be greedy."

Analia scoffed. But she couldn't deny how her eyes flicked over him as he pushed back his chair.

Aaron quickly delegated roles, having Surce consult her tapestries, Branten gather materials for the counterfeit scroll, and Laness and Mor covertly search for the scroll. "If we still can't find it," he finished dryly, "Anna and I will make our Royal appearance in two weeks."

Without further comment, he faded into the shadows.

Analia looked around the table, expecting the tension to finally slacken. Instead, Laness, Surce, and Mor swapped uneasy looks as Branten collected his swans.

"What?" she asked, her voice feeling far too loud. "What else is wrong?"

"It's just…" Laness dropped her eyes to the table, fingers picking at a chip in the wood.

A knot slowly coiled in Analia's stomach. "Laness, what is it?"

"It's all right," Mor told Laness, who appeared to be drowning in guilt. He placed his golden hand atop Analia's. "Has Aaron told you why the two of you will be going in two weeks' time specifically?"

Analia shook her head. Surce's lips thinned, but she didn't try to stop Mor as he began.

Chapter 46

Aaron shoved his hands in his jacket pockets as he wandered through his night-chilled kingdom.

Normally, he would have steered clear of the Pulse at this time, knowing Liss would be packing up her shop. But at some point, he'd stopped subconsciously avoiding her path. Still, his stomach twisted as he absently smiled at his people, many bowing their heads in respect.

Did they know just how little he deserved that respect? How many of them had lived through the war whose ending he'd be "celebrating" in two weeks' time? An anniversary Aaron couldn't bring himself to tell Analia about—although Laness guiltily told him through his bracelet he wouldn't have to worry about that.

He didn't care if Analia knew; even the part that had his grief threatening to swallow him whole. What he cared about was now, there was no shielding her from the monster he became in that kingdom.

Aaron eventually made it back to his house. Mercifully, his family had cleared out, the house quiet around him as he headed for his room. Just to find a note on his pillow.

Aaron didn't have the energy to look at it. He stripped off his jacket and boots, intending to move the note to his bedside table as he sank down on his bed. Instead, he unfolded it, scanning over Analia's neat handwriting.

I don't want to go just to find the scroll. You deserve to have someone with you.
You know where to find me.
A.

Aaron stared at the note for a long, long time. At some point, he drifted off, Analia's note still clutched in his hand. But even that couldn't stop the nightmares, his mind always going back to that tent.

A faint light illuminated the black and silver panels of the tent.

Everything hurt. It hurt to blink, it hurt to swallow, it hurt to breathe. He tried to push himself up, black spots dancing across his vision as his back screamed.

"Easy." Mor, seated on the ground beside his cot, nudged him back down. "Your wounds haven't completely healed yet."

Aaron struggled to push through the fog in his mind. The humans. The damper cuffs. Laness, everything going black...

"Laness," Aaron rasped, struggling to sit up. "Is she—"

"She's fine," said Branten from Aaron's other side. "Aaron, she's fine, stop squirming."

Branten and Mor managed to shove him back down. Aaron tried to protest, but it quickly turned into a cough. Mor reached for a canteen on the ground beside him, Branten propping up Aaron's head to help him drink.

The cold water hit him like a wave of relief. He drained the canteen, eventually falling back on his cot and fixing his gaze on the tent panels.

"How long?" he rasped.

"Three days," Mor said gently.

"And the war?"

"Over," Branten said. But something was off in his voice.

"What is it?" Aaron asked, turning his head to look at him.

But it was Mor who touched his shoulder, his words reaching through his chest and squeezing his heart until it stopped. "I'm so sorry."

Those three words thundered through Aaron's mind as the tent tilted, spun, fuzzed in and out. It faded away completely, replaced by a night-blackened war camp. Countless fires blazed around him, exhausted men raising their heads as Aaron stumbled past into the command tent.

He didn't see the small knot of officers, many of whom were not the ones they had started the war with. He didn't hear conversation come to a halt. He only heard his own ragged, desperate voice, "Where is she? Where is she, where is she, where is she?"

But when Aaron spotted the body wrapped in a silver funeral shroud, when he pulled the material back, it wasn't his mother's face.

Her skin was drained of color, to the point he could see the dark network of her veins. Golden magic still flickered across her skin. And there was nothing behind her smoky-gray eyes.

No. No no no no no—

Aaron's eyes snapped open. He whipped his head from side to side, his bedroom slowly coming into focus.

But it still took him a few moments to look down. A few more to process the sight of Analia pinned beneath him, one of his daggers pressed to her throat.

But she didn't look afraid. On the contrary, her gaze was perfectly calm as it locked on his.

"It was just a dream," she said. "Just a bad dream."

Aaron shuddered so hard his teeth ached. It was a dream. She was alive. And he...

Aaron jerked the knife from her throat, throwing it across the room. He rolled off her, bringing his hands to his face, his entire body shaking.

Gods, it was a nightmare. Just as it was every other night.

But no one had ever seen him in the aftermath before. He'd done everything in his power to make sure of that.

But Analia didn't seem to be leaving any time soon. On the contrary, she propped herself against his pillows, still murmuring as she brushed the hair from his forehead.

Aaron didn't know what to do. He didn't know if he should shove her away, pretend she wasn't there, pull her closer and remind himself she was alive.

Aaron took a steadying breath, filling his nose with smoke and jasmine. But also, something cold.

Aaron peeked between his fingers. Crystal spare him. That beautiful, wonderful woman had opened the window for him.

"You promised me an epic wallow in grief and agony," Analia said softly. "Do your worst, Stelingente."

Aaron had the strangest urge to laugh. Or maybe sob. He definitely didn't want to think twice as he shifted to rest his head in her lap, a single tear rolling down his cheek.

Analia brushed it away with her thumb. And there was no stopping the silent flood that followed.

"You don't have to say anything," she said, stroking his temple. "Not if you don't want to. But I'll listen if you do."

Gods, she understood. She was willing to take on whatever he gave her, even if it was nothing. Even if it was everything.

Aaron caught her free hand, bringing it to his lips. And even though he remained silent, he had no urge to push her away.

Aaron didn't know how long they stayed like that. He only knew that the images circling through his mind began to slow. Eventually, his body relaxed, every tangled emotion settling into a deep, dull ache in the center of his chest.

"Are you all right?" Analia finally asked, her fingers lightly tangled in his hair.

Aaron nodded.

Analia paused. "Do you want me to go?"

No, he never wanted her to leave. He wanted her to stay where he could hear her breathe, feel her heartbeat, remind himself that of all the people he'd lost, she wasn't one of them.

But Aaron nodded. And peeling his head from her lap was one of the hardest things he'd ever done. Even though he knew it wouldn't be fair to ask her to stay when she didn't know the whole truth.

Analia didn't look offended, though. She kissed his forehead, nearly destroying him right there.

Aaron kept perfectly still as Analia climbed off his bed and slipped out the door. Just as Liss had always done.

But Aaron's heart didn't flinch like he expected. Instead, he rolled over, allowing her lingering warmth to lull him back to sleep.

Analia woke the following morning to find a note slid under her door. Unfolding it, she only found three words: *I appreciate you.*

Analia smoothed the creases in the paper as she wandered through the house, but Aaron was nowhere to be found. With a sneaking suspicion, she stepped through Surce's beaded curtain, imagining the big house. Surce had only mentioned in passing how she had curtains in all crucial locations, and thankfully, the magic seemed intuitive enough.

Indeed, a few moments later, Analia padded down the big house's narrow halls, coming to a door she had known would be shut. Aaron's mother's room.

The last time she'd been here, she'd hesitated to even knock. But now, all she could think about was his silent tears.

She didn't have to ask to know that hadn't been his first nightmare. Just as she knew she couldn't leave him alone to brood in the aftermath.

Analia knocked, but there came no reply. She poked her head inside, spotting Aaron seated on his mother's bed, hunched over a book.

"Aaron?"

He briefly looked up. His face was tired and worn, shadows smudged beneath his eyes. Giving her a quick nod, he returned his gaze to his book.

Well, that wasn't promising.

"Careful," she said, coming to sit beside him. "You squint too much and it'll give you wrinkles."

"I'm sure you'll love me anyway."

Analia watched him turn a page. "Did something happen?"

"The DovenU sent me a letter." Aaron gestured to a crumpled note on the bed. "Six hundred women from every kingdom, and none of them had new information on the Crystal."

He turned another page, a bit harder than necessary. Analia, in turn, didn't know if she was unsettled or intrigued. At least his brooding didn't seem to be related to the night before.

"It just doesn't make sense," Aaron muttered. "Ethelind has to know something. She's spent more time looking at Surce's tapestries than I have. But I've been combing through her journals for hours and I can't find anything."

"So," Analia said, eying the stacks of age-worn journals at his feet. "You're obsessing."

Aaron pursed his lips. "Maybe."

It was to be that game, then.

"You know," Analia said, shifting closer on the bed, "you're allowed to take a break."

"I'm fine."

"Then why are you in your mother's room?"

"You get to brood when you go to the roof," he said, hunching his shoulders over the journal. "Why can't I?"

What a stubborn, stubborn man. Unfortunately for him, Analia was even more stubborn.

"All right," she said, settling back against the pillows. "I can't begrudge you your brooding. I only wished to tell you that not all breaks need to be boring."

Aaron made a noncommittal noise.

"In fact," Analia said, nudging the book out of his lap with her feet, "you and I can talk instead."

"I thought we already were."

"No, before I was pestering you. Now, we're talking."

Aaron looked as though he were debating retrieving his book. Analia put her feet in his lap, and finally, his wary eyes moved to her. "Talking about what?"

"Well, you mentioned spending a great deal of time in Surce's studio."

"Yes?"

Analia shrugged. "I was just wondering what you could possibly be staring at."

Aaron looked away. "It's not important."

"Really?" Analia slid her foot up his thigh, reclaiming his attention. "I was just thinking how Surce already had one tapestry of me from decades ago. I can only imagine how many others there might be."

She rested her foot against his stomach, lining it up with the V of his hipbone. Aaron's eyes locked on hers.

"Are you asking," he said slowly, "if I spend my days wistfully staring at your likeness?"

"Oh no," Analia said, "I was just wondering what you saw. Who knows. Maybe there's something new I could show you."

Bracing her feet against him, she stretched. "But if you'd rather sit here and develop wrinkles, I can hardly stop you."

Aaron's eyes moved first to the arch of her hips, then up to the strip of bare stomach she exposed. "And you call me the shameless flirt," he murmured.

His gaze seemed to slide over her every nerve. But Analia kept her expression nonchalant. "I've been trained by the best meaningless flirt I know."

Something darkened in Aaron's gaze. "Is that what you want me to say?" he asked, shifting so he sat beside her. "That it's never been meaningless with you? That I spend my nights fantasizing about the rip of black lace and the soft skin of your thighs?"

Analia fisted her hands in the duvet. "Do you really rip them?"

"I'll tell you mine if you tell me yours," he breathed, lowering his lashes as he leaned toward her.

Analia let him guide her back against the pillows, acutely aware of the heat of his skin, the way he partially propped himself over her. So close. Barely avoiding contact.

"I don't think I have one," she managed.

"Really?" Aaron asked, his lips brushing her neck. "You've never imagined what it would be like to have that perfect kiss? The one that starts slow and sweet, building into a frenzy of lips and heat and passion."

Analia's cheeks flushed. "I never knew you had such a vivid imagination."

"That's not even the full image." He skimmed his nose along her jaw, his voice dropping to a rumble. "Your hand on my chest. My hand on your thigh. Slowly sliding up the sensitive skin, coming closer and closer to exactly where you want me."

Analia's breathing hitched as Aaron's fingers glided up her inner thigh over her leggings. Higher, higher, her legs parting slightly.

"No," he decided, his fingers sliding back down. "Better to draw it out. Better to build the anticipation for the moment my hand finally finds that perfect spot that makes you moan."

Aaron's fingers idly circled along the curve of her thigh, his voice a hot whisper on her cheek. "Pressing. Teasing until you're grinding on my hand, begging for me to be inside you. One finger, two, my hand moving faster. Harder. Your body shuddering as you get closer and closer, until I finally capture your mouth once more, and you fall apart with my name on your lips and my tongue down your throat."

Analia's breath caught as Aaron's hand tightened around her thigh. She was drowning in his words, his touch, the heat that pooled low in her stomach.

Aaron lifted his face to hers, his gaze searing her mouth.

"There," he breathed, brushing a lock of hair behind her ear. "Now you have something to think about at night."

It took a moment for his words to register.

Analia blinked. Once. Twice. Then, she shoved him away, "You truly have no shame."

Aaron fell back on the bed, a slow, wicked grin curling his mouth. "You started this, Analia. You should have known how this was going to end—quit it!"

Aaron laughed, throwing up his arms as she smacked him with a pillow.

"You're unbelievable!"

"I'm unbelievable?" Aaron protested. "You came halfway across my kingdom to seduce me from my studies, just to attack me with a pillow when you succeeded."

Succeeded? Analia looked down, just as Aaron swiped the pillow. She made a noise of protest, trying to snatch it back, but Aaron held it out of her reach.

"Honestly," he said, "You can't blame me. I already have a hard enough time thinking straight around you. But when you flash a chance to earn one of these?" He traced her smile with a corner of the pillow. "This could have ended no other way."

Analia shook her head. But there was no denying how her heart softened as she leaned back against his pillows.

Gods, what had she done to deserve him? She looked up at him, wondering if he even realized his Phoenix Gate smile was curving his mouth.

The quiet that settled around them was soft, comfortable. But Analia's pulse still struggled to slow.

It meant nothing, though. As Aaron said, he was a flirt. Of course he would know what to say to provoke a reaction.

Analia's eyes flicked down, but Aaron was absently fiddling with the pillow conveniently placed on his lap.

"So," he eventually said. "You've been told the significance of our human visit?"

Analia's eyes darted up. "Only the basics."

Mor had only told her it was the anniversary of the war with the human's conclusion—although Laness's squirming told her there was more.

"I'm assuming they didn't inform you of how my mom died during the war."

Chills ran down Analia's spine. "No," she said quietly. "They did not."

Aaron let out a heavy sigh, running his hand through his hair. "To this day, I don't know who killed my mom. And that anger...? That anger is why Mor rules over the humans, not me."

Analia traced the duvet's pattern with a finger. Sometimes, the gods, the Crystal, were unequivocally cruel.

"The humans don't deserve to have as wonderful of a king as you," she told him. "And now, if they try to say otherwise, they can deal with me."

She summoned a tiny flame to each of her fingertips, ignoring the twinge in her gut.

"My lethal shooting star," Aaron sighed.

She was really starting to love that nickname.

"We've got diaries to skim," she said, reaching over him to grab the discarded book.

Wordlessly, they turned their attention to the pages before them. And if Analia happened to lean into him as they read, neither of them commented on it. Nor did they move away.

Chapter 47

Dimitri followed Patryclas across the quiet boardwalk, the recent snowfall crunching beneath his boots.

Ever since returning from the statue of Darmanten, he, Sabi, and Rayner had launched into a flurry of activity: researching the Wraithhouse, gathering supplies, going through every angle of the potentially disastrous scheme Dimitri had outlined. He hadn't even realized it had been a week since he saw Patryclas until the king knocked on his bedchamber door, saying he'd like to show him something.

"Are we there yet?" Dimitri whined, shoving his frozen hands into his cloak pockets.

"Well," Patryclas said, "we're about thirty seconds closer from when you last asked, so I suppose so."

Dimitri sighed loudly.

"Oh, you're fine," Patryclas said, turning on to a narrow side path. "You can make it a few more minutes."

"Why won't you just tell me where we're going?" Dimitri complained.

"Because it's a surprise, Dima."

"But I don't like surprises."

"Well, I think you'll like this one."

Patryclas stopped beside a small building tucked away in a corner of the square. He stepped aside, allowing Dimitri to peer through the geometric display window into the shop beyond. And all he saw was books.

Dimitri hurried up to the window, brushing the snow from the ledge and leaning in to get a closer look.

Gods, there were so many of them. They stood carefully propped and angled on a table in front of the window, cramped together on the shelves of massive bookcases. He even thought he saw some stacked on a side counter.

Patryclas had brought him to a bookshop. An old one, from the looks of it. He was certainly correct in thinking Dimitri would like it, but why bother trekking all the way out here in the cold when there were countless books he could show Dimitri in the library. Unless...

"Is this your family's bookshop?" Dimitri asked, twisting around excitedly.

"It is." Patryclas readjusted Dimitri's hood. "I know I've been busy the past couple weeks, so I thought this might be a nice way to make it up to you."

"You didn't have to do that for me," Dimitri said. After all, he was used to being alone. He knew he couldn't be a king's top priority.

"Who said this was all about you?" Patryclas asked. "Maybe I was the one who was missing our time together."

Dimitri's entire being lit up. "So, what I'm hearing is this is all about *you.*"

"Oh, completely," Patryclas laughed. "I even brought you out in the cold because I missed your relentless complaining."

He moved around Dimitri to open the door, Dimitri hiding his grin in his hands.

"Well, go on," Patryclas said, nudging him forward. "Go explore."

Dimitri didn't hesitate. He stepped inside the empty shop, not needing to glance back to know Patryclas was right behind him as he headed off.

The bookstore was pleasantly warm. Dimitri took his time as he passed through each row of shelves, his fingers skimming over book spines, his eyes trying to take everything in.

Far above his head, multicolored chains of crystals descended from the ceiling. Many had been woven into butterflies, mushrooms, and the like. Tucked away in a back corner, he spotted a fist-sized purple stone, carved in the shape of a heart. The same heart on the inside of his wrist.

This was where Patryclas had grown up. It was where he'd spent all his time sequestered away as he struggled to read. And Dimitri wanted to see it all.

"What's over here?" he asked, heading for a counter in the back of the shop.

"This is where you can purchase your books," Patryclas explained, following a step behind. "My mother usually lingers around here, but I suppose she must have stepped out."

"Do you have records to keep track of everything, like in the library?"

"We do. It's nowhere near as large due to the size difference, but my mother has lists of all the books in her shop, the number of copies, which books have sold, everything."

Dimitri was fascinated. "Can anyone see it?"

"No," Patryclas said, leaning against the counter with a faint smile. "But I suppose you could be an exception."

Dimitri grinned. Pivoting on his heel, he headed back toward the shelves, "I want to see everything first."

"But of course," Patryclas laughed.

Dimitri continued his investigation of the shop. He passed a back staircase that Patryclas said led to a storage area—which Dimitri figured he shouldn't go poking through. Looping around two central marble statues of books, he finally found his way into what appeared to be a reading nook.

Cushioned armchairs and couches created a rectangle around a long, low wooden table. As Dimitri approached, he realized one of the chairs had been carved to look like it was made from stacks of books.

Dimitri laughed, flopping down onto the book throne. "Did you used to practice your reading here?" he asked, looking up at Patryclas.

The king leaned against a nearby bookcase, watching Dimitri with an emotion he couldn't quite read. At his words, Patryclas shook his head.

"Not often," he said, coming to sit on the couch perpendicular to Dimitri's. "There were usually people over here, so I liked to hide in the other corner."

"You were always so shy," a clipped female voice called.

Dimitri jumped. He craned his neck as footsteps descended the back stairs, the speaker stepping into the reading nook a moment later.

The similarities between Patryclas and his mother were uncanny. It went beyond their dark brown hair, brilliant green eyes, and soft curve of their mouths. It was the way they tilted their heads in greeting. The way they formed a tiny line between their brows as they studied Dimitri. Even the long, slender fingers she curled around the large wooden crate in her arms were identical to Patryclas's.

"I was wondering if you were here," Patryclas said, rising to help her with the crate.

"Did you think I left my shop unlocked and unattended?" She wrinkled her nose. Passing her crate to Patryclas, she sharply turned on her heel. "And you. I haven't seen you here before."

Dimitri flinched, somehow feeling like he'd been scolded. "I'm Dimitri."

"Ah, so *you're* Dimitri."

Dimitri squirmed. He shot a quick look at Patryclas, who gave the barest shake of his head. So, she didn't know his true identity.

"I should have guessed as much," she went on without pause, "seeing as my son brought you here. Elene. A pleasure."

She stuck out her hand. Dimitri took it uncertainly, her hand gripping his and giving a sharp shake.

All right, maybe there was one difference between Elene and Patryclas: Elene was downright intimidating. Dimitri glanced to Patryclas once more, but he was preoccupied with the crate he'd placed on the table.

"Mother," he said, poking through its contents, "how big of an order did you get?"

"As big as I needed," she said, swatting his hand away. "I've had an influx of orders the past couple weeks. Sabina seems to be pawning off some of her requests on me, but it's no more than the usual winter rush. You might have remembered that if you came to visit more often."

Elene gave Patryclas a pointed look. For the first time in all the months Dimitri had known him, Patryclas blushed. He ducked his head, "Apologies, Mother."

"Don't worry," Dimitri said without thinking. "He brought me here because he's been neglecting me, too."

Patryclas looked up quickly.

"Is that so?" Elene turned to face Dimitri once more, peering at him more closely. "You enjoy books?"

Dimitri nodded.

"Do you know any of the ones in here?"

She stepped aside, beckoning Dimitri closer. Rising from his seat, he moved to peer into the crate, breathing in the smell of wood and paper.

The books inside were stacked, so Dimitri could see rows of spines. His eyes skimmed down the first line, immediately brightening when he recognized his own poetry collection.

"Ah, so you know that one," Elene said.

"I have my own copy back at the castle."

"Finally! A child with good taste!"

Dimitri let out a startled laugh. "Does that mean you like it, too?"

"Mother loves all poetry," Patryclas explained, having retreated to sit on the couch. "Not only is the entire left section of the shop dedicated to it, but recently, she's started having weekly poetry readings."

"And yet," Elene said, "it was the one genre I could never get you to read."

"Why not?" Dimitri asked, looking up from the crate.

Patryclas tugged on his jacket sleeve, his voice dropping to a mumble. "It never made sense to me."

"Doesn't your Blessing revolve around understanding emotions?"

Elene let out a sharp laugh, "That's what I said."

"You would think that would make him predisposed to interpreting it."

"And yet, the only thing he was predisposed to was hiding on the wrong side of the store."

"I never should've introduced you two," Patryclas muttered. But Dimitri caught the corner of his mouth twitch.

"Oh, don't sulk, my dear," Elene said, moving to kiss his cheek. "You grew up to understand political talk. That's even more confusing than poetry."

Patryclas ran a hand down his face, and Elene turned her head to wink at Dimitri. All right. So maybe she wasn't *completely* intimidating.

"All right, then," Elene said, returning to the crate. "Since you two are here, you can make yourselves useful. Dimitri, you have learned the sections, yes? Good. Grab a stack and help me shelve these."

There was no room for debate.

Dimitri spent the rest of the afternoon helping Elene with her books. He hadn't paid too close attention to her shelf organization when first exploring her shop, but he quickly realized it was completely different from the Moon Castle library. When he asked her about it, all she said was, "I like it this way."

The more Dimitri thought about it, the same could be said about her entire shop. She stocked the books she liked. She organized them the way she liked. Even the design of the physical store was up to her. And Dimitri found the creative freedom surprisingly appealing.

"So," Elene said, coming to join Dimitri and Patryclas at a shelf. "What is it about poetry that you enjoy? The rhyme scheme? The imagery?"

"I like the rhythm of the lines," Dimitri said, reaching up to slide a book onto the shelf.

"Ah, the meter. Tell me why."

"It's a question, Mother, not an interrogation," Patryclas sighed.

Elene ignored him, looking at Dimitri expectantly. Dimitri cocked his head, realizing he'd never thought about it before.

"I like how it feels," he decided, shelving another book. "When everything is consistent, it feels... symmetrical. Purposeful, I think. But then when it breaks and all of that is lost, there's a reason for it."

Patryclas's expression softened. Elene seemed to silently turn over his response, then nodded to herself.

"I could use someone like you," she said, turning back to the shelf. "Thoughtful. Knows how to follow an organizational pattern. Not to mention, you being here would increase the likelihood of my son coming to visit."

Dimitri smiled slightly. "You'll have to take it up with Sabi."

"Sabina needs to learn how to share," Elene muttered.

Patryclas stifled a laugh. Clearly, he, too, could imagine just how well that would go over with Sabi.

But it might be nice to get out of the castle. He could spend his afternoons in the shop, helping Elene with her books and customers, harassing Patryclas, heading back to the castle with him to assist Sabi in the evenings. He would have to find time to visit Rayner as well, but he would figure that out...

Across the shop, there came the sound of the door opening. Patryclas turned, but Elene waved him off, calling out a greeting as she whisked around the corner and out of sight.

"I like your mom," Dimitri decided, shelving his final book.

"I thought you might," Patryclas said. "You two feel things in very similar ways."

"You mean big?"

"Among other things. Although I'm sorry she decided to put us to work all day."

"Please," Dimitri said, "she just gave me a reason to snoop through all her book orders."

Elene's voice drew closer as she spoke with the customer.

"In that case," Patryclas said, pushing off the bookcase, "perhaps we should finally unleash your nosiness on our store records."

Dimitri brightened. He made to follow Patryclas toward the back counter, barely registering Elene's voice about to round the corner behind him.

The customer laughed.

Dimitri's entire body turned to ice.

Patryclas's head whipped around. He reached for Dimitri, undoubtedly to usher him away. But the two rounded the corner.

Deardryn wore a black cloak lined with fur, her lavender dress peeking out from underneath it. The hair around her face was damp with snowflakes, causing her golden curls to straighten. The moment she spotted Patryclas, her expression brightened.

"Patryclas," she said, pushing back her hood. "I wasn't expecting to see you here."

Patryclas recovered remarkably fast. "I'm surprised to see you as well."

Dimitri's hands tightened around one of the shelves. He was trapped. Nowhere to go.

"Sabina informed me it might be faster if I acquired some of my books from your mother."

"And you simply couldn't resist an excuse to take a look around," Patryclas finished.

"You know me too well."

Elene's eyes darted between them, but she remained silent.

"Although forgive me," Deardryn went on, "I don't believe we've met."

Dimitri felt her eyes land on him like a shock to his spine.

"This is Sabi's assistant," Patryclas explained smoothly, resting a hand on Dimitri's shoulder. "He heard I was coming to help my mother unpack her books today and offered his services."

Crystal spare him, what was he supposed to do? He'd never been this close to her in the Moon Kingdom. Even with his disguise, he'd made sure to keep his distance whenever she was near.

"That's incredibly generous of him," Deardryn said. "Especially on a day like this."

Could he slowly back away? Or would any sudden movements catch her attention?

"I know," Patryclas said. "I almost dragged Sylas out of his meeting just so he could shadowjump us here and spare us the walk."

"I had the same thought," Deardryn laughed. "I haven't managed to explore this section of the square, though, so I still had to brave the last few boardwalks."

He couldn't just stay where he was. Any moment, she would turn her attention back to him. He had to move, he had to do something. Crystal spare him, why couldn't he move?

"At any rate," Deardryn said, turning back to Dimitri, "it's nice to finally meet the man behind all my books."

She was looking at him. She was looking directly at him. He had to move.

Dimitri mechanically turned away from the bookcase. He kept his head lowered as he bowed, his voice barely squeezing past his throat. "It's a pleasure, Your Majesty."

Did she recognize his voice? Did she suspect who he was? Dimitri let his back straighten, his eyes sliding up to hers.

Gods, he knew those eyes. He'd spent twenty years learning to read their every look, every thickly veiled emotion.

And he knew what they looked like when she was startled.

Dimitri felt like his body had been slammed into movement. He tore his gaze from hers, his body nearly colliding with the bookcase as he turned toward it once more.

"I'm sorry," Patryclas said suddenly, stepping in front of Dimitri. "We're all just standing here talking and wasting your time, Deardryn. Come, let me help you find your books so you can get back to your work."

With an easy smile, he gestured for his mother and Deardryn to follow, the three talking amiably as they continued down the row. The moment they disappeared around the corner, Dimitri slumped against the bookcase.

She was startled. She was startled when she looked at him. Which meant she hadn't been expecting to see what she did.

Had his disguise started to fade? Did she recognize something in his expression? She had no reason to be startled when looking at someone she'd never met unless something had caught her attention. But what? Crystal spare him, why was she startled?

Dimitri shoved off of the bookcase. His body moved on instinct, heading back toward the crate, just needing something he could do, something that was in his control. But when he peered down into the crate still sitting on the reading nook's table, he found it empty.

They had finished. There was nothing left for him to do. Nothing.

Slowly, Dimitri sank down on the couch, his head falling into his hands.

There was nothing left for him to do. Not with the books. Not with Deardryn. He'd already disguised his appearance, did everything he could to keep his distance. There was nothing else he could have done to prevent this from happening.

He'd always known this moment was inevitable. But how could one woman threaten to take everything away from him? How could one woman have him so afraid?

Dimitri didn't know how much time had passed when there came approaching footsteps. He shrank back into the couch, not daring to look up.

"It's all right, Dima," Patryclas soothed, coming to kneel before him. "It's only me."

He reached out, gently pulling Dimitri's hands from his face. "You're safe, Dima. I promise. My mother escorted her outside. She's gone. It's over."

"She was startled," Dimitri said, blinking hard. "She was startled when she looked at me. I know you sensed it."

Patryclas hesitated a fraction of a moment. "I did."

Dimitri cringed. He made to hide his face once more, but Patryclas tightened his grip on his wrists.

"I did feel it," he repeated, forcing Dimitri to look at him. "And what I felt was so faint, Dima. It was there and gone in a flash. I wouldn't have thought twice about it if I hadn't felt your reaction."

"But why was she startled in the first place?" Dimitri asked miserably.

"Well, I can't give you a definite answer. But if I had to guess, I think she was surprised I had brought you, a seemingly unimportant member of my staff, to my family's shop. Especially when I could have just as easily brought Sabi. Doesn't that seem a little unexpected?"

Dimitri bit his lip. He could see the logic in Patryclas's words. After all, Deardryn herself didn't exactly have a habit of forming any sort of connection with her servants. But gods, the ache in his chest didn't care.

"What do you need, Dimitri?" Patryclas asked softly, moving to sit on the couch beside him.

Dimitri looked up at him, his voice unbearably small. "I just want her to go."

Patryclas's shoulders slumped. He ran a hand down his face, his voice seeming to drag out of him. "I know you do."

Dimitri didn't try to fight as Patryclas pulled him close. He closed his eyes, knowing he was safe to scream or sob or anything else. But all he needed was a moment. Just a moment to process everything that had happened.

Deardryn's arrival. The look in her eyes. The fear.

But also, meeting Elene. Exploring the bookshop. Imagining a future for the first time in he couldn't remember how long.

Not all of it had been bad. It was just... a lot.

"Tell you what," Patryclas said, smoothing back Dimitri's hair. "You go get that poetry book you love, and we'll see if you can make it make sense to me."

"I thought we only had today, not a lifetime," Dimitri mumbled.

Patryclas scoffed. "Go get your book."

Releasing Dimitri, he kissed the side of his head and shooed him away. Dimitri obediently headed off for the poetry section, not immediately noticing his tiny smile.

Today *had* been a lot. But he'd felt it all. And he'd survived.

Grabbing the copy of his poetry collection from the shelf, Dimitri returned to sit beside Patryclas. And as they flipped through the pages, Patryclas becoming increasingly bemused, Dimitri found that image of his future and let it unfold just a little bit more.

Chapter 48

The two weeks leading up to their Human Kingdom visit were a flurry of activity.

Branten ended up creating the counterfeit scroll himself to, in his words, "Avoid crushing the hands of those with big mouths." Meanwhile, Laness, Mor, and Surce scoured their resources, but no new information on the scroll came up.

The night before they were to leave, Analia and Laness lounged on the couch, trading gossip and a bottle of Aaron's finest between them. Eventually, Analia asked if Laness would be joining them the following day, but she shook her head.

"The humans and I have a long, nasty history," she said. "Even before they captured me during the war. I prefer not to go back there unless I have to."

"I think Aaron would prefer the same," Analia mused, turning their empty wine bottle between her fingers. "He's been brooding for two weeks straight."

"That has less to do with the humans than it does with you."

"What do you mean?" Analia asked, sitting up.

Laness flushed and started to stammer an excuse.

"Laness, tell me."

Laness's eyes darted around the room. "This is why Aaron says I shouldn't drink."

"Too late," Analia said, lightly shaking their empty bottle. "Explain."

Laness squirmed. Finally, she sighed, slumping back into the couch.

"Aaron and his family have been the villains of so many stories, Anna. For the most part, Aaron has embraced it. But the idea of becoming the monster in your story, too..."

Laness bit her lip. "Aaron wore my bracelet at all times when he was in the Sun Kingdom. And I have never felt such anguish from him as the night you found out who he truly is."

The wine turned sour on Analia's tongue. "What does that have to do with the humans?"

"When Aaron visits the humans, he's ruthless. Cruel. He becomes every bit the monster history made him out to be because he knows that's the best way to keep them in line. And now, he has to finally show that monster to you."

Laness averted her gaze, fiddling with the bracelets on her arms. Analia looked down into her empty bottle, mentally turning over her time in Sun.

The months of Pryanth's chaos, his cruelty, his kindness with barbed edges. Aaron had seen it all. Just as he'd seen her carry around Pryanth's pendant like a token while she shoved him away.

"Pryanth was supposed to be my safe place," she said, half to herself. "But Aaron was my shelter from his storm. I don't know many monsters who would do that."

The following morning, Analia stood at her vanity, struggling to untangle her hair. At the sound of a knock on her door, she looked up, her comb snagging in a tangle.

"Come in," she sighed, yanking her comb free.

Aaron stepped inside a moment later. He was dressed all in black, the darkness seeming to ripple like living shadows. It only gave way to his family's sigil embroidered in silver threads against his right shoulder: a filled-in constellation of the Crystal. A black-and-silver crown dangled from his wrist, its diamonds and sapphires forming tiny constellations across the metal.

This wasn't the King of Starlight. It was the Heir of Death. And he was mesmerizing.

"Hoping I wasn't dressed yet?" she asked, dragging her attention back to her mirror.

"While that would have been a perk," he said, sounding unusually tired as he sat on her bed, "I actually came to give you one final out."

He really did not want to do this.

Analia kept her voice light as she asked, "Are you that desperate to avoid wedding planning with me?"

Aaron barely cracked a smile. "What would you like, my shooting star?" he asked, leaning back against her pillows. "Elegance? Grandeur? Ice sculptures carved in your likeness, all giving your 'Aaron's being annoying' look?"

Analia snorted. "Is that what typical Star Royal weddings consist of?"

"Honestly? I have no clue. I've never been alive for one, and my mind always glazed over when Ethelind started talking about dinnerware patterns."

"I've always liked the Ash Kingdom's ceremony," Analia said, easing her comb through a tangle. "Everyone gathers around a massive firepit with individual pyres for each guest. The betrotheds stand at the center unlit pile where they say their vows, and then they each light a stick to set the kindling ablaze. The rest of the night is a flurry of dancing and burning sticks as people pass the marriage flame around until every pile is lit."

Analia tipped her head back, remembering the smell of smoke, the way the burning sticks danced through the evening well into the night.

"I like that," Aaron murmured.

Analia caught his eye in the mirror, unable to look away as the tension in his face finally eased. Just as unable as when he'd looked up at her in his mother's room, his eyes smoldering—

"Go from the bottom," he said suddenly.

Analia blinked hard. "What do you mean?"

"You're trying to drag the entire tangle through your hair. If you start from the bottom, you can break it up, piece by piece."

Her hair. He was talking about her hair.

Analia flashed him a dubious look in the mirror, but she complied. Then, she twisted around, "Who taught you that?"

"My mom."

"Really?" Analia moved to the next tangle, painlessly breaking it apart once more. "I feel like there's a story there."

Aaron's expression faltered. He turned on his side, resting his cheek on the back of his hand.

"I told you she lost interest in ruling after the rest of our family died," he said, "but that wasn't strictly true. Sometimes, it felt more like she lost interest in living. She moved through the big house like a ghost, so lost in her thoughts you had to repeat yourself multiple times before her eyes finally focused on you. But most of her time was spent in her room, sometimes reading by the window, other times curled under the covers.

"My grandmother had brought in two servants from the Star Castle to take care of her, but there were some days where she would scream and sob for them to leave her alone. And on those days, I was the only one she would allow to see her. I would comb her hair, make sure she ate, whatever she allowed me to do. And that's how I learned."

His words were a heavy blow to Analia's chest.

"Sometimes," he went on, "she would read to me while I did it. Other times she was completely silent. But sometimes she would just hold me as tight as she could, as if reminding herself I was still alive. And I was always terrified when she finally let go, but she always seemed just a bit more solid after that."

"You gave her something to hold on to," Analia murmured, setting down her comb and starting to braid.

"She gave me something, too."

Aaron rose and came to stand behind her, his arm brushing her side as he retrieved a pin and handed it to her. But all Analia felt was the guilt gnawing her stomach as she thought back over her arrival in his kingdom.

She must have ripped open so many of his scars. Yet, he always stayed.

"I was awful to you when I first arrived here," she said softly.

"Anna..."

"No, don't tell me you understand or that it's all right. You didn't deserve the turmoil I put you through. And I will never be able to tell you how sorry I am for that."

She turned to face him, a lump rising in her throat. But there was no sign of resentment, even lingering hurt on Aaron's face. He only let out a long, tired sigh.

"Analia," he murmured, catching a stray lock of her hair and carefully pinning it back. "I would do it all again. For both of you. But you didn't need me to save you. You did that all on your own."

Maybe. But that didn't erase the fact that sometimes, Aaron's unwavering belief in her was all that kept her going.

Analia touched his cheek. "I appreciate you tremendously."

Aaron's lips parted. He turned his head, brushing a kiss to her palm. Analia turned back to the mirror, the ghost of his lips tingling across her skin.

"You must have truly loved your mom," she said, reaching for another pin.

"There are no words strong enough. Just as there are no words to describe the pain of watching her suffer."

"At that point, you're just dying alongside them."

"Who are you talking about?" Aaron asked curiously.

"My uncle." Analia offered Aaron the braid she'd completed, and he pinched it together as she secured it.

"What's the story there?" he asked.

"Accalon had resisted finding a wife for a long time," she explained. "At first, I think it was because he didn't want some random political marriage. As he continued to get pushed to produce an heir, though, I think it amused him to keep putting it off. But then he met Arienne.

"She was one of the many humans who worked in the mines, and Accalon knew the moment he saw her, that was it. She, however, wasn't so convinced. She put Accalon through his paces, but he only loved her more for it.

"They eventually got married to the shock of the people. Human queens, after all..."

"Unusual," Aaron said, smoothing down her final braid.

"Incredibly. But Accalon never lived by what was usual."

Analia crossed to her wardrobe, Aaron looking away as she changed.

"Arienne quickly became pregnant, my mother also a few months along at the time. Yet, at the end of Aeley's pregnancy and near the end of Arienne's, there was some sort of revolt... outbreak? Accalon would never elaborate.

"Usually, Brenn would have dealt with it, but Aeley had just gone into labor, and he refused to leave her. So, Accalon went to finish it himself. He had promised Arienne he would be back by the end of the day.

"But as one day stretched into three, we think the stress of not knowing what happened to Accalon sent Arienne into premature labor. And... both she and Accalon's son died as a result. He just wasn't ready to be born, and Arienne wouldn't stop bleeding. Leaving Accalon to watch his brother and his wife raise their new child, while he had lost everything. Even when I became more his child than Brenn's."

"You weren't a replacement," Aaron said roughly. He stepped closer once more, his fingers brushing the back of her neck as he tied her gown shut.

Analia bowed her head. "I think," she said after a moment, "at our wedding, Accalon and Elspeth will be immediate friends. They'll spend the entire night in each other's company, dancing and drinking and having a running commentary about the other guests. It will be the one night they don't have to think about wars or their kingdoms or the people they've lost. They can just be... happy."

Analia turned back to face him, just catching the ripple of emotion across his face.

"I think that's exactly what will happen," he said.

Analia looked at their reflection in the mirror. Her gown was made from black, shimmering lace. The long sleeves and skirt obscured most of her skin, but there was something about the translucency of the fabric that still hinted at her body beneath as she moved.

She was elegant. Lethal. The matching pair to the man beside her.

"Time to go?" she asked.

"Almost." Aaron dug around in his pocket. "I told you I didn't know anything about my family's traditions, but that wasn't strictly true. I do know that it starts with a ring."

Aaron pulled out a black velvet ring box. He flipped it open, revealing a silver ring flecked with pearl, set with a circular gray moonstone whose smooth surface gave off a milky blue sheen in the light. Beautiful.

"What do I do?" Analia asked.

"You give me your hand."

Aaron offered his free hand, and Analia didn't hesitate to rest her palm atop his. She shifted her fingers, but Aaron shook his head.

"Close," he said. "But I need your middle finger."

"How come?" Analia asked, her focus going to the fingers Aaron carefully shifted.

"Well, besides getting to flash your jewels with every rude hand gesture, your middle finger is the heart of your hand. Two fingers on this side, two fingers on the other."

Aaron tapped her thumb and pointer finger, then pinky and ring. "Your middle finger is protected by the rest. And that's what I promise to you."

He slid the ring onto her finger, Analia unable to tear her gaze away.

"Do you get a ring?" she asked.

"Not now," he said. "That comes at the wedding ceremony. If my promise has been fulfilled to that point, you give me my ring to promise the same."

Analia didn't need to wait for a wedding ceremony. Even without the ring, Aaron had fulfilled that promise to her. Back in Sun, when he was just her guard. When they weren't speaking after she discovered his secret. Even when she iced him out after her coronation, he had maintained that promise to her.

"So, that was the proposal?" she asked.

Aaron laughed under his breath. "Was that not enough for you?"

Something in his voice had Analia's heart skip a beat.

"What else would you like, my shooting star?" he murmured, sliding his free hand around her waist. "Me on my knees before you? Telling you every single way you inspire me? Your resilience, your determination. Every single scar on your heart that only makes you love even more fiercely. Or perhaps I can wax on about how your smoky eyes and flaming hair threaten to bring me to my knees."

Analia didn't think she was breathing. She gazed up into his face, wondering when he'd come so close. When had his wicked bravado melted away, replaced with something that almost looked like uncertainty.

"What would you say, Analia?" he whispered, sliding his hand out from under hers to cradle her face. "What would your answer be?"

Analia's fingers loosely tangled in the soft fabric of his shirt. She could feel his breath on her mouth, his magic across her senses. The starlight that gifted him the power of death, but cursed him with it as well.

Analia met his gaze, the tenderness in his eyes enough to have her heart aching.

Because it wasn't real. His words, his ring, the look in his eyes. It was all just a part of the performance they would be putting on that day. Even though no one had ever looked at her like that before.

"Much better," she rasped.

For a few moments, Aaron stared at her, motionless. Then, he released her, taking a large step back.

"Then congratulations, Analia," he said, his wicked smirk flashing back into place. "You're stuck with me."

Analia laughed, quickly shaking herself off.

Just another performance.

Chapter 49

Aaron wondered if any other king became nauseated upon entering his kingdom.

The human throne room was dimly lit, shadows flickering across the rafters high above. A crowd had formed along the edges of the room, remaining perfectly silent as Aaron moved between rows of carved pillars, their eyes crawling over his skin.

Gods, there were so many of them. And these were only the humans that lived in the castle.

During the Shattering War, his father had jumped as many Star Kingdom citizens as he could to Starlight: Blessed, Demiblessed, and humans alike. But he hadn't been able to save everyone. Meanwhile, the Human Kingdom had been populating for centuries, to the point Aaron didn't even want to consider how many times over they outnumbered his own kingdom. Especially since it was their numbers and dampers that had given them a chance against the Starlight Kingdom during the war.

It was those very advantages that made them a constant threat.

But that was why he was there, his footsteps slow, unhurried. His unrestrained magic thrumming hard enough the entire castle vibrated.

They all already knew of his power. Just as he knew of their hatred for him. He could feel it in every residual ache across his scarred back.

But that was why he had Mor, now standing on the central dais beside his star-streaked throne. The humans feared the cold calm in his voice as he ordered them to kneel, but they also respected his fairness. Aaron was just the perpetual shadow looming over their kingdom.

Aaron climbed the dais steps. Reaching his throne, he ran his finger along the cold stone arm.

"Well," he said, not turning around, "would you look at this. We have one throne, but two rulers. I suppose two weeks' notice is far too little to assemble a throne."

No one spoke.

"Or perhaps you were busy with celebration preparations," Aaron went on. "We all know what an *outstanding* day it is."

His words sliced through the silence like a blade. The same one that had been buried in his mother's back.

"Rise," he snapped, finally turning to face the humans. They hurried to comply, Aaron catching every uncomfortable shift, every flicker of resentment.

It was clear no one wanted to be there. He should just abolish the tradition entirely.

The thought had barely crossed his mind when a man stepped out of the crowd. Calter: stiff-backed, tight-jawed, head of the council, his cropped hair completely silver despite his forty-odd years.

"Your Majesty," he said, "forgive our offense. We understood that you were to bring your betrothed, but did not anticipate requiring a second throne until your union. We have our brightest blacksmiths designing it as we speak."

"Do you," Aaron said dryly. "I'm sure my betrothed will be thrilled to hear it. Although, I'd hate to speak for her."

Aaron's magic pulsed.

Right on cue, the doors opened.

The crowd turned, whispers surging as Analia stepped inside.

Gods, black was her color. It contrasted her natural features, making her look sharper, more vivid.

He'd barely been able to tear his gaze from her back in her bedroom. Now, as she passed between the dark stone pillars, her face lifted for all to see, she wasn't beautiful. She wasn't the wary Princess of Ash.

She was devastating. She was the terrifying, mesmerizing Queen of Death. One whose smoldering gaze locked on his, moving down his face, his chest, down to his boots and up again.

Holy Crystal above. Aaron subtly braced himself against his throne as she reached the dais, blood rushing through his veins.

"Presenting," Mor said, stepping to the edge of the stairs, "Her Highness Analia Valarus, Princess of Ash and promised Queen of Starlight."

He took her hand, leading her up the dais steps as voices began to buzz. They positively exploded as Aaron took her by the shoulders, guiding her into the seat of the throne.

Aaron smirked. He sat on the armrest, casually lounging back against the throne. "I believe it's customary to bow to your queen."

His magic flashed. The humans scrambled to comply, their voices choking off. Analia watched, expression unreadable. Eventually, she told them to straighten.

"It's an honor to meet you," she said.

There were infinite interpretations in her tone. A fact that the humans clearly hadn't missed as they exchanged looks. Yet, they remained quiet as Calter stepped forward once more.

"Your Majesty," he said, his voice tight. "You've brought a foreigner into our home. Our sacred, hidden home."

"One that would no longer be standing if not for her," Aaron said coldly. "I suggest you thank her, Councilman, instead of questioning your queen."

Calter's lips thinned. He bowed to Analia, mumbling some form of thanks. Analia didn't reply.

"Your Majesty," Laurel, another council member said, pushing through the crowd. "Surely you understand our uncertainties. No foreigner should be aware of our existence, let alone a Royal. You two should not have even been able to meet—unless there are circumstances that we're not aware of."

The crowd stirred. Just as the viper wanted. She may appear unassuming, with her large blue eyes and youthful complexion, but she was by far the most dangerous woman in the kingdom.

"Princess Analia and I met while I was ensuring my kingdoms remained undetected," Aaron said. "She renounced her kingdom, and I returned with her as my betrothed. That is all you'll hear of the story."

Several humans stiffened, unease starting to sharpen.

"I'm no threat to this kingdom's secret," Analia said. Aaron tensed, but Analia touched his hand. "His Majesty had me swear an oath on the Crystal and the gods to protect the secret he would tell me. There are no alliances, no disguised plans, nothing that impacts this kingdom besides my impending joint rule."

For a few moments, no one seemed to take a breath. Finally, the humans slowly, uneasily, settled back into wariness.

A small, petty part of Aaron was annoyed. He shouldn't have to justify himself or Analia. But he knew her addition was clever, necessary even.

"Treasonous whore," a voice muttered. "It's just a matter of time before she burns our kingdom to the ground—"

A silver spear of magic shot through the crowd, choking off the speaker's words as it wrapped around his neck.

"Ancel," Aaron purred, his magic chilling the room as he yanked the fair-haired man toward the dais. "What a pleasure it is to hear your voice. You, after all, have always been one to amaze me. Do you know why?"

Ancel struggled, his face turning red.

"No guesses?" Aaron asked, his magic tightening. "That's a shame. Especially since it's the remarkable looseness of your tongue that has captured my fascination. Fortunately for me, that should make it all the easier to pull from your mouth."

Ancel's eyes widened. He frantically clawed at his neck, his mouth moving wordlessly.

The silent apologies had Aaron's blood freezing until it burned.

He coiled his magic up to Ancel's face, feeling his life force shrink back. It was useless. There was no escaping death. Aaron had learned that the hard way. Perhaps it was one of Ancel's ancestors who had taught him that lesson.

Aaron forced his magic between Ancel's gritted teeth, wrapping around his tongue, the noose around his neck squeezing, squeezing, squeezing—

"No." Analia rested her hand on his thigh.

That small touch hit him like a gods-damned anchor, slamming through the ice that had collected in his veins. He quickly loosened his hold on Ancel, his heart pounding in his ears.

"No?" he repeated, remarkably steady.

"Kill him, and you kill his lesson," Analia said.

Aaron made to tell her he didn't give a fuck about Ancel's lesson, that the true lesson was for everyone else. But Analia wasn't done.

"There's no way of knowing if he's learned to keep his tongue in check if he has none. What he needs is a warning. A reminder of what will happen if such behavior should persist." She ran her finger along the length of Aaron's pinky, sending a shiver down his spine. "Take his finger instead."

Aaron barely hid his shock. Ancel's face contorted as he weighed his options, but Aaron didn't give him time to decide.

Leaning down, he kissed Analia's cheek, his voice deliciously cold in the silence. "Done."

Aaron's magic latched onto Ancel's pinky. Ancel screamed as his finger decayed, the sound ricocheting off the walls, but no one moved to help him. Even as Aaron's magic released him, they remained perfectly still.

Ancel stumbled back, tears streaming down his face as he examined his blackened finger. He no longer tried to conceal his hatred as he looked up at Aaron. But as his gaze moved to Analia, he fell to his knees.

"Thank you, Your Majesty," he blathered. "Thank you for your mercy."

Aaron was unconvinced.

Analia remained perfectly cool as she studied the trembling man before her. "I understand this kingdom prides itself on its lack of magic," she said. "Bear that in mind the next time you address your ruler."

Ancel's mouth worked silently.

"Rise," she snapped.

Ancel scrambled to comply. Two humans finally stepped out of the crowd to usher him away, a savage wave of satisfaction rolling through Aaron's body.

"Magnificent, isn't she?" He slid his arm around Analia's shoulders, wishing he could do far more than that. "Although she has yet to see the extent of her castle."

The crowd jostled, some volunteering their assistance, others trying to duck out of sight. Analia scanned their faces.

"You." She crooked a finger at a man in the center of the pack. "Show me the castle while my betrothed sits council."

Lyonal? Interesting choice.

Aaron was quick to dismiss the room after that. Hundreds of humans shoved toward the doors, voices colliding as they fled. But all things considered, that had gone better than Aaron could have hoped. Now, he just had the headache that was the council to contend with.

Aaron pressed his face to the side of Analia's head, closing his eyes as he breathed in the floral scent of her hair. "You were fantastic," he murmured.

Analia stroked his temple. And Aaron had to stomp down hard on the wave of *what ifs* that surfaced in his mind.

With a sigh, he pulled back. The two rose, Lyonal hurrying to the foot of the dais to meet Analia. Aaron continued toward the group of waiting councilmen, Mor a half step behind.

"You so much as touch her, Lyonal," Aaron called, not looking back, "and I'll be displaying your bones when Analia is done with you."

Lyonal squeaked a reply. Reaching the doors, Aaron finally turned. Just to see Analia smiling up at a pale Lyonal, black flames dancing across her fingertips—holy gods that woman.

A nalia strode through the Human Castle halls, Lyonal hurrying to keep up.

Choosing him to be her guide was easy. There were many hostile faces as she entered the Throne Room; his was just concealed the worst. Either he had enough social power to be bold—meaning if she won him to her side, she also won his lackeys—or he simply had poor self-control. In that case, his inevitable punishment would send just as strong a message.

Regardless, Analia was playing a delicate game. She couldn't let Lyonal's fear turn into hatred. Nor could she try too hard to endear herself to him without it seeming suspicious.

So, she only asked the occasional question on her tour. Offered brief compliments of the castle. And shot a midnight flame over his shoulder to light a sconce when she caught him sizing her up.

Lyonal's eyes widened.

"What's through here?" Analia asked, pushing through a door carved with twining lilies. Lyonal stammered something about a courtyard garden as he hurried after her.

As they traveled deeper and deeper into the castle, Analia kept her senses on high alert. She knew there would be few magic fields to sift through given the humans' dislike of magic, but she was still taken aback by the silence. No hum through the pipes, no flicker in the lamps and sconces. There didn't even seem to be electricity, undoubtedly due to the association with the electrically Blessed.

But also, no scroll. In fact, there was nothing at all outside of Aaron's and Mor's distant networks.

Analia checked, double checked, but her shield was completely lowered. Which meant something was horribly wrong.

It was lunchtime by the time Analia finished her tour. Lyonal escorted her to the King's private suite, looking more than a bit relieved as Analia dismissed him.

Pushing through the heavy wood door, she stepped into a lavish common space decorated in earthy tones. A cart of various juices and covered dishes stood in one corner, the note on top telling her Aaron and Mor had to return to their meeting. Analia selected a dish at random, her mind churning as she sat at a small circular table.

The obvious answer was the scroll was no longer in the castle. Yet, Surce's logic made sense: why get rid of the scroll if it was something they could hold over the Royals' heads? She supposed they could have relocated it, but the certainty of the note and the importance of the scroll suggested there was some kind of magical safeguard here.

In that case, it was most likely dampered. If only she wasn't powerless against them.

Zinia's chamber had immediately snuffed out her flames. She had been oblivious to Aaron's damper until she touched it. Even in Deardryn's temple, the only reason she had located the damper box was because everything else had been magically charged. It had been process of elimination—wait.

The key to finding the damper in Deardryn's temple had been looking for the place of magical emptiness. So, Analia just had to recreate those conditions.

Analia rested her fork against her lips, searching for another way. But she knew there was none. So, she closed her eyes. And using the same radiating technique Aaron had taught her, she set her magic loose.

Heat erupted from her body in an endless wave. It flashed across the common room, spreading across every surface, squeezing through the cracks around the door and flooding the hallways beyond.

Part of her was quietly terrified, knowing it was impossible the humans wouldn't notice the temperature change. But there was nothing she could do about that. Not as her magic coiled up the stairs, storming through the second, third, fourth floors.

Analia's hand clenched around her armrest, the rage that accompanied her magic starting to rise. But she carefully tucked it away in a corner of her mind, remaining focused on the task before her.

The hope was if the scroll was contained within a damper, that damper would block her magic the moment they came in contact. Truthfully, she had no idea if it would work.

As her magic reached the heart of the castle, Analia's stomach jolted. She made to pull back, but before she could, something clamped down on her heat wave.

Onyx hands yanked on her magic, reeling it in, swallowing it down until Analia was choking back a scream. Especially as she felt those hands reaching for more, reaching for her.

Analia slammed the lid back on her magic. The heat radiating off her skin immediately winked out, taking the onyx's hold on her with it.

Analia slumped back, bringing shaking hands to her face. Crystal spare her. That was a terrible, stupid idea. One that left her exhausted and empty.

But there was no time to recover.

Analia shakily pushed herself to her feet. Then, she headed for the door.

Analia followed the path of her magic through the castle. A few humans eyed her warily as she passed, but it was surprisingly easy to ignore them. Quickly finding the spot where her magic had been blocked, her brows rose as she stepped into the sizable library.

She'd originally thought it was too obvious of a spot during her tour. Now, she was certain the central stone statue of intertwined ravens had something hidden inside.

Analia spent a few minutes browsing the shelves, not glancing at the statue as she wandered past. Eventually, she grabbed a worn copy of one of Accalon's favorite books and headed out.

She knew she couldn't risk trying to get the scroll. Even though the library was empty outside of a few young scribes, there was no telling what might happen if she started poking around. Especially if a damper was involved.

Returning to the suite, Analia stifled a yawn as she pushed inside. She half expected to find Aaron and Mor already waiting for her, but the sitting room remained silent and empty. Which meant there was nothing left to do but wait.

Sighing, Analia flopped down on the couch and opened her book. It was another story Accalon had read to her when she was small, this one describing a hidden hollow in the Wind Kingdom where camellia flowers bloomed all year round. Most children preferred to only read books based in their kingdom, but she and Accalon had always loved the mysterious Blessed woman that protected the hollow against invaders. Even now, she could practically hear his voice as he read along, down to the rhythm and pauses of every phrase.

Analia closed her eyes, the memory wrapping around her like an embrace. His voice. This piece of him. Somehow, after all this time, it was still hers.

Analia didn't realize she'd started to doze off until there came the sound of the door opening. She startled upright, her eyes darting around.

"Should I be worried you lost control, or flattered you went to such lengths to get my attention?"

Analia relaxed. Barely sparing Aaron a glance, she asked, "Do you think about your words before saying them, or do you just open your mouth and see what happens?"

"Well, I've always been a fan of surprises."

"That explains your diplomacy strategies."

Mor stifled a laugh as he closed the door behind them. Grinning himself, Aaron tossed his crown on a nearby table, not trying to deny it.

"In all seriousness," he said, coming to sit beside her, "you're all right?"

He rested the back of his hand against her forehead, the amusement in his eyes settling into something softer. Something that had her momentarily unable to respond.

"I'm fine," she promised, hands tightening around her book as she leaned away. "I'm better than fine, in fact."

"Even after that heat wave?" Mor asked, plopping down on her other side.

"Seeing as that heat wave found the scroll, I would say especially so."

Mor sat up straight. Aaron, however, leaned back against the couch, tucking his hands behind his head. "Care to share the details?"

Crystal Bless that man, he wasn't surprised in the slightest.

Storing his reaction away in her heart, Analia quickly filled them in on her investigation.

"There has to be a hidden compartment in the plinth," she finished, thoughtfully toying with her phoenix pin. "That or in the statue itself. I just wish I could have figured that out without notifying the humans in the process."

"The humans barely noticed," Mor assured her.

"Even if they had," Aaron said, "that doesn't change the fact that *you* are *incredible*."

He ruffled her hair. Analia ducked her head, struggling to ignore the tingles that ran down her scalp to her toes.

"Normally," she said, "I would say we try to relocate the scroll with Mor's Blessing. But with that damper?"

"I'm completely blocked," Mor confirmed, his expression far away as he reached out with his own magic. "I can't even get near the statue without the damper lashing out." He shook his head, his gaze coming back into focus. "There's definitely something important in there, though."

Analia added, "And with how primitive that statue is, whatever it is must have been hidden a long time ago."

"Which means we just have to get it the old-fashioned way," Aaron said, as casually as a proposed dinner plan.

Analia couldn't decide if his lack of concern was endearing or exasperating. "But how?" she asked. "I went during a quiet hour, and there were still scribes roaming around. Not to mention, someone could walk in at any moment and see what we're doing."

"The library is staffed around the clock," Mor explained. "The scribes will be an issue no matter what. But right now, everyone else in the castle is getting ready for the celebration."

"Meaning now is our best chance," Aaron finished. He stretched, cracking his back. "We can tag team it. One of us distracts the scribes while the other deals with the plinth."

"That easy, huh?" Analia asked, rubbing her eyes.

"We've dealt with worse," said Mor unconcernedly.

Normally, Analia would've rolled her eyes at that, at the very least point out the ways everything could go wrong. But the heavy, near-empty pit where her magic used to be only had her slumping back against the couch with a frown.

"We can go in a second," Mor went on, rising to his feet. "I just have to grab something first."

Analia struggled upright once more as he headed for an adjoining door. "What about me?"

"You're staying here," Aaron said, nudging her back against the couch. "You've already done more than enough."

"That doesn't mean I can't still help."

"Anna, you look exhausted."

Analia scrunched up her face. "Well thanks."

"You know I don't mean it like that." Aaron lightly tugged on her hair, then rose to retrieve his discarded crown. "Combined with training this morning, you've had two massive magic releases today. That would wear anyone out."

Analia started to protest, but it quickly turned into a yawn. Aaron didn't even have the decency to suppress his laugh.

"Don't worry," he said, "I'll still be needing your help later tonight. But for now, the adjoining doors lead to bedrooms. And the beds aren't half bad."

"Really?" Analia asked, sinking back against the pillows with a sigh. "Is this the part where you tell me they're even better with company?"

"Now what kind of person would I be if I only offered to tell?"

"Uh-huh."

Aaron chuckled. "You know," he said, his voice softening as he came up behind her, "there is one thing I have to tell you."

"That being?"

He leaned down, wrapping his arms around her shoulders. "Well done."

Analia sighed, leaning back against him. Maybe a nap wasn't a *terrible* idea. After all, she needed to be fully functioning if they were going to make it through the celebration. And Aaron was so warm...

Aaron shifted her against him, whispering a warning into her hair. Then, they faded into the shadows, reappearing a moment later on a large, cushy bed.

Analia groaned as she slumped sideways, not bothering with the covers as she pressed her face into the pillow. "Thank you."

Aaron laughed under his breath. "Always."

He touched her hair, a barely there touch. Then, his footsteps retreated, the door softly clicking shut a moment later.

Analia closed her eyes. And she didn't try to stop her mind from drifting into the darkness.

Aaron softly closed his bedroom door, a headache lingering in his temples as he sank down on the couch.

Gods, how was the day not even over yet?

He wasn't a fool: he'd known the council would be even more of a nightmare than usual once they heard about his betrothal. He'd spent hours fending off their questions about his and Analia's story. Even when they'd given up, he still had to listen to their list of complaints and demands, his magic rapidly building in his veins.

Just like his rage. Just like his heartbreak.

But then, there'd been a flash of heat. It moved across the chamber almost too quickly to register, Aaron barely having time to fear Analia had lost control before it disappeared.

He knew if something was wrong, Laness would have felt it and notified him immediately. But that hadn't stopped him from struggling to fill his lungs until he returned to the suite, just to find her half-asleep on the couch.

Safe. In one piece. Letting out a tiny sigh when he'd wrapped his arms around her shoulders, her body relaxing into his...

Mor's bedroom door opened. Aaron started as his brother emerged, a heavy book tucked under his arm.

"Are we distracting them or giving them concussions?" he asked, struggling to refocus.

"See, this is why you're retrieving the scroll." Mor plopped down on the couch beside him, stifling a yawn with his hand. "Where's Anna?"

"Asleep in my room."

"Really?" The amount of implications Mor managed to pack into those two syllables was downright impressive.

"You know," Aaron said, struggling not to squirm, "For someone who claimed we could leave in a second, you seem awfully chatty."

"Does that mean we're *not* going to talk about this?" Mor asked.

"Talk about what?"

"Aaron, from the moment she arrived in Starlight, you haven't been able to tear your eyes from her. You couldn't get here fast enough after you felt her magic during our meeting. Yet, you can't even bring yourself to look at your bedroom right now." Mor leaned forward, his expression solemn. "What are you trying to do here?"

Aaron took a quick breath. Mor's hazel eyes locked on his, quietly asking if this was the game he wanted to play. And Aaron deflated.

He sank back into the couch. "Honestly? I have no idea."

"Do you have no idea," Mor asked, "or are you afraid to admit it?"

Aaron looked away.

"You're allowed to want this," Mor said gently. "To reach for it. The tapestries—"

"The tapestries don't mean anything, Mor," Aaron cut in, raking his hand through his hair. "How many times has Surce told us they're meant to be guides, suggestions of the future, not facts?"

"And yet you haven't told her about them."

"What am I supposed to say? Good morning, Analia. Here's a grand display suggesting a future that you're powerless to impact. Breakfast?"

Mor lightly shoved his shoulder. "Are you never going to tell her, then?"

"I'll tell her once she's made her decision for herself," he said, resting his head back against the couch. "Her choice. Not the one that fate or destiny or the future has cornered her into."

Mor looked as though he were about to speak, but he only dropped his gaze.

"Just say it," Aaron sighed.

"I agree with the sentiment," Mor hedged, absently rubbing the spot where his golden hand met his wrist. "But don't you think she should get to know the full picture before making that choice?"

Aaron released a long, heavy breath. "I'd be lying if I said I hadn't considered that. I just... I just want her to be happy, Mor. I want to give her the opportunity to figure out what she wants and to make that choice without worrying about anyone else."

"You mean *you*."

Aaron dropped his gaze. "That's the only way I can survive."

At least, he told himself he could survive. But just the thought of her walking away, her choice or not, had his lungs constricting, his heart bracing itself.

"Aaron," Mor said, shifting closer, "did you not see the way she looked at you today?"

Oh, he had. He'd spent most of his council meeting obsessing over the blaze in her eyes, picking it apart until he didn't know what was real and what was imagined anymore. But there was one fact that remained.

"It doesn't count," he said. "Today is just pretend."

"Maybe," Mor said. "But what if it's not pretend for her?"

Aaron flinched. From the possibility Mor was right or wrong, he didn't know.

"The way I see it," Mor said, "you have three options." He ticked them off on his golden fingers. "You can tell her about the tapestries and let her make her decision. You can wait for her to make her decision and then tell her. Or, you don't say anything at all and remain in this state of uncertainty indefinitely."

"I want a fourth option," Aaron grumbled.

Mor laughed and patted his shoulder. "You're coming to the end, brother. I can't tell you which is the right choice, but I do know if you don't make one, you're going to regret it."

Aaron rubbed his neck as Mor rose, going to retrieve their counterfeit scroll from the cabinet they'd stored it in before greeting the humans. He'd always appreciated his brothers for their ability to call him out—Branten usually relying on a motivational speech or just physically kicking his ass.

But no one listened like Mor. No one could see all angles like he could, nor present them without it feeling like an ambush.

"Do you really think it might not be pretend?" Aaron asked, so quiet he doubted Mor could hear.

Mor glanced over his shoulder. "I think you need to talk to her."

Aaron dropped his head in his hands. He didn't know how to handle all of this. The humans, the reminders of his mom, everything with Analia. There wasn't enough room in his body to contain it all.

"Let's just go," he sighed.

Chapter 50

Aaron stood in the quiet corridor outside the library, the counterfeit scroll tucked beneath his jacket. Mor had casually ensured the door wouldn't click shut behind him as he strolled inside, creating the perfect gap to peer through as the scribes hurried forward to greet him.

As far as he could tell, their theory had been correct: everyone was too busy with the celebration to visit the library. That, however, didn't include the scribes. They'd eagerly intercepted Mor at the statue, Mor having subtly maneuvered them while they talked so all Aaron could see was the backs of their deep purple robes.

"The council made several references to early trade agreements in our meeting this afternoon," he was saying. "Yet, I've been scanning through my copy of the kingdom's history, and I can't find them. I'm assuming it must be because they were only included in the prior edition."

The three scribes shifted from foot to foot. Young, just like Analia had said. And clearly uncomfortable as the girl on the right accepted the book Mor offered her, turning it over in her hands.

"Your Majesty," she said, looking up at him, "apologies, but I don't believe there is an older edition."

"Yes, there is," Mor said. "I've seen it several times in the history section. It has the same blue cover, but the title is in silver. Come, I'll show you."

Without further comment, he pushed off the statue, heading deeper into the library. The scribes startled, clearly taken aback. But they didn't hesitate to scurry after him. "Yes, yes we must be mistaken, apologies, Your Majesty."

Aaron rolled his eyes. He had no doubt if he'd been the one asking, that interaction would have gone completely differently. But that was the difference between being a feared king and a—mostly—respected one. And in this kingdom, that duality was the only thing keeping everyone in line.

Checking that the coast was clear, Aaron faded into the shadows, reappearing beside the statue and falling to his knees.

Even up close, it didn't look like much. The statue stood about eight feet tall, the rectangular plinth and two intertwined ravens all carved from rough black tourmaline.

If the scroll had been hidden inside, there had to be an access point—and with how heavy the ravens had to be, Aaron doubted it was a lift top. Yet, as he ran his fingers along the rough stone plinth, he found nothing that hinted at a secret compartment. No cracks, no carved symbols, no worn-down sections. Leaning around the statue, he scanned the sections on either side of him, but nothing.

Aaron sat back on his heels. He had to be missing something. Both Analia and Mor had confirmed there was a damper here—although with how far away they'd been, they couldn't have narrowed in on the specific location. But up close...

Aaron flattened his palm against the plinth and reached for his magic. Immediately, a wave of starlight rose up to meet him—more than he anticipated. Deciding to deal with that later, he sent a thin film of starlight creeping across the statue, moving section by section, slowly scanning until—

Aaron yanked his magic back with a jolt.

The leg?

He leaned closer, but it was just textured stone, the natural cracks and grooves forming various patterns across the left raven's outer leg. Familiar patterns...

"Crystal fuck me," Aaron breathed.

The leg wasn't tourmaline. It was onyx. Carved onyx, camouflaged by the natural texture of the surrounding stone.

Experimentally, Aaron poked the leg with a finger, jerking back with a hiss as the damper tried to latch on.

Well, he'd certainly found it. And it made perfect sense.

Whoever hid the scroll must have known even the humans would find an onyx statue suspicious. But with no magic networks of their own, they wouldn't notice one part of the whole was different, even if they brushed against it. And no Blessed would have given it a second look.

Gods, Analia was incredible. The leg was the key.

But how was he supposed to test it? As soon as he touched the leg, it wouldn't just trap his magic, but create a silver flash when it was inevitably released.

"Your Majesty," a scribe said, "we've searched this entire aisle. I don't think it's here."

"Maybe it's in the next section," Mor suggested, slightly louder than necessary.

Aaron took the hint. Gritting his teeth, he reached for the damper.

Immediately, the onyx latched on like a leech. It greedily sucked down his magic, Aaron fighting back a shudder as he struggled with the leg. Tugging, shoving, tapping it with his fingertips. But nothing happened. Nothing unlocked, no secret compartments opened, nothing.

The last of his magic winked out. Running out of ideas, Aaron twisted the leg. Harder, harder, too exhausted and empty to care about the consequences.

Just when he thought all he'd accomplish was breaking the statue, the ravens shifted.

Aaron scrambled to his feet, giving himself better leverage as he shoved against the leg. Once again, it turned the slightest bit.

Aaron leaned against the statue, struggling to quiet his breathing. Crystal spare him, he had to turn the statue? A statue heavy enough that he could barely move it, even with his heightened strength as a Blessed?

Granted, he'd never been one for brute strength—his Blessing and affinity for daggers lent themselves more to speed. He'd have better luck getting Branten to try.

But even if there was time to get him, that would require releasing the damper, and if Mor couldn't play off the sudden release of magic—once, let alone twice?

"Your Majesty, perhaps you were thinking of a prior edition of the Starlight Kingdom's history?"

"No, it was definitely this kingdom," Mor mused. "Perhaps records of those agreements would also be in the Starlight Kingdom's history, so we could try that section."

Aaron closed his eyes, choking back a groan. Then, planting his feet, he shoved.

The statue didn't easily shift into movement, like a doorknob that hadn't been twisted in decades. Slowly, inch by inch, Aaron pushed it around the plinth with a soft scrape, the damper leg acting like an axis for it to rotate around.

Thankfully, the scribes didn't seem to notice the noise, too caught up in their discussion of—gods, he didn't even know anymore. Everything was eclipsed by the burn across his arms, his shoulders, his back. The cold, hollow pit where his magic used to be.

The statue moved another inch. Aaron was just starting to wonder if this was another ruse when the ravens' feet shifted a little more. Revealing the edge of a massive crack in the stone.

Gods, *please.* Aaron shoved even harder, his breath hissing between his teeth as he turned the statue more, more, more—yes.

It wasn't just a crack. It was an opening in the plinth.

Aaron didn't give himself time to think. Not about the burn of his muscles, the sweat that slicked his grip on the damper leg, how much he was going to be feeling this in the morning. He just kept turning the statue.

Thirty degrees. Thirty-five degrees.

The opening started to take shape.

Forty degrees.

It was a cylinder, the same size as the scroll, the feet still blocking him from reaching inside. And as the statue hit forty-five degrees, there came an audible click.

The voices abruptly cut off.

"What was that?" one of the scribes asked.

Crystal spare him. He was trapped. He couldn't flee. Not only would he reveal the compartment, but there was no way they wouldn't notice his released network and know exactly who was behind it.

"The click?" Mor asked, barely missing a beat. "I've been hearing it for weeks. I assumed the library's keepers knew about it and were investigating."

Should he slide the statue back in place? No, then he'd have to do this all over again, and the magic release—

"Yes, Your Majesty, we've been working to identify it," a female scribe said smoothly. "We just have a long list of possibilities with how large the library is."

"We keep thinking we've found it," the male scribe chimed in. "Yet, sooner or later it always returns."

Little liars. Still, Aaron held his breath, not daring to move.

"Well, it sounds like it came from over here," Mor said. And Crystal Bless his brother, his footsteps headed deeper into the library.

For a long, agonizing moment, the scribes remained silent. Finally, one began, "Are you sure—"

She cut off with a grunt as if elbowed in the ribs.

"I believe you're right," the male scribe said. "We'll help you look."

With what sounded like a shove and muttered complaint, the scribes' footsteps scurried after Mor. But Aaron knew his time was just about up.

Tightening his grip on the leg, Aaron's body screamed in protest as he shoved the statue back into movement.

He didn't have to turn it all the way around. He just had to get the toes shifted enough so they didn't cover the opening. Just five more degrees. Four. Three, two.

The statue slid to the ninety-degree mark with another click. Aaron bit back a curse as the scribes piped up once more. "Your Majesty, I think it's coming from over here."

Breathing hard, Aaron sank to his knees on the plinth beside the hole. Its walls were lined with onyx, carved with the same intricate designs now indented in his palms.

Releasing the statue with one hand, Aaron stretched as far as he could toward the hole. As long as he didn't have to fully release the leg, his network would remain plugged, meaning he'd only have to suffer through one magic release. Just one magic release Mor would have to explain away.

Aaron's shoulders screamed as he reached down, past his wrist, his elbow. Closer, closer...

His fingers curled around cold metal. And not wasting a moment, he yanked the scroll free, dropped it on the plinth beside him, pulled the counterfeit scroll from his jacket and tossed it in the hole. Then, the scribes' voices sparking against his nerves, he shoved the scroll under his jacket and hopped off the plinth.

No time to waste.

Aaron threw himself at the statue. All he had to do was get this gods-damned statue back into place, shadowjump away, and finally, he could feel like he'd done something right in this kingdom. He could feel something other than the grief that had been devouring his insides from the moment he'd stepped foot in this castle. So. Close.

But gods, he was so tired. His arms shook as he inched the statue back toward its original position, even slower than before.

Fifty-five degrees. Fifty.

Aaron shuddered as he hit forty-five degrees, just to be rewarded with another click.

"I knew it was over there!" the female scribe called excitedly.

Aaron breathed a curse. He twisted the statue as hard as he could, his heart pounding in his ears.

There would be no explaining an out-of-place statue, the hole underneath, the silver flash of magic as he released the damper. Getting caught wasn't an option. But from the sound of their approaching footsteps, they were only three aisles away.

"Your Majesty," the second female scribe trilled, "this way!"

The statue inched across the plinth. Twenty-five degrees. Twenty.

Aaron could feel his muscles fraying, shredding apart one by one. But he couldn't quit now. Analia had worked so hard to get them to this point. His brother had fought too long and too hard to win this kingdom's trust for him to destroy it now. He himself had lost enough at this kingdom's hands.

Ten degrees.

The footsteps hurried down the second aisle.

Aaron squeezed his eyes shut, biting down on his cheek hard enough to taste blood.

"It must have come from near the statue, Your Majesty."

The statue settled back into place.

Aaron didn't pause. Bracing himself the best he could, he released the statue.

The damper leg flashed with silver light. Aaron threw himself against the statue, trying to block the light with his body, barely choking back his groan as his magic slammed into him like a unit of soldiers.

He couldn't breathe. He couldn't move, his body locking up as his magic rampaged back into his network.

A distant part of his mind heard the scribes speak, their voices growing closer. Closer. Gods, they were right around the corner.

Aaron dug his nails into his palms. And just as the edge of a purple robe poked out around the bookshelf across from him, he dragged himself into the shadows.

Aaron staggered as he reappeared in his suite a moment later. He collapsed on the couch with a groan, his body shaking as it flashed between hot and cold.

Too much magic. Too much turning. Too much everything.

But it was over. He could feel the scroll resting against his chest. He had complete faith Mor would be able to explain any questions away. Which meant despite his aching muscles, their mission was a success.

And it was in great part because of her.

Aaron dragged his gaze to his bedroom door.

No one should have been able to find that damper, but she had. She'd walked into this kingdom with a target on her back, not only standing her ground, but earning a small seed of respect in doing so.

She was absolutely incredible.

And she still didn't know.

Aaron sighed, pressing his face into the back of the couch. He knew Mor was right: he had to talk to her. Not about the tapestries, not yet. But there were countless other things he had to tell her. He just hoped he could unclench his fingers, because time was rapidly running out.

Analia woke to a hand on her shoulder; a voice in her ear telling her it was time to get up. She groaned, pressing her face into the pillow. "You liar."

There was a pause. Then, Aaron leaned closer. "What?"

"You promised you were a delight to wake up to."

Aaron laughed under his breath. "Oh, my shooting star." He shifted so he was stretched out beside her, his hand trailing down her back. "You and I both know my usual delightful means would only end with you smacking me with a pillow. Although, I suppose we could make an exception, just this once."

Analia rolled to face him. She hooked her leg over his, his face inches from hers as she peered up at him through her lashes.

Aaron went perfectly still. He didn't seem to breathe as she trailed her hand up his chest, his neck, curling around his face.

"Smartass," she said, tapping his nose.

Aaron blinked hard. "Tease." He rolled to the edge of the bed. "You should get ready for the celebration. Surce sent you a costume change."

Analia perked up. Her nap had done wonders for her energy levels, even her mood. Or maybe that had to do with the Star Royal still sprawled in her bed.

"I'm assuming it's in the bathing room?" she said, gesturing to the attached door.

Aaron nodded. "Although don't feel like you're forced to change in there."

"Alas, that view is to be saved for my king, not my betrothed."

Analia slid out of bed, feeling Aaron's scorching gaze travel down her back.

"You know," he said, "I noticed you were on top of the covers when I came in. Hoping something other than blankets would come to keep you warm?"

"Oh no," Analia said, "that was simply happenstance. It was the black lace that was supposed to do it."

The bed squeaked as Aaron shot upright. "I, for one, have always been a fan of do-overs."

"What a shame. I've been informed it's time for me to change. If only you had come a little sooner."

Analia kicked the door shut behind her, cutting off Aaron's protest. Grinning to herself, she turned to the garment bag hanging from a towel hook, something silver and metallic peeking out. She pulled the dress free, her eyebrows shooting up. Definitely a statement. But Surce knew what she was doing.

"So," she called, stripping off her gown, "I'm assuming since I can sense the scroll in the sitting room, the mission was a success?"

"That's one way to put it," Aaron muttered, his voice coming closer as he approached the door.

Analia listened to his recount as she changed. By the time he finished, she didn't know if she was more impressed by the Star Royals' safeguards or Mor's stalling abilities.

"How did they not feel your magic release?" she asked, shaking out her newly unpinned hair.

"Oh, they noticed," Aaron said. "But since they didn't see it, Mor was able to play it off as me having one of my tantrums. They're infamous for being felt all throughout the castle."

The bitterness in his voice had Analia's own lips pucker. "So," she said, "what I'm hearing is between you and the castle and me and the roof, we have a formidable brooding radius."

Aaron let out a surprised laugh. "I suppose so."

"We should get an award," Analia said. She pushed through the bathing room door, about to continue. Just to spot the look on Aaron's face.

"Too much?" she asked, suddenly uncertain.

Heat crept across her face as Aaron stared at her, something primal in his eyes.

Her gown was made from a soft silver satin. Thin whirls of white and electric blue twined through the skirts, which stopped at her midthigh. The neckline plunged between her breasts, the back low.

Apparently, that night, she was to be on display in all senses of the word.

Before she could second-guess, Aaron's eyes finally reached hers. He stepped forward, a small, secretive smile playing across his lips.

"You are incredible," he said, the same way he'd comment on the weather. "I just thought you should know."

The knot in Analia's chest slackened. "You're just saying that so your head will no longer be the largest in Elefthia."

"Now why would I want to give up that title? Although I do think that dress is missing something."

"I think it's missing a lot of things," Analia muttered, pulling on the hem.

Aaron chuckled as he went to retrieve a box from the bedside table. Taking something from within, he turned to Analia, who took a step back.

The crown Aaron held was made from hammered silver. Thin curving tendrils radiated out from a large diamond surrounded by small sapphires, amethysts, and fiery opals, replicating an exploding star.

That small, secretive smile was back as Aaron stepped up to her, placing the crown atop her head. "Every queen needs her crown," he told her, rearranging her hair.

Analia's heart stuttered. She was only pretending to be a queen. This was nothing like the crowning ceremony she had fled nearly three months before.

But that didn't change the fact that in the split moment she had forgotten, there was no whisper of *wrong, wrong, wrong*. Instead, she had felt something slide into place. Something she clung to as she followed Aaron toward the door.

Chapter 51

The Throne Room had transformed in the hours since Analia had left. Hundreds of candles flickered throughout the cavernous room, sparkling off the crystal chandeliers and glass tables of food.

The initial suspicion seemed to have mostly faded. But the humans still lingered in the shadows, sneaking looks at Analia and Aaron wedged together on their throne, over to Mor standing off to the side.

At the base of the dais, the members of the council stood in a line, one reading—a toast? Welcome message? Analia couldn't pay enough attention to find out. Not as Aaron lounged beside her, a look of glorious boredom on his face as he played with her fingers.

She'd lost track of how many times he'd apologized to her over the past few weeks for what this night would entail. Every time, she'd assured him it was all right, she trusted him—and that hadn't been a lie. But holy Crystal above, she wasn't prepared for this.

Aaron's fingers left burning trails along the lines of her palm, the dimple of her wrist, the divots between her fingers. His other arm lay curled around her waist, his hand resting suggestively high on her thigh.

In any other circumstance, she'd be trying not to squirm. But there was something about the absence of Aaron's usual wicked amusement, the blank look in his eyes, that had her remain perfectly still.

Eventually, the council's speech came to a close. The crowd broke into a forced applause, Aaron not bothering to look up as he ordered them to dance.

A group of musicians quickly launched into a song, the humans scattering as they hustled to obey. Still, Aaron's expression didn't twitch.

Gods, that look was all wrong on him. It was too harsh. Too cold and empty.

Analia glanced to Mor, his tiny frown telling her this wasn't the usual mask he wore with the humans.

Resting a hand on Aaron's chest, she leaned in to whisper in his ear. "Are we not joining them because you dance as well as you cook?"

Aaron startled slightly. "Smartass," he muttered.

"I understand not wanting to embarrass yourself in front of the humans," she went on, playing with the buttons on his jacket. "Not only would that be a terrible way to lose your kingdom's respect, but you also have people like Branten who would never let you live it down. But just how bad are we talking?"

"Do you honestly think," he asked, "I could have survived this long as king without knowing how to dance?"

Analia's lips grazed his ear. "Who needs to dance when you have daggers?"

Aaron's hand flexed around her thigh. "You're trouble."

"And you're avoiding my question."

Over Aaron's shoulder, Analia caught Mor subtly turn away from them to face the crowd.

"We're not joining them," Aaron told her, "because the first dance is traditionally just for the humans."

"I see," Analia said. "So, I suppose that means it's up to us to have a performance up here."

"Oh, I think you've already started."

Analia yelped as he pulled her onto his lap. Her arms wrapped around his neck, her breath stuttering in her lungs as he lowered his face to hers.

"Tell me, Analia," he murmured. "I've always known I had a role to play tonight. But when did you become so invested in playing along?"

Analia struggled to focus as he slid his hand up her back, his fingers tangling in her hair.

Well, she'd gotten what she'd wanted. That look was gone. Long gone.

But that didn't stop her fingertips from curling into the back of his neck, didn't stop her nose from brushing his as she asked, "Are you asking me to stop?"

"I'm telling you to do what you want with me."

His words were so quiet, she almost hadn't heard over the music. But holy Crystal above, that look in his eyes.

It was a challenge. It might have even been a plea. And Analia didn't think twice.

"If you insist," she said.

Then, she ducked her head to kiss the hollow at the base of his throat.

And something hard pressed against her hip.

Before she could react, Aaron was pulling her to her feet, keeping her in front of him as he ushered her off the dais and into the crowd.

But as they moved into position, as the next song began, it didn't feel like a dance. This was fiercer, smokier. It was the opening to a battle, every step a challenge that had their bodies clashing, withdrawing, sliding against one another until Analia's skin tingled.

But she didn't know what she was fighting for. Not when she craved the fire Aaron's hands trailed across her arms, her shoulders, the bare skin of her back. Not when she could feel his network lace through hers like repair threads in a tapestry.

Song after song, she could feel every human's gaze trained on them. But Analia didn't care. The humans had demanded to know why she was there, and as far as she was concerned, they were providing an answer. Almost painfully so.

"You know," Aaron murmured, his lips tracing the curve of her shoulder, "Ethelind would be scandalized right now."

"Really?" Analia's voice softened into a sigh as Aaron left a deep, lingering kiss where her neck met her shoulder. "But you're doing such a good job playing the moody Star Royal tyrant."

"Maybe." The music shifted into something slower, softer. Aaron turned her to face him, his words brushing the top of her head as he drew her close. "I just wish this mask wasn't as thin as it is."

Analia didn't know what to say to that. For a few minutes, they danced in silence, their movements settling into something smoother. Peaceful.

Analia sighed, resting her head against Aaron's chest.

Somehow, surrounded by hostile stares and impending retribution, she only felt content. A kind of contentment she once could have only dreamed of. But ever since taking Aaron's hand back in Ash, her hopes had a way of finding her.

Maybe that was the true nature of the Starlight Kingdom. It wasn't a place of secrets and mysteries and forgotten magic. It was a kingdom of hope. A hope Aaron was willing to destroy himself to preserve. He needed to preserve it because he was too afraid to hope himself.

"You're not a monster, Aaron," she murmured. "I see you."

Aaron's heart stumbled beneath her ear. Yet, his voice remained steady as he asked, "What exactly do you see?"

Analia's mind flashed back to the Sun armory, where she'd asked him the exact same thing.

"I see someone who is compassionate to a fault," she said after a moment, lifting her head to look at him. "Someone who would do anything for the people he loves, even at his own expense. Someone who hasn't been told nearly enough how deserving he is of the same love he puts out in the world. I see someone who shouldn't let his compassion consume him, because he is far too wonderful to lose."

At her words, something seemed to sag out of Aaron. His head bowed forward until their foreheads touched, his lips forming her name like a prayer.

Analia knew she should remind herself it wasn't real. But staring into Aaron's eyes, she didn't feel the humans' gazes on her. She didn't hear the music, or remember the plan, or recall what happened the last time she'd danced with a man.

All she felt was Aaron's arms around her. His body against hers. The heat spreading across her skin as his cock still pressed against her. And gods, she just wanted more.

"Is this how the fantasy starts?" she breathed.

Aaron's grip on her tightened as she pressed closer, shifting against the hard length of him.

"What are you doing?" he whispered.

"Is it real?" she asked, shifting her hips once more. "The black-lace fantasy?"

She shifted a third time, and Aaron pressed his face to her neck, stifling a moan.

Analia's body crackled. She wanted to hear that sound again. She wanted to know what it was like when he was serious and wicked and unhurried.

Aaron ran his lips up her neck, coming to lightly tug her earlobe with his teeth. Analia whimpered.

Aaron's eyes snapped to hers. Then, the dance floor faded around her, Aaron dragging them out of the shadows on the outskirts of the room.

"Aaron—"

Aaron pinned her against the wall. His hand came up to protect the back of her head, sliding down to her neck, lifting her chin with the stroke of his thumb.

"That," he breathed, bracing his free hand on the wall beside her head and leaning in. "That sound was what I imagined with the black lace. Breaking free the moment my fingers slipped beneath the lace, and I found you drenched for me."

His fingers trailed down her side, her hip, coming to brush the sensitive skin below the hem of her dress. A hem that was suddenly not short enough as his fingers lazily stroked inward.

Analia's nails dug into his shoulders. "I didn't realize we were playing out your fantasy."

"We could play out yours."

His suggestive gaze drifted to her mouth, down her body, landing on the thighs she clamped together. Something in his eyes shuddered. He leaned in, his lips brushing the shell of her ear. "We never established what you wanted me to do with my tongue."

Analia jerked as his mouth moved to her neck, the tip of his tongue darting out to kiss her skin.

"Or maybe lower," Aaron breathed. His lips skimmed down her collarbone. "Or maybe even lower."

Analia squirmed as he pushed his knee between her thighs, imagining his mouth moving down her chest, her stomach. Lower.

"So that's what you want," he breathed, his hand slipping under her dress and around to her hip. "You want my head between your thighs. You want to feel me moaning your name as I worship you with my tongue."

Something in Analia's chest seemed to crack. It was the wall she had built between herself and every smoldering thought, every midnight fantasy that had come unbidden to her mind. She knew she had to reseal it; if she didn't, there would be no way to rebuild.

Aaron's fingers moved back and forth across her hip. And Analia made no move to stop that wall from rumbling harder, harder, harder.

"Aaron," she pleaded.

Aaron shuddered. He leaned in, his lips brushing over hers, "What are we doing, Analia?"

Analia ground against him, her senses alive with smoke and starlight.

She was losing her mind. She didn't care. Not as Aaron hooked her thigh over his, rocking into her exactly where she needed to have her crying out.

"What are we doing, Analia?"

Pieces of that wall rained down around her, hard, fast, unsalvageable.

But she didn't want to rebuild. She wanted it to crumble even faster. She wanted to give in to the desperate ache between her thighs, the yearning in her chest she'd been denying for so long.

Analia gripped his jacket, dragging him across the remaining distance between them. "Just pretend, right?" she breathed.

It was the final barrier between them. Thin, flimsy. And she wanted him to break it. Wanted him, needed him in a way she'd never allowed herself to need someone before.

Analia closed her eyes.

Aaron pulled back.

Analia's eyes snapped open, unable to identify the look that flashed across his face. But he couldn't hide the strain in his voice as he said, "Then we are doing an excellent job."

Did he not realize...?

She started to speak. Aaron turned away, his hand falling from her hip to loosely grip her own, sending her stomach sinking.

And by the time they made it back to their throne, Aaron's empty mask had slid back into place.

Aaron sat on his throne, loosely gripping Analia's hand as he waited for the celebration to end.

Gods, he'd tried so hard to stay in control. All night, he'd focused on his guilt, his disgust with himself for touching her while she still didn't know.

But that hadn't stopped her from playing along. It hadn't stopped him from noticing how her body responded to his. It hadn't stopped her from staring into his eyes, turning over every broken piece he had and still telling him everything he never dreamed he'd hear.

Even then, he held back, letting her take the lead. Just for her to lead them straight into his "black-lace fantasy." And suddenly, he was doing everything he could to feel her back arch, her body melt into his, her lips form those three words.

Just pretend, right?

That had certainly taken care of his hard-on. If only it also prevented him from being hyperaware of how they sat crammed together on his throne, his nerves jumping every time she so much as twitched against him.

Gods, he was a disaster. A miserable, grieving, turned-on disaster.

His magic churned, seemingly in agreement.

This time, Aaron didn't try to suppress it. He latched on, reveling in the cold as he pulled it up and through his veins, just needing the stillness, the silence.

By the time his enka bracelet buzzed, Laness's uneasy voice echoing down their mental line, the ice had frosted over his heart.

The rest of the celebration passed in a frosty blur. He barely remembered his concluding speech, barely felt his own hands as he gripped Analia's and Mor's and pulled them into the shadows. First reappearing in his suite to retrieve the scroll, then back to his dining room.

Cold. Numb. Silent.

Surce, Laness, and Branten sat waiting for them around the table, the scrolls laid out in front of them. As soon as they spotted the scroll in Analia's hand, they launched into a flurry of questions, but Aaron remained silent as Mor filled them in. And he shoved all emotions back down as Analia cast him a long, searching look before moving to the table.

"So," she said, running her fingers over the rings. "Are we ready?"

Everyone exchanged a look, but they nodded. Branten wordlessly rose from his seat, taking up a position at her shoulder.

A small, quiet part of Aaron knew that should have been *him* standing guard—*wanted* it to be him. But as Analia's gaze moved around the room, lingering on his face, he didn't trust himself to so much as twitch.

"All right then," she said, turning away. "Let's do this."

Without further comment, she reached for the scrolls.

The moment Analia opened the first ring, there came a rumble of power. It rolled through the house like the warning before a thunderstorm, strong enough Analia's hands froze on the scrolls.

"Keep going," Surce said, her face pale.

Analia let out a harsh breath. Then, she launched into movement.

Analia's hands flew over the scrolls, snapping the rings together, magic building with every connection until even Aaron's icy cocoon rattled from the power. This was a warning. A promise. Nothing good could have that kind of power.

And only something worse would need to be protected by it.

Analia reached the final row. Her fingers fumbled with the rings, both the scroll and her own hands shaking so hard she could barely connect them.

But finally, the last ring snapped into place.

And that power erupted.

Analia staggered back into Branten, who quickly steadied her. Aaron struggled to maintain his own footing as the floor vibrated beneath his feet, crashes echoing around the room as Laness's flowerpots fell to the ground and shattered. Something ancient hissed through his bones, something whose mere presence was enough to have his soul wanting to flee his body.

Aaron bit down hard on his cheek, keeping his gaze locked on the scroll. Slowly, the rings melted away, the ancient parchment merging together to form a single, tightly curled scroll.

The magic gave one final flare, crackling through Aaron's bones like a lightning strike.

Then, the house fell still. Quiet.

For a long, unnerving moment, no one moved.

Finally, Laness broke the silence. "What the fuck did we just do?"

Surce shook her head as if waking from a dream. "I suppose we'll find out in a moment."

She reached for the scroll, everyone watching her expectantly as she unfurled it. Her topaz eyes rapidly scanned over its contents. Then, she frowned.

"Well?" Branten finally asked.

Surce didn't reply.

The room became a babble of voices, but Aaron remained terrifyingly calm as he moved around the table, accepting the scroll Surce handed him. He did a quick scan. Then, he put the scroll on the table without a word and strode from the room.

The voices rose to a cacophony, but Aaron barely heard them. He could only see the scramble of letters, arranged in no logical order, his magic screaming.

"Aaron."

"Not now, Analia," he ground out, heading for the stairs.

But Analia was faster than he realized. Grabbing his arm, she yanked him away from the stairs. "Come with me."

Analia marched Aaron through the back door, half dragging him through the snow and into the training hollow. Dropping his arm, she grabbed one of her training dummies from the corner pile and shoved it upright before him. "Blast it."

"What?"

"Aaron, I can feel your network. It's building out of control, you need to release it."

Aaron didn't move. Analia stepped up behind him.

"One quick jab, right?" she said. She gripped his arm, shoving it forward.

As his fist automatically coiled and struck the dummy, Aaron let his magic rip free.

Aaron barely remembered the next couple minutes. There was nothing outside of the ice coating his body cracking, melting away until he was gasping for breath, unable to tell if he was burning or freezing. Even as his magic drained to empty, his hands wouldn't stop shaking.

But Analia was steady, her chest pressed to his back, her hand gripping his forearm.

"Better?" she eventually asked.

No, Aaron was far from better. Even though he'd finally thawed, that only left what he'd been trying to numb. But he nodded anyway.

Analia briefly pressed her face to the back of his shoulder. Then, she released him, retreating several paces to sit on his moss patch. Giving him space.

Aaron barely noticed. He sank down on the ground, his head bowing into his hands. "What do you want, Analia?" he asked, more tired than anything.

He heard Analia sit up straight.

"Every time I think I understand what's going on in your head, you seem to flip. And I have no idea why. I have no idea if I did something, or if you're afraid, and if you are afraid, I don't know how to help you because I can't read you. So, please, just tell me what you want."

Analia was quiet for a few heartbeats. "I feel like the moment I get too close," she finally said, "you pull away. Like you're terrified I'll confirm everything history says about you. But I don't think you'd listen to *anyone* deny it, either."

"Well, which is it, Analia?" Aaron asked, finally dropping his hands. "Do you think I'm compassionate and wonderful, or am I a disaster?"

"You're *not* a disaster," she said fiercely. "That's my point."

"And neither are you," said Aaron. "But I still don't know if you're simply afraid, or if this is all just pretend to you."

Analia opened her mouth, but no words came out. Aaron slowly shook his head. He was too tired for this. He was heartbroken and drained and missed his mom.

"I need..." The words tasted foreign on his tongue. What did he need? When was the last time he'd stopped to wonder? "I need a second," he decided.

Analia ran a hand down her face. "Tomorrow?"

Aaron nodded.

"All right, then."

Analia rose, turning to go. Aaron didn't pause before fading into the shadows.

Just before he disappeared, Analia looked back.

"I still care about you," she said, her image fading.

Aaron's heart squeezed. Especially as he didn't know if she heard his response: "And I you."

Aaron reemerged in his mother's room. He sank down on her bed, his mind still horribly cold. But finally, he hadn't said something he'd come to regret.

"You see, Mom?" he mumbled, sinking back against the pillows. "Your son is capable of progress after all."

He just wasn't expecting the blood beneath the callouses that "progress" stripped away.

Chapter 52

Analia could barely sleep that night. The memory of the scrolls' magic crackled through her bones, powerful enough it could have disintegrated her mind, her being, in a single heartbeat.

Yet, right before it had barreled into her, it paused. It wreathed around her, almost as if curious, her own magic rising up to meet it.

Then, it retreated, exploding across the room as she connected the rings.

It was completely overwhelming. Still, all she could think about was the dead look in Aaron's eyes that had taken over the moment they returned to their throne.

Gods, how could she have done that to him? He'd told her all about his history with Liss, just for her to touch him and insinuate it was meaningless. No wonder he was upset. Especially after she'd completely frozen in the hollow.

She knew in that moment she was afraid of answering his questions. But it wasn't until the aftermath that she realized how she was even more terrified of losing him.

Her friend. The man who held her while she broke and helped her put her pieces back together. The man who had never tried to take those pieces for himself.

Even as she started rebuilding on her own, he didn't leave. Because Aaron didn't care about her because she was broken. He cared about *her*.

Which was why he had been jealous of Iphen. Which was why she had been jealous of Vivienne. Which was why she told herself over and over this was nothing but a game because every time she'd found herself in this situation, it had ended in disaster. Worse than disaster.

Yet, that didn't change the fact that the only thing that hadn't been real for her was when she told him it was just pretend.

Analia squeezed her eyes shut, pressing her face into her pillow. She had to talk to him.

The following morning, Analia woke charged with nervous energy. Yet, when she knocked on Aaron's door, he wasn't there. After a quick search, she realized he wasn't even in the house. She was just about to step through the beads to check his mother's room when Surce found her.

"Aaron requested I give you this," she said, passing Analia a folded piece of paper.

Analia opened the note, scanning so fast it took her a moment to process the words.

The Doven U sent word they required my presence immediately. I would have told you in person, but I didn't want to wake you. If you need me, have Laness send a message through our bracelets. We'll talk the moment I get home, I promise. I'm sorry.

A.

"Do you know what they want?" Analia asked, pocketing the note.

"I'm afraid I don't."

Analia nodded, not trying to hide her disappointment. Thanking Surce, she turned to head back down the hall, just needing to move, to—gods, she didn't know what.

"Aaron has never been a perfect man," Surce said suddenly.

Analia looked back.

"He's secretive, provocative, and quite frankly, he talks far too much. But even in his darkest moments, he has always been a blessing to this kingdom."

"Why?" Analia asked.

"Because while Aaron cherishes the sanctuary that our kingdom is, he has always strived for it to be something more. A place of peace and safety. A place where lives can become better than they once were. And he has always understood that protecting these ideals has a price.

"Aaron made me his second to balance whatever pieces of himself he might lose in that war—and there were many. But ever since returning from Sun, those pieces have been coming back to him. And that's because of you."

Surce touched Analia's cheek. "I might balance him, Analia, but you give him hope. Everything else is meaningless without that."

Analia swallowed hard. "He's given me so much more than that."

Surce smiled. "Give him time. He'll come back."

Surce turned and disappeared through her beads with a soft swish, leaving Analia to rest her hand over her heart.

Hope. It all came back to hope.

Aaron's boots were stained with blood. He stepped out of the DovenU's interrogation chambers, giving a short nod to the waiting Dovenesses who would have to clean up his mess. Then, he started off on the long hike up to Zinia's study, eventually finding the warrior queen waiting for him with hood pulled up behind her carved wooden desk.

"So?" she asked.

"I'm surprised you trusted me to take care of this," Aaron said, closing the door and taking the seat across from her.

Zinia grunted. "Don't be petulant, you know I trust you plenty. Now, what did he tell you?"

Aaron rubbed his eyes. He'd been up since dawn when Zinia appeared in his bedroom, rousing him with a terse, "I need you, you're coming with me." He'd barely had time to scribble a note to Analia before they jumped back to Mt. Lanula.

The warrior queen led him through the mountain, the stone shifting from brown, to gray, to purple, the temperature rapidly dropping. Finally, they reached the interrogation chambers.

"He says he knows you," Zinia said. Then, she shoved Aaron inside and closed the door, which didn't open again until he walked out nearly ten hours later, his skin sticky with blood and stomach churning.

"I knew him all right," Aaron said, propping his chin on his fist. "His name was Andrik. One of the Sun Crystal Guards while I was there."

"And how did a Sun guard get all the way here?" she demanded.

"He claimed with this."

Aaron fished a golden pendant from his pocket and tossed it on the table. Zinia turned it over in her fingers, her mounting rage palpable. Almost as strong as Aaron's when he first snatched the bloody chain, recognizing it immediately.

"It's an exact replica of the pendant Analia gave Leona," Zinia hissed. She hurled it back on the table, the golden heart flashing in the light let in by the small side window. "How?"

"He said the pendants have been Blessed with tracker magic," Aaron said, icy calm. "I assume to prevent any jewel thieves from getting far. Although now—"

"They've been tracking Analia," the Doveness finished.

"From the moment she left the Sun Kingdom," Aaron confirmed. "Apparently, the wards around my kingdom were strong enough to block the signal. But as soon as Deardryn sensed the pendant cross the border, she arranged to send Andrik down the river. My contact in Moon saw him go."

"Our wards must not have been strong enough," she said, gripping the table.

Aaron shook his head. The Doveness chair scraped back as she rose to pace the room.

"We have been hidden for two thousand years," she said, her voice thick. "The Starlight Kingdom longer than that. And a pendant almost razed those secrets to the ground."

Aaron watched her pace, his own devastation leaving him completely raw. His kingdom, his everything, was now at risk. But it was the icy terror of what could have happened to Analia if his wards hadn't been strong enough that threatened to take his breath away.

"And you swear she knew nothing of this?" Zinia demanded, twisting on her heel to stare Aaron down.

Aaron's chin jutted up. "Do not try to blame this on her."

The warrior queen held his deadly gaze. Finally, she turned away. "You killed him?"

"And every man he brought with him," Aaron confirmed. "They hadn't sent word of their discovery before your girls found them. Your secret is safe."

"For now," she said, shoulders slumping as she sat back down. "At some point, she'll become suspicious about their lack of communication. Eventually, she'll send more squads. And it will only be a matter of time before she finds your kingdom. Especially since she now has access to Moon territory, which is even closer."

"I know," Aaron said softly. "But there's nothing I can do about that until they come."

Gods, he couldn't even imagine what that would be like.

"Of course there are things you can do, you heartbroken fool! Strengthen the wards around my mountain. Reinforce your own. Don't roll over and show your belly like some mewling pup. You are the King of Starlight. Act like it."

Aaron knew most would be offended by such a speech. But his back straightened.

"Reinforce your own wards," he told her. "I've done enough dirty work for you today."

Zinia let out a dry, tired laugh. "There you are. Now go. Protect your people."

"And you protect yours." He reached across the table, giving her hand a squeeze.

For the briefest moment, the abrasive determination melted from her eyes, replaced by something he never thought he'd see from her: fear.

She stroked the back of his hand, her fingers just as icy as his own.

"Are you going to tell her?" she asked, suddenly tired.

Aaron hesitated.

"Aaron Stelingente, this girl is being hunted and you're not going to tell her?"

"I'll tell her," Aaron said quickly. "Just not today. Not tomorrow, either."

Zinia cocked her head, momentarily confused. Then, her expression softened.

"No," she said, "you wouldn't want to tell her tomorrow, would you?"

"I can only handle one heartbreak at a time," Aaron said, retracting his hand. "I at least want her to enjoy the celebration with everyone else."

The warrior queen didn't respond. Aaron rose from his chair. Just as he was about to fade into the shadows, she looked up, catching his eye.

"She would be so proud of you," Zinia said softly.

Aaron felt as though he'd been punched in the gut. He nodded, not trusting himself to speak as he faded into the shadows, reemerging a moment later on the deserted lakeside.

"Old bat," he muttered, wiping the tears from his eyes. "Always has to get the last word."

Aaron spent the rest of the day strengthening his wards. The day was cold and snowy, only getting worse as the sun began to set, but he didn't mind. It pushed back the memories from that chamber: Andrik's screams, the metallic scent of blood so thick he could taste it.

It would have been cleaner if he'd used his magic, but after everything the night before, the memories stirred up by the Human Kingdom? This was a job for his daggers.

Thus, his questioning began, one cut at a time... one knuckle at a time.

He didn't enjoy what he'd had to do, but he didn't regret it either. That, however, only seemed to make room for the memories buried beneath.

The training hollow. His magic release. Analia's voice, soft and uncertain.

Every time I get close, you push me away.

Liss had said that once, and he'd assumed she was just trying to make a dig.

But maybe they were right. He did push people away. All because he couldn't stand the idea of someone looking at him like he was worth caring about, worth redeeming, after everything he'd done during that war. It was instinct at this point.

But maybe he'd reacted too quickly this time. Maybe he'd been reacting too quickly for a while now. Maybe Liss had pushed him away, but she wasn't the only one to blame. Maybe, it was about gods-damned time he acted like an adult.

Which meant it was time for him to start talking.

Chapter 53

Ember shoved her hands into her robe pockets as she walked through the healer temple, the archmaster healers waiting for her on their dais.

She'd known this was something she had to do ever since Scarsthain—from the moment she was banished, if she was honest. Still, it had taken a few days for her to pluck up the courage to request an audience, a few more for permission to be granted.

In that time, Ember had settled into a near-unnerving calm. But now, as she stopped before the heart-shaped platform, her stomach roiled.

"Ember," Reena said, reclining back in her throne. "You wished to see us?"

"I did, archmasters." Ember bowed to each archmaster healer in turn, her muscles tightening. "Thank you for heeding my request."

"Would you like to tell us what this meeting is about?" Mellaine asked, folding her hands in her lap.

Every instinct scream for Ember to flee. But she bit her cheek, forcing herself to remember Cadmus's words. The biggest obstacle in her path was herself. And she could not just move herself aside, but all the way off the Rosala-forsaken board.

Ember lifted her chin. "I'm here to confess my crimes."

The healers exchanged a quick look. "You may approach," Hollyn said.

Ember's body vibrated with anticipation, but she kept her pace slow and measured as she climbed the dais steps. Coming to stand in the center, she caught Reena's sneer. But Ember was all out of reactions for her.

"I've already confessed to my list of crimes," she said instead, looking at each healer in turn. "I stole a sample of xenol from the school. I conducted unauthorized research.

I withheld information from my superiors. I contacted healers from other kingdoms without permission."

"We've already discussed this," Symonne said.

"We have," Ember agreed, squeezing her hands before her. "But I haven't confessed to being wrong for doing so."

Each archmaster fell still. Their eyes burned across her skin, hot as shame, but she didn't allow herself to pause.

"I understand that by withholding this information, I was jeopardizing King Accalon's case. In our last meeting, this decision was attributed to my friendship with Princess Analia, and while that's partially true, it was also an excuse for my pride."

"Tell us why we had to punish that behavior," Mellaine said, quietly encouraging.

Ember closed her eyes, something fracturing inside her. "Because left unchecked, it could become dangerous. Because while I solved one mystery, that doesn't guarantee I can solve them all. Because the downfall of any healer is when confidence crosses over into pride."

"And what does this all mean?" Mellaine prompted.

The first piece of herself broke away as she whispered, "That I can't do everything by myself."

Ember turned in a slow circle, looking from Mellaine, to Symonne, to Hollyn. As soon as she saw the smirk on Reena's lips, that first piece hit the ground and shattered.

"Well, Ember," Hollyn said, her voice faint in Ember's ears. "I must say, this is unexpected."

All her life, she'd been fighting back against that look. It wasn't contempt or pity, or even disdain. It was a complete lack of surprise.

"Just you standing here shows a promising level of growth," Mellaine said.

It was the look of someone who'd been expecting failure and hadn't been disappointed. It was a look of complete and utter disrespect. Human herbologist healer.

For the longest time, she thought the only way to survive that look was by conquering it. Show no flaws, no failures, nothing those expectations could cling to.

"We'll need time to discuss how to proceed," Symonne said.

But while Ember could control how hard she worked, she couldn't control how that work was perceived. She'd spent the last thirteen years trying to do so, and it had only left her exhausted, defeated, and high on the very pride the healers had to punish her for.

It was a vicious, unrelenting cycle; one where the only person getting dragged along was herself. And she was tired of it.

"We'll summon you back in a few days' time with our answer," Hollyn said. "For now, we thank you for your words—"

"Oh, there's more of them," Ember blurted.

Reena's mouth twisted. Mellaine's face fell. But Ember didn't care. Something had broken inside her at her confession. Now, she was free.

"I stand by the confession I made," she said, backing up to face all four healers. "I know why my pride had to be punished. But you have to know where that pride came from in the first place."

"Ember," Symonne warned. "You have already pled your case."

"Oh, let her speak," Reena said, rolling her neck. "I, for one, would love to hear where she's going with this."

"You would, wouldn't you," Ember said. "After all, you were the one pushing the hardest for my punishment during all of my trial meetings. I solved a Royal's murder, and in return, I got an obligatory reward and a threat to take everything away from me."

"That wasn't a decision we came to lightly," Symonne said, bracing her hands on her armrests. "We took six weeks to consider your case."

"And you would have taken six days to consider it if it were anyone else," Ember said.

The healers went deadly still. Behind them, the golden mask on Rosala's statue flashed like a warning sign.

"What exactly are you trying to suggest?" Hollyn asked, her voice dangerously calm.

Ember didn't flinch. "I'm saying I may feel like I have to prove myself, and that's on me. But we should all take a good look at the environment that made me feel that way."

Ember spread her arms. "The Healer School doesn't just train healers. It trains hierarchies. Ones where herbologists are viewed as less than, and humans are considered magically inferior. You three may protest, but I know Master Mellaine can attest to some of that."

Mellaine's lips thinned. Reena made to protest, but Mellaine raised a sharp hand. "Let her finish."

"She's insulting the very foundation of the healers!"

"I thought you wanted to hear what she has to say, Reena," Mellaine said.

Reena wrinkled her nose. Mellaine turned back to Ember. "Go on."

A heady sort of buzz moved through Ember's body. It was better than approval. It was respect.

"You four," Ember said, voice echoing, "had to punish me because pride is dangerous as a healer. Yet, all I've been trained to do is cling to that pride to survive. I may have been the one to make that choice, but I'm not the first. And I certainly won't be the last.

"Whether or not I'm accepted back into the Healer School, there are changes that need to be made. Because I made a mistake. I let my pride get in my way. I can admit it now. But I shouldn't have been put in a position where that pride was all I had."

Ember's skin was flushed. She met each healer's gaze in turn, staring into Reena's blazing blue gaze the longest.

For so long, she'd allowed everyone else to have all the power. But now?

"Is that all?" Symonne asked stiffly.

"I think so," Ember said. She turned to go, then looked back. "Oh, and thank you."

Ember bowed to each of the healers a final time, delighting in the frozen looks of shock on their faces. Then, she marched out of the temple.

Cadmus waited for her on a bench outside. His cheeks were flushed from the cold, his blue eyes staring distractedly at a nearby street performance. Yet, he immediately turned to her as she sat beside him.

"So?" he asked.

"I did it," Ember said.

Cadmus beamed. He wrapped his arm around her shoulders, pulling her close. "Good for you, Em."

Ember grinned, her heart still hammering against her ribs.

She'd really done it. True, she didn't know what was going to happen next, but at least something was actually going to happen now.

"So," Cadmus said, "when do you get to start your training again?"

"Well, that depends on if I actually get to start training again."

Cadmus froze. He pulled back, his eyes narrowing. "What did you do?"

"I told the truth," Ember said simply.

Cadmus's eyes narrowed even more. "And what truth would that be?"

Ember quickly explained her impromptu speech. Cadmus rubbed his face once she'd finished, seemingly torn between exasperation and pride.

"How do you feel?" he asked.

Ember didn't have to think twice. "Like I don't regret what I said."

"Well," Cadmus said, only slightly pained, "in that case, congratulations."

Ember laughed. A true, easy laugh for the first time in she couldn't remember how long.

Accepting Cadmus's hand, she let him pull her to her feet. Yet, as the two headed off into the kingdom, the distracted look slowly clouded over his eyes once more.

"You're still thinking about Mt. Vasolus, aren't you?" she said.

Cadmus sighed. "I wish I wasn't. But ever since returning from Scarsthain, it's like those whispers have turned to screams."

"Well, that sounds inviting," Ember said sarcastically.

"I know," Cadmus said, "I don't like the idea of going there either. But Em, my uncle didn't go through all that work to keep that symbol hidden forever. He did it so only the right people could find it. It has to mean something."

Ember tugged on a loose thread in her robe. She knew he had a point. But she couldn't shake the crazed look in Brenn's eyes from her mind as he talked about the symbol. That combined with the utter lack of information they'd found had her pulse chanting *danger, danger, danger.*

"I don't like this, Cadmus," she said, lowering her voice as a group of people passed. "Nothing good could be calling to you from that volcano."

"But if something is calling," Cadmus said, "that means there's something we can interrogate."

Ember made to comment on how their last interrogation went so well, but she paused as another group of people passed. Their eyes darted to Cadmus and away in rapid succession, a few bowing their heads while the others shifted uncertainly. Cadmus smiled and greeted each by name, the tension slowly melting as the commoners bowed and moved along.

"You see that?" Cadmus said to Ember as they continued toward the castle. "My people are starting to warm up to me, but they're still torn. My kingdom is struggling, and I'm running out of things to do on my own to help them."

"And you think whatever is in the volcano is your answer?" Ember asked.

"I have no idea. But I know it's important. And if there is the slightest chance this can help, then I have to do it." He looked over at Ember, his expression surprisingly vulnerable. "I let fear run my life for too long. I stood by and watched my own sister suffer as a result, and I can't let that happen to my kingdom as well."

Ember didn't know if she was proud or exasperated. She watched as he started across the street, sunlight glinting off his crown. He'd stopped having to constantly adjust it, his head and neck now steady under its weight.

As she headed after him, she knew just by the set of his shoulders that he had made up his mind.

"When are you going?" she asked.

"A week from today," he said. "I'm going to visit the mines near Vasolus to discuss our reserves, and I'll go after that."

He cast Ember a sidelong look. "Will you try to stop me?"

Once, she would have said absolutely. Now, she shook her head.

Cadmus hesitated. "You don't have to come with me, you know."

She knew that. Just as she knew she couldn't stop him. But that didn't mean she would let him walk into that volcano alone.

"If you think I'd go to some fear-infested bone dungeon," she said, "but not a volcano, then you are sorely mistaken. And also a little insulting."

Cadmus laughed. Ember flashed a grin. But as their paths diverged, she couldn't stop herself from fingering Analia's enka flower bracelet, something dark and heavy shifting inside her.

Chapter 54

The afternoon following Aaron's departure, Analia was greeted by an excited Laness in the dining room.

"It's time to get ready!" she announced.

Analia stared at her blankly.

"Don't tell me…" Laness threw up her hands, making an exasperated noise. Grabbing Analia by the wrist, she dragged her up the stairs, through the beaded curtain, and into Surce's studio, muttering all the while, "I can't believe he didn't tell you."

Apparently, Aaron had established his own form of celebration to mark the end of the war, with the main event occurring at sundown. Every time Analia tried to pry for more information, Surce and Laness told her to wait and see. She did, however, find out Surce had picked out dresses for them. And Analia's was the same black dress she'd seen on her first day at the shop.

As the three got ready, Surce and Laness took turns recounting stories from celebrations past. Branten in particular seemed to always leave a mark on the night—including the year he drunkenly tried to replace a fountain's statue with himself.

By the time they were all ready to go, Analia was thoroughly looking forward to the evening's festivities.

"Before we leave," Laness said, hopping off her stool, "I have something for you, Anna."

She crossed to a nearby shelf where she'd stashed her small leather pack, her red dress trailing behind her. Analia turned from her mirror, just in time to see Laness pull out a chain of woven enka flowers.

"Is that an enka bracelet?" she asked.

"I thought now that you're here, you should have your own bracelet. If you'd like one, I mean."

Laness's green eyes bounced between Analia and the chain, suddenly uncertain.

Analia didn't hesitate to offer her hand. "I would be honored to have one."

Laness beamed. She stepped up beside Analia, wrapping the bracelet around her wrist and pinching it together with her fingers.

"You should know," she warned, "the bracelet can only be bound by truths. One from me, one from you."

Analia pursed her lips. Laness immediately noticed. "It's all right if you don't want to, we can skip that step, the connection just might not be as strong—"

"No, we can do it," Analia said, surprisingly calm.

"You sure?"

Analia nodded. "Just... can you go first?"

Surce surreptitiously retreated to the opposite end of her studio, busying herself with her storage drawers. Laness looked down at the bracelet, her short brown hair falling into her eyes.

"I was on my own from an early age," she finally began. "Despite the lack of magic, it wasn't hard to survive in the Human Kingdom. Vendors had food they tossed out at the end of the day, the abundance of wilderness provided a place to sleep. And the humans were absurdly easy to pickpocket."

Laness grinned, then quickly sobered. "When the war with Starlight broke out, I was thrilled. It meant piles of supplies would be left unattended, and even larger groups of soldiers to steal from. But one day, I stole from the wrong commanding officer."

Analia's stomach sank. She reached for Laness's free hand, the nymph's gaze distant with memories.

"There's more to the story," she eventually said, thoughtfully turning the flowers around Analia's wrist. "That officer left me with more than one type of scar. But that's how I ended up in the humans' prison camp with Aaron."

Laness ran her fingers along the enka chain. With a faint tingle, half of the stems on either side wove together, partially sealing the bracelet. But Analia kept her gaze on Laness.

"I hate that that happened to you," she said.

Laness shrugged a shoulder, more subdued than anything. "Your turn."

Analia's mind wandered back to the Underground, the creature's voice. *A secret for a secret.*

It was the same type of bargain. But as Analia looked into Laness's eyes, her story softly tingling along her wrist, it felt more like an offering.

"After Deardryn told me I'd received my uncle's magic," she said, "she attacked me with her own. She nearly broke my spine. And for a moment, I considered letting her. Because I didn't know how to live with myself after praying for magic for so long, when my uncle needed to die for that to happen."

That was what the twinge was every time she summoned her magic. Always remaining, no matter how much control she gained over her flames.

But as the bracelet sealed around her wrist, as Laness pulled her into a tight hug, that twinge fizzled out.

An offering. A gift. That's what her magic was.

And Accalon would've wanted her to take it.

Analia paused in the dress shop's threshold, the sun just beginning to set as she took in the view.

The entire kingdom seemed to be out and roaming the streets. They wore everything from informal tunics to floor-length gowns, their voices raised over the music that echoed from deeper in the Pulse. Hundreds of bronze braziers had been strategically placed throughout the streets, their heat beating back the winter chill.

"Beautiful," she murmured, Surce and Laness coming up on either side of her.

"So then why are you just standing there?" Branten demanded, bursting out of the crowd before her with a cup in each hand. "This is a party, come on!"

Laness put her hands on her hips as Mor also emerged. "He got away from you, didn't he?"

"For *two seconds*," Mor said despairingly.

"And you'll all be happier for it," Branten said, ushering them all into the crowd.

Analia spent the evening being whisked around the kingdom. Laness, Surce, and Branten periodically split off to visit friends and vendor stands, but Mor made sure to stay with her. He showed her where to get the sweetest puff pastries; beaded necklaces that changed color with the time of day; the hot, spiked cider that Branten made sure to keep her paper cup full of.

By the time the sun had fully set, there was still no sign of messy hair or starlight eyes.

"What's all this?" Analia asked as Mor led her toward a crowded stage.

"This is the Ruhari Releasing," he said, nodding to the people who stepped out of their way. "It's the main event of the entire celebration."

Analia was about to ask what a ruhari was when they reached the stage. People crammed around the rim, scribbling on scraps of paper that littered its surface. Tumbling through it all were what looked to be hundreds of fist-sized fluffballs, ranging in a rainbow of colors. Despite having their tiny eyes and snouts mostly obscured by fur, they didn't seem to have any trouble scurrying around, most letting out little squeaks as they went.

"Those are ruhari?" Analia asked, bracing her hands on the stage and leaning forward.

"Adorable, aren't they?"

Mor placed his hand on the stage palm up, attracting the attention of a nearby teal ruhari. It scurried up his arm on four stubby legs, Mor laughing as it reached his shoulder and nuzzled his neck.

"I've never heard of them before," Analia said, reaching up to stroke its soft, fluffy fur.

"We don't usually see them either. But for some reason, they love to come snuffle about the kingdom around this time of year."

"So what do you do with them?"

"That's the fun part." Mor gently nudged his ruhari back to the stage. "Every citizen gets a slip of paper, where they can write down a fear. Then, they give it to one of these little fluffballs."

"What happens then?" Analia asked.

"I'd hate to ruin the surprise."

Analia raised a brow, and Mor winked.

"Here," he said, passing her a pen and paper scrap. "You work on this. I have to make sure Branten hasn't fallen into the river."

Analia snorted. Mor squeezed her shoulder, then headed back into the crowd, leaving her with her paper scrap and a white ruhari that had wandered over.

"Write down a fear," she mused, tapping her pen against her chin.

The Princess of Ash would have had no problem with that assignment. Now, staring down at her paper, only one fear came to mind.

The ruhari nudged her hand with a velvety snout. Analia smiled and scratched its chin, then quickly scribbled down her fear.

"And now I give this to you?" she asked it uncertainly.

In response, the ruhari picked up her paper in its tiny mouth and scampered away.

"Well, all right then," Analia muttered.

She watched the cluster of ruhari for a few minutes, wondering if she was somehow missing the big surprise. Just as she was about to turn away, the sun disappeared below the horizon.

Immediately, a group of ruhari leaped surprisingly high into the sky. In perfect sync, they puffed out their fur, tumbling on the wind like a cloud of dandelion heads.

Analia craned her head back, letting out a laugh.

"It's even better from higher up."

Analia's delight caught in her throat. She turned.

Aaron stood a few paces away. He wore his usual black-and-blue jacket, his hands shoved in its pockets, his mouth curved in a tentative smile.

"Hi," he said.

Analia eased back against the stage. "Hi."

She'd thought she'd have countless things to say when she saw him. But looking at him now, all those words seemed to whisper out of her mind.

"How was your trip?" she finally asked.

"It was... eventful. I shouldn't discuss it here, though."

"Right."

Analia glanced around, searching for something to say, for someone that could intervene, hating that she was doing it in the first place. What had happened to them?

"I can show you," Aaron blurted. "How it looks higher up, I mean."

He pulled his hand from his pocket and offered it to her. Analia didn't hesitate to slide her fingers through his. But as they faded into the shadows, reappearing a moment later on a railed-off section of the Council Building's roof, there were still no words on her tongue.

Aaron immediately released her hand. He took a step back, his eyes flashing to her face. But he didn't say anything. Neither did she. Instead, they looked away, fixing their eyes on the ruhari above.

She just had to say something. Anything. Her hands gripped the railing, just inches away from his.

"I started this celebration in honor of my mom," he finally said, eyes still on the sky.

"Really?" Analia said, the word momentarily sticking in her throat. "Laness said it was to celebrate the end of the war."

Aaron was quiet for a moment. "I told you how my mom died in the human war," he said. "That I don't know who killed her. I also told you how our visit to the humans was my annual trip to mark the end of our war.

"What I didn't tell you is my mom's death is what enabled our war to come to an end. Meaning the day we spent in the Human Kingdom celebrating..."

"Was the day your mother was killed," Analia finished quietly.

"And today," he said shakily, "is the anniversary of the day I found out she was dead."

Analia's heart ached. Her hand twitched on the rail, painfully aware of the distance between them.

"So," she said, "what I'm hearing is we have been subject to incredibly bad timing."

Aaron laughed slightly, rubbing his eyes. "Today originated as a typical celebration. I added the fears in later for myself, just to get a moment to breathe again. But it's exactly what my mom would have wanted: the beauty in the pain. Just like she was."

"I think a lot of people need something like this," Analia said, her hand inching toward his.

Aaron leaned against the railing, his hand shifting away. "I always struggle when I'm forced to see the humans," he admitted. "But this visit in particular?"

"You were barely holding yourself together," Analia said. "And then I pushed you and told you things that were harsher than they needed to be."

Analia could barely breathe through her wave of guilt.

"Hey." Aaron extended his thumb, then quickly pulled it back. "Don't forget, I disappeared to deal with the DovenU. And then I stayed away longer than I promised because I was terrified of destroying things even more."

Was that what he thought?

Analia finally slid her hand across the railing, her fingertips grazing his. "This wasn't all on you," she told him.

Aaron looked down at their hands. Not moving closer. Not pulling away.

"I suppose it's a good thing I remembered the one conclusion we're allowed to jump to." He shifted his hand, running his thumb along the back of hers. "Did you remember, too?"

Finally, the tension in Analia's shoulders relaxed. "I did," she said. "I hope you also remembered how familiar I am with needing to lose control sometimes."

"You also used to give me some warning when you'd go to the roof," Aaron said, tracing her knuckles with his forefinger. "But this is the first time I've seen you up here in a long time."

Analia made to respond, just as there came a blinding gold flash above. She whipped her head back, golden sparks scattering across the sky.

"Did a ruhari just explode?" she demanded.

"We still don't know why they do that," Aaron said. "Some suspect it's a natural result when they come to the end of their life cycle. Others think it's a way to propagate more ruhari, just as plants do with their seeds. Either way, it doesn't seem to hurt them."

"That's amazing!" Analia leaned out and over the railing as the rest of the ruhari followed suit, filling the sky with a rainbow of flashing lights.

Aaron laughed, his fingers twining with hers. The magic beneath his skin brushed against her own, offering a quiet greeting. Analia smiled over at him, and his eyes widened.

"Would you look at that," he said. "Hundreds of smiles in, and I've never seen you light up like this."

"All you had to do is explode in a million colors."

"Well, if that's all it took."

Analia laughed. A true, delighted laugh, just for him.

Aaron beamed. And Analia knew there wasn't anything she wouldn't do to see that look again.

Aaron beckoned with his free hand, and he led her around to the other side of the observatory. Analia tilted her head back, but Aaron shook his head and pointed down.

For the first time, she noticed the kingdom below. A group of citizens had gathered around the Council Building, calling greetings as they waved.

For a moment, Analia could only stare. Her hand drifted to her phoenix pin, something uncertain and wonderful starting to unfurl in her chest.

"Is this the part where we introduce me as your queen?" she asked, her voice catching in her throat.

"I think this will suffice," Aaron said, sliding his arm around her shoulders.

Analia watched the crowd, blinking back tears as they cheered. For Aaron. For her. She was an outsider, and yet she found more friendly faces in that crowd than in the entire Ash Kingdom.

Aaron leaned in, whispering in her ear. "This is what a kingdom is supposed to feel like."

Analia looked up at him, lost for words. Aaron pressed a quick kiss to her temple, laughing under his breath as someone cheered below.

"Stay or go?" he asked.

"Go," she said. "But in a minute."

Analia turned back to the railing, her heart full to bursting. Aaron waited patiently beside her, soaking in the attention as he waved to his people.

King of one kingdom that adored him, and another that would smile at his head on a spike.

Analia took one final look. Then, she nodded to Aaron, who whispered a warning and whisked her into the shadows. A moment later, they reemerged on his roof, the noise of the kingdom far off, but the lights in the sky still brilliant above their heads.

"I thought you'd want some quiet after all that," Aaron explained, sitting on the edge of the roof. "We can go anywhere else if I was wrong."

Analia shook her head. "Gods, I missed you," she said, sitting beside him. "I miss you every time you're gone."

Aaron's face lit up. He nudged her closer, murmuring in her ear, "Can I tell you a secret?"

Analia nodded.

"I miss you when you're across the room."

Analia's blood sang. "So," she said, "you're saying if I were to move across this roof..."

"My shooting star, I never knew how merciless you are."

Analia laughed, resting her head on his shoulder. For a long time, they were quiet, watching the ruhari flash in the sky. Eventually, she found a pure white one in the crowd. And as she breathed in metal and spice, she watched as her words began to burn.

I don't deserve to be happy.

They were words that haunted her nightmares in Ash, trailed her into the Starlight Kingdom. But as they crumbled to ash, she realized she had already started to burn those whispers herself. That, in fact, she had been happy. For a good while now. To the point that stepping on the roof hadn't felt like her final condemnation as she'd feared.

It had felt like coming home. Especially since she knew Accalon would have wanted those words to burn away.

Analia shifted so her back was to Aaron's chest, his arms sliding around her waist. And she wasn't surprised in the slightest when the stars across her dress rippled, forming the outline of a torch.

Chapter 55

In the week that followed the Ruhari Releasing, Aaron was unable to tear his gaze from Analia. He devoured every movement she made as she spoke, as she trained, as he walked past her in the house. Even his magic reached for her whenever she played her harp.

She was the key he had never realized he was searching for. And it was a special sort of torment to feel the click as the lock disengaged, just for the door to remain unmovable. All he could do was wait as Surce decoded the scroll, memories playing on an endless loop in his mind.

Her lips against his skin. The lightning bolt of pleasure as she ground against him. The tiny moan that had escaped her lips. But it was the look in her eyes when they finally descended the roof that had him spending every night sitting on his mother's bed, staring at the wall.

No one had ever looked at him with such unconcealed affection. But even if he wasn't misinterpreting, did he deserve it? He and his clobbering secrets?

Those two words had ripped through his insides the night of the celebration, making him leave her at her door when all he wanted was to lose himself in the feeling of his lips on hers. But she didn't know.

"Aaron," Surce said, "what are your estimates?"

Aaron blinked hard. He sat at his dining room table, his family gathered around him. He'd told them of the pendant the morning after the celebration, their days now consumed with defense measures: wards, military counts, merchant reports.

Aaron rattled off the numbers Surce was looking for, relieved as everyone turned away. All except Analia.

Gods, even her gaze had his blood rushing through his veins.

"It's been almost a week since the wards were reinforced," Surce said, eyes scanning down the list before her.

"I'm replenishing them first thing tomorrow," Aaron replied, his hands clenching around the edge of his seat.

Surce nodded. The meeting quickly broke off after that, everyone scattering to take care of whatever duties Surce had assigned them—she'd always been better at delegating than he was.

Aaron and Analia rose at the same time. They both turned for the door, nearly bumping into one another as they started to leave. The two jumped back, Analia stammering an apology, Aaron completely electrified.

Quickly reassuring her, he waved her ahead of him, careful to maintain a healthy distance between them as he followed her out of the dining room.

He knew this was his chance to speak. But as they reached the stairs, as the seconds continued to pass, he only felt cornered.

Telling her about the tapestries now, unprompted, would only lead to her feeling lied to—which wouldn't be far off. But had too much time passed for him to avoid that reaction if he told her after she decided? That outcome scared him worst of all.

How was he supposed to risk everything with the one person who had seen through him? Every layer, every flaw, every blackened piece of his soul, and still accepted him.

Was Mor right? Had he waited too long and missed his opportunity? Had their demise become inevitable?

Aaron paused as they reached Analia's door. She turned the knob, Aaron expecting her to push inside without a backward glance. Instead, her shoulders slumped.

"I'm sorry I got us in this mess," she said, her voice cracking.

Aaron was reaching for her before he even processed her words.

"Don't do that," he said, turning her to face him. "Don't blame yourself for this."

"I was the one who brought the pendant here," she argued. "*Pryanth's* pendant. And I knew it had magic, but I never would have thought... I promised to protect your kingdom's secret, and instead I'm bringing Sun to your border."

"This is not your fault," Aaron soothed, his thumb stroking back and forth along her spine. "You had no way of knowing what the pendant could do. Even if you left it behind, that would have just resulted in Deardryn raiding the Ash Kingdom to find out why you weren't moving. This is Deardryn's fault, not yours."

"That doesn't mean I can't be sorry."

Aaron shook his head. He pulled her to his chest, not sure who he was trying to comfort.

His home was dangerously close to being discovered. The peace he had sacrificed himself for was one secret away from shattering. He might have destroyed his very own shooting star.

Aaron didn't know how much more he could take. Especially as Analia peeked up at him, her eyes coming to rest on his mouth.

Gods, she was so close. All he had to do was tilt his head. Just a fraction. Just a single movement and he could finally fit his mouth to hers.

Maybe not *everything* had to fall apart around him. He could learn to live off whatever scraps she gave him—he'd managed to do it with Liss.

Analia's eyes jerked up. Her lips moved, saying something Aaron didn't hear. Then, she stepped out of his grip and into her room, leaving Aaron frozen on the other side of her door.

This was his moment. Back away. Survive. But gods, he was tired of just surviving. He wanted to hope. He wanted to know.

He just had to pray he wouldn't end up shattered in the aftermath.

Analia slumped against her bedroom door, burying her face in her hands.

Gods, how much more of this could she take? His presence, his touch, her every thought consumed by him.

For so long, she'd felt a sense of wrongness, as if her bones had shifted out of place. But sitting on that roof, Aaron's arms around her long after the sky had gone dark, she'd felt it. The click as everything realigned. The rightness that had her feeling like she could finally fill her lungs.

She didn't know what time it was when Aaron eventually helped her to her feet. He led her back through the hatch, down the hall to her room, taking those extra minutes when they both knew he could have shadowjumped them in seconds. Even as they reached her door, he took one more second to look at her.

She knew it would be so easy. Just stretch up on her toes and pick up right where they'd left off in the Human Kingdom.

But she remained perfectly still as Aaron touched her cheek and bid her good night, only hearing his voice from the lakeside as he walked away. *A reminder of what happens when you're not careful.*

That was what their moment in the Human Kingdom had been: a warning. Because even though Analia was happy, healing, putting herself back together, she still managed to hurt him. And she refused to ever do that again.

She had to be patient. Even though every time she saw him, she could only feel his hands on her thighs and his lips on her neck. Even though it had just taken every shred of control she had to step away from him in that hallway and into her room.

And when Aaron knocked on her door the following morning and asked if she would come with him to renew the wards, she knew that control was about to snap.

Analia and Aaron walked through the snowy Starlight Kingdom, hoods pulled up and hands in their pockets. Despite the cold, Aaron had told her he wanted to walk through his kingdom instead of shadowjumping to the lakeside. Now, she watched as he smiled at his people, his face flushed from the cold, snow clinging to his jacket hood.

Every now and again, she caught him casting her looks from the corner of his eye. Yet, he never spoke, leaving her insides to twist tighter and tighter.

Just when she thought she couldn't take it any longer, Aaron put a hand on her arm. He guided her over to the nearby walkway, looking as though he were about to speak. But Analia's gaze was caught by something over his shoulder.

"Watch the ice!" she called.

The woman passing behind Aaron looked up from her collection of papers. She glanced around, letting out a yelp as she spotted the ice-coated steps she'd been about to take.

"Thanks for the warning!" she said, hopping back and twisting to face Analia. "I take this path every day, so you'd think I'd know to be careful—oh, hello again!"

Analia brightened as she recognized the woman from the weapons display. "You remember me."

"I should be saying that to you," the woman said, her eyes darting to the side.

"How could I forget the woman who gave me such a beautiful sheath?"

"You mean accessory," the woman corrected with a laugh. But that was tension creeping into her voice. Just as it was unease that kept her at a careful distance.

Analia glanced to Aaron, wondering if she was imagining things. But Aaron had gone completely still. His eyes darted between Analia and the woman, his face rapidly draining of color.

Analia looked back at the woman, but she had retreated several steps, her dark purple cloak pulled in front of her like a shield.

"What am I missing here?" Analia asked.

The woman bit her lip, not saying anything.

Aaron, meanwhile, seemed to unfreeze. Slowly, he turned to face Analia, his silver eyes wide.

"What you're missing," he said, voice slightly strangled, "is that's Liss."

Chapter 56

Aaron felt as though he'd walked face-first into a brick wall. He barely processed Analia explaining how Liss had given her the black-and-silver sheath dangling from her waist, her own eyes wide with shock.

Analia knew Liss. Was friendly with her, for that matter.

The realization should have left him hurt, betrayed. But as Liss flashed a guilty smile, he only felt confused.

"I'd heard you'd brought an outsider into the kingdom," she explained. "So, naturally, I wanted to scope her out. But I didn't realize..."

Her eyes darted to the gray moonstone ring still on Analia's finger. Crystal spare him. Such a bad idea.

"Anyway," she said quickly, "I didn't even notice either of you until Analia called out, and I see she knows who I am, and you've probably talked to her—I should just go."

Liss backed away, hands raised in front of her. Just as she turned to flee—

"Liss, wait," Aaron called.

Liss turned so quickly she almost lost her footing on the slick walkway. Surprised himself, it took Aaron a moment to glance at Analia. But she had already slipped out of hearing range, giving them their privacy.

For a few long, unbearable moments, both Aaron and Liss searched for words, their eyes darting to everything but each other.

He knew he should say something—he was the one who called her back in the first place. But he was lost in the memories that flashed through his mind, almost too quick to register.

Screaming, sobbing, the ghost of her hands across his skin. They had both been broken by their pasts, each individual piece so sharp he was almost surprised neither of them drew blood when they collided. Over and over and over again, until it was no longer just their pasts that broke them.

"We really fucked things up, didn't we?" he said, half to himself.

Liss's eyes flashed up to his. Then, she scoffed. "It's almost astounding how badly we fucked things up."

Aaron's lips twitched. He felt as though he was waking from a dream, his mind finally settling into reality.

He had loved this woman once. She had broken his heart. But standing there, talking to her after so long, all he felt was regret.

"Gods, Liss," he said, "I'm sorry. Sorry for everything, sorry I didn't apologize sooner."

"I know," she said. "Aaron, I know. And I'm... I'm sorry, too."

Aaron didn't know what he was expecting to happen after hearing those words. There was certainly a flicker of relief. Maybe even a flash of validation. But strongest of all was the release. It rolled down his body, loosening every tensed muscle one by one, somehow making him feel heavier and lighter at the same time.

Across from him, Liss let out a tiny breath, her own expression relaxing. With a faint grin, she moved to hop up on the railing, Aaron leaning beside her.

"So," he said. "Do you think this is a sign of us actually maturing?"

Liss laughed slightly. "Some of us had more work to do than others."

Aaron made a noise of protest.

"Who said I was talking about you?" Liss kicked him in the shins, leaning away as he elbowed her back.

"You know," she went on, voice sobering, "I've spent so much time going over those years in my head. Looking at every angle, turning over every detail. It's reached the point where I don't think I know what was real and what only happened in my head anymore."

"I know what you mean," Aaron sighed.

Liss looked down, her fingers fidgeting in her lap. "Have you come to any conclusions?"

Aaron considered for a moment. "I think neither of us are bad people. We were just bad for each other."

There was a time he wouldn't have been able to choke out the words, even if he was lying. But now, they rolled off his tongue as if they'd been looking for the opportunity to do so.

He'd been thinking for some time now that Liss wasn't the monster he'd built her up to be. That, maybe, he wasn't a complete monster either. Especially as Liss gave him a soft smile.

"You know," she said, "I landed on the same thing. I'd only like to add I was a terror."

"No, you weren't."

"Yes, I was. And you were a moody asshole."

Aaron snorted, not trying to deny it. Liss flashed a teasing grin, but it quickly softened into something more tentative.

"You look happy, Aaron."

Aaron ducked his head, touching his fingertips to his smile. "You know," he said, "I think I am. And you?"

"I would go so far as to say I'm spectacular."

Aaron laughed. "I'm glad to hear it."

He was completely earnest. No, he was relieved. Relieved their chaos had only left a scratch, not a scar. That he trusted the sparkle in her eyes.

"You better treat her right," Liss said, nodding down the walkway.

Aaron followed her gaze to where a group of children—headed by Brookston—had converged on Analia. The little boy tugged her arm to bring her to his level, Analia's laugh carried back to them on the wind.

Gods, he loved that sound.

"Don't worry," he said. "I have no intention of doing otherwise."

"Good. She's a special one. And with such excellent taste in sheaths as well."

"Unbelievable," Aaron muttered.

Liss kicked her legs, positively pleased with herself. Aaron couldn't even blame her. Instead, he looked out across his snow-crusted kingdom, taking in the peace, the quiet.

"Liss," he said after a moment. "I have to be honest. I have no idea what to say."

"That doesn't sound like you," she mused.

"No, it really doesn't."

Liss snickered. Hopping off the railing, she said, "What you say is, 'See you around.'"

She patted his arm. Then, without another word, she breezed off down the walkway, waving to Analia as she passed.

Aaron watched her go, an ancient weight slowly lifting from his shoulders. He didn't think he would be voluntarily seeing her again, not for a very long time at least. But he didn't find himself anxiously anticipating when "See you around," would come to fruition, either.

"Everything all right?" Analia asked, returning to his side.

Aaron nodded, the rip in his chest finally stitching closed. He reached for Analia, her body pleasantly warm from her magic release. And as they faded into the shadows, he didn't stop himself from pulling her closer.

Because Aaron was completely, irrevocably in love with her. Had been for a long time.

As the lakeside came into view, he knew that now, there was no turning back. Not for him, at least. Which meant the moment had finally come.

A nalia didn't immediately step out of Aaron's grip as they reemerged at the lakeside.

Even after everything he'd told her about Liss, she'd still been uneasy when she'd left them to talk. She'd told herself it was on Aaron's behalf. But there was no denying how it immediately melted away when she returned and he gave her his Phoenix Gate smile.

"I still can't believe she sniffed you out," Aaron said, snow crunching beneath his boots as he crouched to replenish the charge points. His magic could only spread so far with each release, meaning they had four more points they had to visit to completely replenish the wards.

"Really?" Analia asked. "From what I can tell, it seems in character for her."

Aaron grinned over his shoulder. "You like her, don't you?"

Analia's cheeks burned. She started to stammer a response, but Aaron cut her off with a laugh.

"It's all right," he said, silver light trailing from his fingers. "I should have expected as much. Even if your personalities didn't click as well as they do, Liss has a universal likability to her."

Analia cocked her head, noting how there was no sign of the usual tension in his voice whenever he spoke of Liss.

"So," she said after a beat, "what's her Blessing?"

"Speed. I found that out the hard way when I drunkenly challenged her to a race and she kicked my ass."

"Let me guess," Analia said. "That was the moment you knew you wanted her."

Aaron snickered, not trying to deny it. He reached back and grabbed Analia's hand, jumping them to the next releasing point.

"I think it was good," he said, half to himself. "Seeing her, I mean. I doubt we'll be going out drinking together any time soon, but I think we both needed that. Especially since she wasn't the only one that handled things poorly."

He bowed his head, eyes on his magic. "I've handled a lot of things poorly."

Something in his voice had Analia's heart skip a beat. She remained quiet as Aaron finished the second point, memories flashing across her mind. Moments that he hadn't just handled poorly, but she had as well. It wasn't until they jumped to the third spot that Analia finally dared to speak.

"Aaron," she said, crouching beside him, "why did you push me away on the Ash turret and in your Sun chambers?"

"Because I was afraid." Magic poured from his hands into the snow. "I'd grown to care about you too much, and I couldn't stand the thought of you finding out who I am, just to run back to Pryanth because he was the lesser evil. So, I took away that choice and tried to remember that Surce's tapestry showed you would take care of yourself that night."

His steady gaze locked on hers. And Analia needed a moment before she could respond.

"What would you have done if I had chosen him?"

Aaron's lips pursed. "I would like to tell you I wouldn't have done anything," he said, reaching for her and jumping them to the fourth spot. "I would have returned to my kingdom and learned to live with your choice. Just as I'd done when you chose the Ash Kingdom.

"But I didn't come to you sooner the day Pryanth slapped you because I had to make sure that when I left my chambers, I wouldn't hunt him down if I so much as heard his name. And knowing what he planned to do to you on your wedding night?" Aaron's eyes blazed. "I would have destroyed that entire kingdom if that's what it took to get to you."

Aaron returned his attention to the wards. Analia pressed her fingertips to her lips, but she didn't try to stop the words from tumbling out.

"I was afraid for you. Every day we weren't speaking in Sun and I would see your injuries that I knew weren't from training."

Aaron went still. Analia could practically feel the line she teetered on.

"I was nervous on the turret and hurt by your lies," she said. "But I was terrified by the thought of something happening to you. And I never felt anything close to that for Pryanth."

Aaron swallowed hard. He took her hand and pulled them into the shadows, whispering in the darkness, "Then why didn't you want me to stay in Ash?"

They reappeared at the final point, the ridges and ravines that separated them from the rest of the Wild Lands rising up before them. Analia could sense the wards tingle beneath them, but Aaron ignored them, his hand still gripping hers, his gaze almost pleading.

Once, she would have told him that she knew his family needed him, just as she had told herself. But that was just an excuse. The first of many, many walls between herself and the realization that it had never been just friendship between them.

Analia looked up at Aaron, her voice shaking. "Because I was too afraid to let you stay."

It took a few moments for Aaron to register her words. He sank back in the snow, his lips forming her name. He was still holding her hand.

Analia remained frozen where she crouched. Gods, what had she done?

Aaron tugged on her hand. She leaned forward, her free hand bracing herself on his chest, his arms pulling her closer.

"Gods, Analia," he breathed, pressing his face to the side of her neck.

Analia tried to squirm away, "I'm sorry—"

"Don't be sorry, Analia. Realize the effect you have on me. How you take my breath away every time you walk in a room. How every time I catch your eyes lingering on me, all I can think about is your skin beneath my hands and your voice screaming my name."

He pulled her onto his lap, his knee grazing the rising ache between her thighs. Analia gasped. Aaron swore against her neck.

"That sound." He pulled back, lifting her chin, his breath hot and unsteady on her mouth. "Tell me why you made that sound. Tell me why I can feel your heart racing and see that mind-shattering blaze in your eyes."

Analia shivered as his thumb brushed the back of her neck. She slid her arms beneath his jacket, hating the layers between them, hating every cautioning whisper that swirled through her mind. Whispers that had been trained by so many, but never him.

"You're safe to tell me, Analia," he whispered. "No matter what your answer is."

"I know," Analia said, her hand finding the back of his neck. "I'm always safe with you."

She lifted her face, her hand guiding Aaron's head down. His eyes were wide and dark, snow clinging to his lashes. She closed her eyes, feeling Aaron pause just a breath away.

"What are we doing, Analia?" he whispered.

It was one simple question. One she had gotten wrong once before—maybe even on purpose. But now, she didn't try to stop the truth from rising up from her chest, her throat, parting her lips.

Aaron went rigid. Analia jolted back, her eyes flying open, "What's wrong?"

Aaron wasn't looking at her. His head had snapped toward the ridge, his nostrils flared.

"Someone," he said, terrifyingly calm, "is at the border."

Chapter 57

Dimitri raced through the Moon Castle. It was the day he was to break into Scarsthain, his friends were waiting for him. But he had to find Patryclas first.

Skidding to a stop before Patryclas's study, Dimitri knocked fast and hard. He didn't immediately notice when Patryclas opened the door, his fist still knocking on its side.

"Dimitri?" Patryclas asked, puzzled. "What's going on?"

"I want to stay in the Moon Kingdom," Dimitri blurted.

Patryclas's eyebrows shot up. He opened the door wider, and Dimitri marched inside, crackling with energy.

He'd been working up the nerve to tell Patryclas since his visit to his mother's bookstore—before that, if he was being honest. Now, it was his final chance. One last opportunity to ask for what he wanted.

Patryclas leaned against the door, watching him curiously. "You were saying?"

"Our bargain is up in a week," Dimitri began, raising his tattooed wrist as he paced. "You told me if I could prove myself a loyal citizen and tell you what I want, you would let me stay."

"I did."

"Well, what I want is to stay here." Dimitri stopped before Patryclas and took a deep breath. "Everything good in my life has fallen apart or come back to hurt me. But I'm tired of being afraid of wanting something. So, what I want is to stay here."

Dimitri looked up into Patryclas's face, willing him to see how much he meant it. He wanted him to feel the happiness that had snuck up on him, even throughout the chaos of Deardryn's scheme. This kingdom was his retreat, his place of peace, and Patryclas was a massive part of that.

"Well," Patryclas said, rubbing his jaw, "that wasn't quite what I was looking for when I asked that question."

Dimitri waited, fighting not to deflate. He knew these people. He knew the way they talked. First came the no. Then...

Patryclas smiled. "But I think we can make arrangements while you identify those final answers."

Something powerful, something wonderful, erupted in Dimitri's chest. He lurched forward, flinging his arms around Patryclas's middle.

Patryclas laughed. He hugged Dimitri back, "Well, this is certainly a welcome surprise."

"Thank you," Dimitri said, quickly pulling away. That was going to take some getting used to. But he'd already learned to trust the fond sparkle in Patryclas's eyes.

"I would be lying if I said I wasn't hoping you would make this choice." He smoothed back Dimitri's hair, leaning down to kiss his forehead. "Welcome home, Dima."

At his words, there came a flash of heat across Dimitri's wrist. When he looked down, his purple heart had finally turned black.

It was done. Their bargain was fulfilled. He was home.

Dimitri cradled his wrist to his chest, the realization settling in his heart. Home. He finally had a home.

Dimitri hurried into Rayner's shop, Sabi already waiting.

"You're late," she complained, hurling a bundle of dark clothing at him.

"I had to do something."

Dimitri stripped off his clothes, shrugging on the far-too-large outfit Sabi had tossed him. Before he could sneak a peek in the mirror, Rayner descended the back staircase, a book under his arm.

"Good, you're here."

He bundled Dimitri into his client chair, propping his book of Moon Royal faces on the table beside him. Thumbing through, he nodded to himself when he found the page he wanted.

"Are you *sure* you're allowed to do this?" Dimitri asked, not for the first time. "Your bargain with Sylas—"

"Dima, are you *fussing* over me?" Rayner asked, eyes sparkling as he looked up from his book. "That's adorable."

Dimitri sat back in his chair with a huff. Still, his mouth twitched as he closed his eyes.

"Keep them open," Rayner said, kneeling before him. "I'm not good at matching if I don't have the full picture."

A thrill ran down Dimitri's spine. He'd never gotten to watch Rayner work, Rayner claiming the attention distracted him. Now, he got to watch Rayner's eyes drag across his face, down his body, setting his nerves tingling.

"Ready?" Rayner whispered.

Dimitri nodded. Then, Rayner's hands were cradling his face.

Magic exploded across Dimitri's skin. It left a burning trail as Rayner's hands moved down his neck, his shoulders, over his chest.

Rayner kept quiet as he worked. Every now and again, his eyes darted to the picture beside Dimitri's head, then back to Dimitri, then away again the moment their gazes locked.

Something about that put Dimitri on edge. Before he could consider it too long, Rayner was waving Sabi over.

"What do you think?" he asked, tilting Dimitri's face from side to side.

Sabi studied Dimitri over Rayner's shoulder. "His nose is too long."

Rayner nodded. He stroked his finger down the bridge of Dimitri's nose, leaving a trail of tingles. "Anything else?"

After a few more adjustments, Rayner finally stepped away, allowing Dimitri to see his reflection in the mirror across the room.

His previously black hair was now a rich dark brown, cut close to his skull. His brows were thick and severe, the planes of his face harsher, harder. He was also about four inches taller, noticeably less scrawny, and dressed in a purple doublet with the Moon Kingdom's sigil of a black moon bisected by two swords across his chest.

"Don't forget this." Rayner passed Dimitri a small glass dropper bottle, its cloudy contents swirling like captured fog.

"Shouldn't it be blue?" Dimitri asked, unscrewing the bottle and peering inside.

"They're glamor drops, not dye," Rayner huffed. "I told you, everything will look the way it's supposed to once the magic touches your eyes. My provider is very talented—although she's not cheap either, so quit trying to spill it."

Dimitri continued to tilt the bottle, watching the contents swirl. "You can afford it."

"Oh, just give it to me."

Rayner swiped the bottle. Stepping closer, he lifted Dimitri's chin with his free hand, guiding his head back.

"Now who's fussing?" Dimitri asked.

"You be quiet."

Rayner leaned in close. Gently lifting Dimitri's lashes with his forefinger, he sent a tiny drop of glamor into his eye, his hands shifting to repeat on the other side.

Dimitri blinked rapidly, the magic cold and tingly across his eyes. He half expected his vision to blur. Yet, he had no problem seeing in the mirror that his amber eyes were now the dark blue of Prince Macsen. A Royal who had access to the Wraithhouse.

"So?" Sabi asked.

"If I get an eye infection," Dimitri said, "I'm blaming Rayner."

Rayner scoffed. Stepping away, he tossed Dimitri a pair of dark robes from a nearby counter, Dimitri slipping them under his cloak. He would be needing those later.

"Don't forget to blink three times to shift the glamor," Rayner said. "I paid extra for that."

Dimitri nodded. Finally, he looked up at his friends, the people he'd chosen, the ones sacrificing everything for him. "Ready?"

Rayner nodded. Beside him, Sabi's face contorted as if tasting something sour. Dimitri started to speak. And obviously losing some internal struggle, Sabi grabbed him and pulled him into a hug.

"You're not allowed to not come back," she told him, abruptly shoving him away. "I don't make friends easily, and I refuse to start from scratch."

"I'm touched," Dimitri drawled.

"I'm devastated," Rayner deadpanned.

Sabi scoffed and swatted his arm. Dimitri snickered. But when he caught Sabi's eye, he gave her a small nod of understanding. Then, with his friends behind him, he headed for the door.

Chapter 58

The Wraithhouse was designed like a massive pit. Dimitri, Rayner, and Sabi stood on the top ring, multiple pairs of stairs cutting through layers of pews and leading down to a large sandy floor.

Countless paintings, statues, and other treasures lay spread out across the top floor. But Dimitri only had eyes for the altar carved from bone, sitting in the center of the sandy pit.

Its long, flat top could have held a full-grown human. Innumerable pulsepearls sat in sockets in the altar's sides, all glowing with a soft pink light. And guarding them were two wraiths, their hoods pulled up as they softly conversed.

"So much for this being the dead hour," Dimitri muttered.

"It's two wraiths," Sabi hissed back. "That's nothing compared to the afternoon rush."

Before Dimitri could stop her, Sabi marched down the stairs, calling an enthusiastic greeting.

"Crystal fuck me," Dimitri muttered.

He fixed his posture, then descended the stairs, Rayner close behind. Time to see if his months in the Moon Castle paid off.

"Magnar," Dimitri called, pitching his voice down. "I'm pleased to see you're here."

The two wraiths had already started to climb the stairs. At Dimitri's call, they turned their attention from Sabi, still talking and gesturing broadly about a third of the way down the steps.

"Your Highness," Magnar, the taller wraith, said with a bow. "Should I have been expecting your visit?"

"Not this time."

Dimitri reached Sabi's side. He stilled her with a hand to her shoulder, then glanced to the second wraith, still staring at Sabi with bewilderment. Magnar elbowed him, and the wraith hurriedly bowed as well.

"My apologies, Your Highness," Magnar said. "Lowtan is still learning his courtesies."

Dimitri tried not to shift on his feet as Magnar and Lowtan reached them. This was the moment any Moon Royal would nod, shadows flickering in a warning behind them. But did the wraiths know that?

"You would be wise to attend to that," Dimitri said.

Lowtan's face tensed. Dimitri ignored him.

"So," he said to Magnar, leaning against a pew. "I see you've met my uncle's head bookkeeper, Sabina. Apparently, she's found a lack of information on your sanctuary and would like to ask some questions."

"It's abysmal!" Sabi said, spreading her arms. "This house is a treasure trove of history and culture and architecture, and its documentation is nonexistent!"

"Would you mind answering her questions?" Dimitri asked, the same way he'd ask a stranger to indulge a child.

The wraiths swapped reluctant looks.

"Your Highness," Magnar began, fiddling with his pulsepearl chain, "we are flattered by the interest, but we have much to do."

"But I purposefully picked a low-traffic time to visit," Sabi said, clasping her hands pleadingly.

"Yes," Magnar said. "Which means this is the only time my acolyte and I have time to work."

"I know the wraiths are a private folk," Sabi said. "You don't have to tell me anything you don't want to. I won't even write it down if you like. See?" Sabi pushed open her dark green cloak. "No paper, no pens."

Dimitri choked back a snort. Like that ever stopped Sabi from absorbing information.

"A private tour, then," he said.

Magnar's eyes darted. "I suppose..."

"No!" Lowtan broke in. "You taught me the secrets of this sanctuary are to stay with our kind."

"Are you defying your Royal?" asked Rayner softly. He sat on the edge of a pew across from Dimitri and a few rows up, his body angled toward the wraiths.

He wasn't a particularly imposing figure, nor did he have any weapons—they weren't permitted inside. But there was something about his faint smirk that had even Dimitri wanting to slowly back away.

Lowtan's fists tightened in his robes. Magnar's nostrils flared slightly. Dimitri remained perfectly still, the air tingling with magic.

"So," Sabi said, completely unfazed. "Shall we start with the wall paintings?"

Magnar's gaze slid back to Sabi. "I suppose we shall."

Sabi beamed. But Dimitri's stomach sank as she turned and led the wraiths up the steps. He didn't like the suspicion in their expressions. He liked the resentment even less.

"Ready?" Rayner breathed, stepping to Dimitri's side.

Lowtan twisted around, "Aren't you two coming?"

Yes, that resentment was definitely a problem.

"I'll wait here," Dimitri said, sitting on his pew. "Sabina tends to be thorough."

Lowtan sneered. He took a step back toward them, "Perhaps I should wait with you—"

"Lowtan!" Sabi trilled. "Magnar said you have to study the history of these objects for your lessons. Come tell me what you know."

Lowtan wavered. Then, with a final dark look at Dimitri, he stalked up the steps to the top floor. Dimitri remained still as Lowtan joined Sabi's tour, Sabi excitedly asking questions as she led them behind a row of bronze wraith statues. Completely blocking their view of the pit below.

"Unstoppable," Rayner murmured, tasting each syllable like a decadent wine.

Dimitri's lips twitched. "Come on," he said, rising to his feet. "Lowtan just sliced our time in half."

Keeping low, Dimitri and Rayner darted down the steps. He half expected an alarm to blare the moment his boot touched sand, but the Wraithhouse remained quiet outside of Sabi's rapid-fire questions.

"This is it, huh?" Dimitri said, dropping to his knees in the sand behind the altar.

"A bit large for my taste," Rayner said, kneeling beside him. "I've also never been a fan of the carving fad."

Dimitri's eyes moved over the altar, taking in the swirling patterns etched around the pulsepearls. Each design was perfectly identical to the one before it, not so much as a variation in depth or length of the lines.

"Look at this," Dimitri said, shuffling farther down the altar. "The entire thing is a perfect mirror of those designs."

"You think it was magically done?" Rayner asked.

"Not in the way you're thinking. Anna told me how dampers have to have special carvings and shit to actually plug a person's magic. But maybe that's not the only way carvings can be used."

"Like protection for precious objects," Rayner mused. He sat back on his heels, flicking his hand at Dimitri. "All right then. Touch it and see what happens."

Dimitri could perfectly imagine Patryclas's look of horror at that idea. But he'd always been impulsive. He tried to grab a pearl, just to feel a quick zap.

"Did you feel that?" Lowtan demanded high above.

"Yes!" Sabi said over Magnar. "A faint draft. I thought it was coming from one of you—oh, look at this archway!"

Dimitri's heart pounded against his ribs.

"That wasn't surprising," Rayner commented.

Dimitri shot him a withering look.

There was no way for them to get one of the pearls. Either the magic would zap their fingers off, or the wraiths would snap their necks after they were notified.

"My apologies, Sabina," Magnar said, "but we must return to our studies."

"But look at the perfect curve of these walls," Sabi said, her pitch rising.

"Sabi's running out of time," Rayner hissed.

"I know, I know!"

Dimitri tugged on his cloak. They couldn't stop the wraiths from knowing when they touched a pearl, and the wards took away any hope of grabbing it and running. If only they could erase the wards—wait.

"Rayner," Dimitri said, nearly falling over in the sand as he turned. "Do you think you could change the appearance of the altar and erase the wards?"

Rayner cocked his head, intrigued. "Maybe. Sabi might have more luck trying to change the pattern—"

"Where is His Highness?" Lowtan asked suddenly. "He and his guard aren't in their seats."

Crystal fuck him.

"Of course you can't see them from here," Sabi said, laughing hysterically. "Your view is cut off by pillars and statues and—oh! Look at this bowl!"

"Try changing just one pattern," Dimitri said, circling his finger in the air around one of the sockets. "Maybe then I can yank one free."

Rayner bit his lip.

"I still don't see them," Lowtan said, his voice moving closer.

"Maybe they moved seats."

"Do it," Dimitri hissed.

Rayner pressed his palm to the altar.

"I knew I felt something!" Lowtan yelled, footsteps pounding overhead. "They're doing something to the altar."

It was the protection magic, not the pulsepearls? Without thinking, Dimitri wrapped his fingers around a pearl. He braced himself for the zap, but it wasn't as strong. The carvings were straightening.

"Lowtan, find them," Magnar barked.

Dimitri desperately yanked on the pearl, his fingers tingling. "I can't get it free!"

"I'm trying," Rayner ground out. "The altar is fighting me."

Lowtan's footsteps pounded down the stairs. Sweat beaded on Rayner's forehead, and the runes straightened a little more.

"I almost have it," Dimitri said, wiggling the pearl.

Above, Sabi screamed. Dimitri whipped his head back.

"Don't stop," Rayner hissed.

Lowtan reached the sand. With a final tug, Dimitri ripped the pearl free, the force causing him to fall backward.

"Get out of here," Rayner hissed, yanking him upright by the collar.

"But Sabi—"

"I promise you, I will get her out. But you have to go."

Lowtan was almost to the altar. Dimitri's fist squeezed around the pearl, feeling it pulse like a heartbeat. "I don't know what to do."

"The pearl will guide you to Scarsthain. When you're there, just follow the magic."

Lowtan appeared on the other side of the altar. Rayner's blazing eyes shifted down to Dimitri's mouth. Dimitri's breath froze in his lungs.

Rayner shoved him away and rose to his feet. "Go!"

Just as he turned away, Dimitri thought he caught a flicker of guilt across his face. Something similar settling in his own stomach, Dimitri closed his eyes.

Scarsthain, Scarsthain, please, Scarsthain.

There came a sharp tug in Dimitri's gut. Something like a cold wind whipped around him, shoving him forward, the ground momentarily disappearing beneath his feet.

Dimitri squeezed the pulsepearl, not daring to open his eyes.

After a few heartbeats, the wind died down; the ground solidified beneath his feet.

Dimitri tentatively opened his eyes, finding himself in a lavish study. Thick scarlet carpet covered the floor, matching the dark wood walls and gold trim. A heavy oak desk stood in the middle of the room, a large, crystalline scale sitting atop it, its sides wavering back and forth.

At first, everything felt eerily calm. Dimitri took a half step forward.

And it felt as though the entire room sucked in a breath.

"Crystal fuck me," Dimitri muttered.

Not wasting time, he stripped off his Royal disguise, switching them for his wraith costume. Then, with three quick blinks, a flurry of tingles moved across his eyes, hopefully meaning they had shifted to the pure black of the wraiths. But there was no time to check.

He could feel a thousand eyes boring into his body, as if the study itself was watching him. Hunting him.

Dimitri shouldered out of the study to find the halls overflowing with wraiths. He shoved through the panicking crowd, heading for a nearby staircase. Countless voices buzzed in his ears, but one word repeated over and over. "Intruder."

How did they know?

Dimitri shoved down the stairs, keeping his hood up. With this many wraiths, they couldn't know every single prison warden's face.

"You!"

Dimitri stumbled as someone grabbed the back of his robes. They yanked him around, Dimitri almost losing his footing on the steps.

"Where are you going?" a female wraith hissed, her dark brown hair peeking out from her hood.

Dimitri didn't give himself time to think.

"There's an intruder!" he said, wrenching away. "I have to check the lower levels."

"On whose orders?"

"You want to waste time going through the chain of command when someone is loose in our prison?"

The wraith glared. Could she see through his glamor? Could she feel the lack of cold radiating from his skin?

Dimitri quickly turned, hurrying down the stairs.

"Fine!" the wraith shouted after him. "But you make sure when he's found, you spill his blood so Scarsthain can taste who tried to infiltrate its walls."

Crystal fuck him, was that how they knew? Because he didn't let the prison *taste* him?

Dimitri wrapped his robes tighter around himself as he charged down high-ceilinged halls, completely devoid of windows. It was too nice, too lived in, to be the prison. This had to be the living quarters of the wraiths, which meant he had to keep moving down.

Dimitri took staircase after staircase, following the crowd. He could feel the cold radiating off their bodies, but there was something else as stone floors turned to dirt. There was a malevolence in the air. Something that tingled across his skin like the moment before a lightning strike.

Dimitri stumbled around a corner, a hallway covered in thick gray carpet stretching out before him. He gripped a doorknob on his right, his heart pounding against his ribs. It took him a moment to notice the words carved into the door.

When three by three by three align, the sleeping shadows will untwine.

Dimitri's hand tightened around the knob, the rest of the words swimming before his eyes as he fought the urge to flee.

It had to be the magic. He was on the right track. So, stomach churning, he pushed through.

Dimitri lost all sense of time as he rocketed through the tunnels. Prisoners screamed. Decay filled his nose. But he followed the power.

Down, down, down. Far enough he would never find his way out again. The prison's lethal promise shivering across his skin. *You are mine.*

Dimitri stumbled around another corner, choking back a sob.

He thought *he* was the hero? Stopping Deardryn, fulfilling Analia's wish? How? When did he ever do anything right?

Patryclas was wrong. The only thing special about him was how he always ruined the lives of those around him. Even in his death, he would be destroying Analia's chance to stop Deardryn.

Dimitri stumbled to a stop, unable to fill his lungs. But he focused on that final thought.

Analia's mission. Stop Deardryn from getting the Crystal: the potential power source of this prison. Meaning if Dimitri was feeling the magic, it was still here. He still had a chance.

He took a deep breath. Let it out slow. One step at a time.

Even as the panic ravaged his insides. Even as he knew something hot should have been expanding deep in his gut.

One step after another. Inhale, exhale.

Dimitri dragged himself toward a massive iron door. The prison screamed in his mind, telling him he was worthless, that everything good he had was destined to crumble. But he forced his shaking hand to grip the central wheel, to turn.

Dimitri stumbled into the chamber beyond. As soon as he was through, the power ceased. And something hot flashed through his insides.

Dimitri wrapped his arms around himself, hobbling toward a small stone pedestal in the center of the room. It was surprisingly nondescript—especially if the Crystal was hidden atop it. But maybe that was the final defense: an unassuming resting place in the heart of a ruthless prison.

Which would mean he'd actually done it. He'd found the Crystal first.

He reached out, his fingers curling around a small woven cradle atop the pedestal, its soft strands shimmering in shades of gold, silver, and bronze. Just to realize it was empty.

The door opened behind him.

"I was wondering when you would arrive, Dimitri."

No.

Dimitri slowly turned. Sylas stood in the shadow of the door, his arms folded. And standing beside him, her words crawling across his skin, was Deardryn.

Chapter 59

Analia and Aaron stood on a snowy ridge, the frothing river far below.

"They must have pulled ashore recently," Aaron said, nodding to the small boat banked on the riverside. "The fresh snow hasn't covered the drag marks yet."

"Multiple pairs of footprints leading away as well," Analia added.

Aaron's lips thinned. His magic snarled around him, the only tell of his fury. But something else tickled Analia's mental shield.

"What do we do?" she asked.

"The only thing we can do," Aaron said. He turned to her, about to continue, but his eyes flew wide. He shoved Analia to the ground, the first dagger scraping her temple as she fell.

Aaron flung out a wave of magic, but it didn't matter. Dagger after dagger flew through his magic like it was mist, Aaron swearing as they slammed into his shoulder, his raised arm, his chest.

Analia cried out. She struggled to catch him as he sank to one knee, drops of red raining down on the snow.

"Aaron, you're—"

"Behind you," he ground out.

What did he—

"Princess Analia Valarus," a horribly familiar voice drawled. "You're a long way from home."

Aaron mouthed a curse.

For a few moments, Analia remained perfectly still, making sure he could support his own weight. Then, she slowly rose to her feet, her voice remarkably steady as she turned. "I'd say the same for you, Lev."

He stood twenty paces away, the gold of his fighting leathers standing out like a beacon against the snow. A dark scruff covered his face, but she would have known that hawkish nose and those sharp brown eyes anywhere. Just as she recognized the five Sun soldiers flanking him.

"You led us on quite the chase," he said, leaning against a tree.

"And you ripped my jacket," Aaron replied, affronted. "I loved this jacket. Surce made it for me herself. How am I supposed to tell her that some petty dinner knives ripped my jacket?"

Lev's eye roll was admittedly impressive. Analia, however, found Aaron's quip oddly comforting.

Yet, she didn't miss how he remained on one knee. He played it off well, but she knew if he didn't rise, it was because he couldn't. Because these Sun soldiers had skewered him. On Deardryn's orders.

For the briefest moment, a rush of calm washed over her. Pure, wonderful calm. Then, her fury struck.

Lev said something, but Analia didn't hear. Instead, Branten's voice whispered through her mind. *It's always easiest to show a man what he expects.*

She scanned her surroundings, taking in the densely packed trees. Too dangerous for flames.

"Please," she said, her voice shaking. "Please don't hurt him."

Aaron ground out something behind her, but she ignored him.

"We don't have to," Lev said, lounging back against his tree. "Those daggers will do all the work for us."

A few of his men stepped forward, and Analia flinched, turning slightly. "Please," she begged, "you don't have to do this. Her Majesty isn't expecting you to find us in all of the Wild Lands. Just let us go."

"No," Lev spat, finally straightening. "I've waited too long to hear that traitor scream. I want to hear your sobs as he pleads for his life. I want you two to suffer for the months of humiliation you put me through."

"What humiliation?" Analia asked, genuinely taken aback.

"From every time I failed to get information on you in time. You ruined me to both Othin and Deardryn. But I'm right on time now."

Lev drew his sword. Analia heard Aaron struggle, unable to rise.

Analia said, "You don't have to—"

"Grab her," Lev barked. "But don't touch the bastard. He's mine."

The Sun soldiers advanced. Analia cringed, angling her back to the trees just a little more.

"What will it be, Analia?" Lev taunted, remaining where he was. "Will you come quietly, or shall we take you screaming?"

Analia's eyes darted from face to face, panicked, afraid. The guards adjusted to her angle.

"Stop!" Analia cried, flinging out her arms. "Stop, stop I'll come. Just don't hurt him."

The soldiers stopped, glancing back at Lev.

"Pathetic," he said. He sheathed his sword. "THIS is why women shouldn't be on the battlefield."

Aaron's fingers brushed her calf. Analia looked back at him, two pairs of hands roughly seizing her by the shoulders.

"Please hold on," she said. "Just a little longer."

Aaron's eyes, tight with pain, met hers. Then, in a blink, he pulled a dagger from his shoulder and threw, one of the guards that had grabbed her gasping with a bloody gurgle.

"Do it," he breathed.

The soldier collapsed behind her.

And the one still gripping her shoulder barely had time to scream as he was engulfed in midnight flames.

Analia shoved him away from the woods and into the remaining three soldiers, pivoting on her heel to face them.

She could smell burning flesh, every lesson from Branten pounding through her body.

Hone every advantage you've got.

Analia ducked under the third guard's swinging sword, shoving away a fourth with a burning palm to his chest. A fifth guard tried to grab her, but she drew her dagger as she twisted away, the blade slashing across his throat.

The third guard advanced on her.

Use them without hesitating.

Analia aimed a ball of midnight flames toward his chest, and the guard threw up his hand. Purple energy flared in his palm, her flames colliding with his magic with an audible smack before ricocheting back toward her.

Analia yelped, jumping out of the way. The guard gave her a savage smile. How did he—it didn't matter.

The guard lunged for her, sword raised.

Relying on fairness doesn't make you honorable, it makes you dead.

Analia dropped to one knee. The guard let out a harsh cry, his sword slashing.

Analia threw a fistful of snow at him.

The guard jerked his head to the side, startled. And Analia slapped her burning hand down on the flat of his blade, softening the steel until it was useless.

"You," the guard said.

Analia blasted him with midnight flames. The guard threw up both hands, shoving her magic back. By the time the magic had cleared, Analia had slipped behind him and stuck her dagger through the back of his neck.

The guard fell to the snow with a wet gurgle. Then, the ridge was silent.

Analia took a step back, breathing hard. She took in the dead bodies around her, her stomach roiling from the smoke, the blood.

"You." Lev stared at her across the field of corpses, his face gone slack. "How did you..."

"It was never going to be a fair fight," Analia said, wiping her bloody dagger on her pants. "One side always has better instincts, better training, better conditions. You just didn't expect that side to be me."

Lev's magic pulsed around him. Combat magic.

"Her Majesty never said—"

"That I have magic?" Analia asked, stepping to her left. "That I'm any more than a quiet little mouse, desperate for a home? To be loved?"

Analia took another step, and Lev shifted to accommodate.

"I'm the captain of the Crystal Guard," he spat. "You don't want to test me."

"Really?" Analia asked. "Seems to me Deardryn didn't think so."

Analia barely had time to duck as Lev drew a dagger from his belt and threw. That was too fast.

"Her Majesty entrusted me to retrieve you," he hissed.

"Is that why she sent five extra men with you?"

Analia stalked closer, flames flickering across her skin. Lev drew his sword, the rasp of metal and leather slicing between them.

"What are you going to do with that, Lev?" Analia taunted, stepping closer. "You saw what happened when your friend tried to swing at me. Maybe you could throw it, but you've already missed once. Come at me yourself, and I will burn you alive."

Analia flicked a spark at him, and Lev jerked away. For the first time, a glimmer of fear entered his eyes. Analia's flames snarled, but she remained horrifically calm.

"You asked what happened to me," she said. "I've had a lifetime of people like you, taking pleasure in trying to stomp out my flames. But turns out, fire tends to consume what tries to smother it."

Lev's eyes widened. Analia sent a jet of flames roaring for him. Lev dove out of the way. Straight over the edge of the ridge Analia had backed him toward.

Analia stepped to the edge, wind whistling in her ears. Far, far below, she could make out a crumpled heap of gold in the snow. Not moving.

"Lesson number one," she said, her hand shaking as she sheathed her dagger. "Always stay aware of your surroundings."

The faintest tap of guilt started up in her chest. But there was no time for that now. Not as she turned.

Aaron had fallen back in the snow. His eyes were squeezed shut, his hands shaking as he tried to pull a dagger from his shoulder.

Analia hurried over to him. "Aaron, Aaron stop." She fell to her knees beside him and pulled his hand away. "You'll bleed out if you do that."

"Take them out," he moaned. "Take them out take them out take them out."

Analia turned to the two blades he'd already pulled out. They rested on the ground beside him, the blades dark with blood against the snow—that wasn't steel.

Analia hurriedly wiped one of the daggers in the snow, revealing a shiny black blade. Onyx. Carved onyx.

The daggers will do all the work for us.

Analia gripped her bracelet, only able to send Laness a single word. *Help.*

"Aaron," she said, struggling for calm as she pressed down on his open wounds. "They're damper blades. You'll be fine once I get them out."

"Not dampers," Aaron panted.

"What?"

"Not dampers." Aaron's voice broke off in a groan, his hands clawing at the protruding hilts.

"Stop moving," Analia said, trying to pin his shoulders. "I'll get them out, I promise."

Aaron struggled for breath, his face deathly pale. But he went still.

Analia quickly counted the blades. Ten still impaled. Two unplugged wounds bleeding fast.

"I got all the soldiers," she said, gripping the first dagger. "Took them down in one go. And I didn't lose control."

"Sorry," Aaron mouthed.

"No," Analia said, pulling free another dagger. "You don't apologize. You just stay still."

Aaron hissed as a blade scraped his collarbone on the way out. Analia shuddered.

"Just five more, Aaron," she said, trying to force her hands to be steady, only feeling his blood on her fingers. "You just have to make it through five more."

Six out.

A cold sweat broke out across Aaron's pale forehead. And a horrible sense of familiarity tingled across the back of Analia's neck.

"No," she whispered. She grabbed the next dagger, her heart pounding. Not again. Please, please not again.

Aaron's eyes fluttered shut.

"No!" Analia smacked his cheek. "You keep your eyes open. I didn't fight for my gods-damned life today just so you could die on me."

Aaron forced his eyes open, the silver clouded over. And Analia couldn't have stopped her words if she tried.

"You asked me about the roof, why I hadn't been on it for so long. I told you a long time ago how I went to the roof because it was my spot with my uncle, but it goes beyond that. It was because all my life, I felt like I was in the wrong place. The wrong castle, the wrong kingdom. And that turret was the closest thing I had to a home.

"For a long time, I stopped going on the roof because I thought I didn't deserve that feeling. Even after I realized that wasn't true, I no longer needed it because I was already home."

Analia shoved the final dagger through her belt, breathing hard. Aaron stared at her blankly, his chest barely moving.

"I can't jump us out of here, Aaron," she told him, her hands sticky with his blood as she pressed down on his wounds. "I can't... I can't save you."

Analia's bracelet tingled. *I'm coming. Too far for one jump. Hold on.*

Aaron went still.

"No!" Analia lunged forward, shaking his shoulders.

She'd already lost so much. Had so much taken away. She couldn't lose him. She couldn't she couldn't she—

Something warm rose up from her stomach like a cresting wave. She didn't know what it was, she didn't care, she didn't think. She latched on, pulling the warmth up through her body, down her hands, into Aaron's chest.

She didn't know what she was doing. Her mind was too fractured to think.

Aaron gasped. He shoved himself upright, hauling Analia to his chest as the world faded to black.

"Aaron," Analia breathed.

He pressed his cold face to her neck. The ground returned beneath her knees. And Aaron's lips moved against her skin. "My shooting star."

Analia's mind flashed back to a starlit night on her turret. A story about shooting stars always searching, always hoping, they would find their way back to each other.

Aaron slumped against her. Analia screamed.

She didn't realize she was in the sitting room until the door flew open. Branten, Mor, and Laness stormed inside, their voices colliding over one another with questions.

But Analia couldn't move. She barely felt Branten lift Aaron to carry him to the couch, Mor kneeling in front of her.

This couldn't be happening. Not again. Not this way, with that plant, not to him.

Analia squeezed her eyes shut, trying to focus. She had to unfreeze.

"Anna," Mor said. "Anna, are you hurt?"

"No," she said, her voice little more than an exhale. But it was something.

"Good." Mor took both her hands in his, squeezing tight. Giving her something to hold on to.

Analia forced her eyes to open. Laness was rushing back into the room, a short, dark-haired woman close behind. The kingdom's healer. But there were no rings around her eyes.

"What happened?" she demanded, small hazel eyes snapping to Analia.

"Damper blades," Analia said, struggling for calm as she pulled one of the daggers from her belt. "I think they were coated with xenol."

The healer swore.

"What happened?" Surce demanded, sweeping inside.

Analia glanced to the healer, and Surce nodded. "Sun ambush," she said.

"Where are they now?" Branten demanded.

Analia met his gaze. "I killed them."

The room went still.

Branten gave her a single, grim nod. "Good."

"Can you heal him?" Surce asked, turning to the healer.

The healer's fingers skimmed over Aaron's chest, his shirt having been cut away. "If I didn't have the dagger, it would be questionable. But I might be able to pull the xenol out using what remains on the blade."

"Do it," Surce said.

"It will be delicate, and it will take time," the healer said. "I need everyone to clear out."

"I'm staying," Analia said, pulling out of Mor's grip. There was no room for arguing.

Analia moved to the couch, listening to the shuffle of feet as everyone cleared out. "Am I in your way?" she asked the healer—who she thought was named Sofika.

"No." Sofika placed Aaron's cold, limp hand in hers. "Be brave, Your Majesty."

Analia didn't know if she was talking to her or Aaron. But she took a deep breath. And it took everything she had to remain quiet as Aaron started to scream.

Chapter 60

Dimitri inched away from the towering Royals, his mind a flurry of curses.

"I know it's you, Dimitri," Deardryn said, moving deeper into the chamber.

Dimitri took another step back. "You don't have permission to be in this chamber."

"Do you think I didn't notice you had vanished from my halls?" she asked, taking her time as she passed between the burning braziers. "That you had a growing friendship with Analia? Do you think I wouldn't recognize your voice and my husband's eyes?"

Dimitri pressed his back to the pedestal, his eyes darting.

"I'll admit," she said, still coming closer, "I wasn't expecting to see them in that bookshop. But I knew you were lurking about somewhere."

Crystal spare him, he knew she'd been startled.

Dimitri tried to slide to the side, but Deardryn's hand shot out. She gripped his face with one hand, the other plunging toward his eye.

Dimitri recoiled. But her fingertip brushed over what felt like a film across his eye, his glamor tingling faintly before completely vanishing.

"There," she said softly, removing his other glamor. "Different hair, different face. But the same amber eyes."

Dimitri wrenched out of her grip, putting the pedestal between them. Only then did he spot the pendant around her neck.

It was made from a simple dark gray stone, a large crack running down the center. Dimitri had polished her entire jewel collection a thousand times, and he'd never seen that pendant. Which meant...

"You found it," Dimitri said, stunned. "You found it!"

Dimitri didn't think. He lunged forward, reaching for the chain.

"Don't touch me."

Deardryn pressed her glowing hand to Dimitri's chest, and he went flying. He slammed against the opposite wall with a bone-cracking thud, stars dancing across his vision.

"You see, Sylas?" Deardryn said, unruffled. "I warned you this would happen."

"Yes, Deardryn," Sylas drawled. "I'm aware. But Patryclas became attached."

Their voices swam through Dimitri's mind. He had to focus. He had to get the Crystal—although it didn't look like the Crystal. Could it be something else?

Dimitri tried to sense the magic, but there was too much interfering power rolling off of Deardryn and Sylas. What should he do?

"I must admit," Deardryn said, turning back to Dimitri, "I was expecting Analia to come herself. She attempted to ruin my family single-handedly, why not another? Although I suppose she had you to do her bidding. Her own personal servant."

Dimitri's temper flared. He struggled to his feet, rounding on Sylas, still leaning against the door. "Why don't you look fucking surprised?"

The shadows at Sylas's feet rippled. "When Magnar informed me a Royal currently having dinner with me stole a pearl from the Wraithhouse, there were only so many people it could have been. Especially when I had the bastard of a foreign king breaking into my castle and trying to spark a war."

Dimitri took an automatic step back, his shoulders hitting the wall.

Bastard. Foreign king. Everything Patryclas somehow knew about him.

He rounded on Deardryn, "You exposed me?"

"I knew who you were from the moment you stepped into my Council Chamber," said Sylas, bored.

Dimitri's breathing sped up. He whipped his head from side to side, shadows creeping across the floor toward him. "But you told me she only came to you about the poison."

"She did tell me that," Sylas said.

Dimitri felt like he was teetering on the edge of a cliff. Because if Sylas knew who he was, that meant Patryclas did as well. And if that was true—no, no he had to be missing something.

"And she also told me why you were here."

"No," Dimitri whispered, wrapping his arms around himself.

"She told me you helped Analia kill her son and escape. That you're wanted for murder."

Murder. Bastard. Failure. All things Patryclas could never—he couldn't even think the word. Not when everything he'd started to cling to was no more than a facade.

"I told him how Analia thought we killed Accalon," Deardryn said. "How she disguised herself in the name of peace, just to burn my son alive."

She stalked forward, Dimitri shrinking back into the wall. "She killed my son, my only son, for a crime he didn't commit. None of us did. And you helped her do it."

"He was going to kill her!" Dimitri exclaimed, but Deardryn ranted over him.

"He was innocent." She pushed him against the wall. "She fled to her own kingdom, got her father sent to this very prison, just so she could take his crown. And she sent you here to defame my character before I could seek my own justice—"

"She's lying!" Dimitri shoved Deardryn's shoulder. He tore past her, vaulting over the pedestal and hurrying toward Sylas's unreadable expression.

"You've known Analia for years," he insisted, swerving away from Deardryn and the rippling shadows. "You and Patryclas. Do you really think Analia could hide that type of hatred from him?"

The shadows paused at Dimitri's feet. A golden whip reached for his mouth, but Dimitri kicked over a brazier, Deardryn stumbling back as her skirts smoldered.

"Analia could have gone to any of the other three kingdoms, but Deardryn just so happens to anticipate the correct one? How fucking likely is that?"

"I was her teacher," Deardryn hissed. "I know her mind."

"Or you know you already sent your demon sucker to the other kingdoms and Sylas was the last to warn."

Dimitri paused a few feet from Sylas, his shadows shifting in a warning. He was Dimitri's only hope. His last hope for something more than a life of misery and servitude. His last hope that he hadn't put himself back together just to be shattered once more.

"The boy has an interesting point," Sylas said, his icy shadows climbing up Dimitri's ankle.

"And every reason to despise me," Deardryn said, remarkably calm a few feet back. "He is the bastard son of my husband. Just close enough to the Royal life to despise me for taking it away from him. For not being his mother.

"Is it not suspicious he aligned himself with the woman that destroyed my temple and murdered my son? Has acted as an ambassador for a case he has nothing to do with?"

Dimitri whirled to face her. Gold-laced pain slapped him across the face; just as sharp as every word she'd ever hurled at him.

Bastard. Servant. Mistake. Dimitri stumbled back, Deardryn's voice ripping open every healing wound.

"He has every reason to defame my character. And you have the evidence to prove it."

"What evidence?" Dimitri forced out, his hand inching toward his pocket.

"I had a spy of my own tracking your movements," Sylas said.

Dimitri's hand came up short. "You what?"

"You didn't think your oath with my husband would be enough for me to let you roam my kingdom unimpeded."

Sylas's shadows climbed up Dimitri's legs, but Dimitri couldn't have moved if he wanted to.

"He informed me of your snooping throughout various landmarks, how you were planning on breaking into the Wraithhouse tonight. He even told me that you were spreading this Crystal nonsense to my people."

The shadows reached Dimitri's waist. But they had nothing to do with the chill that ran through his blood.

He'd only told two people about the Crystal.

Dimitri wanted to close his eyes, shield himself from the blow of Sylas's words.

"Rayner told me everything."

Finally, Dimitri tipped over the edge.

He was consumed by images from the past few weeks: Rayner turning away at the statue. Rayner's look of guilt as Dimitri used the pearl. Rayner telling him about the gods-damned tattoo he'd gotten from Sylas, promising to not use his magic for nefarious reasons.

He'd thought it didn't count tonight because they were protecting the kingdom. Rayner had told him—no, he hadn't said it was fine. He deflected every time Dimitri had asked. Because Rayner had already informed Sylas of their plan and was excused.

Patryclas was a fraud. Rayner was a backstabber. Analia's mission was a failure.

But Dimitri didn't care. Not about anything. He couldn't.

Dimitri plunged his hand into his pocket, finding the pearl. He didn't think. He just let the pearl rip him away into nothingness.

After all, that was all he had left.

Chapter 61

Ember stood off to the side of the snowy mining site, wrapping the loose thread in her healer robes around her finger tight enough to hurt.

For someone who was so eager to get to Mt. Vasolus, Cadmus was certainly taking his Rosala-forsaken time as he spoke with the miners.

Behind them, the volcano rose disconcertingly high against the cold winter sky, making the hairs on the back of her neck stand up. This was such a bad idea. Bad enough she could still feel it through the cold clarity of her devinroot—gods, why hadn't she brought more leaves with her? Such a terrible, stupid, reckless—

"Ready?" Cadmus asked, coming up beside her.

Ember jumped. "How long have you been done?"

"Just long enough to jump my guards back to the castle, tell them I was spending the rest of the day with you, and grab my gear."

Cadmus showed off the rope over his shoulder, then extended his hand. Behind him, a miner shot Ember a withering look as she packed her things.

"You need to be careful," Ember told him as she took his hand.

"Why?" he asked, pulling them into the shadows. "It's not a lie."

"You're also a bachelor king spending all your time with a female healer—and a good looking one at that."

"A healer sworn to celibacy."

"Which only infuriates your suitors more."

"Just imagine the scandal when they realize I view you as a sister."

Ember snickered despite herself as they reemerged at the peak of the volcano. Cadmus barely spared his surroundings a second look as he knelt to unravel his rope. Ember, meanwhile, took one look at the gaping mouth of the volcano, sobered, and took a few hasty steps back.

"You know," she said, hovering over his shoulder, "you could make an announcement clearing the air. Spare half the kingdom the turmoil. I bet if we hurry, we can make it back before that miner girl giving me the side-eye can spread the gossip—"

"We're doing this, Ember."

"But why?" Ember whined. "I don't want to burn alive, Cadmus."

"We're not going to burn alive," Cadmus sighed.

"Oh, *you* won't," Ember said. "You're an Ash Royal. You have magic fire blood. I'm a human that specializes in plants. Plants don't like fire, Cadmus. I took off Anna's enka bracelet because I don't want our only link to her to get scorched."

Cadmus had the audacity to laugh under his breath. "The only way you would burn to death was if the volcano was active. Arms up."

Ember begrudgingly raised her arms as Cadmus turned on his knees, looping the rope around her middle. "It's active enough to spew fire during your ceremonies," she said.

"And yet, that's the only time."

Cadmus gave her a meaningful look. One that had Ember's heart curling in on itself.

"No," she said, slowly lowering her arms. "Don't tell me you are risking my life on a legend."

"Which one of us has been close enough to the volcano to verify it?" Cadmus countered.

"Rosala spare me," Ember muttered.

"During the Ancient Ones' rule," Cadmus recited over her, eyes back on what she realized was a belay rig, "Mt. Vasolus was the most active of all the volcanoes that make up the Belt. We can see the history of eruptions through the ravines and valleys carved by lava flow, proving just how dangerous it was to live in this territory.

"But Azar was Blessed with flames. When he first saw Mt. Vasolus, he knew this was his kingdom. Yet, he also knew he couldn't build a kingdom just to let it burn.

"It's said he climbed to the top of Mt. Vasolus, braving the heat and toxic gas to descend into the lava chamber. For a long time, nothing happened. Then, a massive eruption of lava burst forth from the volcano's mouth, sending Azar's men fleeing for their lives.

"They thought their king was dead. But hours later, a figure stained with soot and ash stepped into their camp, his clothing burned away but otherwise intact."

"And it was Azar," Ember muttered, kicking the coiled rope at her feet.

"It was," Cadmus said, finally rising. "And while he refused to say what he did or how he survived, what we do know is Mt. Vasolus has never erupted since. We also know that's why our kingdom's sigil is the phoenix rising from a plume of smoke."

"It's a great story," Ember said, "But that's all it is. And everything else screams stay away."

"Ember, what do you smell?"

Ember's eyebrows shot up. Cadmus cocked his head at her, and she reluctantly took a deep breath through her nose.

"Mountain air," she said. "Cold. Faintly smoky."

"Exactly. No harsh gases. Now, come here."

Cadmus nudged her closer to the gaping hole of the volcano. Ember cringed back against his hand, away from the gaping darkness that threatened to tug her down, down, down.

"Feel that?" he said. "No heat. And look." He guided Ember down into a crouch beside him at the edge of the hole. "You can look down, and there's no bubbling lava."

"No," she agreed. "Just an infinite fall ready to break our spines."

She could practically hear Cadmus's eyes roll. He shifted closer, his hand coming to squeeze her shoulder.

"I can feel the call of the volcano," he said. "It's so strong I can barely block it out. This is where we're meant to be, Em. You just have to trust me."

She did trust him. She also had instincts screaming *Run, run, run.*

"I hate you," she muttered.

Cadmus laughed. "You ready to go down?"

"Can't we just yell down from up here?" she begged, one final time.

"You can," Cadmus said, rising to his feet. "But I'm going."

Ember muttered under her breath.

Not long later, she was attached to the belay with various absurdly complicated knots. She tugged on her rope, mildly impressed even as her stomach rolled.

"How is this going to get us in and out?" she asked. "There's no one to pull us up and lower us."

"I wouldn't be so sure of that."

Ember looked up. Cadmus gave her a rare grin, then stuck his fingers in his mouth and whistled.

There came the sound of scurrying feet. Then, Ember watched, wide-eyed, as a swarm of fire sprites scampered up the volcano from Rosala-knew where and gathered around them.

"This is our team?" Ember asked. "Tiny beings made of fire holding on to flammable rope?"

"This rope was made by a Blessed," Cadmus said. "And they are far stronger than they look."

Cadmus smiled down at the fire sprites as they lined up beside one of the ropes and took hold. Ember's grip tightened on her own rope, her hands red and numb from the cold.

"Ready?" Cadmus asked her, infuriatingly calm.

It was her last chance. She knew Cadmus would never force her to follow him. She could turn and run as fast as she could, and he wouldn't hold it against her.

For that very reason, Ember gave a shallow nod. One she prayed to Rosala she wouldn't regret as she sat at the edge of the volcano's mouth. Then, she pushed off into the darkness.

As soon as she was in open air, a scream rose in Ember's throat.

Immediately, the rope around her waist pulled taut, her scream turning into a strangled gasp as she was smoothly lowered.

"You all right?" Cadmus asked beside her.

"We're going to die."

"We're not going to die."

"*I'm* going to die."

"Ember, open your eyes."

Ember hadn't realized she'd squeezed them shut. Slowly, she peeked beneath her lids, her eyes flying wide despite herself.

The walls of the volcano were a breathtaking gradient of red, scarlet, and purple, lit by the opening above. She reached out to touch the layers of rock, letting out a sound of delight as she felt the lava flow lines beneath her fingers.

"Amazing, isn't it?" Cadmus asked.

"There are so many different fungi!" she exclaimed, scratching her itchy markings.

Cadmus looked as though he was torn between amusement and exasperation. Yet, by the time they landed on the first rocky ledge, something had clouded over his eyes. He immediately moved to the edge and stepped off, forcing Ember to follow.

As they continued to be smoothly lowered into the volcano, Ember's anxiety began to ebb. Yet, she couldn't shake the feeling that something was wrong.

Ember traced her fingers along the lava flow lines, noticing some had a faint glow to them. She kicked her legs, swinging closer to the wall. Were those runes?

"We're getting close," Cadmus said. "I can feel it."

Ember looked down at him, Cadmus somehow having dropped faster than her. Then, her stomach lurched.

She landed on the ledge beside him and pointed down. "Is it because we're looking for that?"

Far, far below, she could just make out a pool of golden flames.

"That's not lava," Cadmus said, drifting toward the edge. "That's Ash magic."

Ember was about to protest when every hair on her body stood up. A hot current blew up from the depths of the volcano, swirling around them like the ghost of a laugh.

"Very good, Ash King," a low, soft voice purred. "Although your legend is missing some crucial details."

"Who's there?" Cadmus called. He stepped toward the edge of the ledge, but Ember grabbed him by the back of his jacket and yanked him back. They had to leave. Now.

"Someone who can fill in your history." The voice somehow sounded perfectly close, yet far away.

Ember desperately tugged on the rope, but nothing happened.

"You are correct, Azar did descend into the volcano. Yet, what he found was a sealed-off lava chamber, the volcano having released its final eruption. That fabled blast of lava was actually his own magic as he cleared away the rock, enabling him to leave his own pool of fire behind."

"He did that just to create a ritual?" Cadmus asked, his voice growing distant. He tried to step off the ledge again, but Ember tightened her grip on him.

"A ritual, and a prison," the voice replied. "But I've found my own ways of reaching the surface."

Ember desperately tugged on the rope once more, Cadmus squirming in her grip. She was right, the symbol had been a warning—where were the fire sprites?

"So, it has been you calling to me," Cadmus said.

"Indeed it has. Come closer, my king."

There came another exhale of heat. Cadmus lunged forward. Ember's boots scrambled for purchase, but Cadmus pulled her over the edge, landing on the next ledge ten feet below.

"Cadmus," she gasped, heart pounding, "Cadmus stop. We have to leave."

"Oh, sweet healer," the voice purred, sending vibrations through the volcano's walls, "don't rush him. Your king has a question he'd like to ask."

Cadmus swayed on his feet, his expression far away.

Was this magic? A curse? Rosala spare her, she had to snap him out of it.

"Cadmus, don't listen to him," Ember said, shaking his shoulders. "We have to leave."

"Why have you been calling me?" Cadmus asked as if he hadn't heard her.

Ember wanted to cry.

"My curse. The curse of questions, the curse of answers, the curse of power. I'd thought my voice had finally made a breakthrough, but then that ungrateful king took my power. Fortunately, I still found a way."

The ledge shook beneath Ember's feet. Holding on to Cadmus with one hand and the rope with the other, she tried to climb up the wall, but the rock crumbled beneath her boots.

"Which king?" Cadmus called into the pit.

"Is that the question you'd like answered?"

"No!" Ember yelled before Cadmus could open his mouth. "Just tell us what the mark means and let us go."

"Oh, sweetling, I'm not holding you here. It's your king's rope that needs to be tugged to pull you out."

Ember whipped toward Cadmus. She tried to grab his rope, but he pushed it behind himself and away from her reach. His foot found the edge of the ledge.

"Cadmus, please," Ember begged. But what little she could see of his face was completely blank. Ember turned back to the pit, her words firing past her lips. "Tell us what the mark means."

"I may only answer a question from your king."

Ember bit back a scream. She whirled on Cadmus, who was already asking. "What is the symbol on my father's wrist?"

"It's the sign of my bargain."

"No!" Ember lunged toward Cadmus, but it was too late.

A ribbon of flame snapped up from the pit, slicing through Cadmus's rope, coming to curl around his wrist.

Cadmus barely had time to yell before he was yanked over the edge.

Ember didn't think. Her hands flew across the knots, detaching herself from her rope and replacing it with Cadmus's. Then, she leaped over the edge.

"So many bargains," the voice purred. "And yet, they always want the same thing: power."

Ember angled herself toward the flash of gold, Cadmus's scream of pain echoing around her. She was moving too slow. Rosala spare her, she needed help.

"You'd be amazed by what they were willing to bargain. But I always have just one request: access to their minds. And so, so many said yes without a second thought."

Ember slammed her hand against the wall, sending every last drop of magic she had into the stone.

"Your father didn't so much as hesitate. But you, Cadmus Valarus, only wanted a question answered."

The creature laughed. Fungus spread across the walls. Cadmus continued to fall.

"Don't worry, little king. You'll have time to change your mind."

Fungus burst forth from the walls. It wrapped around Cadmus as he tumbled past, slowing his descent just enough for Ember to slam into him. They hit the wall with a crack, Ember wrapping her arms around him and giving the rope a sharp tug.

This time, there came a gut-jerking tug. Then, they started to rise.

Ember shifted to deal with the flames around Cadmus's wrist. But they released him without protest, the creature's laugh echoing below as they were pulled up maddeningly slow.

"Farewell, my king. We'll speak again soon."

Ember's grip tightened on Cadmus. His head fell against her shoulder, his voice so faint she could barely make it out. "I'm all right."

Ember's magic tingled in her fingers, but she forced it back. Growing plants was one thing. Healing would have to wait—thank Rosala, his pulse and breathing were strong.

"Why did you only have the signal attached to your rope?" she asked.

"I thought you'd panic. I'm sorry."

They reached the lip of the opening. Ember hauled herself and Cadmus over, the fire sprites hurrying to their sides.

Cadmus gently reassured them he was all right and thanked them for their help, his face terrifyingly pale. The sprites didn't seem fully convinced. But they lined up to pat his and Ember's ankles, then scattered back down the volcano face.

Finally, he turned to Ember, "I'm sorry—"

Ember launched herself at him. "Never," she said, gripping the front of his jacket, "do that again."

Cadmus released a breath, pressing his face to the top of her head. "You were right," he said.

"But so were you." Ember pulled back and wiped her eyes. "Cadmus, there is a creature in that volcano that has been corrupting Ash rulers for who knows how long. We have to tell someone."

"Who?" he asked. "I'm the king, and you saw me down there. I don't even have the mark, and it could have compelled me to do anything."

He made to say more, but Ember's insides had turned to ice.

"Cadmus," she said, her voice distant in her own ears. "Let me see your wrist."

Cadmus's lips parted. He didn't try to stop her as she grabbed his wrist, her heart sinking at the curved, asymmetrical star now tattooed into his skin.

"But I didn't give it permission," he said, his hand shaking in hers. "I didn't say it could have access to my mind."

"But that doesn't mean it won't try," Ember said. "Cadmus, we have to do something. We have to tell the council. I can't... I can't protect you from this."

Cadmus clutched his wrist, eyes darting as if looking for a way out. But there was nothing. And Cadmus knew it. He flipped his hand in hers, squeezing so tight her fingers ached. "I know."

Ember opened her mouth to argue, her blood buzzing for the next fight. Then, his words registered.

She cocked her head, not quite sure what to say. "Well, all right, then."

The faintest smile flickered across Cadmus's lips. He took a slow, deep breath through his nose, the pulse at his throat beginning to slow, Ember's following suit.

"Thank you for rescuing me," he said quietly.

Ember could only nod. Cadmus gave her a look of understanding, then moved to start collecting their rope. But Ember couldn't force her body to move and help him.

She looked up at the sky, wondering if she had ever been so afraid.

And that was when she saw the line of approaching sun dragons in the distance.

Chapter 62

Aaron felt like he had been flattened by a rolling pin. Every part of him ached: his muscles, his bones, even the now empty pit inside him where his magic usually slumbered.

More importantly, someone was holding his hand.

Aaron cracked open his eyes. Analia sat on the floor beside his couch, her cheek resting against their hands as she slept. He tried to twitch his fingers, just to suck in a breath as his body protested.

Analia's eyes popped open. She shifted up on to the edge of the couch, her free hand grabbing a glass off the table.

"Here," she said, bringing the glass to his lips.

Aaron gratefully swallowed the water, tasting the tangy residue of a healing potion on his lips. A quick glance down told him he was wearing a shirt and pants not covered in blood, which meant someone must have taken care of that as well.

Analia made to refill the glass with a crystalline pitcher, but Aaron shook his head. He sank back against the couch, Analia placing the empty glass on the table.

She was still holding his hand.

"Are you all right?" she asked, resting the back of her free hand against his forehead.

"Well," he mumbled, "I seem to be having the pleasure of talking to you, so I'm alive at the very least—"

"Idiot!" Analia exploded.

Aaron's fluttering eyelids snapped open.

"You stupid, self-sacrificing idiot! Have you completely lost it?"

"I think I have," Aaron said, raising a leaden arm to rub his eyes. "I'm seeing Anna, but I'm hearing Laness."

"It's not funny, Aaron!"

"No, frankly it's a little disconcerting—"

"You've been out for two days!"

Aaron's entire body went cold. *You've been out a long time, brother. She's gone.*

Aaron peered at Analia more closely. Her hair was haphazardly braided back, pieces sticking out in all directions. She'd changed into a soft black shirt, her purple-and-gray pants matching the smudges beneath her eyes. And Aaron suddenly felt incredibly small.

"I'm sorry," he whispered.

"You should be sorry!"

"But you stayed?" he asked. "You didn't do anything reckless or stupid or—"

"Self-sacrificing?" Analia suggested. "No, you did enough of that for the both of us."

Aaron didn't know if he felt guilty or relieved. She was still holding his hand.

"What were you thinking?" Analia asked, almost desperately.

"I was thinking I couldn't let you get hit, that my magic should be able to deflect them, and I was wrong about the latter." Aaron struggled into an upright position. "I was thinking we couldn't have gotten out of there if both of us went down."

"Then you should have let them hit me."

Aaron's nostrils flared. "Never."

"Aaron, both of us could have dealt with them, but only you were able to jump us out of there. I was the expendable one, not you."

Aaron's heart flinched. "And yet," he said, spreading his arms, "here we are."

"And only the gods know how," Analia muttered.

"I know how," Aaron said. "You."

Analia glowered, but Aaron went on. "I took those knives because I trusted you to get us out of there."

"And what would have happened to your kingdom if you were wrong and died?" Analia argued, pushing the hair from her face. She was still holding his hand.

"I was gambling on you being able to handle it," he said. "And I was right."

"You were stupid."

"Stupid, but correct."

Aaron grinned, Analia visibly struggling to maintain her indignation.

"Anna," he said, squeezing her hand, "everything is all right. You, me, the kingdom." He lowered his voice to a whisper as he added, "And you were incredible."

A crack formed in Analia's stony expression. "Because you were right?"

"Impeccably so." In ways he would have never anticipated, in fact.

Analia deflated, still holding his hand. Aaron winked, but Analia didn't smile.

"You can't automatically prioritize me over yourself," she told him. "I'm not interested in heroics or whatever that was. I need to know I can trust you're making the smart decision, not the one that will make you feel less guilty."

Clever girl. And she only knew the half of it.

"You can trust me," Aaron told her softly. "I promise."

Analia let out a long breath, her head drooping forward. Gods, she must have been exhausted.

Aaron squeezed her hand. "Are you still angry?" he asked tentatively.

"I was never angry. I was *terrified.*" Her voice broke on the last word. And Aaron knew she wasn't just talking about that moment.

"Come here."

"I don't want to hurt you."

"You won't hurt me."

Aaron pulled Analia closer, finally dropping her hand to fold her into his arms. She leaned into him gingerly, Aaron pressing his face to the side of her neck. He closed his eyes, breathing her in, not even caring about the ache across his chest. Because they'd survived.

"How did we go from you nearly dying to me being comforted?" Analia finally asked.

Aaron chuckled. "My selfish shooting star, you think this is all for you?"

His mouth glided across her neck, her throat, stopping as he felt her pulse against his lips. Strong. Alive. Quickening? Oh gods.

He was a fool. A gods-damned fool. Drowning in smoke and jasmine; the feel of her soft skin against his mouth.

He didn't remember deciding to kiss her throat. He just felt his control slip as Analia sighed, lifting her chin to expose more of her neck to him.

A fool. A fool whose hand traveled down her spine, his lips whispering against her skin. "What are you thinking about?"

"I'm wondering," she murmured, "if this is how your black-lace fantasies begin."

Crystal spare him, they were back to this.

"Now, why are you thinking about that?" he asked, his voice remarkably steady.

"Because," she said, her fingertips trailing up his neck and tangling in his hair, "it's how mine do."

She was going to destroy him. Either from the maddening stillness of her body against his, or the images in his mind of her in bed, her hand between her thighs, imagining it was his—he had to know.

"Then what?" he asked, burying his face in her hair. "What happens next?"

"Your hand slips beneath my shirt," Analia said, her voice shaking slightly.

Aaron obediently complied, her skin burning against his fingers as he trailed up her spine. "And then?"

"I press closer. And you put your hand on my thigh."

"Here?" Aaron placed his hand close to her knee.

Analia shook her head.

"Here?" Aaron slid his hand higher, his thumb drawing slow, lazy circles on the inside of her thigh. "Or maybe here?"

Analia let out a tiny gasp as his hand inched higher. And that sound went right to his cock and squeezed. He slid his hand even higher, Analia's body shifting as his thumb circled closer, closer—

"There," she breathed, his thumb dangerously close to the apex of her thighs. "Your hand pauses there."

"And then?"

Analia nearly undid him right there as her eyes, dark with desire, slid down to his mouth.

"Tell me yours," she whispered.

He was a fool. A gods-damned fool straining against his pants.

"Usually," he said, "you start here."

Aaron pulled her onto his lap. Analia dragged her hand from his hair, tightening her grip around his neck, "And then?"

"And then you wrap your legs around me."

"And then?"

Analia rocked against him, sending a shock of pleasure down his spine.

"And then," he gasped, pressing his face to her neck, "I find that spot on your neck. The one that has you letting out that tiny sound that drives me insane—yes."

Aaron's tongue darted out to kiss the tiny hurt his teeth had left to get that whimper.

He was a fool. A burning, throbbing fool as Analia's nails dug into his shoulders, her uneven breaths on his skin—"And then?"

But Aaron's mouth remained on her neck, kissing and mouthing until Analia's back arched and his body was alive with how his name became a plea on her tongue. She ground against him, Aaron nearly losing himself as he trailed his mouth up her neck.

"And then," he whispered, "once your body is wild for me, needing me, I ask you what you want. And you pull away, just enough to put your hand on my chest and say—"

"You," Analia breathed, staring up into his eyes.

Aaron's leash snapped. His hand flew from her waist, "And then I lift your chin—"

"And you lean in—"

"And it's soft—"

"Sweet."

But when Aaron's lips finally captured hers, it was anything but. It was an unleashing. Every restraint, every prison bar and suppressing thread scorched away by the crush of Analia's mouth on his.

Analia pressed him down on the couch, Aaron's hands roving across her shoulders, her back, her hips. He needed to feel her. All of her. Not just the hand she rested against his cheek, her sigh against his mouth—Crystal spare him, why had he waited so long?

Aaron ran his tongue along the seam of her lips, and she immediately opened for him. He swept into her mouth, a groan rumbling in the back of his throat as he finally tasted her.

"Gods, Analia," he gasped, pulling away and pressing his face to her neck. "You taste…" Aaron kissed her neck, and Analia's breath hitched. "Can't get enough."

Analia's hand tightened in his hair, trying to bring his mouth back to hers. But Aaron rolled her onto her side, kissing down her neck, her collarbone, flicking his tongue against the hollow of her throat.

He'd imagined this moment so many times: Analia lying before him, her skin flushed, eyes dark with need. It had become instinct to shove the thoughts back down, too afraid of their sharpened edges. But now, all he wanted was to let them play out. He wanted to taste her on his tongue, feel her writhe against him, wanted to hear her scream.

"Gods, Analia," he said, his mouth moving over her breast, finding her nipple through her black shirt. "How are you real?"

Analia's response cut off in a gasp as he drew her nipple into his mouth. He mouthed her through the fabric, Analia moaning his name, and he was drowning, drowning, drowning.

"Aaron, please," she said, squirming down his body. "I need you back here."

She drew his face back to hers, lightly sucking his lower lip into her mouth. Aaron could have died right there. He pulled the band from her braid, tangling his hand in her hair.

The final intact shred of his sanity still whispered she didn't know. But Aaron didn't care. Not when kissing her felt like waking up. Like he'd spent his entire life drifting through a dull, hazy dream.

But now, his senses were alive with smoke and jasmine, the brush of her tongue against his.

As Analia smiled, momentarily breaking their kiss, Aaron knew he never wanted to fall back asleep. Because Analia was the open window that drove away his nightmares. And Aaron?

A door opened upstairs.

Analia jolted away with a wet smack. Aaron gasped for breath, completely dazed. He reached to pull her back down, only freezing when he spotted Surce descending the stairs into the sitting room.

Aaron stifled a groan as Analia and Surce exchanged a few quick words. Eventually, Analia rose from the couch, Aaron resisting the urge to pull her back down as she headed for the stairs. She only looked back once before quickly ascending, Surce remaining silent until there came the click of her bedroom door closing.

"I see you have recovered," she said mildly.

Aaron refused to blush under her topaz stare. Even as it pointedly flicked down. He struggled into a sitting position, "Two days out of commission and the first thing you do is scold me."

"Two days out of commission and the first thing you do is paw at the girl like some sex-crazed barbarian."

Aaron winced.

"You're only alive because of her," Surce went on, sitting beside him. "The daggers that impaled you?" She pulled one from her dress belt and threw it down on the table before them. "Not only are they forged from dampers, but the blades were coated with xenol. They attracted all of your magic, enabling the xenol to consume it and immediately attack your life force. You are only alive because of how quickly Analia moved."

"Clever girl," Aaron said, suddenly queasy.

"And you are a fool," Surce hissed. "What would this kingdom have done if we lost you?"

"It was me or Analia."

"And you chose her."

"I trust her," Aaron said. "But she didn't trust herself." He dropped his gaze, "Didn't trust her magic, at least."

Surce's eyes narrowed dangerously. "Are you insinuating you allowed yourself to be impaled, numerous times, by fatal blades, so Analia would be forced to fully embrace her abilities?"

"Well," Aaron said, shifting uncomfortably, "while I would love to claim I'm that diabolical, no. That was just a fortuitous outcome."

Aaron's mind flashed back to those hazy final memories. How Analia had slammed her hand on his chest, and something warm raced through his veins. Something that allowed him to muster just enough magic to shadowjump them out before everything went black.

Aaron quickly explained to Surce. "It shouldn't be possible," he finished, his voice beginning to rasp.

"It shouldn't be possible she received her magic the way she did," Surce said, steepling her fingers in her lap. "Just as it shouldn't be possible she was born without a Blessing."

Aaron rubbed his forehead. Pieces slowly came together in his mind, forming an image that had his stomach sinking.

"You don't think," he began, his voice breaking off in a cough. His lingering high had finally faded, making room for every bruised, aching piece of him to shove to the forefront.

"Rest, Aaron," Surce said, finally softening as she guided him back on the couch. "You need to regain your strength. Not only if you're correct, but for the conversation to come."

"Conversation?"

"Does she know?"

Guilt stampeded through Aaron's insides.

"Tell her," she said, rising from the couch. "You're only making it worse for yourself."

"I know," Aaron said, sagging into the couch.

Surce patted his cheek. She made to exit the room, but turned back in the doorway leading to the dining room.

"Analia remained at your side the entire time you were unconscious," she said. "We could barely drag her away long enough to wash the blood from her."

With that, she exited, leaving Aaron to deal with the hope and shame warring in his chest.

Analia stepped into the sitting room a few hours later, her hair damp from the bath. Aaron still dozed on the couch, his eyes half-closed.

As soon as he heard her footsteps on the stairs, his eyes flicked open, immediately locating her, settling on her mouth.

A flush crept across Analia's skin. No one had ever kissed her like that before; like she was the answer to an unspoken prayer. Her mind had been completely incoherent when she pulled away, barely able to make it to her room before she slumped against the wall. Even now, her heart pounded as she sat on the edge of the couch.

"How are you feeling —"

"No, no, no," Aaron interrupted, struggling to sit up. "No more couch-side vigils. I'm fine."

"And I suppose that's why you're still on the couch?"

"I like it here," Aaron said. "I finally understand why Branten's spent so many a drunken night on this thing."

"And it has nothing to do with how you nearly fainted when you tried to make it to the bathing room without help?"

Aaron grimaced. He turned his face into the back of the couch, grumbling something about Branten's big mouth. Analia tried to smile, but her skin prickled.

"Why don't you want me to stay?" she asked.

Had she misunderstood? Had their kiss—their blistering, mind-shattering kiss—not meant anything to him? Their kiss that happened immediately upon his waking up after two days, injured, delirious—oh gods.

Before her mind could spiral any further, Aaron was reaching for her, cradling her face in his hands.

"My shooting star," he sighed, resting his forehead against hers. "You have no idea how badly I want you to stay."

Analia relaxed. Her eyes drifted down, watching Aaron smile. He leaned in, his lips brushing hers as she closed her eyes.

"But I want you to be comfortable more," he said. "In your own bed, where you can actually get some sleep."

"I can't do that," she whispered.

"Why not?"

"Because now I hear the thud as those daggers find you. I feel your blood on my hands."

Her fingers skimmed across his chest, not needing to look to know each point of entry. She saw it every time she closed her eyes.

Guilt flashed in Aaron's eyes. Then concern. Back to guilt. Finally landing on resolve.

"What do you need, Analia?" he asked.

Analia didn't think. She nudged him back on the couch, a line forming between his brows as he complied. But he remained perfectly still as she nestled beside him, resting her hand over his heart.

"This is all I need," she told him.

Something in Aaron's expression crumpled. He pulled her close, pressing his face into her hair. *Right, right, right.*

"What do you want, Aaron?" Analia murmured.

She expected him to consider. Instead, he immediately brushed her hair aside, his lips soft against the skin behind her ear. One, two, three, four, following a trail of phantom burns.

"That," he said, shifting her in his arms. "I've been wanting to do that for a long time."

Analia would never be able to describe the release she felt in that moment. She melted into him, his words soft against her temple.

"There's one more thing I need to tell you."

"Sleep first," Analia mumbled.

Aaron took a breath. Paused. "Sleep first," he agreed.

Analia hummed, snuggling into metal and spice.

"Sweet dreams," he murmured.

And for the first time in she didn't remember how long, Analia wasn't afraid to close her eyes.

Chapter 63

Analia felt as though she'd woken from a dream, just to slip into another one.

Early afternoon light filtered in through the sitting room's windows. Aaron remained fast asleep beside her on the couch, her back pressed to his chest, his knees tucked behind hers. At some point, his hand had found its way under her shirt, his fingers now resting against her stomach.

Analia sighed, turning to snuggle into his chest. She could feel herself drifting off once more to the slow, even beat of his heart, his body warm around her. Hot, even. Burning.

Analia frowned. She peeked up at him, noting how for the first time in two days, his features were completely relaxed. But the flush hadn't left his cheeks. Nor had the heat receded when she rested the back of her hand against his forehead.

Analia reluctantly slid free of his arms. Sifting through the clutter on the table, she found the small blue bottle whose contents Surce dripped on Aaron's lips each morning. Yet, when she tipped it toward herself, she found it empty.

Analia pursed her lips, then glanced back at Aaron. It was possible Surce had already given him his dose while they were asleep. But with how high his fever was still running?

Deciding not to risk it, she grabbed the notepad from the edge of the table, scribbling a note saying she was going to Surce's studio to get more potion. She placed the note on the couch beside Aaron's head, intending to quietly slip away. But then, she leaned down, pressing a quick kiss to his cheek.

Aaron stirred. Analia stroked his hair, murmuring to him until he sighed and settled once more. Finally, Analia crept out of the room.

With every step, she braced herself for her dream to end, to be transported back to normalcy.

But what if this *was* normal? Not just the memory of Aaron's kiss, the phantom heat and weight of his arm around her, but the soft glow spreading throughout her body.

Even if it wasn't, it was still hers. At least in this moment.

Analia pressed her fingertips to her smile. Reaching Surce's beads, she passed through the curtain, imagining Surce's studio.

To her surprise, the circular space was completely deserted.

"Surce?" she called, stepping deeper into the room.

Nothing stirred. A half-finished tapestry lay across Surce's loom, the threads so dark Analia couldn't begin to imagine what it could be.

Shrugging to herself, she moved toward the back where Surce had a collection of drawers. Although, maybe rifling through the seamstress's things wasn't the brightest idea.

Analia paused, halfway across the room. Yes. Definitely best to wait for Surce back at the house.

Analia retreated back the way she'd come, floorboards squeaking beneath her feet. As she passed the loom, her sleeve snagged on one of the hooks. Cursing under her breath, Analia carefully extracted herself, her eyes absently wandering up to the tapestries. And her body went cold.

They were all tapestries of her. Sitting on her turret roof, glowering at her unlit candle. Crouching in an Ash corridor, her expression hollow as she adjusted her funeral robes. Her open palm holding the Ash ring.

Countless moments of her life stretched across the studio walls. Her breath trembled in her lungs as she caught sight of one depicting Accalon smiling at her on the roof. But he wasn't the only person featured.

"Anna!" Aaron tore through the curtain of beads. Analia turned in time to see him stumble, his face flushed. But she couldn't bring herself to worry about him; couldn't feel anything at all.

"What is this?" she asked.

She stared into his face, desperate to see a look of shock. But as Aaron's eyes darted around the room, there was only panic.

"You knew," she breathed.

"Analia, let me explain—"

"You knew about everything."

She turned back to the tapestries, each image of herself and Aaron slamming into her like a physical blow.

Ring hunting in Sun. Her coronation day. Them sitting on their throne in the Human Kingdom. Gods, there was even one showing their goodbye at the Phoenix Gate, his fingertips touching her smile.

"I didn't want you to find out this way," Aaron said, coming up beside her. "I was going to tell you last night."

"How convenient."

Her eyes moved from one tapestry to the next, unable to look away even as cracks skittered across her heart. Especially when her eyes landed on two sticks, their burning ends touching one another to create a triangle.

Analia's hand flew to her throat. Aaron swore, following her gaze.

"I swear," he said, stepping into her line of sight, "I have never seen that one."

"But you've seen the others," she said, her voice shaking. "You haven't seen that one, but you've seen the others."

Aaron looked away, backing up to steady himself against the loom. "Mostly."

Analia swayed on her feet. All she wanted was to back away, cover her eyes, pretend she hadn't seen. But she could not—would not—go back to a life of hiding.

"How long?" she asked.

Aaron looked away.

"Aaron, how long have you known?"

Aaron's entire body sagged. "Since before I met you."

Something worse than betrayal sliced through Analia's chest. She stumbled back a step, her arms wrapping around her middle.

"Analia, I promise," he said desperately, "I wasn't trying to hurt you."

"How could you?" she asked, her voice breaking.

There was a time this realization would have had her flames blazing. But now?

"Was any of this real?" she asked, her voice breaking. "All the times you comforted me and pushed me and believed in me. Were you just playing the part the tapestries outlined—"

"Gods, Analia, no." Aaron struggled to stand on his own. "I have never faked or forced the way I feel about you. Not when holding you, not when kissing you, not even when I smile at you. It's all real."

Somehow, that made her feel worse.

"And you've known about it all along," she said. "You used these tapestries to help you create the outcome you wanted—"

"How could you *say* that?" Aaron asked, disbelieving.

"How could you keep this from me?"

"I wanted you to have a choice!"

Aaron took a step toward her, his face crumpling as she flinched back. Gods, how did his pain still hurt her?

"The moment you saw the tapestries," he said, struggling for calm, "you wondered if I was only playing my role, and I don't blame you. It was that very pressure to do so that I was trying to spare you from. I was trying to allow you to choose not what the gods wanted, what fate wanted, but what *you* wanted."

"What I wanted was for you to be *honest* with me. I told you as much on the walkway, and you promised me…"

Tears filled Analia's eyes. Aaron retreated to sit on Surce's stool, his hand coming to his chest.

How had it been less than an hour since she'd woken in his arms?

"How could you take this choice from me?" she asked.

Aaron's head snapped up, "You will *always* have a choice with me."

"Only the choices you want me to have."

Aaron sucked in a breath.

"You told me back on the bridge there were no more reasons to hide," she said. "But you still keep giving me pieces. What am I supposed to do with that, Aaron? How am I supposed to trust anything you say when I don't know if you are picking and choosing what information to tell me?"

"I wasn't trying to do that."

"Why is this choice so important to you—"

"Because I wanted you to choose me!"

Analia's jaw dropped. Aaron gripped the loom, looking as though he hadn't been expecting his words.

He stared into her face, trying to read her reaction. Analia, in turn, found the last shred of hope she had and felt it crumble.

"So," she said, terrifyingly calm, "this was about what *you* wanted."

Aaron's face drained of color. "No," he whispered.

But Analia's voice became louder. "This was about me making the choice you could deal with the easiest."

Aaron's lips moved, forming words Analia couldn't hear over the crackle of her flames. Her temperature began to rise, her magic pressing for release, to spit all the words she knew would hurt Aaron most. It would be so. Easy.

Analia released a long, heavy breath. Then, she turned, silently heading for the beads.

She could hear Aaron struggle to his feet, his footsteps coming after her, "Analia, I'm sorry—"

"Don't come after me, Aaron," Analia said.

Then, she walked away from the man who had helped put her heart back together, just to break it again. Through the beads, no destination in mind, his anguished voice calling her name.

Surce's shop appeared around her, mercifully quiet and empty. Analia stumbled through racks, shoving through the door just to slump back against the building's facade. She buried her face in her hands, the winter wind biting against her skin.

Gods, how had she ended up here again? Brenn, Rois, Pryanth, Deardryn. How many more people had to betray her for her to finally learn the lesson?

Analia shook her head, the cold band of Aaron's ring rubbing her cheek.

She'd told herself she was only wearing it to maintain their ruse, that it had nothing to do with the flood of warmth she felt every time she looked at it. The exact same thing she'd told herself when wearing Pryanth's pendant back in Sun.

Analia wanted to scream. Aaron's ring, Pryanth's pendant. How did she not notice the parallels sooner? Why did she keep doing this to herself?

Analia gripped the ring, wanting nothing more than to pry it from her finger and hurl it across the kingdom. But she couldn't bring herself to move.

How many times had she told herself, told Aaron, that he was nothing like Pryanth? How many times had he proven that to her?

Even now, heartbroken and furious, she knew he was telling the truth when he said he wasn't trying to hurt her. Just as she knew she didn't want to become the person that let her scars rule her life.

But where did that leave her? There were still the tapestries and decisions and choices—gods, she just needed to think.

Analia dropped her hands, trying to catch her breath. Just to spot the lavender orb of light hovering near her face.

Tingles ran across the back of her neck. Her mind flashed back to Mt. Lanula, Laness and Hyla explaining how the winllows guided those who needed the DovenU the most.

Had she truly reached the point where she had nowhere left to go?

The winllow drifted closer, moving around her head in a question. Analia glanced at the orb, then back at the shop.

She only hesitated a moment.

Reaching for her enka bracelet, she sent a silent message down the line.

I'm all right. With the DovenU. Don't let him come until I call.

Then, not giving Laness time to respond, she reached out her hand to the orb.

A aron ripped through the curtain of beads, yelling Laness's name.

He didn't feel the lingering pain in his body as he raced down his second-floor hallway and down the stairs. Didn't feel the fever that had turned him into a stammering fool. All he knew was he was an idiot. An absolute fucking idiot.

Aaron jumped the final steps, his family already gathered in the sitting room. Laness barreled forward to meet him, "What happened—"

"Where is she—"

"I felt the shift. It was so perfect, and then—"

"She found them," Aaron said, feeling himself breaking apart, piece by piece.

"Found what?" Branten demanded from the arm of the couch.

Aaron barely heard him as he spotted Surce, leaning against the fireplace. He rounded on her, "How could you leave them out?"

"Leave what out?" Branten asked.

Aaron said, "I told you I would tell her, I was about to, why didn't you let me handle it?"

"You know this isn't my doing," Surce said, infuriatingly calm. "The room decided to show her."

No, no it had to be her fault. He couldn't handle it not being her fault because that would mean it was his, and he couldn't survive that.

"Show her what?" Branten said, shoving between them. "Aaron, what's going on?"

He looked to Aaron expectantly, but Aaron couldn't open his mouth. Not when speaking those words aloud would destroy the last shred of composure he had. He could barely tolerate the sound of Laness quietly explaining to Branten and Mor, each word breaking off another piece of himself to fall and shatter.

"She saw them?" Branten repeated.

"Is she all right?" Mor asked from beside the bookcase.

"I don't know," Aaron said miserably. "She ran off, and I can't find her."

"She's all right," Laness said quickly. "But she... she told me not to let you come after her."

The world seemed to freeze around him. He slowly backed toward the couch, that last piece of himself dangling by a thread as he sat.

"She's done," he breathed. He barely registered Mor coming to sit beside him.

It was official: he'd destroyed the best thing that ever happened to him, just as he always did.

"But you two were just cuddled up on the couch not two hours ago!" Branten exclaimed, looking like he didn't know what to do with himself as he moved around the room. "A few tapestries were enough to take that away?"

"Branten, it was everything," Aaron moaned. "Things even I hadn't seen."

Aaron dropped his head in his hands. He waited for the chorus of "I told you so," knowing he deserved it completely.

"Oh, Aaron," Laness said. She came to curl up against his side, her arms wrapping around him. "I am so, so sorry."

Aaron was too tired to shove her away. He took a shuddering breath, a tear tracing down his cheek.

Mor squeezed his shoulder. "She will come back."

It was the firm belief in his voice that finally had Aaron shattering.

Branten and Surce joined them on the couch as Aaron curled in on himself.

He'd always known a person to scream when in pain, getting louder as it intensified. He should have been heard all across Elefthia. But he couldn't move. He couldn't make a sound.

He had been selfish. So fucking selfish. He had caused the same anguish ripping through his chest to shimmer in Analia's eyes as she tried not to cry. He'd *done that* to her.

"What have I done?" he whispered. "What have I done, what have I done, what have I done, what have I done?"

Analia marched into Zinia's study, the winllow having transported her into the center of the mountain's courtyard.

The warrior queen sat expectantly behind her desk, hood pulled up and fingers laced atop the table.

Analia faintly registered her lack of magic network, but shoved the thought aside as she reached the desk and thrust out her hand. A column of midnight flames shot from her palm, coiling up in a tight corkscrew, and uncoiling back down until completely extinguished.

Zinia studied her for a long, long time. Analia thought she caught a flicker of sorrow in her eyes, but it was gone too quick to tell.

Finally, she sat back in her chair. "Looks like you'll be needing a room."

Analia's voice was empty. "Yes, my lady."

"Find Hyla. She'll do the rest."

Analia nodded. She turned and headed for the door.

"Analia," Zinia called after her.

Analia glanced back. She couldn't see most of Zinia's face through the shadow of her hood. But there was no mistaking the satisfaction in her gray eyes as she said, "Well done."

Analia blinked hard. And it wasn't until she was safely locked away in her room that she let her sobs break free.

PART 4: CONSTELLATION

Chapter 64

Dimitri expected it to hurt when everything fell apart. Unbearably so. But all he felt was a cold, empty silence.

He hadn't had a destination in mind when he escaped Scarsthain. He just felt a tug, and a moment later, he stood at the base of Darmanten's statue in the flower maze.

For the entirety of that day, he sat on the statue's plinth, staring unseeingly at the snowy garden before him.

He didn't care. He couldn't care. There was nothing left to care about. But he still couldn't let Deardryn catch him.

Dimitri let his servant's instincts guide him back into the central kingdom. After all, the last place they would look was right under their noses.

Step, step, step.

He moved through streets and boardwalks as if in a dream, seeing the lives continue around him like paintings in a gallery. Or perhaps he was the painting: observed, unable to make contact. Nothing more than a collection of lines and color.

He didn't care. There was nothing to care about as he climbed the inn's wooden porch steps, not immediately noticing someone was speaking to him.

"Reliable oak. It's got great shock resistance, which is good for inns like this where you have drunken idiots constantly slamming through."

Dimitri turned. A little girl perched on the railing, her light brown hair falling over her shoulders in twin braids. She wore a pale pink dress, the hem splattered with mud.

"You again," he said.

The singing girl from the boardwalk scowled. "Is that any way to speak to a child?"

"You're not a child," Dimitri sighed. "You're just the size of one."

The little girl wrinkled her nose. "Well you're no fun."

"And your analysis of doors was riveting."

Dimitri turned away. Tired. Numb.

"Hey." Hopping off the railing, the girl wedged herself between him and the door. "I'm trying to help you, you know."

"I don't take advice from strangers." Dimitri moved her out of his way by the shoulders, then slammed her beloved door in her face.

The following day, Dimitri wandered to a different inn. Not because of the girl—he didn't care. It was smarter to keep moving, that was all. Still, he could have sworn something like relief flickered across the cold, heavy fog inside him when he stepped into the new inn. But it only lasted so long.

"See, this door is painted, not stained. Bad sign."

Dimitri turned in his seat beside the fire. The girl sat in the chair beside him, her cheeks flushed from the heat.

"What are you doing here?" he hissed.

"You slammed the door in my face."

"I thought you'd like to see how the hinges work."

"I told you," the girl said, leaning toward him and lowering her voice, "I'm trying to help you."

"Great. So you're annoying and crazy."

"Well, we tend to find one another."

Dimitri tightened his grip around his wooden armrest. Then, he turned away without comment. There was no point getting angry. There was no point at all.

"This is pathetic," the girl said. "You can barely contain yourself when listening to my silly stories on the boardwalk, yet I call you annoying and crazy, and you just let your temper fizzle out without comment. Did Deardryn truly break you that bad?"

How did she know about that? It didn't matter.

Without a word, Dimitri stood and walked away through crowded tables. He flagged over the innkeeper, "That girl isn't paying for a room." Then, he ascended the stairs to his own room, not looking back as the innkeeper shooed the little girl away.

The following morning, Dimitri spotted his fading Moon Royal features in his cracked mirror. It wasn't a surprise: he had only needed the appearance for a night, so Rayner had used less magic.

Just thinking his name had Dimitri flinching back. He should be happy he was regaining his normal appearance—no, he didn't care. He certainly didn't feel a deep, piercing ache at the thought of losing his final link to Rayner.

"You're giving up," the girl said that night, hovering behind him as he chopped wood out back in exchange for his room. "You came to this kingdom to stop Deardryn—"

"How do you know that?"

"But you can't stop her if you give in. Is that what you want? For her to prove that you will forever be the bastard servant she forced you to be?"

"I tried to stop her, and I failed. Again. So back. Off."

The following morning, Dimitri's hair was back to blonde.

"Look, I understand," the girl said, already waiting for him at his next inn. "You feel like you've been betrayed by people you've grown to love—"

"I *was* betrayed."

By Rayner. Someone who made no attempt to hide his lack of loyalty. And Dimitri had liked him for it.

"Fine, you were betrayed," the girl said, the wind blowing back her gray cloak hood. "You thought you finally found people that loved you when all you've known in your life is ridicule—"

"How do you know this?"

"You thought you finally had a home, and now, you have to mourn those things all at once. It's devastating."

"Don't tell me how I feel," Dimitri growled, turning to find a new inn.

"Fine," she said, trailing after him. "I won't tell you how you feel. But I will tell you this is the worst part. You can't get any lower, which means you can either stay here and be miserable forever, or you can start climbing back up."

The girl continued talking. And Dimitri ignored her all the way to his next inn.

Step, step, fucking step.

The next day, Dimitri's appearance was back to normal. It had been a week and one day since Rayner last maintained his Moon Kingdom appearance, meaning their oath had been broken.

Dimitri moved aside his shirt, the lock tattoo on his collarbone now completely gray. But he sensed no blood magic coming to strike him down. Why? Because they had mutually decided to break it?

Dimitri scoffed. Snatching his poetry collection from the chipped bedside table, he headed for the door, hoping Rayner had more than just a grayed-out tattoo. He descended the stairs, about to push through the ajar stairwell door. Then, he caught the conversation on the other side.

"No, Your Majesty," the ancient innkeeper mumbled. "I haven't seen anyone like that."

"Are you sure?"

The voice blasted through Dimitri like a winter wind. It pinned him against the wall; ripped through the last vestiges of the numbness, the silence.

He'd known the Royals would come for him. Deardryn wouldn't let him spread her secret, just as Sylas wouldn't let him create chaos in his kingdom. It was only a matter of time before they found him. He just didn't expect it to be Patryclas.

The two continued talking, but Dimitri couldn't hear them. Every one of his senses was eclipsed by the explosion that radiated out from his chest.

The girl had been wrong. This was the worst part: everything inside him disintegrating under the sheer force of emotion. Fury. Heartbreak. Grief. Confusion. Loneliness. It was too much to contain, but there was nowhere for it to go.

"Please," Patryclas said, his voice sounding far away. "If you do see him, notify me and only me immediately. Keep him safe until I arrive."

"Of course, Your Majesty."

What did that mean? What did any of it mean?

Dimitri struggled to control his breathing as Patryclas's footsteps headed for the door.

Why send for just Patryclas? Why keep him safe? Why go to such lengths to pretend to love him? Why? Why why why why?

Dimitri didn't realize he was running until the inn door slammed behind him, cutting off the innkeeper's yells.

Why did Rayner betray him? Why did Rayner pretend to care? Why did any of them pretend to care?

"You're doing it again!" the girl said, racing after him from Crystal knew where. "You're running away."

"Leave me alone," Dimitri snarled, speeding up.

The girl didn't so much as flinch. She matched his pace as he flew through the backstreets of the square, the boardwalk bouncing beneath their feet.

"You ran away from Othin when he tried to reach out. You ran away from Analia in Sun. You ran away from the Sun Kingdom itself. And now you're running away from Patryclas."

"I went back to Analia," Dimitri snapped. He wove behind a line of deserted warehouses. Faster, he had to go faster.

"You did," the girl conceded. "Just to immediately run off to the Moon Kingdom."

"It's not like that!"

"You allowed yourself to care about her and Aaron. Then you ran away from them. Twice."

"No!" Dimitri darted up a pair of steps built into the back of a warehouse.

"Yes," the girl said, following. "And now you're doing the same thing to Patryclas. What would Analia say?"

"I failed her!" Dimitri leaped on to the warehouse roof and whirled to face the girl. "It doesn't matter what she would say, because I failed her. I failed her in every way, over and over again, and there is nothing I can do to fix it, so why the fuck should I try?"

Dimitri towered over the girl, practically pulsating with rage and devastation. He waited for her to flee. Instead, she planted her feet, folded her arms, and shook her head at him.

"How blind are you?" she asked.

Dimitri recoiled.

"Do you honestly think Analia only cares about you because she gave you an assignment?"

"I also helped her escape the castle."

"Oh, I see. So you think she feels indebted to you."

Dimitri wanted to brush her words aside. Instead, he shrunk back as the girl stepped closer.

"Holy Crystal above," she said. "You don't believe Analia cares about you. You convinced yourself your connection to her is dependent on this side mission you've assembled—yes, it was your doing. She didn't ask you to stay and play spy."

Dimitri shook his head, backing toward the edge of the roof. He couldn't hear this. He couldn't stare at the mirror this girl held up to his face. It was too dark. Too sad and ugly.

"What do you think Analia cares about more?" the girl asked, her tone softening as she followed him. "This mission, or you being all right?"

"I don't know," Dimitri whispered.

"Yes, you do. You're just afraid to say it out loud. Because if Analia doesn't care if you fail, that would mean someone truly cares about you. And that would mean...?"

"I have something to lose outside of my control," Dimitri breathed. A new kind of hollowness crept over him as he stared off over her head.

"Would you look at that." The girl sat on the edge of the roof and primly folded her hands in her lap. "Now we're getting somewhere."

She patted the roof beside her.

Somehow, Dimitri's feet moved, his body coming to sit beside her. And the words he'd been too terrified to even acknowledge finally spilled past his lips.

For the rest of the day, the two sat talking on the edge of the roof. Dimitri didn't know what it was about this strange little girl, but somehow, she had every tangled, heart-aching thought tumbling out of his mouth without hesitation.

How he was terrified of being abandoned. How he had thought the only way to avoid that feeling was to have no one at all.

But then, he'd found Analia and Aaron. He'd tried so hard to keep them at a distance, knowing they could destroy him. He just didn't know how wonderful it could feel to have them as well.

For the first time, he was wanted, cared for. And it was *terrifying*. So, he pulled away. Just to fall into the same trap with Patryclas.

But maybe it wasn't a trap. Maybe it was what he wanted, and he had a history of wants coming back to hurt him. Maybe it was all right that he wanted the connection and affection that Patryclas offered.

Maybe it was all right that he didn't want to be alone anymore.

"I ran because I wanted to stay," Dimitri finished, his throat raw.

"Well, in that case," the girl said, "you ran in the wrong direction."

Something settled in Dimitri's chest like a key in a lock.

"Why do you have to make sense?" he asked, annoyed.

"I've walked through many, many doorways," the girl said, tracing her fingers through the shadows on the roof between them. "Some even you would appreciate."

"Unlikely." Muscles aching, Dimitri pushed himself to his feet.

"Where are you going?" she asked, looking up at him.

"I'm going to tell a friend I have an answer to his question."

The girl grinned.

Dimitri crossed back to the steps, his body unbearably heavy. But at least he knew what he had to do; what he wanted to do.

His head was just about to disappear over the edge when he looked back. "What's your name?"

The girl looked up, eyes flashing gold in the light. "Loliette."

Chapter 65

Analia woke to Hyla flinging open her door.

"Time to train," the Doveness announced, dropping a bowl of something on Analia's bedside table. Whisking around the room, she pulled one of the DovenU's magic camouflage bodysuits from a chest and tossed it toward the bed.

Analia didn't try to catch it. She curled into a tighter ball beneath her covers, her body aching as if covered in a network of bruises. She just wanted to sleep, forget where she was, why she was there.

"Get up," Hyla said, snapping her fingers in Analia's face.

Analia reared back, spitting a curse.

"If you thought you could come to our mountain to sulk," Hyla said, "you were horribly mistaken. Now, get. Up."

She yanked the covers back, looking thoroughly unimpressed as Analia glared. A part of her was tempted to summon her flames. But Hyla only folded her arms and tapped her foot. And Analia realized she was too tired to care.

Dragging herself into a sitting position, she reached for the bowl on her bedside table. "What is this?" she asked, poking her spoon around the mush.

"Fuel." Hyla didn't continue until Analia stuck a bland, clumpy spoonful in her mouth. "You need something that will give you energy if you're going to train. So, you get porridge."

"You sound like Branten," Analia grumbled, choking down another bite.

Hyla's nose wrinkled. "Hurry up."

A few minutes later, Analia followed Hyla through curving walkways inset in the mountain's walls, spiraling down to the training courtyard below. She expected to feel eyes on her as she passed numerous groups of women, but to her surprise, they barely looked up.

"Here," Hyla said, stopping in an empty section in the courtyard.

Analia glanced around, spotting plenty of sparring Dovenesses, but no training dummies. "Here what?" she asked.

"Here," Hyla said, "is the spot you will train."

Analia stared blankly. Hyla put her hands on her hips.

"I told you, Analia. This is not a place to sulk and wallow. This is a place to rebuild. And you can't do that if the only moving you do is running away from the reason you're here."

"I know the reason I'm here," Analia said, folding her arms. "I am painfully, intimately familiar with the reason I'm here."

"Fine," Hyla said, stepping closer. "You acknowledge why you're here. But have you faced it? Have you accepted it?"

Hyla took another step closer. Analia held her ground, flames starting to crackle. "Don't act like you know what I've done or what I've been through."

"Don't act like you want to do anything other than crawl back into bed and hide from the world."

Hyla tried to shove her. Analia ducked out of the way, quickly retreating a few steps.

"I'm not quitting," she hissed.

"Good." Hyla shifted her weight. "Now fight back."

Hyla's fist flashed out. Analia caught her wrist, just for Hyla's foot to sweep into her ankle, knocking her feet out from under her.

Analia hit the ground hard. She scrambled back to her feet, breathing hard.

"The DovenU does not focus on brute strength," Hyla said, slinking around Analia. "We work with speed and cunning. We watch our opponents, learn their movements and patterns, and then we strike where they're weakest."

Hyla grabbed Analia by the hair. Analia whipped her arm back, bringing her forearm down on Hyla's arm, but Hyla flipped her grip and grabbed her wrist.

"Your weakness," Hyla said, spinning Analia around and bringing her close, "is you rely on the basics, not your instincts, and that makes you predictable."

Hyla stepped away from Analia's stomping foot. Analia squirmed, but Hyla locked her arm behind her back and flipped her to the ground. Analia's suit absorbed much of the impact, but she still bit down hard on her tongue.

"Rely on your instincts, Analia," Hyla said.

She kicked toward Analia's ribs. Analia snatched at her foot, Hyla dodging out of the way. Her foot came down in a wide stance, and Analia didn't think.

She sent a stream of black flames toward Hyla's side. The Doveness dodged out of the way; right into Analia's foot, waiting to trip her. Hyla stumbled but quickly regained her footing.

"Better," she said, coming forward to offer Analia a hand up. "Stop trying to stay in control."

She pulled Analia to her feet. Then, their true training began.

Hyla was a whirlwind of deadly efficiency, each movement elegant and precise. Analia quickly realized her victory on the ridge was that of a child playing war compared to the enemy before her.

Eventually, Hyla called for a break. Analia took a step back, wiping the sweat from her brow. She expected Hyla to walk away without comment. Instead, she gave Analia a nod of approval.

From that point on, Analia's days were consumed by training. It wasn't Branten's structured, step-by-step routine. This was all practical learning, Hyla never letting up, punishing Analia's mistakes and praising her successes.

Slowly, Analia's mind slipped into something calm and analytical. She learned to read Hyla's movements, sometimes even managing to predict them while still thinking multiple steps ahead. But as her instincts took over, that only made room for her thoughts to wander.

Aaron hadn't told her. He'd known about those tapestries for decades, and he hadn't told her. Because he wanted her to choose him?

Analia aimed a punch toward Hyla's stomach. Hyla grabbed her wrist, pulling her in close, but Analia used the momentum to headbutt Hyla's chin. Hyla retreated.

They were destined. Everything that had happened between them wasn't happenstance or perfect timing. Their story was woven in the stars. And he. Hadn't. Told her.

Why? Was it a test to see if she would run away? Or was he hoping she would? Were all the times he told her he was a monster attempts at scaring her off so he could escape his fate?

No. That wasn't him. That wasn't her. Which meant he truly had been trying to give her the biggest picture he could. But he should have given her the whole picture.

Analia's cheek burned as Hyla slapped her—"Instincts, Analia."

Analia blinked hard, then dodged a flying elbow.

I wanted you to choose me.

How could he say he was doing this for her if that was his motive?

Although, look at how she'd reacted after finding out. She'd barely given him a chance to speak before abandoning him, just as so many had before. All she could think was she'd been betrayed once again. Her trust had been built up and shattered, once again.

But had he truly betrayed her? He'd certainly withheld information. But could he have done so not just to make sure she chose him because she wanted him, but also because he knew the scar tissue those tapestries would slice through?

She didn't know. She didn't know if there was a "right" way for either of them to handle the tapestries. All she knew was Aaron had never stopped fighting for her. Just as she had fought for him on that ridge. And then she'd fled without a second thought.

Analia's eyes burned. But this time, Aaron wasn't there to wipe her tears. He wasn't there to hold her together, kiss her like she was something to cherish, offer her something to hold on to. Because she. Ran. Away.

"Say it again."

Analia blinked hard. She'd been blindly punching Hyla's raised palms, the Doveness having adjusted her stance without complaint to take each blow.

"Say it again, Analia," Hyla said. "What did you do?"

Analia hadn't realized she'd spoken aloud, but the words didn't pause on her tongue. "I ran away."

Another punch.

"Why?" Hyla demanded.

Punch, punch.

"Because I was afraid."

"Of what?"

"Myself."

Analia wasn't expecting that response. She didn't know what it meant. But her fists flew faster, harder, her tears finally spilling free.

She. Ran. Away. Away from the tapestries, away from Aaron. But where was she running to?

Eventually, Analia's fists slowed. Hyla kept her palms raised, catching each blow without so much as a wince.

Finally, Analia let her fists drop. She looked down at her hands, her knuckles split and stinging with that final question.

Where was she running to?

Analia had no answers as Hyla approached. She wiped the tears from her face, waiting for the rebuke. But Hyla only put a hand on her shoulder.

"You faced it," she told her. "You said it out loud, and you faced it. It won't be the last time you'll have to, but this was the hardest time."

Analia hung her head, her heart aching. Hyla squeezed her shoulder.

"Be proud of yourself, Analia. You just proved to yourself how strong you are."

Gods, she didn't feel strong. She felt broken and battered and defeated.

Another tear slid down Analia's cheek. But she nodded to Hyla, who gave her a small smile. Then, she turned, and Analia followed perhaps the best teacher she ever had back toward the tunnels.

A fate woven in the stars.

Aaron stood at the window in his mother's room, listening to the fists hammering on the door.

"We know you're in there," Branten's muffled voice called.

"We just want to talk to you," Mor said.

Aaron sighed, fogging the chilly glass. The knocking grew louder.

"Come on, Aaron," Branten said. "Stop feeling sorry for yourself and open the door."

"You know he's not going to stop until you do," Mor added.

From this angle, he could see Mt. Lanula far in the distance. Was that what his mother was always looking at when she sat at this window? Wondering if she had nowhere left to go? Or had the winllows come for her, but she'd decided to stay?

She'd stayed for him and died for him; Analia had left because of him. It all ended the same way.

"Aaron, we just want to help you," Mor said. "You shouldn't have to sit in there alone."

Aaron fingered the letter in his hand, tracing the countless creases he had made as he folded, unfolded, and refolded it again.

She was safe. She didn't want to see him. He was a fool.

"This is ridiculous!" There came a thud as Branten pressed against the door, the knob jiggling hard. "Are you really going to hide in this room forever? When has that ever worked out for you?"

Aaron silently turned and crossed the room.

"You are a fighter, Aaron. That's how you survived the Underground, and that's what makes you a damn good king. Now start being a good brother and let us in—"

Aaron opened the door and stepped aside. Branten toppled inside, Mor managing to catch himself on the doorframe before he could follow.

Aaron rocked back on his heels. "You were saying?"

Branten quickly righted himself.

"See?" Mor said. "I told you he would be dressed."

"Great," Branten said. "Now all he needs is his boots so he can go after her already."

"Analia told me to stay away," Aaron said, turning to sit on the bed.

"Five days ago!" Branten exclaimed.

"Aaron," Mor said, pushing off his mother's desk, "we all know you're no stranger to loss. But this isn't something you have to lose."

Aaron looked down, his fingers absently folding and refolding his note. "I know."

Branten began, "You can't just—you know?"

Aaron nodded. "I was an idiot for not showing her the tapestries. But I've been an even bigger idiot for not offering her any answers in the aftermath."

Mor asked, "Does that mean...?"

Aaron creased the letter one final time, then slipped it into his pocket. "I was just about to go when you two started harassing me."

Well, he'd been trying to collect enough courage to do so. But now, speaking it aloud?

"Really?" Mor asked.

Aaron nodded. Branten whooped and tackled him back on the bed with a hug. "Bring her home, brother!"

"If she's ready," Mor cautioned, sitting beside them.

"Of course if she's ready—how irresponsible do you think we are?"

Mor pointedly cleared his throat. Aaron snorted.

In the days he'd spent in his mother's room, he finally let that dark storm in the back of his mind play out. It rampaged through his thoughts, dragging forward every fear and doubt he'd ever tried to suppress.

Sometimes he yelled. Other times he sobbed into his hands. But for most of it he sat silently, a part of him forgetting how to move. But finally, he let that storm rage all the way out.

In the aftermath, he'd found the one, simple truth. He loved her. He'd failed her. He'd failed himself. Now, he owed it to both of them to see if there was anything he could rebuild.

Branten and Mor still bickered. Aaron clapped them on the back and rolled to his feet.

"Don't worry," he said, accepting the boots Mor passed him. "I already figured out how to find out without having to see her."

He just didn't know what would happen if she *did* want to see him.

Chapter 66

"Your king won't stop pestering me," Zinia said by way of greeting.

Analia's brows twitched up. She stood in the doorway of the warrior queen's lavish study, Hyla having informed her that her presence was requested immediately.

"How does he know I'm here?" she asked, moving to take the seat across from Zinia. Had Laness told him? She didn't think she had to specify...

"Because I told him."

"What?" Analia spluttered. "How, why, when?"

"As soon as you arrived. I knew that doe-eyed fool would be worried—don't give me that pout, you should have informed him yourself."

Analia fought the urge to hang her head. "Why are the king's worries any concern of yours?" she asked instead.

"Because that boy king has been the most persistent pain in my rear, and he will always have a prominent place in my heart."

Something finally clicked in Analia's mind. Her gaze scanned over the warrior queen, taking in her gray eyes, her obscured neck and features, sensing not even a whisper of magic.

"So," she said, leaning back in her chair. "Where's your damper?"

Zinia didn't appear the slightest bit fazed. She lifted her jeweled goblet to her lips, "Why would I need one of those?"

"Because if I were to sense your magic before you discerned my motives, you would have no way of making sure the Starlight Kingdom remained ignorant that you're still alive."

"Oh," Zinia said, "the Starlight Kingdom is quite aware of my existence on this mountain."

"Just as they are aware of your claim to the throne," Analia said. "A claim that would undoubtedly be dredged up if I were to start talking, which would not only threaten Aaron's rule, but also pressure you into reclaiming a throne you never wanted."

Zinia's mouth tightened. Analia held her stare, unflinching as the silence thickened around them.

Finally, Zinia put down her goblet. "Very good," she said. Then, she pushed back her hood.

The warrior queen was somehow exactly and nothing like what Analia expected. Her sandy-brown hair sat coiled in a knot atop her head, drawing attention to her high forehead and sharp, pointed chin. Despite her wrinkles, her face was still regal. Imperious. The chunks of onyx pierced through her earlobes only solidifying the image.

"I believe," Ethelind Stelingente said, her mouth curving in a sharp smile, "you forgot to bow."

Analia hurried to comply, but Aaron's grandmother flicked her hand. "Oh, don't bother. You and your little squabble have wasted enough of my time as is."

Analia's cheeks burned. "How much has Aaron told you?"

"He told me nothing," Ethelind said. "He didn't have to. Even my girls still sucking their thumbs could figure out the tapestries are the only thing that could get you angry enough to come here."

"Does everyone know about the tapestries?" Analia demanded.

"Now that you do? Yes."

Analia threw up her hands.

"Is that why you're angry?" Ethelind asked, rising from her chair and striding toward the window. "Because Aaron didn't tell you about the tapestries when you wanted him to?"

"I had a right to know."

"And he had a right to keep them to himself, seeing as he was involved in many of those tapestries."

Analia pressed her lips into a line. She knew Ethelind had a point, but that only made the heat creeping up her spine burn hotter.

"In my experience," Ethelind said, pulling back the curtains, "when people are angry, they stay and fight. Sometimes with other people, many times with themselves. But you fled. Which means there was something you were running away from."

The warrior queen turned, catching Analia in her vice-like stare. Analia squirmed. She was tempted to brush her off, let herself cling to her crackling flames. It was so much easier than the alternative. But gods, it was also exhausting.

"I ran from the tapestries," she finally said, leaning her head back against her chair. "I ran from everything they suggested because I was afraid Aaron would become one more person that broke my heart."

"The potential for heartbreak is a part of life, child," Ethelind said, softening a fraction.

"Is it a part of life to be hated by your own father?" Analia asked, more tired than anything. "The one person who is supposed to love you unconditionally? If he can stop loving me, who can't?"

Analia briefly closed her eyes. She wasn't surprised by the lump rising in her throat; the blow as it hit home. This pain had become a part of her the moment Brenn turned on her when she was seven. She had just finally spoken it aloud.

Ethelind was quiet for a moment.

"When Aaron first came to me after returning from Sun," she finally said, "he spent the first hour rambling about you. And from everything I've heard, that sack of hot air was never your father. Not in the way that mattered.

"That was your uncle, and he never stopped. That tornado of a healer girl has never stopped. Aaron has never stopped, even now when you're apart and sulking."

"I'm not—"

"I didn't say I was talking about you."

Analia looked down at her hands.

"I will be the first to tell you how exasperating that boy can be," Ethelind went on. "But along with that, he is the most trustworthy individual I have encountered in all my years."

She pushed off the windowsill, coming to stand before Analia. "The question is not if you care about him—because we both already know the answer to that. Instead, you must decide if you are willing to trust him. Fully. Completely."

Analia rubbed her bruised knuckles, her own words echoing through her mind. *If he can stop loving me, who can't?*

Once, even acknowledging that fear would have destroyed her completely. A part of her still couldn't believe she'd actually said the words aloud.

But her confession hadn't hurt. It hadn't destroyed her. If anything, it felt like she had broken free.

Analia looked up at Ethelind, reading the challenge in her eyes. "I think it could be the easiest thing in the world."

Ethelind clasped her hands. "Will you see him, then?"

Analia nodded.

"Thank the Crystal." Ethelind turned toward the back door. "Aaron!"

Analia's chair squeaked as she jerked to her feet.

The back door swung open.

"I do hope you realize the volume of your bellow doesn't impact the speed with which I arrive—"

Aaron stepped inside. Immediately spotting Analia, he recoiled, his shoulders hitting the doorframe. Analia's heart thundered in her ears.

"Why?" Aaron demanded, wheeling on Ethelind.

"Why won't you come faster?" Ethelind asked. "What an excellent question."

"Why didn't you tell me she'd be here?"

"I didn't tell her you would be here, either."

Analia couldn't move as Ethelind strode toward Aaron, patting his chest. "I've become bored of being a stomping ground for your squabble. Talk, leave, make up, stop pestering me. And Analia?"

Ethelind turned, completely ignoring Aaron as he tried to protest. She pulled something from her robes and tossed it toward Analia, who reflexively caught it. The disk from her trial?

"Why?" Analia asked, looking up at Ethelind.

The warrior queen gave her a small smile. "Because you passed."

Those words seemed to expand in Analia's chest.

"I was never told what the purpose of the disk was outside of the trial," Ethelind went on, "but now that Aaron has told me of Surce's issues decoding the scrolls, I have to assume it somehow plays a role." Ethelind stepped around Aaron to open the door. "I expect you two to be gone by the time I return."

With that, she swung the door shut with a decisive clunk.

Analia and Aaron were left in the sudden quiet, the wide expanse of space stretching between them like a ward line.

"I didn't know she would do that," Aaron finally said, running his hand through his hair.

"I know," Analia said.

"I'm sorry."

"I know."

Aaron shifted his weight, still lingering by the door. Analia watched him from behind the desk, not sure if she wanted to look away or drink in his features. When was the last time they'd been apart for so long?

"Why did you come, Aaron?" she asked, not meanly.

"First, to apologize. But also…" He dropped his eyes to his hands. "I knew you must have countless questions. And I wanted to offer answers."

"All of them?"

Aaron nodded. Analia didn't know how to feel about that. She moved to the window, resting her fingertips against the chilly glass.

The snowy mountain stretched out before her, its icy peaks sparkling in the sunlight.

It would be so easy to stay here. She knew if she told Aaron to leave, he respected her enough to do so without protest. Which meant it was completely up to her.

"You tell me everything," she said, finally turning to face him, "and I'll tell you my choice."

Aaron looked slightly taken aback. Recovering quickly, he met her gaze, giving her a single nod.

"So," he said, coming forward and offering his hand. "Shall we go then?"

Analia nodded. She took his hand. And Aaron whispered a warning as he pulled her into the shadows.

Chapter 67

Aaron always wondered how he would feel when he finally showed Analia the tapestries. But he never anticipated the feeling of peace as he stepped out of the shadows into Surce's studio, Analia's hand in his.

He knew this was what he had to do. Not because Analia had already seen, not because of his promise, but because he wanted to. Even as he took in every secret he had, laid out on the walls in unnerving detail, he knew. It was time. He was ready.

"I promise," he said, "this is every single one. Even the ones I didn't know about before."

Analia nodded. She released his hand, moving to examine the closest collection of tapestries.

"There are so many," she murmured, but she didn't sound angry.

Aaron decided to take that as encouragement. He sat down on the bench, giving himself a moment to find the most coherent way through his story.

Finally, he began.

"I told you that Talitha established the Human Kingdom as a way to end the Blessed-Human Civil War. What I didn't tell you were the contingencies of that agreement."

Analia glanced at him, but she didn't interrupt.

"We can go over them all at another time if you wish. What's relevant is Talitha's neighboring base would only hold a few people at a time, enabling the humans to be free from the Blessed as much as possible. The agreement remained uncontested for millennia, until my father jumped everyone he could from the Star Kingdom here during the Shattering War.

"As you can imagine, the humans were furious. They said a few Blessed did not encapsulate an entire kingdom, and thus we were breaking our bargain. I have no idea how Ethelind maintained peace for so long. But after twenty-two years of negotiations, the humans declared our time was up. And with nowhere else to go, there was only one option: war.

"At this time, Branten, Mor, and I were freshly released from the Underground. I had just started tapping into my magic once more, and consequently, I was devastating on the battlefield. I must have killed hundreds on my own. Stopping their hearts, rotting their lungs, draining their life forces. And my magic never waned. I was naive enough to think I had it under control, but Branten and Mor knew the truth.

"They tried to caution me numerous times, going so far as to corner me in the command tent. They told me if I wasn't careful, I would lose myself in my magic. What they didn't know was I already had.

"My magic has always been powerful. But after over a decade of suppressing it and not even half that time learning to wield it? I'm just grateful that Branten and Mor read my temper and backed off as quickly as they did that day. Because the truth was, no one could have stopped me at that point. I had finally unleashed my magic to protect my home, and I was completely at its mercy. Until the day I found myself surrounded on the battlefield, and I didn't hesitate to unleash my magic.

"The next few moments were a blur. When my magic finally cleared and my senses faded back in, I was the only person left standing in a ring of bodies. And not all of them were enemies."

Analia froze beside a tapestry of silver light and bloody boots. Aaron's stomach churned, but he went on.

"I don't know if it was the grief or shock, but I finally slammed my magic back down and fell to my knees. Eventually, Branten and Mor found me and knelt with me in the center of my carnage. But all I could think was 'What have I done?'

"I didn't speak for three days after that. The only reason I *did* say anything was because the war wasn't over yet, and I knew my people still needed me. So, I returned to the battlefield, my magic carefully locked away. But my fear of losing control again caused me to hesitate. And that's what eventually enabled the humans to capture me."

Aaron couldn't bring himself to look at the tapestry of his mangled back that Analia had moved to. "My time in the human camp was long and bloody. They knew by killing me they would save a great deal of their men, but I was also the Prince of Starlight. I was valuable. So, they shackled me with damper cuffs and left me to rot at the post. Whips, burning pokers, broken bones. I was told I was gone for two weeks, but I couldn't tell you if that was true or not. All I knew was the pain. And that was when Laness showed up.

"Despite her own impending death, she chattered at me incessantly. She refused to stop until I finally responded, at which point she would launch into a new conversation. She was infuriating, and she saved my life.

"The day they came to execute Laness, she fought like a demon. She barely managed to steal the key and unlock one of my cuffs, but I was able to do the rest. In the confusion caused by the flash of my returning magic, I grabbed Laness and shadowjumped back to our command tent. And the last thing I remember is hearing my mother's scream."

Aaron swallowed hard. "I was unconscious for three days. When I finally woke up, Branten and Mor were there, and I immediately asked what happen. They told me that the war was over. They told me that we had won. We had won because my grief-stricken mother had finally taken to the battlefield to avenge the last piece of family she had left, not just ending the war but her life. That had been two days before I woke. And all I wanted to do was storm the Human Kingdom and set my magic free, not stopping until every human was dead because no one knew who planted the sword between my mom's shoulder blades. But of course, Ethelind stopped me.

"She told me that the battle was over. If my mom's sacrifice was going to mean anything, we had to try for peace. And I... I don't remember much of what happened after that. It's all just a blur of screaming and sex and sobbing and silence. So much silence. I don't know when it crept over me, but I know it took everything away in its wake.

"My family tried so hard to help me through that time, and I told you how I thought Liss had finally burned the numbness away. Yet, I don't think it truly faded until I met Surce. That woman took one look at me, and before I could even untie her from the stake, she said she had a tapestry for me. And long story short, it was of you. Dark and fierce and heartbroken, but alive. You know it as the tapestry of your wedding night. But I... I know it as my lifeline.

"That tapestry is what I imagined as I slowly mastered my magic. It's what I clung to when I thought the grief would destroy me. Because I knew from the look on your face you were just as broken as I was. But you were still fighting. And you kept showing up in Surce's tapestries."

Aaron finally lifted his gaze, finding Analia had moved to the tapestry of her wedding night, her fingertips resting against her woven cheek.

"You asked me," he said, "if I orchestrated them, and I swear to you on the Crystal, the gods, and my family's graves that I did not. Most of the time, I didn't recognize them until they were already happening. Regardless, when Surce wove the tapestry of the scroll and we realized it was in Sun, I immediately volunteered to retrieve it. Not just for my people, but also out of the hope that somehow, I could find you. And when I did, you were nothing like what I was expecting.

"You were so... sad. You were curling in on yourself the same way I had. But then you verbally scorched me and marched away. And fuck if you didn't give me hope in that moment."

Analia let out something that could have been a laugh.

"When we were in Sun, I told myself I was only drawn to you because of the tapestries. I was infatuated with the person I'd imagined, and you were betrothed so I had to let it go. Especially since I didn't realize that first tapestry was of your wedding night until I saw your dress. Regardless, that didn't stop me from looking for every reason to talk to you, be around you, learn who you really are. And when you smiled at me for the first time?"

Aaron tipped back his head with a grin. "I knew I was playing a dangerous game. I just didn't realize how badly I was losing. Not until I saw Pryanth's hand branded across your cheek. And when I saw what the Devourist did to you? Anna, I almost ripped off my damper and killed the thing, consequences be damned. And that was when I knew I had gotten too close. I needed to pull away, fast.

"But when I found you lying motionless at Deardryn's feet in that temple? When you lifted your head to look at me? I knew I hadn't been sent to the Sun Kingdom to find the scroll. I had been sent to find you.

"Yet, the last thing I wanted was to be one more thing you had to deal with, so I left you in Ash without protest. And part of me was relieved. I'd already lost everything: my family, my kingdom, my reputation. I'd learned to live with that, but I was terrified of that happening to you. Especially if you didn't want it.

"So, I jumped back to my sitting room where everyone was waiting. And I immediately fell to my knees. Not because of the magic I'd used, but because I'd finally found you, the woman in the tapestries, and I'd let you go. And before I could speak, Laness shook me by the shoulders and yelled I was an idiot.

"For the next eight weeks, she constantly buzzed around me, feeding me updates, begging me to just go get you already. Every time, I told her you had the bracelet and would call when you were ready. But that didn't stop me from missing you every second you were gone.

"On your coronation day, I was the one that sought Laness out. And the moment she said you called for me, I was gone. I almost blurted everything to you the moment you hugged me. But the only thing I wanted more than you was for you to have the freedom to choose what makes you happy. I thought if you'd known about the tapestries, you would feel an obligation to fate, the gods, the Crystal—maybe even me. So, I promised myself I would tell you after.

"In the meantime, I tried to show you as much as I could. My power, my darkness, my danger. But every time, you stayed."

Aaron shook his head. "I tried to stay away, and I couldn't. I tried to just be your friend, and I couldn't. I tried not to love you, and I couldn't."

Analia finally turned to look at him, her lips parted. Aaron met her gaze.

"I won't lie and tell you my intentions have been purely selfless," he said. "We both know I wanted to ensure you were choosing me, not fate. But I wanted you to have that same security.

"You have endured so much heartbreak, Analia. Heartbreak you did nothing to deserve. All I wanted was for you to know what it feels like to live without fear.

"I wanted you to believe me when I say I choose you. I wanted you to trust that your heart will always be safe with me. I wanted you to have no reason to doubt when I finally told you how deeply, unshakably I love you.

"At some point, I lost track of what truly matters, which is what you want for yourself. All I know is you are my hope, Analia. I have spent a lifetime waiting for you, and I would wait another if that's what it took to have even a fraction of the time we've shared. And I swear to you, that is everything."

Aaron sat back on the bench, letting her know he was finally done. He'd expected it to be hard to tell that story, painful even. But he felt oddly weightless as those final secrets lifted from his shoulders. Now, all there was left to do was wait.

For a long time, Analia remained quiet. She turned to the tapestry of their burning sticks, trailing her finger along the triangle. Aaron was just starting to think she might not say anything at all when she finally spoke.

"When I went to the DovenU, I thought I was angry—and I was. But that wasn't what I felt when I first saw the tapestries. I was... afraid. I was afraid because almost every relationship I've had where love is *expected*..."

"Hasn't ended well," Aaron finished.

Analia's fingers curled around her pin. "I ran because I knew you couldn't just break my heart; you could destroy me."

"Never," Aaron whispered.

"I knew you would say that, too. But there was still me. My fear. And what if I inadvertently broke us anyway?"

Aaron's hands gripped the bench. "What does that mean?"

"It means," Analia said, turning to face him, "I have a choice. And I'm choosing to be happy."

Aaron could have sworn his heart stopped as she finally came toward him.

"It means I love how you care so deeply for your people. I love how unwavering your faith is in those you care for, even when giving them something to hold on to. I even love how you can't keep your mouth shut to save your life."

Aaron breathed out a laugh as Analia perched on his lap.

"But most of all," she said, "I love the care and consideration you give to your secrets. I love that every time you offer one to me, I know just how much you trust me. The same way I trust you—which I never thought I'd be able to say about anyone.

"But you showed me time and time again how you are not just worthy of it, but I could trust that trust." Analia shook her head. "I don't even know if that makes sense."

"It does," Aaron said hoarsely.

"Good," Analia said, touching his chest. "Because the point is I choose you, too. You, your kingdom, your darkness. No matter the danger or consequences."

Analia looped her arms around his neck. "You're not alone anymore, Aaron. You know what that means?"

Aaron's lips parted, but no words came out. Somehow, he shook his head.

"It means you should kiss me," she said. "Because I love you, too."

Chapter 68

Analia looked up at Aaron from his lap, her arms around his neck, his expression uncomprehending as he stared at her.

For so long, she'd convinced herself this moment could only come when she was back in one piece. No jagged edges. No bloody scars.

But after a week with the DovenU, she was starting to think that maybe there was no such thing as healed. There was only healing. Healing and trying.

"It's real, Aaron," she said, fighting back a laugh. "I love you."

Slowly, he lifted his gaze, Analia fluttering her eyelashes as their eyes met.

Aaron's shoulders shook with something that could have been a laugh or a sob. "What am I going to do with you?" he asked.

Before she could respond, his arms were wrapping around her, guiding her to his chest as his lips found hers.

Where their first kiss had been burning, frantic, Aaron's mouth was now achingly sweet on hers.

It was an introduction. One where no secrets, no uncertainties, no ghosts from their pasts lingered between them. It was just them.

Analia threaded her fingers through his hair, letting out a sigh as his hand came to cradle the side of her face. *Right, right, right.*

She didn't know how long it was before he was pulling away. He ran his lips along her cheekbone, forming a heartbreakingly tender line. "Are you sure?" he asked.

"I feel like you should have asked that before kissing me."

Aaron chuckled and kissed her nose. "Smartass."

He looked down at her, offering his Phoenix Gate smile. No, not *Phoenix Gate—*

"I love you," he whispered.

Analia blinked hard, leaning her cheek against his chest. "And I love you."

Aaron's arms tightened around her. "Say it again."

"I love you."

"Again."

Analia didn't try to fight her laugh. "I love you. I love you I love you I love—"

Aaron's lips were back on hers, all restraint gone. This was all lips and tongues and clashing teeth. And it set her body ablaze.

Not from magic. Not from rage.

From him. Him as he hardened against her, her hands flashing across his chest, his shoulders, around to his back.

There was no more hesitation. This was solid. A certainty. A rightness that had her wrapping her legs around him, rocking against him until both of them were moaning.

"Fuck, Anna." Aaron tore away from her kiss, his pupils nearly swallowing the silver of his eyes as they darted around. "Not here."

Not here? Analia gasped for breath, struggling to keep up. By the time she spotted the tapestry over his shoulder and remembered where they were, Aaron's arms had slid down to her waist, his mouth hot and swollen against hers. "Fair warning."

Then, fingers digging into her hip, he pulled them into the shadows. And it was there in the darkness, nothing but his arms around her and his lips against hers that he whispered, "I love you, my shooting star."

Analia didn't have time to respond before they reemerged on Aaron's bed. He pressed three quick kisses to her mouth. Then, he nestled his face against her neck, breathing her in like she was the last threads of his control.

But Analia only felt a sudden stillness creep over her. It dampened the flush across her skin, her eyes drifting to the opposing wall.

It wasn't the terror that had once consumed her any time she thought of her wedding night. That bed, the bedframe, the forearm pressed against her throat. If anything, it was the gentle tap of fingertips against her awareness, still managing to whisper, *Remember this?*

"Anna?"

Analia blinked hard as Aaron pulled back. He let his arms fall to his sides, offering a sweet smile as their eyes met. "Hi."

Analia mouthed a hello.

"Are you all right?" he asked.

Analia nodded.

"Do you know it's all right if you're not?"

Another nod.

Aaron was quiet for a few moments, his eyes scanning over her face. "What do you want, my shooting star?" he asked softly.

Analia latched on to those words like an anchor.

Shooting star, not flame to his life. Silver eyes, not honey. His hands at his sides, offering instead of taking. *What do you want?*

Back in Surce's studio, her answer was this. No hesitation. But there was something about seeing this room, his bed, everything suddenly feeling real that had her—not changing her mind. Just feeling... stuck.

"Can I touch you?" she asked suddenly.

A shadow passed over Aaron's face, so quick she almost missed it. But he didn't hesitate. "Yes."

Analia's eyes darted down, but Aaron's hands remained at his sides, fingers absently tracing the duvet's pattern. Then, she reached for him.

Analia started with his face. She ran her fingers along his jaw, over to the curve of his cheekbone, down the straight slope of his nose.

Aaron watched her quietly as she traced the small, contented smile on his lips, remaining perfectly still as she moved down to his chin, his throat, those whispers stirring as she reached his tunic laces.

Analia paused. Aaron wiggled his eyebrows, surprising a tiny laugh out of her.

"May I?" she asked.

"Dear gods, please."

Analia's lips twitched, those whispers settling once more. With a soft tug, she undid his laces, something like anticipation glinting in his eyes as he helped her pull it off. But he didn't touch her as she guided him back on the bed.

Analia sat back, her knees on either side of him as she took in his bare torso. Pale, not tan. Muscled and toned, decorated with scars—nowhere near as many as his back.

Aaron. Safe.

"How did you get this?" she asked, her finger hovering above his chest as she traced a short, thin scar.

Aaron shifted beneath her, almost a squirm, but his voice remained nonchalant. "Branten."

"From the Underground?"

"More like two years ago when I tried to roll his drunken ass off my couch."

Analia laughed again, something finally relaxing in her chest. Something that had her flattening her hand above his chest, Aaron's nod of permission a bit too fast to be casual, her fingertips lightly touching down on the gap between his collarbones.

Aaron released a tiny breath. Analia ran her fingers up his collarbone, back down to his chest, his body warm and hard and smooth.

How long had she been wanting to touch him like this? No tunic, no jacket, no cloak. She traced a curved scar below his sternum, Aaron making a low, rumbling noise in his chest. But still, he did not move.

And Analia wanted to hear that sound again. She wanted to memorize every plane, every line and muscle. With her fingers. With her lips. With her tongue.

"Gods, Analia," Aaron breathed. "Who gave you permission to look at me like that?"

Analia slid her gaze up his stomach, his chest, sparks flickering in her blood as she spotted the flush in his cheeks. "Like what?"

"Like you're realizing touch isn't limited to your fingers."

Analia's heart skipped a beat. "Is that what you want?"

"I told you, Analia. You can do what you want with me. Lips, fingers, tongue—"

Aaron cut off in a curse as Analia leaned down and drew his nipple into her mouth. She flicked her tongue, Aaron squirming beneath her.

But his hands remained at his sides, fisting into the duvet. Waiting for permission. And Analia felt those whispers start to burn as she trailed her lips down his chest, tracing his rib with her tongue.

He tasted like salt. He felt like freedom. No sign of honey eyes or flashing tempers as she trailed her fingers down the taut muscles of his stomach. As he twisted his hands in the duvet, his eyes moving over her like he wanted to devour her image.

Aaron, Aaron, Aaron.

Analia's fingers slid lower, past his navel, down his stomach. She wanted this. She was ready. He was already so close to that low, rolling ache. She just had to shift a little bit, bring her hand a little lower.

And once again, she froze as her hand found his waistband.

Crystal strike it all, it was such a small flinch. But it was there.

"We can stop at any point," Aaron said softly. "I'm content just getting to look at you."

His hands clenched the duvet in a white-knuckle grip. He was shaking beneath her hands. He was hard as granite. And Analia knew with absolute certainty that if she gave the word, he would sit up, flash his Phoenix Gate smile, and they would go from there.

"Whatever you want, Analia," he promised.

Gods, those words weren't supposed to ache.

Analia pressed her cheek to his chest, taking a deep breath. Spice. The faint metallic scent of his magic. *Him.*

This was her choice. A choice that Pryanth had tried to take from her—in more ways than one. She had stopped him, but he had scarred her anyway.

And she had survived; had healed and rebuilt enough to reclaim this choice. One that, in the future, she might want or even need to say no to—which she knew Aaron wouldn't question.

But right now? Right now, she refused to let Pryanth take one more thing from her. Especially not Aaron.

Analia collected every last memory she had of her wedding night. Then, she let them burn in midnight flames.

This was not a prince's chamber. It was a king's.

Analia sat up. Before Aaron could speak, she took his hand, guiding it up and under her shirt.

"I want you," she said simply, letting her hand drop.

Aaron remained completely still: his hand resting between her rib cage, his eyes locking on hers. "Are you sure?" he asked, one final time.

When head, heart, and gut are aligned, that is when the path is clearest.

Analia felt the click from that question in every fiber of her being. "Yes."

"Thank the fucking Crystal." Aaron surged up, his mouth colliding with hers.

Aaron's kiss was devastating. It reached straight through her as his tongue swept into her mouth, finding those flickering sparks and igniting them into a blaze.

She didn't know how they managed to undress. But somehow, she was pulling him down on top of her, his hands sliding up her stomach to her breasts. Analia's nails dug into his back, his lips finding the spot on her neck that had her letting out a gasp.

"Fuck, Analia," he panted. He propped himself up on an elbow, his eyes moving down her face, the swell of her breasts, her stomach, the apex of her thighs, all the way down to her toes and up again. "Are you a punishment or a reward?"

Analia shifted her hips, her own gaze dragging up the considerable length of him. "Depends who's asking."

Aaron's chuckle was dark and wicked. "Good answer."

He ducked his head, drawing her nipple into his mouth. Analia's back arched, her mind bathed in flames. The flames of a desire that had been building and tempered and building for weeks—*months*. Scorching away any thoughts of taking things slow, savoring this moment.

They had time for that later. They had a lifetime. Now... now she wanted him unleashed.

Analia circled her hips against him. "Aaron, please."

Aaron shuddered, not needing to be asked twice. He dragged his lips down her ribs, her stomach.

He sat back between her thighs, his hands pushing them wider, wider, wider.

Analia thought she might unravel right there as his gaze dragged down her center, then lifted to hers. "Yes?"

"Yes," she breathed.

Aaron ducked his head. And the first stroke of his tongue had her world crack down the center.

There was no soft, teasing touches. There was just the brutal heat of his mouth, the caress of his tongue as he licked and kissed his way up her core. Analia writhed against him, Aaron's hand flattening against her stomach.

Flames rose up under her skin. Higher, higher, so high that once, she would have been terrified.

But Analia wasn't afraid. Not as his lips closed around her clit. And she couldn't have stopped those flames from erupting if she wanted as he gave a long, soft suck.

Analia cried out as the release blazed through her. Hot, relentless, all-consuming.

But Aaron wasn't done yet. He worked her in long, devastating strokes, Analia arching off the bed as she let out something between a moan and a plea.

She needed *him. Now.*

Aaron slid his tongue inside her. Analia plunged her fingers into his hair, her fist coiling tight, Aaron flicking his tongue over her clit in retaliation. And those flames were consuming her once more as her body tightened, threatened to shudder apart—gods, punishment or reward.

Analia slumped back against the bed, breathing hard. Nowhere near done as Aaron sat up, eyes wide and dark and blazing.

"Gods, Analia." He reached out, running a shaking knuckle along her cheek, the other hand running up his cock. "I need, I—please, I need—"

Analia didn't let him finish before she was reaching for him. Fingertips skimming down his cock, coiling around to give a long, hard pump. Aaron swore, rocking in her hand.

Gods, yes. Inside her. *Now.*

She guided him to her entrance, slick with desire. But Aaron had other ideas. He pulled her legs up over his shoulders, lifting her hips. And Analia's mind, her body, her very being all funneled down into that spot as he slid in to the hilt, both of them crying out.

"All right?" he asked, his chest heaving.

Analia rolled her hips, testing the fullness. "Aaron, please."

Aaron released a harsh breath. He withdrew slightly, his hips flexing in a shallow thrust. He watched her carefully with each thrust, moving a little farther, a little deeper each time. Holding on to that last shred of control. For her.

Analia reached up, her own heart full as she rested her palm over his. "Yes."

Aaron's expression rippled, a shooting star set free. And finally—*finally*—*his control snapped.*

Analia was beyond thoughts. Beyond words. Beyond any sense as Aaron found his rhythm. Fast. Deep. Hers.

He was hers as she ran her fingers along his face, his chest, anywhere she could reach.

Her choice. Her love. Her fate. Her friend.

He was *right.*

"I love you," he whispered. And it was her undoing.

Analia tightened her muscles around him, hard as she could.

Aaron shouted her name, his body going rigid as he came. And the embers of Analia's world—her old, rotting, blackened world—finally broke apart to reveal the flames at their core. They blazed through her as she followed him over the edge, destroying, cleansing, forming something new.

Not ashes to rise from, but threads. Weaving between their hearts, their souls. Looping into the final knot of their tapestry.

Not of a broken king and grieving princess. Not even a shooting star.

It was a constellation. A torch. It was—he was—*they were*—something to hold onto.

Finally, the two fell still. Aaron gently lowered her legs from his shoulders, slumping forward to press his face to her neck.

Analia ran her hand down the raised scars on his back. Soft. Soothing as she closed her eyes, savoring the heat and weight of him.

She didn't know how much time had passed when Aaron started to pull away.

"Hey." Analia caught his face in her hands, forcing him to pause, to look at her. "Worth it."

Then, she kissed him. Kissed him for every day they'd been apart. Kissed him for every decade he'd had to wait and wonder. Kissed him until every shadow from their pasts had finally drifted away.

Aaron was the first to pull away. He wiped his eyes, letting out a broken little laugh as she tried to tug him back down. He kissed her cheek, her chin, the corner of her mouth. Then, he finally rolled away, his arms coming around her as he nestled her against his chest.

Analia looked up into his face. His silver eyes, bright as the stars that had watched over her on her turret. The stars that had been her only company after her uncle's death. The stars they had looked up at on a snowy evening, searching for something greater than a shooting star.

"My constellation."

Chapter 69

"I've been trying to figure out the moment I fell in love with you," Aaron said.

He leaned against the kitchen island, watching Analia flip eggs in a sizzling pan. Apparently, Mor had been teaching her how to cook in his spare time. He'd also taught her not to let Aaron touch anything, but he didn't mind.

It had been a long time before either of them fell asleep the night before, transitioning from talking to kissing to moaning like steps in a dance. When Aaron finally closed his eyes, he was terrified he would discover it had all been a dream.

But he'd woken up to find her head resting against his chest. He'd already been inside her twice that morning, first when she pounced on him, then in the bathing room when he took her slow and deep and aching. He kept waiting for her to disappear, but she never did.

Somehow, this beautiful, incredible, mesmerizing woman was real. And she was his.

Analia asked, "Have you found your answer?"

Aaron blinked, his gaze having wandered down her black-and-silver nightgown. "I think it was the day we went to Selbi's apothecary. That was the first time I ever saw you stand up to Pryanth, which was reason enough. But the thought of you putting me in my place as well?"

Aaron tipped his head back with a smile.

"To be fair," Analia said, "I think there are plenty of people who would like to. You just don't stop talking long enough for them to do so."

Aaron laughed, "Oh, undoubtedly. But what truly gave me no chance was the passion in your eyes as you defended the orphans. All I could think about was you doing that for my kingdom."

Analia beamed as she twisted to pass him the teakettle. "I don't know if I have a specific moment," she said, turning back to the stove.

"Oh?" Aaron asked as he filled their mugs. "I suppose there are just too many to choose from."

Analia flicked a pinch of salt at him.

"I don't think I allowed myself to even consider it while in Sun," she said. "Even when I told you to go in Ash, I refused to believe it."

"Believe what?"

"That loving you was inevitable."

Aaron gripped his mug, not caring as the heated porcelain burned his fingers. "Gods, I love you."

Analia ducked her head, Aaron not even needing to see her flush to know it was there.

"Does that mean we've reached the part where I ask what this means?" she asked.

Aaron laughed under his breath. He stepped up behind her, sliding his arms around her waist. "What would you like it to mean?"

Analia hummed, pretending to consider. "Well," she said, "I think it means I get to move into your room because your bed is far bigger."

"Excellent choice," he agreed, resting his chin on her shoulder. "What else?"

"And I think it means I get to do this."

Analia turned in his arms, pressing a lingering kiss to his mouth. She started to pull away, but Aaron played chase, deepening their kiss until she was melting into him.

Gods, this was what he wanted. No secrets, no lies, no looming choice. Just this moment.

The peace. The bliss. He didn't even care when Analia accidentally brushed the back of his head with her hot spatula. He only let her go when the eggs made a menacing pop.

"I'll warn you," he said, slightly breathless as Analia turned back to the stove. "If you do that, there will be consequences."

"That better be a guarantee."

Aaron chuckled, nuzzling the side of her neck. "What else?"

"This ring," Analia said, raising her free hand.

Aaron frowned. "That ring feels tainted." He reached up, turning the gray moonstone ring around her finger. "If you want a ring, I can get you a new one."

"Not yet," Analia said, interlacing their fingers. "I want some time with you to myself. Not because of the Crystal or the laws or the tapestries. But because I choose you—"

Aaron barely let her get the words out. In one smooth movement, he spun her around and lifted her in his arms. Analia laughed, just managing to shove the pan off the stove before he carried her to the island.

Gods, he loved that sound. He loved those words.

I choose you.

Aaron sat her on the island, his hands skimming down the length of her as he slid to his knees. He was going to devour her. He was going to hear her scream, breakfast be damned.

Aaron kissed her ankle, her calf, the inside of her knee. His lips moved up the curve of her thigh. Just as there came a hammering on his front door.

Aaron swore under his breath.

Analia laughed, loosely wrapping her legs around his shoulders. "You should probably check that."

Aaron was thoroughly tempted to disagree. Instead, he reluctantly disentangled himself and headed for the door, summoning a look of defeat as he swung it open.

Branten, Mor, Laness, and Surce clustered together on the other side. As soon as they saw him, their expressions fell.

"No," Branten said, disbelieving. "Don't tell me..."

Aaron hung his head. He stepped aside, his family crowding into the entryway in a tangle of questions.

It took them a few moments to register the sizzling coming from the kitchen. Then, they surged forward, voices coming to an abrupt halt as they froze in the doorway.

Over Laness's head, Aaron saw Analia wave as she assembled her plates. Their heads whipped back and forth between her and Aaron several times. Finally, Branten whirled and jabbed a finger at Aaron, "You fucking bastard!"

Aaron smirked, Laness and Branten erupting into cheers.

Analia turned to him, hands on her hips. "What did you do?"

"My shooting star," Aaron crooned, stepping through the crowd, "how you accuse me."

He lifted her chin, and the cheers quickly turned to groans as he kissed her.

"Oh gods," Branten said. "Are we going to have to deal with that now?"

"Look at them," said Laness, disgusted. "They're practically glowing."

But when Aaron pulled back, they were beaming. Analia leaned around him to look at them, her cheeks flushed. "I guess this means you four are stuck with me now."

Mor, Branten, Laness, and Surce all exchanged a look.

"What?" Analia asked.

"We're trying to figure out who owes who," Laness confided.

"I said it would take them three months," Surce said.

"And we all said you weren't allowed to bet because of your tapestries," Branten retorted.

"You bet on us?" Aaron asked.

"I think Mor was technically closest," Laness mused.

"Oh really?" Aaron turned to his brother, who took a step back and raised his hands.

"We were also," he said loudly, "trying to figure out if we call Analia Her Majesty now."

Analia's eyes widened. "Oh gods, no titles, we're not even—I'm not—"

"We can talk about legality another time," Aaron said, fighting back a laugh as he touched the small of her back. "For now, it's breakfast time—although you cockblockers can fend for yourselves."

Laness and Branten snickered. Mor came forward to take Analia's place at the stove, and the rest of them gathered around the island in a tangle of voices and questions and laughter.

For once, Aaron remained mostly quiet, just allowing himself to soak in the noise. This was all he ever wanted. And somehow, it was his.

It wasn't until their plates were cleared that Aaron brought himself to redirect.

"You all should know," he said, "it wasn't just Analia that returned from the DovenU. Turns out, Ethelind had a gift."

The rest of the table cast Analia a quick look.

"It's all right," she said. "I figured the secret out on my own."

"Of course you did," said Mor fondly.

"Since when does Grandma Ethy give out gifts?" Branten demanded, offended.

Aaron replied, "Since Analia earned this one." He pulled the decoder from his pocket and slid it to Surce. "I believe this should help you immensely with the scroll."

Surce's eyes gleamed. She turned over the disk with long, nibble fingers, "What does this do?"

"According to Ethelind," Aaron said, "it should help you decode the scroll."

"Although you should know we have no idea how it works," Analia added.

Surce rolled the disk between her fingers, a cat playing with its prey. "I'll learn."

"I still don't know why you didn't just ask Mor to do this," Analia said. She stood behind Aaron's bedroom door, holding it open for him as he pushed her wardrobe through.

"Now where would be the fun in that?" he grunted.

Analia rolled her eyes. She maneuvered around the door to help him push, but just like every other time, he waved her off. With one last shove, he maneuvered the wardrobe into the empty space beside his own.

"And with that," he said, looking back with a smile, "you're home."

Analia felt his words settle in her heart. She stepped into his arms, resting her head against his chest. "I love you."

"And I you." Aaron kissed the side of her head. For a few moments, he was quiet. Then, he brought his lips to her ear, "You should know I almost certainly destroyed all semblance of organization in your wardrobe."

Analia laughed. She pulled away and opened the wardrobe, taking in the scattered piles of clothing and tangled hangers.

"You're helping me," she informed him.

"I would love nothing more."

Analia grabbed the closest pile and carried it to their bed, Aaron following a step behind.

"You know," she said as they folded, "we haven't discussed the finer points of what this means."

"This?" Aaron asked innocently.

Analia whacked him with a tunic. Aaron caught it, a wicked grin on his face as he pulled her into a kiss.

She would never get used to this. The ice and flames Aaron sent skittering across her skin; the way she could drown in every kiss and touch and still starve for more.

"You see?" Aaron asked, finally breaking away. "There are many 'thises' to consider. It's completely understandable I was confused."

"Is that so?" Analia let him guide her back against the bed, her fingers tangling in the front of his shirt. "Just how many, exactly?"

"Well, there's this."

Aaron leaned in once more, his kiss deep, luxurious. She wrapped her legs around him, pulling him closer, heat spreading across her skin as he hardened against her.

But Aaron broke away, softly clicking his tongue. "My impatient shooting star." He shifted onto his side, his arms sliding under and around her as he pulled her back against him. "I thought you wanted to know what the other 'thises' are."

He ran his lips along her neck in a soft, lazy caress, his voice dropping to a croon. "Don't you want to know?"

Crystal spare her, they were playing *this* game. Analia lifted her chin, offering more of her neck. But Aaron only slid his hand down her stomach, his fingers running along the hem of her shirt.

"I don't hear an answer, Analia." He nipped her ear.

Analia's hips jerked, her voice coming out as a gasp. "Yes."

Aaron chuckled. The sound vibrated through his chest and into her bones; a soft and wicked sound that had her melting into him.

"Good," he murmured. "Because I've always been a fan of this."

His hand slipped beneath her shirt. Analia arched into his touch as he circled her peaked nipple, the scrape of his calluses dragging a moan from her lips.

Not enough. Nowhere near enough.

But Aaron's movements remained slow, unhurried as he explored, his mouth a breath away from her neck. "So responsive." He ran a knuckle along the curve of her breast. "So greedy." He brushed a kiss to the corner of her jaw. "Does that mean you like this 'this'?" His hand moved to her other breast, flicking her nipple.

Analia ground against him, a silent plea, Aaron letting out a hiss in return.

"Now why are you trying to ruin my fun?" he asked, tightening his arms around her, struggling to hold her still. "Shouldn't I get my turn?"

Analia momentarily stilled, her attention caught. "Your turn?"

"Oh, Analia," he purred, "don't tell me you've already forgotten."

He paused, making sure she remained still. Then, his hand resumed its exploring, his voice dropping to a whisper. "You straddling me. Trailing your hands, your mouth, over my skin." His hand wandered down to her stomach. "Tasting me. Taunting me. Taking my breath away with your resilience."

He circled her navel, Analia's breath hitching as his hand continued lower, lower—gods, lower.

"You didn't think I had forgotten?" he breathed. "That none of my 'thises' would include showing you just what you had done to me? That I wouldn't want to take my turn?"

His hand curled around her waistband. Considering. Toying with her.

Analia arched her hips, trying to force him lower, down to the building ache between her thighs. "Aaron, *please.*"

Aaron shuddered, from his name on her lips, her plea, she didn't know. She didn't care. Not as his hand slipped beneath her waistband, her muscles going taut as his fingers finally found her. He slid between her folds, his curse hot against her neck as he discovered the wetness waiting for him.

"Look at you," he said. "I might just start to think you like this 'this' as much as I do."

He dragged his finger up, Analia squirming as he idly circled. Teasing, brushing, never quite—

Analia cried out as he pressed down, the sensation lighting up her nerves like a beacon. *Right, right, right.*

Aaron smiled against her neck. "Tell me," he murmured, trailing his finger back down, "are there any more 'thises' I've forgotten?"

Analia's lips parted; her attention locked on his finger sliding down to her entrance. Pausing as if waiting for something. Infuriating enough that her mind remembered how to process his words, dragging up the memory of how they'd gotten there in the first place.

"What about being your queen?"

Aaron hummed in approval. "I believe that is up to you."

He slid his finger inside her, her head falling back against his shoulder with a moan.

"You should know," he said, his voice unsteady as he pumped in and out, "if you were to be queen, you would be queen of this kingdom. *Our* kingdom." His finger moved harder, deeper. "My equal."

He slid a second finger inside her, filling her until all there was—all she knew—was him. His fingers as she ground on his hand, his words, his offer.

For so long, she'd fought for that title in Ash. Not because she wanted it, not because her people wanted her, but because it was her right.

But this kingdom had welcomed her before her connection to Aaron. They'd cheered for her as she stood on that rooftop. They *accepted* her.

Aaron crooked his fingers, dragging them over that electric spot. Analia's hips bucked as she cried out, release shimmering around her like heat in a desert. She twisted her head, trying to capture his mouth with hers.

But Aaron was gone. His body sliding down hers, his hands shoving her leggings down, flattening her hips so she lay on her back. And then his fingers were joined by his mouth, his lips whispering against her core. "Cum for me, Your Majesty."

His lips sealed around her clit, his teeth scraping ever so slightly. And Analia was crying out, her hand fisting in his hair, release flashing over her and sending her awareness scattering apart.

But Aaron didn't stop. He pulled her harder against him, ravaging her core, building her up and up until she was plunging over the edge once more and all there was was love and light and lightning.

Analia slumped back against the pillows, her body trembling. Aaron finally pulled back. He kissed the inside of her thigh, his eyes moving up to hers as he brought his fingers to his mouth and sucked them clean.

Crystal fucking spare her.

Analia reached for him, but he was already moving back up beside her.

"I've been dreaming of that all morning," he murmured, nestling her against him once more.

Analia closed her eyes, lifting her chin as his lips found hers. Soft. Sweet. Tasting of her pleasure as his tongue brushed hers.

Analia's fingers skimmed down his chest, his stomach. "Does that mean I get to do what I've been dreaming about?"

She dragged her palm up the hard length of him, loving the way she could feel his groan against her mouth. She reached for his laces. Just as he went completely rigid.

Analia pulled back, "Did I—"

"No," Aaron said quickly, pulling her back to him. But all color had drained from his face.

Ice trickled down Analia's spine. "What's wrong?"

Aaron brought his hand up, revealing his enka bracelet. "It's Laness," he said, his lips barely moving. "They're in trouble. All of them."

Chapter 70

Ember paced the length of her chamber in the Ash Castle, Cadmus quietly tracking her from a nearby armchair.

The week following their descent into Mt. Vasolus had passed in a blur. Cadmus had somehow gathered enough magic to jump them back to the Council Chamber, barely gasping out a warning to the councilmen about the approaching sun dragons before losing consciousness. In the ensuing chaos, Ember was shoved into Cadmus's chambers and told to keep an eye on him. Even after he'd fully recovered, he'd asked her to stay put in the castle where it was safe.

It was there that Ember heard pieces of the battle raging outside the castle gates. How Sun had used their dragons to fly deep into Ash Kingdom territory. How Ash forces managed to box them in, but after Sun reinforcements used the mountain range to sneak up behind them, the Sun army was on the move once more.

She knew there was more to the story. But those details were lost in the haze of her devinroot withdrawal.

It hadn't been her idea. But seeing as she was trapped in Cadmus's chambers, and her devinroot—which she technically wasn't supposed to have in the first place—was locked in the apothecary?

The first few days had been the worst: uncontrollable tremors, racing thoughts, nightmares every time she closed her eyes. It was no wonder she wasn't supposed to use the plant. Even seven days in, she felt like her bones had become brittle, her legs threatening to collapse beneath her weight.

"Em, are you sure you're all right?" Cadmus asked from his chair, not for the first time.

"I told you, I'm fine."

Ember's legs tingled. She staggered into the wall, Cadmus immediately rising to help. He guided her down on the edge of his bed, his hands tightening on her arms as she tried not to shake.

"Em, how bad is that pl—"

"It's nothing," Ember snapped, her eyes darting. "I was already weaning myself off, it's honestly not that bad anymore."

Cadmus bit his lip. Ember braced herself for his response, but he only turned to the guards that had been stationed in his chambers and ordered them to fetch Ember some water.

Ember perked up. But only one of the two guards slipped out the door, leaving her to stifle a groan.

After Cadmus had told the council about Mt. Vasolus, they had decided to leave two guards with him at all times. Not just for protection in case Sun breached the castle, but also because they had no idea what Cadmus might do with his mark. Cadmus had begrudgingly agreed, and at first, so had Ember.

But now, those guards also prevented her from leaving to retrieve her enka bracelet from the apothecary. Meaning she had no way of telling Analia what was going on.

Ember was just considering distracting the guard so Cadmus could shadowjump to get it when someone knocked on the door. Raising a brow, Cadmus moved to open the door, his body blocking the visitor from view.

The two exchanged a few quick, hushed words, Ember's fuzzy mind barely paying attention. Something about the square, Spark Street, Sun soldiers—wait.

Ember shoved to her feet, her legs shaking. Seemingly sensing her approach, Cadmus backed up, closing the door with one hand and steadying her with the other.

"You can't let them take Spark Street," Ember said, gripping his arm. "If they destroy the apothecary, we lose the bracelet."

"I know," Cadmus soothed. "That's why I'm going."

The remaining guard straightened. "Your Majesty—"

"My kingdom is under attack," Cadmus said, crossing to his armoire and grabbing his boots. "We tried the council's way and it's not working. I have to go."

"But I've been ordered—"

"You've been ordered by the council. Now, you're being ordered by your king. Stand down."

Cadmus stood from tying his boots, his expression hard. The guard glanced rapidly between Cadmus and Ember—the latter of whom had retreated to sit on a nearby chair. Finding no way to protest, he bowed his head. "May I at least accompany you in the field, Your Majesty?"

Cadmus nodded. He flexed his fingers, golden sparks briefly flickering across his fingertips. Then, he crossed the room, coming to lightly grip Ember's shoulders.

"Stay here, please," he said, his voice softening. "Don't get caught up in this."

Ember's mind was struggling to keep up with what "this" even was. But she knew one thing for sure.

"Cadmus, you have to get the bracelet," she said. "We have to tell her what's happening."

"I'll try," he said, "I promise, I'll try. But Em, there's nothing she can do. My priority is protecting the kingdom. You have to understand that."

Ember ran her tongue along her dry mouth, tasting something bitter. Still, she nodded.

"Thank you," Cadmus sighed, relieved.

He gave her shoulders a quick squeeze. Then, he retreated back through the room, the guard coming forward to meet him. Resting his hand on the guard's shoulder, Cadmus cast Ember one final look. But he didn't say a word as the two faded into the shadows.

For a few moments, Ember sat quietly in the empty room, Cadmus's sudden absence forming an ache in her chest. It would be so easy to just stay where she was, just as she'd promised. But she knew that wasn't an option.

Sending Cadmus a silent apology, she rose to her feet and slipped out the door.

Ember moved down the corridor on shaky legs. She had to do this. This was still Analia's home; she deserved to know. She deserved the option to fight for it if she wished—especially since she had a Rosala-forsaken Star Royal on her side.

Reaching the door she was looking for, Ember took a moment to lean against the wall and catch her breath. She'd barely knocked when the door flew open, Lucilla's golden head popping out of the opening. "What can I do?"

As it turned out, Lucilla was only just learning how to shadowjump. She also had never been inside the apothecary—which Ember only found out after telling Lucilla her plan. As a result, Lucilla jumped them two streets down from the apothecary. And not two feet behind a Sun soldier fighting off three Ash soldiers at once.

Ember clapped a hand over Lucilla's mouth. She dragged Lucilla into a nearby alleyway and down behind a dumpster, her body no longer shaking from just withdrawal.

The entire square had been turned into a battlefield. All around, there came the clang of sword-on-sword, nearly drowned out by yells and screams—Rosala spare her, they weren't just from soldiers. Magic thrummed through the air, hard enough her teeth vibrated.

How could she have brought a twelve-year-old here? Royal magic or not, she shouldn't have to see this.

Blood stained the snowy streets. One of the nearby Sun men stabbed through an Ash soldier's throat with his spear and kicked her away. The smell of burning flesh and screams filled the air as the Ash Royals joined the battle deeper in the square.

"Lucilla," Ember said, her body flashing between hot and cold. "Lucilla, we have to go back."

"I don't have enough magic to jump," she said.

Ember expected her face to be stark with panic, but her blue eyes were hard and focused.

"We'll just have to try and sneak back to the castle then."

"But we can make it to the apothecary," Lucilla said, leaning out beyond the dumpster to peer down their alley. "The side roads are clear; we just have to sneak around—"

Ember pulled Lucilla back, a stray arrow whizzing past where her head had been a moment earlier.

"Lucilla," Ember tried again, "it's not safe for either of us. Cadmus said he'd get the bracelet."

"You said he said he would *try*," Lucilla countered.

The Sun soldier dodged a downward cut, smacking the butt of his spear into one Ash soldier and skewering the other.

"If we have to run," Lucilla said, "we might as well get the bracelet."

The two soldiers exchanged a flurry of blows. As skilled as the Ash soldier was, she was no match for the deadly golden blur backing her toward a nearby building. As soon as she was down, there would be no stopping the Sun soldier from finding their hiding spot.

Ember took a single moment to think. Then, she grabbed Lucilla's hand, "Let's go."

Staying low, the two darted out from behind the dumpster. They had just rounded a building when there came a gurgling scream.

"Don't look back," Ember panted, squeezing Lucilla's hand as her head turned. "There's nothing you can do for her. Keep moving."

Lucilla pressed her lips together, but her pace didn't falter. Ember, however, could barely stay on her feet, the ground seeming to tilt and spin beneath her.

But she couldn't slow down, couldn't lose her footing. That Sun soldier was on the move, and there was no telling which way he'd gone.

"It will be faster if we cross the main street here," Lucilla panted. "The alleyways start to curve too much up ahead."

"I know," Ember said. "And it will be even faster if we cut through the marketplace."

"I thought we needed to stay under cover."

"I thought you could shadowjump us straight to the apothecary."

Ignoring Lucilla's grumbled response, Ember pulled her to a stop a few feet from the end of the alleyway. She peeked around the corner, ears pricked for any sound of movement. But the street was empty, the sound of fighting still a little ways in the distance.

"Now," Ember hissed.

The two darted across the street and into the abandoned marketplace. Half of the support poles holding up the green canvas had become dislodged by the snow and wind, causing the tarp to shift and sag precariously above their heads.

Ember and Lucilla kept low as they darted between wooden racks, but there came no sound of pursuit.

Three more racks and they would see the apothecary. Two more and they'd be free. One more and—

"Hey!"

Ember and Lucilla whirled at the edge of the marketplace. The Sun guard from before charged through the racks toward them, his fighting leathers stained with gore, his spear already drawn. He was moving too fast.

"On your left!" Lucilla screamed.

The soldier's eyes widened. He turned instinctively, bashing his shin on a rack. He swore, and Ember launched into movement. She grabbed the nearest support pole and pulled as hard as she could.

The pole ripped free from the snow, the force strong enough to tug the remaining dislodged poles with it. All around, there came the sound of collapsing poles, the Sun soldier crying out in alarm as he was trapped under the snow-weighted fabric.

"Move!" Ember said, pushing Lucilla forward.

They crossed a final street, the sound of the Sun soldier thrashing and cursing chasing after them. But they reached the apothecary, mercilessly untouched, the myriad of plants standing tall in the massive windows.

Ember grabbed the knob and pulled herself to a stop. She just had to get inside, grab her bracelet from her back room, and then shadowjump out of there. But something was wrong. She was pulling on the door, and nothing was happening.

"Hurry!" Lucilla said.

Rosala spare her.

"Another Sun soldier's coming!" Lucilla cried.

"It's locked," Ember moaned.

The captured Sun soldier yelled to his friend. It was only a matter of time before he was free, and then there would be two of them—and Rosala spare her, she needed to think.

"Dane keeps the spare key around back," Ember said. "I can grab it and then—"

Footsteps pounded toward them.

"Go," Lucilla said. "I can distract them."

Ember started to protest, but Lucilla ducked out of her grip and darted straight toward the approaching Sun soldiers. She raised her arms, calling out a challenge. Then, she sent a jet of golden flames toward the Sun soldiers, who dove out of the way.

Lucilla darted around them and back toward the marketplace, sending taunting whips of fire behind her. She was either the bravest little girl Ember had ever met, or the most reckless. Regardless, she couldn't risk her getting hurt.

Ember hurried around the apothecary, bracing her hand on the exterior for support. She grabbed the key hidden behind the loose window frame. Then, she returned to the door, fingers fumbling the key, just needing to hear the click as the lock disengaged—yes!

Ember flung open the door.

"Where do you think you're going?"

A hand grabbed Ember by the back of her jacket—the one day she wasn't wearing her healer robes.

If she'd been thinking straight, she might have turned to show him her healer markings. If her mind hadn't been scattered from withdrawal, she might have remembered the healers were a neutral party; she was protected.

Instead, Ember screamed. Her voice filled the shop, magic erupting from her body in a single, terrified wave.

The plants on the window doubled, tripled, quadrupled in size. Vines and leaves and stems snapped out to grab the Sun soldier, the man shrieking as he was ripped away.

Ember fell to her knees. Too much magic. Not enough energy. Nowhere near enough control. But she had to get that bracelet.

Ember staggered to her feet, tripping over her own plants as they coiled across the floor. She shoved forward, thorns scratching her skin, vines tightening around her limbs. She just needed to reach her back room.

Behind her, there came a metallic rasp as the Sun soldier unsheathed his sword. She glanced back to see him struggling to maneuver it around, but it would only be a matter of time before he was slashing free. And Ember had nothing.

Squeezing her hands into fists, she tried to direct the plants away from her and toward the Sun guard. But she couldn't focus. Rosala spare her, she couldn't regain control of her magic.

A massive root wrapped around her ankle. Ember crashed to her knees, the root rapidly climbing up her calf, her knee, her thigh. Just ten steps from her back room.

Ember thrashed, but she couldn't break away.

The root made it up to her hips, her stomach, squeezing tighter, tighter, tighter.

There came a flash of heat. Golden flames engulfed the root trapping her, reducing it to ash within seconds.

Ember fell forward, barely catching herself on her elbows as she gasped for breath. A distant part of her heard Lucilla yelling that one had split off, she was sorry, please get up. But all she could focus on was the pain in her ribs; the black spots that danced across her vision.

"You have to get the bracelet!" Lucilla yelled, somewhere in the front of the shop. "Ember—"

Lucilla's voice cut off in a cry of alarm. Ember didn't remember telling herself to move, but suddenly, she was struggling to her feet, her vision blurred.

Lucilla was in the front of the shop, desperately squirming in a Sun soldier's grip. Burns covered the left side of his face, his hair mostly singed away.

Ember stepped toward Lucilla, but she shook her head furiously. "The bracelet!"

Right. The bracelet.

The second man slashed through a nearby curtain of vines.

Ember's entire body ached, but she turned and staggered toward her back room. Lucilla would shadowjump away, she would be fine.

She plowed through the ajar door, barely feeling the ache in her shoulder. Tumbling over her desk chair, she flung open one of her drawers—where was it, where was it, where was it—there!

Ember snatched the enka bracelet from a pile of plant clippings. She shoved it on her wrist, the plant's magic tingling across her skin.

"Whatever nymph is on the other line," she said under her breath, "tell Analia we need her. Sun has invaded Ash—"

Ember barely registered the pain across the back of her head before everything went black.

Chapter 71

The dining room was a flurry of activity as Laness recounted both Ember's and Dimitri's warnings. She'd barely gotten two sentences out before Aaron shadowjumped to his room, returning with his and Analia's fighting leathers a moment later.

"It's all happening so fast," Laness finished. She paced around the room, the enka flowers in the windowsills blooming and withering in her wake.

"She had to have coordinated this," Mor agreed, staring down at the map of Elefthia Surce had placed on the table. "She must have sent her forces the moment Dimitri found her in Scarsthain with the Crystal. But if the point is getting back at Analia, why invade Ash when she knows she's not there?"

"Her reasoning doesn't matter," Analia said, surprisingly calm. She'd always thought she'd be outraged if Deardryn procured the Crystal first. But her mind had settled into a cold, sharp focus the moment Laness had finished her report.

"Anna's right," Aaron said, one foot on his chair as he tied his boot. "There's nothing we can do about Deardryn and Scarsthain. But we can help Ash."

"After what they did to Anna?" Branten demanded from the table.

"They certainly don't deserve Analia's help," Mor murmured.

"But Aaron's right," Laness said. "Regardless of what they've done, we can't let Deardryn swipe another seat of power."

"But we risk revealing ourselves if we assist," Surce pointed out.

"Not necessarily." Aaron brought his booted foot back to the ground and stood up straight. "Analia and I will go in first. We'll assess, then report back with our bracelets. If we're lucky, Analia and I can handle things on our own. If we need help from more than Laness, Branten, and Mor, then we reconvene."

Aaron looked to Analia for confirmation. She glanced around the room, taking in her family's reluctant expressions, all on her behalf.

But Laness and Aaron were right: they couldn't let Deardryn gain another step. And Analia couldn't allow the home of thousands of people to be destroyed, even if it had never been a home to her.

Analia slid Aaron's dagger into her boot. "That's the best plan we can hope for."

Aaron gave her a grim nod.

"You can't use your magic while you're there," Surce reminded him.

"Oh, Surce," he drawled, "it's adorable you think I'll need it."

Surce rolled her eyes.

"We'll have to shadowjump inside the castle," Analia decided. "It's the only safe place since we don't know how far the fighting has spread."

"The wards won't let me in," Aaron reminded her.

"But they *will* let me. The council undoubtedly tried to turn the wards against me, but if I know my brother, he won't have let them."

At least, she hoped that was the case.

"Don't forget you'll have to make it look as though Anna is doing the jumping," said Mor, eyes still on the map.

"Good point." Aaron offered his hand to Analia, but she hesitated, her gaze dropping to her ring.

The last thing she wanted was to take it off. Especially since they had just reached the point where she could wear it, implications and promises and all. It was a part of her now, just like the phoenix pin tucked away in her pocket beneath her leathers.

The thought of the council forcing her into hiding once again had her flames seething.

But Aaron's secret, this kingdom's secret, were too important to risk.

"We shouldn't give the council anything to pounce on." Turning to Laness, she reluctantly slid off her ring and offered it to her. "Hold on to this for me?"

"Of course." Laness pocketed the ring, her expression softening a fraction.

Analia glanced to Aaron, not sure what his reaction would be. But he only nodded, his expression tight as he offered his hand once more. Analia slid her fingers through his, giving a quick squeeze.

"All right," he said, looking around the room. "Anything else?"

Laness, Branten, Mor, and Surce all swapped quick looks, but no one spoke.

"In that case," Aaron said, "we'll be back."

He squeezed Analia's hand. Then, he started to pull her into the shadows. Just as the dining room was about to fade—

"You should know," Laness said suddenly, wringing her hands. "Ember's message was abruptly cut off. All I felt was a spike of fear, but I haven't been able to get in contact with her since."

Analia's eyes widened in horror as the dining room disappeared.

"We will find her," Aaron said, pulling her close. "I promise you, Analia, we will find her. But for now, you have to stay with me."

"I know."

Analia squeezed her eyes shut, trying to force her pulse to slow. She had to focus. Focus on the warmth of Aaron's fingers; focus on how he relinquished control of their jump so she could guide them.

Back to the Ash Castle. Back to a people that had driven her away. But also, to her siblings, and a best friend who needed her.

Analia pulled them forward, her mind latching on to the crackle of Ash magic ahead of her in the darkness. In a few moments, its warmth glided over her skin without resistance, and Analia had never loved her brother more.

But then, it turned its attention toward Aaron.

In one swift move, it rose up in front of him in a burning, swirling wall, ready to shove him back. Far back.

Aaron tensed, his own network beginning to churn.

"It's all right," Analia soothed, reaching for the flames with a mental hand. "He won't hurt this kingdom. He's safe."

The magic crackled.

Analia stroked Aaron's cheek with her free hand, trailing her magic across his skin. "It's all right," she murmured. "You can let him through."

The boundary magic hesitated, unconvinced. But Analia didn't try to force it.

She'd never been told how to influence the wards—she didn't even know if she had the ability to do so after her coronation. But her instincts told her to stay calm. Quiet.

Finally, the magic shifted. Slowly, almost warily, the wall of magic split down the center, creating an opening for them to pass through. Aaron reclaimed control of their jump, and a moment later, the noisy Council Chamber materialized around them.

The entire council was in session. Aeley sat in Cadmus's seat, surrounded by military captains including Balstaire, captain of the Crystal Guard. They all spoke over one another as they pointed at a massive map of the Ash Kingdom on the council table, various figurines presumably marking the location of Ash and Sun forces arranged across it.

For a few moments, no one noticed their arrival. But finally, Aeley looked up. She immediately recoiled, sounds of surprise moving around the table as the others noticed.

"Princess Analia," Ganze spluttered from the head of the table. "What are you—"

"We can skip the outrage and rebukes, Ganze," Analia said, striding toward the table.

Ganze's pale, exhausted face flushed with color. "That is how you greet us after over three months?"

"Don't worry, councilmen," Analia said, brushing past a guard to reach the war map. "I'll be gone as soon as the kingdom is secure."

"You can't walk out on your kingdom for a second time!" Laird exclaimed. "You have a duty—"

"They have us surrounded on three sides," Analia murmured, scanning the map.

Ganze said, "Where do you think you can run off to—where have you been?"

"She won't bother with the western quadrant," Aaron said, coming to peer over her shoulder. "It would be a waste to go all the way around the central kingdom when her goal is already in reach."

"She'll leave it as an escape route to demonstrate her mercy," Analia agreed.

"Especially if she can convince our forces otherwise and create an opening straight into the heart of the kingdom."

"Who is this man!" Laird demanded, slamming his hands down on the table.

"'This man' is your salvation." Analia finally looked up at the crowd. "Aaron has spent more time in the Sun Kingdom military than anyone in this room. He knows their strategies, their numbers, and their weak points. But if you would rather have your pride and resentment outweigh your loyalty to this kingdom, we will leave."

"You have no right to lecture us on loyalty," Ganze hissed. "Not when it is your affairs with the Sun Kingdom that got us here."

Analia started to reply.

"Why should we trust you?" Councilwoman Tris asked from across the table.

"You were betrothed to a Sun Royal!" someone called.

"How do we know that's not where you ran off to!" Laird yelled, jabbing a finger. "This could be how Deardryn plans to destroy us from the inside."

Voices broke out over one another. Analia felt Aaron tense at her back, his suppressed network churning. But Analia only pressed her lips into a line.

None of this was new to her. But she didn't deserve it either. Never had. If they didn't want her help, she wouldn't give it to them, and she would give them no one to blame but themselves. *That's* what Accalon would have wanted.

"Enough!" Aeley finally said, her voice cold and commanding.

The voices immediately died down. Analia met her mother's eyes, close enough to feel the cold of her flickering frost magic.

"Analia has always been a disgrace," Aeley said, "but she's not a fool. She knows Deardryn would never take her back after she killed Pryanth."

A soldier made to speak, but Aeley raised her hand to silence him. "Why have you come back, Analia?" she asked.

"Because," Analia said, holding her stare. "While this may not be my home, it was my uncle's."

Ganze and Laird muttered at that, but Aeley and Councilwoman Marie nodded.

"It's your choice," Analia said, facing the table at large. "Do we stay, or do we leave?"

For a long, long moment, the chamber remained silent. Analia's gaze moved from face to face, some meeting her stare, most looking away.

Finally, Ganze's chair scraped across the floor, his body stiff as he sat once more. "Tell us what you know, then," he said.

Analia felt a wicked lash of satisfaction. She promptly turned her back on Ganze to face Balstaire. "What's our latest report?"

Balstaire shifted from foot to foot, rattling off Sun's position.

"We're not outnumbered," he finished, "but Sun has separated our forces and is picking them off one at a time. Any time we get close to shoving them back, they have their dragons fly in new forces and retrieve the exhausted ones."

"Where's my brother?" Analia asked.

"We last saw him fighting in the streets," a short, muscular woman said.

"With how many guards?"

"None, Your Highness—Your Majesty."

"You left your king unprotected?" Analia asked sharply.

"He ordered us to spread out," Balstaire said. "Go where we were needed."

"Where you're needed is with your king." Analia turned to Aeley. "I'm assuming he ordered you not to intervene?"

"He knows I won't risk weakening his authority," Aeley said tightly.

"Good thing he gave me no such orders." Analia turned back to Balstaire. "Send a squadron of six soldiers to find my brother. They're to stay with him at all times, and if he tries to dismiss them, they can remember they were ordered by the rightful heir."

Balstaire nodded once. He flicked his hand at a nearby female captain, who immediately darted from the room.

"Where's Lucilla?" Analia asked Aeley.

"She's been safe in her chambers."

"Good. As for the rest of the units—"

"This is unacceptable," Ganze exploded. "You cannot storm into this kingdom, overturn our council, and start delegating demands when you stripped yourself of that authority."

"I couldn't be a Royal without magic," Analia shot back. "But I was for two decades. I couldn't marry a Royal of an enemy kingdom, but I did that as well. I couldn't murder him on our wedding night, return to this kingdom and dethrone my own father, just to walk away from my coronation ceremony. Yet, I did it all."

Analia paced to the center of the table. "This kingdom is under attack. Yet you sit here squabbling over broken traditions instead of fighting to save your home."

"A home you abandoned," Laird hissed. "You expect us to respect someone who swore an oath to the Crystal and the gods to have no loyalty to us?"

"If I hadn't done so, you would be cursing my name as I reigned over you."

Voices rumbled. Analia thrust out her hand, a column of midnight flames shooting forth from her palm. The voices abruptly cut off.

"This kingdom disowned me from the time I was seven," she said, her temperature climbing. "My claim to the throne created a future of contention for this kingdom. Either a queen you resented sat on the throne, or the rightful heir rejected it. You may blame our current state on me, my magic, or even my father's rumors. But to blame any of these options, you must also blame yourselves.

"It is the duty of the council to serve your kingdom and Royals, and you *failed*. You failed by letting my father's disdain spread throughout the kingdom. You failed by falling victim to your own prejudices against me. You failed when I entered this chamber and you prayed for *my* failure.

"You may not have sparked the divide within this kingdom, but you assisted in fanning the flames. But now, I'm presenting you with an opportunity to begin to redeem yourselves. So, you can either sit down and listen to what I have to say, or you can leave."

No one moved.

Analia folded her arms and waited.

Finally, one by one, the council sank back into their chairs.

Analia turned to her mother. "And you?"

Aeley met Analia's gaze. For the first time, she didn't look at Analia like a disappointed mother. She looked at Analia like an equal. "What does your friend know?"

It took Analia a moment to name the emotion blazing inside her. Triumph. It was triumph as she nodded to Aaron and stepped aside.

Aaron's report was quick and thorough. After some hesitation, the other officers started asking questions and nodding along with Aaron's responses. Eventually, there came a faint pulse on Analia's wrist.

Ember got in contact. She's being held hostage in the Candlelight Music Hall. There's something blurry about her thoughts, though.

Analia thoughtfully rubbed her bracelet as the soldiers wound down.

"Balstaire," she said, "where would you say the fighting is densest?"

"The south end of the square, Your Majesty."

"Aaron will head there," Analia decided. "I want a scout specifically designated to tracking where those dragons recoup."

"And you?" Laird asked.

Analia smiled thinly. "I have a mission of my own."

She looked to Aeley, who gave a shallow nod. Analia sharply dismissed the room, taking a great deal of pleasure in the rush to comply. Aeley was the last to leave, taking a moment to pause beside Analia.

"Accalon would be proud," she said tightly. Then, unable to meet her gaze, Aeley exited, leaving Analia momentarily lost for words.

"Even after all that," she said, "she can't give me a direct compliment."

"Well," Aaron said, turning her to face him. "I'm plenty proud of you."

Analia didn't think she was in the mood for his usual antics. Still, she didn't resist as he lifted her chin, anticipating the crush of his mouth on hers.

But Aaron only kissed the corner of her mouth. Then the other. Then, he pulled back, a line forming between his brows.

"What are you...?" Analia began.

"They're turned the wrong way," he said, puzzled. He nudged the corner of her mouth with his thumb, surprising a laugh out of her.

"You're ridiculous," she said, still laughing.

"And you love me for it," he agreed, leaning in for real this time.

Analia slid her arms around his neck. She didn't care that someone could walk in at any moment, what that could mean. She only pulled him closer, his mouth hot and sinful against hers.

"I can't believe you're leaving me like this," he said, dragging his mouth to her neck. "I'm going to be on the battlefield, and all I'll be able to think about is the filthy things you could order me to do with that tone of yours."

"Really?" Analia skimmed her fingers down his chest. "Do you think I'll be ordering your fingers, your tongue, or your co—"

"Analia!"

Analia laughed as he groaned, pressing his hips into hers. She loved how she could feel him harden through his leathers. Loved that she knew all she had to do was lay back against the table and he would sink into the building ache between her thighs. What a slap to the face that would be to the councilmen.

But Aaron seemed to regain control. With a quick kiss to the corner of her mouth, he pulled away.

"Laness told me your mission," he said over his shoulder, heading for the door. "If Cadmus needs a guard, so do you."

Analia knew she wasn't going to win that battle.

"Should we bring in Branten?" she asked, trailing after him.

"No. Rois will work just fine."

"Why him?"

"Because," Aaron said. "Not only is he already here, but he's the only one I trust to actually prioritize your safety."

Analia tilted her head as she followed Aaron out the door, but she didn't protest.

Just as Aaron had hoped, finding Rois took no time at all. It took even less time to convince him to join Analia, even as his eyes darted between her and Aaron.

She grabbed both men by the hand, pretending to be the one that pulled them into the shadows. A moment later, they appeared in the square, the Candlelight Music Hall looming a few streets over.

Before they could get their bearings, a group of Sun soldiers charged around the corner.

Analia ducked around the first, stabbing her dagger up into the base of his skull. One of them tried to grab her by the hair, but Analia brought her arm around and back on his, jabbed her elbow into his stomach, then sent a wave of flames to finish him.

"Anna, you're *killing* me," Aaron complained, kicking away the final fallen soldier.

Rois muttered something about scouting the rest of the way, then disappeared around the corner.

"You're too easily distracted," Analia said, her heart pounding as Aaron backed her against the wall.

"And you are too incredibly arousing." Aaron ran his lips down her cheek. "My deadly shooting star."

Analia tilted her head, her lips finding his in a lingering kiss.

"Come back to me," she whispered, bringing her hand to his cheek.

Aaron leaned into her touch. "I'm always searching."

Indeed, when Analia opened her eyes a few moments later, Aaron's gaze was fixed on something down the alleyway.

"Is that a greenhouse?" he asked.

Analia twisted to follow his gaze, the greenhouse's windows reflecting the firelight.

"It is," she said. "Ember told me the nymphs had just finished building it when I left."

"And it has mirrors?" Aaron asked. "To help direct the sunlight?"

Analia's eyes narrowed. "What are you thinking?"

"I'm thinking I'm about to solve your dragon problem." Aaron stole a quick kiss, paying Rois no mind as he reappeared. "Good luck."

Then, he slipped away into the shadows.

"So," Rois said after a moment. "You're with him?"

Analia looked up at him, braced for his reaction. But all she saw was a flicker of something that looked a lot like regret.

"Come on, Rois," she said, patting his arm as she passed. "We have a hostage to save."

Chapter 72

Aaron stepped out of the shadows in the southern square, right in the center of a group of Sun soldiers.

"Where did you—" one began.

Aaron stabbed his dagger through the soldier's throat. A second soldier snatched at him, but Aaron stomped on his foot, bringing his knee up as the soldier doubled over. Kicking him back into the third guard, Aaron spun, grabbing the final soldier by the arm and hurling him against a nearby statue of Azar.

He didn't get up again. And Aaron dispatched the second and third with brutal efficiency.

Aaron wiped the blood from his dagger on his leathers. A few feet away, an Ash soldier stared at him, his mouth hanging open.

"Where did you come from?" he asked.

"If you'd been paying attention to your surroundings, you would know that."

Thank the Crystal he hadn't.

"So," Aaron said. "Where's your king?"

"But you're not an Ash—"

"Ah, there he is."

Aaron patted the Ash soldier on the shoulder, then headed off toward the golden flames visible on a raised walkway. He could feel the low buzz of combat in his blood, his magic begging to be released. But Aaron kept it carefully locked away as he dispatched two soldiers blocking the steps, then ascended.

Cadmus stood farther down the walkway, surrounded by Ash and Sun soldiers. One of the Sun men tried to run Cadmus through with his spear from behind, but Cadmus gave an irritated flick of his hand.

Golden flames flashed up in a ring around the Ash soldiers. The flames expanded outward, the heat washing over Aaron's face, the Sun soldiers not caught in the blaze quickly retreating. As soon as they were off the walkway, Cadmus let the flames wink out.

"That's certainly efficient," Aaron called, strolling through the ring of smoldering bodies.

Cadmus glanced over, seemingly unsurprised by Aaron's arrival. "If only it were unlimited."

"Where would be the fun in that? Nice wound, by the way." Aaron nodded to the bloody gash running alongside Cadmus's breastplate strap.

"Like I said," Cadmus said. "Limited supply."

Down on the street, a fresh wave of Sun soldiers shoved toward the stairs.

"So," Cadmus said, adjusting his armor. "Since you're here and these soldiers say they have orders from the rightful heir, I take it my sister is nearby."

"She's currently leading a prison break."

"Good. Although how did you... Ember." Cadmus shook his head, not even surprised. "Is she all right?"

Aaron hesitated the briefest second. "She's as good as you can expect her to be."

Cadmus bit his lip, but he nodded. "Well, I'm glad you're here—behind you!"

Aaron was already lifting his arm, catching the Sun soldier's blade on the metal reinforcements on his forearm. Cadmus engulfed him with flames, and the soldier reeled back with a curse. The Ash soldiers hurried forward as the rest of the Sun group crested the stairs.

"So," Aaron said, completely unfazed. "What's going on here?"

"We've cleared most of the square," Cadmus said. "But every time we're about to push them back beyond the wall, the dragons come."

Cadmus gestured up in the sky where a unit of sun dragons circled.

Aaron nodded. "Rotating squadrons. There are only so many dragons, but most of the military has flying experience. You'd have better luck attacking the dragons than eliminating the soldiers."

"We've tried," Cadmus said, "but they're nearly impenetrable."

"Their hide is like iron," Aaron agreed. "You're only going to get some real damage at the wing joint, behind the leg, and through the eye—if you can get through the extra eyelids."

"And they have fangs and claws to keep us away from those areas."

"And now, you have me. Duck."

Cadmus did as ordered. Aaron slid a dagger from his boot and threw, the tip burying itself in the approaching Sun guard's throat.

The guard fell to his knees. Aaron came forward to retrieve his dagger, the guard collapsing behind him as he turned back to Cadmus. "Shall we go then?"

Dimitri opened his eyes in a Moon Castle hallway.

The wraith he must have used as an anchor stood a little ways away, pulse-pearl softly glowing around her neck as she washed a windowpane. She didn't bother looking up as Dimitri marched past. Nor did she notice when Dimitri's stolen pulsepearl rolled down his fingers and beneath the floor-length purple curtains.

"You dropped something," he said, not breaking stride.

He didn't look back as the wraith let out a tiny gasp. Hopefully, she would find a way to return the pulsepearl to its owner. Dimitri, in the meantime, had other plans.

Based on the paintings and carved wooden doors, he'd appeared on the third floor. He just had to make it down one flight and he'd be at Patryclas's study. Then, he would get the answers he needed. At the very least, he could say goodbye.

Dimitri rubbed his aching chest as he rounded the corner. Just for someone to slam him face-first into a nearby door.

"What are you doing here?"

Dimitri's calm melted within seconds, replaced by a hatred so hot it was cold.

"Rayner," he hissed.

Rayner grabbed Dimitri's wrist, pulling it up and between his shoulder blades. "How did you get in here?" he demanded.

"Really?" Dimitri asked, inching his free hand up the door. "That's all you have to say to me?"

Rayner's fingers twitched. He pressed Dimitri harder against the door, hissing something Dimitri didn't hear. He only felt that tiny flinch replay across his wrist. After everything that backstabbing bastard had done, he had the audacity to be hurt?

"Where's Sabi?" Dimitri demanded.

"She's safe. I promised you I'd get her out—"

"You betrayed me!"

Dimitri twisted the doorknob. The two tumbled through the door into the sitting room beyond, Dimitri curling into a ball and rolling out of Rayner's grip. Popping to his feet, he stomped down on Rayner's reaching hand. Then, he fled.

How dare Rayner act like his promises meant anything? How dare he sharpen every memory they shared until they could draw blood? How dare Dimitri still miss him anyway?

Footsteps hurried toward him. Dimitri leaped up on a windowsill, pointing his feet inward and pulling the curtains closed around him. The one time it paid off to be short and skinny.

Dimitri held his breath as Rayner's footsteps rounded the corner. Twenty years of sneaking around the Sun Castle, learning the best places to hide, all came down to this moment. Would Rayner pause? Would he look to the side? Or would he keep moving?

Rayner's footsteps slowed as they approached. Dimitri's fist tightened around the thick velvet curtain. Keep moving. Just keep fucking moving.

Rayner's footsteps reached the window.

Dimitri held his breath.

And Rayner passed without pause.

Dimitri didn't relax. He remained where he was, not moving, not breathing, waiting for the hall to be silent once more. Then, he counted to twenty. Finally, he slowly pulled the curtain back.

Rayner leaned against the opposite wall, arms folded. "Did you really think I wouldn't notice only one window had its curtains drawn?" he asked.

Dimitri's eyes moved across Rayner's preferred ordinary features, down to his black-and-purple attire, back up to his face, every detail having his stomach roiling. He stared into Rayner's eyes, the only aspect that couldn't be obscured by his magic.

"I hate you," he said. Slowly. Deliberately.

Rayner's eyes darted away. And Dimitri did what he did best: he ran. Down the hall, around the corner, the stairs coming into view.

"Dimitri!"

Around a group of startled servants. Between the massive potted plants flanking the walls leading to the stairs. Away from the man who had shattered his trust and toward the one who put it back together again.

"For the Crystal's sake."

A hand brushed Dimitri's shoulder. He darted around the closest plant, Rayner chasing after him until Dimitri got the plant between them.

"Really, Dima?" Rayner asked, his face mostly obscured by tall, broad leaves. "We're playing this game?"

"Why not?" Dimitri asked. "You've always liked playing games with your fucking king."

"A king who has given orders to capture you on sight."

Rayner feinted to the left, but Dimitri quickly readjusted their positions.

"From spy to guard," he said. "That must be exhilarating."

"I'm trying to get you out before anyone else sees you!"

"Oh fuck off." Dimitri darted to the next plant. Rayner tried to grab him, but Dimitri wriggled free. He just had to maneuver Rayner around, and he'd be at the stairs.

"I give you my word, Dimitri, I'm trying to help you."

"Your word?" Dimitri let out a sharp, painful laugh. "What the fuck is that worth?"

"Everything."

"Is that why your word stabbed me in the back?"

"I never gave you my word."

Dimitri froze. Rayner's hand darted out from around the plant on his right, and he leaped back just in time.

"I gave you my word I would get Sabi out, and I did," Rayner continued, inching to the left. "Just as I gave Sylas my word I wouldn't use my magic for nefarious reasons."

"All I'm hearing is I was never important enough to be one of your technicalities, even though you did your best to convince me otherwise."

And he had fallen for it. Totally, completely, irrevocably. The back of Dimitri's throat burned.

"No," Rayner said, "that's not—oh Crystal strike this down."

Rayner burst through the plant with a rustle and a rip. Dimitri yelped and stumbled back, but the ground disappeared beneath his feet.

Dimitri tumbled backward down the stairs. He landed in a crumpled heap on the floor below, his body aching, his vision blurred.

He had to get up; had to find Patryclas. Dimitri struggled into a sitting position. Rayner tackled him back down.

"What do you want, Dima?" he asked, shoving his knee into Dimitri's back. "An apology? You're not going to get it."

How was this the same person who had claimed to crave his company? Who had draped glowing feathers across his shoulders and sat with him when his world felt like it was crumbling beneath him?

"I didn't want to betray you, but I would do it again. I won't choose your life over mine."

A sob rose in Dimitri's throat. He reached for the balcony bars in front of him, determined to drag whatever pieces of himself remained away. But the entryway wasn't deserted like he thought.

"Let go of me!"

Analia thrashed in Rois's grip as he marched her toward the music hall entrance, his hood pulled up to obscure his face.

"Stop fighting," he snapped.

The two struggled into the shadows across from the Candlelight Music Hall, the two guards stationed at the top of the steps straightening at the commotion.

"Who's there?" the taller guard called, stepping to the edge of the stairs.

"Look who I found," Rois said.

Analia swore as Rois shoved her into the light. He pulled on her braid, jerking her face up for the guards to see.

"Is that...?" The first soldier inched down the steps, the other remaining at the door.

"Princess Analia," Rois said, tasting the words like a fine wine. "I figured the dragons wouldn't mind an extra passenger."

"Crystal fuck me," the first soldier breathed.

"Her Majesty said Analia was not in the kingdom," the second guard said, his voice low and flat.

"She thought she could sneak back in," Rois laughed, marching Analia across the street. Analia struggled, the street dangerously slick beneath her boots.

"I can't believe we have Analia fucking Valarus," the first guard said, his greedy gaze moving along her body. "Do you have any idea how much gold we'll get as a reward?"

"Do you know how quickly my brother will be here to burn you alive?" Analia retorted.

The first soldier laughed. "She's a feisty one! How exciting."

Analia spat at him, earning a grin in return. But the second soldier's eyes were fixed on Rois, piercing through the shadows of his hood.

"What happened to your fighting leathers?" he asked.

"You think I would have gotten close enough to grab her in those?" Rois scoffed.

"You have her now," the second guard said. "Why keep your hood up?"

"I've been a little busy."

They reached the steps. The first soldier moved aside, head cocked. Rois tried to shove Analia up, but she went boneless, sliding down in his grip.

"Oh for the Crystal's sake," he muttered.

Analia screamed in outrage as he picked her up and tossed her over his shoulder like a doll. She pounded her fists against his back as he climbed the steps, his grip unyielding on her thighs.

"What did I tell you," Rois said, nearing the top of the stairs.

"She's not cuffed," the first guard said suddenly.

He came closer, his icy fingers wrapping around Analia's wrist. She grabbed his hand with her free one and twisted. The soldier yelped and released her, just to slap the back of her head.

"Why is she not cuffed?" the second guard repeated, his voice sharpening.

"Didn't have time," Rois said, only missing half a beat.

"Without those damper cuffs," the second guard said, "the girl would have no reason not to use her magic on you. Yet your cloak isn't so much as singed."

"Don't give her any ideas," Rois snapped.

The second guard didn't flinch. Instead, his footsteps approached the edge of the stairs, his voice terrifyingly quiet. "Take off your hood, soldier."

"Don't interfere with my capture—"

The first soldier ripped off his hood from behind. Analia felt Rois go rigid as silence fell across the steps.

"He's not ours," the second guard breathed.

Analia pushed off Rois's back with her hands, his grip loosening so she could flip over his shoulder.

The first guard only made it two steps before he was engulfed in midnight flames.

Analia landed awkwardly on the edge of a step, her momentum sending her tripping down the rest until she splashed into the melted snow at the bottom.

"Very graceful, Your Highness," Rois commented.

Analia turned to find Rois standing at the top of the steps, his sword drawn. The second guard lay dead behind him, blood slowly pooling around him.

"Maybe I should torch you after all," she grumbled.

Rois laughed slightly as she climbed back to his side. "Did I hurt you?" he asked.

Analia shook her head. She and Rois had quickly outlined their plan once Aaron had left, both agreeing that it was better to get as close as possible before dispatching the guards so they couldn't alert the others.

Now, she tentatively looked up into his face, waiting for his usual concern. But Rois only nodded and turned for the door.

"Ready?" he asked.

Analia fought back her smile. "Let's go."

As soon as they opened the door, Analia knew they'd found the right spot. Injured soldiers waiting for transport lined the music hall lobby, the air sharp with the scent of blood. Those still able to walk moved around the scattered cots, a handful going up and down the spiral staircase leading to the balconies.

As soon as Analia and Rois stepped inside, every pair of eyes snapped to them.

The two shared a quick look. Then, with shouts erupting all around them, they took off in opposite directions.

Chapter 73

Aaron crouched on the roof of the greenhouse, bow and arrow in hand. After explaining his plan to Cadmus and the nymphs, he'd climbed up to track the sun dragons' flight patterns. If he was right, the next rotation would appear over the phoenix statues on the music hall roof in three. Two. One.

Six dragons soared into view. Aaron pulled the arrow back to his cheek, carefully taking aim. It wasn't his favorite weapon—nor was he a particularly good shot. But he just had to be close.

Aaron let the arrow fly. It shot across the square, grazing the lead dragon's wing and dropping harmlessly to the street below.

The unit turned, streaking straight toward him.

Closer, just a little closer. Now.

Aaron banged his fist three times on the ceiling. Immediately, the glass blazed with golden light as Cadmus summoned a flare of magic. The light bounced off their configuration of mirrors, sending a blinding light through the ceiling and window facing the dragons.

The dragons squealed in alarm. Two veered off to either side, their riders struggling to keep their saddle. One shot straight up, the other backpedaling fast. But the final two still headed straight for him, both riders and mounts squinting in the light.

"That's it," Aaron murmured. "Try and get me."

It would only be a few moments before the others recovered and joined in—although this was still a far better outcome than he'd been anticipating.

Aaron rose to his feet as the dragons drew near.

Closer, closer.

The dragons swooped over the roof across the street.

Crystal spare him, this was such a bad idea. But it was too late to go back now. Especially since the lead dragon was already across the street.

Just as it reached the edge of the roof, Aaron jumped.

He faded into the shadows, praying he got the timing right. Twisting in the darkness, he reappeared exactly where he'd disappeared, his body dropping down right behind the saddle on the sun dragon's back.

The rider, a balding man Aaron vaguely recognized, twisted around to face him.

"Hello!" Aaron said brightly. "And goodbye." He shoved the guard from the saddle, sending him tumbling on to the roof and off the side.

The second dragon's rider yelled something behind him, Aaron looking back in time to see him draw his spear. But Cadmus had already made it outside, sending a stream of golden flames that had the dragon veering away and crashing into a nearby building.

Aaron couldn't believe that had actually worked. He shifted, trying to pull himself forward into the saddle.

The dragon bucked. Aaron swore as he slid backward, grabbing the reins just in time. He tried to pull the dragon to a stop, but it ignored him, flipping and thrashing as it rose higher into the air.

Aaron whipped from side to side, his shoulders wrenching as he desperately gripped the reins. He just had to maneuver into the saddle so he could get a firm position. But the kingdom was growing smaller and smaller below him.

The dragon rolled. Aaron bit down hard on his tongue, nearly losing his seat. But surprisingly, that was helpful. As soon as the dragon straightened out, Aaron launched himself forward, momentarily releasing the reins with one hand to pull himself into the saddle by its horn.

"All right," Aaron growled, settling in the saddle. "Now we're doing this my way."

The dragon rolled on its back and dropped. Wind shrieked in Aaron's ears as they hurtled toward the music hall roof a dozen feet below, the phoenix statue's wings and beak rising up to meet him.

"Crystal strike me down," Aaron muttered.

There was no way he would survive impact. Not with the dragon crushing him from above and the statue piercing him from below.

Well, Branten had said he spent seven months learning how to fall on his ass. Might as well see just how good he'd gotten.

Aaron waited until the statue was within arm's reach. Then, heart pounding, he loosened his legs.

Pain exploded across Aaron's back as he slammed into the statue and tumbled down the other side. Still gripping the reins, he pulled them around the statue and crossed them in front of him. The dragon twisted to avoid collision but was pulled up short by the looped reins.

Aaron gasped for breath as the dragon hissed, its tiny legs scrabbling for purchase against the music hall. That was far, far too close.

Quickly tying the reins in a knot, Aaron moved around the statue to face the dragon.

"You know," he said. "It's a shame you were actively trying to kill me. I think we could have been friends."

The dragon snapped at him. Aaron didn't flinch.

"You have two options," he said, his ribs shrieking as he slid a dagger from his boot. "You can either fly me back to your main camp, or you can never fly again."

The dragon hissed. It gave one final tug on the statue, the stone groaning ominously. Aaron's grip tightened on his dagger. But somehow, the statue held.

Finally, the dragon sagged.

Aaron grinned, taking a quick peek down at the street below. Spotting Cadmus, the two nodded at one another. Then, Aaron turned back to the dragon. "I'm ready when you are."

Analia should have been used to running for her life. She darted along the edge of the entryway, dodging blades, ducking grasping hands. Reaching a side door, she shoved inside and slammed it behind her.

She and Rois had known they wouldn't stay undetected for long. They'd agreed it was better to split up, allowing them to search more ground and force the Sun soldiers to spread out.

Now, Analia raced down the dim winding hallways meant for performers. Laness had told her Ember was in the dressing rooms, which meant the catwalks above the main performance area were the fastest way to her. Hopefully, the Sun soldiers hadn't had time to learn the labyrinthian turns of these hallways, and she could lose them on her way. But Analia quickly realized her sense of direction might not be as solid as she'd originally thought.

She'd thought she'd known where she was going, having spent years running through these halls with Ember. Yet, she kept anticipating turns and doors that weren't there.

A soldier popped out in front of her. Analia plowed into him, jabbing her dagger up under his chin as she tumbled over him. She scrambled back to her feet. Keep moving. She had to keep moving.

Analia ran on. The music notes on the walls turned to silhouettes of dancers. Had she gone too far?

Analia paused at a four-way path, her head whipping from side to side.

"Corner her!"

Guards quickly closed in from three sides. It was too close quarters to use her magic. There were too many to fight off without her flames. There was only one option left.

Analia turned left, her boots pounding on the polished floors. Left, right, so many footsteps behind her.

Analia shoved open a final door, stumbling out into the deserted main performance room. She looked to the massive stage across the room, over to the mezzanine where she and Rois had first met, then up to the glass catwalks above.

Muffled shouts came from the other side of the door. Analia grabbed a nearby cart of programs and shoved it against the door. Then, flames roaring, she hurried to the closest mounted ladder.

She was a quarter of the way up when the banging started. Halfway up when the wooden door started to crack. Analia propelled herself upward, her hands scraping along the metal rungs. She pulled herself onto the catwalk as the door shattered, chunks of wood flying as soldiers hacked and slashed their way through.

Analia raced across the catwalk. Normally, the glass provided an exhilarating, mind-bending view of the performers below. Now, Analia struggled to keep her footing on the slick surface as she headed for the stage.

She was so close. She just had to keep moving.

"Hello, Princess."

Analia gasped as someone yanked her back by the hair, nearly taking her feet out from under her. She craned her head back, not recognizing the woman who had grabbed her. Her green eyes were flecked with gold, matching her fighting leathers and the lighter streaks in her braided-back hair.

"Such a fuss over one little girl," she said, stroking her fingers down Analia's cheek.

Her fellow soldiers swarmed on to the catwalk.

Analia's heart pounded in her ears. Gods, how could she get out of this?

"You should be glad it's me that caught you," the woman went on. "All those brutes have been talking about is if the queen would notice if they fucked you first. At least the scars I give you will heal."

Analia coughed as the soldier bent her over the railing, forcing the air from her lungs.

The remaining soldiers were mere feet away. She was trapped.

"I hope you've enjoyed the chaos you've caused," the soldier hissed, flagging down her fellow soldiers.

"I never have," Analia whispered.

Then, she brought her hands up, locking on to the soldier's forearms and burning straight through her leathers. The soldier shrieked. She reared back in surprise, and Analia shoved her down the catwalk. She only stumbled a few steps before a fellow soldier steadied her, but it was too late.

Analia sent a wave of midnight flames toward their feet. They stumbled back, avoiding the blaze.

"You think this will stop us for long?" one of them yelled.

Analia retreated to a connecting catwalk, gasping for breath. Just as there came a low, reverberating groan.

The soldiers looked down at the flames; at the fissures rapidly spreading across the heated glass.

Before they could even turn to flee, the walkway shattered with an ear-splitting crack.

Analia raised her arm against the heat, the soldiers screaming as they fell. No time for guilt.

Analia hurried over the stage and into the backstage area. Sliding down the closest ladder, she entered the hall of dressing rooms, barely registering the ache of bruises the guard had left on her arms and stomach.

She moved down the hall, hammering on the locked doors, calling Ember's name, only finding empty rooms.

Where was Rois?

Analia banged on the final door in this section. Before she could call out, something rustled on the other side.

"Ember?"

"Anna?"

Analia gripped the doorknob, melting the lock inside and kicking the door open. Ember huddled on one of the cushy chairs, her light brown hair darkened with blood. Her skin had turned a pale, waxy shade, her blue-gray eyes unfocused as they darted around the room.

"What did they do to you?" Analia asked, crossing to Ember and kneeling before her.

"Not them," Ember mumbled. "Withdrawal."

"What?" Analia rested the back of her hand against Ember's burning forehead. "Em, we have to get you out of here."

"They just have me?" Ember asked, scratching her markings.

"As far as I know," Analia soothed, helping Ember up. "Can you walk?"

"Yes, but Anna, it wasn't just me there."

"Rois and I will take care of it. Can you move any faster?"

Analia stumbled out the door and down the hall, Ember leaning on her for support. They just had to make it outside. They could use the back door, Rois would eventually figure it out, and then Aaron would come and everything would be fine. They would be safe.

"Anna," Ember said, finally supporting her own weight. "I think they got your—"

The two froze as footsteps raced toward them. Countless. From all different directions.

"We're surrounded," Analia said faintly.

Dimitri watched through the balcony bars as Deardryn and Patryclas stepped into the entryway.

"I've enlisted my soldiers to assist in the search," Deardryn was saying. "It's only a matter of time before Analia's mole is brought to justice."

Dimitri's eyes latched on to Deardryn with deadly concentration. On top of him, Rayner went completely still.

"So you've been saying," Patryclas mused. "Will that be my husband's justice, or yours?"

"Why ask such a question?"

"Why did it agitate you?"

Deardryn paused midstep. Something flickered across her face, too quick for Dimitri to catch. Then, she turned her back to Dimitri to face Patryclas, who leaned against the fountain.

"I've always been intrigued by your Blessing," she said, perfectly conversational as she stepped up beside him. "How is it that one man can untangle the complex network of emotions that runs through not just one person, but every person around him? How overwhelming must that be?"

"It takes practice," Patryclas said, green eyes wary. "Just like every form of magic."

"That must make it as fallible as every other Blessing."

Patryclas's lips thinned.

"I'm not trying to insult you," Deardryn soothed, resting her hand over his on the fountain rim. "On the contrary, I'm even more impressed by your consistent accuracy. But it does explain how Dimitri deceived you for so long."

Something pulsed inside Dimitri, hot and fast. He squirmed beneath Rayner's weight, his lips parting.

Rayner pressed his hand over Dimitri's mouth. "Are you trying to get yourself killed?" he hissed.

Dimitri bit down on Rayner's hand, hard enough to taste blood. Rayner hissed, but didn't pull away. Instead, he brought his free hand behind Dimitri's ear.

"You feel that?" he whispered. He circled his finger, and something prickled down Dimitri's spine. "One hard tap to these nerves, and you're done. You can either listen quietly and collect some intel, or I can drag your unconscious body away."

How was he supposed to stay silent? How could he stay still when the source of all his misery was right there. Going after one of the only good things he had left.

He couldn't let Deardryn poison Patryclas against him. But he couldn't stop her from a cell, nor if he was dead.

Slowly, reluctantly, Dimitri sagged. Rayner removed his hand from Dimitri's neck, but he kept the other near his mouth.

Below, Patryclas was saying, "Still, I'm surprised you were able to come to that conclusion so quickly." He casually withdrew his hand from Deardryn's to adjust his doublet. "After all, with all the information your kingdom has compiled, I would think that would make it even harder to find a straightforward answer."

"You would think that. Heading Elefthia's Center of Research does demand a certain attention to detail. Yet, I've found that skill actually assists in identifying patterns that are... overlooked."

"Indeed. I have never met a kingdom more apt at collecting the facts needed to tell a story. I only presumed you would take into account the facts I gave you, seeing as though I have, as you say, an impressive degree of accuracy."

"I would in any other circumstance," Deardryn said, trailing her hand through the water. "I, however, have twenty years of experience with not just Dimitri's heart, but his mind."

Rayner pressed his hand to Dimitri's mouth, smearing sticky blood across his lips. But Dimitri remained perfectly still, his breaths synced to the pulse inside him.

"I've been wondering about that experience," Patryclas said, moving to inspect one of the moonstone pillars. "After speaking with you, I expected him to be vindictive, even cruel. And while there was certainly anger, even hatred, overpowering it all was a despair that almost took my breath away. The same despair that radiates off you when you speak of him."

Deardryn and Dimitri tensed at the same moment.

"I don't think you understand," Deardryn said slowly. "The child despises me."

"And you despise him." Patryclas turned back to Deardryn. "You're not a monster for feeling that way. He's the product of the trust your husband broke. His presence in your castle is a constant reminder of how, once again, Othin chose someone else over you."

For a moment, Deardryn looked as though she were going to correct him. Instead, she raised a hand, turning her face away. "Stop."

"You have every reason to be devastated. But you have no right to displace that pain onto Dimitri."

Patryclas advanced toward Deardryn, green eyes blazing. "You let your hatred break an innocent little boy. You taught him he was worthless, unlovable, in an attempt to alleviate your pain. And I know from your flicker of guilt that you know this was wrong, but you didn't care."

Tears stung Dimitri's eyes as Patryclas voice shook with emotion. Gods, it hadn't been fake. None of it.

"Why were you in Scarsthain, Deardryn?" Patryclas asked.

"I was apprehending Dimitri."

"Who was there because he thought you would be there."

Deardryn's eyes narrowed. "How do you know that?"

Patryclas didn't respond. Rayner's grip on Dimitri's shoulder tightened. The pulsing light in Dimitri's stomach grew.

"You've been listening to him," Deardryn said slowly. "I thought it was odd you brought him to your family's bookstore, but I never would have guessed..." Deardryn's hand gripped the stack of golden bracelets on her wrists, almost compulsively. "You're not just attached to him. You *love* him."

"Do not say that as if it's impossible," Patryclas spat.

"You're the reason Sylas has been resisting me," Deardryn went on as if she hadn't heard.

Patryclas made to speak, but Deardryn turned away to pace around the fountain.

"I can't allow her to keep interfering with my plans," she muttered to herself, her eyes darting. "Not like this. I can't have anyone whispering in Sylas's ear about caution and uncertainties."

Dimitri watched Deardryn pace, his brows furrowing. Something was different about her. Something was... off.

Patryclas retreated to the far side of the entryway, his back to the wall and eyes on Deardryn.

"I've already summoned the guards, Deardryn," he said. "If you come peacefully, you can be spared the harshness of our dungeon."

Deardryn turned to him with a sneer. "You mean the guards that have been sent out on patrol?" she asked. "How long do you think it will take them to get here, Patryclas? Ten minutes? Twenty?"

"No matter," Patryclas said with a shrug. "I'll simply hold you here myself."

"You?" Deardryn scoffed. "With what, the ceremonial dagger your hand is inching toward."

"No," Dimitri breathed, Rayner's grip tightening on him.

"Face it, Patryclas," Deardryn said, advancing toward him. "Every part of you, from your Blessing to your very being, promotes peace."

"I thought we had that in common," Patryclas said, shifting to the right.

"We do. But peace has always been cultivated by bloodshed. And I cannot maintain it if the blood spilled is my own."

With that, Deardryn sprang.

Dimitri lunged forward, his scream muffled by Rayner's hand. But Patryclas was much faster than he appeared.

He slid to the side, sending Deardryn crashing into the wall. She stumbled back, and Patryclas grabbed her arms. He spun her around, pulling her against him.

Deardryn thrashed. Dimitri strained. And Patryclas remained perfectly still, his head bowed and eyes closed.

"He needs my help!" Dimitri exclaimed against Rayner's hand.

"Dimitri, look," Rayner said, sitting upright and pinning Dimitri against his chest.

Dimitri blinked rapidly. Below, Deardryn's struggling had slowed. Her usual composure had slid back into place, perhaps something even softer than that.

"That's it," Patryclas soothed, releasing one of Deardryn's arms to stroke her hair. "Give it all to me. The anger, pain, fear."

Dimitri thrashed, expecting Deardryn to do the same. Instead, the Dragoness gasped for breath, her hair falling forward into her face. But she didn't try to escape Patryclas's hold.

"That's it," Patryclas soothed. "I can take it. Just give it to me."

Deardryn drooped. Patryclas kept his eyes shut, his expression tight as if in pain. Was he... taking on her emotions?

"Did you know he could do that?" Rayner breathed in Dimitri's ear.

Dimitri started to shake his head. But then, his mind flashed back to the Full Moon Festival. The way Patryclas had rubbed his chest, exactly where Dimitri felt his own chest caving in. He'd expected the feeling to get worse, for the guilt to finally destroy him for good. But instead, the pain had eased.

"He did it to me," Dimitri breathed, his body starting to shake. "He did it to help me."

He had taken on Dimitri's panic, his soul-crushing grief, just so he didn't have to hurt. And he hadn't asked for anything in return. Because it hadn't been a favor or a bargain. None of this had been a bargain to Patryclas.

Slowly, disbelievingly, Dimitri relaxed back against Rayner.

Patryclas was safe. Deardryn was taken care of. It was finally over.

This was his moment to finally run forward instead of away. He could feel everything he ever wanted balancing at the edge of his fingertips.

"There you go," Patryclas murmured, his hand moving down Deardryn's arm. "It's almost over. You just have to..."

Patryclas froze, hand on Deardryn's wrist. "What is—"

Deardryn's calm shattered. She twisted, slamming her glowing hand down on Patryclas's chest.

"No!" Dimitri screamed.

And Rayner was thrown back by a wave of golden light.

Chapter 74

"You have to go," Analia said quickly, turning to Ember.

Ember's eyes bulged. "I'm not leaving you!"

The footsteps were one hallway away.

Ember gripped Analia's arm, "I won't leave you just so Sun can hurt you again."

Analia blinked back tears. "I'll be fine," she promised. "But you can't help me if you're thrown in a cell with me."

"Cornered at last, Princess."

Analia angled herself in front of Ember as guards advanced down either end of the hall. She scanned their ranks. Too many to burn. Even if she could, they were in far too close quarters. She might accidentally hurt Ember.

Analia reached behind her, finding Ember's cold, clammy hand. She gave a single squeeze, her fingers stretching to tap the enka bracelet on Ember's wrist. Then, she let go and straightened.

"It certainly took you long enough," Analia said, looking to the head guard. "All this for one little princess?"

"Hand over the hostage," he said, his expression flat.

"Hostage," Analia snorted. "I never realized the Sun Kingdom was so skeptical of the gods that they were willing to anger one of them."

A few soldiers shifted uncomfortably. The Sun Kingdom was infamous for having the greatest amount of people who questioned the gods' existence, but clearly, that uncertainty only went so far.

"I think the gods will forgive the necessary means of war," the captain said.

"Even Rosala?" Analia maneuvered Ember around to face the guard. "Even though her rings are white, she is chosen by Rosala. She's supposed to be protected by all kingdoms in exchange for her healing."

Mutters rose behind her, but Analia didn't turn. The captain of the guard scratched his chin, pretending to consider. But Analia caught the dart of his eyes.

"I was informed she was participating in active rebellion," he said.

"Oh yes," Analia said sarcastically, "I'm sure she could do some real damage on the battlefield."

Ember started to shake in Analia's grip as more voices rose, but she remained silent.

"I'm done," Analia said, not dropping the head soldier's gaze. "I know when I'm trapped. But I, at least, intend on upholding my vow to the healers and Rosala."

The soldier considered. Ember shifted in Analia's grip, and Analia held her breath.

There was nothing she could do if Ember protested. There were too many guards to fight off; there was no chance she could calm them once more. They would both be doomed.

Gods, she just needed Ember to stay quiet. Escape to fight another day.

"Chessa," the captain snapped. "Escort this healer out. Either leave her outside or bring her to the temple, I don't care."

A short, lithe soldier with olive skin darted forward. Ember cast Analia a final helpless look over her shoulder, but didn't fight as Chessa took her by the arm.

Analia watched her friend go, a lump rising in her throat. Swallowing hard, she looked back to the captain. "I suppose this is the part where you take me away?"

He smirked. And Analia barely registered his fist flash toward her jaw before everything went black.

Aaron and his dragon flew over the walls surrounding the central kingdom, heading west. Passing over a small, cozy-looking town, they spiraled down toward what had once been a grassy hillside. Now, the Sun army had turned it into a command center.

Countless soldiers milled between gold-and-white command tents. Even more gathered around wagons of supplies and barrels of ale, the hillside surrounded by trenches. In the center of it all was a marble statue shaped like a pair of wings.

"I see your dragon friends are still on the battlefield," Aaron commented, glancing around the empty sky.

The dragon huffed.

"I suggest you go back and join them," Aaron said, running his finger along one of the dragon's wing joints. Then, seeing no reason to wait, he swung his leg over the dragon's side and dropped.

Aaron tucked into a ball, rolling with the impact and coming up on his feet in the center of the Sun Kingdom camp.

By the time the soldiers realized he was dressed in black, not gold, it was too late.

Aaron's body moved on instinct. He slashed and stabbed his way through the Sun ranks, yells echoing in his ears, warm, sticky blood spraying in his face.

It didn't matter he was surrounded. He had been trained in the Underground. He was the heir of death. These lives were his to take.

Aaron punched a soldier in the jaw. He tackled a second, hamstringing a third unarmored soldier with his dagger as he tumbled past.

Someone slashed at him from behind, finding the slit in his leathers at the elbow. Aaron hissed. He snatched a sword from a fallen soldier and turned to face his opponent. She only lasted a few quick blows, but the rest were pressing in.

Blades ricocheted off his metal enforcements, sending him stumbling. He caught his opponent's spear by the shaft and pulled him in, sending his dagger through the soldier's eye. But the attacks kept coming, blade after blade slashing toward his face, his chest, his neck.

He could feel himself slowing down with each block and strike, blood flowing from countless cuts, as many as the soldiers that lay dead around him. He couldn't take on an entire army by himself. Even with his magic.

A soldier planted his boot in Aaron's stomach, sending him flying back into the marble wings.

Aaron gasped for breath, his already injured ribs shrieking as the Sun army closed in. He lifted his dagger as the first soldier approached.

Before either could swing, the soldier was engulfed in a wave of golden flames.

Aaron's knees nearly gave out as Cadmus marched toward the hill, a dozen Ash soldiers in tow. They had been following Aaron's dragon from the moment he'd landed on its back, Cadmus shadowjumping them to keep pace.

Now, the Ash soldiers charged into battle. Aaron gave himself a moment to catch his breath. Then, he followed.

There were a few minutes where Aaron thought they might actually win. Outnumbered as they were, the Ash soldiers were fresh with the element of surprise.

Cadmus's flames engulfed their supply wagons. Sun soldiers lay scattered on the ground, some moaning, most completely still. But everything went wrong when they tried to charge the command tents.

The Sun army condensed around Ash, creating pockets of combat. A Sun soldier hurled an Ash man into a burning wagon. Two Ash men tried to break through to help, but they were quickly dragged to the ground, disappearing under a wave of golden leathers. Cadmus waded through the crowd, but his flames were sputtering, his expression tight with pain.

Aaron kicked aside a soldier, trying to reach him. He'd only taken two steps when something plowed into him from behind. He slammed to the ground, someone landing on top of him and pressing the breath from his lungs.

"There you are," a familiar voice said.

Aaron gritted his teeth as Dannel yanked his head back.

"It almost feels like a full-circle moment," Dannel went on. "You spent your time in Sun humiliating me, and now I have you flat on your face for all your men to see."

Aaron squirmed, but Dannel pressed him harder to the dirt.

"I must have truly wounded you, Dannel," Aaron gasped. "Over five months and you're still thinking about me. Although you should know, if you wanted my attention, you could have just—"

Dannel slammed his fist into Aaron's lower back. Aaron hissed a curse.

"Look at that," Dannel said. "You do stop talking."

A group of soldiers converged on Cadmus. He tried to summon his magic, but his flames immediately flickered out.

Aaron thrashed, his magic surging. He had to help Cadmus. He couldn't—

The starlight in Aaron's veins thinned. His eyes widened in horror as Dannel secured the damper cuffs behind his back, his magic rapidly funneling away.

"Enjoy the afterlife," Dannel whispered.

The last thing Aaron saw was Cadmus disappearing under a wave of gold before Dannel's hand was on the back of his neck, and everything went black.

Chapter 75

When Dimitri had first entered Gritta's Inn, he was thirteen. He hadn't known it was a drug den, he hadn't known it would cost gold he'd never been given. He just wanted to escape Pryanth's torment, Deardryn's resentment, the unpredictable affection and ice of his father.

Even now, he couldn't bring himself to remember the details of that night. But there was no forgetting how something warm had rapidly expanded in his chest, building and building until he couldn't contain it anymore.

He hadn't been lying when he'd told Analia the Crystal didn't Bless bastards. It cursed them. Because when the magic finally erupted from Dimitri's body, it wasn't the blue of Othin's shielding magic.

It was gold.

The same gold as the magic spears Pryanth would hurl at him when they were small.

The same gold of the sunstones' light that would flicker whenever he was afraid.

The same gold that launched Rayner halfway down the hall.

It was Sun magic. Royal magic. Magic he had shoved down until it was so small that even Analia's emerging sensory abilities couldn't distinguish him from the Sun Royals around him. Magic that Deardryn couldn't let roam free in her kingdom.

Indeed, Deardryn didn't look surprised as Dimitri slid down the railing, flickering with light. She raised her hands defensively, but Dimitri raced past her.

"Patryclas," he choked out, skidding to his knees beside Patryclas, slumped against the wall. "You have to get up. You have to come with me."

Dimitri was vaguely aware of Deardryn fleeing out the front door, but he didn't care. He shook Patryclas's shoulder, gasping for air.

"I sensed your emotions on the balcony," Patryclas breathed, his eyes shut. "I wish you didn't have to see this."

"No!" Dimitri snapped. "This is not happening. You are not dying. You're not leaving me right after you told me I was finally home."

Patryclas mumbled something, but Dimitri ignored him. He closed his eyes, reaching for the well inside him he'd done everything to suppress. There was no time for moderation or control or whatever else they taught in the magic lessons he'd never received. There was only Patryclas and the gaping void opening up around him.

Golden light flooded forth from Dimitri's palms. Patryclas gasped.

Heal, heal, he had to heal, not do more damage. But holy Crystal above, damage was all that remained.

Patryclas's life force had been reduced to a shallow puddle. But beyond that, Deardryn must have manipulated her additional healer Blessing. Organs deteriorating, blood flow slowing, everything was shutting down.

"I can fix it," Dimitri said, near hysterical. "I have to fix it—"

His magic abruptly winked out.

"No!"

Dimitri frantically reached for his magic, dragging the golden light up and out of his palms. He just had to replenish enough life force for Patryclas to hold on for the healers, he could do it.

The magic winked out again.

"Dammit!" Dimitri summoned more magic. "I can do it."

"Dima," Patryclas whispered, golden light flashing across his pale face. "Dima, Dima stop."

"I'm sorry," Dimitri gasped, tears flowing down his cheeks. "I'm sorry I'm sorry I'm sorry—"

"Dimitri, stop." Patryclas pulled Dimitri against his chest. "It's all right, sweet boy. You will be all right."

He was dying. His heart was struggling to beat beneath Dimitri's ear. Yet, Patryclas was comforting him. Dimitri should have been comforting him, but Patryclas was comforting him because he was dying. He was dying, dying, dying.

"It was an honor to love you, Dimitri," Patryclas whispered, so faint Dimitri almost didn't hear.

Dimitri cried harder.

"Make sure you tell Sylas..."

Patryclas's words broke off in a wheezing cough.

"I will," Dimitri said. "I promise. I..." Dimitri's voice broke. "Love you."

They were such small words, but he'd never spoken them all the same.

"Don't turn it off, Dimitri," Patryclas said, momentarily tightening his grip. "Don't let this big feeling ruin all the wonderful ones."

Crystal spare him, how was he going to survive this?

"I won't," Dimitri whispered. He took a long, deep breath. "I figured out what I want."

Patryclas's head drooped against his shoulder. Dimitri wanted to scream.

"I want to stop Deardryn," he said instead, his words rambling over his tongue. "And when that's done, I want to have a bookshop. Just like your mom."

Patryclas mouthed the words against his shoulder, his breathing slowing.

"I'll sell all kinds of books," he said. "Well, maybe I'll get someone to help me because most people still find me prickly. But I want to be able to choose all the books I sell and where they go and what the shop looks like and everything. I want to be able to point someone directly to the right book because I've read them all and know exactly where everything is. That's what I want. A future. Here. With you and Sabi and…"

Dimitri's voice choked off. He waited for Patryclas's response. But Patryclas didn't say a word. He didn't move.

"Patryclas?" Dimitri asked, his voice unbearably small. He pulled back, his hands moving to lift Patryclas's lolling head, his eyes closed. He just had to open his eyes. He just had to see—

The castle door burst open.

Dimitri barely registered the guards swarming inside, Deardryn shrieking, hands latching on to him. He barely remembered screaming, thrashing, clawing at the guards until his nails were broken and bloody, his enka bracelet tearing and falling from his wrist.

All he remembered was being dragged away from the closest thing he'd ever had to a father. Not knowing if he was dead or alive.

Chapter 76

Analia had no problem recognizing the basalt walls of her Ash Castle cell. What she didn't know was how much time she'd spent in the dungeon.

She'd woken up in darkness, having been stripped of her fighting leathers, her wrists shackled behind her with damper cuffs. The only good news was the guards hadn't bothered taking the enka bracelet off her ankle, and its magic still worked despite her cuffs.

While Laness couldn't link everyone's bracelets together, she could pass along everyone's news.

Aaron, too, had been captured and thrown into the Ash dungeons. Ember had found Rois, her thoughts still jumbled from withdrawal. But the most groundbreaking news came from Surce, who'd finally managed to decode a section of the scroll.

As time ticked on, Analia didn't bang on the door and scream for someone to let her out—although she could hear those who did. Instead, she sat quietly, shifting her leg every now and again so she could feel her phoenix pin in her pocket. She didn't know why the guards hadn't taken it, but she didn't complain. She only waited.

When the Sun soldiers finally swung open her door, Analia's heart gave a tiny squeeze. It was official: Sun had conquered the Ash Castle, maybe even the central kingdom.

She didn't resist as the soldiers yanked her to her feet and marched her out the door. Instead, she quickly oriented herself by the cell numbers she marched past. If they took two more lefts, they would pass the Royal vault entrance, and she could try to break free. But the plan evaporated as another group of guards rounded the corner with Aaron.

He, too, had been stripped of his fighting leathers, leaving the black tunic and pants he wore beneath. Deep purple bruises marred the left side of his face. His ankles had been cuffed in addition to his wrists, the chain rattling against the stone floor as he carefully stepped forward.

The moment their eyes locked, Analia's icy composure cracked down the center. But the two of them remained quiet as they were marched along, Aaron's only twitch of emotion the slight flare of his nostrils as he spotted the bruise on her jaw.

The guards led them up the dungeon stairs and back into the castle. Analia expected to be escorted into the Throne Room, but the Sun soldiers marched past without pause. Instead, they shoved Analia and Aaron up the stairs, climbing higher and higher until Analia's heart pounded with rage. Nevertheless, she couldn't suppress her flinch as the guards marched her inside her uncle's chambers.

The cleared-out room had been turned into a makeshift study. A massive map of the Ash Kingdom took up one wall, an ornate desk and chairs turned to face it. A soft gold carpet had been placed down, making Deardryn's footsteps near silent as she strode toward them.

Her long-sleeved gown was made from black velvet, small, blood-red rubies stitched across the bodice. The form-fitting cut was certainly flattering. Yet, the colors had her golden complexion looking dull, almost tired.

"Little dragoness," she said, her expression perfectly serene. "I must admit, I was surprised to hear you were discovered scuttling through my kingdom."

Analia didn't move.

"I see you have disposed of my pendant," Deardryn went on. "Since my searchers have yet to return and you're standing before me, I presume you disposed of them, too?"

Analia remained silent.

Deardryn softly clicked her tongue. "Come now, Analia. I taught you better than relying on silence. Although I suppose I can't blame you. Not after what happened in this room."

Analia's eyes moved inexorably to the spot she'd found her uncle's body. Deardryn watched her carefully, but Analia had no reaction to give. She couldn't feel anything at all.

"This is cruel," Aaron said softly. "Even for you."

Deardryn's expression flashed through a flurry of emotions, too quick to read. Then, she turned to the guards. "Where is Analia's phoenix pin?"

Analia's shoulders tightened.

"Last I saw," one of Analia's guards drawled, "it was in her pocket."

Deardryn nodded softly, then took a step forward.

"Do *not*," Aaron spat.

Deardryn ignored him.

"I told the guards to let you keep it," she told Analia as she approached. "Four months in my kingdom, and I never saw you without it. Yes, it was your uncle's. But at some point, it became yours as well."

Analia cringed as Deardryn stopped before her, her guard tightening his grip on her shoulders.

"It's a part of you," the Sun Queen said. She slid her hand into Analia's pocket and grabbed her pin. "You should have a reminder of who you are."

Analia leaned away, but Deardryn had no problem attaching her pin to her tunic. Carefully. Almost meaningfully. Using the same hands she had pressed to Accalon's chest as she tried to suck his magic from his veins.

Just for a moment, the Dragoness's eyes locked on hers. And Analia felt those memories ignite.

"Good," Deardryn murmured. Stepping back, she turned to the guards. "Move them to the left wall. Away from doors and windows."

Analia's mind spun as the guards shoved her and Aaron against the map wall, their cuffed hands trapped between their backs and the wall.

There were too many emotions. Too many memories trying to suck her down. She didn't even notice the guards retreating until the door clunked shut behind them.

"That's quite the security system you've got," Aaron commented, lounging back against the wall.

"I invite you to try and escape," Deardryn said, pouring a glass of wine from a decanter on the desk. "You certainly have the numbers. Even on your own, you managed to strangle one of my men with your wrist chain when he came to feed you. But now, you not only have an extra shackle, but no magic, no weapons. And I'm sure Analia hasn't forgotten what I have."

Deardryn flicked her hand, sending a ribbon of golden light tingling across Analia's cheek. Analia's face spasmed. Aaron froze. Deardryn smiled languidly and sipped her wine.

It was a purely insolent, diminishing move. One that had Analia's body burning with phantom flames and Aaron's jaw tightening. But Analia took a slow, steadying breath.

"Fascinating," Deardryn murmured, studying Analia through half-lidded eyes. "You have grown. In more ways than one."

Deardryn put down her goblet on her crowded desk, her movement allowing Analia to spot the damper box. After she'd destroyed her last Ash ring, she doubted Deardryn would be willing to risk the box, just to make a petty jab at power. What was she up to?

"You wouldn't happen to have any of my daggers in that clutter, would you?" Aaron asked conversationally.

"Aaron Stelingente," Deardryn murmured. Taking her time, she crossed the room and stroked his cheek. "Even as my guard, you had your mother's arrogance. As well as your father's charm. Analia truly stood no chance, did she?"

Aaron remained perfectly still. But Analia's face twitched.

Deardryn laughed to herself. "Oh, yes, my dear, I knew. Stories are far easier to read when you are not a part of them. Even when you two were bickering he couldn't keep his eyes off you.

"That's why I made him your guard. I was hopeful his fascination—or perhaps infatuation—would make him clumsy, giving me a glimpse into what either of you were up to. I must say, he remained remarkably controlled."

Deardryn tucked Analia's hair behind her ear. "Even now, he's able to hide every shred of hatred he has for me. And yet, there's no concealing the fury in his eyes when I so much as touch you." Deardryn paused, her fingers thoughtfully resting against Analia's temple. "I wonder..."

Without warning, Deardryn backhanded Analia across the face. Analia's head hit the wall. Aaron tensed, even as there came no crack, as Deardryn's hand continued to hover in front of Analia's face.

"Fascinating," Deardryn murmured, honey gaze on Aaron.

Analia's heart pounded in her ears. She had to stay calm; figure out what Deardryn was after and escape. But all she could smell was the sweet scent of Deardryn's skin, flooding her mind until she was drowning in memories.

"That is true love, my dear," Deardryn said, her voice sounding far away. "The fierce, uncontrollable urge to protect someone. To ensure their safety and well-being. To destroy any threat to those constitutions."

Analia shuddered as Deardryn drew a glowing fingertip down her cheek. Trapped in a cage. Her uncle's magic. Aaron, bleeding on the ground.

"He'll never break, though," Deardryn said. She pressed down hard, Analia sucking in a breath as magic jolted through her body. "He knows I won't kill you. Not yet."

Don't make me have to kill you.

Once, the memory of those words would have sent her crumbling. But now, Analia squared her shoulders.

"Why, Deardryn?" she asked. "Is it because you know you need me, or because you remember what happened the last time we met?"

Deardryn's lip curled. She twisted the bracelets on her wrist, her eyes briefly going out of focus. "Look how sharp your fangs have become."

She shoved Analia back against the wall, then paced back toward the table. Aaron leaned into her, but Analia kept her narrowed gaze on Deardryn.

"There's always going to be hatred in our hearts," Deardryn said, lifting something from the table. "You killed my son, and I didn't save your uncle when I could have. Some may argue it would be best for us to kill each other now and claim our justice while we can. But I told you once before, Analia. I am patient. And I always think ahead."

Deardryn advanced toward Analia, a damper blade glinting in her hand. "You were right, little dragoness. You are still of use to me. Even if you come to me now, with another man's promises in your ear after burning my only child alive on your wedding bed."

Golden light flickered around Deardryn. Analia tried to slip out of her path. In one swift move, Deardryn pinned her to the wall with a hand to her shoulder.

"We'll deal with that in due time," she said, terrifyingly calm as she leaned in. "For now, I want to see just how sharp those fangs really are."

Deardryn raised her dagger.

Analia thrashed.

And Aaron struck.

Grabbing the unlit torch from the nearby sconce in his bound hands, he spun and smacked Deardryn's wrist. Deardryn hissed and dropped the dagger.

"Don't touch her," Aaron spat.

"Fine."

Deardryn slammed her glowing palm between Aaron's shoulder blades. He flew forward, slamming into the perpendicular wall.

Analia captured the fallen dagger under her boot. She dragged it toward herself, trying to kick it up the wall. Before she could grab it, Deardryn was on her.

"Always up to something," Deardryn said, snatching the dagger. "Even when I'm trying to help you."

She spun Analia around, pressing her face against the wall. Analia thrashed, but Deardryn only tightened her grip.

"You're only helping yourself," Analia spat.

"That doesn't exclude you from also benefiting. After all, my needing your magic means you get to access it once more."

"You mean in the few moments before your Devourist tries to suck me dry?"

"Always so stubborn," Deardryn said, surprisingly frustrated. "Analia, if you're ever going to outsmart me, you must learn to release your preconceived notions when reality no longer supports them.

"I have no Devourist with me. I have my damper box, but no obsidian. And my dagger, if plunged into your body, would block your magic, which is the opposite of what I'm claiming to want. Think."

Analia strained against Deardryn's grip. She could hear Aaron struggling off to the side, unable to break free of whatever magical restraints Deardryn had forced upon him. She was on her own.

Gods, she wanted to be furious. This was the woman who'd manipulated her for four months, just to slice a dagger down her spine. But she had also treated Analia like her own. And even as she rapidly searched for ways to outmaneuver her, the grief at losing that hurt worst of all.

"What else can the dagger do?" Analia asked.

"Very good." Deardryn drew the cold tip of the blade down Analia's arm. "These damper cuffs aren't like your typical shackles. There are no locking mechanisms that can only be opened with one specific key. In fact, many keys can open these cuffs. As long as they are dampers."

Deardryn slid the dagger through the crack where the two ends of the cuff met under her left wrist. There came a click, and Deardryn loosened the cuff.

An ominous rumble moved down Analia's arm into her stomach. "Wait," she began.

"I told you I need your magic," Deardryn said, moving to the next. "I lured you out of hiding for that very reason. Now, let us see how much has been stored after two days."

"No!" Analia and Aaron yelled in unison.

Deardryn opened the last cuff. Analia tried to yank her hands back, but Deardryn easily lifted the cuffs from her skin.

And magic slammed back into Analia. It thundered through her body with bone-crushing pressure, every drop of magic trying to return to her network at the same time—Crystal spare her, it was too much.

Analia wanted to scream. She wanted to die. She was a sealed cup trying to contain an ocean, the pressure building, building, building.

But somehow, she closed her eyes. She slumped against the wall, not trying to fight as her magic clawed back into her network.

She was tired of fighting her magic, herself. She just had to let it flow. Back into her skin, down to her feet until she could smell the carpet burning, all around her until the map crumbled to ash beneath her palms.

Finally, Analia turned, the last of her flames flickering around her. "Is that sharp enough for you?"

Accalon's chamber thrummed with power. Aaron braced himself against the side wall, his starlight eyes wide with awe. Deardryn had retreated to the center of the room to grip the table.

"Extraordinary," she breathed, cautiously moving forward. "Even without a fully recovered network, you have that much power."

"And you gave it back to me."

Analia shot a stream of flames from her fingertips, but Deardryn batted it aside.

"You gave me a taste of your power back in my temple," Deardryn said. "But this is what I've been waiting for."

Aaron shifted against the wall to Analia's right.

"You keep saying that," Analia said, inching to the left. "Even before my flames came in, you insisted I had magic, just because you felt it leave my uncle's body."

"That magic was the most powerful Blessing I have ever encountered, Analia. It's not the type of magic to sit dormant."

"But it is the type of magic to help you find the Crystal."

Deardryn's face twitched. "I was wondering how he knew about that," she murmured.

Deardryn's back was completely turned to Aaron. He took a few slow steps, his ankle chain muffled by the carpet.

"Do you mean Dimitri?" Analia asked, stepping closer.

"Your power intrigues me, Analia," Deardryn said, nudging her back with a finger between her collarbones. "But what I'm more interested in is your sensing abilities."

Analia fought not to glance at Aaron as he reached the table. Why would Deardryn want anything to do with her sensory abilities if she'd already tracked down the Crystal in Scarsthain? Unless Deardryn knew more than Analia thought.

"How are my sensory abilities any different from yours?" she asked.

"Because you can still sense the different types of Blessings."

Analia's blood went cold. Deardryn started to turn back toward her table.

"That's impossible," Analia blurted. Deardryn turned back. "My flames have come in. I've specialized."

"And yet, you still react to my magic."

Aaron quietly nudged two chairs apart, his eyes on the damper dagger.

"You can't lie to me, Analia," Deardryn said. "I could see it in your eyes the moment my magic touched your skin. It wasn't fear. It was recognition. You remembered not the feeling of indistinct power, but the glow of my magic in the temple, in my rings, all throughout my castle. Just like you remember it now."

Deardryn trailed a thin ribbon of magic down Analia's arm. Analia shuddered, the soft, languid thrum sinking into her skin. She looked up at the Dragoness, wanting to deny it. But confusion and fear pushed her words aside.

"Tell me," Analia said. "Tell me why I can still sense them."

Deardryn's lips twisted. "My dear, that's an obvious answer, as impossible as it seems. We know for a fact the Blessed can only recognize their own magic."

Aaron looked at Analia quickly, the chairs now pushed apart.

Analia could feel Deardryn's words circling around her, just out of reach.

She should've been used to impossibilities at this point. Not being Blessed by the Crystal. Receiving her magic through her uncle. Aaron being the long-lost heir to the Star Kingdom. The existence of his kingdom in the first place.

Yet, the moment Deardryn's words clicked home, Analia burst out laughing. "You think I have access to every Blessing?"

Deardryn scowled. "Royal Blessings, at least."

Analia laughed harder, nearly doubling over. It was all she could do.

"Do not disrespect your queen," Deardryn hissed.

Her hand snapped out. Analia instinctively caught her wrist, her mind flashing back to another chamber; another tan hand that had aimed for her cheek.

"Never," she said, sobering instantly, "touch me again."

Analia squeezed Deardryn's wrist, tight as she could.

But Deardryn didn't flinch. Instead, she stared into Analia's face, studying her with almost unnerving consideration.

"Excellent," she murmured.

Analia scoffed. She threw Deardryn's arm aside, "I don't have multiple Blessings."

"The sundial doesn't lie."

"What does the sundial have to do with this?" Analia demanded.

"What do you think it's measuring when determining a person's worthiness?" Deardryn brushed back her hair with a sharp gesture. "That dial is activated by the magic of whoever stands on it, and it has never glowed so bright. Not even for me."

Aaron turned away from the table, his hands carefully reaching out behind him.

"But the dial only measures power," Analia insisted. "There's no way of proving I don't just have a powerful Blessing."

That had to be it. It couldn't be another secret about her uncle she hadn't seen coming.

"You mean to say there have been no unusual occurrences in the last five months?" Deardryn asked. "No strong winds or rushing water or flickering shadows that couldn't be explained?"

Analia started to respond.

Aaron's chains softly clinked against the table.

Deardryn whirled, "You!"

Aaron dove clear as Deardryn aimed a wave of golden light for him. He tucked into a backward somersault, bringing his cuffed hands in front of him.

Deardryn made to strike again, but Analia grabbed her wrist from behind, redirecting the blow. Golden light slammed into the front right leg of the table, strong enough to snap it away. Analia tightened her grip, Deardryn letting out a screech as her gold bracelets melted into her skin.

Deardryn flipped her hand free and elbowed Analia in the face. Analia fell back, spitting blood.

Deardryn whipped back toward Aaron as there came a snap, the chain connecting his cuffs now dangling from one wrist. He lunged toward the table, but Deardryn grabbed a chair and swung it into his side. Aaron hit the ground hard.

Deardryn advanced on him, but quickly jumped back as a ball of midnight flame shot past her skirts. It collided with the back right leg of the table, demolishing the wood in seconds. Unbalanced, the table crashed to the ground.

Aaron rolled out of the way just in time, trinkets raining down around him. He reached for the dagger, but Deardryn flung out her hands.

"Enough!"

Golden light exploded throughout the chamber.

Analia cried out as the force slammed her against the window. But the physical pain was a mere pinprick compared to the magic plunging inside her, reaching for her very soul and ripping it away with a single mighty tug.

She had only felt this type of pain once before. Back in the Sun temple, when she'd told Deardryn of Pryanth's death. It was the type of pain that left no physical mark, but still managed to take something from her beyond energy and magic and life force. Something vital.

At that point, she'd just wanted it to be over. The constant battles and failures and fear.

But at some point, she'd finally found her way off that battlefield. She'd found safety, acceptance, a home and people worth fighting for.

A fresh wave of midnight flames erupted from her body, colliding with the golden light. The two magics canceled each other out, Analia's teeth vibrating from the resulting shock waves.

She pushed herself off the window, advancing through the haze of residual magic. She immediately paused when she caught sight of Deardryn pinning Aaron to the wall, a glowing golden hand around his throat.

"Your power truly is astounding," Deardryn panted, not looking back. "But I've seen enough of your flames. I've decided it's time to give your other Blessings an incentive."

"Let him go," Analia said, her voice trembling with rage.

"Try and stop me, little dragoness."

Deardryn tightened her hand around Aaron's throat. He tried to shove her away, but Deardryn easily pinned his arms to his sides with a band of golden light.

Analia charged forward, her blood boiling so hot it was cold.

Not Aaron. Deardryn had already slaughtered his family, destroyed his home, taken everything from him. She didn't get to hurt him anymore.

Analia raised her burning hand.

"Not so fast, Analia," Deardryn chided. "You can't use your flames when I'm this close to him. If I burn, he burns."

She was right. Analia curled her hand into a fist, forcing her flames to extinguish. She needed a plan.

"Try another way," Deardryn said.

"I don't have any other magic!" Analia exclaimed.

Aaron met Analia's gaze over Deardryn's shoulder. Even with her hand around his throat, with her magic sucking his life away, all she could see was the unwavering faith in his eyes.

Analia didn't know if she wanted to scream or sob. She rushed to the remnants of the table. Spotting two of Aaron's daggers, she shoved them in her boots, then grabbed the damper blade.

"Hurry, Analia," Deardryn called. "No one, no matter how powerful, can withstand my magic for long."

Analia charged back toward Deardryn, looping around to her side. She'd barely raised the dagger when Deardryn clicked her tongue.

"That's not going to do anything."

A ribbon of Sun magic swatted the dagger from Analia's hand. It ricocheted off the wall to Analia's right, thudding down beside Aaron's boot.

"Time's almost up," Deardryn said.

Tears burned in Analia's eyes. "Please," she begged. "I don't have any other magic, there's nothing there, I can't—"

Analia broke off as there came a snap. Aaron tried, but he couldn't stifle his gasp of pain. And that tiny sound ripped Analia's heart in half.

It was the same sound he'd made when she crouched over him in the snow, her fingers stained with his blood. She barely remembered what had happened in those minutes, hadn't thought twice about the warm glow she had latched onto in that moment. But now, her mind flashed through memories.

The incredibly strong wind when she fought with Aaron after her trial. The way her tub would start to fill before she could touch it when she was upset. Her uncle, always so careful to keep his magic locked away, but also insisting on lighting the sconces each morning as if he needed the release.

Accalon. Her everything when she had nothing.

It didn't matter Brenn spiked Accalon's drink. Deardryn had admitted she'd left him to die. Just as she continued to take, and take, and take.

Deardryn's magic flared.

Something snapped in Analia's chest.

And she shoved Deardryn across the chamber with a gust of wind.

Chapter 77

Analia didn't give herself time to think. Not about the devastation of another secret ripping through her insides.

Instead, she rushed to Aaron, who coughed and slid down the wall. She was about to fall to her knees when Deardryn's magic struck her from the side. She slammed into the wall, pain flaring across her shoulder.

"Very good, little dragoness."

Deardryn knelt by the destroyed table, searching through the wreckage for something. Analia pushed herself upright on shaking legs, positioning herself in front of Aaron as he struggled to catch his breath.

"When does this stop, Deardryn?" she asked raggedly. "You established my sensory abilities; you established I have access to different magics." Analia nearly choked on the words. "I know you stole something from Scarsthain. There's nothing else for you to want."

"Close," Deardryn said. "I only want one more thing from you. I want you to open this."

Deardryn opened her damper box and pulled out a dark gray pendant. She lifted it for Analia to see, and Analia couldn't fight back her surprise. It was the same dark gray rock with the crack down the center from Surce's tapestry.

Aaron's fingers brushed her ankle, and she didn't have to look at him to know he, too, recognized it. The tapestries had been showing them the answer all along.

"That seems too ordinary of a jewelry piece for your taste," Analia commented.

"I know you're trying to goad me into sharing more details," Deardryn said, rising to her feet. "It's a traditional technique, but you're finally thinking on the right path." She stepped up to Analia, smoothing a hand down her hair. "Never be the first to reveal what you know. Knowledge is a weapon best wielded in the shadows. But fortunately for you, I intend on explaining."

She paused, waiting for Analia to ask the obvious question. But Analia kept her face blank, even as her heart ached at Deardryn's nod of approval.

"I knew from the moment Dimitri disappeared from my castle he was with you. He was a clever ally for you to make, one with an easy motive to twist onto your side."

"Dimitri is my friend," Analia said. "Not a business partner."

Deardryn waved aside the comment, turning to pace the room. Analia eyed the door, knowing she could easily make it out and run. Just as she knew Deardryn was aware she would never leave Aaron, who rose shakily to his feet.

"Dimitri accused me of stealing the Crystal," Deardryn went on, leaning against the window. "And since you knew of my visit to Scarsthain, I presume he informed you I succeeded."

"And since you're dangling that rock in my face instead of the Crystal," Analia said, "I presume there's a problem."

Deardryn was quiet for a moment, turning the stone between her fingers.

"Let me guess," Aaron rasped. "The Crystal is sealed inside the rock, and you need all seven Royal Blessings to crack it. And you know none of the other Royals would help you do so, which brings us here."

"I see you're not one for a drawn-out story," Deardryn commented.

"Almost having a drawn-out death does that to a person."

Deardryn smiled slightly. Analia flinched, and Aaron touched his fingertips between her shoulder blades.

"Regardless," Analia said, taking a few steps forward, "you have a problem. We've already established I can stop you from using Aaron as leverage. You played your final card too soon."

She could sense the casing around the Crystal in Deardryn's hand. If she could summon the winds again, she could knock it out of Deardryn's hand, grab it and Aaron, and escape. But when Analia reached for her magic, all she felt was flames.

"I see your advantage is evading you," Deardryn commented.

Analia made to retort, but Deardryn waved a hand. "Don't worry, it makes no difference. I still have, as you say, a card to play."

Analia's stomach did a slow role. "What do you..."

"Guards!"

Analia didn't want to turn as the door opened. She didn't think she could bear to see what had Aaron suck in a breath behind her. She wanted to close her eyes, cover her ears.

"Analia!"

Slowly, mechanically, Analia turned.

Guards pinned Cadmus and Lucilla against the far wall, Analia unable to sense their networks. Dampered. Both bore minor bruises and scratches, but where Cadmus was still and watchful, Lucilla had turned into a she-demon. She kicked and screeched at her guard, eventually angling her head to bite down on his hand.

The guard yelled and slapped her across the face. The crack had barely sounded when Analia blasted him with midnight flames.

Lucilla kicked his burning, screaming body away, but Deardryn quickly pinned her to the wall with a loop of magic around her waist.

"Joshel," Deardryn said, completely unfazed. "Gag the prisoners and leave. Take your fallen soldier with you, too."

Analia took a step forward, and the magic around Lucilla tightened. She was forced to watch as Joshel did as ordered, Deardryn sending a second golden restraint around Cadmus as the Sun guard departed.

"Why?" Analia asked, her voice flat, dead, as she turned to Deardryn. There was no other way to express the demolition in her chest.

"Precaution," Deardryn said. "You destroyed my Ash ring, meaning if you won't open the casing, I need a new sacrifice to do it myself."

Lucilla screamed something through her gag as she shoved against her bonds. Analia couldn't bring herself to look.

Her siblings were trapped. Turned into sacrificial hostages, just as she'd feared after breaking Deardryn's Ash ring.

"Even if you do obtain Ash magic," she said, "you still don't have Star and Moon magic."

"But I do."

Analia's last shred of triumph crumbled as Deardryn returned to her damper box, lifting Aaron's damper by the chain.

"Your love lost it in my temple when he was escaping," Deardryn explained. "He'd been wearing it for so long that the magic hadn't fully returned to his network. I was able to seal away what little remained, not only procuring Star magic, but also a new idea about how to collect magic."

Aaron swore under his breath as he moved to stand at Analia's shoulder.

"You still don't have Moon," Analia insisted.

Deardryn tilted her head. "Are you confident about that?"

Those words stung more than they should have.

"Dimitri has been in the Moon Kingdom for months," Analia said, folding her arms. "He's heard nothing about a Moon death."

"Dimitri was on the run for over a week after we apprehended him in Scarsthain. There is much he has not heard."

Analia searched Deardryn's expression, trying not to sway on her feet.

This could all be a massive bluff. But even if it weren't, this was the perfect opportunity for Deardryn to procure an Ash ring. One of her siblings could still die today.

And it would be all her fault.

"What's it going to be, Analia?" Deardryn asked. "Will you cooperate? Or will your sibling die?"

She met Analia in the center of the room and offered the Crystal.

The chamber went deadly quiet.

Crystal spare her, what was she supposed to do? Analia looked to Aaron, but he shook his head. He couldn't make this choice for her. But how was she supposed to make it herself?

Cadmus made a small, muffled noise. Her eyes moved inexorably to his. He looked to Deardryn, then Lucilla, and finally gave a small nod.

At some point, her brother had become a king. And Analia could barely breathe through the spike of pain as she extended her hand to Deardryn. "Give me the Crystal."

Deardryn's composure cracked for the briefest moment. Analia wasn't surprised to see the triumph. But before she could decide if she had truly seen a flash of fear, Deardryn pressed the Crystal into her palm.

For a few long moments, Analia stared down at the rock in her hand, completely at a loss. She could feel the power churning beneath her finger as she ran it down the central crack, but otherwise, nothing happened.

"Let it feel your magic," Deardryn said. "This magic won't reach out to you. You need to reach for it."

Analia didn't know how. She didn't know how to summon the Sun magic that had revived Aaron's life force, or the Wind magic that had shoved Deardryn across the chamber, much less the other Royal magics. Every time she reached for her magic, all she felt was flames. Her uncle's flames.

This was his magic, not her own. It was the one thing she had spent her life wishing for, and she had to lose her uncle to get it.

For so long, she hated that wish, hated herself for having it, hated herself because maybe her uncle would still be alive if she hadn't tried so hard to chase after it.

There was a point she would have rather died than endure the guilt of knowing it was his magic running through her network.

But she knew Accalon. She knew he would want her to have it in his death. What she hadn't realized until that moment, was he would also want her to use it. Use it to protect the people she loved, just as he always had.

Analia looked first to her siblings, the bruises against their skin, the magic flickering around them. Aaron, his face ashen, Deardryn's fingers blossoming across his throat. All because she couldn't protect them. Until now.

Analia's flames parted. Power rose up from the depths of her being in a terrifying, overwhelming wave. She didn't give herself time to consider how this power would consume her; how it would destroy her from the inside out. Instead, she focused it all into her palm, the room growing hotter and hotter, the air crackling with power.

"Crystal spare us all," Aaron breathed.

Then, the stone split.

Analia barely registered the crack when pure white energy erupted from her hand, pouring into her.

This wasn't the release of magic after a few days of being dampered. This was centuries' worth, finally unleashed. Bone-crushing, mind-shattering, soul-devouring power. This was a magic that had built and toppled worlds.

Deardryn had been right: this magic didn't reach out to her. It claimed her. Used her as fuel for its fury.

And all she could do was scream.

Chapter 78

Analia was glowing. Analia was glowing and she was screaming and Aaron was screaming.

Deardryn launched herself away from the blinding white light, which refracted a million colors across the chamber. The massive window shattered in an explosion of glass. Fissures spiderwebbed across the ceiling.

But Aaron didn't care. Not as Analia fell to her knees, her body contorting as she screamed.

"Don't," Deardryn shrieked. "You can't interfere!"

Aaron. Didn't. Care.

He lunged for her, his throat raw as he screamed her name. Golden light flung him back against the wall. It looped around his middle, warning tingles racing across his skin.

He could see Deardryn's mouth moving, saying Analia should be all right, she was strong enough to survive. But all he heard was Analia screaming, screaming like her soul was being torn from her body one shred at a time.

He desperately looked to the Ash siblings. Lucilla was sobbing, trying to cover her ears with her shoulders. Cadmus reached for Deardryn's damper box with his foot, just managing to pull it toward himself. Deardryn immediately rushed toward him.

Aaron didn't waste a second. He grabbed Analia's flung damper blade from his waistband—gods he loved that woman—and bent his trapped arms up, touching the blade to the magic. The onyx immediately absorbed the golden light, and Aaron was free.

Sliding to the ground, he looped his ankle chain over the point where it met his left cuff. Then, he tugged with his leg.

The chain snapped free. And clutching his dagger, Aaron shoved to his feet and charged toward the eruption. He unlocked his first shackle in seconds, almost managing to get the second when a massive chunk of ceiling broke free.

Aaron tried to dodge, but stone slammed him down, several cracks radiating throughout his body. He struggled, reaching for Analia, the magic seeming to peel back his skin layer by layer. But she was just out of reach.

Aaron was forced to watch, helpless, as the glow around Analia intensified. He cringed away, but his eyes never left her.

Not as the light flared. Not as she collapsed forward. Not as the magic slowly receded back into her palm, her outstretched arm limp across the floor. Not as she lay completely still, white light briefly flickering across her skin until even that was gone.

"Anna?" Aaron breathed in the sudden quiet.

Analia didn't move.

Deardryn remained frozen beside Cadmus, her eyes wide.

"Anna," Aaron said, slightly louder, "Anna, please."

He couldn't see if her chest was moving. He couldn't hear her breathe.

Aaron dug his fingers into the carpet, trying to drag himself forward. This couldn't be happening. The tapestries couldn't lie, so many hadn't come true yet, this wasn't allowed to happen. His heart, his soul, couldn't have been stitched back together just to be ripped apart once more.

Aaron barely recognized his voice as it tore from his throat, "Analia!"

Analia's foot twitched. Aaron held his breath as a shudder ran down the length of her body.

Deardryn took a step forward. Cadmus tensed. Lucilla wailed, flinging herself at her binds, the magic crackling up her torso.

"Lucilla, stop," Analia whispered.

Lucilla froze.

Aaron's heart stuttered.

"She survived," Deardryn breathed. "The magic recognized her as its own."

Aaron watched numbly as Deardryn knelt beside Analia, brushing the hair from her face with something like tenderness. Analia tried to pull the Crystal to her chest, but Deardryn gently plucked it from her fingers.

Aaron couldn't bring himself to care. He dropped his head to the floor, tears stinging his eyes.

She was alive. She'd survived. And he would never pray to the Crystal ever again.

"What is this?" Deardryn breathed.

Somehow, Aaron forced his heavy head to rise. Deardryn held the Crystal up to her face. It looked exactly as pictured in every legend: an almost translucent color, made up of countless layers and angles and folds. Except this Crystal was very clearly only a slice of the whole.

"You didn't think Talitha was dumb enough to hide the Crystal in one place," Analia rasped.

The entire chamber fell still as she struggled into a sitting position. She looked up at Deardryn, unflinching under her mounting fury.

"The Crystal was separated into pieces," she said. "Talitha hid each of them away to avoid the exact plan you've been trying to enact. I suppose your research didn't tell you that."

Deardryn's nostrils flared.

A savage, bloodthirsty satisfaction crackled through Aaron's veins. Especially as Analia tactfully withheld the fact that, according to Surce's translations, there were three pieces to find. Meaning Deardryn still had a long way to go.

"You knew," Deardryn breathed, hand going to her wrist. "You knew and you didn't tell me."

"I also know that now, I'm coming with you."

Aaron, Cadmus, and Lucilla sucked in a breath. Deardryn merely brushed back her hair. "Is that so?"

"You need me now more than ever," Analia said, rising unsteadily to her feet.

"Anna, stop," Aaron whispered.

Analia ignored him. "You've just seen firsthand what this Crystal is capable of. Do you think you can survive that?"

Cadmus yelled something through his gag, eyes wide.

"I have my own methods of dealing with the Crystal," Deardryn said coolly.

"You mean your rings?" Analia steadied herself against the wall. "I possess all seven Royal Blessings, and I barely survived. Even if you get your Ash ring, do you think your stolen magic has any chance of withstanding that sort of power?"

Deardryn's eyes darted down to the Crystal.

Aaron's pulse sped up. He desperately shoved at the rock, finally pushing it off himself. "Analia, you don't have to do this—"

"You have two choices, Deardryn," Analia said over him. "You can take the ultimate risk that you, too, can wield the Crystal's magic. But even if you don't die in the process, you know you will never be able to wield it like I can. And at that point, you'll have also risked the possibility that you can't track me down again."

"Why am I supposed to believe you're suddenly interested in helping me?" Deardryn asked.

"I'm not," Analia retorted. "But I'm not foolish enough to believe you would let me or my family escape unscathed. You would likely raze this entire castle to the ground with the Crystal in your attempts to keep us here. And I won't let you harm them."

"Analia, please," Aaron pleaded, his heart ripping at the seams as he failed to rise. "You don't have to do this. We can find another way—"

"That's the deal," Analia said, raising her voice over his. "You let my family and Aaron go, and I will come quietly."

"Don't even think about it," Aaron spat at Deardryn.

"Aaron, please." Analia's voice cracked, and Aaron felt it mirrored in his entire being. How was he supposed to let her walk away?

Deardryn thoughtfully ran her fingers along the Crystal shard, then slipped it into a pocket. Yet, when she looked up, her expression was completely blank.

"Your loyalty is inspiring, Analia," she said, her voice flat.

Analia didn't move as Deardryn approached Aaron. She retrieved the damper blade that had fallen from his hand, his second wrist cuff still intact. Then, she moved to the Ash siblings.

As soon as their gags were out, Cadmus and Lucilla erupted into protests. Analia raised a hand and cringed away, tears in her eyes.

"I can't let her hurt you," she whispered.

"You can't trust her!" Lucilla yelled.

Deardryn looked down at her, her movements stiffer than before. "She is a clever one."

She waved her hand, dismissing the bonds. Then, she plunged the damper blade into Cadmus's stomach.

At least, it should have been Cadmus's stomach.

With a screech, Lucilla shoved her brother aside, the dagger sinking into her throat.

Analia watched the dagger pierce Lucilla's throat in slow motion. She didn't scream. She didn't engulf Deardryn with magic—she had none left. All she did was stare, transfixed by the crimson stain flowing down Lucilla's neck.

Lucilla. Her sister. The one making the horrible wet gurgling noise across the room. Dying. Because of her.

Analia was vaguely aware of Cadmus and Deardryn grappling off to the side, the former screaming, screaming, screaming. She looked up into Lucilla's eyes, red and swollen from crying. And somehow, over Cadmus and Deardryn's yells, Analia heard her sister's, her twelve-year-old sister's, final five words.

"I just wanted to help."

Tears stung Analia's eyes. "You did," she whispered, nearly choking on the words. "I'm so sorry."

Lucilla smiled faintly as she slumped to the ground. And she did not move again.

Finally, Analia unfroze. She launched herself toward Lucilla, screaming her name.

Arms wrapped around her from behind, pulling her back, lowering her to the ground.

"There's nothing you can do, Anna," Aaron whispered, tears in his own eyes. "She's gone. I am so, so sorry."

"She was a *child*."

"I know."

"She was just a child." Analia pressed her face to Aaron's chest, feeling like her very being was collapsing in on itself.

Her sister was dead. She was captured by invaders in the one place she was supposed to be safest, turned into a bargaining chip, bruised and bloodied. And then she sacrificed herself. Somehow, they'd reached a point where she thought that was the only way to help.

"How did we get here?" Analia asked, her voice breaking.

"I... I don't know."

Aaron tightened his arms around her. And for one minute, one terrible, agonizing, impossible minute, he was able to hold her together.

It was nowhere near enough time. Analia didn't think there would ever be enough time to feel this. But somehow, she managed to catch her breath. Her hand moved down their tangled limbs, her fingers brushing the silky petals of the bracelet around his ankle. Aaron's hand found one of the daggers in her boot.

Neither of them moved as the chamber went still. Analia heard Cadmus gasp for breath. She heard Deardryn rise from the floor and approach.

"Look at me, Analia."

Analia didn't move. She didn't fight as Deardryn grabbed her head and forced her to look up. She didn't look at Cadmus magically pinned against the wall once more; at the damper dagger in Deardryn's free hand, golden light flickering over her sister's blood.

"Do not try to corner me," Deardryn said, velvet soft. "Now, I have all my magics, and an excellent reason to keep you with me."

But that wasn't triumph in her eyes. If anything, she looked pale, almost rattled.

Analia didn't have enough energy, enough room in her body or mind, to wonder why.

Deardryn tried to tug Analia to her feet. Aaron tightened his grip, letting out a vicious curse. For a few moments, the two grappled, each pulling Analia in different directions. Analia could feel herself being ripped apart from the inside out.

Finally, Aaron released her with one hand. Deardryn jerked Analia away and to her feet. Just as Laness appeared at Aaron's side, dressed in her DovenU camouflage.

Deardryn reared back, "Where did you—"

Aaron threw his dagger.

Deardryn twisted, the blade sinking into her upper arm.

Laness pulled Aaron to his feet. Deardryn hissed, ripping the dagger free, golden light flaring around her.

Aaron looked to Cadmus, crouched beside Lucilla's body.

"Go!" Cadmus yelled.

Deardryn struck. Aaron dodged, grabbed his fallen dagger, then looked up. His eyes met Analia's for a fraction of a moment. Then, he and Laness were gone.

Deardryn's chest heaved, her expression wild. "See?" she said, whipping around to face Analia. "I suppose he doesn't love you after all."

Analia didn't try to stop her face from crumpling. She turned away, keeping her back to Deardryn as she called the guards. She didn't turn as they entered and marched her brother away. She didn't turn as Deardryn hauled her after them. Through the halls, down the stairs into the entryway.

Not until they were fading into the shadows did Analia let her fury show.

Chapter 79

Aaron clung to Laness as they shot back across Elefthia.

Laness had been steadily moving from enka patch to enka patch toward them ever since they were captured, the nymph barely having reached the Ash Kingdom when Analia touched Aaron's bracelet to summon her. Thankfully, in the confusion of the Sun Castle being conquered, no one had noticed a nymph slip through the Phoenix Gate and past the Ash Kingdom's wards. At that point, jumping into Accalon's chambers had been easy. So pathetically fucking easy.

"Take off my cuff," Aaron ground out. "I can get us home. Just take off the cuff."

Aaron barely had time to register the woods materialize around him. Laness drew one of the damper blades that had skewered him, and in seconds, Aaron's remaining cuff dropped away.

Aaron didn't care about the blow as his magic slammed into him. He pocketed the cuffs, grabbed Laness, and dragged them into the shadows.

Home, home, home. Although how was it home when she was no longer there?

Aaron didn't feel the ground solidify beneath his feet. Laness caught him as he staggered, shoving him on to his sitting room couch and propping him up against the armrest.

"It worked?" she whispered.

"It worked," Aaron mouthed. He couldn't speak the words. Even though he'd known they were coming from the moment Surce decoded that scroll.

Aaron closed his eyes as Branten, Mor, and Surce stampeded into the room. So loud. So many voices. But none of them were hers.

Laness tried to answer their flurry of questions, but Branten roared over the noise. "Where is Anna?"

"With Deardryn!" Laness yelled back.

"What?" Mor demanded, stumbling back.

"Then go get her!" Branten yelled.

"We can't," Aaron breathed.

"Why not?" demanded Mor and Branten.

"Because this was all according to plan."

Silence.

Surce knelt in front of Aaron. She lifted his chin with a finger, and he finally opened his eyes.

"What did you do?" she breathed.

Aaron couldn't respond.

"It was Analia's plan," Laness said, coming to stand beside him. "She came up with it the moment I told her what you decoded."

"She knew Deardryn had a shard," Aaron said, leaning his aching body against the back of the couch. "The probability of all of us escaping alive, let alone with the Crystal, was slim to none."

"What does this have to do with anything?" Branten demanded.

"Don't you see?" Laness said. "Analia is now on the inside."

"And she's not coming back until she gets that shard," Aaron said.

Branten, Mor, and Surce wore identical looks of horror. Aaron could feel their fear writhe in his own stomach, but stronger than that was the fierce wave of pride.

"Why didn't you tell us?" Mor asked, collapsing on the couch beside Aaron.

"Analia made me swear not to say anything," Laness said. "She knew you and Branten in particular would panic."

"I might have said something," Aaron said vaguely. "But I was busy being a prisoner."

Branten scoffed. Surce studied Aaron carefully, then shook her head, unsurprised.

"And how are you with all of this?" she asked.

"Devastated," Aaron said. "I watched her almost die I don't know how many times. But if anyone is a survivor, it's her."

Everyone looked down.

Aaron's eyes moved around the room, knowing she wasn't going to be there; his chest still cracking down the center as he spotted no dark red hair. No smoky-gray eyes.

She was gone. Trapped. With Deardryn.

"Isn't this the part where one of you idiots gives me a hug?" he rasped.

Mor let out a small, choked noise. Then, he pulled Aaron in, the rest of his family piling on. Aaron closed his eyes, letting his family hold him together.

"She'll be all right," Mor murmured.

Aaron sighed, his breath almost steady. "I know."

Ember crouched behind a statue's pedestal, peeking over the top as a group of guards escorted Cadmus past. Deardryn and Analia followed a couple moments later, both unsettlingly expressionless.

After being escorted from the music hall, Ember had met up with Rois—gods, where had he found her? In an alleyway, maybe? She was almost two weeks clean of devinroot, but her mind felt just as hazy as day one.

But she'd managed to tell Rois the full story—including Lucilla's capture. The guard had wanted to find a safe place to leave Ember, but he couldn't argue as Ember gestured to the carnage around them and asked, "Where?"

So, he reluctantly brought her along as he snuck back into the Ash Castle. They'd staked out this corridor ever since Deardryn claimed it as her study wing.

They had watched as Analia and Aaron were marched inside, followed by Lucilla and Cadmus. They had heard the yells, the explosion of power, Aaron's and Analia's gut-wrenching screams. Ember had barely been able to stop Rois from charging inside.

Even now, he was taut as a bow string as the Sun guard passed. Deardryn had stationed her guards at the end of the hall, but Ember had no doubt they, too, had heard. Just as she knew Deardryn would kill them before they could leave the floor as a result.

"We have to help them," Rois breathed in Ember's ear.

"We can't," Ember said, forcing back tears. "Not by going after them, at least. The best thing we can do is remain undetected and collect information."

"But—"

"We can't do this, Rois," Ember whisper yelled. "We need help."

Rois clenched his jaw. The Sun unit disappeared around the corner, their footsteps fading away.

"I'm getting Lucilla," Rois said. "They don't get to toss her body into a random funeral pyre as if she meant nothing."

Ember knew she should stop him. There would be no way to explain a body suddenly vanishing.

But she didn't move as Rois rose because he was right. Lucilla deserved more. And it was Ember's fault she was even there in the first place.

Ember pressed her shaking fingers to her lips, tears welling up in her eyes.

Lucilla's capture was her fault. Lucilla being in that chamber was her fault. Lucilla being in a position where she could be killed was her fault. It was her fault that that beautiful, clever, mischievous little girl now lay dead and forgotten on the stone floor.

But Ember didn't have time to fall apart. She would grieve Lucilla's loss, but that little girl had sacrificed herself to protect her siblings. And she wouldn't let that sacrifice be in vain.

Analia might be out of reach, but she knew Aaron would tear apart the world if that was what it took to reach her. For now, she had to focus on helping who she could, and that was Cadmus.

Which meant Ember needed a plan.

And she needed help.

Analia didn't try to fight as Deardryn dragged her through the shadows. She could feel the Dragoness's magic was running out, to the point she could barely hide her stumble as they emerged before a massive black gate. The Crescent Moon Gate.

Sylas wordlessly stepped through, his black castle looming behind him. Deardryn shoved Analia toward him, and he took her by the shoulders.

Right before he pulled her into the shadows, she looked up, spotting a shooting star arcing above her head.

Analia held that image close to her chest as Sylas unceremoniously dropped her in her dungeon cell and disappeared. A pair of guards got to work shackling her to the wall, but Analia didn't put up a fight.

She sat against the wall as the guards slammed her cell door shut behind them, her fingers finding the enka bracelet around her ankle.

Is he all right? She asked silently.

Laness response was immediate and tired. *He will be. He says he loves you and to come back to him.*

Analia smiled to herself. *Tell him I'm always searching.*

Analia let the connection drop, her hand coming to toy with her phoenix pin.

Deardryn thought she hadn't been paying attention; that she had failed to learn any of her lessons. No matter how much she sharpened her fangs, she was still only a piece on Deardryn's board.

Astute, but still controllable. Clever, but not clever enough to be a threat.

To Deardryn, Analia wasn't the intended Queen of Starlight—she was a princess. And she was.

The princess who had killed her husband with her uncle's flames, and walked away from her crown. The princess who Deardryn had brought into the heart of her schemes.

She was the Princess of Ash.

And she was going to watch those schemes burn.

Chapter 80

Dimitri didn't know how long he'd been locked in his cell. He'd lost track of how many trays of slop had been delivered and taken away, most left untouched, Dimitri not remembering the ones he picked at.

It reached the point that the guards had taken to kicking his ribs to see if he would move.

Sometimes he did. Most of the time he didn't. A part of him hoped they would kick him again.

Anything was better than the jagged hole ripping through his chest. Because Patryclas was dead. Probably dead. Certainly dead.

He'd felt the damage Deardryn had inflicted. There was no surviving that.

It took Dimitri a long, long time to collect the courage to check the heart on the inside of his wrist, expecting it to be gray. But the tattoo remained black.

Why? Did they only fade when the oath was broken? Did it not matter if one of the swearers was dead? Or could Patryclas—Dimitri couldn't think the words. He couldn't hope; not when being wrong would slam him into this feeling all over again. And he couldn't survive that twice. Just as Patryclas couldn't have survived those injuries.

He was dead. He had to be dead. There was no way he wasn't dead. And the pain in Dimitri's entire body had him wondering if he was on the way to the same fate.

He had promised Patryclas he wouldn't turn off the feeling, no matter how big it got. But Dimitri didn't know how anyone survived this. The crushing feeling that he had not only lost someone precious, but in doing so, he'd lost a part of himself.

Sometimes crying helped. Sometimes it didn't. There were honestly only three things that kept him breathing.

The fact that Analia had survived the loss of her uncle. The dream that Patryclas had helped him find. And the burning, blazing, all-consuming certainty that Deardryn would pay.

When his cell door swung open, Dimitri didn't bother looking up. Only when the clatter of a food tray didn't come did he partially uncurl his body.

Sylas leaned in the shadowy entrance of his cell. He had never seen the Moon King so disheveled: his clothes rumpled; his hair mussed. But it was the lost look in his eyes that had Dimitri unable to look away.

"Deardryn attacked Patryclas," he said. A statement, not a question.

Dimitri nodded mutely.

"She's a traitor."

He nodded again.

"She framed you."

A third nod.

Sylas hung his head, his shoulders heaving. Dimitri lowered his gaze, his lungs tightening, waiting for Sylas to turn and go without further comment.

Instead, the Moon King straightened. Expression hardening, he stepped out of the cell, holding the door open.

"Come with me."

Author's Note

Thank you so much for reading *Kingdom of Smoke and Starlight*! I hope you enjoyed reading it as much as I enjoyed writing it. If you did, I would appreciate it so incredibly much if you left a review on Goodreads or Amazon. You truly have no idea how much even a sentence, a star rating, helps us authors.

This book has such a special piece of my heart. I often say KOMAM is the book I needed to write, but KOSAS? KOSAS is the book I wanted to write. Analia and Aaron's story specifically is what got me excited to write again back in June 2021 after two years of doubting I was a good enough writer to even write a book. Yet, here we are, two books later!

I think one of the most magical aspects of the fantasy genre is how it enables us to explore such dark, painful topics through a creative lens. My psychology degree wonders if the fantastic elements that are unable to be experienced in real life gives us the distance we need to feel comfortable digging in, but the human in me thinks it all boils down to the feeling of being understood.

We might not be a rejected princess with too much magic, but we know what it feels like to be told "You're not good enough." We know how it feels to have so much anger and hurt that we don't know how to process it all. We know how scary it is to embrace who we are.

I think there's a feeling of being seen when we read about characters who have been hurt in the same way we have, regardless of the methods. And while I definitely did my fair share of breaking, especially in KOMAM, I wanted to write a story that explored the then what? Once we finally allow ourselves to break, how do we put ourselves back together again?

I hope in reading KOSAS, you not only felt seen through all the pain, but you also got some catharsis as characters started to heal. Maybe even a little hope. I know I did while writing. If nothing else, though, I hope you at least got some payoff now that Analia and Aaron are finally together because my gods.

Those two dummies. I think we can all agree they had a lot of stuff they needed to work through before they could be together, but the amount of times I had to dial back a scene because even I was impatient for them to just make out already is too high to count.

But of course, since I'm the writer, they're not out of the woods yet. No one is, which brings us to my poor sweet Dima. The latest victim of my "I must break you so you can rebuild into something even stronger" cycle. Don't worry, there's a lot that still needs to unfold in his story. And you can start to see how in book 3, *Kingdom of Dreams and Decay*, coming soon.

In the meantime, if you'd like to stay up to date on all my book-related chaos, plus some sneak peeks and inevitable rambles, you can join my newsletter at abigailehrhardt.com.

Once again, thank you for reading, and I'll see you in KODAD!

Glossary

The Ancient Ones: three dark, malevolent beings that ruled over Elefthia during ancient times.

Ash Kingdom: founded by Azar Valarus, this kingdom is ruled over by the Ash Royals and is known for its forges, creativity, and volcanoes, specifically Mt. Vasolus.

Ash Royal: descendants of Azar Valarus—one of the Defiants and rulers of the Ash Kingdom. All are Blessed with fire magic, which can range in a variety of colors.

The Belt: a string of volcanoes located in the Ash Kingdom.

The Bend: a network of drug dens, brothels, and other nefarious businesses on the outskirts of the Sun Kingdom.

Bless: the act of bestowing Blessings.

Blessed: the humans—and their descendants—whom the Crystal gifted magic to. All Blessed are guaranteed to have an extended life span, faster healing, and heightened strength and reflexes, as well as the same magic as their parents. It's a fifty-fifty chance for either magic if both parents have magic.

Blessing: a word that has become synonymous with a person's magic, extended life span, faster healing, and heightened strength and reflexes.

Copper fleck: the smallest unit of currency.

The Crystal: the Ancient Ones' most powerful weapon. Translucent and palm-sized, the Crystal is responsible for magic flooding Elefthia, bestowing Blessings, and sealing away the Ancient Ones. At some point during Talitha's reign, it disappeared.

Crystal Guard: existing in all kingdoms, the Crystal guard is made up of the seven strongest warriors in each kingdom, charged with protecting the Royals.

Damper: created from onyx, after various carvings and charms, a damper can act like a magical plug, drawing all of a person's magic to itself and not releasing it until removed. The longer the damper is worn, the longer it takes for the magic to return.

Darmanten: one of the five major gods, he is the god of day and night.

The Defiants: seven humans that stepped up during the war against the Ancient Ones, ultimately sealing the Ancient Ones away, enabling the Crystal to release magic into Elefthia, and founding the seven kingdoms.

Demiblessed: those with one Blessed, one human parent.

Devinroot: a plant that grows off of magic and is a highly addictive stimulant.

Devourist: the demons that made up the majority of the Ancient Ones' army.

Doveness: the name of a member of the DovenU

The DovenU: a secret tribe of female warriors located in Mt. Lanula.

Elefthia: the name of the continent the once seven, now six kingdoms are found on.

Elladine: one of the five gods, she is the goddess of death and younger sister of Rosala and Kierra.

Enka flowers: a flower whose magic can create communication pathways between people.

Everflame: a flame created by Azar, which cannot be extinguished and provides the majority of the Ash Kingdom's magically powered light.

Ferrin: one of the five gods, he is the god of time and prophecy.

Gold piece: the highest unit of currency.

Gritta's: a drug den in the Sun Kingdom.

Healers: Blessed, Demiblessed, and, in extremely rare cases, humans, that have been chosen by Rosala to receive healer magic from the Crystal. Healers swear vows of celibacy and political neutrality.

Healer markings (sometimes referred to as "markings" or "rings"): the rings inked around a healer's eyes, which depict their level of training. There are four rings: herbology, internal, external, and mystery, which are marked in white as apprentices, but turn the healer's kingdom's colors upon completion of their apprenticeship.

Human: while Royals, Blessed, Demiblessed, and healers are all human, the term has predominantly come to refer to magicless humans, or to the race as a collective.

Kierra: one of the five gods, she is the goddess of life, and older sister of Rosala and Elladine.

Magic network: the internal network that a Blessed's or Demiblessed's magic runs through.

Mist Kingdom: founded by Noelani Sai, the Mist Kingdom is ruled by the Mist Royals and is considered to be the most devout of the kingdoms.

Mist Royal: descendants of Noelani Sai—one of the Defiants—Mist Royals rule over the Mist Kingdom. All are Blessed with water magic.

Moon Kingdom: founded by Mahina Ruanega, the Moon Kingdom is ruled by the Moon Royals and is known for its bogs, tattoos, and secretive people.

Moon Royal: descendants of Mahina Ruanega—one of the Defiants—Moon Royals rule over the Moon Kingdom. They possess Blessings that allow them to manipulate darkness—although they are intentionally vague about what that specifically entails.

Mt. Lanula: one of the three major mountains of Elefthia, located in the Wild Lands.

Mt. Raegyr: one of the three major mountains of Elefthia, located in the center of the Star Kingdom.

Mt. Vasolus: one of the three major mountains of Elefthia, Vasolus is a volcano located in the Ash Kingdom.

Nymphs: appearing incredibly human-like outside of their slit pupils and pointed ears, nymphs derive their life source from a specific plant—although they have a general affinity for all plants.

The Phoenix Gate: the gate in the center of the wall surrounding the Ash Castle, created by King Accalon Valarus during the early years of his kingship.

Pulsepearl: a small pink pearl that is the source of a wraith's magic and life force. They also enable the holder to relocate to any location where there is another pulsepearl.

Rosala: one of the five gods, she is the goddess of healing, and older sister of Elladine, and younger sister of Kierra.

Royal: the descendants of the seven Defiants and rulers of the once seven, now six kingdoms of Elefthia.

Sand Kingdom: founded by Theistan Rubarena, the Sand Kingdom is ruled over by the Sand Royals, and is known for its red deserts, and general practice of not using animals for work or food.

Sand Royal: descendants of Theistan Rubarena—one of the Defiants—Sand Royals rule the Sand Kingdom. They are Blessed with earth manipulation.

Scarsthain: the highest-security prison in Elefthia, located on the border between Star and Moon territory. It's home to the foulest, most deadly of criminals, and is known for its brutality.

Scarsworn dagger: ceremonial daggers only found in the Moon Kingdom that allow people to make magical, blood-based oaths that manifest as tattoos on the swearers' skin.

The Serpent's Tail: one of the three major rivers of Elefthia, which runs from the Wind Kingdom at the northeast, down to the Sun Kingdom, southeast to the Mist Kingdom, and then southwest to the Moon Kingdom.

The Shattering: the climax of the seven-year war between the Star Kingdom and the six kingdoms. The Star Royal line was completely eradicated after Royals from all six kingdoms sent a deadly blast of magic through the Star Castle, so powerful that King Hester's bone fragments were all that survived. This effectively ended the Star Kingdom's rule over the other kingdoms.

Silver chip: the unit of currency valued higher than a copper fleck, and lower than a gold piece.

Solemnai: a celebration that happens every three months in the Sun Kingdom. The tradition was started by Queen Deardryn Oshar to help bridge the gap between the commoners and Royals.

The Solstice Ceremony: occurring once a year, the Solstice Ceremony takes place at the foot of Mt. Raegyr. Here, the reigning Royal from each kingdom releases a blast of magic into the ground to maintain the magic flow across Elefthia.

Soul gate: the Soul Gate can only be opened on the Summer Solstice and the days following and preceding. Each gate can only be opened by the magic of the reigning Royal, and permits direct access to the Star Kingdom where the Solstice Ceremony takes place.

Star Kingdom: founded by Talitha Stelingente, the Star Kingdom was once ruled by the Star Royals. After the Shattering, it became the one piece of neutral ground the six kingdoms could gather on.

Star Royal: descendants of Talitha Stelingente—leader of the Defiants—and rulers of the Star Kingdom. Star Royals are given the Blessing of death.

Sun dragon: dragons that are exclusively found in the Sun Kingdom. Their bodies are long and serpentine, covered in scales in varying shades of gold that are as strong as steel. They have small, white wings, short, stubby legs, and large, golden eyes.

Sun Kingdom: founded by Helia Oshar, the Sun Kingdom is ruled by the Sun Royals, and is known for its research, scholars, and library full of forbidden texts.

Sun Royal: descendants of Helia Oshar—one of the Defiants—Sun Royals rule over the Sun Kingdom. Their Blessings revolve around the life force, enabling them to heal the minds, souls, life forces, and magic networks that healer magic cannot reach.

Sunstone: golden fist-sized stones that can sense Sun magic and glow in response. They provide most of the magic-based light in the Sun Kingdom.

The Unleashing: the moment that the Defiants procured the Crystal and used it to release magic into Elefthia for the first time.

The Wild Lands: the southernmost section of Elefthia, where the Crystal dumped all of the Ancient Ones' dark, malevolent power. It is wisely left alone as a result.

Wind Kingdom: founded by Raiden Cruchendai, the Wind Kingdom is ruled by Wind Royals, and is known for its mountains and cold temperatures.

Wind Royal: descendants of Raiden Cruchendai—one of the Defiants—Wind Royals rule over the Wind Kingdom. Their Blessings revolve around air manipulation.

Wraiths: predominately found in the Moon Kingdom, wraiths are spectral beings that commonly possess the offered bodies of recently deceased humans. Their known to have all-black eyes, a chill that radiates off of them, and their magic and life force are connected to their pulsepearls.

The Wraithhouse: the largest religious sanctuary for wraith-kind, located in the central Moon Kingdom.

Xenol: a plant that is able to eat away a person's magic, and eventually, a person's life force.

Acknowledgements

It's pretty widely understood that your second book is going to kick your ass—and my god did KOSAS do just that. Part of it was my fault for deciding to write the first draft during my senior year of college, but most of it is because I have an uncanny ability to write myself into plot hole corners. It's a gift, what can I say? And KOSAS would not be here today if not for all of the people who helped me through not only said gift, but every other hurdle of writing this story.

First, a massive thank you to all of my unbelievably talented, thoughtful, badass beta readers. Marlena, your ability to alternate between chaotic reader reaction keyboard smashes and unbelievably insightful commentary that was essential in shaping Analia's arc—and maintaining basic common sense—is mind boggling. Kyra, it's a good thing you're entertained by me because you're stuck with me. Not just because you provided such essential reader reactions, but because you've proven yourself capable of dealing with the utter nonsense that pops out of my mouth on a daily basis, (signed Gabby). KJ, the Elected Dictator of the Dimitri Defense Squad, your ability to notice the tiny shit I miss and match my chaotic energy remains unparalleled. Auntie Vikki—I don't even know where to put your thank you because you've been involved in literally every aspect of this book. Beta reading, proof reading, artwork—because we all know I'm useless there. Not to mention you spent collectively three plus hours helping me solve the raven statue plot hole—still can't believe tourmaline was the answer. And now that you have the almighty punctuation book, I'm pretty sure you've become unstoppable. Jokes aside, though, thank you so so much for helping put this book together.

To Noah: editor extraordinaire, namer of the scarsworn dagger, the man who so patiently puts up with me. Thank you for all of the incredible work you put into this story, and helping it become something I'm truly proud of.

To Clara, my second proofreader, thank you for being there to catch all of my... questionable punctuation choices. I did better this time, though!

Moving over to the art side of things, first up we have Liz from Raven Pages Design. I can't express how much fun I had brainstorming the ebook and paperback covers, the dust jacket, and interior art with you. There's something magical that happens when you find someone who vibrates on the same chaotic frequency as you, and I think all of your stunning designs can speak to that.

To Maria, thank you so so much for the under jacket design! I still can't get over the little shooting stars around the text.

As for my friends—Kenna, Christi, Cynthia, and Kylee to name a few—thank you for dealing with me in general. Whether it's helping me with social media posts, choosing understanding over irritation when I go radio silent in the writing cave, or just being excited and supportive, you all mean the world to me.

To my immediate family—you better have skipped certain sections. Skimmed at the very least. Even if you didn't, we're not breaking my delusion.

In all seriousness, though, thank you for relentlessly believing in me and my books. Special thanks to Mom who has a knack for selling my books on flights and to the various strangers you encounter and inevitably befriend.

Finally, thank you, dear reader. Thank you for reading my books. Thank you for giving me a chance. Thank you for all of your messages and comments telling me how much you love my characters and informing me I better not hurt any of them or else. Releasing a book can be a lonely, scary thing, but you all make it worthwhile.

About the Author

A bigail Ehrhardt has been writing absurdly elaborate stories since she was nine years old, to the point her teachers had to confine her plots to forty-five minute time frames. It still didn't help. Now, her stories are just as fantastical, just as intricate, but (hopefully) a lot easier to follow.

As a baby, Abigail was diagnosed with bilateral retinoblastoma, a rare cancer of the retinas. After having one eye removed and the other severely damaged, she quickly realized books were her key to unlocking a world that was no longer designed for her. Now, she writes stories of her own, featuring a healthy dose of magic, romance, and wounded dreamers.

You can find her in Connecticut, where she's probably hoarding nail polish, adopting far too many plants, and becoming more emotionally attached to the side characters than protagonists of whatever book she's reading.

instagram.com/abigailehrhardt.author/

facebook.com/profile.php?id=61553660026246

tiktok.com/abigailehrhardt.author